W9-BLP-740

The Editor

CARLA KAPLAN is the Davis Distinguished Professor of American Literature at Northeastern University. She is the author of *The Erotics of Talk: Women's Writing and Feminist Paradigms, Zora Neale Hurston: A Life in Letters,* and *Miss Anne in Harlem: The White Women of the Black Renaissance* (forthcoming). She is also editor of *Every Tongue Got to Confess: Negro Folk Tales from the Gulf States* and *Dark Symphony and Other Works by Elizabeth Laura Adams.*

A NORTON CRITICAL EDITION

Nella Larsen
PASSING

AUTHORITATIVE TEXT

BACKGROUNDS AND CONTEXTS

CRITICISM

Edited by

CARLA KAPLAN

DAVIS DISTINGUISHED PROFESSOR OF AMERICAN
LITERATURE, NORTHEASTERN UNIVERSITY

W • W • NORTON & COMPANY • *New York* • *London*

W. W. Norton & Company has been independent since its founding in 1923, when William Warder Norton and Mary D. Herter Norton first published lectures delivered at the People's Institute, the adult education division of New York City's Cooper Union. The Nortons soon expanded their program beyond the Institute, publishing books by celebrated academics from America and abroad. By mid-century, the two major pillars of Norton's publishing program—trade books and college texts—were firmly established. In the 1950s, the Norton family transferred control of the company to its employees, and today—with a staff of four hundred and a comparable number of trade, college, and professional titles published each year—W. W. Norton & Company stands as the largest and oldest publishing house owned wholly by its employees.

This title is printed on permanent paper containing
30 percent post-consumer waste recycled fiber.

The text of this book is composed in Fairfield Medium with the display set in Bernhard Modern.
Composition by Binghamton Valley Composition.
Manufacturing by the Maple-Vail Book Group, Binghamton.
Book design by Antonina Krass.
Production manager: Benjamin Reynolds.

Library of Congress Cataloging-in-Publication Data

Larsen, Nella.
Passing : authoritative text, backgrounds and contexts, about Nella Larsen, criticism / Nella Larsen ; edited by Carla Kaplan.
p. cm. — (A Norton critical edition)
Includes bibliographical references.
ISBN-13: 978-0-393-97916-9 (pbk.)
1. African American women—Fiction. 2. Racially mixed people—Fiction.
3. Passing (Identity)—Fiction. 4. Identity (Psychology)—Fiction.
5. Female friendship—Fiction. 6. Human skin color—Fiction.
7. New York (N.Y.)—Fiction. 8. Married women—Fiction.
9. Psychological fiction. 10. Larsen, Nella—Criticism and interpretation.
I. Kaplan, Carla. II. Title.

PS3523.A7225P37 2006
813'.52—dc22
2006047244

W. W. Norton & Company, Inc., 500 Fifth Avenue, New York,
N.Y. 10110-0017
www.wwnorton.com
W. W. Norton & Company Ltd.
15 Carlisle Street, London W1D 3BS

1 2 3 4 5 6 7 8 9 0

Contents

Introduction:
Nella Larsen's Erotics of Race

Our passion for categorization, life neatly fitted into pegs, has led to unforeseen, paradoxical distress; confusion, a breakdown of meaning. Those categories which are meant to define and control the world for us have boomeranged into chaos; in which limbo we swirl, clutching the straws of our definitions. We find ourselves bound, first without, then within, by the nature of our categorization.
— JAMES BALDWIN, *Notes of a Native Son*

Nella Larsen seems to have experienced ambition and ambivalence in equal measure. So it is interesting to imagine what she would have made of the recent explosion of interest in her writing, reputation, and life. *Quicksand* and *Passing*, her two published novels, were favorably received in 1928 and 1929. But they certainly never generated the celebrity now accorded Larsen as one of the central figures of the African-American, modernist and feminist literary canons. With approximately two hundred scholarly articles and more than fifty dissertations now dedicated to her work,[1] Larsen's status among early twentieth-century black women writers is rivaled only by Zora Neale Hurston's, in spite of Larsen's comparatively slim output and the fact that after 1930 she ceased to publish and dropped out of New York's literary circles altogether.[2] Larsen's writing, and *Passing* especially, is now hailed for helping create modernist psychological interiority, expanding our uses of irony, challenging marriage and middle-class domesticity, complexly interrogating gender, race, and sexual identity, and for redeploying traditional tropes—such as that of the tragic mulatta[3]—with a contemporary and critical twist. Most importantly, Larsen's work is now prized for its portrayal of black, female subjectivity and for its depiction of the social and psychological vertigo caused when identity categories break down. *Passing* offers one of our most chilling pictures of the dangers—*and* the pleasures—of the "chaos" Baldwin describes above.

1. See the Selected Bibliography in this edition for a listing of works focused on *Passing*.
2. See the Chronology included in this edition.
3. For representative samples of this tradition, see "The Tragic Mulatto(a)" section included in this edition.

Larsen came to prominence as the Harlem Renaissance was waning, at the apex of a cultural craze for Harlem that imbued blackness with a specific cultural capital. Like many of her contemporaries, Larsen was anxious to cash in on the fleeting "vogue" for blackness, while, as Langston Hughes put it, "books by Negro authors were [still] being published with much greater frequency and much more publicity than ever before or since in history."[4] "Editors not only welcome us," Larsen remarked in one interview, "they actually seem to be on the lookout for us. They seem eager to give us an opportunity to show ourselves. . . . It may be just a fad on their part, but I think it's an awfully good fad."[5] While the "vogue" opened certain doors, skeptics such as Hughes and Larsen knew that mainstream interest was sure to shift again, and soon. I "had a swell time while it lasted," Hughes remembered. "But," he added, "I thought it wouldn't last long."[6] By 1929, Larsen was already "beginning to feel that the reading public is getting rather bored with Negro books."[7] "I've met a man from Macmillans," she wrote her friend Dorothy Peterson, "who asked me to look out for any Negro stuff and send them to him." She encouraged Peterson to "write some poetry, or something" quickly, before the fad ended.[8]

In *Quicksand*, Larsen had mocked these conditions and the exoticizing interest which asks that black Americans offer a primitive, essential, emotionally authentic antidote to the ills of modernity. "The role that Helga [Crane, the light-skinned protagonist of *Quicksand*] was to play" was clear. She was to "make an impression . . . like a veritable savage . . . [to be] a foreigner, and different," to wear "bright things . . . exotic things." While Helga initially welcomes the attention, being treated as an exotic soon leaves her feeling "like nothing so much as some new and strange species of pet dog being proudly exhibited. . . . A decoration. A curio. A peacock."[9] Such expectations, Larsen was keenly aware, could confront black women at almost any time: "I went to lunch the other day with some people that I know very little (fays) [Harlem slang for whites or ofays]," Larsen wrote to Carl Van Vechten, "[and] in the course of our talk it developed that they

4. Langston Hughes, "When the Negro Was in Vogue," *The Big Sea* (New York: Hill and Wang, 1940), p. 228.
5. Nella Larsen interview with Marion L. Starkey. "Negro Writers Come Into Their Own," unpublished ms. in Alfred A Knopf Collection, Harry Ransom Humanities Research Center, University of Texas, as quoted by George Hutchinson, *In Search of Nella Larsen: A Biography of the Color Line* (Boston: Harvard University Press, 2006), Chapter 18, p. 21. I am grateful to George Hutchinson for sharing his book while it was still in manuscript.
6. Hughes, *The Big Sea*, p. 228.
7. Nella Larsen to Carl Van Vechten, July 28, 1929. The James Weldon Johnson Collection, Beinecke Library, Yale University.
8. Nella Larsen to Dorothy Peterson, Thursday the 21st [1927], James Weldon Johnson Collection, Beinecke Library, Yale University. See pp. 164–65 for the full text of this letter.
9. Nella Larsen, *Quicksand and Passing*, ed. Deborah E. McDowell (New Brunswick: Rutgers University Press, 1986), pp. 68–70; 73. All future references to *Quicksand* are to this edition and will be cited parenthetically.

would have been keenly disappointed had they discovered that I was not born in the jungle of the Virgin Isles, so I entertained them with quaint stories of my childhood in the bush, and my reaction to the tom-tom undertones in jazz. It was a *swell* luncheon."[1]

In *Passing*, Larsen took her assault on racial prejudice even further. Where *Quicksand* destabilizes racial *attitudes*, *Passing* questions the very *idea* of race, exposing it as one of our most powerful—and dangerous—fictions. Discussing the phenomenon of passing with her husband Brian, Irene Redfield poses the question of why passers "always come back."[2] " 'Why?' Irene wanted to know. 'Why?' " " 'If I knew that,' " Brian responds, " 'I'd know what race is' " (38). Brian's question of "what race is," the novel suggests, cannot really be answered. While portraying the absurd contradictions on which our ideas of race are built, *Passing* probes our longing for the very identities that it questions. The novel reminds us of the (sometimes tragic) gap between what we think we believe in and what in fact we want. Race, *Passing* intimates, always lives in that gap.

With the publication of *Quicksand*, in 1928, Larsen had earned enough money to move to a more fashionable location in Harlem's coveted Dunbar apartments[3] and enough recognition to be awarded the Bronze Medal Harmon Award (a prize for "Distinguished Achievement Among Negroes"). Her first novel had created opportunities for her to rethink her career goals[4] and "she wanted to finish the [next] book for Knopf while interest in her work was high enough to secure good sales," biographer Thadious Davis writes.[5] *Passing* appeared on April 26, 1929.[6] A handsomely produced $2.00 book with a black cloth binding and orange trim, the novel was marketed

1. Nella Larsen to Carl Van Vechten, June 14, 1929, Carl Van Vechten Papers, James Weldon Johnson Collection, Beinecke Library, Yale University.
2. While passers may have returned rarely in real life, the passing novel generally turns on the moment of regret, the narrative crisis in which the passer either returns or longs to return to his/her race, underscoring the idea that one *has* a true (and a false) race and also the fallacy of white superiority. For newspaper coverage of actual cases of passing and for representative samples of the passing novel and its "moment of regret," see the "Contemporary Coverage of Passing and Race" and "Selections from Stories and Novels of Passing: 'The Moment of Regret' " included in this edition.
3. Among the well-known black figures who also lived at the Dunbar Apartments were Rudolph Fisher, W. E. B. Du Bois, and Paul and Eslanda Robeson.
4. Larsen had earned a nursing degree in 1915 and worked as a nurse at the Tuskegee Institute, in Alabama, and for the New York City Department of Health. From 1921 to 1926 she worked as a librarian at the Harlem branch of the New York Public Library, now the Schomburg Center for Research in Black Culture. In the 1940's, Larsen returned to nursing, working as a chief nurse Gouverneur Hospital and then as supervisor of nurses for Metropolitan Hospital, both in New York City, until her retirement in September of 1963, just a few months before her death in March of 1964.
5. Thadious Davis, *Nella Larsen: Novelist of the Harlem Renaissance: A Woman's Life Unveiled* (Baton Rouge: Louisiana State University Press, 1994), p. 285.
6. This date is in dispute. Some list the novel's original release date as April 26, others as April 19th. Given that the novel's first New York reviews appear on the 27th and 28th, the 26th seems the more likely date.

with a wraparound blurb from Carl Van Vechten, to whom (along with his wife Fania Marinoff) *Passing* was also dedicated.[7] With a nod to the "vogue" for blackness, Van Vechten's blurb described the novel as "a strangely provocative story, superbly told. The sensational implications of PASSING should make this book one of the most widely discussed on the Spring list."[8]

It was no small thing for Larsen to launch her book with this endorsement from Van Vechten. In 1926, Van Vechten's fifth novel, *Nigger Heaven*, had ignited a firestorm. Having lauded the "wealth of novel, erotic, picturesque material" available to the artist who tackles "the squalor of Negro life, the vice of Negro life," and warned black writers to "write about this exotic material" of Harlem's streets and cabarets before "white authors . . . exploit it until not a drop of vitality remains,"[9] Van Vechten evidently decided to exploit the material himself. *Nigger Heaven* is a fairly predictable story of a sad love affair between a black, female Harlem librarian and her would-be writer lover as they battle racism in New York, against a violent and sometimes sensationalized backdrop of Harlem's nightlife. This backdrop made the novel both controversial and a best-seller, much read in New York circles and even—to Van Vechten's delight—banned in Boston. The title, meant as an ironic metaphor for social segregation (a "nigger heaven" being a segregated balcony in a theater or orchestra hall), occasioned such outrage that many of Van Vechten's harshest critics never, in fact, read the book.[1] W. E. B. Du Bois spoke for many of Van Vechten's detractors (and not a few of Van Vechten's black friends as well)[2] when he complained that Van Vechten had used "cheap melodrama" to portray Harlem as just the "wildly, bar-

---

7. The book's dust jacket treated the novel as Clare Kendry's story, describing her as "the heroine of this novel . . . a beautiful colored girl who crosses the color line into the white world. Her life as a white woman brings her superior advantages of almost every kind, and yet after a time there comes an inexplicable longing to go back to her own people."

8. The publisher's advertisement for the book went further, describing it as "an ASTONISHING and SENSATIONAL novel" and claiming that its subject was "so explosive that for a long time the advisability of its publication was seriously debated."

9. Van Vechten's statement comes from his response to a multimonth symposium in *The Crisis*, entitled "The Negro in Art: How Shall He Be Portrayed?" a symposium that included responses to questions about the artist's social responsibility from W. E. B. Du Bois, Alfred Knopf, Joel Spingarn, Sherwood Anderson, Charles Chesnutt, Countee Cullen, Jessie Fauset, Langston Hughes, Sinclair Lewis, Georgia Douglas Johnson, Julia Peterkin, Walter White, H. L. Mencken, Du Bose Heyward, and others. Van Vechten's response was made all the more ironic by the little-known fact that he was the ghostwriter of the symposium's questions.

1. "Irony is not anything that most Negroes understand," Van Vechten lamented. Interview for Columbia Oral History Project, 1960, as quoted by Nathan Irvin Huggins, *Harlem Renaissance* (New York: Oxford University Press, 1971), p. 113. Langston Hughes agreed, writing in his memoirs that "the strange inability on the part of many of the Negro critics to understand irony, or satire . . . partially explains the phenomenon of that violent outburst of rage that stirred the Negro press for months after the appearance of Carl Van Vechten's *Nigger Heaven*" (*The Big Sea*), p. 268.

2. Countee Cullen, for example, did not speak to Van Vechten for more than a dozen years after the publication of *Nigger Heaven*.

baric drunken orgy" white revelers imagined. For Du Bois this title was not solidarity or irony, but an "affront" and a "blow in the face."[3] Supporters, however, such as James Weldon Johnson, Langston Hughes and Zora Neale Hurston insisted that the book made a "significant and powerful"[4] contribution to race debates. "To say that Carl Van Vechten has harmed Negro creative activities is sheer poppycock," Hughes insisted.[5]

Larsen felt that Van Vechten's black world was more authentic than any yet depicted by blacks.[6] "Its too close, too true," she wrote Van Vechten. "[It's] as if you had undressed the lot of us and turned on strong light. Too, I feel a kind of despair. Why, oh why, couldn't we have done something as big as this for ourselves?"[7] By leading with Van Vechten's blurb and her dedication to him and Marinoff, Larsen was staking her ground as an anticonservative, a modern believer in irony and unconventionality, neither a practitioner of the standard "tragic mulatto" story[8] nor a novelist in the genteel mold of her competitor Jessie Fauset. To any reader familiar with the *Nigger Heaven* controversy, Larsen's dedication signaled an identification with the "dangerous . . . abhorrent . . . compelling . . . arresting . . . mysterious . . . not safe" (20–21; 47) ways of racially ambidextrous characters, an identification that would have been triply reinforced had Larsen not been pressured to drop her original title for the novel—"Nig"—and replace it with *Passing* instead.

The extent to which Larsen was criticizing prevailing racial assumptions, announcing an identification with Clare Kendry ("the character she most admires," as George Hutchinson puts it) and attempting to unsettle her readers, was rarely noted by early reviewers. Fascinated with Larsen's mixed racial heritage (Danish on her mother's side and West Indian on her father's), reviewers writing mostly for white readers take for granted that Irene Redfield's disapproval of Clare Kendry's passing and attempted return to Harlem speaks for the novel as a whole. They pronounced the novel "ade-

3. W. E. B. Du Bois, "Books," *The Crisis* 24 (December 1926): 31–32.
4. James Weldon Johnson, *Opportunity*, October 1926.
5. *The Big Sea*, p. 272.
6. Larsen thought similarly of Gertrude Stein's controversial *Melanctha*. In a letter to Stein (undated), Larsen wrote that "I have talked with our friend Carl Van Vechten about you. Particularly about you and *Melanctha*, which I have read many times. And always I get from it some new thing. A truly great story. I never cease to wonder how you came to write it and just why you and not some one of us should so accurately have caught the spirit of this race of mine." Nella Larsen to Gertrude Stein, no date, James Weldon Johnson Collection, Beinecke Library, Yale University.
7. Nella Larsen to Carl Van Vechten [postmarked August 12, 1926], Carl Van Vechten Papers, The New York Public Library, as quoted by Davis, p. 21. Mary Love, the main character in Van Vechten's novel, was modeled, in part, on Nella Larsen.
8. See The Tragic Mulatto/a section in this edition. The "tragic mulatto" story generally responds to the notorious "one-drop rule" for determining blackness by sentimentally depicting how what Sterling Brown calls this single "drop of midnight" could doom the mulatto American to a "tragic end." *The Negro in American Fiction*, p. 144.

quate,"[9] "interesting,"[1] or "earnest and courageous" but "somewhat short of achievement,"[2] "adroit" in some of its technique if not altogether "convincing,"[3] a "good novel" when it "rises above race categories,"[4] or manages to show that the Negro . . . is, in all vital essentials, no different from the white."[5] Reviewers writing for mostly black readerships, on the other hand, praised the novel. In *The Crisis*, W. E. B. DuBois pronounced *Passing* "one of the finest novels of the year."[6] Alice Dunbar-Nelson called the novel a "masterpiece" of "subtle artistry," "compact and terse . . . a book that will linger."[7] *Opportunity's* reviewer described *Passing* as "a novel of achievement and promise," commending its "economy of words" and "its calm clear handling of a theme which lends itself to murky melodrama."[8] The novel shows, Aubrey Bowser wrote in *The New York Amsterdam News*, that "society makes a fool of itself" when it comes to race.[9] While Bowser is right about society making a fool of itself, he also gets the novel's main message about race exactly wrong, believing that Larsen agrees with him that "a person should be either one thing or the other," when the point of Larsen's pairing of Clare Kendry and Irene Redfield is that fixing identity is not only impossible but also deadly. Larsen's refusal to soft pedal society's race foolishness may account for the novel's relatively unimpressive sales. While Knopf was able to take the novel into a third printing, the print runs were small (under 2,000 copies a run), and both sales and review attention were lackluster beyond New York City.

He never acted like a nigger or a whiteman. That was it. That was what made the folks so mad.

—WILLIAM FAULKNER, *Light in August*

Refusing to act out one's racial identity was particularly risky in the 1920s, with the nation in the grip of especially violent attempts to

9. Margaret Cheney Dawson, "The Color Line," *The New York Herald Tribune Books*, April 28, 1929. See p. 87 in this edition.
1. "M. L. H.," *The Wilson Bulletin* 41, no. 4 (December 1929): 169. See p. 102 in this edition.
2. Anonymous, "The Dilemma of Mixed Race: Another Study of the Color-Line in New York," *The New York Sun*, May 1, 1929. See p. 88 in this edition. See also Esther Hyman's review of *Passing*, pp. 93 in this edition.
3. Anonymous, "Beyond the Color Line," *The New York Times Book Review*, April 28, 1929. See p. 85 in this edition.
4. W. B. Seabrook, "Touch of the Tar-brush," *The Saturday Review of Literature*, May 18, 1929. See p. 91 in this edition.
5. Mary Griffin, "Novel of Race Consciousness," *The Detroit Free Press*, June 23, 1929. See p. 96 in this edition.
6. W. E. B. DuBois, *The Crisis* 36 (July 1929). See p. 97 in this edition.
7. Alice Dunbar-Nelson, "As in a Looking Glass," *The Washington Eagle*, May 3, 1929. See p. 90 in this edition.
8. Mary Fleming Labaree, *Opportunity*, 7 (August 1929). See p. 99 in this edition.
9. Aubrey Bowser, "The Cat Came Back," *The New York Amsterdam News*, June 5, 1929. See p. 94 in this edition. Bowser reads Clare Kendry simply as "despicable," taking for granted both that Irene's view is reliable and that she speaks for Larsen.

regulate social and racial "types." While other sexual and social taboos were falling by the wayside in this famously rebellious time, fixed racial lines were being drawn more sharply than at any other period of American history. Never before or since has the color line been treated with such hysteria. So-called "Americanization" organizations were hell-bent on holding people to strict racial categories and extending segregation's legal and economic reach by making all movement across racial lines seem both undesirable and unnatural. Groups like the American Legion proclaimed the ideal of an all-white, non-immigrant nation. "We want and need every One Hundred Per Cent American. And to hell with the rest of them," American Legion Commander Frederic Galbraith trumpeted. Undergirded by dozens of anti-ethnic, antimiscegenation, and anti-immigration laws passed during the decade, naturalization ideology fed the membership rolls of the Klan and the American Legion, which reached their zenith with appeals to racial purity. More lynchings were perpetrated in the Twenties than at any other time (51 in 1922 alone).[1]

If you were sitting in your kitchen on an autumn day in 1925, drinking coffee and casually leafing through *The New York Times*, the paper would offer a high-spirited America proud of its prosperity. You would find ample examples of the Twenties as it has so often been described: forward-looking, energetic, a bit wild and reckless in its modernizing, but successful and sure-footed. But that same *New York Times* on that same fall day could also have shown you a different, darker Twenties, revealing a nation obsessed with maintaining race and ethnic lines at any and all costs.

The phenomenon of passing was perceived to increase dramatically in the Twenties, generating both fascination and terror. Some papers claimed that 5,000 black people a year were "crossing the color line" to join the "white fold,"[2] while others put the number much higher, as high as 75,000 people a day in Philadelphia alone.[3] Charles S. Johnson, the sociologist, founding editor of *Opportunity* and later President of Fisk, calculated that 355,000 blacks had passed between 1900 and 1920.[4] Such reports fueled the already widespread anxiety that economic and social factors were conspiring to push blacks across "the color line" and that such crossings were, increasingly, difficult to detect. The matter of knowing "when . . . a

1. On modernism's relationship to this racial ideology see also my "Undesirable Desire: Citizenship and Romance in Modern American Fiction," *Modern Fiction Studies* 43, no. 1 (Spring 1997).
2. Emilie Hahn, "Crossing the Color Line," *New York World*, July 28, 1929. See p. 117 in this edition.
3. "75,000 Pass in Philadelphia Every Day," *The Afro-American*, December 19, 1931. See p. 123 in this edition.
4. Editorial, *Opportunity* 3, no. 34 (October 1925): 291, as quoted by Werner Sollors, *Neither Black Nor White, Yet Both: Thematic Explorations of Interracial Literature* (New York: Oxford University Press, 1997), p. 281.

Caucasian [is] not a Caucasian" was "a conundrum which is no joke," as one reporter put it.[5]

Alongside numerous editorials suggesting how to stop passers—by exposing them or removing "the prime [economic] incentive that actuates" passing[6]—were a spate of theories about how to detect blackness and rout out the passers.[7] Larsen both mocks such theories and suggests that if they had any merit, and if there were any genuine differences between black and whites, reliable detection would be the province of blacks alone, whites being either too foolish or too racially illiterate to detect difference. When Irene, for example, first wonders if she has been found out, passing at the rooftop café of the Drayton Hotel, she determines that her fears are "Absurd! Impossible!" because "white people were so stupid about such things for all that they usually asserted that they were able to tell; and by the most ridiculous means, fingernails, palms of hands, shapes of ears, teeth, and other equally silly rot" (11). Even Hugh Wentworth, modeled on Van Vechten, finds it impossible to "tell the sheep from the goats" (55). Whether the problem is that there is no difference or, instead, that he cannot discern it, is suspended by Irene's insistence that whatever marks racial difference, while "not definite or tangible" (55), does exist. It is, she tells Wentworth, "just—just something. A thing that couldn't be registered" but which blacks, such as herself, can "pick" in "less than five minutes" (56). This idea that differences are real even when they cannot "be registered" goes to the heart of the nation's historic "one-drop rule" of hypo-descent, which the 1920 census had reinforced and underscored by dropping the category "mulatto" and insisting that every American "be one thing or the other," black or white. Such moves made the job of policing "the color line" both more urgent and more difficult.

Failures to police "the line," Americans were warned, could engender an array of horrors—from the danger of lynching one's own brother,[8] to apparent whites giving birth to black infants, the "hellish" fear of "reversion" that Gertrude Martin refers to in Passing: "it might go way back and turn out dark no matter what colour the father and mother are. . . . It's awful the way it skips generations and then pops out" (26).[9]

5. "When Is a Caucasion Not a Caucasian?" The Independent 70 (March 2, 1911): 478. See p. 105 in this edition.
6. Louis Fremont Baldwin, From Negro to Caucasian, Or How the Ethiopian Is Changing His Skin (San Francisco: Pilot Publishing Company, 1929), p. 4. See p. 112 in this edition.
7. For an excellent history of such theories of detection, see "The Bluish Tinge in the Half-moon; or, Fingernails as Racial Sign," and "Passing: or Sacrificing a Parvenu," in Sollors, pp. 143–61 and 246–84.
8. See "Careful Lyncher! He May Be Your Brother," The Philadelphia Tribune, January 21, 1932, included in this edition, p. 124.
9. On this fear of racial "reversion" see Caleb Johnson, "Crossing the Color Line" on p. 121 in this edition. See also Sollors, "Natus AEthiopus/ Natus Albus," pp. 48–77.

In this context, the formulaic plot of the passing story with its inevitable attempt, as Brian puts it, to "come back,"[1] could play multiple roles. On the one hand, the longing to return could signal racial pride and prove that economic advantage and nothing else motivates such crossings. "A good many colored folks that try to be white find that it isn't as pleasant as they imagined in would be," Booker T. Washington is reported to have remarked. "White folks don't really have a good time, from the Negro point of view. They lack the laughing, boisterous sociability which the Negro enjoys."[2] On the other hand, the moment of regret might have gone some distance towards alleviating national anxieties over tens of thousands of undetectable passers. While they might get across "the line" undetected, readers could be reassured that eventually, like Clare Kendry, they would "always" at least try to "go back."

As any casual reader of 1920's newspapers would know, extraordinary measures were taken throughout the decade, nonetheless, to try to keep people from crossing racial lines in any way. In a round-up of national news in *The New York Times*, for example, a reader might find a short paragraph on the ongoing trial of Ossian Sweet, a Detroit black man terrorized by a white mob bent on forcing his family to move out of their all-white neighborhood.[3] In the sports and editorial pages were jubilant articles proclaiming racial justice in the federal government's persecution of black heavyweight champion Jack Johnson, whose marriage to a white woman was prosecuted under the Mann Act and viewed by the press as either kidnap or coercion, since it was self-evident to white reporters that no white woman would have chosen a black man of her own free will. Extensive local coverage was even given to white Edith Sproul's marriage to black Sidney Peterson (brother of Larsen's friend, Dorothy), although neither of the principals was a celebrity. The biracial marriage of George Schuyler and white Texas heiress Josephine Cogdell—which was to become nationally famous in the 1930's—was a carefully guarded secret in the 1920s, and Cogdell confined herself almost exclusively to Harlem in that decade, on the grounds that a white woman married to a black man (even secretly) would be unsafe elsewhere in the country.[4] But dominating the front pages, in both black and white papers, as Larsen reminds her readers, was the ever present, always

---

1. As Robert Bone puts it, "the invariable outcome [of passing] . . . is disillusionment with life on the other side . . . a new appreciation of racial values, and an irresistible longing to return to the Negro community" *The Negro Novel in America* (New Haven: Yale University Press, 1958), p. 98. For examples of this ubiquitous moment of regret and longing to return, see the "Selected Writings about Passing" included in this edition.
2. As quoted by Caleb Johnson, "Crossing the Color Line."
3. Where the Sweet case was buried towards the back of white newspapers, it shared the front pages of black newspapers with the Rhinelander and Johnson cases.
4. See Kathryn Talalay, *Composition in Black and White: The Life of Philippa Schuyler* (New York: Oxford University Press, 1995).

sensationalized Rhinelander case. Pressured by his family, millionaire Leonard "Kip" Rhinelander had filed an annulment suit to end his marriage to Alice Jones, on the grounds that she had deceived him into believing she was white. Jones was forced to endure seeing her name dragged through "the sewer and the slime"[5] with her love letters to Kip read out in court as evidence that she had seduced a poor hapless white boy.

Such violations, and this trial was lousy with them, served to remind black women across the nation of the dangers of crossing race lines. At one point in the trial, Alice Jones Rhinelander, at this time one of the wealthiest women in the nation, was forced to strip naked to the waist in court so the jury could draw their own conclusions about whether or not Rhinelander could have been deceived about Alice's "true" race. This was then—as it would still be today—an almost unthinkable humiliation, and while Alice Jones did win her legal case, her marriage and reputation were both ruined. She was hounded by groups like the Klan, which threatened violence and revenge. Newspaper readers in 1925 would readily have drawn the obvious conclusion: that this was the treatment black women, or even women *suspected* of being black, should expect. Hence, Larsen's allusion to this trial—"what if Bellew should divorce Clare? Could he? There was the Rhinelander case" (71)—foreshadows not merely a possible end to Clare's marriage but her ruination and humiliation as well.

The kind of racial hysteria, violence, and humiliation that Larsen marks with her reference to the Rhinelander case led to a natural turning inward in many black communities and some unsurprising waning of black interest in integration. Instead, many black Harlem intellectuals urged notions of racial allegiance and race loyalty which insisted that the races were, and should remain, fundamentally distinct. Citing "incompatible personalities, irreconcilable ideals, and different grades of culture," W. E. B. Du Bois, for example, discouraged intermarriage. In many Harlem circles, former debates over the nature of race were replaced by fierce calls to racial loyalty. Alain Locke, one of the Harlem Renaissance's most important race theorists and the editor of the influential volume *The New Negro*, advocated "racial solidarity" and what he called "the admirable principle of loyalty." According to Locke, "pride in itself is race pride, and race pride seems a rather different loyalty from the larger loyalty to the joint or common civilization."[6] Crossing race lines under such social conditions, many blacks argued, was self-hating and dangerous at best. It was considered treasonous at worst.

5. "Davis Flays Kip's Lawyer in Plea for Alice," *The Chicago Defender*, December 5, 1925.
6. Alain Leroy Locke, *Race Contacts and Interracial Relations: Lectures on the Theory and Practice of Race*, ed. Jeffrey C. Stewart (Washington, D.C.: Howard University Press, 1992), pp. 95, 96–97). Also quoted in Hutchinson, pp. 81–82.

The passing narrative could underscore this ethic of allegiance and loyalty by representing the moment of regret—the passer's awareness that the privileges and benefits of whiteness are nothing but a "mess of pottage"[7]—as an ethical and moral crisis, a growing consciousness of "crossing the line" as betrayal. Langston Hughes's short story "Passing," for example, works just this way. It begins with a son's apology for cutting his own mother. "Dear Ma," he writes, "I felt like a dog, passing you downtown last night and not speaking to you. You were great, though. Didn't give a sign that you knew me."[8] Numerous passing narratives weigh the benefits of passing against this particular moral cost. Reporting the case of a mother whose passing daughter's neglect does her in—"the doctor said it was her [the mother's] heart. It was. Not a disease—a broken heart"—The Chicago Whip concludes that it does not "pay to 'pass.' "[9]

But in Clare Kendry's case, passing, which clearly does not "pay," is treated as morally complex, not just a mistake or a betrayal. Clare initially asserts that "all things considered . . . it's even worth the price" (20). But as her "pale life" presses on her, her "longing" for blackness grows into a "wild desire," "an ache, a pain that never ceases" (7). And she comes to feel that Irene's "way" of staying with her own people "may be the wiser and infinitely happier one" (34). Clare's change of heart, however, unlike that of virtually every other passer in the tradition, is not the outcome of a crisis of conscience. Clare regrets passing because she desperately misses black folks. To Clare's immense frustration, Irene misreads this passion for blackness as a mere "hankering." And Clare responds that "you don't know, you can't realize how I want to see Negroes, to be with them again, to talk with them, to hear them laugh," (51), language which—as I discuss later—is echoed not only in Quicksand but also in Larsen's own correspondence. To say that Clare changes her mind is not to say that she is represented as either racially unethical or immoral, although those are the terms she uses in describing herself to Irene as "without any proper morals or sense of duty" (58). In fact, Larsen complicates Clare's racial ethics, first, by having all judgments of Clare rendered via Irene's unreliable narration, and, second, by weaving together the novel's racial and sexual plots in ways that complicate all judgment.

In Irene's view, Clare is very much at fault, racially. From the very beginning of the novel, Irene judges Clare as having "no allegiance" and being "selfish, and cold, and hard" (6). Clare, she insists repeatedly,

7. James Weldon Johnson, The Autobiography of an Ex-Colored Man (New York: Dover, 1995), p. 100.
8. Langston Hughes, "Passing," The Ways of White Folks (New York: Vintage, 1990). See p. 281 in this edition.
9. Don Pierson, "Does It Pay to 'Pass?' " The Chicago Whip, August 20, 1927. See p. 107 in this edition.

"cared [not] at all about the race" nor had any "great, or even real affection" for it. "No, Clare Kendry cared nothing for the race. She only belonged to it," Irene decides (36). Believing irrevocably in her own infallible "instinctive loyalty" to [her] race (71), Irene finds it "completely sardonic" (69) that she cannot forego that responsibility towards someone she's convinced has none of it:

> The sardony of it! She couldn't betray Clare, couldn't even run the risk of appearing to defend a people that were being maligned, for fear that that defence might in some infinitesimal degree lead the way to final discovery of her secret. She had to Clare Kendry a duty. She was bound to her by those very ties of race, which, for all her repudiation of them, Clare had been unable to completely sever (36).

From the first, however, we see that even as she is misjudging Clare as "selfish, and cold, and hard," Irene is remembering, if she will only acknowledge it, Clare's fierce racial "allegiance" and personal "loyalty" to fellow blacks. "Driven to anger," Irene recalls, Clare "would fight with a ferocity and impetuousness that disregarded or forgot any danger, superior strength, numbers, or other unfavourable circumstances. How savagely she had clawed those boys the day they hooted her [black] parent and sung a derisive rhyme" (6). The stakes are too high for Irene to admit to herself that Clare, not she, is the real "race woman," with genuine racial affection and loyalty. To admit as much would be to recognize how complex allegiance can be, riven with contradiction and even seeming betrayal. To admit Clare's loyalties and longings would also be to face, as Irene is wholly unprepared to do, her own lack of feeling: "[perhaps] the woman before her was yet capable of heights and depths of feeling that she, Irene Redfield, had never known. Indeed, never cared to know. The thought, the suspicion, was gone as quickly as it had come" (47). Nor does Irene want to admit her own hypocrisy, as someone who passes for convenience.[1]

Clare is right to scoff at what Irene considers the "right thing" (46) or the "safe" thing to do in terms of race. It is Irene's racial ideology, not Clare's, which is truly problematic. More than problematic, Irene—race woman, devotee of "security," fixity, and a world of black and white, right and wrong—proves deadly. Nothing is worse, as it turns out, than the kind of race "loyalty" Irene adheres to, one that can buck no gray areas, no complications, no messy desires, no instabilities, slippages, or contradictions, a "loyalty" which insists, in Bowser's words, that people be "either one thing or the other."[2]

Larsen condemns Irene's racial ideology, in part, by having Irene's

---

1. As did Larsen on occasion. See her letter to Carl Van Vechten, May 14, 1932, included in this edition, p. 170.
2. See p. 94 in this edition.

language mimic "to a surprising degree" the discourse of some of the most notorious white racists of her day. In her insistence that race is real and that one is "bound" to it, Irene's language resonates not as much with the "race men" of the Harlem Renaissance like Locke and DuBois, but rather, with racist men like Lothrop Stoddard, author of *The Rising Tide of Color against White World Supremacy*, follower of scientific racist and eugenecist Madison Grant, and an architect of a range of racist policies. At the Negro Welfare League dance, especially, in conversation with Hugh Wentworth, Irene sounds peculiarly like Stoddard. Where Irene maintains that race is distinguished by things "that couldn't be registered," by things "not definite or tangible," which nevertheless "bound" (56; 55) one to racial "loyalty," Stoddard's well-known view was that while racial "characteristics" and "endowment" were "elusive of definition" and "difficult to describe" there were, nonetheless, "definite" distinctions which bound one to "racial duty."[3] If nothing else raises suspicions about Irene's credibility, this should certainly do so.

In the context of 1920's race debates especially, Larsen's nuanced handling of Clare's passing and Irene's "allegiance" demonstrates that ideologies which conceptualize race as an ethics, whether originating in black pride or white racism, vary enormously, depending, in large part, upon whether they attempt an answer to Brian's question of "what race is." Those who are determined to do so and who believe that this question can be answered are most likely to increase the violence that surrounds racial categorization.

But this does not mean that all race loyalty must be seen either as immoral or as equally so. Larsen advocates a very specific form of race loyalty while at the same time challenging the idea that we should apply ethics or morals to racial allegiance. Her loyalty is distinguished, in part, by a steadfast refusal to answer Brian's question and specify absolutely to what one's loyalty might be sworn. *Passing* destabilizes available ideas of race but at the same time is animated by the very race fascinations and longings it seems designed to critique. Larsen accomplishes this, in large measure, by having Clare and Irene be both "strangers . . . in their racial consciousness" (44) and, at the same time, attracted to each other and, thereby, to one another's competing conceptions of race. As Biman Basu writes, "racial transgression is itself eroticized . . . the political economy of passing cannot be separated from its economy of desire."[4] Hence, an erotics of race takes the place of the ethics of race that we find in most other passing stories.

3. Lothrop Stoddard, *The Rising Tide of Color against White World Supremacy* (New York: Scribner's, 1920), pp. xiv, 276.
4. Biman Basu, "Hybrid Embodiment and an Ethics of Masochism: Nella Larsen's *Passing* and Sherley Anne Williams's *Dessa Rose*," *African American Review* 36, no. 3 (Fall 2002): 383–401.

Irene's response to Clare's "appealing" and "seductive" "way," is, as Deborah McDowell has compellingly argued,[5] an "onrush of affectionate feeling" for the "lovely," "beautiful," "incredibly beautiful," "tempting," arresting," "languorous," "tortured loveliness" she believes she disapproves of. Irene's powerful erotic response to Clare allows also a positive response to unfixed, uncategorizable racial identity—"I'm sorry, but just at the minute I can't seem to place you" (12)—which Irene otherwise cannot, or will not, allow herself to approve. By the same token, Clare's "longing to be with you again, as I have never longed for anything before," (7) allows Clare, who eschews all categories, received ideologies, and fixed identities, to embrace what she has repudiated and renounced. If Larsen's ironization of Irene's reliability has undercut her cut-and-dried views, Clare's "wild desire" for the kind of blackness Irene embodies restores some of its potential legitimacy, or at least its desirability. Through the growing attraction between Irene and Clare, Larsen can depict characters who long for things they do not believe in and who believe in things which they find they do not want. The novel's dynamics of contradictory but compelling desire unmask racial ethics as foundationless.

The racial erotic that Larsen creates in *Passing* allows her to stand back from every available position on race. In this context, her choice of an epigraph for the novel is particularly salient. One of the most well-known poems of the Harlem Renaissance, Countee Cullen's "Heritage,"[6] like *Passing*, refuses to answer Brian's question of "what race is" either in favor of a definite and tangible essence or a mere social construction, a race debate that raged throughout the Harlem Renaissance. Nor does it accept the solution to that dilemma so often adopted by other Harlem Renaissance writers. For many, conceiving of race as an ethics suspended the debate over racial ontology by shifting the ground towards practice. Whatever race might be, the argument went, one had a moral obligation to one's "own" people. "Heritage," however, persistently raises ethical questions only to leave them, as does *Passing*, decidedly unresolved. Many Harlem Renaissance race writings simultaneously argue for both an essentialist and a constructionist position. But "Heritage" winks at that simultaneity. Unable to decide, finally, whether his remote African heritage endows him with tangible difference or is instead a mere idea, "a book one thumbs/Listlessly, till slumber comes," the speaker struggles for "peace" and wonders if consciously playing "a double part" might answer to his "need" to resolve his identity. Having no choice but to career between contrary identity positions, the speaker considers embracing the contradictions of his being and making his lack of choice a choice in itself.

What Cullen's speaker considers but cannot quite bring himself to do, Larsen's novel advances, without seeming to make an argument and without any of the didacticism so common to other "race novels" of the period. *Passing* refuses essentialism, stands back from social constructionism, and is persistently critical of the idea that a racial ethic can ever either appropriately adjudicate between these positions or manage to sidestep them. If it is tragic that Clare and Irene cannot choose one another and if it is their flirtation with such a choice which engenders the novel's tragic ending, choice itself is thereby thematized. While no racial *positions* are unequivocally endorsed in this novel, racial *choices*—if they are based on genuine longings and desires rather than on conventionalized moral attitudes—do provide some of the only positive moments this novel is willing to offer.

Interestingly enough, one of the narratives to most closely approximate Larsen's complex representation of racial choice—of race *as* choice—is a story of Jessie Fauset's, the writer from whom Larsen often tried hardest to differentiate herself. Fauset's "The Sleeper Wakes" features the blond, blue-eyed Amy, left with a middle-class black family when she is five years old, a family who is unable to tell her with certainty whether she is "white or colored" (Fauset, 287).[7] At seventeen, Amy runs away to join the white world, just as a young man in another type of story might run off to join the circus. Not until she identifies with her husband's black servant, however, does Amy both come to feel "I *am* colored" (Fauset, 296) and to see the white world for the cold, hard, insolent, acquisitive place it is. "Perhaps there *was* some root," Amy thinks, "some racial distinction" between blacks and whites (Fauset, 305). The story's turning point is Amy's "decision" (Fauset, 305) to leave whiteness behind. "She wanted to be colored, she hoped she was colored" (Fauset, 305) she maintains, as she gives in to the "stifled hidden longing" for blackness that she had long suppressed.

This "longing" for blackness resonates with Larsen's representation of Clare Kendry. And like Fauset, Larsen depicts the full realization of that longing as her story's turning point. Larsen also represented that longing in striking terms in *Quicksand*. Helga Crane initially refuses to identify with the most sensationalized notions of racial essence, as we see in a nightclub scene rich with allusions to Cullen's "Heritage":

> . . . they danced, ambling lazily . . . or violently twisting their
> bodies, like whirling leaves . . . shaking themselves ecstatically

7. This story is included in full on p. 285 in this edition.

to a thumping of unseen tomtoms. . . . She was drugged, lifted, sustained, by the extraordinary music, blown out, ripped out, beaten out . . . and when the music died, she dragged herself back to the present with a conscious effort; and a shameful certainty that not only had she been in the jungle, but that she had enjoyed it . . . she hardened her determination. . . . She wasn't, she told herself, a jungle creature.[8]

But soon thereafter, living abroad, Helga finds herself "homesick . . . [for] her people."[9] Her "longing heart" gives in to "the irresistible ties of race"[1] and she experiences a moment of revelation, "knowledge of almost sacred importance,"[2] as she finds herself identifying with the black father who had abandoned her family:

> For the first time Helga Crane felt sympathy rather than contempt and hatred for that father, who so often and so angrily she had blamed for his desertions of her mother. She understood, now, his rejection, his repudiation, of the formal calm her mother had represented. She understood his yearning, his intolerable need for the inexhaustible humor and the incessant hope of his own kind, his need for those things, not material, indigenous to all Negro environments. . . . And as she attended [white] parties, the theater, the opera, and mingled with [white] people on the streets, when she longed for brown laughing ones, she was able to forgive him . . . [and] she found her thoughts straying with increasing frequency to . . . Harlem, its dirty streets, swollen now, in the warmer weather, with dark, gay humanity . . . why couldn't she have two lives.[3]

This passage is particularly poignant in light of what we now know of Larsen's own biography, including her black father's abandonment of the family, her white mother's remarriage to a white man, and her mother's abandonment, in turn, of her too-dark daughter. And so it should not be surprising that her character's longing for blackness is echoed in Larsen's own correspondence. In a letter to Gertrude Stein, for example, Larsen writes: "I've got a nostalgia, a yen to see the teeming streets of Harlem and hear some real laughter."[4] Larsen's case against judging Clare's passing stands on its own in the novel. But within the larger context of writings such as these and race debates in Harlem, it is a particularly striking and bold argument.

8. Nella Larsen, *Quicksand and Passing*, p. 59.
9. Ibid., pp. 92, 95.
1. Ibid., p. 92.
2. Ibid., p. 93.
3. Ibid., pp. 92–93.
4. Nella Larsen to Gertrude Stein, January 26, 1931, James Weldon Johnson Collection, Beinecke Library, Yale University. See p. 169. in this edition.

Larsen's use of passing, then, while it may seem familiar, is both original and complex. Rather than a trope that reinforces an ethics of race, as passing usually does, Larsen uses passing to critique a tradition of treating racial "allegiance" as a moral dilemma rather than the matter of preference, longing, and choice that Larsen imagines it could be. Passing, as Claudia Mills notes, is particularly useful for the creation of morality tales. "In circumstances of oppression," Mills writes, "a refusal to pass is commendably courageous, and perhaps passing is condemnably cowardly."[5] But by taking the passing trope out of the moral realm altogether, Larsen rewrites the tradition from the ground up, making it not only more useful to black *women*, but making it more useful to a modern, even postmodern, conception of identity as well. Had Larsen used passing either to answer Brian's question or to lionize some and condemn others, her novel might have proved more accessible to a contemporary audience. It would, however, not have received the enormous attention from scholars that it now invites.

Contemporary scholarship on passing, much of which has at least touched on this novel, generally remains divided. There are those who see passing as a "radical and transgressive practice"[6] that demonstrates the instability and fictionality of race and destabilizes or "wreaks havoc"[7] on identity categories. Hence, Paul Gilroy argues that passing puts "rooted identity . . . that most precious commodity . . . in grave jeopardy."[8] And as Juda Bennett puts it, "all passing stories question the meaning of race."[9] On the other hand, there are those who believe that passing reinforces identity categories by suggesting that there are meaningfully racialized states of being to pass *between* and, thus, that passing is "implicated in the very discourse" it critiques.[1] As Kate Baldwin puts it, "passing works to uphold the very categories it would seek to sever."[2] By using both Irene and Clare and by enmeshing them in mutual desire, Larsen's passing refuses to signify on either side of this debate, instead taking the debate itself as its subject to scrutinize and interrogate. Larsen's passing, thus, neither "destabilizes" race nor "upholds" it. Nor does it dismantle race. Passing, in Larsen's hands, is best described as a performative

---

5. Claudia Mills, " 'Passing': The Ethics of Pretending to Be What You Are Not," *Social Theory and Practice* 25, no. 1 (Spring 1999): 48.
6. Sara Ahmed, " 'She'll Wake Up One of These Days and Find She's Turned into a Nigger': Passing through Hybridity," *Theory, Culture, and Society* 16, no. 2 (1999): 90.
7. Maria Carla Sanchez, ed., *Passing: Identity and Interpretation in Sexuality, Race, and Religion* (New York: NYU Press, 2001), p. 2.
8. Paul Gilroy, *Against Race: Imagining Political Culture beyond the Color Line* (Cambridge: Harvard University Press, 2000), p. 105.
9. Juda Bennett, *The Passing Figure: Racial Confusion in Modern American Literature* (New York: Peter Lang, 1996), p. 25.
1. Ahmed, p. 89.
2. Kate Baldwin, "The Recurring Conditions of Nella Larsen's *Passing*," *Theory@Buffalo* 4 (1998): 52. See p. 463 in this edition.

which "poisons"[3] race, rendering all available conceptions of it incoherent and, in the words of Irene Redfield, "Absurd," "Impossible," and "ridiculous."

Given the complexity and contemporaneity of Larsen's view of race, it is not surprising that such rich critical attention now focuses on *Passing*. This volume is intended to provide readers with a sense of that criticism and also to help them situate Larsen's achievement in an historical and cultural context.

Among the many issues taken up by current critics of this novel are questions of whether *Passing* is principally a story of race, or sex, or class. The reader interested in that question might want to compare Deborah McDowell's essay to Jennifer Brody's, for example. Another critical issue covered by the selections in this volume is the question of how to read the ending, whether or not Larsen depicts Irene as directly responsible for the novel's tragic outcome. The Davis and McDowell essays included below both weigh in on this question. Some of the essays included here consider the novel in relationship to historical events of the day, such as the Rhinelander case, as do the selections by Mark Madigan and Miriam Thaggert. Others, such as the essays by Baldwin, duCille, Rottenberg, Wald, and Wall, consider how Larsen uses and alters the trope of passing. The homoerotic subplot of the novel is taken up by many of the critics included here, and special attention is given to this topic by Butler and McDowell. Larsen has often been called, in Mary Helen Washington's words, a "mystery." Her biography has proved particularly contentious, with three competing versions of her life currently available. Included in this edition are essays by Larsen's two principal biographers, Thadious Davis and George Hutchinson, and perhaps, through them, readers can grasp something of the nature of the quarrel over her life. Readers interested in situating Larsen's work in its larger literary history will find useful materials in the following sections: "The Tragic Mulatto(a)," "Selections from Stories and Novels of Passing: 'The Moment of Regret,'" and "Selected Writings from the Harlem Renaissance." Those interested in historical backgrounds will find the "Contemporary Coverage of Passing and Race" and "The Rhinelander/Jones Case" sections especially useful. Those interested in Nella Larsen's historical reception will want to make use of the "Reviews" section, and those interested in her life will find biographical materials and a selection of her letters under

---

3. See Judith Butler's *Gender Trouble: Feminism and the Subversion of Identity* (New York: Routledge, 1990).

"About Nella Larsen." As this volume goes to press, there are no doubt more articles, book chapters, and dissertations being written about Nella Larsen and *Passing*. The bibliography for this volume includes those written up to this time of which the bibliographers and the editor were able to locate copies.

Acknowledgments

I would like to acknowledge and thank the many extraordinary scholars who have done exceptional work on Nella Larsen and her writing; critical recuperation is a collaboration of many generations, and we who benefit from reconfigured canons have much to appreciate. I am especially grateful to Deborah McDowell for opening up so many of our readings of this text and to Thadious Davis and George Hutchinson for bringing Nella Larsen back to life. I would also like to thank George Hutchinson for kindly sharing Larsen documents with me and for his generosity one hot August day at the Beinecke.

For assisting in the preparation of this volume by providing various kinds of support, both material and moral, I am grateful to the Beinecke Library, my wonderful agent Brettne Bloom, the Dorothy and Lewis B. Cullman Center for Scholars and Writers of the New York Public Library, the Guggenheim Foundation, Amy Kaplan, Clair Kaplan, Rosalyn Kaplan, Bernard Kaplan, Kathleen McHugh, Marilyn Neimark, Carla Peterson, Ramón Saldívar, Diana Lachatanere and the rest of the staff at The Schomburg Center for Research in Black Culture, Alisa Solomon, Thomas Tanselle of the Guggenheim Foundation, B. Kaye Watson, and all of the students at Yale, NYU, and USC with whom I've discussed this novel over the years. I particularly thank my beloved significant adversary Steve Larsen, for being himself.

I am grateful to former Deans Beth Meyerowitz and Joseph Aoun at the University of Southern California for providing research support and, at Northeastern University, to President Joseph Aoun, Provost Ahmed Abdelal, Professor Mary Loeffelholz and, especially, Dean James R. Stellar, who did all they could to see that this volume did not suffer too much in the transition from Los Angeles to Boston.

At Norton I was unbelievably lucky to work with Kathryn Talalay and Carol Bemis—they were the conscientious, insightful, fun, and patient editors whom writers dream about. I also thank Brian Baker and the rest of the staff at Norton.

This volume could not have been completed without the fine work, persistent digging, and consistent good spirits of my three top-notch research assistants: Ruth Blandon, Lucia Hodgson, and Emily Zietlow. Hania Musiol is also to be thanked for coming on board at the end to proofread.

A Note On the Text

Originally titled "Nig," the novel's title was changed to *Passing* prior to publication. It is unknown whether this change was made at the publisher's behest or Larsen's. Knopf printed three editions of the novel, which sold some 3,000–4,000 copies in 1929. The text of this edition is based on the first printing, which included the final paragraph. The third printing of the novel omitted this paragraph and it has, consequently, been omitted in many subsequent reprintings of the novel. However, since it is unknown whether the paragraph was dropped at Larsen's request or as a printer's error, the paragraph is included here, as it originally appeared. Larsen's original spelling and punctuation have been retained throughout this text.

The Text of
PASSING

for
Carl Van Vechten
and
Fania Marinoff[1]

1. Writer, music critic, and photographer Carl Van Vechten (1886–1964) and actress Fania Marinoff (1887–1972) were two of Larsen's best friends. Van Vechten and Marinoff were known as "honorary Negroes" for their support of the Harlem Renaissance. Because of their controversial status as white patrons and especially because of the controversy generated by Van Vechten's 1926 novel *Nigger Heaven*, dedicating her novel to Van Vechten and Marinoff was a bold move on Larsen's part. *Passing* was originally titled "Nig," partly in reference to *Nigger Heaven*, but the title was changed prior to publication. The Hugh Wentworth character in *Passing* is partly modeled on Van Vechten and his wife, Bianca, on Van Vechten's wife, Marinoff. "I think you're the grandest friend that I've ever had," Larsen once wrote in a letter to Van Vechten.

One three centuries removed
From the scenes his fathers loved,
Spicy grove, cinnamon tree,
What is Africa to me?
—COUNTÉE CULLEN[2]

2. See p. 308 in this edition for complete version of Countee Cullen's (1903–1946) poem "Heritage." "Heritage" was published in Cullen's first published volume of poetry, *Color*, which appeared in 1925.

PART ONE: ENCOUNTER

One

It was the last letter in Irene Redfield's little pile of morning mail. After her other ordinary and clearly directed letters the long envelope of thin Italian paper with its almost illegible scrawl seemed out of place and alien. And there was, too, something mysterious and slightly furtive about it. A thin sly thing which bore no return address to betray the sender. Not that she hadn't immediately known who its sender was. Some two years ago she had one very like it in outward appearance. Furtive, but yet in some peculiar, determined way a little flaunting. Purple[3] ink. Foreign paper[4] of extraordinary size.

It had been, Irene noted, postmarked in New York the day before. Her brows came together in a tiny frown. The frown, however, was more from perplexity than from annoyance; though there was in her thoughts an element of both. She was wholly unable to comprehend such an attitude towards danger as she was sure the letter's contents would reveal; and she disliked the idea of opening and reading it.

This, she reflected, was of a piece with all that she knew of Clare Kendry. Stepping always on the edge of danger. Always aware, but not drawing back or turning aside. Certainly not because of any alarms or feeling of outrage on the part of others.

And for a swift moment Irene Redfield seemed to see a pale small girl sitting on a ragged blue sofa, sewing pieces of bright red cloth together, while her drunken father, a tall, powerfully built man, raged threateningly up and down the shabby room, bellowing curses and making spasmodic lunges at her which were not the less frightening because they were, for the most part, ineffectual. Sometimes he did manage to reach her. But only the fact that the child had edged herself and her poor sewing over to the farthermost corner of the sofa suggested that she was in any way perturbed by this menace to herself and her work.

Clare had known well enough that it was unsafe to take a portion of the dollar that was her weekly wage for the doing of many errands for the dressmaker who lived on the top floor of the building of which

3. Reflecting on decades of admonishments to black women to wear drab colors such as blue, brown, and grey, Helga Crane of Larsen's *Quicksand* insists on surrounding herself with brighter, more exotic colors and wonders why "didn't someone write *A Plea for Color*." Alice Walker's *The Color Purple* takes its title from this long-running debate over which colors are fitting for black women.
4. Carl Van Vechten was well known for his expensive and extravagant foreign writing papers, many of which were also oversized. Hence this reference may have been a semi-private joke intended for Van Vechten and Marinoff, who were both frequent correspondents of Larsen's.

Bob Kendry was janitor. But that knowledge had not deterred her. She wanted to go to her Sunday school's picnic, and she had made up her mind to wear a new dress. So, in spite of certain unpleasantness and possible danger, she had taken the money to buy the material for that pathetic little red frock.

There had been, even in those days, nothing sacrificial in Clare Kendry's idea of life, no allegiance beyond her own immediate desire. She was selfish, and cold, and hard. And yet she had, too, a strange capacity of transforming warmth and passion, verging sometimes almost on theatrical heroics.

Irene, who was a year or more older than Clare, remembered the day that Bob Kendry had been brought home dead, killed in a silly saloon-fight. Clare, who was at that time a scant fifteen years old, had just stood there with her lips pressed together, her thin arms folded across her narrow chest, staring down at the familiar pasty-white face of her parent with a sort of disdain in her slanting black eyes. For a very long time she had stood like that, silent and staring. Then, quite suddenly, she had given way to a torrent of weeping, swaying her thin body, tearing at her bright hair, and stamping her small feet. The outburst had ceased as suddenly as it had begun. She glanced quickly about the bare room, taking everyone in, even the two policemen, in a sharp look of flashing scorn. And, in the next instant, she had turned and vanished through the door.

Seen across the long stretch of years, the thing had more the appearance of an outpouring of pent-up fury than of an overflow of grief for her dead father; though she had been, Irene admitted, fond enough of him in her own rather catlike way.

Catlike. Certainly that was the word which best described Clare Kendry, if any single world could describe her. Sometimes she was hard and apparently without feeling at all; sometimes she was affectionate and rashly impulsive. And there was about her an amazing soft malice, hidden well away until provoked. Then she was capable of scratching, and very effectively too. Or, driven to anger, she would fight with a ferocity and impetuousness that disregarded or forgot any danger; superior strength, numbers, or other unfavourable circumstances. How savagely she had clawed those boys the day they had hooted her parent and sung a derisive rhyme, of their own composing, which pointed out certain eccentricities in his careening gait! And how deliberately she had—

Irene brought her thoughts back to the present, to the letter from Clare Kendry that she still held unopened in her hand. With a little feeling of apprehension, she very slowly cut the envelope, drew out the folded sheets, spread them, and began to read.

It was, she saw at once, what she had expected since learning from the postmark that Clare was in the city. An extravagantly phrased wish to see her again. Well, she needn't and wouldn't, Irene told herself, accede to that. Nor would she assist Clare to realize her foolish desire to return for a moment to that life which long ago, and of her own choice, she had left behind her.

She ran through the letter, puzzling out, as best she could, the carelessly formed worlds or making instinctive guesses at them.

". . . For I am lonely, so lonely . . . cannot help longing to be with you again, as I have never longed for anything before; and I have wanted many things in my life. . . . You can't know how in this pale life of mine I am all the time seeing the bright pictures of that other that I once thought I was glad to be free of. . . . It's like an ache, a pain that never ceases. . . ." Sheets upon thin sheets of it. And ending finally with, "and it's your fault, 'Rene dear. At least partly. For I wouldn't now, perhaps, have this terrible, this wild desire if I hadn't seen you that time in Chicago. . . ."

Brilliant red patches flamed in Irene Redfield's warm olive cheeks.

"That time in Chicago." The words stood out from among the many paragraphs of other words, bringing with them a clear, sharp remembrance, in which even now, after two years, humiliation, resentment, and rage were mingled.

Two

This is what Irene Redfield remembered.

Chicago. August. A brilliant day, hot, with a brutal staring sun pouring down rays that were like molten rain. A day on which the very outlines of the buildings shuddered as if in protest at the heat. Quivering lines sprang up from baked pavements and wriggled along the shining car-tracks. The automobiles parked at the kerbs were a dancing blaze, and the glass of the shop-windows threw out a blinding radiance. Sharp particles of dust rose from the burning sidewalks, stinging the seared or dripping skins of wilting pedestrians. What small breeze there was seemed like the breath of a flame fanned by slow bellows.[5]

It was on that day of all others that Irene set out to shop for the things which she had promised to take home from Chicago to her two small sons, Brian junior and Theodore. Characteristically, she had put it off until only a few crowded days remained of her long visit. And only this sweltering one was free of engagements till the evening.

Without too much trouble she had got the mechanical aeroplane

---

5. This foreshadows the violence of Clare Kendry's white husband, Bellew, and suggests his moral responsibility for the novel's tragic ending: "One moment Clare had been there, a vital glowing thing, like a flame of red and gold."

for Junior. But the drawing-book, for which Ted had so gravely and insistently given her precise directions, had sent her in and out of five shops without success.

It was while she was on her way to a sixth place that right before her smarting eyes a man toppled over and became an inert crumpled heap on the scorching cement. About the lifeless figure a little crowd gathered. Was the man dead, or only faint? someone asked her. But Irene didn't know and didn't try to discover. She edged her way out of the increasing crowd, feeling disagreeably damp and sticky and soiled from contact with so many sweating bodies.

For a moment she stood fanning herself and dabbing at her moist face with an inadequate scrap of handkerchief. Suddenly she was aware that the whole street had a wobbly look, and realized that she was about to faint. With a quick perception of the need for immediate safety, she lifted a wavering hand in the direction of a cab parked directly in front of her. The perspiring driver jumped out and guided her to his car. He helped, almost lifted her in. She sank down on the hot leather seat.

For a minute her thoughts were nebulous. They cleared.

"I guess," she told her Samaritan, "it's tea I need. On a roof somewhere."

"The Drayton,[6] ma'am?" he suggested. "They do say as how it's always a breeze up there."

"Thank you. I think the Drayton'll do nicely," she told him.

There was that little grating sound of the clutch being slipped in as the man put the car in gear and slid deftly out into the boiling traffic. Reviving under the warm breeze stirred up by the moving cab, Irene made some small attempts to repair the damage that the heat and crowds had done to her appearance.

All too soon the rattling vehicle shot towards the sidewalk and stood still. The driver sprang out and opened the door before the hotel's decorated attendant could reach it. She got out, and thanking him smilingly as well as in a more substantial manner for his kind helpfulness and understanding, went in through the Drayton's wide doors.

Stepping out of the elevator that had brought her to the roof, she was led to a table just in front of a long window whose gently moving curtains suggested a cool breeze. It was, she thought, like being wafted upward on a magic carpet to another world, pleasant, quiet, and strangely remote from the sizzling one that she had left below.

The tea, when it came, was all that she had desired and expected.

6. A hotel modeled principally on Chicago's Drake hotel. Thadious Davis notes that the nearby Morrison Hotel in Chicago was particularly famous for its rooftop restaurant in the 1920's.

In fact, so much was it what she had desired and expected that after the first deep cooling drink she was able to forget it, only now and then sipping, a little absently, from the tall green glass, while she surveyed the room about her or looked out over some lower buildings at the bright unstirred blue of the lake reaching away to an undetected horizon.

She had been gazing down for some time at the specks of cars and people creeping about in streets, and thinking how silly they looked, when on taking up her glass she was surprised to find it empty at last. She asked for more tea and while she waited, began to recall the happenings of the day and to wonder what she was to do about Ted and his book. Why was it that almost invariably he wanted something that was difficult or impossible to get? Like his father. For ever wanting something that he couldn't have.

Presently there were voices, a man's booming one and a woman's slightly husky. A waiter passed her, followed by a sweetly scented woman in a fluttering dress of green chiffon whose mingled pattern of narcissuses, jonquils, and hyacinths was a reminder of pleasantly chill spring days. Behind her there was a man, very red in the face, who was mopping his neck and forehead with a big crumpled handkerchief.

"Oh dear!" Irene groaned, rasped by annoyance, for after a little discussion and commotion they had stopped at the very next table. She had been alone there at the window and it had been so satisfyingly quiet. Now, of course, they would chatter.

But no. Only the woman sat down. The man remained standing, abstractedly pinching the knot of his bright blue tie. Across the small space that separated the two tables his voice carried clearly.

"See you later, then," he declared, looking down at the woman. There was pleasure in his tones and a smile on his face.

His companion's lips parted in some answer, but her words were blurred by the little intervening distance and the medley of noises floating up from the streets below. They didn't reach Irene. But she noted the peculiar caressing smile that accompanied them.

The man said: "Well, I suppose I'd better," and smiled again, and said good-bye, and left.

An attractive-looking woman, was Irene's opinion, with those dark, almost black, eyes and that wide mouth like a scarlet flower against the ivory of her skin. Nice clothes too, just right for the weather, thin and cool without being mussy, as summer things were so apt to be.

A waiter was taking her order. Irene saw her smile up at him as she murmured something—thanks, maybe. It was an odd sort of smile. Irene couldn't quite define it, but she was sure that she would have classed it, coming from another woman, as being just a shade too provocative for a waiter. About this one, however, there was something that made her hesitate to name it that. A certain impression of assurance, perhaps.

The waiter came back with the order. Irene watched her spread out her napkin, saw the silver spoon in the white hand slit the dull gold of the melon. Then, conscious that she had been staring, she looked quickly away.

Her mind returned to her own affairs. She had settled, definitely, the problem of the proper one of two frocks for the bridge party that night, in rooms whose atmosphere would be so thick and hot that every breath would be like breathing soup. The dress decided, her thoughts had gone back to the snag of Ted's book, her unseeing eyes far away on the lake, when by some sixth sense she was acutely aware that someone was watching her.

Very slowly she looked around, and into the dark eyes of the woman in the green frock at the next table. But she evidently failed to realize that such intense interest as she was showing might be embarrassing, and continued to stare. Her demeanour was that of one who with utmost singleness of mind and purpose was determined to impress firmly and accurately each detail of Irene's features upon her memory for all time, nor showed the slightest trace of discernment at having been detected in her steady scrutiny.

Instead, it was Irene who was put out. Feeling her colour heighten under the continued inspection, she slid her eyes down. What, she wondered, could be the reason for such persistent attention? Had she, in her haste in the taxi, put her hat on backwards? Guardedly she felt at it. No. Perhaps there was a streak of powder somewhere on her face. She made a quick pass over it with her handkerchief. Something wrong with her dress? She shot a glance over it. Perfectly all right. *What* was it?

Again she looked up, and for a moment her brown eyes politely returned the stare of the other's black ones, which never for an instant fell or wavered. Irene made a little mental shrug. Oh well, let her look! She tried to treat the woman and her watching with indifference, but she couldn't. All her efforts to ignore her, it, were futile. She stole another glance. Still looking. What strange languorous eyes she had!

And gradually there rose in Irene a small inner disturbance, odious and hatefully familiar. She laughed softly, but her eyes flashed.

Did that woman, could that woman, somehow know that here before her very eyes on the roof of the Drayton sat a Negro?

Absurd! Impossible! White people were so stupid about such things for all that they usually asserted that they were able to tell; and by the most ridiculous means, finger-nails, palms of hands, shapes of ears, teeth, and other equally silly rot.[7] They always took her for an Italian, a Spaniard, a Mexican, or a gipsy. Never, when she was alone, had they even remotely seemed to suspect that she was a Negro. No, the woman sitting there staring at her couldn't possibly know.

Nevertheless, Irene felt, in turn, anger, scorn, and fear slide over her. It wasn't that she was ashamed of being a Negro, or even of having it declared. It was the idea of being ejected from any place, even in the polite and tactful way in which the Drayton would probably do it, that disturbed her.

But she looked, boldly this time, back into the eyes still frankly intent upon her. They did not seem to her hostile or resentful. Rather, Irene had the feeling that they were ready to smile if she would. Nonsense, of course. The feeling passed, and she turned away with the firm intention of keeping her gaze on the lake, the roofs of the buildings across the way, the sky, anywhere but on that annoying woman. Almost immediately, however, her eyes were back again. In the midst of her fog of uneasiness she had been seized by a desire to outstare the rude observer. Suppose the woman did know or suspect her race. She couldn't prove it.

Suddenly her small fright increased. Her neighbour had risen and was coming towards her. What was going to happen now?

"Pardon me," the woman said pleasantly, "but I think I know you." Her slightly husky voice held a dubious note.

Looking up at her, Irene's suspicious and fears vanished. There was no mistaking the friendliness of that smile or resisting its charm. Instantly she surrendered to it and smiled too, as she said: "I'm afraid you're mistaken."

"Why, of course, I know you!" the other exclaimed. "Don't tell me you're not Irene Westover. Or do they still call you 'Rene?"

In the brief second before her answer, Irene tried vainly to recall where and when this woman could have known her. There, in Chicago. And before her marriage. That much was plain. High school? College? Y. W. C. A. committees? High school, most likely. What white girls had she known well enough to have been familiarly addressed as 'Rene by them? The woman before her didn't fit her memory of any of them. Who was she?

"Yes, I'm Irene Westover. And though nobody calls me 'Rene any more, it's good to hear the name again. And you—" She hesitated,

---

7. This question of whether or not there were visible, detectable signs of race—and of who could and could not read them—was central to debates over passing in the 1920s. Larsen refers to current theories of racial detection again, later in the novel, when Irene and Hugh Wentworth discuss the "ways . . . not definite or tangible" of reliably telling the "sheep and the goats" apart (see p. 55). See also the section "The Contemporary Coverage of Passing and Race" in this edition.

ashamed that she could not remember, and hoping that the sentence would be finished for her.

"Don't you know me? Not really, 'Rene?"

"I'm sorry, but just at the minute, I can't seem to place you."

Irene studied the lovely creature standing beside her for some clue to her identity. Who could she be? Where and when had they met? And through her perplexity there came the thought that the trick which her memory had played her was for some reason more gratifying than disappointing to her old acquaintance, that she didn't mind not being recognized.

And, too, Irene felt that she was just about to remember her. For about the woman was some quality, an intangible something, too vague to define, too remote to seize, but which was, to Irene Redfield, very familiar. And that voice. Surely she'd heard those husky tones somewhere before. Perhaps before time, contact, or something had been at them, making them into a voice remotely suggesting England. Ah! Could it have been in Europe that they had met? 'Rene. No.

"Perhaps," Irene began, "you—"

The woman laughed, a lovely laugh, a small sequence of notes that was like a trill and also like the ringing of a delicate bell fashioned of a precious metal, a tinkling.

Irene drew a quick sharp breath. "Clare!" she exclaimed, "not really Clare Kendry?"

So great was her astonishment that she had started to rise.

"No, no, don't get up," Clare Kendry commanded, and sat down herself. "You've simply got to stay and talk. We'll have something more. Tea? Fancy meeting you here! It's simply too, too lucky!"

"It's awfully surprising," Irene told her, and seeing the change in Clare's smile, knew that she had revealed a corner of her own thoughts. But she only said: "I'd never in this world have known you if you hadn't laughed. You are changed, you know. And yet, in a way, you're just the same."

"Perhaps," Clare replied. "Oh, just a second."

She gave her attention to the waiter at her side. "M-mm, let's see. Two teas. And bring some cigarettes. Y-es, they'll be all right. Thanks." Again that odd upward smile. Now, Irene was sure that it was too provocative for a waiter.

While Clare had been giving the order, Irene made a rapid mental calculation. It must be, she figured, all of twelve years since she, or anybody that she knew, had laid eyes on Clare Kendry.

After her father's death she'd gone to live with some relatives, aunts or cousins two or three times removed, over on the west side: relatives that nobody had known the Kendry's possessed until they had turned up at the funeral and taken Clare away with them.

For about a year or more afterwards she would appear occasionally among her old friends and acquaintances on the south side[8] for short little visits that were, they understood, always stolen from the endless domestic tasks in her new home. With each succeeding one she was taller, shabbier, and more belligerently sensitive. And each time the look on her face was more resentful and brooding. "I'm worried about Clare, she seems so unhappy," Irene remembered her mother saying. The visits dwindled, becoming shorter, fewer, and further apart until at last they ceased.

Irene's father, who had been fond of Bob Kendry, made a special trip over to the west side about two months after the last time Clare had been to see them and returned with the bare information that he had seen the relatives and that Clare had disappeared. What else he had confided to her mother, in the privacy of their own room, Irene didn't know.

But she had had something more than a vague suspicion of its nature. For there had been rumours. Rumours that were, to girls of eighteen and nineteen years, interesting and exciting.

There was the one about Clare Kendry's having been seen at the dinner hour in a fashionable hotel in company with another woman and two men, all of them white. And dressed! And there was another which told of her driving in Lincoln Park[9] with a man, unmistakably white, and evidently rich. Packard limousine, chauffeur in livery, and all that. There had been others whose context Irene could no longer recollect, but all pointing in the same glamorous direction.

And she could remember quite vividly how, when they used to repeat and discuss these tantalizing stories about Clare, the girls would always look knowingly at one another and then, with little excited giggles, drag away their eager shining eyes and say with lurking undertones of regret or disbelief some such thing as: "Oh, well, maybe she's got a job or something," or "After all, it mayn't have been Clare," or "You can't believe all you hear."

And always some girl, more matter-of-fact or more frankly malicious than the rest, would declare: "Of course it was Clare! Ruth said it was and so did Frank, and they certainly know her when they see her as well as we do." And someone else would say: "Yes, you can bet it was Clare

---

8. While parts of the south side of Chicago remained all-white in the 1920s the south side's "black belt" (between Twelfth Street on the north, Fifty-fifth Street on the south, Wentworth Avenue on the west, and Indiana Avenue on the east) was already making the phrase "south side" synonymous with blacks, as it remains today in Chicago. According to George Hutchinson's research, Larsen's family, during her Chicago years, tended to live in mixed or border areas on the edges of the black belt. For more specifics on Larsen's Chicago, see The Chicago Commission on Race Relations, *The Negro in Chicago* (Chicago: University of Chicago Press, 1922) and Louis Wirth and Eleanor H. Bernert, *Local Community Fact Book of Chicago* (Chicago: The University of Chicago Press, 1949). I am grateful to the Chicago Historical Society for directing my attention to these resources.

9. A tony north-side neighborhood virtually all white and well-educated in the 1920s, and anchored by venerable institutions such as the Chicago Historical Society and the Lincoln Park Zoo.

all right." And then they would all join in asserting that there could be no mistake about its having been Clare, and that such circumstances could mean only one thing. Working indeed! People didn't take their servants to the Shelby for dinner. Certainly not all dressed up like that. There would follow insincere regrets, and somebody would say: "Poor girl, I suppose it's true enough, but what can you expect. Look at her father. And her mother, they say, would have run away if she hadn't died. Besides, Clare always had a—a—having way with her."

Precisely that! The words came to Irene as she sat there on the Drayton roof, facing Clare Kendry. "A having way." Well, Irene acknowledged, judging from her appearance and manner, Clare seemed certainly to have succeeded in having a few of the things that she wanted.

It was, Irene repeated, after the interval of the waiter, a great surprise and a very pleasant one to see Clare again after all those years, twelve at least.

"Why, Clare, you're the last person in the world I'd have expected to run into. I guess that's why I didn't know you."

Clare answered gravely: "Yes. It is twelve years. But I'm not surprised to see you, 'Rene. That is, not so very. In fact, ever since I've been here, I've more or less hoped that I should, or someone. Preferably you, though. Still, I imagine that's because I've thought of you often and often, while you—I'll wager you've never given me a thought."

It was true, of course. After the first speculations and indictments, Clare had gone completely from Irene's thoughts. And from the thoughts of others too—if their conversation was any indication of their thoughts.

Besides, Clare had never been exactly one of the group, just as she'd never been merely the janitor's daughter, but the daughter of Mr. Bob Kendry, who, it was true, was a janitor, but who also, it seemed, had been in college with some of their fathers. Just how or why he happened to be a janitor, and a very inefficient one at that, they none of them quite knew. One of Irene's brothers, who had put the question to their father, had been told: "That's something that doesn't concern you," and given him the advice to be careful not to end in the same manner as "poor Bob."

No, Irene hadn't thought of Clare Kendry. Her own life had been too crowded. So, she supposed, had the lives of other people. She defended her—their—forgetfulness. "You know how it is. Everybody's so busy. People leave, drop out, maybe for a little while there's talk about them, or questions; then, gradually they're forgotten."

"Yes, that's natural," Clare agreed. And what, she inquired, had they said of her for that little while at the beginning before they'd forgotten her altogether?

Irene looked away. She felt the telltale colour rising in her cheeks. "You can't," she evaded, "expect me to remember trifles like that over twelve years of marriages, births, deaths, and the war."

There followed that trill of notes that was Clare Kendry's laugh, small and clear and the very essence of mockery.

"Oh, 'Rene!" she cried, "of course you remember! But I won't make you tell me, because I know just as well as if I'd been there and heard every unkind word. Oh, I know, I know. Frank Danton saw me in the Shelby one night. Don't tell me he didn't broadcast that, and with embroidery. Others may have seen me at other times. I don't know. But once I met Margaret Hammer in Marshall Field's.[1] I'd have spoken, was on the very point of doing it, but she cut me dead. My dear 'Rene, I assure you that from the way she looked through me, even I was uncertain whether I was actually there in the flesh or not. I remember it clearly, too clearly. It was that very thing which, in a way, finally decided me not to go out and see you one last time before I went away to stay. Somehow, good as all of you, the whole family, had always been to the poor forlorn child that was me, I felt I shouldn't be able to bear that. I mean if any of you, your mother or the boys or—Oh, well, I just felt I'd rather not know it if you did. And so I stayed away. Silly, I suppose. Sometimes I've been sorry I didn't go."

Irene wondered if it was tears that made Clare's eyes so luminous.

"And now 'Rene, I want to hear all about you and everybody and everything. You're married, I s'pose?"

Irene nodded.

"Yes," Clare said knowingly, "you would be. Tell me about it."

And so for an hour or more they had sat there smoking and drinking tea and filling in the gap of twelve years with talk. That is, Irene did. She told Clare about her marriage and removal to New York, about her husband, and about her two sons, who were having their first experience of being separated from their parents at a summer camp, about her mother's death, about the marriages of her two brothers. She told of the marriages, births, and deaths in other families that Clare had known, opening up, for her, new vistas on the lives of old friends and acquaintances.

Clare drank it all in, these things which for so long she had wanted to know and hadn't been able to learn. She sat motionless, her bright lips slightly parted, her whole face lit by the radiance of her happy eyes. Now and then she put a question, but for the most part she was silent.

Somewhere outside, a clock struck. Brought back to the present, Irene looked down at her watch and exclaimed: "Oh, I must go, Clare!"

A moment passed during which she was the prey of uneasiness. It had suddenly occurred to her that she hadn't asked Clare anything

1. Chicago-area department store with a high-end reputation.

about her own life and that she had a very definite unwillingness to do so. And she was quite well aware of the reason for that reluctance. But, she asked herself, wouldn't it, all things considered, be the kindest thing not to ask? If things with Clare were as she—as they all—had suspected, wouldn't it be more tactful to seem to forget to inquire how she had spent those twelve years?

If? It was that "if" which bothered her. It might be, it might just be, in spite of all gossip and even appearances to the contrary, that there was nothing, had been nothing, that couldn't be simply and innocently explained. Appearances, she knew now, had a way sometimes of not fitting facts, and if Clare hadn't—Well, if they had all been wrong, then certainly she ought to express some interest in what had happened to her. It would seem queer and rude if she didn't. But how was she to know? There was, she at last decided, no way; so she merely said again. "I must go, Clare."

"Please, not so soon, 'Rene," Clare begged, not moving.

Irene thought: "She's really almost too good-looking. It's hardly any wonder that she—"

"And now, 'Rene dear, that I've found you, I mean to see lots and lots of you. We're here for a month at least. Jack, that's my husband, is here on business. Poor dear! in this heat. Isn't it beastly? Come to dinner with us tonight, won't you?" And she gave Irene a curious little sidelong glance and a sly, ironical smile peeped out on her full red lips, as if she had been in the secret of the other's thoughts and was mocking her.

Irene was conscious of a sharp intake of breath, but whether it was relief or chagrin that she felt, she herself could not have told. She said hastily: "I'm afraid I can't, Clare. I'm filled up. Dinner and bridge. I'm so sorry."

"Come tomorrow instead, to tea," Clare insisted. "Then you'll see Margery—she's just ten—and Jack too, maybe, if he hasn't got an appointment or something."

From Irene came an uneasy little laugh. She had an engagement for tomorrow also and she was afraid that Clare would not believe it. Suddenly, now, that possibility disturbed her. Therefore it was with a half-vexed feeling at the sense of undeserved guilt that had come upon her that she explained that it wouldn't be possible because she wouldn't be free for tea, or for luncheon or dinner either. "And the next day's Friday when I'll be going away for the week-end, Idlewild,[2] you know. It's quite the thing now." And then she had an inspiration.

2. One of the nation's first black summer resorts, and the midwest's answer to Oak Bluffs on Martha's Vineyard, another affluent black resort community. Idlewild, North of Grand Rapids Michigan, was founded in 1912 and catered to middle- and upper-middle-class black professionals. Scholar and critic Robert Stepto writes that while it mainly drew families from Chicago and Detroit, "you could always spy license plates informing you that there were black folks in town from just about anywhere within a two-day drive." "Idlewild and Other Seasons," *Callaloo,* Volume 14, number 1 (1991).

"Clare!" she exclaimed, "why don't you come up with me? Our place is probably full up—Jim's wife has a way of collecting mobs of the most impossible people—but we can always manage to find room for one more. And you'll see absolutely everybody."

In the very moment of giving the invitation she regretted it. What a foolish, what an idiotic impulse to have given way to! She groaned inwardly as she thought of the endless explanations in which it would involve her, of the curiosity, and the talk, and the lifted eyebrows. It wasn't she assured herself, that she was a snob, that she cared greatly for the petty restrictions and distinctions with which what called itself Negro society chose to hedge itself about; but that she had a natural and deeply rooted aversion to the kind of front-page notoriety that Clare Kendry's presence in Idlewild, as her guest, would expose her to.[3] And here she was, perversely and against all reason, inviting her.

But Clare shook her head. "Really, I'd love to, 'Rene," she said, a little mournfully. "There's nothing I'd like better. But I couldn't. I mustn't, you see. It wouldn't do at all. I'm sure you understand. I'm simply crazy to go, but I can't." The dark eyes glistened and there was a suspicion of a quaver in the husky voice. "And believe me, 'Rene, I do thank you for asking me. Don't think I've entirely forgotten just what it would mean for you if I went. That is, if you still care about such things."

All indication of tears had gone from her eyes and voice, and Irene Redfield, searching her face, had an offended feeling that behind what was now only an ivory mask lurked a scornful amusement. She looked away, at the wall far beyond Clare. Well, she deserved it, for, as she acknowledged to herself, she *was* relieved. And for the very reason at which Clare had hinted. The fact that Clare had guessed her perturbation did not, however, in any degree lessen that relief. She was annoyed at having been detected in what might seem to be an insincerity; but that was all.

The waiter came with Clare's change. Irene reminded herself that she ought immediately to go. But she didn't move.

The truth was, she was curious. There were things that she wanted to ask Clare Kendry. She wished to find out about this hazardous business of "passing," this breaking away from all that was familiar and friendly to take one's chance in another environment, not entirely strange, perhaps, but certainly not entirely friendly. What, for example, one did about background, how one accounted for oneself. And how one felt when one came into contact with other Negroes. But she couldn't. She was unable to think of a single question that in

---

3. For a black family to have a (seemingly) white houseguest at such a resort would have been considered scandalous, not least because of assumptions that a white houseguest of black friends would, necessarily, be of a questionable social and class background.

its context or its phrasing was not too frankly curious, if not actually impertinent.

As if aware of her desire and her hesitation, Clare remarked, thoughtfully: "You know, 'Rene, I've often wondered why more coloured girls, girls like you and Margaret Hammer and Esther Dawson and—oh, lots of others—never 'passed' over. It's such a frightfully easy thing to do. If one's the type, all that's needed is a little nerve."

"What about background? Family, I mean. Surely you can't just drop down on people from nowhere and expect them to receive you with open arms, can you?"

"Almost," Clare asserted. "You'd be surprised, 'Rene, how much easier that is with white people than with us. Maybe because there are so many more of them, or maybe because they are secure and so don't have to bother. I've never quite decided."

Irene was inclined to be incredulous. "You mean that you didn't have to explain where you came from? It seems impossible."

Clare cast a glance of repressed amusement across the table at her. "As a matter of fact, I didn't. Though I suppose under any other circumstances I might have had to provide some plausible tale to account for myself. I've a good imagination, so I'm sure I could have done it quite creditably, and credibly. But it wasn't necessary. There were my aunts, you see, respectable and authentic enough for anything or anybody."

"I see. They were 'passing' too."

"No. They weren't. They were white."

"Oh!" And in the next instant it came back to Irene that she had heard this mentioned before; by her father, or, more likely, her mother. They were Bob Kendry's aunts. He had been a son of their brother's, on the left hand.[4] A wild oat.

"They were nice old ladies," Clare explained, "very religious and as poor as church mice. That adored brother of theirs, my grandfather, got through every penny they had after he'd finished his own little bit."

Clare paused in her narrative to light another cigarette. Her smile, her expression, Irene noticed, was faintly resentful.

"Being good Christians," she continued, "when dad came to his tipsy end, they did their duty and gave me a home of sorts. I was, it was true, expected to earn my keep by doing all the housework and most of the washing. But do you realize, 'Rene, that if it hadn't been for them, I shouldn't have had a home in the world?"

Irene's nod and little murmur were comprehensive, understanding.

Clare made a small mischievous grimace and proceeded. "Besides, to their notion, hard labour was good for me. I had Negro blood and

4. Born to a white father and black mother.

they belonged to the generation that had written and read long articles headed: 'Will the Blacks Work?' Too, they weren't quite sure that the good God hadn't intended the sons and daughters of Ham to sweat because he had poked fun at old man Noah once when he had taken a drop too much. I remember the aunts telling me that that old drunkard had cursed Ham and his sons for all time."[5]

Irene laughed. But Clare remained quite serious.

"It was more than a joke, I assure you, 'Rene. It was a hard life for a girl of sixteen. Still, I had a roof over my head, and food, and clothes—such as they were. And there were the Scriptures, and talks on morals and thrift and industry and the loving-kindness of the good Lord."

"Have you ever stopped to think, Clare," Irene demanded, "how much unhappiness and downright cruelty are laid to the loving-kindness of the Lord? And always by His most ardent followers, it seems."

"Have I?" Clare exclaimed. "It, they, made me what I am today. For, of course, I was determined to get away, to be a person and not a charity or a problem, or even a daughter of the indiscreet Ham. Then, too, I wanted things. I knew I wasn't bad-looking and that I could 'pass.' You can't know, 'Rene, how, when I used to go over to the south side, I used almost to hate all of you. You had all the things I wanted and never had had. It made me all the more determined to get them, and others. Do you, can you understand what I felt?"

She looked up with a pointed and appealing effect, and, evidently finding the sympathetic expression on Irene's face sufficient answer, went on. "The aunts were queer. For all their Bibles and praying and ranting about honesty, they didn't want anyone to know that their darling brother had seduced—ruined, they called it—a Negro girl. They could excuse the ruin, but they couldn't forgive the tar-brush.[6] They forbade me to mention Negroes to the neighbours, or even to mention the south side. You may be sure that I didn't. I'll bet they were good and sorry afterwards."

She laughed and the ringing bells in her laugh had a hard metallic sound.

"When the chance to get away came, that omission was of great value to me. When Jack, a schoolboy acquaintance of some people in the neighbourhood, turned up from South America with untold gold, there was no one to tell him that I was coloured, and many to tell him about the severity and the religiousness of Aunt Grace and Aunt

---

5. From Genesis, 9:20–27. One of Noah's sons, Ham, is cursed with slavery as punishment for witnessing his father's nakedness and drunkenness. This story was both used as justification for slavery and became the basis, in some black folklore, for an association between Jews and blacks.

6. Slang for black; either having black ancestry or being dark skinned.

Edna. You can guess the rest. After he came, I stopped slipping off to the south side and slipped off to meet him instead. I couldn't manage both. In the end I had no great difficulty in convincing him that it was useless to talk marriage to the aunts. So on the day that I was eighteen, we went off and were married. So that's that. Nothing could have been easier."

"Yes, I do see that for you it was easy enough. By the way! I wonder why they didn't tell father that you were married. He went over to find out about you when you stopped coming over to see us. I'm sure they didn't tell him. Not that you were married."

Clare Kendry's eyes were bright with tears that didn't fall. "Oh, how lovely! To have cared enough about me to do that. The dear sweet man! Well, they couldn't tell him because they didn't know it. I took care of that, for I couldn't be sure that those consciences of theirs wouldn't begin to work on them afterwards and make them let the cat out of the bag. The old things probably thought I was living in sin, wherever I was. And it would be about what they expected."

An amused smile lit the lovely face for the smallest fraction of a second. After a little silence she said soberly: "But I'm sorry if they told your father so. That was something I hadn't counted on."

"I'm not sure that they did," Irene told her. "He didn't say so, anyway."

"He wouldn't, 'Rene dear. Not your father."

"Thanks. I'm sure he wouldn't."

"But you've never answered my question. Tell me, honestly, haven't you ever thought of 'passing'?"

Irene answered promptly: "No. Why should I?" And so disdainful was her voice and manner that Clare's face flushed and her eyes glinted. Irene hastened to add: "You see, Clare, I've everything I want. Except, perhaps, a little more money."

At that Clare laughed, her spark of anger vanished as quickly as it had appeared. "Of course," she declared, "that's what everybody wants, just a little more money, even the people who have it. And I must say I don't blame them. Money's awfully nice to have. In fact, all things considered, I think, 'Rene, that it's even worth the price."[7]

Irene could only shrug her shoulders. Her reason partly agreed, her instinct wholly rebelled. And she could not say why. And though conscious that if she didn't hurry away, she was going to be late to dinner, she still lingered. It was as if the woman sitting on the other side of the table, a girl that she had known, who had done this rather dangerous and, to Irene Redfield, abhorrent thing successfully and had

---

7. See James Weldon Johnson's *Autobiography of an Ex-Colored Man* for the claim that it was all a "mess of pottage." Clare changes her mind, coming to believe it was *not* "worth the price" a few pages later in the novel.

announced herself well satisfied, had for her a fascination, strange and compelling.

Clare Kendry was still leaning back in the tall chair, her sloping shoulders against the carved top. She sat with an air of indifferent assurance, as if arranged for, desired. About her clung that dim suggestion of polite insolence with which a few women are born and which some acquire with the coming of riches or importance.

Clare, it gave Irene a little prick of satisfaction to recall, hadn't got that by passing herself off as white. She herself had always had it.

Just as she'd always had that pale gold hair, which, unsheared still, was drawn loosely back from a broad brow, partly hidden by the small close hat. Her lips, painted a brilliant geranium-red, were sweet and sensitive and a little obstinate. A tempting mouth. The face across the forehead and cheeks was a trifle too wide, but the ivory skin had a peculiar soft lustre. And the eyes were magnificent! dark, sometimes absolutely black, always luminous, and set in long, black lashes. Arresting eyes, slow and mesmeric, and with, for all their warmth, something withdrawn and secret about them.

Ah! Surely! They were Negro eyes![8] mysterious and concealing. And set in that ivory face under that bright hair, there was about them something exotic.

Yes, Clare Kendry's loveliness was absolute, beyond challenge, thanks to those eyes which her grandmother and later her mother and father had given her.

Into those eyes there came a smile and over Irene the sense of being petted and caressed. She smiled back.

"Maybe," Clare suggested, "you can come Monday, if you're back. Or, if you're not, then Tuesday."

With a small regretful sigh, Irene informed Clare that she was afraid she wouldn't be back by Monday and that she was sure she had dozens of things for Tuesday, and that she was leaving Wednesday. It might be, however, that she could get out of something Tuesday.

"Oh, do try. Do put somebody else off. The others can see you any time, while I—Why, I may never see you again! Think of that, 'Rene! You'll have to come. You'll simply have to! I'll never forgive you if you don't."

At that moment it seemed a dreadful thing to think of never seeing Clare Kendry again. Standing there under the appeal, the caress, of her eyes, Irene had the desire, the hope, that this parting wouldn't be the last.

"I'll try, Clare," she promised gently. "I'll call you—or will you call me?"

---

8. This is just the sort of racial clue that Irene will later call "absurd."

"I think, perhaps, I'd better call you. Your father's in the book, I know, and the address is the same. Sixty-four eighteen. Some memory, what? Now remember, I'm going to expect you. You've got to be able to come."

Again that peculiar mellowing smile.

"I'll do my best, Clare."

Irene gathered up her gloves and bag. They stood up. She put out her hand. Clare took and held it.

"It has been nice seeing you again, Clare. How pleased and glad father'll be to hear about you!"

"Until Tuesday, then," Clare Kendry replied. "I'll spend every minute of the time from now on looking forward to seeing you again. Good-bye, 'Rene dear. My love to your father, and this kiss for him."

The sun had gone from overhead, but the streets were still like fiery furnaces. The languid breeze was still hot. And the scurrying people looked even more wilted than before Irene had fled from their contact.

Crossing the avenue in the heat, far from the coolness of the Drayton's roof, away from the seduction of Clare Kendry's smile, she was aware of a sense of irritation with herself because she had been pleased and a little flattered at the other's obvious gladness at their meeting.

With her perspiring progress homeward this irritation grew, and she began to wonder just what had possessed her to make her promise to find time, in the crowded days that remained of her visit, to spend another afternoon with a woman whose life had so definitely and deliberately diverged from hers; and whom, as had been pointed out, she might never see again.

Why in the world had she made such a promise?

As she went up the steps to her father's house, thinking with what interest and amazement he would listen to her story of the afternoon's encounter, it came to her that Clare had omitted to mention her marriage name. She had referred to her husband as Jack. That was all. Had that, Irene asked herself, been intentional?

Clare had only to pick up the telephone to communicate with her, or to drop her a card, or to jump into a taxi. But she couldn't reach Clare in any way. Nor could anyone else to whom she might speak of their meeting.

"As if I should!"

Her key turned in the lock. She went in. Her father, it seemed, hadn't come in yet.

Irene decided that she wouldn't, after all, say anything to him about Clare Kendry. She had, she told herself, no inclination to speak of a person who held so low an opinion of her loyalty, or her discretion. And certainly she had no desire or intention of making the slightest effort about Tuesday. Nor any other day for that matter.

She was through with Clare Kendry.

Three

On Tuesday morning a dome of grey sky rose over the parched city, but the stifling air was not relieved by the silvery mist that seemed to hold a promise of rain, which did not fall.

To Irene Redfield this soft foreboding fog was another reason for doing nothing about seeing Clare Kendry that afternoon.

But she did see her.

The telephone. For hours it had rung like something possessed. Since nine o'clock she had been hearing its insistent jangle. Awhile she was resolute, saying firmly each time: "Not in, Liza, take the message." And each time the servant returned with the information: "It's the same lady, ma'am; she says she'll call again."

But at noon, her nerves frayed and her conscience smiting her at the reproachful look on Liza's ebony face as she withdrew for another denial, Irene weakened.

"Oh, never mind. I'll answer this time, Liza."

"It's her again."

"Hello. . . . Yes."

"It's Clare, 'Rene. . . . Where *have* you been? . . . Can you be here around four? . . . What? . . . But, 'Rene, you promised! Just for a little while. . . . You can if you want to. . . . I am *so* disappointed. I had counted so on seeing you. . . . Please be nice and come. Only for a minute. I'm sure you can manage it if you try. . . . I won't beg you to stay. . . . Yes. . . . I'm going to expect you . . . It's the Morgan. . . . Oh, yes! The name's Bellew, Mrs. John Bellew. . . . About four, then. . . . I'll be so happy to see you! . . . Goodbye."

"Damn!"

Irene hung up the receiver with an emphatic bang, her thoughts immediately filled with self-reproach. She'd done it again. Allowed Clare Kendry to persuade her into promising to do something for which she had neither time nor any special desire. What was it about Clare's voice that was so appealing, so very seductive?

Clare met her in the hall with a kiss. She said: "You're good to come, 'Rene. But, then, you always were nice to me." And under her potent smile a part of Irene's annoyance with herself fled. She was even a little glad that she had come.

Clare led the way, stepping lightly, towards a room whose door was standing partly open, saying: "There's a surprise. It's a real party. See."

Entering, Irene found herself in a sitting-room, large and high, at whose windows hung startling blue draperies which triumphantly dragged attention from the gloomy chocolate-coloured furniture. And Clare was wearing a thin floating dress of the same shade of blue, which suited her and the rather difficult room to perfection.

For a minute Irene thought the room was empty, but turning her head, she discovered, sunk deep in the cushions of a huge sofa, a woman staring up at her with such intense concentration that her eyelids were drawn as though the strain of that upward glance had paralysed them. At first Irene took her to be a stranger, but in the next instant she said in an unsympathetic, almost harsh voice: "And how are you, Gertrude?"

The woman nodded and forced a smile to her pouting lips. "I'm all right," she replied. "And you're just the same, Irene. Not changed a bit."

"Thank you." Irene responded, as she chose a seat. She was thinking: "Great goodness! Two of them."

For Gertrude too had married a white man, though it couldn't be truthfully said that she was "passing." Her husband—what was his name?—had been in school with her and had been quite well aware, as had his family and most of his friends, that she was a Negro. It hadn't, Irene knew, seemed to matter to him then. Did it now, she wondered? Had Fred—Fred Martin, that was it—had he ever regretted his marriage because of Gertrude's race? Had Gertrude?

Turning to Gertrude, Irene asked: "And Fred, how is he? It's unmentionable years since I've seen him."

"Oh, he's all right," Gertrude answered briefly.

For a full minute no one spoke. Finally out of the oppressive little silence Clare's voice came pleasantly, conversationally: "We'll have tea right away. I know that you can't stay long, 'Rene. And I'm so sorry you won't see Margery. We went up the lake over the week-end to see some of Jack's people, just out of Milwaukee. Margery wanted to stay with the children. It seemed a shame not to let her, especially since it's so hot in town. But I'm expecting Jack any second."

Irene said briefly: "That's nice."

Gertrude remained silent. She was, it was plain, a little ill at ease. And her presence there annoyed Irene, roused in her a defensive and resentful feeling for which she had at the moment no explanation. But it did seem to her odd that the woman that Clare was now should have invited the woman that Gertrude was. Still, of course, Clare couldn't have known. Twelve years since they had met.

Later, when she examined her feeling of annoyance, Irene admitted, a shade reluctantly, that it arose from a feeling of being outnumbered, a sense of aloneness, in her adherence to her own class and kind; not merely in the great thing of marriage, but in the whole pattern of her life as well.

Clare spoke again, this time at length. Her talk was of the change that Chicago presented to her after her long absence in European cities. Yes, she said in reply to some question from Gertrude, she'd been back to America a time or two, but only as far as New York and Philadelphia, and once she had spent a few days in Washington. John Bellew, who, it appeared, was some sort of international banking agent, hadn't particularly wanted her to come with him on this trip, but as soon as she had learned that it would probably take him as far as Chicago, she made up her mind to come anyway.

"I simply had to. And after I once got here, I was determined to see someone I knew and find out what had happened to everybody. I didn't quite see how I was going to manage it, but I meant to. Somehow. I'd just about decided to take a chance and go out to your house, 'Rene, or call up and arrange a meeting, when I ran into you. What luck!"

Irene agreed that it was luck. "It's the first time I've been home for five years, and now I'm about to leave. A week later and I'd have been gone. And how in the world did you find Gertrude?"

"In the book. I remembered about Fred. His father still has the meat market."

"Oh, yes," said Irene, who had only remembered it as Clare had spoken, "on Cottage Grove near—"

Gertrude broke in. "No. It's moved. We're on Maryland Avenue—used to be Jackson[9]—now. Near Sixty-third Street. And the market's Fred's. His name's the same as his father's."

Gertrude, Irene thought, looked as if her husband might be a butcher. There was left of her youthful prettiness, which had been so much admired in their high-school days, no trace. She had grown broad, fat almost, and though there were no lines on her large white face, its very smoothness was somehow prematurely ageing. Her black hair was clipt, and by some unfortunate means all the live curliness had gone from it. Her over-trimmed Georgette *crêpe* dress was too short and showed an appalling amount of leg, stout legs in sleazy stockings of a vivid rose-beige shade. Her plump hands were newly and not too competently manicured—for the occasion, probably. And she wasn't smoking.

Clare said—and Irene fancied that her husky voice held a slight edge—"Before you came, Irene, Gertrude was telling me about her two boys. Twins. Think of it! Isn't it too marvellous for words?"

Irene felt a warmness creeping into her cheeks. Uncanny, the way

9. According to Thadious Davis, this is Nella Lasen's "personal joke," since her family owned a building on Maryland Avenue "whose name had been changed from Jackson at the time of the 1893 World's Columbian Exposition."

Clare could divine what one was thinking. She was a little put out, but her manner was entirely easy as she said: "That is nice. I've two boys myself, Gertrude. Not twins, though. It seems that Clare's rather behind, doesn't it?"

Gertrude, however, wasn't sure that Clare hadn't the best of it. "She's got a girl. I wanted a girl. So did Fred."

"Isn't that a bit unusual?" Irene asked. "Most men want sons. Egotism, I suppose."

"Well, Fred didn't."

The tea-things had been placed on a low table at Clare's side. She gave them her attention now, pouring the rich amber fluid from the tall glass pitcher into stately slim glasses, which she handed to her guests, and then offered them lemon or cream and tiny sandwiches or cakes.

After taking up her own glass she informed them: "No, I have no boys and I don't think I'll ever have any. I'm afraid. I nearly died of terror the whole nine months before Margery was born for fear that she might be dark. Thank goodness, she turned out all right. But I'll never risk it again. Never! The strain is simply too—too hellish."

Gertrude Martin nodded in complete comprehension.

This time it was Irene who said nothing.

"You don't have to tell me!" Gertrude said fervently. "I know what it is all right. Maybe you don't think I wasn't scared to death too. Fred said I was silly, and so did his mother. But, of course, they thought it was just a notion I'd gotten into my head and they blamed it on my condition. They don't know like we do, how it might go way back, and turn out dark no matter what colour the father and mother are."

Perspiration stood out on her forehead. Her narrow eyes rolled first in Clare's, then in Irene's direction. As she talked she waved her heavy hands about.

"No," she went on, "no more for me either. Not even a girl. It's awful the way it skips generations and then pops out. Why, he actually said he didn't care what colour it turned out, if I would only stop worrying about it. But, of course, nobody wants a dark child."

Her voice was earnest and she took for granted that her audience was in entire agreement with her.

Irene, whose head had gone up with a quick little jerk, now said in a voice of whose even tones she was proud: "One of my boys is dark."

Gertrude jumped as if she had been shot at. Her eyes goggled. Her mouth flew open. She tried to speak, but could not immediately get the words out. Finally she managed to stammer: "Oh! And your husband, is he—is he—er—dark, too?"

Irene, who was struggling with a flood of feelings, resentment, anger, and contempt, was, however, still able to answer as coolly as if she had not that sense of not belonging to and of despising the company in which she found herself drinking iced tea from tall amber glasses on that hot August afternoon. Her husband, she informed them quietly, couldn't exactly "pass."

At that reply Clare turned on Irene her seductive caressing smile and remarked a little scoffingly: "I do think that coloured people— we—are too silly about some things. After all, the thing's not important to Irene or hundreds of others. Not awfully, even to you, Gertrude. It's only deserters like me who have to be afraid of freaks of the nature. As my inestimable dad used to say, 'Everything must be paid for.' Now, please one of you tell me what ever happened to Claude Jones. You know, the tall, lanky specimen who used to wear that comical little moustache that the girls used to laugh at so. Like a thin streak of soot. The moustache, I mean."

At that Gertrude shrieked with laughter. "Claude Jones!" and launched into the story of how he was no longer a Negro or a Christian but had become a Jew.

"A Jew!" Clare exclaimed.

"Yes, a Jew. A black Jew, he calls himself. He won't eat ham and goes to the synagogue on Saturday. He's got a beard now as well as a moustache. You'd die laughing if you saw him. He's really too funny for words. Fred says he's crazy and I guess he is. Oh, he's a scream all right, a regular scream!" And she shrieked again.

Clare's laugh tinkled out. "It certainly sounds funny enough. Still, it's his own business. If he gets along better by turning—"

At that, Irene, who was still hugging her unhappy don't-care feeling of rightness, broke in, saying bitingly: "It evidently doesn't occur to either you or Gertrude that he might possibly be sincere in changing his religion. Surely everyone doesn't do everything for gain."

Clare Kendry had no need to search for the full meaning of that utterance. She reddened slightly and retorted seriously: "Yes, I admit that might be possible—his being sincere, I mean. It just didn't happen to occur to me, that's all. I'm surprised," and the seriousness changed to mockery, "that you should have expected it to. Or did you really?"

"You don't, I'm sure, imagine that that is a question that I can answer," Irene told her. "Not here and now."

Gertrude's face expressed complete bewilderment. However, seeing that little smiles had come out on the faces of the two other women and not recognizing them for the smiles of mutual reservations which they were, she smiled too.

Clare began to talk, steering carefully away from anything that might lead towards race or other thorny subjects. It was the most brilliant exhibition of conversational weight-lifting that Irene had ever seen. Her words swept over them in charming well-modulated streams. Her laughs tinkled and pealed. Her little stories sparkled.

Irene contributed a bare "Yes" or "No" here and there. Gertrude, a "You don't say!" less frequently.

For a while the illusion of general conversation was nearly perfect. Irene felt her resentment changing gradually to a silent, somewhat grudging admiration.

Clare talked on, her voice, her gestures, colouring all she said of wartime in France, of after-the-wartime in Germany, of the excitement at the time of the general strike in England,[1] of dressmaker's openings in Paris, of the new gaiety of Budapest.

But it couldn't last, this verbal feat. Gertrude shifted in her seat and fell to fidgeting with her fingers. Irene, bored at last by all this repetition of the selfsame things that she had read all too often in papers, magazines, and books, set down her glass and collected her bag and handkerchief. She was smoothing out the tan fingers of her gloves preparatory to putting them on when she heard the sound of the outer door being opened and saw Clare spring up with an expression of relief saying: "How lovely! Here's Jack at exactly the right minute. You can't go now, 'Rene dear."

John Bellew came into the room. The first thing that Irene noticed about him was that he was not the man that she had seen with Clare Kendry on the Drayton roof. This man, Clare's husband, was a tallish person, broadly made. His age she guessed to be somewhere between thirty-five and forty. His hair was dark brown and waving, and he had a soft mouth, somewhat womanish, set in an unhealthy-looking dough-coloured face. His steel-grey opaque eyes were very much alive, moving ceaselessly between thick bluish lids. But there was, Irene decided, nothing unusual about him, unless it was an impression of latent physical power.

"Hello, Nig," was his greeting to Clare.

Gertrude who had started slightly, settled back and looked covertly towards Irene, who had caught her lip between her teeth and sat gazing at husband and wife. It was hard to believe that even Clare Kendry would permit this ridiculing of her race by an outsider, though he chanced to be her husband. So he knew, then, that Clare was a Negro? From her talk the other day Irene had understood that he didn't. But how rude, how positively insulting, for him to address her in that way in the presence of guests!

In Clare's eyes, as she presented her husband, was a queer gleam, a jeer, it might be. Irene couldn't define it.

The mechanical professions that attend an introduction over, she inquired: "Did you hear what Jack called me?"

"Yes," Gertrude answered, laughing with a dutiful eagerness.

---

1. In May 1926, the British railway, transport, steel, and coal mining unions went on a week-long General Strike.

Irene didn't speak. Her gaze remained level on Clare's smiling face. The black eyes fluttered down. "Tell them, dear, why you call me that."

The man chuckled, crinkling up his eyes, not, Irene was compelled to acknowledge, unpleasantly. He explained: "Well, you see, it's like this. When we were first married, she was as white as—as—well as white as a lily. But I declare she's gettin' darker and darker. I tell her if she don't look out, she'll wake up one of these days and find she's turned into a nigger."

He roared with laughter. Clare's ringing bell-like laugh joined his. Gertrude after another uneasy shift in her seat added her shrill one. Irene, who had been sitting with lips tightly compressed, cried out: "That's good!" and gave way to gales of laughter. She laughed and laughed and laughed. Tears ran down her cheeks. Her sides ached. Her throat hurt. She laughed on and on and on, long after the others had subsided. Until, catching sight of Clare's face, the need for a more quiet enjoyment of this priceless joke, and for caution, struck her. At once she stopped.

Clare handed her husband his tea and laid her hand on his arm with an affectionate little gesture. Speaking with confidence as well as with amusement, she said: "My goodness, Jack! What difference would it make if, after all these years, you were to find out that I was one or two per cent coloured?"

Bellew put out his hand in a repudiating fling, definite and final. "Oh, no, Nig," he declared, "nothing like that with me. I know you're no nigger, so it's all right. You can get as black as you please as far as I'm concerned, since I know you're no nigger. I draw the line at that. No niggers in my family. Never have been and never will be."

Irene's lips trembled almost uncontrollably, but she made a desperate effort to fight back her disastrous desire to laugh again, and succeeded. Carefully selecting a cigarette from the lacquered box on the tea-table before her, she turned an oblique look on Clare and encountered her peculiar eyes fixed on her with an expression so dark and deep and unfathomable that she had for a short moment the sensation of gazing into the eyes of some creature utterly strange and apart. A faint sense of danger brushed her, like the breath of a cold fog. Absurd, her reason told her, as she accepted Bellew's proffered light for her cigarette. Another glance at Clare showed her smiling. So, as one always ready to oblige, was Gertrude.

An on-looker, Irene reflected, would have have thought it a most congenial tea-party, all smiles and jokes and hilarious laughter. She said humorously: "So you dislike Negroes, Mr. Bellew?" But her amusement was at her thought, rather than her words.

John Bellew gave a short denying laugh. "You got me wrong there, Mrs. Redfield. Nothing like that at all. I don't dislike them, I hate them. And so does Nig, for all she's trying to turn into one. She wouldn't have a nigger maid around her for love nor money. Not that I'd want her to. They give me the creeps. The black scrimy devils."

This wasn't funny. Had Bellew, Irene inquired, ever known any Negroes? The defensive tone of her voice brought another start from the uncomfortable Gertrude, and, for all her appearance of serenity, a quick apprehensive look from Clare.

Bellew answered: "Thank the Lord, no! And never expect to! But I know people who've known them, better than they know their black selves. And I read in the papers about them. Always robbing and killing people. And," he added darkly, "worse."

From Gertrude's direction came a queer little suppressed sound, a snort or a giggle. Irene couldn't tell which. There was a brief silence, during which she feared that her self-control was about to prove too frail a bridge to support her mounting anger and indignation. She had a leaping desire to shout at the man beside her: "And you're sitting here surrounded by three black devils, drinking tea."

The impulse passed, obliterated by her consciousness of the danger in which such rashness would involve Clare, who remarked with a gentle reprovingness: "Jack dear, I'm sure 'Rene doesn't care to hear all about your pet aversions. Nor Gertrude either. Maybe they read the papers too, you know." She smiled on him, and her smile seemed to transform him, to soften and mellow him, as the rays of the sun does a fruit.

"All right, Nig, old girl. I'm sorry," he apologized. Reaching over, he playfully touched his wife's pale hands, then turned back to Irene. "Didn't mean to bore you, Mrs. Redfield. Hope you'll excuse me," he said sheepishly. "Clare tells me you're living in New York. Great city, New York. The city of the future."

In Irene, rage had not retreated, but was held by some dam of caution and allegiance to Clare. So, in the best casual voice she could muster, she agreed with Bellew. Though, she reminded him, it was exactly what Chicagoans were apt to say of their city. And all the while she was speaking, she was thinking how amazing it was that her voice did not tremble, that outwardly she was calm. Only her hands shook slightly. She drew them inward from their rest in her lap and pressed the tips of her fingers together to still them.

Husband's a doctor, I understand. Manhattan, or one of the other boroughs?"

Manhattan, Irene informed him, and explained the need for Brian to be within easy reach of certain hospitals and clinics.

"Interesting life, a doctor's."

"Ye-es. Hard, though. And, in a way, monotonous. Nerve-racking, too."

"Hard on the wife's nerves at least, eh? So many lady patients." He laughed, enjoying, with a boyish heartiness, the hoary joke.

Irene managed a momentary smile, but her voice was sober as she said: "Brian doesn't care for ladies, especially sick ones. I sometimes wish he did. It's South America that attracts him."

"Coming place, South America, if they ever get the niggers out of it. It's run over—"

"Really, Jack!" Clare's voice was on the edge of temper.

"Honestly, Nig, I forgot." To the others he said: "You see how henpecked I am." And to Gertrude: "You're still in Chicago, Mrs.—er—Mrs. Martin?"

He was, it was plain, doing his best to be agreeable to these old friends of Clare's. Irene had to concede that under other conditions she might have liked him. A fairly good-looking man of amiable disposition, evidently, and in easy circumstances. Plain and with no nonsense about him.

Gertrude replied that Chicago was good enough for her. She'd never been out of it and didn't think she ever should. Her husband's business was there.

"Of course, of course. Can't jump up and leave a business."

There followed a smooth surface of talk about Chicago, New York, their differences and their recent spectacular changes.

It was, Irene thought, unbelievable and astonishing that four people could sit so unruffled, so ostensibly friendly, while they were in reality seething with anger, mortification, shame. But no, on second thought she was forced to amend her opinion. John Bellew, most certainly, was as undisturbed within as without. So, perhaps, was Gertrude Martin. At least she hadn't the mortification and shame that Clare Kendry must be feeling, or, in such full measure, the rage and rebellion that she, Irene, was repressing.

"More tea, 'Rene," Clare offered.

"Thanks, no. And I must be going. I'm leaving tomorrow, you know, and I've still got packing to do."

She stood up. So did Gertrude, and Clare, and John Bellew.

"How do you like the Drayton, Mrs. Redfield?" the latter asked.

"The Drayton? Oh, very much. Very much indeed," Irene answered, her scornful eyes on Clare's unrevealing face.

"Nice place, all right. Stayed there a time or two myself," the man informed her.

"Yes, it is nice," Irene agreed. "Almost as good as our best New York places." She had withdrawn her look from Clare and was searching in her bag for some non-existent something. Her understanding was rapidly increasing, as was her pity and her contempt. Clare was so daring, so lovely, and so "having."

They gave their hands to Clare with appropriate murmurs. "So good to have seen you." . . . "I do hope I'll see you again soon."

"Good-bye," Clare returned. "It was good of you to come, 'Rene dear. And you too, Gertrude."

"Good-bye, Mr. Bellew." . . . "So glad to have met you." It was Gertrude who had said that. Irene couldn't, she absolutely couldn't bring herself to utter the polite fiction or anything approaching it.

He accompanied them out into the hall, summoned the elevator.

"Good-bye," they said again, stepping in.

Plunging downward they were silent.

They made their way through the lobby without speaking.

But as soon as they had reached the street Gertrude, in the manner of one unable to keep bottled up for another minute that which for the last hour she had had to retain, burst out: "My God! What an awful chance! She must be plumb crazy."

"Yes, it certainly seems risky," Irene admitted.

"Risky! I should say it was. Risky! My God! What a word! And the mess she's liable to get herself into!"

"Still, I imagine she's pretty safe. They don't live here, you know. And there's a child. That's a certain security."

"It's an awful chance, just the same," Gertrude insisted. "I'd never in the world have married Fred without him knowing. You can't tell what will turn up."

"Yes, I do agree that it's safer to tell. But then Bellew wouldn't have married her. And, after all, that's what she wanted."

Gertrude shook her head. "I wouldn't be in her shoes for all the money she's getting out of it, when he finds out. Not with him feeling the way he does. Gee! Wasn't it awful? For a minute I was so mad I could have slapped him."

It had been, Irene acknowledged, a distinctly trying experience, as well as a very unpleasant one. "I was more than a little angry myself."

"And imagine her not telling us about him feeling that way! Anything might have happened. We might have said something."

That, Irene pointed out, was exactly like Clare Kendry. Taking a chance, and not at all considering anyone else's feelings.

Gertrude said: "Maybe she thought we'd think it a good joke. And I guess you did. The way you laughed. My land! I was scared to death he might catch on."

"Well, it was rather a joke," Irene told her, "on him and us and maybe on her."

"All the same, it's an awful chance. I'd hate to be her."

"She seems satisfied enough. She's got what she wanted, and the other day she told me it was worth it."

But about that Gertrude was sceptical. "She'll find out different," was her verdict. "She'll find out different all right."

Rain had begun to fall, a few scattered large drops.

The end-of-the-day crowds were scurrying in the direction of street-cars and elevated roads.

Irene said: "You're going south? I'm sorry. I've got an errand. If you don't mind, I'll just say good-bye here. It has been nice seeing you, Gertrude. Say hello to Fred for me, and to your mother if she remembers me. Good-bye."

She had wanted to be free of the other woman, to be alone; for she was still sore and angry.

What right, she kept demanding of herself, had Clare Kendry to expose her, or even Gertrude Martin, to such humiliation, such downright insult?

And all the while, on the rushing ride out to her father's house, Irene Redfield was trying to understand the look on Clare's face as she had said good-bye. Partly mocking, it had seemed, and partly menacing. And something else for which she could find no name. For an instant a recrudescence of that sensation of fear which she had had while looking into Clare's eyes that afternoon touched her. A slight shiver ran over her.

"It's nothing," she told herself. "Just somebody walking over my grave, as the children say." She tried a tiny laugh and was annoyed to find that it was close to tears.

What a state she had allowed that horrible Bellew to get her into!

And late that night, even, long after the last guest had gone and the old house was quiet, she stood at her window frowning out into the dark rain and puzzling again over that look on Clare's incredibly beautiful face. She couldn't, however, come to any conclusion about its meaning, try as she might. It was unfathomable, utterly beyond any experience or comprehension of hers.

She turned away from the window, at last, with a still deeper frown. Why, after all, worry about Clare Kendry? She was well able to take care of herself, had always been able. And there were, for Irene, other things, more personal and more important to worry about.

Besides, her reason told her, she had only herself to blame for her disagreeable afternoon and its attendant fears and questions. She ought never to have gone.

Four

The next morning, the day of her departure for New York, had brought a letter, which, at first glance, she had instinctively known came from Clare Kendry, though she couldn't remember ever having had a letter from her before. Ripping it open and looking at the signature, she saw that she had been right in her guess. She wouldn't, she told herself, read it. She hadn't the time. And, besides, she had no wish to be reminded of the afternoon before. As it was, she felt none too fresh for her journey; she had had a wretched night. And all because of Clare's innate lack of consideration for the feelings of others.

But she did read it. After father and friends had waved goodbye, and she was being hurled eastward, she became possessed of an uncontrollable curiosity to see what Clare had said about yesterday. For what, she asked, as she took it out of her bag and opened it, could she, what could anyone, say about a thing like that?

Clare Kendry had said:

> 'RENE DEAR:
>
> However am I to thank you for your visit? I know you are feeling that under the circumstances I ought not to have asked you to come, or, rather, insisted. But if you could know how glad, how excitingly happy, I was to meet you and how I ached to see more of you (to see everybody and couldn't), you would understand my wanting to see you again, and maybe forgive me a little.
>
> My love to you always and always and to your dear father, and all my poor thanks.
>
> CLAIRE.

And there was a postscript which said:

> It may be, 'Rene dear, it may just be, that, after all, your way may be the wiser and infinitely happier one. I'm not sure just now. At least not so sure as I have been.
>
> C.

But the letter hadn't conciliated Irene. Her indignation was not lessened by Clare's flattering reference to her wiseness. As if, she thought wrathfully, anything could take away the humiliation, or any part of it, of what she had gone through yesterday afternoon for Clare Kendry.

With an unusual methodicalness she tore the offending letter into tiny ragged squares that fluttered down and made a small heap in her black *crêpe de Chine* lap. The destruction completed, she gathered them up, rose, and moved to the train's end. Standing there, she dropped them over the railing and watched them scatter, on tracks, on cinders, on forlorn grass, in rills of dirty water.

And that, she told herself, was that. The chances were one in a million that she would ever again lay eyes on Clare Kendry. If, however, that millionth chance should turn up, she had only to turn away her eyes, to refuse her recognition.

She dropped Clare out of her mind and turned her thoughts to her own affairs. To home, to the boys, to Brian. Brian, who in the morning would be waiting for her in the great clamorous station. She hoped that he had been comfortable and not too lonely without her and the boys. Not so lonely that that old, queer, unhappy restlessness had begun again within him; that craving for some place strange and different, which at the beginning of her marriage she had had to make such strenuous efforts to repress, and which yet faintly alarmed her, though it now sprang up at gradually lessening intervals.

PART TWO: RE-ENCOUNTER

One

Such were Irene Redfield's memories as she sat there in her room, a flood of October sunlight streaming in upon her, holding that second letter of Clare Kendry's.

Laying it aside, she regarded with an astonishment that had in it a mild degree of amusement the violence of the feelings which it stirred in her.

It wasn't the great measure of anger that surprised and slightly amused her. That, she was certain, was justified and reasonable, as was the fact that it could hold, still strong and unabated, across the stretch of two years' time entirely removed from any sight or sound of John Bellew, or of Clare. That even at this remote date the memory of the man's words and manner had power to set her hands to trembling and to send the blood pounding against her temples did not seem to her extraordinary. But that she should retain that dim sense of fear, of panic, was surprising, silly.

That Clare should have written, should, even all things considered, have expressed a desire to see her again, did not so much amaze her. To count as nothing the annoyances, the bitterness, or the suffering of others, that was Clare.

Well—Irene's shoulders went up—one thing was sure: that she needn't, and didn't intend to, lay herself open to any repetition of a humiliation as galling and outrageous as that which, for Clare Kendry's sake, she had borne "that time in Chicago." Once was enough.

If, at the time of choosing, Clare hadn't precisely reckoned the cost, she had, nevertheless, no right to expect others to help make up the reckoning. The trouble with Clare was not only that she wanted to have her cake and eat it too, but that she wanted to nibble at the cakes of other folk as well.

Irene Redfield found it hard to sympathize with this new tenderness, this avowed yearning of Clare's for "my own people."

The letter which she just put out of her hand was, to her taste, a bit too lavish in its wordiness, a shade too unreserved in the manner of its expression. It roused again that old suspicion that Clare was acting, not consciously, perhaps—that is, not too consciously—but, none the less, acting. Nor was Irene inclined to excuse what she termed Clare's downright selfishness.

And mingled with her disbelief and resentment was another feeling, a question. Why hadn't she spoken that day? Why, in the face of Bellew's ignorant hate and aversion, had she concealed her own origin? Why had she allowed him to make his assertions and express his misconceptions undisputed? Why, simply because of Clare Kendry, who had exposed her to such torment, had she failed to take up the defence of the race to which she belonged?

Irene asked these questions, felt them. They were, however, merely rhetorical, as she herself was well aware. She knew their answers, every one, and it was the same for them all. The sardony[2] of it! She couldn't betray Clare, couldn't even run the risk of appearing to defend a people that were being maligned, for fear that that defence might in some infinitesimal degree lead the way to final discovery of her secret. She had to Clare Kendry a duty. She was bound to her by those very ties of race, which, for all her repudiation of them, Clare had been unable to completely sever.

And it wasn't, as Irene knew, that Clare cared at all about the race or what was to become of it. She didn't. Or that she had for any of its members great, or even real, affection, though she professed undying gratitude for the small kindnesses which the Westover family had shown her when she was a child. Irene doubted the genuineness of it, seeing herself only as a means to an end where Clare was concerned. Nor could it be said that she had even the slight artistic or sociological interest in the race that some members of other races displayed. She hadn't. No, Clare Kendry cared nothing for the race. She only belonged to it.

"Not another damned thing!" Irene declared aloud as she drew a fragile stocking over a pale beige-coloured foot.

"Aha! Swearing again, are you, madam? Caught you in the act that time."

Brian Redfield had come into the room in that noiseless way which, in spite of the years of their life together, still had the power to disconcert her. He stood looking down on her with that amused smile of his, which was just the faintest bit supercilious and yet was somehow very becoming to him.

2. Evidently "sardony" is Larsen's coinage, a noun form of sardonic. Deborah McDowell changes the word to "irony" in her edition of the novel on the grounds that it may have been a printer's error. Most subsequent editions restore "sardony."

Hastily Irene pulled on the other stocking and slipped her feet into the slippers beside her chair.

"And what brought on this particular outburst of profanity? That is, if an indulgent but perturbed husband may inquire. The mother of sons too! The times, alas, the times!"

"I've had this letter," Irene told him. "And I'm sure that anybody'll admit it's enough to make a saint swear. The nerve of her!"

She passed the letter to him, and in the act made a little mental frown. For, with a nicety of perception, she saw that she was doing it instead of answering his question with words, so that he might be occupied while she hurried through her dressing. For she was late again, and Brian, she well knew, detested that. Why, oh why, couldn't she ever manage to be on time? Brian had been up for ages, had made some calls for all she knew, besides having taken the boys downtown to school. And she wasn't dressed yet; had only begun. Damn Clare! This morning it was her fault.

Brian sat down and bent his head over the letter, puckering his brows slightly in his effort to make out Clare's scrawl.

Irene, who had risen and was standing before the mirror, ran a comb through her black hair, then tossed her head with a light characteristic gesture, in order to disarrange a little the set locks. She touched a powder-puff to her warm olive skin, and then put on her frock with a motion so hasty that it was with some difficulty properly adjusted. At last she was ready, though she didn't immediately say so, but stood, instead, looking with a sort of curious detachment at her husband across the room.

Brian, she was thinking, was extremely good-looking. Not, of course, pretty or effeminate; the slight irregularity of his nose saved him from the prettiness, and the rather marked heaviness of his chin saved him from the effeminacy. But he was, in a pleasant masculine way, rather handsome. And yet, wouldn't he, perhaps, have been merely ordinarily good-looking but for the richness, the beauty of his skin, which was of an exquisitely fine texture and deep copper colour.

He looked up and said: "Clare? That must be the girl you told me about meeting the last time you were out home. The one you went to tea with?"

Irene's answer to that was an inclination of the head.

"I'm ready," she said.

They were going downstairs, Brian deftly, unnecessarily, piloting her round the two short curved steps, just before the centre landing. "You're not," he asked, "going to see her?"

His words, however, were in reality not a question, but, as Irene was aware, an admonition.

Her front teeth just touched. She spoke through them, and her tones held a thin sarcasm. "Brian, darling, I'm really not such an idiot that I don't realize that if a man calls me a nigger, it's his fault the first time, but mine if he has the opportunity to do it again."

They went into the dining-room. He drew back her chair and she sat down behind the fat-bellied German coffee-pot, which sent out its morning fragrance, mingled with the smell of crisp toast and savoury bacon, in the distance. With his long, nervous fingers he picked up the morning paper from his own chair and sat down.

Zulena, a small mahogany-coloured creature, brought in the grapefruit.

They took up their spoons.

Out of the silence Brian spoke. Blandly. "My dear, you misunderstand me entirely. I simply meant that I hope you're not going to let her pester you. She will, you know, if you give her half a chance and she's anything at all like your description of her. Anyway, they always do. Besides," he corrected, "the man, her husband, didn't call you a nigger. There's a difference, you know."

"No, certainly he didn't. Not actually. He couldn't, not very well, since he didn't know. But he would have. It amounts to the same thing. And I'm sure it was just as unpleasant."

"U-mm, I don't know. But it seems to me," he pointed out, "that you, my dear, had all the advantage. You knew what his opinion of you was, while he—Well, 'twas ever thus. We know, always have. They don't. Not quite. It has, you will admit, its humorous side, and, sometimes, its conveniences."

She poured the coffee.

"I can't see it. I'm going to write Clare. Today, if I can find a minute. It's a thing we might as well settle definitely, and immediately. Curious, isn't it, that knowing, as she does, his unqualified attitude, she still—"

Brian interrupted: "It's always that way. Never known it to fail. Remember Albert Hammond, how he used to be for ever haunting Seventh Avenue, and Lenox Avenue, and the dancing-places, until some 'shine' took a shot at him for casting an eye towards his 'sheba?'[3] They always come back. I've seen it happen time and time again."

"But why?" Irene wanted to know. "Why?"

"If I knew that, I'd know what race is."

"But wouldn't you think that having got the thing, or things, they were after, and at such risk, they'd be satisfied? Or afraid?"

"Yes," Brian agreed, "you certainly would think so. But, the fact

3. 'shine' . . . 'sheba': derisive slang for a black man and for a beautiful black woman, respectively; Seventh . . . and Lenox: commercial streets, known as places to see and be seen and central locations for the famous Harlem speakeasy district that included The Cotton Club, Connie's Inn, Small's Paradise, and other famous cabarets.

remains, they aren't. Not satisfied, I mean. I think they're scared enough most of the time, when they give way to the urge and slip back. Not scared enough to stop them, though. Why, the good God only knows."

Irene leaned forward, speaking, she was aware, with a vehemence absolutely unnecessary, but which she could not control.

"Well, Clare can just count me out. I've no intention of being the link between her and her poorer darker brethren. After that scene in Chicago too! To calmly expect me—" She stopped short, suddenly too wrathful for words.

"Quite right. The only sensible thing to do. Let her miss you. It's an unhealthy business, the whole affair. Always is."

Irene nodded. "More coffee," she offered.

"Thanks, no." He took up his paper again, spreading it open with a little rattling noise.

Zulena came in bringing more toast. Brian took a slice and bit into it with that audible crunching sound that Irene disliked so intensely and turned back to his paper.

She said: "It's funny about 'passing.' We disapprove of it and at the same time condone it. It excites our contempt and yet we rather admire it. We shy away from it with an odd kind of revulsion, but we protect it."

"Instinct of the race to survive and expand."

"Rot! Everything can't be explained by some general biological phrase."

"Absolutely everything can. Look at the so-called whites, who've left bastards all over the known earth. Same thing in them. Instinct of the race to survive and expand."

With that Irene didn't at all agree, but many arguments in the past had taught her the futility of attempting to combat Brian on ground where he was more nearly at home than she. Ignoring his unqualified assertion, she slid away from the subject entirely.

"I wonder," she asked, "if you'll have time to run me down to the printing-office. It's on a Hundred and Sixteenth Street. I've got to see about some handbills and some more tickets for the dance."

"Yes, of course. How's it going? Everything all set?"

"Ye-es. I guess so. The boxes are all sold and nearly all the first batch of tickets. And we expect to take in almost as much again at the door. Then, there's all that cake to sell. It's a terrible lot of work, though."

"I'll bet it is. Uplifting the brother's no easy job. I'm as busy as a cat with fleas, myself." And over his face there came a shadow. "Lord! how I hate sick people, and their stupid, meddling families, and smelly, dirty rooms, and climbing filthy steps in dark hallways."

"Surely," Irene began, fighting back the fear and irritation that she felt, "surely—"

Her husband silenced her, saying sharply: "Let's not talk about it, please." And immediately, in his usual, slightly mocking tone he asked: "Are you ready to go now? I haven't a great deal of time to wait."

He got up. She followed him out into the hall without replying. He picked up his soft brown hat from the small table and stood a moment whirling it round on his long tea-coloured fingers.

Irene, watching him, was thinking: "It isn't fair, it isn't fair." After all these years to still blame her like this. Hadn't his success proved that she'd been right in insisting that he stick to his profession right there in New York? Couldn't he see, even now, that it *had* been best? Not for her, oh no, not for her—she had never really considered herself—but for him and the boys. Was she never to be free of it, that fear which crouched, always, deep down within her, stealing away the sense of security, the feeling of permanence, from the life which she had so admirably arranged for them all, and desired so ardently to have remain as it was? That strange, and to her fantastic, notion of Brian's of going off to Brazil[4] which, though unmentioned, yet lived within him; how it frightened her, and—yes, angered her!

"Well?" he asked lightly.

"I'll just get my things. One minute," she promised and turned upstairs.

Her voice had been even and her step was firm, but in her there was no slackening of the agitation, of the alarms, which Brian's expression of discontent had raised. He had never spoken of his desire since that long-ago time of storm and strain, of hateful and nearly disastrous quarrelling, when she had so firmly opposed him, so sensibly pointed out its utter impossibility and its probable consequences to her and the boys, and had even hinted at a dissolution of their marriage in the event of his persistence in his idea. No, there had been, in all the years that they had lived together since then, no other talk of it, no more than there had been any other quarrelling or any other threats. But because, so she insisted, the bond of flesh and spirit between them was so strong, she knew, had always known, that his dissatisfaction had continued, as had his dislike and disgust for his profession and his country.

A feeling of uneasiness stole upon her at the inconceivable suspicion that she might have been wrong in her estimate of her husband's character. But she squirmed away from it. Impossible! She couldn't have been wrong. Everything proved that she had been right. More than right, if such a thing could be. And all, she assured herself, because she understood him so well, because she had, actually, a spe-

---

4. See the 1925 newspaper article "Writer Says Brazil Has No Color Line," included in the "Contemporary Coverage of Race and Passing" section of this edition.

cial talent for understanding him. It was, as she saw it, the one thing that had been the basis of the success which she had made of a marriage that had threatened to fail. She knew him as well as he knew himself, or better.

Then why worry? The thing, this discontent which had exploded into words, would surely die, flicker out, at last. True, she had in the past often been tempted to believe that it had died, only to become conscious, in some instinctive, subtle way, that she had been merely deceiving herself for a while and that it still lived. But it *would* die. Of that she was certain. She had only to direct and guide her man, to keep him going in the right direction.

She put on her coat and adjusted her hat.

Yes, it would die, as long ago she had made up her mind that it should. But in the meantime, while it was still living and still had the power to flare up and alarm her, it would have to be banked, smothered, and something offered in its stead. She would have to make some plan, some decision, at once. She frowned, for it annoyed her intensely. For, though temporary, it would be important and perhaps disturbing. Irene didn't like changes, particularly changes that affected the smooth routine of her household. Well, it couldn't be helped. Something would have to be done. And immediately.

She took up her purse and drawing on her gloves, ran down the steps and out through the door which Brian held open for her and stepped into the waiting car.

"You know," she said, settling herself into the seat beside him, "I'm awfully glad to get this minute alone with you. It does seem that we're always so busy—I do hate that—but what can we do? I've had something on my mind for ever so long, something that needs talking over and really serious consideration."

The car's engine rumbled as it moved out from the kerb and into the scant traffic of the street under Brian's expert guidance.

She studied his profile.

They turned into Seventh Avenue. Then he said: "Well, let's have it. No time like the present for the settling of weighty matters."

"It's about Junior. I wonder if he isn't going too fast in school? We do forget that he's not eleven yet. Surely it can't be good for him to—well, if he is, I mean. Going too fast, you know. Of course, you know more about these things than I do. You're better able to judge. That is, if you've noticed or thought about it at all."

"I do wish, Irene, you wouldn't be for ever fretting about those kids. They're all right. Perfectly all right. Good, strong, healthy boys, especially Junior. Most especially Junior."

"We-ll, I s'pose you're right. You're expected to know about things like that, and I'm sure you wouldn't make a mistake about your own boy." (Now, why had she said that?) "But that isn't all. I'm terribly afraid he's picked up some queer ideas about things—some things— from the older boys, you know."

Her manner was consciously light. Apparently she was intent on the maze of traffic, but she was still watching Brian's face closely. On it was a peculiar expression. Was it, could it possibly be, a mixture of scorn and distaste?

"Queer ideas?" he repeated. "D'you mean ideas about sex, Irene?" "Ye-es. Not quite nice ones. Dreadful jokes, and things like that."

"Oh, I see," he threw at her. For a while there was silence between them. After a moment he demanded bluntly: "Well, what of it? If sex isn't a joke, what is it? And what is a joke?"

"As you please, Brian. He's your son, you know." Her voice was clear, level, disapproving.

"Exactly! And you're trying to make a molly-coddle out of him. Well, just let me tell you, I won't have it. And you needn't think I'm going to let you change him to some nice kindergarten kind of a school because he's getting a little necessary education. I won't! He'll stay right where he is. The sooner and the more he learns about sex, the better for him. And most certainly if he learns that it's a grand joke, the greatest in the world. It'll keep him from lots of disappointments later on."

Irene didn't answer.

They reached the printing-shop. She got out, emphatically slamming the car's door behind her. There was a piercing agony of misery in her heart. She hadn't intended to behave like this, but her extreme resentment at his attitude, the sense of having been wilfully misunderstood and reproved, drove her to fury.

Inside the shop, she stilled the trembling of her lips and drove back her rising anger. Her business transacted, she came back to the car in a chastened mood. But against the armour of Brian's stubborn silence she heard herself saying in a calm, metallic voice: "I don't believe I'll go back just now. I've remembered that I've got to do something about getting something decent to wear. I haven't a rag that's fit to be seen. I'll take the bus downtown."

Brian merely doffed his hat in that maddening polite way which so successfully curbed and yet revealed his temper.

"Good-bye," she said bitingly. "Thanks for the lift," and turned towards the avenue.

What, she wondered contritely, was she to do next? She was vexed with herself for having chosen, as it had turned out, so clumsy an opening for what she had intended to suggest: some European school for Junior next year, and Brian to take him over. If she had been able to present her plan, and he had accepted it, as she was sure that he would have done, with other more favourable opening methods, he would have had that to look forward to as a break in the easy monotony that seemed, for some reason she was wholly unable to grasp, so hateful to him.

She was even more vexed at her own explosion of anger. What could have got into her to give way to it in such a moment?

Gradually her mood passed. She drew back from the failure of her first attempt at substitution, not so much discouraged as disappointed and ashamed. It might be, she reflected, that, in addition to her ill-timed loss of temper, she had been too hasty in her eagerness to distract him, had rushed too closely on the heels of his outburst, and had thus aroused his suspicions and his obstinacy. She had but to wait. Another more appropriate time would come, tomorrow, next week, next month. It wasn't now, as it had been once, that she was afraid that he would throw everything aside and rush off to that remote place of his heart's desire. He wouldn't, she knew. He was fond of her, loved her, in his slightly undemonstrative way.

And there were the boys.

It was only that she wanted him to be happy, resenting, however, his inability to be so with things as they were, and never acknowledging that though she did want him to be happy, it was only in her own way and by some plan of hers for him that she truly desired him to be so. Nor did she admit that all other plans, all other ways, she regarded as menaces, more or less indirect, to that security of place and substance which she insisted upon for her sons and in a lesser degree for herself.

Two

Five days had gone by since Clare Kendry's appealing letter. Irene Redfield had not replied to it. Nor had she had any other word from Clare.

She had not carried out her first intention of writing at once because on going back to the letter for Clare's address, she had come upon something which, in the rigour of her determination to maintain unbroken between them the wall that Clare herself had raised, she had forgotten, or not fully noted. It was the fact that Clare had requested her to direct her answer to the post office's general delivery.

That had angered Irene, and increased her disdain and contempt for the other.

Tearing the letter across, she had flung it into the scrap-basket. It wasn't so much Clare's carefulness and her desire for secrecy in their relations—Irene understood the need for that—as that Clare should have doubted her discretion, implied that she might not be cautious in the wording of her reply and the choice of a posting-box. Having always had complete confidence in her own good judgment and tact, Irene couldn't bear to have anyone seem to question them. Certainly not Clare Kendry.

In another, calmer moment she decided that it was, after all, better to answer nothing, to explain nothing, to refuse nothing; to dispose of the matter simply by not writing at all. Clare, of whom it couldn't be said that she was stupid, would not mistake the implication of that silence. She might—and Irene was sure that she would—choose to ignore it and write again, but that didn't matter. The whole thing would be very easy. The basket for all letters, silence for their answers.

Most likely she and Clare would never meet again. Well, she, for one, could endure that. Since childhood their lives had never really touched. Actually they were strangers. Strangers in their ways and means of living. Strangers in their desires and ambitions. Strangers even in their racial consciousness. Between them the barrier was just as high, just as broad, and just as firm as if in Clare did not run that strain of black blood. In truth, it was higher, broader, and firmer; because for her there were perils, not known, or imagined, by those others who had no such secrets to alarm or endanger them.

The day was getting on toward evening. It was past the middle of October. There had been a week of cold rain, drenching the rotting leaves which had fallen from the poor trees that lined the street on which the Redfields' house was located, and sending a damp air of penetrating chill into the house, with a hint of cold days to come. In Irene's room a low fire was burning. Outside, only a dull grey light was left of the day. Inside, lamps had already been lighted.

From the floor above there was the sound of young voices. Sometimes Junior's serious and positive; again, Ted's deceptively gracious one. Often there was laughter, or the noise of commotion, tussling, or toys being slammed down.

Junior, tall for his age, was almost incredibly like his father in feature and colouring; but his temperament was hers, practical and determined, rather than Brian's. Ted, speculative and withdrawn, was, apparently, less positive in his ideas and desires. About him there was a deceiving air of candour that was, Irene knew, like his father's show of reasonable acquiescence. If, for the time being, and with a charming appearance of artlessness, he submitted to the force of superior strength, or some other immovable condition or circumstance, it was because of his intense dislike of scenes and unpleasant argument. Brian over again.

Gradually Irene's thought slipped away from junior and Ted, to become wholly absorbed in their father.

The old fear, with strength increased, the fear for the future, had again laid its hand on her. And, try as she might, she could not shake it off. It was as if she had admitted to herself that against that easy surface of her husband's concordance with her wishes, which had, since the war had given him back to her physically unimpaired, covered an increasing inclination to tear himself and his possessions loose from their proper setting, she was helpless.

The chagrin which she had felt at her first failure to subvert this latest manifestation of his discontent had receded, leaving in its wake an uneasy depression. Were all her efforts, all her labours, to make up to him that one loss, all her silent striving to prove to him that her way had been best, all her ministrations to him, all her outward sinking of self, to count for nothing in some unperceived sudden moment? And if so, what, then, would be the consequences to the boys? To her? To Brian himself? Endless searching had brought no answer to these questions. There was only an intense weariness from their shuttle-like procession in her brain.

The noise and commotion from above grew increasingly louder. Irene was about to go to the stairway and request the boys to be quieter in their play when she heard the doorbell ringing.

Now, who was that likely to be? She listened to Zulena's heels, faintly tapping on their way to the door, then to the shifting sound of her feet on the steps, then to her light knock on the bedroom door.

"Yes. Come in," Irene told her.

Zulena stood in the doorway. She said: "Someone to see you, Mrs. Redfield." Her tone was discreetly regretful, as if to convey that she was reluctant to disturb her mistress at that hour, and for a stranger. "A Mrs. Bellew."

Clare!

"Oh dear! Tell her, Zulena," Irene began, "that I can't—No. I'll see her. Please bring her up here."

She heard Zulena pass down the hall, down the stairs, then stood up, smoothing out the tumbled green and ivory draperies of her dress with light stroking pats. At the mirror she dusted a little powder on her nose and brushed out her hair.

She meant to tell Clare Kendry at once, and definitely, that it was of no use, her coming, that she couldn't be responsible, that she'd talked it over with Brian, who had agreed with her that it was wiser, for Clare's own sake, to refrain—

But that was as far as she got in her rehearsal. For Clare had come softly into the room without knocking, and before Irene could greet her, had dropped a kiss on her dark curls.

Looking at the woman before her, Irene Redfield had a sudden inexplicable onrush of affectionate feeling. Reaching out, she grasped Clare's two hands in her own and cried with something like awe in her voice: "Dear God! But aren't you lovely, Clare!"

Clare tossed that aside. Like the furs and small blue hat which she threw on the bed before seating herself slantwise in Irene's favourite chair, with one foot curled under her.

"Didn't you mean to answer my letter, 'Rene?" she asked gravely.

Irene looked away. She had that uncomfortable feeling that one has when one has not been wholly kind or wholly true.

Clare went on: "Every day I went to that nasty little post-office place. I'm sure they were all beginning to think that I'd been carrying on an illicit love-affair and that the man had thrown me over. Every morning the same answer: 'Nothing for you.' I got into an awful fright, thinking that something might have happened to your letter, or to mine. And half the nights I would lie awake looking out at the watery stars—hopeless things, the stars—worrying and wondering. But at last it soaked in, that you hadn't written and didn't intend to. And then—well, as soon as ever I'd seen Jack off for Florida, I came straight here. And now, 'Rene, please tell me quite frankly why you didn't answer my letter."

"Because, you see—" Irene broke off and kept Clare waiting while she lit a cigarette, blew out the match, and dropped it into a tray. She was trying to collect her arguments, for some sixth sense warned her that it was going to be harder than she thought to convince Clare Kendry of the folly of Harlem for her. Finally she proceeded: "I can't help thinking that you ought not to come up here, ought not to run the risk of knowing Negroes."

"You mean you don't want me, 'Rene?"

Irene hadn't supposed that anyone could look so hurt. She said, quite gently, "No, Clare, it's not that. But even you must see that it's terribly foolish, and not just the right thing."

The tinkle of Clare's laugh rang out, while she passed her hands over the bright sweep of her hair. "Oh, 'Rene!" she cried, "you're priceless! And you haven't changed a bit. The right thing!" Leaning forward, she looked curiously into Irene's disapproving brown eyes. "You don't, you really can't mean exactly that! Nobody could. It's simply unbelievable."

Irene was on her feet before she realized that she had risen. "What I really mean," she retorted, "is that it's dangerous and that you ought not to run such silly risks. No one ought to. You least of all."

Her voice was brittle. For into her mind had come a thought, strange and irrelevant, a suspicion, that had surprised and shocked her and driven her to her feet. It was that in spite of her determined selfishness the woman before her was yet capable of heights and depths of feeling that she, Irene Redfield, had never known. Indeed, never cared to know. The thought, the suspicion, was gone as quickly as it had come.

Clare said: "Oh, me!"

Irene touched her arm caressingly, as if in contrition for that flashing thought. "Yes, Clare, you. It's not safe. Not safe at all."

"Safe!"

It seemed to Irene that Clare had snapped her teeth down on the word and then flung it from her. And for another flying second she had that suspicion of Clare's ability for a quality of feeling that was to her strange, and even repugnant. She was aware, too, of a dim premonition of some impending disaster. It was as if Clare Kendry had said to her, for whom safety, security, were all-important: "Safe! Damn being safe!" and meant it.

With a gesture of impatience she sat down. In a voice of cool formality, she said: "Brian and I have talked the whole thing over carefully and decided that it isn't wise. He says it's always a dangerous business, this coming back. He's seen more than one come to grief because of it. And, Clare, considering everything—Mr. Bellew's attitude and all that—don't you think you ought to be as careful as you can?"

Clare's deep voice broke the small silence that had followed Irene's speech. She said, speaking almost plaintively: "I ought to have known. It's Jack. I don't blame you for being angry, though I must say you behaved beautifully that day. But I did think you'd understand, 'Rene. It was that, partly, that has made me want to see other people. It just swooped down and changed everything. If it hadn't been for that, I'd have gone on to the end, never seeing any of you. But that did something to me, and I've been so lonely since! You can't know. Not close to a single soul. Never anyone to really talk to."

Irene pressed out her cigarette. While doing so, she saw again the vision of Clare Kendry staring disdainfully down at the face of her father, and thought that it would be like that that she would look at her husband if he lay dead before her.

Her own resentment was swept aside and her voice held an accent of pity as she exclaimed: "Why, Clare! I didn't know. Forgive me. I feel like seven beasts.[5] It was stupid of me not to realize."

"No. Not at all. You couldn't. Nobody, none of you, could," Clare moaned. The black eyes filled with tears that ran down her cheeks and spilled into her lap, ruining the priceless velvet of her dress. Her long hands were a little uplifted and clasped tightly together. Her

5. Biblical reference to the seven-headed beast who appears several times in Revelations.

effort to speak moderately was obvious, but not successful. "How could you know? How could you? You're free. You're happy. And," with faint derision, "safe."

Irene passed over that touch of derision, for the poignant rebellion of the other's words had brought the tears to her own eyes, though she didn't allow them to fall. The truth was that she knew weeping did not become her. Few women, she imagined, wept as attractively as Clare. "I'm beginning to believe," she murmured, "that no one is ever completely happy, or free, or safe."

"Well, then, what does it matter? One risk more or less, if we're not safe anyway, if even you're not, it can't make all the difference in the world. It can't to me. Besides, I'm used to risks. And this isn't such a big one as you're trying to make it."

"Oh, but it is. And it can make all the difference in the world. There's your little girl, Clare. Think of the consequences to her."

Clare's face took on a startled look, as though she were totally unprepared for this new weapon with which Irene had assailed her. Seconds passed, during which she sat with stricken eyes and compressed lips. "I think," she said at last, "that being a mother is the cruellest thing in the world." Her clasped hands swayed forward and back again, and her scarlet mouth trembled irrepressibly.

"Yes," Irene softly agreed. For a moment she was unable to say more, so accurately had Clare put into words that which, not so definitely defined, was so often in her own heart of late. At the same time she was conscious that here, to her hand, was a reason which could not be lightly brushed aside. "Yes," she repeated, "and the most responsible, Clare. We mothers are all responsible for the security and happiness of our children. Think what it would mean to your Margery if Mr. Bellew should find out. You'd probably lose her. And even if you didn't, nothing that concerned her would ever be the same again. He'd never forget that she had Negro blood. And if she should learn—Well, I believe that after twelve it is too late to learn a thing like that. She'd never forgive you. You may be used to risks, but this is one you mustn't take, Clare. It's a selfish whim, an unnecessary and—

"Yes, Zulena, what is it?" she inquired, a trifle tartly, of the servant who had silently materialized in the doorway.

"The telephone's for you, Mrs. Redfield. It's Mr. Wentworth."[6]

"All right. Thank you. I'll take it here." And, with a muttered apology to Clare, she took up the instrument.

"Hello. . . . Yes, Hugh. . . . Oh, quite. . . . And you? . . . I'm sorry,

6. Mr. Wentworth, Hugh Wentworth: modeled on Carl Van Vechten. Wentworth's wife Bianca, is modeled on Fania Marinoff, Van Vechten's wife. For disagreement about whether or not Wentworth is Van Vechten, see Kathleen Pfeifer, *Race Passing and American Individualism* (Amherst: University of Massachusetts Press, 2003).

every single thing's gone. . . . Oh, too bad. . . . Ye-es, I s'pose you could. Not very pleasant, though. . . . Yes, of course, in a pinch every-thing goes. . . . Wait! I've got it! I'll change mine with whoever's next to you, and you can have that. . . . No. . . . I mean it. . . . I'll be so busy I shan't know whether I'm sitting or standing. . . . As long as Brian has a place to drop down now and then. . . . Not a single soul. . . . No, don't. . . . That's nice. . . . My love to Bianca. . . . I'll see to it right away and call you back. . . . Good-bye."

She hung up and turned back to Clare, a little frown on her softly chiselled features. "It's the N. W. L. dance," she explained, "the Negro Welfare League,[7] you know. I'm on the ticket committee, or, rather, I *am* the committee. Thank heaven it comes off tomorrow night and doesn't happen again for a year. I'm about crazy, and now I've got to persuade somebody to change boxes with me."

"That wasn't," Clare asked, "Hugh Wentworth? Not *the* Hugh Wentworth?"

Irene inclined her head. On her face was a tiny triumphant smile. "Yes, *the* Hugh Wentworth. D'you know him?"

"No. How should I? But I do know about him. And I've read a book or two of his."

"Awfully good, aren't they?"

"U-umm, I s'pose so. Sort of contemptuous, I thought. As if he more or less despised everything and everybody."

"I shouldn't be a bit surprised if he did. Still, he's about earned the right to. Lived on the edges of nowhere in at least three continents. Been through every danger in all kinds of savage places. It's no won-der he thinks the rest of us are a lazy self-pampering lot. Hugh's a dear, though, generous as one of the twelve disciples; give you the shirt off his back. Bianca—that's his wife—is nice too."

"And he's coming up here to your dance?"

Irene asked why not.

"It seems rather curious, a man like that, going to a Negro dance."

This, Irene told her, was the year 1927 in the city of New York, and hundreds of white people of Hugh Wentworth's type came to affairs in Harlem, more all the time. So many that Brian had said: "Pretty soon the coloured people won't be allowed in at all, or will have to sit in Jim Crowed sections."[8]

"What do they come for?"

"Same reason you're here, to see Negroes."

---

7. Larsen's fictional cross between the two most important national black "uplift" organiza-tions: the National Urban League, founded in 1911 and The NAACP, founded in 1909.
8. Originating with minstrel shows, the term "Jim Crow" was first widely used to deride and stereotype blacks, gradually becoming synonymous with all practices of racial segregation, from train cars to water fountains. "coloured people won't be allowed in": Many of the most famous Harlem nightclubs and cabarets, like the popular jungle-themed Cotton Club on 142nd and Lenox, employed only black performers but admitted only whites as patrons.

"But why?"

"Various motives," Irene explained. "A few purely and frankly to enjoy themselves. Others to get material to turn into shekels.[9] More, to gaze on these great and near great while they gaze on the Negroes."

Clare clapped her hand. " 'Rene, suppose I come too! It sounds terribly interesting and amusing. And I don't see why I shouldn't."

Irene, who was regarding her through narrowed eyelids, had the same thought that she had had two years ago on the roof of the Drayton, that Clare Kendry was just a shade too good-looking. Her tone was on the edge of irony as she said: "You mean because so many other white people go?"

A pale rose-colour came into Clare's ivory cheeks. She lifted a hand in protest. "Don't be silly! Certainly not! I mean that in a crowd of that kind I shouldn't be noticed."

On the contrary, was Irene's opinion. It might be even doubly dangerous. Some friend or acquaintance of John Bellew or herself might see and recognize her.

At that, Clare laughed for a long time, little musical trills following one another in sequence after sequence. It was as if the thought of any friend of John Bellew's going to a Negro dance was to her the most amusing thing in the world.

"I don't think," she said, when she had done laughing, "we need worry about that."

Irene, however, wasn't so sure. But all her efforts to dissuade Clare were useless. To her, "You never can tell whom you're likely to meet there," Clare's rejoinder was: "I'll take my chance on getting by."

"Besides, you won't know a soul and I shall be too busy to look after you. You'll be bored stiff."

"I won't, I won't. If nobody asks me to dance, not even Dr. Redfield, I'll just sit and gaze on the great and the near great, too. Do, 'Rene, be polite and invite me."

Irene turned away from the caress of Clare's smile, saying promptly and positively: "I will not."

"I mean to go anyway," Clare retorted, and her voice was no less positive than Irene's.

"Oh, no. You couldn't possibly go there alone. It's a public thing. All sorts of people go, anybody who can pay a dollar, even ladies of easy virtue looking for trade. If you were to go there alone, you might be mistaken for one of them, and that wouldn't be too pleasant."

9. Slang for cash, derived from the ancient Hebrew; this suggestion that Jews may have especially benefited from the Harlem "vogue" could be a not uncommon anti-Semitism on Larsen's part, a reference to the numbers of Jews among Harlem whites, or to the consumer protests in Harlem which sometimes targeted businesses that were perceived to be owned by Jews.

Clare laughed again. "Thanks. I never have been. It might be amusing. I'm warning you, 'Rene, that if you're not going to be nice and take me, I'll still be among those present. I suppose, my dollar's as good as anyone's."

"Oh, the dollar! Don't be a fool, Clare. I don't care where you go, or what you do. All I'm concerned with is the unpleasantness and possible danger which your going might incur, because of your situation. To put it frankly, I shouldn't like to be mixed up in any row of the kind." She had risen again as she spoke and was standing at the window lifting and spreading the small yellow chrysanthemums in the grey stone jar on the sill. Her hands shook slightly, for she was in a near rage of impatience and exasperation.

Clare's face looked strange, as if she wanted to cry again. One of her satin-covered feet swung restlessly back and forth. She said vehemently, violently almost: "Damn Jack! He keeps me out of everything. Everything I want. I could kill him! I expect I shall, some day."

"I wouldn't," Irene advised her, "you see, there's still capital punishment, in this state at least. And really, Clare, after everything's said, I can't see that you've a right to put all the blame on him. You've got to admit that there's his side to the thing. You didn't tell him you were coloured, so he's got no way of knowing about this hankering of yours after Negroes, or that it galls you to fury to hear them called niggers and black devils. As far as I can see, you'll just have to endure some things and give up others. As we've said before, everything must be paid for. Do, please, be reasonable."

But Clare, it was plain, had shut away reason as well as caution. She shook her head. "I can't, I can't," she said. "I would if I could, but I can't. You don't know, you can't realize how I want to see Negroes, to be with them again, to talk with them, to hear them laugh."

And in the look she gave Irene, there was something groping, and hopeless, and yet so absolutely determined that it was like an image of the futile searching and the firm resolution in Irene's own soul, and increased the feeling of doubt and compunction that had been growing within her about Clare Kendry.

She gave in.

"Oh, come if you want to. I s'pose you're right. Once can't do such a terrible lot of harm."

Pushing aside Clare's extravagant thanks, for immediately she was sorry that she had consented, she said briskly: "Should you like to come up and see my boys?"

"I'd love to."

They went up, Irene thinking that Brian would consider that she'd behaved like a spineless fool. And he would be right. She certainly had.

Clare was smiling. She stood in the doorway of the boys' playroom, her shadowy eyes looking down on Junior and Ted, who had sprung apart from their tusselling. Junior's face had a funny little look of resentment. Ted's was blank.

Clare said: "Please don't be cross. Of course, I know I've gone and spoiled everything. But maybe, if I promise not to get too much in the way, you'll let me come in, just the same."

"Sure, come in if you want to," Ted told her. "We can't stop you, you know." He smiled and made her a little bow and then turned away to a shelf that held his favourite books. Taking one down, he settled himself in a chair and began to read.

Junior said nothing, did nothing, merely stood there waiting.

"Get up, Ted! That's rude. This is Theodore, Mrs. Bellew. Please excuse his bad manners. He does know better. And this is Brian junior. Mrs. Bellew is an old friend of mother's. We used to play together when we were little girls."

Clare had gone and Brian had telephoned that he'd been detained and would have his dinner downtown. Irene was a little glad for that. She was going out later herself, and that meant she wouldn't, probably, see Brian until morning and so could put off for a few more hours speaking of Clare and the N. W. L. dance.

She was angry with herself and with Clare. But more with herself, for having permitted Clare to tease her into doing something that Brian had, all but expressly, asked her not to do. She didn't want him ruffled, not just then, not while he was possessed of that unreasonable restless feeling.

She was annoyed, too, because she was aware that she had consented to something which, if it went beyond the dance, would involve her in numerous petty inconveniences and evasions. And not only at home with Brian, but outside with friends and acquaintances. The disagreeable possibilities in connection with Clare Kendry's coming among them loomed before her in endless irritating array.

Clare, it seemed, still retained her ability to secure the thing that she wanted in the face of any opposition, and in utter disregard of the convenience and desire of others. About her there was some quality, hard and persistent, with the strength and endurance of rock, that would not be beaten or ignored. She couldn't, Irene thought, have had an entirely serene life. Not with that dark secret for ever crouching in the background of her consciousness. And yet she hadn't the air of a woman whose life had been touched by uncertainty or suffering. Pain, fear, and grief were things that left their mark on people. Even love, that exquisite torturing emotion, left its subtle traces on the countenance.

But Clare—she had remained almost what she had always been, an attractive, somewhat lonely child—selfish, wilful, and disturbing.

Three

The things which Irene Redfield remembered afterward about the Negro Welfare League dance seemed, to her, unimportant and unrelated.

She remembered the not quite derisive smile with which Brian had cloaked his vexation when she informed him—oh, so apologetically—that she had promised to take Clare, and related the conversation of her visit.

She remembered her own little choked exclamation of admiration, when, on coming downstairs a few minutes later than she had intended, she had rushed into the living-room where Brian was waiting and had found Clare there too. Clare, exquisite, golden, fragrant, flaunting, in a stately gown of shining black taffeta, whose long, full skirt lay in graceful folds about her slim golden feet; her glistening hair drawn smoothly back into a small twist at the nape of her neck; her eyes sparkling like dark jewels. Irene, with her new rose-coloured chiffon frock ending at the knees, and her cropped curls, felt dowdy and commonplace. She regretted that she hadn't counselled Clare to wear something ordinary and inconspicuous. What on earth would Brian think of deliberate courting of attention? But if Clare Kendry's appearance had in it anything that was, to Brian Redfield, annoying or displeasing, the fact was not discernible to his wife as, with an uneasy feeling of guilt, she stood there looking into his face while Clare explained that she and he had made their own introductions, accompanying her words with a little deferential smile for Brian, and receiving in return one of his amused, slightly mocking smiles.

She remembered Clare's saying, as they sped northward: "You know, I feel exactly as I used to on the Sunday we went to the Christmas-tree celebration. I knew there was to be a surprise for me and couldn't quite guess what it was to be. I am so excited. You can't possibly imagine! It's marvellous to be really on the way! I can hardly believe it!"

At her words and tone a chilly wave of scorn had crept through Irene. All those superlatives! She said, taking care to speak indifferently: "Well, maybe in some ways you will be surprised, more, probably, than you anticipate."

Brian, at the wheel, had thrown back: "And then again, she won't be so very surprised after all, for it'll no doubt be about what she expects. Like the Christmas-tree."

She remembered rushing around here and there, consulting with this person and that one, and now and then snatching a part of a dance with some man whose dancing she particularly liked.

She remembered catching glimpses of Clare in the whirling crowd, dancing, sometimes with a white man, more often with a Negro, frequently with Brian. Irene was glad that he was being nice to Clare, and glad that Clare was having the opportunity to discover that some coloured men were superior to some white men.

She remembered a conversation she had with Hugh Wentworth in a free half-hour when she had dropped into a chair in an emptied box and let her gaze wander over the bright crowd below.

Young men, old men, white men, black men; youthful women, older women, pink women, golden women; fat men, thin men, tall men, short men; stout women, slim women, stately women, small women moved by. An old nursery rhyme popped into her head. She turned to Wentworth, who had just taken a seat beside her, and recited it:

"Rich man, poor man,
Beggar man, thief,
Doctor, lawyer,
Indian chief."

"Yes," Wentworth said, "that's it. Everybody seems to be here and a few more. But what I'm trying to find out is the name, status, and race of the blonde beauty out of the fairy-tale. She's dancing with Ralph Hazelton at the moment. Nice study in contrasts, that."

It was. Clare fair and golden, like a sunlit day. Hazleton dark, with gleaming eyes, like a moonlit night.

"She's a girl I used to know a long time ago in Chicago. And she wanted especially to meet you."

" 'S awfully good of her, I'm sure. And now, alas! the usual thing's happened. All these others, these—er—'gentlemen of colour' have driven a mere Nordic from her mind."

"Stuff!"

" 'S a fact, and what happens to all the ladies of my superior race who're lured up here. Look at Bianca. Have I laid eyes on her tonight except in spots, here and there, being twirled about by some Ethiopian? I have not."

"But, Hugh, you've got to admit that the average coloured man is a better dancer than the average white man—that is, if the celebrities and 'butter and egg' men who find their way up here are fair specimens of white Terpsichorean art."[1]

"Not having tripped the light fantastic[2] with any of the males, I'm

---

not in a position to argue the point. But I don't think it's merely that. 'S something else, some other attraction. They're always raving about the good looks of some Negro, preferably an unusually dark one. Take Hazelton there, for example. Dozens of women have declared him to be fascinatingly handsome. How about you, Irene? Do you think he's—er—ravishingly beautiful?"

"I do not! And I don't think the others do either. Not honestly, I mean. I think that what they feel is—well, a kind of emotional excitement. You know, the sort of thing you feel in the presence of something strange, and even, perhaps, a bit repugnant to you; something so different that it's really at the opposite end of the pole from all your accustomed notions of beauty."

"Damned if I don't think you're halfway right!"

"I'm sure I am. Completely. (Except, of course, when it's just patronizing kindness on their part.) And I know coloured girls who've experienced the same thing—the other way round, naturally."

"And the men? You don't subscribe to the general opinion about their reason for coming up here. Purely predatory. Or, do you?"

"N-no. More curious, I should say."

Wentworth, whose eyes were a clouded amber colour, had given her a long, searching look that was really a stare. He said: "All this is awfully interestin', Irene. We've got to have a long talk about it some time soon. There's your friend from Chicago, first time up here and all that. A case in point."

Irene's smile had only just lifted the corners of her painted lips. A match blazed in Wentworth's broad hands as he lighted her cigarette and his own, and flickered out before he asked: "Or isn't she?"

Her smile changed to a laugh. "Oh, Hugh! You're so clever. You usually know everything. Even how to tell the sheep from the goats. What do you think? Is she?"

He blew a long contemplative wreath of smoke. "Damned if I know! I'll be as sure as anything that I've learned the trick. And then in the next minute I'll find I couldn't pick some of 'em if my life depended on it."

"Well, don't let that worry you. Nobody can. Not by looking."

"Not by looking, eh? Meaning?"

"I'm afraid I can't explain. Not clearly. There are ways. But they're not definite or tangible."

"Feeling of kinship, or something like that?"

"Good heavens, no, no! Nobody has that, except for their in-laws."

"Right again! But go on about the sheep and the goats."

"Well, take my own experience with Dorothy Thompkins. I'd met her four or five times, in groups and crowds of people, before I knew she wasn't a Negro. One day I went to an awful tea, terribly dicty.

Dorothy was there. We got talking. In less than five minutes, I knew she was 'fay.'[3] Not from anything she did or said or anything in her appearance. Just—just something. A thing that couldn't be registered."

"Yes, I understand what you mean. Yet lots of people 'pass' all the time."

"Not on our side, Hugh. It's easy for a Negro to 'pass' for white. But I don't think it would be so simple for a white person to 'pass' for coloured."

"Never thought of that."

"No, you wouldn't. Why should you?"

He regarded her critically through mists of smoke. "Slippin' me, Irene?"[4]

She said soberly: "Not you, Hugh. I'm too fond of you. And you're too sincere."

And she remembered that towards the end of the dance Brian had come to her and said: "I'll drop you first and then run Clare down." And that he had been doubtful of her discretion when she had explained to him that he wouldn't have to bother because she had asked Bianca Wentworth to take her down with them. Did she, he had asked, think it had been wise to tell them about Clare?

"I told them nothing," she said sharply, for she was unbearably tired, "except that she was at the Walsingham. It's on their way. And, really, I haven't thought anything about the wisdom of it, but now that I do, I'd say it's much better for them to take her than you."

"As you please. She's your friend, you know," he had answered, with a disclaiming shrug of his shoulders.

Except for these few unconnected things the dance faded to a blurred memory, its outlines mingling with those of other dances of its kind that she had attended in the past and would attend in the future.

Four

But undistinctive as the dance had seemed, it was, nevertheless, important. For it marked the beginning of a new factor in Irene Redfield's life, something that left its trace on all the future years of her existence. It was the beginning of a new friendship with Clare Kendry.

She came to them frequently after that. Always with a touching

---

3. Harlem slang for whites, a derivative of "ofay"; dicty: Harlem slang for snooty, haughty, or pretentious upper-class mannersisms—one who is "dicty" is one who puts on airs.
4. Slippin' me: i.e., tricking me or trying to put something over on me.

gladness that welled up and overflowed on all the Redfield household. Yet Irene could never be sure whether her comings were a joy
or a vexation.

Certainly she was no trouble. She had not to be entertained, or
even noticed—if anyone could ever avoid noticing Clare. If Irene
happened to be out or occupied, Clare could very happily amuse herself with Ted and Junior, who had conceived for her an admiration
that verged on adoration, especially Ted. Or, lacking the boys, she
would descend to the kitchen and, with—to Irene—an exasperating
childlike lack of perception, spend her visit in talk and merriment
with Zulena and Sadie.

Irene, while secretly resenting these visits to the playroom and
kitchen, for some obscure reason which she shied away from putting
into words, never requested that Clare make an end of them, or
hinted that she wouldn't have spoiled her own Margery so outra-
geously, nor been so friendly with white servants.

Brian looked on these things with the same tolerant amusement
that marked his entire attitude toward Clare. Never since his faintly
derisive surprise at Irene's information that she was to go with them
the night of the dance, had he shown any disapproval of Clare's presence. On the other hand, it couldn't be said that her presence
seemed to please him. It didn't annoy or disturb him, so far as Irene
could judge. That was all.

Didn't he, she once asked him, think Clare was extraordinarily
beautiful?

"No," he had answered. "That is, not particularly."

"Brian, you're fooling!"

"No, honestly. Maybe I'm fussy. I s'pose she'd be an unusually
good-looking white woman. I like my ladies darker. Beside an A-
number-one sheba,⁵ she simply hasn't got 'em."

Clare went, sometimes with Irene and Brian, to parties and
dances, and on a few occasions when Irene hadn't been able or
inclined to go out, she had gone alone with Brian to some bridge
party or benefit dance.

Once in a while she came formally to dine with them. She wasn't,
however, in spite of her poise and air of worldliness, the ideal dinner-
party guest. Beyond the aesthetic pleasure one got from watching
her, she contributed little, sitting for the most part silent, an odd
dreaming look in her hypnotic eyes. Though she could for some purpose of her own—the desire to be included in some party being made
up to go cabareting, or an invitation to a dance or a tea—talk fluently
and entertainingly.

She was generally liked. She was so friendly and responsive, and

5. See p. 38, n. 3.

so ready to press the sweet food of flattery on all. Nor did she object to appearing a bit pathetic and ill-used, so that people could feel sorry for her. And, no matter how often she came among them, she still remained someone apart, a little mysterious and strange, someone to wonder about and to admire and to pity.

Her visits were undecided and uncertain, being, as they were, dependent on the presence or absence of John Bellew in the city. But she did, once in a while, manage to steal uptown for an afternoon even when he was not away. As time went on without any apparent danger of discovery, even Irene ceased to be perturbed about the possibility of Clare's husband's stumbling on her racial identity.

The daughter, Margery, had been left in Switzerland in school, for Clare and Bellew would be going back in the early spring. In March, Clare thought. "And how I do hate to think of it!" she would say, always with a suggestion of leashed rebellion; "but I can't see how I'm going to get out of it. Jack won't hear of my staying behind. If I could have just a couple of months more in New York, alone I mean, I'd be the happiest thing in the world."

"I imagine you'll be happy enough, once you get away," Irene told her one day when she was bewailing her approaching departure. "Remember, there's Margery. Think how glad you'll be to see her after all this time."

"Children aren't everything," was Clare Kendry's answer to that. "There are other things in the world, though I admit some people don't seem to suspect it." And she laughed, more, it seemed, at some secret joke of her own than at her words.

Irene replied: "You know you don't mean that, Clare. You're only trying to tease me. I know very well that I take being a mother rather seriously. I *am* wrapped up in my boys and the running of my house. I can't help it. And, really, I don't think it's anything to laugh at." And though she was aware of the slight primness in her words and attitude, she had neither power nor wish to efface it.

Clare, suddenly very sober and sweet, said: "You're right. It's no laughing matter. It's shameful of me to tease you, 'Rene. You are so good." And she reached out and gave Irene's hand an affectionate little squeeze. "Don't think," she added, "whatever happens, that I'll ever forget how good you've been to me."

"Nonsense!"

"Oh, but you have, you have. It's just that I haven't any proper morals or sense of duty, as you have, that makes me act as I do."

"Now you are talking nonsense."

"But it's true, 'Rene. Can't you realize that I'm not like you a bit? Why, to get the things I want badly enough, I'd do anything, hurt anybody, throw anything away. Really, 'Rene, I'm not safe." Her voice as well as the look on her face had a beseeching earnestness that made Irene vaguely uncomfortable.

She said: "I don't believe it. In the first place what you're saying is so utterly, so wickedly wrong. And as for your giving up things—" She stopped, at a loss for an acceptable term to express her opinion of Clare's "having" nature.

But Clare Kendry had begun to cry, audibly, with no effort at restraint, and for no reason that Irene could discover.

PART THREE: FINALE

One

The year was getting on towards its end. October, November had gone. December had come and brought with it a little snow and then a freeze and after that a thaw and some soft pleasant days that had in them a feeling of spring.

It wasn't, this mild weather, a bit Christmasy, Irene Redfield was thinking, as she turned out of Seventh Avenue into her own street. She didn't like it to be warm and springy when it should have been cold and crisp, or grey and cloudy as if snow was about to fall. The weather, like people, ought to enter into the spirit of the season. Here the holidays were almost upon them, and the streets through which she had come were streaked with rills of muddy water and the sun shone so warmly that children had taken off their hats and scarfs. It was all as soft, as like April, as possible. The kind of weather for Easter. Certainly not for Christmas.

Though, she admitted, reluctantly, she herself didn't feel the proper Christmas spirit this year, either. But that couldn't be helped, it seemed, any more than the weather. She was weary and depressed. And for all her trying, she couldn't be free off that dull, indefinite misery which with increasing tenaciousness had laid hold of her. The morning's aimless wandering through the teeming Harlem streets, long after she had ordered the flowers which had been her excuse for setting out, was but another effort to tear herself loose from it.

She went up the cream stone steps, into the house, and down to the kitchen. There were to be people in to tea. But that, she found, after a few words with Sadie and Zulena, need give her no concern. She was thankful. She didn't want to be bothered. She went upstairs and took off her things and got into bed.

She thought: "Bother those people coming to tea!"

She thought: "If I could only be sure that at bottom it's just Brazil."

She thought: "Whatever it is, if I only knew what it was, I could manage it."

Brian again. Unhappy, restless, withdrawn. And she, who had prided herself on knowing his moods, their causes and their remedies, had found it first unthinkable, and then intolerable, that this, so like and yet so unlike those other spasmodic restlessnesses of his, should be to her incomprehensible and elusive.

He was restless and he was not restless. He was discontented, yet there were times when she felt he was possessed of some intense secret satisfaction, like a cat who had stolen the cream. He was irritable with the boys, especially Junior, for Ted, who seemed to have an uncanny knowledge of his father's periods of off moods, kept out of his way when possible. They got on his nerves, drove him to violent outbursts of temper, very different from his usual gently sarcastic remarks that constituted his idea of discipline for them. On the other hand, with her he was more than customarily considerate and abstemious. And it had been weeks since she had felt the keen edge of his irony.

He was like a man marking time, waiting. But what was he waiting for? It was extraordinary that, after all these years of accurate perception, she now lacked the talent to discover what that appearance of waiting meant. It was the knowledge that, for all her watching, all her patient study, the reason for his humour still eluded her which filled her with foreboding dread. That guarded reserve of his seemed to her unjust, inconsiderate, and alarming. It was as if he had stepped out beyond her reach into some section, strange and walled, where she could not get at him.

She closed her eyes, thinking what a blessing it would be if she could get a little sleep before the boys came in from school. She couldn't, of course, though she was so tired, having had, of late, so many sleepless nights. Nights filled with questionings and premonitions.

But she did sleep—several hours.

She wakened to find Brian standing at her bedside looking down at her, an unfathomable expression in his eyes.

She said: "I must have dropped off to sleep," and watched a slender ghost of his old amused smile pass over his face.

"It's getting on to four," he told her, meaning, she knew, that she was going to be late again.

She fought back the quick answer that rose to her lips and said instead: "I'm getting right up. It was good of you to think to call me." She sat up.

He bowed. "Always the attentive husband, you see."

"Yes indeed. Thank goodness, everything's ready."

"Except you. Oh, and Clare's downstairs."

"Clare! What a nuisance! I didn't ask her. Purposely."

"I see. Might a mere man ask why? Or is the reason so subtly feminine that it wouldn't be understood by him?"

A little of his smile had come back. Irene, who was beginning to shake off some of her depression under his familiar banter, said, almost gaily: "Not at all. It just happens that this party happens to be for Hugh, and that Hugh happens not to care a great deal for Clare; therefore I, who happen to be giving the party, didn't happen to ask her. Nothing could be simpler. Could it?"

"Nothing. It's so simple that I can easily see beyond your simple explanation and surmise that Clare, probably, just never happened to pay Hugh the admiring attention that he happens to consider no more than his just due. Simplest thing in the world."

Irene exclaimed in amazement: "Why, I thought you liked Hugh! You don't, you can't, believe anything so idiotic!"

"Well, Hugh does think he's God, you know."

"That," Irene declared, getting out of bed, "is absolutely not true. He thinks ever so much better of himself than that, as you, who know and have read him, ought to be able to guess. If you remember what a low opinion he has of God, you won't make such a silly mistake."

She went into the closet for her things and, coming back, hung her frock over the back of a chair and placed her shoes on the floor beside it. Then she sat down before her dressing-table.

Brian didn't speak. He continued to stand beside the bed, seeming to look at nothing in particular. Certainly not at her. True, his gaze was on her, but in it there was some quality that made her feel that at that moment she was no more to him than a pane of glass through which he stared. At what? She didn't know, couldn't guess. And this made her uncomfortable. Piqued her.

She said: "It just happens that Hugh prefers intelligent women."

Plainly he was startled. "D'you mean that you think Clare is stupid?" he asked, regarding her with lifted eyebrows, which emphasized the disbelief of his voice.

She wiped the cold cream from her face, before she said: "No, I don't. She isn't stupid. She's intelligent enough in a purely feminine way. Eighteenth-century France would have been a marvellous setting for her, or the old South if she hadn't made the mistake of being born a Negro."

"I see. Intelligent enough to wear a tight bodice and keep bowing swains whispering compliments and retrieving dropped fans. Rather a pretty picture. I take it, though, as slightly feline in its implication."

"Well, then, all I can say is that you take it wrongly. Nobody admires Clare more than I do, for the kind of intelligence she has, as well as for her decorative qualities. But she's not—She isn't—She hasn't—Oh, I can't explain it. Take Bianca, for example, or, to keep to the race, Felise Freeland. Looks *and* brains. Real brains that can hold their own with anybody. Clare has got brains of a sort, the kind that are useful too. Acquisitive, you know. But she'd bore a man like Hugh to suicide. Still, I never thought that even Clare would come to a private party to which she hadn't been asked. But, it's like her."

For a minute there was silence. She completed the bright red arch of her full lips. Brian moved towards the door. His hand was on the knob. He said: "I'm sorry, Irene. It's my fault entirely. She seemed so hurt at being left out that I told her I was sure you'd forgotten and to just come along."

Irene cried out: "But, Brian, I—" and stopped, amazed at the fierce anger that had blazed up in her.

Brian's head came round with a jerk. His brows lifted in an odd surprise.

Her voice, she realized, *had* gone queer. But she had an instinctive feeling that it hadn't been the whole cause of his attitude. And that little straightening motion of the shoulders. Hadn't it been like that of a man drawing himself up to receive a blow? Her fright was like a scarlet spear of terror leaping at her heart.

Clare Kendry! So that was it! Impossible. It couldn't be.

In the mirror before her she saw that he was still regarding her with that air of slight amazement. She dropped her eyes to the jars and bottles on the table and began to fumble among them with hands whose fingers shook slightly.

"Of course," she said carefully, "I'm glad you did. And in spite of my recent remarks, Clare does add to any party. She's so easy on the eyes."

When she looked again, the surprise had gone from his face and the expectancy from his bearing.

"Yes," he agreed. "Well, I guess I'll run along. One of us ought to be down, I s'pose."

"You're right. One of us ought to." She was surprised that it was in her normal tones she spoke, caught as she was by the heart since that dull indefinite fear had grown suddenly into sharp panic. "I'll be down before you know it," she promised.

"All right." But he still lingered. "You're quite certain. You don't mind my asking her? Not awfully, I mean? I see now that I ought to have spoken to you. Trust women to have their reasons for everything."

She made a little pretence at looking at him, managed a tiny smile, and turned away. Clare! How sickening!

"Yes, don't they?" she said, striving to keep her voice casual. Within her she felt a hardness from feeling, not absent, but repressed. And that hardness was rising, swelling. Why didn't he go? Why didn't he?

He had opened the door at last. "You won't be long?" he asked, admonished.

She shook her head, unable to speak, for there was a choking in her throat, and the confusion in her mind was like the beating of wings. Behind her she heard the gentle impact of the door as it closed behind him, and knew that he had gone. Down to Clare.

For a long minute she sat in strained stiffness. The face in the mirror vanished from her sight, blotted out by this thing which had so suddenly flashed across her groping mind. Impossible for her to put it immediately into words or give it outline, for, prompted by some impulse of self-protection, she recoiled from exact expression.

She closed her unseeing eyes and clenched her fists. She tried not to cry. But her lips tightened and no effort could check the hot tears of rage and shame that sprang into her eyes and flowed down her cheeks; so she laid her face in her arms and wept silently.

When she was sure that she had done crying, she wiped away the warm remaining tears and got up. After bathing her swollen face in cold, refreshing water and carefully applying a stinging splash of toilet water, she went back to the mirror and regarded herself gravely. Satisfied that there lingered no betraying evidence of weeping, she dusted a little powder on her dark-white face and again examined it carefully, and with a kind of ridiculing contempt.

"I do think," she confided to it, "that you've been something—oh, very much—of a damned fool."

Downstairs the ritual of tea gave her some busy moments, and that, she decided, was a blessing. She wanted no empty spaces of time in which her mind would immediately return to that horror which she had not yet gathered sufficient courage to face. Pouring tea properly and nicely was an occupation that required a kind of well-balanced attention.

In the room beyond, a clock chimed. A single sound. Fifteen minutes past five o'clock. That was all! And yet in the short space of half an hour all of life had changed, lost its colour, its vividness, its whole meaning. No, she reflected, it wasn't that that had happened. Life about her, apparently, went on exactly as before.

"Oh, Mrs. Runyon. . . . So nice to see you. . . . Two? . . . Really? . . . How exciting! . . . Yes, I think Tuesday's all right. . . ."

Yes, life went on precisely as before. It was only she that had changed. Knowing, stumbling on this thing, had changed her. It was as if in a house long dim, a match had been struck, showing ghastly shapes where had been only blurred shadows.

Chatter, chatter, chatter. Someone asked her a question. She glanced up with what she felt was a rigid smile.

"Yes . . . Brian picked it up last winter in Haiti. Terribly weird, isn't it? . . . It *is* rather marvellous in its own hideous way. . . . Practically nothing, I believe. A few cents. . . ."

Hideous. A great weariness came over her. Even the small exertion of pouring golden tea into thin old cups seemed almost too much for her. She went on pouring. Made repetitions of her smile. Answered questions. Manufactured conversation. She thought: "I feel like the oldest person in the world with the longest stretch of life before me."

"Josephine Baker?[6] . . . No. I've never seen her. . . . Well, she might have been in *Shuffle Along*[7] when I saw it, but if she was, I don't remember her. . . . Oh, but you're wrong! . . . I do think Ethel Waters[8] is awfully good. . . ."

There were the familiar little tinkling sounds of spoons striking against frail cups, the soft running sounds of inconsequential talk, punctuated now and then with laughter. In irregular small groups, disintegrating, coalescing, striking just the right note of disharmony, disorder in the big room, which Irene had furnished with a sparingness that was almost chaste, moved the guests with that slight familiarity that makes a party a success. On the floor and the walls the sinking sun threw long, fantastic shadows.

So like many other tea-parties she had had. So unlike any of those others. But she mustn't think yet. Time enough for that after. All the time in the world. She had a second's flashing knowledge of what those words might portend. Time with Brian. Time without him. It was gone, leaving in its place an almost uncontrollable impulse to laugh, to scream, to hurl things about. She wanted, suddenly, to shock people, to hurt them, to make them notice her, to be aware of her suffering.

"Hello, Dave. . . . Felise. . . . Really your clothes are the despair of half the women in Harlem. . . . How do you do it? . . . Lovely, is it Worth or Lanvin? . . . Oh, a mere Babani. . . ."[9]

"Merely that," Felise Freeland acknowledged. "Come out of it, Irene, whatever it is. You look like the second grave-digger."[1]

6. One of the most famous black performers in America, Josephine Baker (1906–1975) had her start as a chorus girl in productions such as *Chocolate Dandies* and *Shuffle Along*. In 1925, she became one of the most renowned American artists in Europe when she moved to France. A lifelong civil rights activist, Baker refused to perform for segregated audiences.

7. The first all-black 1921 musical, written by Aubrey Lyles and Flournoy Miller, with music by the team of Noble Sissle and Eubie Blake. It was a smash hit that ran for more than five hundred performances in New York and rerouted traffic. In addition to Josephine Baker, the cast included Florence Mills, Lottie Gee, Hall Johnson, William Grant Still, and others. "Shuffle Along" sometimes vies with the triumphant return of the 359th regiment as the inaugural event credited with launching the Harlem Renaissance.

8. Ethel Waters (1896–1977), one of the most well-known blues and jazz singers, an actress, and a very popular recording artist, whose career began as "Sweet Mama Stringbean" in vaudeville. Waters moved to New York in 1919.

9. According to Mae Henderson, Worth, Lanvin, and Babani were all "well-known designers associated with the great houses of haute couture in Paris during the early twentieth century."

1. The second grave-digger in Shakespeare's *Hamlet* (Act V, Scene i) fails to guess the first grave-digger's riddle.

"Thanks, for the hint, Felise. I'm not feeling quite up to par. The weather, I guess."

"Buy yourself an expensive new frock, child. It always helps. Any time this child gets the blues, it means money out of Dave's pocket. How're those boys of yours?"

The boys! For once she'd forgotten them.

They were, she told Felise, very well. Felise mumbled something about that being awfully nice, and said she'd have to fly, because for a wonder she saw Mrs. Bellew sitting by herself, "and I've been trying to get her alone all afternoon. I want her for a party. Isn't she stunning today?"

Clare was. Irene couldn't remember ever having seen her look better. She was wearing a superlatively simple cinnamon-brown frock which brought out all her vivid beauty, and a little golden bowl of a hat. Around her neck hung a string of amber beads that would easily have made six or eight like one Irene owned. Yes, she was stunning.

The ripple of talk flowed on. The fire roared. The shadows stretched longer.

Across the room was Hugh. He wasn't, Irene hoped, being too bored. He seemed as he always did, a bit aloof, a little amused, and somewhat weary. And as usual he was hovering before the bookshelves. But he was not, she noticed, looking at the book he had taken down. Instead, his dull amber eyes were held by something across the room. They were a little scornful. Well, Hugh had never cared for Clare Kendry. For a minute Irene hesitated, then turned her head, though she knew what it was that held Hugh's gaze. Clare, who had suddenly clouded all her days. Brian, the father of Ted and Junior.

Clare's ivory face was what it always was, beautiful and caressing. Or maybe today a little masked. Unrevealing. Unaltered and undisturbed by any emotion within or without. Brian's seemed to Irene to be pitiably bare. Or was it too as it always was? That half-effaced seeking look, did he always have that? Queer, that now she didn't know, couldn't recall. Then she saw him smile, and the smile made his face all eager and shining. Impelled by some inner urge of loyalty to herself, she glanced away. But only for a moment. And when she turned towards them again, she thought that the look on his face was the most melancholy and yet the most scoffing that she had ever seen upon it.

In the next quarter of an hour she promised herself to Bianca Wentworth in Sixty-second Street, Jane Tenant at Seventh Avenue and a Hundred and Fiftieth Street, and the Dashields in Brooklyn for dinner all on the same evening and at almost the same hour.

Oh well, what did it matter? She had no thoughts at all now, and all she felt was a great fatigue. Before her tired eyes Clare Kendry was talking to Dave Freeland. Scraps of their conversation, in Clare's husky voice, floated over to her: ". . . always admired you . . . so much about you long ago . . . everybody says so . . . no one but you. . . ." And more of the same. The man hung rapt on her words, though he was the husband of Felise Freeland, and the author of novels that revealed a man of perception and a devastating irony. And he fell for such pish-posh! And all because Clare had a trick of sliding down ivory lids over astonishing black eyes and then lifting them suddenly and turning on a caressing smile. Men like Dave Freeland fell for it. And Brian.

Her mental and physical languor receded. Brian. What did it mean? How would it affect her and the boys? The boys! She had a surge of relief. It ebbed, vanished. A feeling of absolute unimportance followed. Actually, she didn't count. She was, to him, only the mother of his sons. That was all. Alone she was nothing. Worse. An obstacle.

Rage boiled up in her.

There was a slight crash. On the floor at her feet lay the shattered cup. Dark stains dotted the bright rug. Spread. The chatter stopped. Went on. Before her, Zulena gathered up the white fragments.

As from a distance Hugh Wentworth's clipt voice came to her, though he was, she was aware, somehow miraculously at her side. "Sorry," he apologized. "Must have pushed you. Clumsy of me. Don't tell me it's priceless and irreplaceable."

It hurt. Dear God! How the thing hurt! But she couldn't think of that now. Not with Hugh sitting there mumbling apologies and lies. The significance of his words, the power of his discernment, stirred in her a sense of caution. Her pride revolted. Damn Hugh! Something would have to be done about him. Now. She couldn't, it seemed, help his knowing. It was too late for that. But she could and would keep him from knowing that she knew. She could, she would bear it. She'd have to. There were the boys. Her whole body went taut. In that second she saw that she could bear anything, but only if no one knew that she had anything to bear. It hurt. It frightened her, but she could bear it.

She turned to Hugh. Shook her head. Raised innocent dark eyes to his concerned pale ones. "Oh, no," she protested, "you didn't push me. Cross your heart, hope to die, and I'll tell you how it happened."

"Done!"

"Did you notice that cup? Well, you're lucky. It was the ugliest thing that your ancestors, the charming Confederates ever owned. I've forgotten how many thousands of years ago it was that Brian's great-great-grand-uncle owned it. But it has, or had, a good old hoary history. It was brought North by way of the subway. Oh, all right! Be English if you want to and call it the underground. What I'm coming to is the fact that I've never figured out a way of getting rid of it until about five minutes ago. I had an inspiration. I had only to break it, and I was rid of it for ever. So simple! And I'd never thought of it before."

Hugh nodded and his frosty smile spread over his features. Had she convinced him?

"Still," she went on with a little laugh that didn't, she was sure, sound the least bit forced, "I'm perfectly willing for you to take the blame and admit that you pushed me at the wrong moment. What are friends for, if not to help bear our sins? Brian will certainly be told that it was your fault.

"More tea, Clare? . . . I haven't had a minute with you. . . . Yes, it is a nice party. . . . You'll stay to dinner, I hope. . . . Oh, too bad! . . . I'll be alone with the boys. . . . They'll be sorry. Brian's got a medical meeting, or something. . . . Nice frock you're wearing. . . . Thanks. . . . Well, good-bye; see you soon, I hope."

The clock chimed. One. Two, Three. Four. Five. Six. Was it, could it be, only a little over an hour since she had come down to tea? One little hour.

"Must you go? . . . Good-bye. . . . Thank you so much. . . . So nice to see you. . . . Yes, Wednesday. . . . My love to Madge. . . . Sorry, but I'm filled up for Tuesday. . . . Oh, really? . . . Yes. . . . Good-bye. . . . Good-bye. . . ."

It hurt. It hurt like hell. But it didn't matter, if no one knew. If everything could go on as before. If the boys were safe.

It did hurt.

But it didn't matter.

Two

But it did matter. It mattered more than anything had ever mattered before.

What bitterness! That the one fear, the one uncertainty, that she had felt, Brian's ache to go somewhere else, should have dwindled to a childish triviality! And with it the quality of the courage and resolution with which she had met it. From the visions and dangers which she now perceived she shrank away. For them she had no remedy or courage. Desperately she tried to shut out the knowledge from which had risen this turmoil, which she had no power to moderate or still, within her. And half succeeded.

For, she reasoned, what was there, what had there been, to show that she was even half correct in her tormenting notion? Nothing. She had seen nothing, heard nothing. She had no facts or proofs. She was only making herself unutterably wretched by an unfounded suspicion. It had been a case of looking for trouble and finding it in good measure. Merely that.

With this self-assurance that she had no real knowledge, she redoubled her efforts to drive out of her mind the distressing thought of faiths broken and trusts betrayed which every mental vision of Clare, of Brian, brought with them. She could not, she would not, go again through the tearing agony that lay just behind her.

She must, she told herself, be fair. In all their married life she had had no slightest cause to suspect her husband of any infidelity, of any serious flirtation even. If—and she doubted it—he had had his hours of outside erratic conduct, they were unknown to her. Why begin now to assume them? And on nothing more concrete than an idea that had leapt into her mind because he had told her that he had invited a friend, a friend of hers, to a party in his own house. And at a time when she had been, it was likely, more asleep than awake. How could she without anything done or said, or left undone or unsaid, so easily believe him guilty? How be so ready to renounce all confidence in the worth of their life together?

And if, perchance, there were some small something—well, what could it mean? Nothing. There were the boys. There was John Bellew. The thought of these three gave her some slight relief. But she did not look the future in the face. She wanted to feel nothing, to think nothing; simply to believe that it was all silly invention on her part. Yet she could not. Not quite.

Christmas, with its unreality, its hectic rush, its false gaiety, came and went. Irene was thankful for the confused unrest of the season. Its irksomeness, its crowds, its inane and insincere repetitions of genialities, pushed between her and the contemplation of her growing unhappiness.

She was thankful, too, for the continued absence of Clare, who, John Bellew having returned from a long stay in Canada, had withdrawn to that other life of hers, remote and inaccessible. But beating against the walled prison of Irene's thoughts was the shunned fancy that, though absent, Clare Kendry was still present, that she was close.

Brian, too, had withdrawn. The house contained his outward self and his belongings. He came and went with his usual noiseless irregularity. He sat across from her at table. He slept in his room next to hers at night. But he was remote and inaccessible. No use pretending that he was happy, that things were the same as they had always been. He wasn't and they weren't. However, she assured herself, it needn't necessarily be because of anything that involved Clare. It was, it must be, another manifestation of the old longing.

But she did wish it were spring, March, so that Clare would be sailing, out of her life and Brian's. Though she had come almost to believe that there was nothing but generous friendship between those two, she was very tired of Clare Kendry. She wanted to be free of her, and of her furtive comings and goings. If something would only happen, something that would make John Bellew decide on an earlier departure, or that would remove Clare. Anything. She didn't care what. Not even if it were that Clare's Margery were ill, or dying. Not even if Bellew should discover—

She drew a quick, sharp breath. And for a long time sat staring down at the hands in her lap. Strange, she had not before realized how easily she could put Clare out of her life! She had only to tell John Bellew that his wife—No. Not that! But if he should somehow learn of these Harlem visits—Why should she hesitate? Why spare Clare?

But she shrank away from the idea of telling that man, Clare Kendry's white husband, anything that would lead him to suspect that his wife was a Negro. Nor could she write it, or telephone it, or tell it to someone else who would tell him.

She was caught between two allegiances, different, yet the same. Herself. Her race. Race! The thing that bound and suffocated her. Whatever steps she took, or if she took none at all, something would be crushed. A person or the race. Clare, herself, or the race. Or, it might be, all three. Nothing, she imagined, was ever more completely sardonic.

Sitting alone in the quiet living-room in the pleasant firelight, Irene Redfield wished, for the first time in her life, that she had not been born a Negro. For the first time she suffered and rebelled because she was unable to disregard the burden of race. It was, she cried silently, enough to suffer as a woman, an individual, on one's own account, without having to suffer for the race as well. It was a brutality, and undeserved. Surely, no other people so cursed as Ham's dark children.

Nevertheless, her weakness, her shrinking, her own inability to compass the thing, did not prevent her from wishing fervently that, in some way with which she had no concern, John Bellew would discover, not that his wife had a touch of the tar-brush—Irene didn't want that—but that she was spending all the time that he was out of the city in black Harlem. Only that. It would be enough to rid her forever of Clare Kendry.

Three

As if in answer to her wish, the very next day Irene came face to face with Bellew.

She had gone downtown with Felise Freeland to shop. The day was an exceptionally cold one, with a strong wind that had whipped a dusky red into Felise's smooth golden cheeks and driven moisture into Irene's soft brown eyes.

Clinging to each other, with heads bent against the wind, they turned out of the Avenue[2] into Fifty-seventh Street. A sudden bluster flung them around the corner with unexpected quickness and they collided with a man.

"Pardon," Irene begged laughingly, and looked up into the face of Clare Kendry's husband.

"Mrs. Redfield!"

His hat came off. He held out his hand, smiling genially.

But the smile faded at once. Surprise, incredulity, and—was it understanding?—passed over his features.

He had, Irene knew, become conscious of Felise, golden, with curly black Negro hair, whose arm was still linked in her own. She was sure, now, of the understanding in his face, as he looked at her again and then back at Felise. And displeasure.

He didn't, however, withdraw his outstretched hand. Not at once.

But Irene didn't take it. Instinctively, in the first glance of recognition, her face had become a mask. Now she turned on him a totally uncomprehending look, a bit questioning. Seeing that he still stood with hand outstretched, she gave him the cool appraising stare which she reserved for mashers,[3] and drew Felise on.

Felise drawled: "Aha! Been 'passing,' have you? Well, I've queered that."[4]

"Yes, I'm afraid you have."

"Why, Irene Redfield! You sound as if you cared terribly. I'm sorry."

"I do, but not for the reason you think. I don't believe I've ever gone native[5] in my life except for the sake of convenience, restaurants, theatre tickets, and things like that. Never socially I mean, except once. You've just passed the only person that I've ever met disguised as a white woman."

"Awfully sorry. Be sure your sin will find you out and all that. Tell me about it."

"I'd like to. It would amuse you. But I can't."

Felise's laughter was as languidly nonchalant as her cool voice. "Can it be possible that the honest Irene has—Oh, do look at that coat! There. The red one. Isn't it a dream?"

Irene was thinking: "I had my chance and didn't take it. I had only

2. New York shorthand for Fifth Avenue, the city's most exclusive shopping district.
3. Sexually aggressive men.
4. Ruined, undermined, or made it go awry.
5. Larsen, by ironically flipping the usual meaning of this phrase—a white expression for going black—to mean passing for white, takes a subtle jab at primitivism's exoticization of blacks.

to speak and to introduce him to Felise with the casual remark that he was Clare's husband. Only that. Fool. Fool." That instinctive loyalty to a race. Why couldn't she get free of it? Why should it include Clare? Clare, who'd shown little enough consideration for her, and hers. What she felt was not so much resentment as a dull despair because she could not change herself in this respect, could not separate individuals from the race, herself from Clare Kendry.

"Let's go home, Felise. I'm so tired I could drop."

"Why, we haven't done half the things we planned."

"I know, but it's too cold to be running all over town. But you stay down if you want to."

"I think I'll do that, if you don't mind."

And now another problem confronted Irene. She must tell Clare of this meeting. Warn her. But how? She hadn't seen her for days. Writing and telephoning were equally unsafe. And even if it was possible to get in touch with her, what good would it do? If Bellew hadn't concluded that he'd made a mistake, if he was certain of her identity—and he was nobody's fool—telling Clare wouldn't avert the results of the encounter. Besides, it was too late. Whatever was in store for Clare Kendry had already overtaken her.

Irene was conscious of a feeling of relieved thankfulness at the thought that she was probably rid of Clare, and without having lifted a finger or uttered one word.

But she did mean to tell Brian about meeting John Bellew.

But that, it seemed, was impossible. Strange. Something held her back. Each time she was on the verge of saying: "I ran into Clare's husband on the street downtown today. I'm sure he recognized me, and Felise was with me," she failed to speak. It sounded too much like the warning she wanted it to be. Not even in the presence of the boys at dinner could she make the bare statement.

The evening dragged. At last she said good-night and went upstairs, the words unsaid.

She thought: "Why didn't I tell him? Why didn't I? If trouble comes from this, I'll never forgive myself. I'll tell him when he comes up."

She took up a book, but she could not read, so oppressed was she by a nameless foreboding.

What if Bellew should divorce Clare? Could he? There was the Rhinelander case.[6] But in France, in Paris, such things were very easy. If he divorced her—If Clare were free—But of all the things that

---

6. The sensational trial in which Leonard "Kip" Rhinelander, goaded by his wealthy family, sought divorce from his wife, Alice Jones, on the grounds that she had misled him into believing she was white. While Jones won her court case, the marriage ended in divorce, and the trial and its coverage were both brutal and humiliating for Jones. See "The Rhinelander/Jones Case" section in this edition, pp. 129–98, and pp. 387–93 and 507–32.

could happen, that was the one she did not want. She must get her mind away from that possibility. She must.

Then came a thought which she tried to drive away. If Clare should die! Then—Oh, it was vile! To think, yes, to wish that! She felt faint and sick. But the thought stayed with her. She could not get rid of it.

She heard the outer door open. Close. Brian had gone out. She turned her face into her pillow to cry. But no tears came.

She lay there awake, thinking of things past. Of her courtship and marriage and Junior's birth. Of the time they had bought the house in which they had lived so long and so happily. Of the time Ted had passed his pneumonia crisis and they knew he would live. And of other sweet painful memories that would never come again.

Above everything else she had wanted, had striven, to keep undisturbed the pleasant routine of her life. And now Clare Kendry had come into it, and with her the menace of impermanence.

"Dear God," she prayed, "make March come quickly."

By and by she slept.

Four

The next morning brought with it a snowstorm that lasted throughout the day.

After a breakfast, which had been eaten almost in silence and which she was relieved to have done with, Irene Redfield lingered for a little while in the downstairs hall, looking out at the soft flakes fluttering down. She was watching them immediately fill some ugly irregular gaps left by the feet of hurrying pedestrians when Zulena came to her, saying: "The telephone, Mrs. Redfield. It's Mrs. Bellew."

"Take the message, Zulena, please."

Though she continued to stare out of the window, Irene saw nothing now, stabbed as she was by fear—and hope. Had anything happened between Clare and Bellew? And if so, what? And was she to be freed at last from the aching anxiety of the past weeks? Or was there to be more, and worse? She had a wrestling moment, in which it seemed that she must rush after Zulena and hear for herself what it was that Clare had to say. But she waited.

Zulena, when she came back, said: "She says, ma'am, that she'll be able to go to Mrs. Freeland's tonight. She'll be here some time between eight and nine."

"Thank you, Zulena."

The day dragged on to its end.

At dinner Brian spoke bitterly of a lynching that he had been reading about in the evening paper.

"Dad, why is it that they only lynch coloured people?" Ted asked.

"Because they hate 'em, son."

"Brian!" Irene's voice was a plea and a rebuke.

Ted said: "Oh! And why do they hate 'em?"

"Because they are afraid of them."

"But what makes them afraid of 'em?"

"Because—"

"Brian!"

"It seems, son, that is a subject we can't go into at the moment without distressing the ladies of our family," he told the boy with mock seriousness, "but we'll take it up some time when we're alone together."

Ted nodded in his engaging grave way. "I see. Maybe we can talk about it tomorrow on the way to school."

"That'll be fine."

"Brian!"

"Mother," Junior remarked, "that's the third time you've said 'Brian' like that."

"But not the last, Junior, never you fear," his father told him.

After the boys had gone up to their own floor, Irene said suavely: "I do wish, Brian, that you wouldn't talk about lynching before Ted and Junior. It was really inexcusable for you to bring up a thing like that at dinner. There'll be time enough for them to learn about such horrible things when they're older."

"You're absolutely wrong! If, as you're so determined, they've got to live in this damned country, they'd better find out what sort of thing they're up against as soon as possible. The earlier they learn it, the better prepared they'll be."

"I don't agree. I want their childhood to be happy and as free from the knowledge of such things as it possibly can be."

"Very laudable," was Brian's sarcastic answer. "Very laudable indeed, all things considered. But can it?"

"Certainly it can. If you'll only do your part."

"Stuff! You know as well as I do, Irene, that it can't. What was the use of our trying to keep them from learning the word 'nigger' and its connotation? They found out, didn't they? And how? Because somebody called Junior a dirty nigger."

"Just the same you're not to talk to them about the race problem. I won't have it."

They glared at each other.

"I tell you, Irene, they've got to know these things, and it might as well be now as later."

"They do not!" she insisted, forcing back the tears of anger that were threatening to fall.

Brian growled: "I can't understand how anybody as intelligent as you like to think you are can show evidences of such stupidity." He looked at her in a puzzled harassed way.

"Stupid!" she cried. "Is it stupid to want my children to be happy?" Her lips were quivering.

"At the expense of proper preparation for life and their future happiness, yes. And I'd feel I hadn't done my duty by them if I didn't give them some inkling of what's before them. It's the least I can do. I wanted to get them out of this hellish place years ago. You wouldn't let me. I gave up the idea, because you objected. Don't expect me to give up everything."

Under the lash of his words she was silent. Before any answer came to her, he had turned and gone from the room.

Sitting there alone in the forsaken dining-room, unconsciously pressing the hands lying in her lap, tightly together, she was seized by a convulsion of shivering. For, to her, there had been something ominous in the scene that she had just had with her husband. Over and over in her mind his last words: "Don't expect me to give up everything," repeated themselves. What had they meant? What could they mean? Clare Kendry?

Surely, she was going mad with fear and suspicion. She must not work herself up. She must not! Where were all the self control, the common sense, that she was so proud of? Now, if ever, was the time for it.

Clare would soon be there. She must hurry or she would be late again, and those two would wait for her downstairs together as they had done so often since that first time, which now seemed so long ago. Had it been really only last October? Why, she felt years, not months, older.

Drearily she rose from her chair and went upstairs to see about the business of dressing to go out when she would far rather have remained at home. During the process she wondered, for the hundredth time, why she hadn't told Brian about herself and Felise running into Bellew the day before, and for the hundredth time she turned away from acknowledging to herself the real reason for keeping back the information.

When Clare arrived, radiant in a shining red gown, Irene had not finished dressing. But her smile scarcely hesitated as she greeted her, saying: "I always seem to keep C. P. time,[7] don't I? We hardly expected you to be able to come. Felise will be pleased. How nice you look."

Clare kissed a bare shoulder, seeming not to notice a slight shrinking.

"I hadn't an idea in the world, myself, that I'd be able to make it; but Jack had to run down to Philadelphia unexpectedly. So here I am."

7. "Colored People's Time"—i.e., late.

Irene looked up, a flood of speech on her lips. "Philadelphia. That's not very far, is it? Clare, I—?"

She stopped, one of her hands clutching the side of her stool, the other lying clenched on the dressing-table. Why didn't she go on and tell Clare about meeting Bellew? Why couldn't she?

But Clare didn't notice the unfinished sentence. She laughed and said lightly: "It's far enough for me. Anywhere, away from me, is far enough. I'm not particular."

Irene passed a hand over her eyes to shut out the accusing face in the glass before her. With one corner of her mind she wondered how long she had looked like that, drawn and haggard and—yes, frightened. Or was it only imagination?

"Clare," she asked, "have you ever seriously thought what it would mean if he should find you out?"

"Yes."

"Oh! You have! And what you'd do in that case?"

"Yes." And having said it, Clare Kendry smiled quickly, a smile that came and went like a flash, leaving untouched the gravity of her face.

That smile and the quiet resolution of that one word, "yes," filled Irene with a primitive paralysing dread. Her hands were numb, her feet like ice, her heart like a stone weight. Even her tongue was like a heavy dying thing. There were long spaces between the words as she asked: "And what should you do?"

Clare, who was sunk in a deep chair, her eyes far away, seemed wrapped in some pleasant impenetrable reflection. To Irene, sitting expectantly upright, it was an interminable time before she dragged herself back to the present to say calmly: "I'd do what I want to do more than anything else right now. I'd come up here to live. Harlem, I mean. Then I'd be able to do as I please, when I please."

Irene leaned forward, cold and tense. "And what about Margery?" Her voice was a strained whisper.

"Margery?" Clare repeated, letting her eyes flutter over Irene's concerned face. "Just this, 'Rene. If it wasn't for her, I'd do it anyway. She's all that holds me back. But if Jack finds out, if our marriage is broken, that lets me out. Doesn't it?"

Her gentle resigned tone, her air of innocent candour, appeared, to her listener, spurious. A conviction that the words were intended as a warning took possession of Irene. She remembered that Clare Kendry had always seemed to know what other people were thinking. Her compressed lips grew firm and obdurate. Well, she wouldn't know this time.

She said: "Do go downstairs and talk to Brian. He's got a mad on."

Though she had determined that Clare should not get at her thoughts and fears, the words had sprung, unthought of, to her lips. It was as if they had come from some outer layer of callousness that had no relation to her tortured heart. And they had been, she realized, precisely the right words for her purpose.

For as Clare got up and went out, she saw that that arrangement was as good as her first plan of keeping her waiting up there while she dressed—or better. She would only have hindered and rasped her. And what matter if those two spent one hour, more or less, alone together, one or many, now that everything had happened between them?

Ah! The first time that she had allowed herself to admit to herself that everything had happened, had not forced herself to believe, to hope, that nothing irrevocable had been consummated! Well, it had happened. She knew it, and knew that she knew it.

She was surprised that, having thought the thought, conceded the fact, she was no more hurt, cared no more, than during her previous frenzied endeavours to escape it. And this absence of acute, unbearable pain seemed to her unjust, as if she had been denied some exquisite solace of suffering which the full acknowledgment should have given her.

Was it, perhaps, that she had endured all that a woman could endure of tormenting humiliation and fear? Or was it that she lacked the capacity for the acme of suffering? "No, no!" she denied fiercely. "I'm human like everybody else. It's just that I'm so tired, so worn out, I can't feel any more." But she did not really believe that.

Security. Was it just a word? If not, then was it only by the sacrifice of other things, happiness, love, or some wild ecstasy that she had never known, that it could be obtained? And did too much striving, too much faith in safety and permanence, unfit one for these other things?

Irene didn't know, couldn't decide, though for a long time she sat questioning and trying to understand. Yet all the while, in spite of her searchings and feeling of frustration, she was aware that, to her, security was the most important and desired thing in life. Not for any of the others, or for all of them, would she exchange it. She wanted only to be tranquil. Only, unmolested, to be allowed to direct for their own best good the lives of her sons and her husband.

Now that she had relieved herself of what was almost like a guilty knowledge, admitted that which by some sixth sense she had long known, she could again reach out for plans. Could think again of ways to keep Brian by her side, and in New York. For she would not go to Brazil. She belonged in this land of rising towers. She was an American. She grew from this soil, and she would not be uprooted. Not even because of Clare Kendry, or a hundred Clare Kendrys.

Brian, too, belonged here. His duty was to her and to his boys.

Strange, that she couldn't now be sure that she had ever truly known love. Not even for Brian. He was her husband and the father of her sons. But was he anything more? Had she ever wanted or tried for more? In that hour she thought not.

Nevertheless, she meant to keep him. Her freshly painted lips narrowed to a thin straight line. True, she had left off trying to believe that he and Clare loved and yet did not love, but she still intended to hold fast to the outer shell of her marriage, to keep her life fixed, certain. Brought to the edge of distasteful reality, her fastidious nature did not recoil. Better, far better, to share him than to lose him completely. Oh, she could close her eyes, if need be. She could bear it. She could bear anything. And there was March ahead. March and the departure of Clare.

Horribly clear, she could now see the reason for her instinct to withhold—omit, rather—her news of the encounter with Bellew. If Clare was freed, anything might happen.

She paused in her dressing, seeing with perfect clearness that dark truth which she had from that first October afternoon felt about Clare Kendry and of which Clare herself had once warned her—that she got the things she wanted because she met the great condition of conquest, sacrifice. If she wanted Brian, Clare wouldn't revolt from the lack of money or place. It was as she had said, only Margery kept her from throwing all that away. And if things were taken out of her hands—Even if she was only alarmed, only suspected that such a thing was about to occur, anything might happen. Anything.

No! At all costs, Clare was not to know of that meeting with Bellew. Nor was Brian. It would only weaken her own power to keep him.

They would never know from her that he was on his way to suspecting the truth about his wife. And she would do anything, risk anything, to prevent him from finding out that truth. How fortunate that she had obeyed her instinct and omitted to recognize Bellew!

"Ever go up to the sixth floor, Clare?" Brian asked as he stopped the car and got out to open the door for them.

"Why, of course! We're on the seventeenth."

"I mean, did you ever go up by nigger-power?"

"That's good!" Clare laughed. "Ask 'Rene. My father was a janitor, you know, in the good old days before every ramshackle flat had its elevator. But you can't mean we've got to walk up? Not here!"

"Yes, here. And Felise lives at the very top," Irene told her.

"What on earth for?"

"I believe she claims it discourages the casual visitor."

"And she's probably right. Hard on herself, though."

Brian said "Yes, a bit. But she says she'd rather be dead than bored."

"Oh, a garden! And how lovely with that undisturbed snow!"

"Yes, isn't it? But keep to the walk with those foolish thin shoes. You too, Irene."

Irene walked beside them on the cleared cement path that split the whiteness of the courtyard garden. She felt a something in the air, something that had been between those two and would be again. It was like a live thing pressing against her. In a quick furtive glance she saw Clare clinging to Brian's other arm. She was looking at him with that provocative upward glance of hers, and his eyes were fastened on her face with what seemed to Irene an expression of wistful eagerness.

"It's this entrance, I believe," she informed them in quite her ordinary voice.

"Mind," Brian told Clare, "you don't fall by the wayside before the fourth floor. They absolutely refuse to carry anyone up more than the last two flights."

"Don't be silly!" Irene snapped.

The party began gaily.

Dave Freeland was at his best, brilliant, crystal clear, and sparkling. Felise, too, was amusing, and not so sarcastic as usual, because she liked the dozen or so guests that dotted the long, untidy living-room. Brian was witty, though, Irene noted, his remarks were somewhat more barbed than was customary even with him. And there was Ralph Hazelton, throwing nonsensical shining things into the pool of talk, which the others, even Clare, picked up and flung back with fresh adornment.

Only Irene wasn't merry. She sat almost silent, smiling now and then, that she might appear amused.

"What's the matter, Irene?" someone asked. "Taken a vow never to laugh, or something? You're as sober as a judge."

"No. It's simply that the rest of you are so clever that I'm speechless, absolutely stunned."

"No wonder," Dave Freeland remarked, "that you're on the verge of tears. You haven't a drink. What'll you take?"

"Thanks. If I must take something, make it a glass of gingerale and three drops of Scotch. The Scotch first, please. Then the ice, then the ginger ale."

"Heavens! Don't attempt to mix that yourself, Dave darling. Have the butler in," Felise mocked.

"Yes, do. And the footman." Irene laughed a little, then said: "It seems dreadfully warm in here. Mind if I open this window?" With that she pushed open one of the long casement-windows of which the Freelands were so proud.

It had stopped snowing some two or three hours back. The moon was just rising, and far behind the tall buildings a few stars were creeping out. Irene finished her cigarette and threw it out, watching the tiny spark drop slowly down to the white ground below.

Someone in the room had turned on the phonograph. Or was it the radio? She didn't know which she disliked more. And nobody was listening to its blare. The talking, the laughter never for a minute ceased. Why must they have more noise?

Dave came with her drink. "You ought not," he told her, "to stand there like that. You'll take cold. Come along and talk to me, or listen to me gabble." Taking her arm, he led her across the room. They had just found seats when the door-bell rang and Felise called over to him to go and answer it.

In the next moment Irene heard his voice in the hall, carelessly polite: "Your wife? Sorry. I'm afraid you're wrong. Perhaps next—"

Then the roar of John Bellew's voice above all the other noises of the room: "I'm *not* wrong! I've been to the Redfields and I know she's with them. You'd better stand out of my way and save yourself trouble in the end."

"What is it, Dave?" Felise ran out to the door.

And so did Brian. Irene heard him saying: "I'm Redfield. What the devil's the matter with you?"

But Bellew didn't heed him. He pushed past them all into the room and strode towards Clare. They all looked at her as she got up from her chair, backing a little from his approach.

"So you're a nigger, a damned dirty nigger!" His voice was a snarl and a moan, an expression of rage and of pain.

Everything was in confusion. The men had sprung forward. Felise had leapt between them and Bellew. She said quickly: "Careful. You're the only white man here." And the silver chill of her voice, as well as her words, was a warning.

Clare stood at the window, as composed as if everyone were not staring at her in curiosity and wonder, as if the whole structure of her life were not lying in fragments before her. She seemed unaware of any danger or uncaring. There was even a faint smile on her full, red lips, and in her shining eyes.

It was that smile that maddened Irene. She ran across the room, her terror tinged with ferocity, and laid a hand on Clare's bare arm. One thought possessed her. She couldn't have Clare Kendry cast aside by Bellew. She couldn't have her free.

Before them stood John Bellew, speechless now in his hurt and anger. Beyond them the little huddle of other people, and Brian stepping out from among them.

What happened next, Irene Redfield never afterwards allowed herself to remember. Never clearly.

One moment Clare had been there, a vital glowing thing, like a flame of red and gold. The next she was gone.

There was a gasp of horror, and above it a sound not quite human, like a beast in agony. "Nig! My God! Nig!"

A frenzied rush of feet down long flights of stairs. The slamming of distant doors. Voices.

Irene stayed behind. She sat down and remained quite still, staring at a ridiculous Japanese print on the wall across the room.

Gone! The soft white face, the bright hair, the disturbing scarlet mouth, the dreaming eyes, the caressing smile, the whole torturing loveliness that had been Clare Kendry. That beauty that had torn at Irene's placid life. Gone! The mocking daring, the gallantry of her pose, the ringing bells of her laughter.

Irene wasn't sorry. She was amazed, incredulous almost.

What would the others think? That Clare had fallen? That she had deliberately leaned backward? Certainly one or the other. Not—

But she mustn't, she warned herself, think of that. She was too tired, and too shocked. And, indeed, both were true. She was utterly weary, and she was violently staggered. But her thoughts reeled on. If only she could be as free of mental as she was of bodily vigour; could only put from her memory the vision of her hand on Clare's arm!

"It was an accident, a terrible accident," she muttered fiercely. "It *was*."

People were coming up the stairs. Through the still open door their steps and talk sounded nearer, nearer.

Quickly she stood up and went noiselessly into the bedroom and closed the door softly behind her.

Her thoughts raced. Ought she to have stayed? Should she go back out there to them? But there would be questions. She hadn't thought of them, of afterwards, of this. She had thought of nothing in that sudden moment of action.

It was cold. Icy chills ran up her spine and over her bare neck, and shoulders.

In the room outside there were voices. Dave Freeland's and others that she did not recognize.

Should she put on her coat? Felise had rushed down without any wrap. So had all the others. So had Brian. Brian! He mustn't take cold. She took up his coat and left her own. At the door she paused for a moment, listening fearfully. She heard nothing. No voices. No footsteps. Very slowly she opened the door. The room was empty. She went out.

In the hall below she heard dimly the sound of feet going down the steps, of a door being opened and closed, and of voices far away.

Down, down, down, she went, Brian's great coat clutched in her shivering arms and trailing a little on each step behind her.

What was she to say to them when at last she had finished going down those endless stairs? She should have rushed out when they did. What reason could she give for her dallying behind? Even she didn't know why she had done that. And what else would she be asked? There had been her hand reaching out towards Clare. What about that?

In the midst of her wonderings and questionings came a thought so terrifying, so horrible, that she had had to grasp hold of the banister to save herself from pitching downwards. A cold perspiration drenched her shaking body. Her breath came short in sharp and painful gasps.

What if Clare was not dead?

She felt nauseated, as much at the idea of the glorious body mutilated as from fear.

How she managed to make the rest of the journey without fainting she never knew. But at last she was down. Just at the bottom she came on the others, surrounded by a little circle of strangers. They were all speaking in whispers, or in the awed, discreetly lowered tones adapted to the presence of disaster. In the first instant she wanted to turn and rush back up the way she had come. Then a calm desperation came over her. She braced herself, physically and mentally.

"Here's Irene now," Dave Freeland announced, and told her that, having only just missed her, they had concluded that she had fainted or something like that, and were on the way to find out about her. Felise, she saw, was holding on to his arm, all the insolent nonchalance gone out of her, and the golden brown of her handsome face changed to a queer mauve colour.

Irene made no indication that she had heard Freeland, but went straight to Brian. His face looked aged and altered, and his lips were purple and trembling. She had a great longing to comfort him, to charm away his suffering and horror. But she was helpless, having so completely lost control of his mind and heart.

She stammered: "Is she—is she—?"

It was Felise who answered. "Instantly, we think."

Irene struggled against the sob of thankfulness that rose in her throat. Choked down, it turned to a whimper, like a hurt child's. Someone laid a hand on her shoulder in a soothing gesture. Brian wrapped his coat about her. She began to cry rackingly, her entire body heaving with convulsive sobs. He made a slight perfunctory attempt to comfort her.

"There, there, Irene. You mustn't. You'll make yourself sick. She's—" His voice broke suddenly.

As from a long distance she heard Ralph Hazelton's voice saying: "I was looking right at her. She just tumbled over and was gone before you could say 'Jack Robinson.' Fainted, I guess. Lord! It was quick. Quickest thing I ever saw in all my life."

"It's impossible, I tell you! Absolutely impossible!"

It was Brian who spoke in that frenzied hoarse voice, which Irene had never heard before. Her knees quaked under her.

Dave Freeland said: "Just a minute, Brian. Irene was there beside her. Let's hear what she has to say."

She had a moment of stark craven fear. "Oh God," she thought, prayed, "help me."

A strange man, official and authoritative, addressed her. "You're sure she fell? Her husband didn't give her a shove or anything like that, as Dr. Redfield seems to think?"

For the first time she was aware that Bellew was not in the little group shivering in the small hallway. What did that mean? As she began to work it out in her numbed mind, she was shaken with another hideous trembling. Not that! Oh, not that!

"No, no!" she protested. "I'm quite certain that he didn't. I was there, too. As close as he was. She just fell, before anybody could stop her. I—"

Her quaking knees gave way under her. She moaned and sank down, moaned again. Through the great heaviness that submerged and drowned her she was dimly conscious of strong arms lifting her up. Then everything was dark.

Centuries after, she heard the strange man saying: "Death by misadventure, I'm inclined to believe. Let's go up and have another look at that window."[8]

8. "Centuries . . . that window: These last two sentences were present in the first printings of the novel but omitted in Knopf's third printing and have been, subsequently, omitted in some reprints of the novel. It is unknown whether these sentences were dropped in that printing at Larsen's request or simply as a printer's error. Misadventure means an unfortunate event, something untoward or unlucky.

BACKGROUNDS AND CONTEXTS

Reviews

MARY RENNELS

"Passing" Is a Novel of Longings"†

I can't say whether I'd "pass" or not. And you really ought to have an opinion before you give your answer to "Passing."

It is the story of two negresses, both light enough to pass for white. One does. She marries a white husband. She always has hankering for her race, freedom, rhythm. The other marries a dark husband, has a dark child, "passes" when convention makes it more convenient . . . but is happy in her Harlem life.

After years of separation the two women meet. The one who went white longs for the comforts of the one who stayed black. So she comes to Harlem. Trouble results because the "faker" fell in love with the true one's husband. When the faker fell out of the seventh-story window, the problem was solved for Miss Larsen.

My objection to the book is that Nella Larsen didn't solve the problem. Knocking a character out of a scene doesn't settle a matter.

The problem presented of the negro "passing" is vital to me—and Nella Larsen knows how to present it so. It is more a question than it is literature.

ANONYMOUS

Beyond the Color Line††

Nella Larsen is among the better negro novelists. She writes a good, firm, tangible prose, and her dialogue is convincing except when she is trying to give you an idea of how intellectual people talk at a party. While she is neither as rhythmical nor as pungent as Claude McKay,[1]

---

† From *The New York Telegram*, April 27, 1929; Magazine Section, p. 2.
†† From *The New York Times Book Review*, April 28, 1929: n.p. © 1929, *The New York Times*. Reprinted by permission.
1. Jamaican writer Claude McKay's militant poetry and radical novels were influential and controversial.

and nowhere near as much a creature of the five senses, she still manages to capture color, scent and atmosphere in her simple, direct sentences. She is not especially concerned with presenting, her milieu; apparently she is willing to take for granted that her reader knows that negroes live in Harlem and Chicago. Unlike other negro novelists, and white novelists who write about negroes, she does not give her following a bath in primitive emotionalism. She is not seeking the key to the soul of her race in the saxophone to the exclusion of all else.

What she is after in "Passing" is the presentation of two psychological conflicts. Both are set forth from one point of view, that of Irene Redfield, a negro woman who, although she has a skin light enough to "pass" for Caucasian, prefers to maintain her racial integrity. The first conflict concerns the attitude of Irene Redfield toward another woman of some negro blood, a quite lovely girl who is "passing" for white. The second problem of "Passing" is the lovely girl's unquenchable desire for negro company, even when it is liable to endanger the life with a white man that she has built up for herself.

Not only has "Passing" the unity imparted by keeping the action to within the perceptive limits of one person; it also has a time unity, gained by employing the "flashback" method of the motion picture: Miss Larsen is quite adroit at tracing the involved processes of a mind that is divided against itself, that fights between the dictates of reason and desire. She follows the windings of Irene Redfield's thought without chasing the fleeting shades of cerebral processes into blind alleys; hence she is not a good stream-of-consciousness writer, but rather a good recorder of essentials.

There are two criticisms to be made of "Passing." The most serious fault with the book is its sudden and utterly unconvincing close, a close that solves most of the problems that Miss Larsen has posed for herself by simply sweeping them out of existence through the engineered death of Clare Kendry, the girl who is passing. The second fault may not be a fault at all; it may merely reveal a blind spot in the reviewer. But fault or not, Clare Kendry, seems a little too beautiful to be true; she seems to be Miss Larsen's apotheosis of half-caste loveliness, a person out of the proverbial band-box. But perhaps she is not as lovely as all that; perhaps she just seems that way to Irene, through whose eyes she comes to the reader.

But in spite of the suspiciously "made" ending, and in spite of Clare's posed beauty, "Passing" is on the whole an effective and convincing attempt to portray certain aspects of a vexatious problem. The fact that it is by a girl who is partly of negro blood adds to the effectiveness.

MARGARET CHENEY DAWSON

The Color Line†

Passing

Among white people there seem to be two common attitudes toward Negroes, one that they are a different order of beings with utterly foreign feelings and thoughts the other that they are, in a sad, luscious way, entirely romantic. Nothing startles the white man so surely as the discovery of a simple, dignified routine in the life of educated Negroes. . . . Mr. and Mrs. Redfield went down to breakfast . . . they discussed Junior's education . . . later she shopped, wondered what to wear that evening . . . the maid announced callers . . . tea was served. This technique has been used in Negro fiction before, but not, I think, in the unselfconscious, taken-for-granted way in which Miss Larsen uses it in "Passing." Indeed, she seems so unaware of its effectiveness that she throws all the emphasis of her story onto those spectacular phases of the race problem which are more commonly supposed to be interesting. Nevertheless, it remains one of the most arresting things in her book.

"Passing" refers to the quiet slipping across the color line practiced by so many fair-skinned Negroes, and the story concerns particularly the fate of Clare Kendry, white-faced, golden-haired beauty, whose passage was completely successful until a yearning for her own kind led her to take fatal risks. Opposed to this precarious, rootless existence and passionately anxious for a recognized stability, stands Irene Redfield, Clare's old schoolmate. Between these two the race issues develop, then become tangled and obscure. At first, Irene protects Clare out of race loyalty; later because she fears that detection and divorce from the ignorant Mr. Kendry (a white man) would leave Clare free to finish the seduction of her own husband, Brian. Throughout she holds a curious attitude toward Clare—another interesting aspect to the white reader— a mixture of contempt and admiration, envy and disgust. In the end when Kendry discovers Clare at a Harlem party, Irene's emotions merge into shear hatred—Clare must not be free, Clare must not come back to the people she has disowned. They called Clare's fall from the window "death by misadventure." But Irene herself was not quite sure.

Any novel that deals with a public problem can be judged either for the sharpness of its point in controversy or for distinction of style. As a piece of writing, "Passing" can only be called adequate. Perhaps the

† From *The New York Herald Tribune Books*, April 28, 1929: n.p. Copyright © 1929 by The New York Times Co. Reprinted with permission.

romanticism that associates the Negro with powerful rhythms and broad good humor is false as far as this newer generation is concerned. It is doubtless well that we be pricked to consciousness of growing society and responsibility among them. But the flat, unimpassioned sentences are a disappointment to an expectancy of beauty. However, that strange excitement arising from the mere mention of race, as from the word sex, holds one's interest to the end.

ANONYMOUS

The Dilemma of Mixed Race: Another Study of the Color-line in New York†

To many recent studies of the mixed race situation, usually called the negro problem, is added "Passing," by Nella Larsen (Alfred A. Knopf; $2.50). The author's mother was a Dane, her father a negro of the Danish West Indies. Her mother later married a Dane, and the first child was brought up with a white half sister. The elder studied nursing and became head nurse at Tuskegee,[1] but remained there only a year. She returned to New York, entered a library school, and was for some time children's librarian of the New York Public Library.

A year ago her first novel, "Quicksand," was published and gained the annual prize award from the Harmon Foundation "for distinguished achievement among negroes." Like "Passing," it was a work of intense race consciousness—or of that double consciousness which torments the half-casts the world over. The sad fact is that the status of the half-caste is not a problem but a dilemma. This writer has no solution to suggest, though she passionately resents the injustice of the fact.

"Passing," more particularly, is a study of the dilemma of the "negro" whose blood is nearly all white, whose appearance is nearly all white, and who is tempted to step over the strict bounds of "colored" society into the freedom of the white world. It can be done, and is done often, in the way of ordinary social contacts. But to cut loose altogether from the brothers and sisters of the tarb[r]ush[2] is another matter. Here is an extreme case. A beautiful white "negress" succeeds in "passing" with a white husband. Luckily their only child is white. The husband is an average New York business man, who hates all "niggers," though some odd instinct leads him to call his wife Clare "Nig" by way of pet

---

† From *The New York Sun*, May 1, 1929: n.p.
1. Founded in 1880 by Booker T. Washington as a normal and industrial school, Tuskegee University is one of the oldest black institutions in the nation.
2. I.e., black.

name. They are well-to-do, Clare has everything a woman wants in the way of comforts and luxuries, and is accepted in white society.

But something is at work in her. Having crossed the bridge, she cannot be happy on the other side. In the end she is betrayed by her uncontrollable longing for Harlem and those whom she recognizes, after all, as her own people. She reestablishes a secret connection by way of a girlhood friend, Irene—who is light enough to "pass" at good hotels and other places where the dark negro is made unwelcome. But Irene has never thought of climbing from the lower race to the higher; the idea is repugnant to her; She has married a superior negro, slightly darker than she, a successful physician. They are both people of cultivation, and live in a society which a little consciously observes all the niceties of the well-bred white world. But the husband is too proud to be content in the polite Jim Crow[3] atmosphere of Harlem. He had always wanted to go South, to some place like Brazil, where the man of mixed race can respect himself and be respected. The wife, clinging to the idea of New York as their own place, has held him back, and now from his unhappiness and Clare's and Irene's jealousy a dreadful thing emerges.

This we shall not relate, since it is a last act artfully led up to and cannot fairly be given away in a summary. We are not sure that, as a piece of action, it is altogether credible. But the moral and racial forces at work upon the chief actors are such as may easily lead to tragedy. Perhaps the whole affair labors somewhat short of achievement because of a certain artificiality in this writer's style. She has gone to Mrs. [Edith] Wharton and the elegant sophisticates for her lessons in writing. She insinuates, she interpolates, she relucts. Her Clare and her Irene converse in accents of impeccable refinement. A third woman of light color, their friend Gertrude (knowingly married by a white man), is more forthright and mammyish. But the only thoroughly vulgar person on the stage is Clare's white husband— back-slapper, nigger-hater and bounder-at-large.

However you may judge the book as a work of art, you must be aware of an earnest and courageous attempt in it to deal with the whole theme, not a part of it selected as suitable for racial defense or propaganda. Resentment there is of the white man's refusal of social rights to a mixed race which owes its existence to his own passions; and of his more or less furtive and informal pursuit of a people he formally despises—as witnessed by the clientele of Harlem night clubs and cabarets. But there is recognition also of a powerful call of the negro blood which decisively binds the near-white grandchild or great-grandchild of the black man to the more primitive race.

3. See p. 49, n. 8.

ALICE DUNBAR-NELSON

As in a Looking Glass†

Nella Larsen delights again with her new novel, *Passing*, Alfred A. Knopf ($2.00), New York. It is apparently slighter in structure than the previous one, *Quicksand*, and you are apt to think as you are reading it, that it is of comparative unimportance. What could be more commonplace than the story of a fair girl, a waif almost, who finds that life is easily switched from one key to another, and takes the dominant key? Clare succeeds, marries, and is apparently happy. She has a strange urge to return to her own people, and therein lies danger, disaster, tragedy. Slight the story, you feel as you read it, slight, if absorbing.

Then the denouement comes. It is so surprising, so unexpected, so startling, so provocative of a whole flood of possibilities, so fraught with mystery, of a "Lady or Tiger"[4] problem, that you are suddenly aware that you have been reading a masterpiece all along, and that the subtle artistry of the story lies in just this—its apparent inocuousness, with its universality of appeal. You feel as you lay the book down that the real tale begins at the end; that there has been only a preface in the printed pages, and the novels goes on in the mind of the reader, speculation, piecing together of fragments to make a whole, ending of a situation, completion of a life, following up of the emotional life of Irene and Brian.

The real situation is not that Clare "passed." It is that she came back into the life of Irene and that she loved Brian. She did not a have to be a near-white woman to do this, nor did the others have to be colored. It is a situation that is so universal that race, color, country, time, place have nothing to do with it. Of course, the author was wise in hanging the situation onto a color complex: the public must have that now. But the book would have been just as intriguing, just as provocative, just as interesting if no mention had been made of color or race. Clare might have been any woman hungry for childhood friends; Irene and her brown skinned friends any group out of the class of the socially elite.

Nella Larsen has written a book that will linger in your memory longer than some more pretentious volumes. It is compact and terse;

---

† From *The Washington Eagle*, May 3, 1929: n.p.
4. Frank R. Stockton's 1882 Story "The Lady or The Tiger?" featured the dangers and moral dilemmas of choosing one path—or door—over another.

stripped of non-essentials of language or incident or description. It is hardly more than a bare outline. But it etches itself on your memory, like stark trees against a wintry sunset. The language is lucid, fluid; the descriptions, when there are any, done with a sweeping stroke of the brush that simulates the Japanese method.

Clare is an adventuress; Irene, the ordinary woman, afraid of life, wrapped in home, child, husband, gone Berserker when these latter are threatened—but why anticipate? The best way to enjoy *Passing* is to read it, and then discuss it, and ask about ten of your friends for their version of the ending, and get the ten different versions you are bound to get. But at all events, read it.

W. B. SEABROOK

Touch of the Tar-brush†

Negro writers seldom posses a sense of form comparable to that of Miss Nella Larsen. Her new novel, "Passing," is classically pure in outline, single in theme and in impression, and for these reasons—if for no others—powerful in its catastrophe. The whole tragedy is prepared and consummated in less than fifty thousand words, without the clutter of incident and talk which impede the progress of most novels, and without a single descent, so far as this reviewer could perceive, into sentimentality. The sharpness and definition of the author's mind (even when her characters are awash in indecision) are qualities for which any novel reader should be grateful.

"Passing" tells the story of the life and death of Clare Kendry, who was white "with a touch of the tar-brush." Clare Kendry married a man who did not know she had Negro blood. She could have lived her life through placidly on the assurance of her husband's ignorance if she had not felt herself disturbed and fascinated by the race she had abandoned. She went back to her own people furtively in spite of the danger which she always recognized and one night in Harlem, at a party, her white husband found her. In the scene which followed she leaned (or was pushed) backward from a window. Her lifeless body in its red, shining dress was picked up by the Negroes in the courtyard six floors below.

Miss Larsen prefers to tell Clare Kendry's story through another character, that of an old schoolmate who was Clare's link between the white and Negro worlds. Sometimes this character is opaque enough to irritate us by hiding the figure of Clare, the shimmering centre of

† From *The Saturday Review of Literature,* May 18, 1929: 1017–18. Reprinted by permission of *The Saturday Review.*

the tragedy. Particularly is this true in the last section of the book, when it becomes apparent that Clare has consummated her career of betrayal by falling in love with Brian, the Negro husband of her old schoolmate. In this final passage the old schoolmate (whose name is Irene Redfield) wearies us a little with her suffering. As a matter of technique, Miss Larsen should either have told us the story of Clare Kendry directly, without the device of an intervening personality, or else have made the device-character interesting enough to mean something to us. As it is, we are impatient with Irene Redfield's tortures because they cut off our view of Clare.

It is in the creation of that character, not always perfectly realized but always strongly felt, that Miss Larsen's best achievement lies. Form alone could not do this. Clare Kendry, as intrepid and lovely as the most romantic of heroines, has made her declaration:

> Spicy grove, cinnamon tree,
> What is Africa to me?

She has built her life on it, but Africa is not so easily dismissed from the blood and bone. In describing the gradual surrender of Clare to the fascination of the Negro, her final return and death. Miss Larsen has made an unusually powerful appeal to the sensibilities and imaginations of her readers.

In some other respects the author has not been so successful. Although the writing is of good quality in general, it does occasionally lapse into the sort of jargon we call "literary." There is no reason, for example, for Miss Larsen to say "the rich amber fluid" when she means tea. Or to say "thanking him smilingly as well as in a more substantial manner for his kind helpfulness and understanding," when she means that the lady tipped the taxi-driver. These occasional elaborations are disconcerting in a work which otherwise seems so clear and chaste. Similarly, one wonders whether the author does not slightly exaggerate the wit and elegance of the salons of Harlem. Such wit and tone as Miss Larsen describes ("brilliant, crystal-clear and sparkling" with "nonsensical shining things" being thrown into "the pool of talk") have not been common this side the water, or indeed anywhere else since the eighteenth Century. And when examples of this esprit are given ("you're as sober as a judge," is the first of them) one wonders what Madame du Deffand would have had to say about them.

These occasional evidences of self-consciousness are undoubtedly due to the fact that Miss Larsen, like most other Negro writers, is aware of a mixed audience; a large proportion of her readers must be white people, which is to say, either uncomprehending or hostile. But there is a great deal less of this self-consciousness in Miss Larsen than in most writers of her race. She has produced a work so fine, sensitive, and distinguished that it rises above race categories and becomes that rare object, a good novel.

ESTHER HYMAN

Passing†

There is a growing attitude of rebellion on the part of critics against the assumption that the Negro problem is a romantic problem; that the case of the individual of mixed blood, desperately seeking poise in a world wherein he is perforce abnormal, is a dramatic case. Nevertheless, the position of the individual out of harmony with his surroundings, set apart from the ordinary run of human beings, is indeed pregnant with pathos, and to the writer—the analyst of human emotions—full of dramatic possibilities.

Miss Nella Larsen has felt the innate drama of her protagonists, but her well-planned story, written with a quiet and careful artistry, has not completely fulfilled the promise inherent in her theme. Her three central characters are well realized—Irene, who could have passed for white, but whose fierce racial consciousness makes her contemptuous of those who go outside their own kind; Clare, fair and beautiful, married to a man ignorant of her Negro blood, to whom the call of Harlem eventually proves irresistible; Brian, darker than the others, longing for South America with its easier tolerance, but held in check by his wife, Irene, who clings for herself and for her husband and sons to the security of the life she already knows. But there is not sufficient depth to the background against which these are painted. Even in these days of tolerance and broadmindedness towards artistic forms a mere forty thousand words are not sufficient to develop a theme of importance against a firm and satisfying background.

The device of taking for granted the reader's interest in and knowledge of life among Harlem's cultured upper class would be successful in a short story and is not without effectiveness here. But the dramatic climax lacks conviction, not so much because of its inherent improbability as because of the insufficiency of the preparation—it needs a very decided push, such as could scarcely escape the attention of a crowd of people with gaze concentrated upon the victim, to send a woman hurtling through a window. Against a more richly-painted background these creations of Miss Larsen would have stood out as memorable figures.

† From *The Bookman* 69 (June 1929): 427–28.

The author is fond of the fashionable affectation of the deliberately and elaborately split infinitive. A worse fault is her lack of sympathy with a very real problem. Irene's passionate devotion to the Negro race to which she only partly belongs is a natural enough defensive instinct; but Clare's case is as real, and infinitely more deserving of compassion. Ninety percent white, her longing to identify herself with the people among whom all her maturity has been spent is at least as understandable as her later craving to return to Harlem society. If Miss Larsen had presented Clare directly, instead of obliquely through Irene, she would have made of her a more satisfying character. As it is, her problem is never clearly stated and in the end is evaded.

It is this perfunctory background that accounts for the reader's dissatisfaction with well told and at times a really moving story related in a careful, well-balanced prose, and revealing with sincerity and at times with subtlety a group of finely differentiated characters. This is a contribution of value to the growing list of "border line" literature.

AUBREY BOWSER

The Cat Came Back†

Mankind is divided into races by differences of color, features and hair. This is about the best that science can do, for science is concerned only with material things. Society is not satisfied with scientific distinctions, for it classes as Negroes many people who are whiter than those classed as Caucasians. A white-skinned person with fair hair and gray eyes may be called a Negro, while a black Arab or a woolly-haired Abyssinian is classified as white. Thus society makes a fool of itself.

The ethnological distinction of race, though accurate enough in a physical sense and serviceable as a generalization, is a poor guide in dealing with questions of race as they are. Race is a matter of mind rather than body, of background rather than foreground. A white baby reared by a Negro family will grow up as much of a Negro as his dark foster-brothers and a black baby reared by white people will grow up hating Negroes.

There is nothing discernibly Negro in the poems of Alexander Pushkin, in the novels of Alexander Dumas pere, in the dramas of Dumas fils. As a matter of fact, the senior Dumas had no sympathy

† From *The New York Amsterdam News*, June 5, 1929: n.p. Reprinted by permission of *The New York Amsterdam News*.

whatever for Negroes; he hated them. Thinking to please him, a Parisian hostess invited a black relative of his to meet him at dinner, and Dumas was furious at what he called an insult.

Race, as a matter of mind rather than blood, has afforded a theme for many novels. Most of them have fallen flat because they were arguments rather than stories. When an author's aim is to prove something his story fails. Art is not supposed to prove anything, nor is life, they are sufficient in themselves.

Nella Larsen almost avoids these pitfalls in "Passing," her latest book—almost. She doesn't try to hoist the race problem on her shoulders and she manages to keep the viewpoint of the story-teller. But she succumbs to the grudge that most Negroes have against a Negro who goes over the race line and cannot stay there. The grudge is justifiable, for a person should be either one thing or the other, but it hampers the story-teller.

Thus her heroine, like most of the chief characters in race-line novels, is portrayed as a despicable character. Clare Kendry is a pretty girl with a magnetic personality: but she has no morals in either the obvious or the higher sense. Entirely selfish, she is out to do everybody. She will wrong people who have been kind to her as readily as she wrongs those who have treated her badly.

She leaves her race and marries a white man without telling him she is colored. He gives her everything and she ought to be satisfied; but in the first chapter of the book we find her slipping around with other white men. Even then she is not satisfied; she wants clandestine relations with colored people. She gets them, too; serpents like her get everything they want.

If race were a physical thing, Clare Kendry, with such an infinitesimal drop of Negro blood, would have been glad to stay with white people. But she had been reared as a Negro and she couldn't get away from Mother Ethiopia; her mental and social background drew her back to colored people like a swimmer caught in an undertow. Her white husband hated Negroes violently, danger was always at her shoulder, but she took chance after chance; she couldn't keep away from Harlem. As in the old song, "the cat came back."

The colored woman from whose viewpoint the story is told had always been kind to Clare, even in Clare's childhood when everyone else despised her. If it had been in Clare's nature to treat anyone right, it would have been this woman. But no; she stole this woman's husband as readily as she would anyone else's.

How did it all end? Well, one time Clare took too long a chance. If you wish to know what happened then, ask Nella Larsen.

This novel is more logical than "Quicksand," Nella Larsen's first book, which was spoiled by a ridiculous ending. Yet "Quicksand" is a better book from a purely literary viewpoint. "Quicksand," especially in the opening chapters, had a limpid, refreshing style, as clear as a crystal stream.

"Passing" falls into the modern affectation of broken sentences with deleted verbs. It stutters. The author has also taken less pains with her work. The story opens with a letter from Clare Kendry to Irene Redfield. Three chapters later Irene receives another letter from Clare, but "she couldn't remember ever having a letter from her before."

The best thing about "Passing" is that it tells a story for the sake of the story and not for the sake of the race problem.

MARY GRIFFIN

Novel of Race Consciousness†

Why do white men and women visit Harlem? For various reasons, according to Nella Larsen author of "Quicksand" and now of "Passing." "A few purely and frankly to enjoy themselves. Others to get material to turn into shekels. More, to gaze on these great and near great while they gaze on the Negroes."

Harlem, as Nella Larsen describes it, is not a whirling, seething, entertaining place, but home—a spot to those who live there much like the rest of the world, except perhaps for a consciousness of race that does not permeate those of us whose skins are white. It seems a possessing desire with Nella Larsen to show the white world, now more interested in Negro affairs than ever before, that the Negro man or woman is, in all vital essentials, no different from the white. She herself is half white—being the child of a Danish mother and a Negro father. Her father died when she was only 2 years old and her mother married again, this time a man of her own nationality and race. With her step-sister, Nella attended a private school whose pupils were for the most part German and Scandinavian. At 16 she visited her Danish relatives and at 19 returned to this country to enter a school for nursing. Since that time she has shifted her interests to books—first as a librarian, then as a novelist. Her first novel, "Quicksand," appeared in 1928 and brought her recognition in the form of the award of the second prize in literature and a bronze medal from the Harmon foundation for "distinguished achievement among Negroes."

Nella Larsen's mixture of blood has given her a double perception which few purely Negro or purely white authors can hope to attain.

† From *The Detroit Free Press*, June 23, 1929: n.p.

She portrays the dissatisfaction and furtiveness of those "light" colored, who "pass" for white, even to the extent of marrying whites. They care nothing for their race (only belong to it) when they are young, but soon or late Miss Larsen sees them lured back to Harlem. She shows the disapproval and at the same time the half-admiration that those who could pass for white, but do not, hold for those who do. This second type is willing to go "native" only to the extent of getting theater tickets and enjoying the luxuries of fine restaurants. They may wish to protect their children from knowledge of race prejudice until they are grown, but they are never ashamed of their race. If they are educated, there may even be a drop of humor in the situation: the Negro knows what the white thinks of him—always has, while the white doesn't . . . not quite, at least.

There is all too meager an understanding between the dark and light races. Perhaps such studies as Miss Larsen's will help erase racial prejudice.

W. E. B. DU BOIS

Passing†

Nella Larsen's "Passing" is one of the finest novels of the year. If it did not treat a forbidden subject—the inter-marriage of a stodgy middle-class white man to a very beautiful and selfish octoroon—it would have an excellent chance to be hailed, selected and recommended. As it is, it will probably be given the "silence", with only the commendation of word of mouth. But what of that? It is a good close-knit story, moving along surely but with enough leisure to set out seven delicately limned characters. Above all, the thing is done with studied and singularly successful art. Nella Larsen is learning how to write and acquiring style, and she is doing it very simply and clearly.

Three colored novelists have lately essayed this intriguing and ticklish subject of a person's right to conceal the fact that he had a grandparent of Negro descent. It is all a petty, silly matter of no real importance which another generation will comprehend with great difficulty. But today, and in the minds of most white Americans, it is a matter of tremendous moral import. One may deceive as to killing, stealing and adultery, but you must tell your friend that you're "colored", or suffer a very material hell fire in this world, if not in the next. The reason of all this, is of course that so many white people in

† From *The Crisis* 36 (July 1929): 234, 248–50. W. W. Norton wishes to thank the Crisis Publishing Co., Inc., the publisher of the magazine of the National Association for the Advancement of Colored People, for use of *The Crisis Magazine* materials.

America either know or fear that they have Negro blood. My friend, who is in the Record Department of Massachusetts, found a lady's ancestry the other day. Her colored grandfather was a soldier in the Revolutionary War, and through him she might join the D. A. R. But she asked "confidentially", could that matter of "his—er—color be left out?"

Walter White in "Flight" records the facts of an excursion of a New Orleans girl from the colored race to the white race and back again. Jessie Fauset in "Plum Bun" considers the spiritual experiences and rewards of such an excursion, but the story of the excursion fades into unimportance beside that historical document of the description of a colored Philadelphia family. That characterization ought to live in literature.

Nella Larsen attempts quite a different thing. She explains just what "passing" is: the psychology of the thing; the reaction of it on friend and enemy. It is a difficult task, but she attacks the problem fearlessly and with consummate art. The great problem is under what circumstances would a person take a step like this and how would they feel about it? And how would their fellows feel?

So here is the story: Irene, who is faintly colored, is faint with shopping. She goes to a hotel roof for rest and peace and tea. That's all. Far from being ashamed of herself, she is proud of her dark husband and lovely boys. Moreover, she is deceiving no one. If they wish to recognize her as Spanish, then that is their good fortune or misfortune. She is resting and getting cool and drinking tea. Then suddenly she faces an entirely different kind of problem. She sees Clare and Clare recognizes her and pounces on her. Clare is brilliantly beautiful. She is colored in a different way. She has been rather brutally kicked into the white world, and has married a white man, almost in self-defense. She has a daughter, but she is lonesome and eyes her playmate Irene with fierce joy. Here is the plot. Its development is the reaction of the race-conscious Puritan, Irene; the lonesome hedonist, Clare; and then the formation of the rapidly developing triangle with the cynical keen rebel, Irene's husband.

If the American Negro renaissance gives us many more books like this, with its sincerity, its simplicity and charm, we can soon with equanimity drop the word "Negro". Meantime, your job is clear. Buy the book.

ANONYMOUS

Passing†

Claire Kendry, an exotic, restless girl of provocative charm, leaves Harlem and has no difficulty in passing for white. After several years of marriage, Claire, longing for the warmth and color of life among her own race, revives her childhood friendship with Irene Redfield, and makes contacts in Harlem that endanger her own secret and the happiness of Irene's marriage.

Miss Larsen is the author of *Quicksand*, a novel concerned with a cultured negro girl trying to adjust herself to life.

MARY FLEMING LABAREE

Passing††

Nella Larson's "Quicksand" was a novel of achievement and promise. The same may be said of her second novel.

There should be as many ways of telling a story as there are story-tellers—and there are, when it comes to the truly great among them. For the giant uses his chosen method with so subtle an artistry, with so dazzling a power, with so passionate an earnestness, that the method is not merely enriched but transformed into something more and different, thus becoming his very own.

Of the various modes of classifying story-methods, the most obvious and least painless is to set down

    I. Direct
    II. Indirect

and let it go at that.

In her new novel, Miss Larsen has forsaken the direct telling of "Quicksand" for an indirect telling, thereby losing the advantage of straight impact upon the sense and sensibility of her readers. Had the material been used directly as the life of Clare Kendry, had Miss Larsen christened her story, "The Girl Who Passed," it might have marched more vividly before our eyes, more nearly searched our hearts. Yet in that case, we should, perhaps, have missed some of the

---

† From *The Open Shelf*, July 1929: 110.
†† From *Opportunity* 7 (August 1929): 255.

shades of intellectual and emotional reaction to the fact of *passing*, in the lives that touch upon and are touched by the "having" Clare.

We see Clare chiefly through the eyes of Irene Redfield, in this fashion acquiring what may be the norm of reaction to *passing*, by a cultured woman of the Negro social group, in a great metropolitan area in the United States of America, today. We are given the reactions of sundry other individuals and types—both Negro and Caucasion. Witness Gertrude, the butcher's wife, Dr. Brian Redfield who needed *something* more, Hugh Wentworth literary godling, the golden Felise. And we cannot forget John Bellew, husband of the beautiful eager Clare who wanted to barter and at the same time eat her cake. He symbolizes the extreme of wooden-headed white reaction to dark blood.

The background of "Passing"? It is less diversified, less rich if you will, than the background of "Quicksand." There we had a southern college, Chicago, New York, Copenhagen, and again the South—this time a small town church and parsonage. In "Passing" we have concentrated Harlem, with only a flashback to Chicago. But it is the story not the physical background that counts here. It is the story plus the psychological background and ether.

I like "Passing" for its calm clear handling of a theme which lends itself to murky melodrama. But this quality of calmness and clearness does not and has not entailed the blinking of a single element in the stupid Nordic complex and its unlovely sequelae. The tragedy is told with an economy of words, but is full import is unmistakable. A throb of *the urge to speak out* runs through it.

Also, in the novel under discussion, we have a competent piece of story-telling: both plot and people move logically to their appointed end. Yet somehow, it fails to be a great story, and with the given ingredients, it might have been great and greatly moving. I wish with all my heart that instead of bringing forth another novel next year, Mrs. Imes would, after a decade of brooding, give the world its needed epic of racial interaction between thinking members of the American social order belonging to both African and European stocks.

Novels may be transcripts or interpretations of life; and life being so mammoth an affair must be viewed in sections, large or small. These sections may be marked off horizontally like well-behaved geologic strata or cut perpendicularly into segments, like a birthday cake.

A ripe artist of gargantuan powers and stature may cut perpendicularly, study life in all its layers, set before us its tremendous light and shadow, paean and threnody, with delicate precision or a passionate "Behold!"

There is no layer or segment of humanity that is *verboten* to the maker of novels, if he be an honest workman. And the honest reader need not flinch from honest fact or honest interpretation of any phase of life. Yet certain literary somebodies and other literary nobodies would have us believe that only life in the raw or bloody-rare is life at all and worth writing up. The pity of it!—if "Walls of Jericho" and "Home to Harlem"[5] perched upon our bookshelves with "Plum Bun" and "Passing" nowhere to be seen.

Doctors, lawyers, men of affairs, their wives and daughters are neither less valuable nor less richly human members of society than jazz boys and girls, roustabouts and drunks—though it takes a more gifted, understanding and highly experienced artist to make them breathe and move and speak so that we know them for what they really are, so that we ourselves breathing, moving and speaking with them, come to perceive more clearly what we ourselves really are— of one blood with them and all humanity.

ANONYMOUS

Do They Always Return?†

Here is an excellent novel which suggests that the "near whites" always return to their own race for genuine happiness, comfort and understanding. It is interesting to note that this was also apparent in "Plum Bun" by Jessie Redmon Fauset.

Clare Kendry, the "near white," is married to a white man. The situation is complicated by the fact that the husband has an orthodox southern viewpoint concerning Negroes. Moreover, Clare's white husband calls her "Nig" because as she grows older she becomes darker.

The unsuspecting husband explains to Clare's "near white" friends that as long as he is assured that Clare is not colored he might even call her "nigger." It is apparent that he regards the nickname as having no significance other than a humorous one.

Irene Redfield might also 'pass'; but she chooses not to, and makes an interesting comparison with Clare. Irene is the unwilling confidant of Clare who seeks her companionship in order to escape the tenseness of her racial camouflage.

Clare's husband finally discovers that her blood is not really "blue" but black. The discovery is made in circumstances which result in Clare's death.

At the beginning, the story moves slowly. However, the injection of innumerable situations where the reader's interest is usually intense renders the work one of merit.

5. *Walls of Jericho* by Rudolph Fisher and *Home to Harlem* by Claude McKay treat the street life of Harlem.
† From *New York News*, September 28, 1929: n.p.

"M. L. H."

Passing†

Two aspects of this interesting book, well-reviewed by now, stand out to one reader. Miss Larsen has gone to particular pains, it seems to us, to impress again upon her readers that the social life of the upper middle class Negro contains all the refined detail of luxurious living of the corresponding white strata. This is evident in her minute descriptions of how Irene orders her dinners, arranges her teas, and manages her large household.

The second outstanding fact is that the book contains, especially in its last half, an absorbing account of the inner life of a somewhat divided personality. Criticisms have been raised about the "made" ending of the novel. This seems to us far more convincing and unforced than other parts. The emotions of Irene and the events during and approaching the crisis, the actual denoument itself are no new thing in the vocabulary of the followers of psychological experiences. Irene's experience seems to outtop the other events and steal the title of "main character" away from Clare.

ANONYMOUS

Passing††

To readers of the recent novels of American negro life the title of this story has a technical meaning. A man or woman of part negro blood may be sufficiently fair to be mistaken for a person of wholly white descent, and to assimilate purposely is known as "passing." The book shows the process in several degrees. Irene Redfield, the principal character, found it convenient to "pass" in the restaurants and theatres of Chicago, but was proud, being married to a darker-skinned doctor, that her social acquaintances should not mistake her. Clare Kendry, Irene's schoolfellow, was more reckless: having "passed" so far as to deceive and marry a Nordic whose hatred of her race was a mania, she was drawn back by an instinct to visit Irene and mingle with the dark intellectuals. Apart from her husband's unconsciously offensive outbursts, Clare's difficulty was to continue a part which no longer attracted her even socially. Irene's regard for her passes

† From *The Wilson Bulletin* 41, no. 4 (December 1929):169.
†† From *The Times Literary Supplement,* December 12, 1929: 1060. © *The Times Literary Supplement.*

through three definite stages. At the first reunion she is drawn to Clare by a contemptuous pity. At the second encounter she is fascinated by the woman's charm and daring. At the third stage Irene's husband is involved in Clare's intimacy, and Irene herself fatally puzzled how Clare can be separated from him. To let the white man know might be the simplest way, despite the danger that he may thrust Clare permanently among them through the divorce Court. Finally chance makes Irene betray her rival without a word. The dialogue is, despite occasional racial slang, written with reserve.

Contemporary Coverage of Passing and Race

ANONYMOUS

When Is a Caucasian Not a Caucasian?†

This is a conundrum which is no joke. It is a very serious matter with many of the first Creole families of Louisiana. To us outside who look on it is absurdly amusing, as the antics of those who make fools of themselves always are, no matter how serious to the participants.

Louisiana was settled by the French. The French used to have less fear of race admixture than English settlers. Many Creoles, like Cubans, have a dark complexion, and have been suspected of negro blood, which they angrily deny. LoIuisiana has an elaborate terminology for the successive dilutions, from the mulatto and the quadroon downward—or upward—which we printed some weeks ago. When the dilution reaches the sixteenth fraction it is almost indistinguishable, and at the sixty-fourth no test can discover it. For all practicable purposes the man is a Caucasian—but not for Louisiana law.

Of all States, Louisiana ought to be the last to enact a law forbidding intermarriage of a white person with any one who has the least infusion of negro blood. There is no knowing where it might hit, for in Louisiana beyond doubt many pass for white in whose genealogy research would discover a few drops of negro blood. Such a case has lately stirred up the State.

A young woman of a good family, a graduate of a fashionable ladies' seminary in New Orleans, was killed by being run over in the street. A newspaper spoke of her as colored. That was a mortal offense. Her brother brought suit for slander, and the editor, by referring to ancient records, showed that one of her ancestors was recorded as colored. That put the whole family into a horrible plight. They had always thought of themselves as white, and had associated

† From *The Independent,* 70 (March 2, 1911): 478–79.

105

only with white people. Now nobody would associate with them. They must sink, tho visibly white, to the rank and caste and associations of negroes. Hitherto they had been good enough to associate with anybody. Now, with no fault of their own, and no change in themselves, they were thrust, with all their whiteness, into the outer blackness.

The dead girl had a sister happily married to a man of German origin. There was no question that he was a full Caucasian. But he had imbibed the Louisiana prejudice and terror of invisible and infinitesimal nigritude. He discovered—and his wife did—from the newspaper account that she had this bar sinister. He could not continue to live with such a banned woman. Besides, the law forbade it. He was liable to imprisonment for maintaining marital relations with her. He appealed to the court to have his marriage annulled, and the court could do no less. So she was sent adrift with the rest of her family. Thus in this case two legal maxims had illustration, one by its truth, "Summa lex, summa injuria,"[1] and the other by its extreme contradiction, "De minimis lex non curat."[2] The law does care a great deal for the smallest things. It cares in Louisiana for what is so attenuated as to be invisible.

Now such a law and such enforcement is barbarous beyond expression. It puts a suspicion in multitudes of families. It is against all common sense as against all Christianity. Who knows where, thru personal malice, it may strike next? The story is told in the Sun— very likely so—of a similar case in one of the parishes. A suit for slander was brought for calling a family colored. The sheriff looked up the records and found the charge sustained. As the investigation amused him, he looked farther and found one of his own ancestors recorded as colored—but a fortunate fire soon after destroyed the proof.

Now, what should be done? If Louisiana must maintain its infamous law against intermarriage, it should at least set a line where the prepotent negro blood is to be held as washed out. Set it at one-eighth, or one-sixteenth, or one-thirty-second, or one-sixty-fourth, but at least set it somewhere. If we do not misremember, South Carolina has such a law. It is adding stupidity to cruelty to allow the taint to go on forever.

And once more, we advise all white negroes in Louisiana, or anywhere else in the South to change their residence and leave their pedigree behind. There is such a case now in Baltimore, where the doctors can't tell whether a girl is white or black. Let them leave as white people and be received as white people. We do not doubt there are thousands of such people, both North and South, who have, by

---

1. "Extreme law is the greatest injury," Latin.
2. "The law does not care for small things," Latin.

changing their home, changed their race and color. We have known such cases, and not all Creoles. Thus, as the bleaching process goes on, the conundrum will cease to concern them, When is a Caucasian not a Caucasian?

ANONYMOUS

Writer Says Brazil Has No Color Line†

Melville Herskovitz, writing in the October issue of the *American Mercury* under the title of "The Color Line" has, among other things, the following to say about race relations in Brazil.

In Brazil anyone who has white blood is white. A Negro is merely a person who is a Negro in the biological sense. They had slavery in Brazil, and later than we had it, but the change came about easily and was not forcibly imposed upon the slave owners. There had been no social degradation in the old days if one's ancestors had been freed slaves and there was thus an easy mingling among the resulting people of all racial types and much cross breeding. In consequense of the different sociological line-up there is no stigma attacthed to Negro blood, such as obtains here. Mixed Negroes feel no discrimination — they mingle with people on similar social levels, and there is no race problem in Brazil.

DON PIERSON

Does It Pay to "Pass?"††

Five years ago a beautiful little girl left a small Georgia town to come to Chicago. Flaxen hair. Clear limpid blue eyes—almost violet in the deep blueness. Skin as white as milk. Smooth as satin. Graceful. Cultured. Educated. A product of one of the best schools in Atlanta for our girls. In this Georgia town she was well liked. Loved by many. Though there were whisperings about the race of her father it was not strange for this town where many such things have "just happened" in the dead dark past.

Her mother was dark—almost black. She had worked for one of the first families of the so-called aristocracy for years—dating back to those dark days of slavery. She was inordinately proud of her beau-

† From *The Chicago Defender*, October 1925: n.p. Used with permission of *The Chicago Defender*.
†† From *The Chicago Whip*, August 20, 1927: n.p.

tiful daughter. She lavished the best upon her. She pushed the girl forward. She with mother's pride in the glory of her child remained in the background. Yet, the girl did not mix much. She was known by all but mixed with few. Pleasant but aloof. Not friendless but with few if any intimates. She seemed to drift with those whom Dame Rumor had put the same sort of Caucasian stamp on face and mind. Then came a love affair. The mother objected. The man was not good enough. Not rich enough. Not the "type." It was the girl's first love. To her, it was her only love. She disappeared from the little town, leaving for Chicago. Her mother's heart was torn with grief. Her crinkly hair whitened. Her face lined with anguish. A life's hope was dashed to earth. Perhaps some pale faced man in that same town also shed a tear.

That was five years ago. A few weeks ago that black mother in that small Georgia town found out that her daughter was in Chicago. Working. Yearning. Grieving over a lost love. She was "passing." Working in a big department store. Some of the townsfolks told the aged mother and she attempted the long and to her perilous journey to Chicago to get one glimpse of her "baby" so that she could die in peace. She was taken by kind friends unknown to the girl to the department store. The old lady was a curiosity in the modern city. A real old "Aunt Dinah" come to life. As she tottered down the crowded aisles of the busy store the girls giggled and made fun of her. The girl who was "passing" joined in the jests as was her wont at other times—not suspecting that the old lady was her own mother who had traveled many miles in Jim Crow[3] coaches to once more see her "baby." Then she recognized the face. Stark fear spread over her face. She saw exposure. Disgrace. Scorn. All would be lost if she recognized this old "mammy" as her mother or even took the chance of recognizing her at all. She saw all of her plans of marriage to the pale-faced brother of one of the girls who worked at her side go glimmering. She saw all of her future dashed to earth as she thought once before. She now followed the dictates of her mother's early training. So she quietly slipped from behind the counter and went down to the rest room. The aged woman asked for her by the name she had given her as a baby. No such person worked there the old "Aunty" was told between cruel jests and gibes. Her dark face paled and she left the big store with her white head bowed still lower. Her "baby" was lost.

Within a week after she had returned to her home in that small town in Georgia, she died. The doctor said it was her heart. It was. Not a disease—a broken heart.

---

3. See p. 49, n. 8.

JUANITA ELLSWORTH

From White Negroes†

There is no more interesting race problem than that represented by the informal passing of the individual members of one race to membership in another race. This phenomenon is as old as the human race; it has apparently occurred between all races that have been in contact for any length of time. Significant occurrence of this kind take place when Negroes pass into membership in the Caucasian race. Surprising to most people is the fact that "passing" often takes place accidentally. That is to say, a light-skinned Negro is surprised on occasion to find himself or herself accepted as a white person. If the new recognition is allowed to stand, economic opportunity and a new status result. The economic advantage that comes from "passing" is great; it is sometimes the chief reason for deliberately seeking the transition from one race to another.

The following illustrations relate to only one side of this situation. Only those individuals who hold their racial identity as Negroes could be approached by the interviewer. A study of those clinging to their white blood would be revealing, but very difficult. Because of the consequences which would naturally follow any self-admitted black blood in those who have severed any relations with it, information would be almost impossible to obtain. Interesting situations are revealed in the following illustrations.

Miss "A," who is a young college graduate, became a teacher in ——— school where there are many little Spanish children. "Soon after my appointment the principal came into the room one day and asked me to interpret the conversation of two of these children. I declared my ignorance of the Spanish language and the principal was surprised. Turning to me she said, 'Aren't you Spanish?' 'No,' I replied. 'What are you then?' she asked. I told her and she looked astounded. A few hours later I was summoned to the office and asked to resign. She said that a terrible mistake had been made as I had been mistaken for Spanish. You can see that the disadvantage of my acknowledging my race is only too obvious. However, on the other hand, I could never have been happy there had I been forced into deception."

Miss "B" is head girl in a large and responsible business concern. In securing the position no question of her race was asked and she vouchsafed no information. When asked why, she replied, "Do you honestly believe I could have gotten that position or any decent one

---

† From *Sociology and Social Research* (May–June 1928): 449–54. Reprinted by permission of *Sociology and Social Research*.

if it were known what I am? I'd likely be offered a maid's job. As it is I am paid the highest salary and given more authority than any girl in the office. My attitude toward my associates is restrained. Sometimes I am inclined to be bitter when I reflect that the girls who profess the deepest devotion would turn in a minute if they knew of my one-eighth black blood. I never accept any of the office hospitality. I offer the subterfuge that my mother being ill prevents my entertaining and I can't accept others' hospitality when I can't reciprocate. The idea of my cutting loose from my race is even more preposterous to me than abandoning my family. I'd work as black any time if I were given the same opportunities and advantages."

Dr. "C," who has associated almost strictly with white students during his college days, explains his actions as follows: "It didn't take me long to realize that if I was going to have any fun—really—I'd have to forget any black ancestry I had. Too, in my associations here I was not always being depressed by any possibilities of insults and discriminations. Negro students don't get anything out of white colleges but work and pity. (My passing as white was intentional and deliberate and I'd do it over again. The advantages were my unhampered participation in activities and the human treatment I received. Of course, I couldn't really leave my race permanently because I have too many fond remembrances. When I get ready to marry I'll pick out a girl just like myself—not that I admire a light girl better than others but because when we go to shows and travel we can do so without any discrimination."

Mrs. "D," a young woman who has just recently married, stated that she had, in working prior to her marriage, never had any unpleasant or unusual experiences. "The most appalling thing that ever happened to me, however," she stated, "occurred at the time of my marriage. When my husband and I appeared at the bureau to secure our marriage license they told me white women weren't allowed to marry Negroes in this state. My husband became furious and it was only after heated words and witnesses that my statement was accepted. Too, when my husband and I go out, the curious attention that we attract makes my husband disgusted. You can see then that my color, although an advantage when I used it to 'get by,' has proved rather a nuisance to me since. I sometimes feel inclined to wear a sign, 'I am a Negro,' so that my husband would not be the recipient of such hostile glances from every white man that notices us."

* * *

These white Negroes have achieved success in an environment which puts a premium upon being white and a reproach upon being colored. Nearly all the persons who have crossed the color line, as indicated in the cases cited, have done so because of the economic opportunities afforded thereby. The crossing of the color line was not due to a dissatisfaction with the Negro group, but to a desire for the advantages open to white persons but closed to colored persons.

ANONYMOUS

3,000 Negroes Cross the Line Each Year†

Says Bishop Martin in Addressing N.A.A.C.P.; No Favors But Equal Opportunity

That five thousand Negroes of light color "pass" and become to all intents and purposes white people, was the assertion of Bishop J. W. Martin, of the A. M. E. Zion Church, addressing a mass meeting last night of the National Association for the Advancement of Colored People now in 19th Annual Conference here.

"Fully five thousand Negroes of lighter hue are forced over the line" each year, in order to get a chance to win their daily bread at the kind of work they love best and for which they are best fitted," declared Bishop Martin.

"I know the Mayor of a certain town who is a white man now, but as a boy was as good a Negro as the community had and his brother is to this day a good colored preacher. We want the doors of all professions and trades, of all skilled and unskilled labor opened to us and we want them opened wide enough for us to get without having to 'pass'.

"An equal opportunity to spend and to be spent along with any and all groups in this country is the demand made in behalf of the Negro by the National Association for the Advancement of Colored People. We want no special favors, no extraordinary kindnesses, no granting of handicaps, but a just chance to shoot from taw[4] and keep on shooting until the game is ended.

The National Association for the Advancement of Colored People has proved its right to live and move and have its being by formulating and carrying forward a program of the highest good for the rich and the poor, the high and the low, the more favored and the less favored alike.

"How we colored people live in the United States of America depends upon where and under what conditions we are forced to live. Go into many of our towns and you might lay down the rule that where the pavement ends there the blacks begin. Now this is not of our own choosing but is the result of conditions forced upon us. Restricted districts, prohibitive purchase price for houses, exorbitant

† From *The Philadelphia Tribune*, July 12, 1928: n.p. Reprinted by permission of *The Philadelphia Tribune*.
4. To be given an equal chance.

rents threat and abuse, are only some of the means employed for adding insult to our already sorely injured group.

"When it comes to public parks and playgrounds; leisure and recreation, the Negro is often not even thought of in connection with them; and this is doubly true in that section of our country where we live in large numbers and where the need therefore is greatest. What we are going to do about it I know not, but this I do know, the fight is on, the National Association for the Advancement of Colored People has taken the field, and will never leave until the lives of our boys and girls of our men and women are held more precious; until we can have a chance to live out all the days of our appointed time. Lynchings and mob violence, ghettoes and chain gangs are the result of small value put on the lives of certain citizens of our republic.

"The arm of the Government must be made long enough and strong enough to reach to the most out-of-the-way place and rescue. Will it ever come? We will watch and wait, but hustle while we wait."

LOUIS FREMONT BALDWIN

From Negro to Caucasion, Or How the Ethiopian Is Changing His Skin.†

A concise presentation of the manner in which many Negroes in America who, being very fair in complexion, with hair naturally or artificially free from kink, have abandoned their one-time affiliations with Negroes, including their own relatives, and by mingling at first commercially or industrially, then socially with Caucasians, have ultimately been absorbed by the latter.

In sending you this little booklet, and asking you to peruse it, the author feels that he may be inviting your adverse comment, to which you might care to give public expression, of a nature that is not only sceptical of the facts presented, but emphatically dissenting from his attempt to defend a practice rather generally in vogue, but carried on so clandestinely as to be unpardonably offensive, upon discovery.

It is clear that he must have ignored the old adage that "Discretion is the better part of valor," when he ventures to justify, on any grounds

† From Louis Fremont Baldwin, *From Negro to Caucasian, Or How the Ethiopian Is Changing His Skin* (San Francisco: Pilot Publishing Company, 1929; prepared and published at the request of the Society for the Amalgamation of the Races, New York), pp. 1–9; 35–40; 62–65. From the General Research and Reference Division, Schomburg Center for Research in Black Culture, The New York Public Library, Astor, Lenox, and Tilden Foundations.

whatsoever,—the intermingling of the black, yellow and white races matrimonially, as being beneficial to the evolution of the human family, in the light of the unanimous disapproval of such intermingling throughout America and the Western World.

LOUIS FREMONT BALDWIN
Author

Introduction

It was only after the writer had held a very confidential interview with one of the persons referred to in the pages that follow, that he came to the decision to bring this matter to public notice, reaching the conclusion that the information, of which he is in possession, if given out, would prove simply interesting to some, surprising to others and very doubtful to others. The precaution that had to be exercised in investigating matters of this nature, becomes all the more apparent, because of the uncomfortable uncertainty which the accuser feels, when he decides to launch his accusation against the suspected; and the narration that follows shows how extremely delicate a matter it is even to entertain a suspicion along these lines, which if expressed and unfounded, would prove lamentably regrettable on the one hand and offensive to the point of insulting on the other.

In presenting the situation which the pages to follow reveal, the author feels that he is giving information, with which the white people of America are totally unfamiliar; he believes that it never dawns upon them that the Negro is barred from occupying positions such as salesmen, clerks, stenographers, bank-tellers and the like. It is a matter on which they have had occasion to give little if any thought—and in cases where any notice at all has been given, it has been passed off lightly as having no especial significance, but just a matter of custom, to which all parties concerned naturally assented.

It is believed that a perusal of what follows will convince the reader that it is not an acceptable condition to ALL PARTIES concerned, and the deprivation resulting from its prevalence, to say nothing of its effect upon the earning capacity of the aggrieved, accounts for the tremendous increase in the number engaged in the practice, described in the text as, "PASSING."

The author has with scrupulous care endeavored to state nothing but actual facts, growing out of his personal interviews and investigations, and presents the instances within noted, as typical of hundreds coming under his personal review, and hundreds aye,—thousands more known to others who have furnished the data that makes verification possible, and positive new cases appearing with alarming frequency.

Since no reader of this book will deny that it is natural for the individual to remove the obstacles that interfere with his civic and economic progress, by such methods as seem to him available, and since this method—that of passing from a "Negro to a Caucasian"—necessarily carries with it relations of the most intimate character, will it not prove a step in the right direction for the dominant race to endeavor to eradicate its racial and color prejudices,—open wider the doors of opportunity, and thus remove the prime incentive that actuates Negroes "to pass as white."

It is not asserted that this would prevent race-in-termingling, but it would then be practiced under conditions free from deception and thereby more conducive to the benefits, Divinely planned to result from well regulated "Mixing of the Races."

How far the author succeeds in impressing the public with the extent to which this practice has been and is now being carried on, depends entirely upon the credulity of the reader, but be assured that since in "mysterious ways, wonders are performed," it may be that because of being subjected to such discrimination, deprivation, and oppression, the Negro perceives this attempt at "becoming white" to be the method,—and the only method, of finding a solution to the vexatious problems that confront him on every hand.

—The Author.

How Negroes Are Becoming White

It is the desire of the writer to bring to the attention of the public a certain phase of the troublesome Negro problem destined to prove of much public concern, though at present little or no thought is given to it, undoubtedly due to the fact, that the procedure to be described, is being carried on so clandestinely as to be unobserved by all,—all, except a very few,—increasing rapidly however,—who have been or are now engaging in the practice, together with their relatives and friends.

The few who are aware of this, are in the main Negroes—or ex-Negroes, the name by which I designate those who "HAVE BECOME WHITE." It has never dawned upon the dominant race, that there has been such a large influx of the Negro race into his own, as a direct result of the practice of—

"Passing"

This name originated during the days of Slavery; by employing this means, an escape from Slavery to Freedom was greatly facilitated; those whose physical characteristics did not enable them to employ this means to effect their escape, not infrequently traveled as men, when they were women, and vice versa, for the reward offered in the advertisements, informing the public that this or that slave had escaped, invariably read:—

> Buxom Nigger woman (or man) not very black, the property of ———, answers to the name of ———. Fifty Dollars reward for her (or his) return dead or alive will be paid by ——— owner, address ———.

Naturally—the runaway if a woman, disguised as a man, wending (his) way along the road, with a hoe, or a shovel or scythe slung across the shoulder would not appear to be the "Buxom Nigger Woman" not very black who had run away, and for whose capture the reward was advertised.

Then Chattel Slavery, Now Social Bondage

But while the practice is still known by the same name, it serves a rather different purpose for the present generation, the purpose is different mainly in that instead of it being used as a means to escape from chattel slavery, it is used to effect an escape from an industrial, commercial, political and social bondage, in which Negroes are now living, quite as drastic as was the chattel slavery, in which their fore-fathers lived. This newer slavery is the logical successor of that former kind, to rid the country of which, were spent thousands upon thousands of lives and millions upon millions of treasure. What will have to be spent to abolish this present form of bondage, that furnishes so many Negroes with an irresistible desire "TO PASS", the writer will not venture to predict.

It is well to contrast the "MOTIVE" for PASSING now, with the motive of former days; then it was meant to be but temporary, serving only the purpose of landing the "PASSER" beyond the reach of his erstwhile master, after which he gladly sought out "his own people" with whom to mingle, as he strove to pursue the even tenor of his way, in the various walks of the life of an escaped slave.

But now,—PASSING is deliberately planned to be permanent, those attempting it having made a resolve to abandon forever all relations and associations that might in any way connect or identify them with the people whose dark skins and kinky hair subject them to an ostracism, as humiliating as it is unbearable.

*   *   *

Detection Difficult

As a matter of fact, to detect one trying "to pass" is most difficult; white people are not inclined to think of a Negro in terms of intelligence or equality. The idea of Sambo and Dinah lingers fondly in their memories. If one uses good English, shows marked intelligence, and culture, wonder is expressed at such a one being a Negro; consequently one possessing these attributes, and physical features alienating him from the Negroid type at the same time, runs little or no risk of being detected.

It must also be considered that there is an extreme delicacy about accusing a person of being a Negro. It is so degrading to be thus identified that people hesitate to make the accusation. Even in cases where the resemblance is close, the observer will ask—"You seem to be a Negro? and if you are, I can't rent you the apartment or give you the position, as the case may be.

Unless therefore there are distinct evidences that the individual in question is a Negro, he may go his way without interference.

It is perfectly plain that the Negro race gets a whiter complexion from the admixture of the blood of white ancestors; it is also plain that he gets his straight hair from this same source supplemented by the blood of the American Indian. This excludes, of course, those who obtain these characteristics by the use of the artificial methods referred to in these pages.

*   *   *

Other assertions about being able to detect one drop of Negro blood from an appearance of the finger nails, or from a microscopic examination of the back, along the line of the backbone, are equally unfounded.

It does not appear that that young scion of a New York millionaire [Leonard "Kip" Rhinelander], who took unto himself a wire, from whom he was made to seek divorce, when, largely because her father was a cab-driver, the information became public that she was a Negress, it does not appear that he could detect her Negro blood from either of these tests, and he evidently had ample opportunity to apply either or both.

*   *   *

Promiscuous Mating Not Advocated

As intimated elsewhere in these pages, the impression is general—though unwarranted—that naught but detrimental consequences will follow the introduction of this dark, or yellow, or black blood into the white race, whereas the author contends that the intermingling of bloods, through well regulated intercourse, is not only inevitable, but actually productive of a type of humanity differing from and superior to, an off-spring that results from a non-intermingling.

The contention is emphasized, that racial intermingling is INEVITABLE, and while man has directed all of his energies to prevent and thwart it, it is slowly and subtly worming its way into the lives of those who, apprehensive of its prevalence, chafe at the progress it is making, in spite of their efforts to prevent.

※ ※ ※

EMILIE HAHN

Crossing the Color Line†

Social and Economic Ambitions Lead Negroes to "Pass"
at Rate of 5,000 a Year to White Fold

In a small town in Texas two automobiles, one driven by a Negro and the other by a white man, collided. The white man was responsible, but this was Texas, and he demanded redress for the damage done to his car. He felt so strongly about it, in fact, that he pulled a gun and was threatening to shoot when another man intervened. This bystander said that he had seen the wreck and that the white man was in the wrong. The crowd that had gathered took his word for it and the aggrieved driver put away his gun and pursued his way in peace. Had he discovered that the evidence had been given by a "light nigger" his fury would have known no bounds. The masquerader, after having averted the catastrophe, went home to the Jim Crow section of town.

Suppose that some day he should decide not to go home, but to join the ranks of the privileged Caucasians. His life would be much easier. At present his status is very uncertain. With the increasing confusion of race-mixture in the United States the Government finds it

† From *New York World*, July 28, 1929: n.p.

necessary to change the definition of Negroes every ten years for the benefit of the census-takers. In 1910 the Department of Commerce report stated: "The census's classification is necessarily based upon perceptibility, qualified by the ability of the enumerator to perceive."

In other words, it is up to the census-taker to decide offhand just how much black blood runs in the veins of a suspiciously high-yellow[5] citizen. The problem seems to have developed in complexity in the last few years, for, in 1890, the Government had much more definite ideas.

"Be particularly careful," read the directions, "to distinguish between blacks, mulattoes, quadroons and octoroons. The word 'black' should be used to describe those persons who have three-fourths or more black blood; 'mulatto," those persons who have three-eights to five-eights black blood; 'quadroons,' those persons who have one-fourth black blood, and 'octoroon,' those persons who have one-eighth or any trace of black blood."

Even these directions are not explicit enough; another part of the records gives this guide: Black, 10–16 or more; mulatto, 6–16 to 10–16; quadroon, 3–16 to 6–16; octoroon, less than 3–16.

It all looks very pretty and scientific, but as a matter of fact the proposition is not so simple. Any conscientious census-taker would be baffled by the problem, for there is no law governing the color of a child of race-mixture, or of his children after him. I was brought up in the belief that any family with a trace of Negro blood, be it ever so slight a taint, would produce one child of the darkest possible hue every fourth generation. This romantic idea probably owes a large part of its existence to Mendel, although I believe that in some parts of the country the legend is changed to the extent that it is every seventh generation, rather than every fourth, that is thus unfortunately affected.

The truth is that after the first generation the results are impossible to prophesy. A "mulatto"—that is, the child of a white and a black—runs pretty generally to type, but second-generation children and the succeeding generations are likely to develop any sort of variation. The features may resemble that of one race, while the color is that of the other, and there are all possibilities in between. It is common to see a "high-brown" of very fair skin with the characteristic thick lips and dark eyes of the Negro; on the other hand, many a black man has the features of the Nordic—light eyes, narrow lips and prominent slender nose. Sometimes in a family of mixed pedigree a child will be born that resembles in all ways a child of pure white blood. It is just as likely that a family with the same pedigree will produce a black child of Negroid features.

It is likely that many of the pale masqueraders are never discovered. The National Association for the Advancement of Colored

---

5. Light-skinned black.

People has estimated that bout 5,000 people a year decide to drop all claim to Negro blood and enter the world of the white man. Financially speaking, it is decidedly to their advantage to do so. An educated colored man finds the economic struggle exceedingly difficult. If a Negro is a lawyer or any kind of scientist he has a hard time getting a job, and when he has found it he is usually underpaid. If such a man is light enough to pass as a white it is only natural that he find some way of making a permanent adjustment.

The statistics of the association are not official. Naturally those who intend to "pass" do not inform their people before doing it. The only way of arriving at any estimate is to watch the discrepancy in the number of light-skinned Negroes that have been born and accounted for up to the time of their disappearance, and the number of those who are actually there to be counted. In the Negro districts of our cities there are not as many light Negroes as would be expected.

Often the Negro who can "pass" will pretend to be white only for the moment, when it seems expedient. Certain difficulties and annoyances are always facing colored people in this country. The Jim Crow rule which prevails on Pullmans, for instance makes it very uncomfortable for a Negro to travel: the restrictions of theatres and restaurants are always with them.

I remember that when I was a child in the St. Louis public schools there was a red-haired girl in my class who kept very much to herself. One day a rumor spread that her mother was a Negress, and that the authorities had just discovered it. For two or three days the little boys spent the recess hour chanting "Nigger! Nigger!" and then she disappeared. I do not know if she attended the Negro school hereafter; it was two or three miles from her house. But I am willing to wager that she found some way, ultimately, of leaving her environment and living more comfortably elsewhere.

Color Line
Can Be Recrossed

Some years ago, in the West, I knew a boy who looked like a Spaniard. I was not aware that he was a Negro, although as a matter of fact he never denied it. He never spoke of such things. He was very quiet; he said that he came from the South; he mixed with white people and no one thought of questioning him. At last he disappeared and for several years I heard no more of him. The next time I saw him he was a Negro and had allied himself with Negro propagandists. He has never again tried to "pass," but if he should want to, he could certainly get away with it. I suppose he did it for several years trying to make up his mind which he would be, and then a pride of race swung the balance. It is somewhat inconsistent to speak of race pride in a matter like this. Surely the boy was more white than Negro. But one drop of Negro blood settles the matter in the mind of the American.

There was a reporter on a Middle Western newspaper at the same time that my brother worked there and they became acquainted. After a time they both left the paper and my brother's friend went to another city,where he continued his newspaper work. He has become mildly successful and more or less well known. I have only lately discovered that he is, according to our standards, a Negro. He first started to "pass" when he came to the Western town on business. He had often tried to write for publication, but had no success until he sold a story to a local paper. He did not say that he was a Negro and the editor was enthusiastic about his work, offering him a job immediately. Why not? He took it and has since lived as a white man, without even changing his name. He married a white girl from a Southern State. It is likely that he has qualms at times. He is not unknown, and many Negroes are aware of his masquerade, but such cases are an old story to them. They will not interfere.

Line Blurred

Beyond Recognition

If I have happened on such cases how many more are probably in existence? There must be many people whose positions in the white world are firmly intrenched. Our whole idea of segregation is based on one line of difference. At first there was a definite distinction between white and black. With increasing miscegenation the dividing line shifted; whites were distinguished from all other people by the expedient of putting together all those with any black blood and labeling them Negroes.

Now, after some generations of confusion, there are two extremes, the white and the black, of pure direct descent. In between is a rapidly growing company of people who represent the mixture in all possible proportions. There is no more reason to call them Negroes than there is to call them whites. The distinction between the full-blooded Negro and the mulatto does not exist in the mind of the white man who claims that it is so obscure as to be imperceptible.

The same rule can work the other way. Where the difference between a white and a light Negro is imperceptible, it is only natural that such a distinction will be ignored by an individual who will profit by stepping across the line and joining the privileged race. Our own jealousy guarded segregation is a myth.

CALEB JOHNSON

From Crossing the Color Line†

It is estimated that nearly 10,000 persons of fractional Negro ancestry each year "cross the color line" from Negro to white society. The Negroes call them "passers." Some of them are octoroons; others are "mustifees," the offspring of an octoroon and a white person and actually and legally white. Contrary to general impression, white ancestry is the dominant strain, as the author points out here in reporting the scientific investigations of Dr. Davenport of the Carnegie Institution

One out of every ten persons in the United States bears the visible tinge of the "tar brush," according to the last Federal Census. No statistics are available, naturally, of the number of persons who do not acknowledge their Negro ancestry but pass for white in their home communities and elsewhere, but it is a large and rapidly increasing number.

Crossing the color line is so common an occurrence that the Negroes have their own well-understood word for it. They call it "passing." It is less and less difficult for the young man or woman of African descent, whose skin, hair and features are not decidedly Negroid, to "pass" without fear of detection. The "passer's" Negro relatives and friends can be relied upon not to give the "passer" away. Their attitude is that it is a good joke on the white folks; coupled with this there seems to be a sense of pride that one of their race has achieved the social equality denied to themselves.

In New York, where only one person out of thirty-four is an acknowledged Negro, it is a matter of common repute among the colored folks of Harlem that more than ten thousand of their number have "passed," and are now accepted as white in their new relations, many of them married to white folks, all unsuspected. In Chicago, with a Negro population of one in twenty, and in Philadelphia, where one in thirteen is a Negro, the proportion of annual "passings" is said to be even larger.

* * *

Scientific investigations by the Carnegie Institution of Washington have thrown new light on the results of the mating of white with Negro or part Negro, and have set at rest some of the popular misconceptions about these mixed relations. The belief that the white-and-black hybrid is less fecund than either pure white or pure black

† From *Outlook and Independent* 158 (August 26, 1931): 526ff.

is regarded as incorrect by the Carnegie investigators, who present evidence to the contrary in an imposing list of very large families, offspring of two mulatoes, mulatto and Negro, mulatto and quadroon, and the like. This theory (that the Negro race will eventually die out from infertility because of the increasing white mixture) seems to be based on a false analogy between the human white Negro hybrid, the mulatto, and the ass-horse hybrid, the mule, notoriously sterile, and it has been cherished by many who believed that by such a dying-out process alone will the Negro problem be solved.

The results of this scientific investigation indicate that the Negro race is not dying out from infertility but is bleaching out through admixture with the white race. The white strain is the dominant one and this fact has a direct bearing upon the increasing number of Negroes with three-quarters or more of white blood who "pass" every year and marry into white families.

* * *

While there are no statistics to support the conclusion; there is strong reason for the belief that many more women than men cross the color line from Negro to white. This partly due to the fact that sexual attraction is stronger between the light male and the darker female than in the opposite direction. It is a matter commented on by numerous scientific observers, who agree that the male Negro almost universally prefers a woman of his own color or darker, while the primitive sex-appeal of the octoroon girl is highly potent with the average young white male. Moreover, the social act of "passing" is easier for the girl than for the man.

As a rule, a young octoroon girl finds more opportunity to study the ways of white folks, observe their intimate personal habits, learn to speak and act as they do, than does the young colored man no darker than his near-white sister. The girl's opportunity comes through domestic service, as cook, nursemaid or in some other intimate household capacity. And, if she is not too scrupulous, she can always find a man who will assist her financially in her step across the color line. The farther she goes from the community in which she is known as colored, the less likely is she to be discovered and denounced by some white person who knows her.

* * *

It took six hundred years for the Moors to lose their identity in the mass of the Spanish population and to change the complexion of Spain from that of the blond Visigoths to the dark brunet Spaniard of today. Ten per cent of Americans today are recognizably Negroid; an incalculable percentage carry the blood in their veins though classed as white. It seems not inconceivable that the American Negro will eventually vanish, completely absorbed into the general body of mixed bloods of all races which will constitute the American people of the future.

ANONYMOUS

75,000 Pass in Philadelphia Every Day†

Most Recent Influx is from the State of Virginia.
WHITE BY DAY;
NIGHTS, COLORED
Ga. Jurist's Son Amassed Fortune.

There are fully 75,000 persons of color who are passing for white, here.

These figures include the thousands of near-white Virginians who have flocked to this city since that state began to crusade for so-called racial purity.

Virginia Near-Whites

These Virginia near-whites have had it easier than other groups of our people who have gone over to the Nordics. Their white blood was merely under suspicion in the Old Dominion State. Moving to Pennsylvania allowed them to get from under the old threats and dangers, without actually having to make new group connections.

But these near-white Virginians are only a small part of the total number of persons of mixed colored and white blood who are passing in this section of the East.

It was the fashion even during slavery days, for certain white masters to send their colored children here to be educated. Others, to insure the greater freedom of their colored blood-kin, sent them to this old Quaker City to live. Nearly all of these went over to the whites.

Added to these were the thousands of free persons of fair complexions who, during slavery, found Philadelphia the nearest and most convenient haven of their "passing" operations.

White by Day—Colored by Night

Recent additions to these original groups have been almost too widespread to trace. In good times thousands of fair persons of color hereabouts merely go white during their working hours in Philadelphia shops and stores and factories, and then return at evening to the bosoms of their colored relations. Others find it to their profit and liking to go over permanently to the local white group.

† From *The Afro-American*, December 19, 1931: n.p. Reprinted by permission of the Afro-American Newspaper Archives and Research Center.

Almost any member of our group knows from ten to a score of his acquaintances who are counted in the Nordic group. Most of these "lost" ones give as the chief reason for their passing, the superior business and economic advantages on the white side of the line.

Personally we know dozens of these individuals, nearly all of them occupying positions in the community which would have been beyond their reach as members of our group.

Amassed Fortune

One of these "passers," the colored son of an eminent Georgia jurist, moved here about 30 years ago, and has amassed a considerable fortune. His children and grandchildren have all married white.

A peculiar incident in connection with this particular "passer" happened here in Philadelphia not so long ago. This colored son of the famous Georgia jurist has a white brother who is still living, and a pillar of respectability in his native town.

Recently, the wife of this brother visited Philadelphia and was shown numerous social honors. One of the Philadelphia newspapers, because of her Colonial connections, interviewed her at length on the historical associations connected with the old Georgia city of her birth.

No Mention

No mention, however, was made of the near-white brother who is passing. People here don't believe that he gives a hang about these "Colonial" connections of his. It is known, however, that he has more "coin of the realm" than all of his Georgia white relations put together.

ANONYMOUS

Careful Lyncher! He May Be Your Brother†

Careful lyncher! he may be your brother. . . .

At last it seems as if this "you can tell by their walk, you can tell by their talk, you can tell by their uncouth manners" theory of the white man is breaking down.

The last two or three weeks have brought an additional amount of proof to substantiate the conception of most Negroes, that the superior whites are "not so smart as they think."

The front page of a prominent Negro weekly told, last week, of how a Negro woman bore the illustrious first Secretary of the United States treasury, Alexander Hamilton, two sons. One of the sons mar-

† From *The Philadephia Tribune*, January 21, 1932: n.p. Reprinted by permission of *The Philadelphia Tribune*.

ried into a white family and went his merry way. The other married a "very light "Negro woman, and one of the sons of this union "turned white" and is now living in a Jersey town, married to a "white" woman.

And the miracle of it is, the superior whites, whose perfect beings are said to react naturally when "one drop" of Negro blood heaves into view—never found out!

Two weeks ago a Lieutenant of the United States Army was found shot; most probably murdered, on a lonely road. His record showed brilliant service. He had been steadily promoted on merit and suddenly it is found that he was a Negro.

A number of women of the "superior" group had fallen along the army man's paths. He married one from Georgia who "hated niggers". . . . and they never found out.

There's a moral in these cases for Southerners, who seem so very bent upon lynching Negroes: be careful how you do it—the man may be your brother.

ANONYMOUS

Blonde Girl Was 'Passing'†

Mother on Stand in N.Y. Court Tearfully Relates Story of Tragedy

A blonde dancing girl in a burlesque show was killed by her white husband a few weeks ago, when she refused to leave her job.

The story told by the *Amsterdam News* is as follows:

Through the testimony of an aged woman, Mrs. Elizabeth Jones, it was brought out that the murdered woman, Jean Thomas, 33 Post Avenue, was not only a Negro but was the daughter of the aged witness, who had posed as a servant in the home of the couple. The accused husband, William Thomas, emitted a cry and slumped in his chair when the revelation was made. He declared that he had thought his wife "pure white."

The elderly mother's testimony was unexpected. She had been called to the stand by the prosecution to testify that she had often heard the husband threaten to kill his wife unless she consented to give up her appearances in the burlesque shows. She had just finished her testimony when the defense attorney decided to ask her one more question.

"Why," he asked, "are you so interested in this case and the fate of Jean Thomas?"

† From *The Boston Chronicle*, January 23, 1932: n.p.

The old woman did not answer immediately, Looking down for a few minutes, she murmured slowly:

"Jean was my daughter."

Thomas cried out and short recess was called while he was carried to the anteroom to get over his shock. Speaking to the attendants there, he stated:

"I have been married to Jean for four years and until that woman made her statement I never had the faintest suspicion that my wife was not pure white. I saw the old woman around the house, but I thought she is a servant of some kind."

ANONYMOUS

Virginia Is Still Hounding 'White' Negroes Who 'Pass'†

Wage Drive Against "Near-White" Negroes Who Register Births As "White"—Woodson's Book Cited As Aid to Nefarious Work.

The State of Virginia, through its 'Bureau of Vital Statistics, Dr. W. A. Plecker, director, is still hounding "white" Negroes who "pass," according to a report in the Eugenical News. "The Virginia Bureau of Vital Statistics, discovered soon after the organization of the bureau in 1912," begins the report, "that near-white Negroes were registering their births as white. The bureau began to investigate the matter through its local registrars, physicians, and others, and discovered a spontaneous and widespread movement of those people to secure official recognition as white through birth, death, and marriage registration.

"We began a systematic effort to combat this movement by securing accurate and dependable information as to the racial origin of such families and groups of families, through living informants familiar with the facts, and through our old birth, death, and marriage records covering period of 1853 ot 1896. We also secured much information by referring to the old tax records listed by paces, going back to the early part of the 19th century. (Dr. Carter G.) Woodson's 'Free Negro Heads of Families In the United States in 1830,' also furnishes exceedingly valuable information.

"An act of the 1924 legislature was secured defining a colored person as one with any ascertainable degree of Negro blood, and

† From *The Pittsburgh Courier*, June 29, 1935: n.p. Reprinted by permission of GRM Associates, Inc., agents for *The Pittsburgh Courier*. From the issue of June 29, 1935. Copyright © 1935 by *The Pittsburgh Courier*; copyright renewed 1963 by *The Pittsburgh Courier*.

forbidding marriage of such a person to a white one. It also makes it a felony to make registration certificate false as to color or race.

"Starting with groups of mixed breeds from 200 to 1200 in number claiming their colored admixture to be Indian with no Negro, we found it not difficult to secure definite evidence of Negro as the basic stock. In most instances no evidence whatever could be found of Indian mixture. In other cases, individual families and connections, the beginning of new, larger groups originating from one white-Negro crossing have been definitely studied and evidence filed by counties. New information is being constantly secured, and the starting of new problems are being discovered, studied, and facts filed for permanent preservation.

"Our Bureau places its source material at the disposal of those desiring information in connection with marriage, schools at attendance, etc."

The Rhinelander/Jones Case†

ANONYMOUS

Society Youth Weds Cabman's Daughter††

Leonard Kip Rhinelander and New Rochelle Girl Married by That City's Mayor Moves into Humble Home And Will Continue to Live with the Bride's Parents—Her Sister a Butler's Wife.

Leonard Kip Rhinelander, son of Philip Rhinelander, was married on Oct. 14 to Miss Alice Beatrice Jones, daughter of a Pelham taxicab driver and odd-job man, it became known yesterday.

The wedding took place in the New Rochelle City Hall and was performed by Mayor Harry Scott. No member of the Rhinelander family, one of the oldest in Manhattan, was there. The witnesses were two New Rochelle officials.

A sister of the bride is the wife of a butler employed in Pelham. His employer is Mrs. Joseph Arthur, whose housekeeper said yesterday that the butler was a negro. She explained that he had worked in the Arthur household since he was 15 years old and that no one there had ever questioned his race.

Another sister, formerly Grace Jones, is the wife of "Footsy" Miller, a chauffeur, whose home is next that of the Rhinelander bride's parents, Mr. and Mrs. George Jones. The Joneses occupy one of three small frame dwellings on the outskirts of New Rochelle. For the present, the Leonard Kip Rhinelanders will live with the Joneses. They went there immediately after the wedding ceremony.

In giving the necessary date to the Westchester County Clerk, the bride said that she was 23 years of age, white, born in Pelham and the daughter of George Jones and the former Elizabeth Brown. The record disclosed that Jones said he was born in Leicestershire. England, and that his wife was a native of Lincolnshire. They were

† For an explanation of this case, which hit the front pages of all the major newspapers, see pp. xvii–xviii of the Introduction in this Norton Critical Edition.
†† From *The New York Times*, November 14, 1924: n.p. Copyright © 1924 by The New York Times Co. Reprinted with permission.

married in England thirty years ago, and have lived in New Rochelle for twenty-nine years. Jones's ancestors at one time lived in the West Indies.

Young Rhinelander gave his age as 22, said he was white, and the son of Philip Rhinelander. He gave his mother's maiden name as Adeline Kip, another of the New York families that go back to the days when the Dutch called this city New Amsterdam.

Mayor Scott, in confirming the fact that he had officiated at the quiet little ceremony, said that the witnesses who had appeared were William R. Harmon, City Clerk of New Rochelle, and Harry Cole, who serves as private secretary to Mayor Scott. Immediately after the ceremony the couple stepped into Rhinelander's limousine and motored out to the Jones home at 763 Pelham Road. Two days ago the couple signed a lease on a suite in the Pintard Apartments, a big dwelling at 605 Main Street. New Rochelle, and will soon move in there.

According to the information available, young Rhinelander met Miss Jones in Stamford, Conn., about three years ago, and since that time has maintained correspondence with her. A grocer whose store is just a step from the Jones home told last night of often seeing the young man going to the Jones domicile with flowers.

The mother of young Rhinelander died in 1916 from burns received when a lamp exploded in the family's country home at Tuxedo Park. He has two brothers, T. J. Oakley Rhinelander and Philip Rhinelander 2d. He is known to be wealthy in his own right. Philip Rhinelander, his father, is prominent in many clubs and is a member of several historical societies, membership in which is confined to descendants of those who settled America.

ANONYMOUS

Poor Girl to Fight Hubby's Parents†

With the possible intentions of challenging the stupidity of the ultra-exclusives and the public in general, who expressed so much undue amazement over the Rhinelander marriage, the young millionaire has filed action for the annulment of his recent marriage to the charming Miss Beatrice Jones, a member of our group, and she in turn filed answer.

According to authoritative reports such actions were taken merely to relieve the newlyweds of the mortification they have suffered since

† From *The Chicago Defender*, December 26, 1924: 1, 5. Used with permission of *The Chicago Defender*.

their secret marriage has been divulged. The undue publicity has been extremely humiliating. The continual gossiping and annoyances had long ago driven the loving couple into seclusion. Something had to be done to put an end to the inevitable lashing of gossips and the press. Hence the annulment proceedings.

The annulment was filed in the Westchester supreme court at White Plains, Wednesday, Nov. 26. It has been broadcasted by the press thereby satisfying hoodlums, scandal mongers, the petty jealousies of society and hushing the affair to a marked degree.

Despite the filing of the annulment the young millionaire has informed his wife to have courage and believe in him. He states that regardless of the outcome he still loves her and will return to her as soon as he is able. It is alleged he was kidnapped by his father and forcibly kept from his wife. He writes to her daily.

The basis for the belief that Mr. Rhinelander is sincere is a letter he sent his wife at the time he involuntarily took action for the annulment. He consulted his wife and told her exactly what was being done and informed her to fight the case to the end. He advised her to get the best lawyer obtainable. The text of the letter as divulged by Mrs. Rhinelander's attorney, Judge Swineburne, read:

"Honey Bunch, Old Scout—I hope you will win the case. Get the best lawyer at any cost. Believe in me, dear, as everything is exactly as I explained to you.

"Leonard Rhinelander."

The fact that the young couple married secretly in New Rochelle, Oct. 14, indicates that they did not desire publicity. The young millionaire knew what he was doing. He went into the marriage compact with his eyes open. He was fully acquainted with his wife's parentage and ancestry. He was aware that the publicity would be humiliating. Not so much because of a Race issue, as he has boldly defied that question, but because of the social gap that existed between them.

The Rhinelanders have the distinction of being among the most exclusive and wealthiest families both here and abroad. Many members of the so-called "Four Hundred," whom the average person looks upon as being in the highest of high society circles, would feel themselves honored if only permitted to rub elbows with the Rhinelanders.

Realizing the barriers that would be built up by the ultra-exclusives of which he was a member, Mr. Rhinelander introduced Miss Jones into Newport society during the time that they were engaged. They took a long motor trip the latter part of last summer visiting many large cities and resorts. As the dashing couple appeared in society they were the topic of discussion and naturally, being in the company with Mr. Rhinelander, it was expected that the then Miss Jones was also a member of a family of high social standing.

The millionaire loved Miss Jones for many years before they married according to Mrs. Katherine Walton, a white woman friend of the bride who said she had never seen such perfect love. "Alice married young Rhinelander for love." Mrs. Walton declared. "They both loved each other. She was in love with her husband long before she knew he had money."

"In fact she never learned he was wealthy until Rhinelander inherited $500,000 from the estate of his mother. Rhinelander was especially attentive to Alice's mother, Mrs. George Jones and she cared for him and treated him like a son," declared Mrs. Walton.

Mrs. Walton claims to have known all about the annulment long before it was published. She states that Rhinelander has no intentions of leaving his bride. The annulment is said to have been about the best method to dispose of the outrageous publicity. The public will soon forget and the happy couple will be together again.

According to Judge Swineburne, who represents Mrs. Rhinelander, the bride's father on numerous occasions attempted to prevent the millionaire from marrying his daughter. The judge states: "Mrs. Rhinelander's father called on the young man many times before the wedding and pleaded with him not to marry his daughter. He told him he had his daughter's interests at heart in making his plea, saying that such an alliance must come to a bad end."

At this point Mr. Rhinelander is said to have pointed out that there was nothing that could prevent him from marrying Miss Jones, as he loved her and would stand by her regardless of what happened.

"Mr. Jones stated," said the Judge. "That his family were working people and that there was a social gulf between his daughter and the distinguished Rhinelander which could not be bridged."

It has been pointed out that the affair will soon blow over. The young couple will go West or to Europe: remarry if necessary and carry out their future plans as anticipated. As Judge Swineburne stated, this is not the first time that the millionaire's father has yanked him from Miss Jones. He was sent West over two years and also to Europe in an effort to make him forget her, but he always returned to the girl he loved.

ANONYMOUS

From Calls Rhinelander Dupe of Girl He Wed†

Husband's Counsel Says He Will Prove Bride Was Negro and Practiced Fraud. Quotes Her Love Letters. Youth Ignores Wife as Trial of Annulment Suit Opens in Crowded Courtroom.

Leonard Kip Rhinelander of New York City, who is suing for the annulment of his marriage to Alice Beatrice Jones Rhinelander of New Rochelle, on Oct. 14, 1924, on the grounds that she deceived him as to her race and that she had colored blood, sat unmoved today in a crowded court room before Supreme Court Justice Joseph Morschauser and a jury and heard his counsel, former Supreme Court Justice Isaac N. Mills, read excerpts from letters written to him by the defendant which described the relationship between them. He heard his wife termed the mistress of another man before he met her, and heard Judge Mills described the alleged negro ancestry of his wife, her sisters and her father.

He was listening to the opening address of Judge Mills to the jury in the case which has caused a furore in social circles since last Fall, when it became known that young Rhinelander, descendant of a proud old family of French Huguenots and bearer of one of New York's noted names, had married the daughter of a New Rochelle taxi driver, George Jones, a man alleged to be a negro.

Mrs. Rhinelander's father, a long-faced, dark-skinned man, with long wavy hair, sat fingering his chin as he heard the revelations contained in letters which Judge Mills said he would produce as documentary evidence that the defendant, then Alice Beatrice Jones, had lured young Rhinelander into marrying her. The defendant informed Rhinelander in one of her letters, Judge Mills said, that she was keeping herself only for him, "although there is a Harvard man————and I've had a chance to have a hundred dates."

Through it all Rhinelander, his wife, her father and her mother sat with faces in which not a muscle moved.

* * *

† From *The New York Times,* November 10, 1925: 1. Copyright © 1925 by The New York Times Co. Reprinted with permission.

ANONYMOUS

From Loved Rhinelander, Wife's Letters Say†

Twenty-six Notes Are Read in Suit to Annul Marriage to Negro Girl. He Thought Her White Rhinelander Testifies That Otherwise He Would Not Have Wed Her.

The love letters of Alice Jones Rhinelander, the negro wife of Leonard Kip Rhinelander, who is suing her for annulment of their marriage, were read before a crowded court room here today. They were the fervid, illiterate letters of a woman to whom Rhinelander was a Prince Charming, and although at times their contents were erotic, they conveyed the impression that she was very much in love with him.

He had taken her from the humble home of her negro taxicab driver father to the Hotel Marie Antoinette, had driven her there in his car, remained with her there five days and her experience had made an indelible impression on her mind. She referred to that hotel affair time and again in her letters; it was there, she wrote, that she first began to love him.

Not all the letters contained unpleasant, crudely expressed sentiments of her warm attachment to Rhinelander. There were some letters of very real feeling, letters which showed sincerity. She wrote poetry to him, poetry with a truly negro rhythm which was so superior to her ordinary forms of expression that it seemed as if she must have copied the lines from a popular song:

Kisses, dear, from you, can cheer me when I'm blue.
Your gentle lips have always thrilled me through:
I need carressing, too;
There's happiness I can't express,
In each kiss from you.

Said She Prayed for Him.

She prayed for him, she said, wanted him to save his money and not be so extravagant, to study hard as that would help both of them, to take care of his health.

"I often thank the Lord for the lucky day when I met Leonard K. Rhinelander," she wrote him.

The letters were introduced by former Judge Isaac N. Mills, counsel for Rhinelander, to show that Alice was always the aggressor, that she sought to be with him, was the active and he the passive member in their affairs.

---

† From *The New York Times*, November 13, 1925: 1, 3. Copyright © 1925 by The New York Times Co. Reprinted with permission.

Lee Parsons Davis, her counsel, made loud but apparently academic objections to the reading of "this filth" as he characterized it, but was smilingly overruled by Justice Morschauser, Mr. Davis does not object to strenuously as appears on the record, for he has a lot of letters from Rhinelander to his wife, which are said to be as unpleasant as hers. These will be introduced and also pictures to which she referred in her letters, pictures of her taken in the Marie Antoinette.

During the entire day Rhinelander sat on the stand expressionless, his eyes shielded by his glasses so that no one could guess what his thoughts were as he listened to the recital of his one adventure, which ended when he found that he had married a negress. During the most embarrassing moments his face did not change. He stared straight before him at the rail of the witness stand.

Some distance in front of him at the end of the counsel table his wife leaned on the arm of her chair, her head supported on her hand. She seemed to have lost the tense attitude of the day before, she drooped lower and lower as the day wore on, and never looked around, except once or twice when her white mother bent forward and whispered to her. She did not weep, and what she thought as she listened to the unrestrained vulgarity of her letters, it was impossible to tell.

Earlier in the day Rhinelander had said that he believed his wife to be white when he married her, that she had told him so, and that once she had said she was "of Spanish extraction." If he had not believed her, he would never have married her, he said, and he was not convinced of her negro blood until her birth certificate was shown to him. Her counsel insists he must have been blind.

Rhinelander was his usual well-dressed self. He wore a brown suit, a fancy waistcoat, an orange and black tie, and spats. He and his butler brother-in-law, Robert Brooks, were quite the dandies of the courtroom. Brooks appeared yesterday, with his black curly hair slicked down until it shone, dressed in a neat blue suit and wearing a purple and red tie, which was not gaudy but noticeable. He sat with his wife, Emily, Mrs. Rhinelander's sister, who is unmistakably a negress, next to Mr. and Mrs. Jones.

The voyage Rhinelander took to Alaska, the months he spent at the ranch school in Arizona, and his return to New York, were described rapidly by him. His eyes blinked as he tried to start each sentence, and then it boiled out. But his English was good and his memory accurate. He considered himself engaged on his return, he said, and told of gaining control, on his coming of age, of $30,000 left him by his grandfather.

"Did you intend to marry her?" Justice Mills asked him.

"I did."

Says He Loved Her.

"Did you love her?"

"I did."

"Was there any talk at any time before your marriage of the question of color?"

"There was," said Rhinelander, "Between May and December, 1924. In the presence of Alice and Mr. and Mrs. Jones, Mrs. Jones told me that they had done everything in their power to prevent Emily from marrying Brooks, but seeing it was of no avail they denied Emily and Brooks the house for two years, telling me they were not colored, they were English. They were born in England. They said. "The first we ever saw a colored person was on our arrival in America, walking on Sixth Avenue. We were surprised and didn't know what they were. Alice said of course they were not colored; they never associated with colored people and never would."

"Did you ever talk with Alice with regard to being of Spanish extraction?" asked Judge Mills.

"Yes," he said. "She told me she had become acquainted with a Harvard man in the Adirondacks and he asked Alice, 'What are you?' and Alice said, 'I'm of Spanish extraction.' "

He told of his marriage and of living at the Jones house for a time, and the attempt to start housekeeping in an apartment. The reporters came around, and when he told Alice what was in the paper, she said, "It is a terrible lie: It isn't true."

Later she told reporters, said Rhinelander, that she was not colored, and that she would sue the newspapers for libel. But she never did, he said. Finally he left her because of the doubt in his own mind, which had been firmed when he saw his wife's birth certificate stating her color as black.

"If you had known what is now conceded to be true before you had married Alice, that she is of colored blood, would you have married her?" asked Judge Mills.

"No," said Rhinelander decidedly.

"Did you believe her to be white?"

"Yes, I always believed her to be white."

Twenty-six Letters Read.

Then the reading of letters began again and lasted all of the day. Twenty-six of the fifty letters which Judge Mills intends to put into the record had been read when court adjourned, and he will probably take most of tomorrow getting the rest of them into the record. They were nearly all alike, even in those parts which cannot be reproduced, for there was a constant reiteration of the same thing.

*   *   *

ANONYMOUS

From Rhinelander Bares Love Secrets†

Young Kip Stammers as He Tells of Pursuing Alice during Three Years' Wooing Admits He Spent Many Hours with His Wife's Family, Who Made No Effort to Hide Their Racial Connections

With the gnawing sense of condemnation racking through his tortured brain while gripped in the merciless bands of acid-test questioning, Leonard Kip Rhinelander wilted on the witness stand Tuesday and not only admitted that it was his father's lawyer who forced the suit for annulment of his marriage to Alice Jones, a member of our group, but that he had sworn falsely to five statements in the bill of particulars.

The annulment suit has been in the White Plains court for more than a week and beginning Monday Rhinelander has been under the rapid fire cross-examination of Mrs. Rhinelander's attorney, Lee Parsons Davis, the court has been filled with members of both groups. At the beginning of the trial Rhinelander's attorney, former Judge Mills, introduced slimy evidence which dragged his wife's name in the mire by reading many of her intimate letters to the millionaire.

On the stand Kip willingly admitted that he objected to his attorney reading these letters, which apparently had been stolen from his trunk and that he protested vigorously against the annulment suit. When Rhinelander made these admissions his attorney, with a look of disgust, slumped far down in his chair after turning his back on the witness.

Admits Pursuing Wife

Kip also admitted that it was he who pursued his wife and forced his attentions upon her, also knowing three years before their marriage that there must have been some question as to her not being white, but he was so much in love with her that he did not care. Startling revelations were brought out in his testimony as he was led into many traps by his wife's attorney which have completely torn down the flimsy fortification presented to the jury last week by his own attorney. Kip related how he had often played poker with Robert Brooks, Mrs. Rhinelander's sister's brown-skinned husband, and had had dinner several times at the Brooks home.

Rhinelander denied he gave his wife an automobile for a wedding present and insisted his present was a diamond ring. He gave Jacobs, his attorney, a note to take his automobile out of the garage in New

† From *The Chicago Defender*, November 21, 1925: 1ff. Used with permission of *The Chicago Defender*.

Rochelle, he admitted, but said he gave his attorney no authority to take the furnishings out of his wife's apartment.

✳   ✳   ✳

Is It Color?

Young Kip Rhinelander is trying to have his marriage to Alice Beatrice Rhinelander annuled on the grounds that she is not a white woman, and that she deceived him as to her racial identity before their marriage. Rhinelander and his wife were about the same complexion before the marriage and they are now and since neither has changed physically, they must be of the some complexion now. When they were married, legally, they became as one. Then what can be Rhinelander's contention now? Can he invoke the law on one hand and repudiate it on another?

A white woman in Illinois recently adopted a boy of our Race. In doing so, she made him her heir as though he were "born of her in lawful wedlock," declares the Illinois law. It is the law that makes a person in this country a member of one race or another. By law, Kip should belong to Mrs. Rhinelander's race, or she to his, it doesn't matter which. He is seeking the aid of the law to change nature's own product. Is it color or money?

But it doesn't happen to be Mrs. Rhinelander's color that is giving rise to the suit. It is something far more sinister, and will be brought out before the case is ended. We call all persons white who are the color of Mrs. Rhinelander.

ARCHIE MORGAN

From Kip's "Soul Message" Notes Read†

Annulment Suit Enters Final Stages as State Completes Its Evidence. Kip's Young Bride Weeps When She Is Forced to Expose Her Body before Judge and Jury

It seems utterly impossible to believe that there ever existed a stronger, more absolute, more genuine love than that of Leonard Kip Rhinelander, heir to $100,000,000, and his non-white bride Alice Jones Rhinelander, who due to his father's demand calling for an annulment of his marriage to her a year ago. The trial in the White Plains court has entered its third week, and not only startling and shocking revelations have been made, but imprintable evidence written into the records; yet when the unnatural method of love making of this young

† From *The Chicago Defender*, November 28, 1925: 1, 4. Used with permission of *The Chicago Defender*.

couple was exposed Monday, this born aristocrat stoutly denies any stigma is attached to their love except in the opinion of others.

The Rhinelander trial has been the most sensational of its kind in court record. The testimony at the beginning of this week with the disrobing of Mrs. Rhinelander and the reading of Kip's two unprintable mystery letters which threatened to halt the suit last Thursday has been of a nature that revealed the most outrageous and disgusting filth that probably has ever been heard in a courtroom. After the trying ordeal of Monday when Kip was released from the fiery cross-examination of his wife's attorney, Mrs. Rhinelander was unable to take the stand Tuesday and seemingly was still suffering from the humiliation she was subjected to Monday when she was obliged to show a portion of her body and limbs to prove that her husband could not have been ignorant of her racial descent because of her color. However, Tuesday, Robert Brooks, Mrs. Rhinelander's sister Emily's brown-skinned husband testified: also a Mrs. Barbara Reynolds, newspaper reporter for the New Rochelle Standard Star, which first exposed the whole affair, tossed a bomb into the plaintiff's accusations by testifying that when she interviewed Rhinelander on Nov. 13 of the last year he boldly admitted to her question that he had married a Colored girl and asked to keep it out of the papers because if his father knew it, it would mean his life happiness.

Clears Courtroom

After an adjournment of two days, the trial was resumed Monday morning and Rhinelander was again subjected to severe question by Davis.

"Did you tell this jury your relations with Alice Rhinelander were natural?" he asked.

"Yes," answered the witness.

"Did you mean that answer?"

"Yes."

Davis then read the extract from the court record in which Rhinelander had made that assertion to the jury. At this point Justice Morschauer definitely ordered the courtroom cleared of all women, except those whose duties required their presence meaning newspaper women.

Alice and her parents, Mr. and Mrs. George Jones, had been among the first to leave.

The first letter, dated July 11, 1922, at the Cliff hotel, San Francisco, was written just before Rhinelander sailed for Honolulu.

The second letter, which will go down in court annals as "Exhibit M." was dated June 6, 1922. It was written before the other at the Cliff hotel in San Francisco. It was almost entirely unprintable.

* * *

"Keeping up with the Joneses" has been for the past 12 months what might be termed the international pastime due to the unusual importance of the famous and never to be forgotten Rhinelander annulment suit. It is doubtful if ever in the annals of American history that a case of such significant importance has ever been contested, and many a decade will be cast into oblivious before there will be another.

To begin with, Leonard Kip Rhinelander, heir to $100,000,000, who married Alice Beatrice Jones, a member of our group, is a direct descendant of the famous Huguenots. If there ever existed such a thing as blood of distinction it is evident that none could be more properly classed as such than that which flowers through the tender veins of this young scíon of society.

There are hundreds of millionaires in American and hundreds of thousands of independently rich Aristocrats, but of this vast number of so-called members of purest of blue bloods there probably are none who can trace their ancestral deliveragance, which will correspond with that pure strain of aristocracy of which Mr. Rhinelander is identified. Yet as paradoxically [sic] as it may seem, this dashing young aristocrat loved, and knowingly took upon himself a bride whose blood was "tainted" with that of a former sub-dominant race.

No family in US has played a more unique and interesting part in the history of American than that of the Rhinelanders. Back in the days when the Edict of Nantes came to vex the spirit of the world, Phillip Jacob Rhinelander lived in the ancient castle of Schoenberg at Oberwesel on the Rhine. Philip emigrated to the US to escape the religious persecution of his time and in 1636 settled in the town of New Rochelle, in Westchester County, the same county in which the annulment suit is being tried.

The family played for more than 200 years a part in the history of this country, which doubtful can be equaled by that of any of the older families of all America. It was a family, which held romance millions and action. Unlike the average rich American who accumulated their fortunes by the sweat of their own brow, since the making of this "Land of Promise," the Rhinelanders have always been rich. They were wealthy persons of distinction when the Astors were trading furs in Canada and the Vanderbilts digging potatoes in Long Island.

Again this case is of international interest due to "keeping up with the Joneses." The Rhinelander attorneys spent several months in England seeking data on the ancestors of Mrs. Alice Jones Rhinelander's parents. The Joneses are English born and all Great Britain is deeply interested in this case. The papers have been carrying daily accounts of it. Also publications in France, Germany, Russia, Denmark, Sweden, and other countries.

The world's society thrives on romance—of tales of Normandy,

Picardy, Hollywood, Brittany, Araby, and even Waikiki/. But the romance of Leonard Kip Rhinelander and Alice Beatrice Jones has overstepped all. This romance undoubtedly will furnish rich material for some of our great coming motion pictures.

The Joneses

Forty some years ago there landed in this country George Jones, his wife Beatrice and a little 6-year old white girl. They were from England. Mrs. Jones was white, so was the child, which was an off-spring of Mrs. Jones' former marriage to a white man named Brown. Within his bosom, Mr. Jones carried an old leather wallet which bulged with shillings representing his life savings while a coachman in the same family in England that Mrs. Jones had worked for, and the contact of which is responsible for the culmination of the present family tie. Jones was born in Leicestershire, England. His father was a West Indian and died when Jones was 2 years old. His mother was white. She was Mary Botty, born at Coventry, England.

Garbed as the usual immigrants, the trio found quarters on the lower east side. Finally, Mr. Jones found employment in the Bronx and they moved there only to transfer their place of abode to New Rochelle, the township settled by the Rhinelanders. This was back in 1891. They arrived March 19 of the same year.

Jones was first a valet, he served the late John E. Risley, American ambassador to Denmark, who took him to New Rochelle. Later, he became a coachman for a wealthy family and they moved into a humble home at 763 Pelham Rd. This was an exclusive white section and Jones was always looked upon by members of the community as "The Colored Cab Driver."

He obtained his first citizenship papers in the city court at Mount Vernon on March 30, 1895, and his second papers on May 24, 1912. Citizenship was granted him by Supreme Court Justice Morschauser, in whose court and before home at the time of this writing, the present annulment suit is being heard.

Things were more or less uneventful in the Jones home until the arrival of their first child Emily, who was born Dec. 4, 1895. It cannot be distinctly remembered what became of the little white child which was Mrs. Jones daughter by her white husband, but it is said that she had been stopping with another family and is now married and living in Connecticut.

However, Alice, the present Mrs. Rhinelander, was born in the Pelham Rd. home June 18, 1899. Grace, youngest, was born July 19, 1903. The Joneses were well liked to everybody and in the girls' early school days they were generally referred to as the little "Colored kids over on Pelham Rd."

The little brown-skinned Beau Brummells had often heard of the good-looking sisters, but the only chance that they had to see them was when the girls frequented the public library. The Jones girls went to the Pentard Ave. School, which was in their district and were the only members of our group to attend the school at that time.

Unfortunately, the Joneses did not finish grammar school. They had been raised in an atmosphere of labor and were large for their age. When Emily, the oldest, was 15, she stopped going to school and obtained employment as a maid for a family named Wilson.

One bright sunny morning in May 1916, after having transferred to the Trinity School from the Jefferson school, Alice is reported to have played on the road and was tardy. She was scolded by her teacher and Alice began to pout. That afternoon the little Jones kid was absent and remained so. She quit school and had not finished the sixth grade.

Became Maid

Alice was 16 when she is said to have accepted a position as maid for Mrs. Alice V. Cady of Rochelle Park and worked there for six months. Grace, the youngest, followed the footsteps of her sisters and she and Alice are said to have worked as waitresses for a long period at the Manor club in Pelham Manor.

Due to the independence acquired because of their early start in earning a living, Alice and Grace eventually became identified with that vivacious feminine set so often referred to as "flappers." They are said to have sought gayety and found it. "Strutting parties" as Mrs. Rhinelander calls them in her letters to her husband were frequented but no members of our group were there. No, Alice and Grace were "white." Their mother told them so. And so they moved in white society.

Old Mrs. Jones is said to have been extremely prejudiced against color, though married to a man of "Negro" blood. This perhaps was not noticed until the girls began having company, which was early. True in form, there was blood calling and the girls had a few admirers who were not white.

Two young high school boys, Ossie Turner and Johnny Thomas, both of whom were of prominent New Rochelle families liked Grace, and on several occasions called upon her at home. Though Grace is said to have admired them both, her mother is alleged to have protested vigorously against her associating with them, so Grace had to ask the young men politely not to call upon her again.

Alice, the present Mrs. Rhinelander, is said never to have kept company with any member of our group, though Ira Moses, a garbage man, is said to have liked her. Moses is now married and lives at 311 Mechanic St., New Rochelle. At that time, Moses collected garbage where Alice is said to have worked as a cook.

Knowing that she was not white and because of her unusual politeness, Moses one day became bold enough to attempt to force his attentions upon her. It is said he received a cold reception. The following day when he knocked at the kitchen door to collect the trash, he was met with a barrage of language that would have made a [word illegible] doughboy of the trenches stand in amazement.

At the time of this writing it is rumored that Moses perhaps will be called to testify at the annulment suit at White Plains that he at one time kept company with Mrs. Rhinelander. It is claimed that Moses has a picture of Alice and her intimate friends are said to know how he came in possession of it.

Family "Black Sheep"

Back in the spring of 1914, when Emily the oldest, was 18 years old, she worked as a maid for the Wilson family. The Wilsons were well acquainted with the Arthurs, large real estate holders of the exclusive section of Pelham, for whom Robert Brooks, Emily's present husband had worked since he was a boy of 15. Bob, at this time, was 22 years old.

Mrs. Arthur, then a widow, whose husband Joseph was a playwright and author of "Still Alarm" now being shown in motion pictures, had a collection of good books, one of which Mrs. Wilson desired to borrow. Mrs. Wilson sent Emily on this mission one afternoon and she met Bob. He was the first Colored man she had ever become acquainted with.

Whether it was love at first sight is a question, but after a year of courtship she married Bob against the protests of her mother. Emily was then said to have been branded the "black sheep" of the family and was ostracized from the Jones home for more than three years.

However, it was March 1915 that Bob and Emily obtained their marriage license from the city hall and were quietly married by and at the home of Rev. J. B. Bodie in Hortet Ave. About three persons witnessed the ceremony.

Having been put out by her mother because of her marriage to Bob, the newlyweds came to New York and for a week until Bob made other arrangements they roomed with Mr. and Mrs. Max Green at 216 W. 132nd St.

Finally, Bob secured a position for Emily as maid at the Arthurs and they moved from the Green's back to Bob's former room. Three years elapsed before Robert, the baby, was born. During this period, it is said that Emily had practically been disowned by her mother, though her sisters and father thought different.

Upon the arrival of the baby, Mrs. Jones' heart softened. The whole family was so elated over the little bunch of loveliness that Emily was again accepted into the Jones home. So was Bob.

❊　❊　❊

Grace Met Kip First

When Grace, the youngest Jones girl was 18, she married William Miller, an Italian. That was four years ago. They now live at the Jones home in Pelham Rd. It was Grace who first met Rhinelander and introduced him to Alice. After a most romantic courtship of three years, Alice and Kip gave vent to love, which resulted in an unprecedented surprise to society.

At the time of this writing the annulment suit of this marriage is being contested in the White Plains court. It is generally believed that the young millionaire will return to his wife regardless of the results of the case. He has testified on the stand that he did not want to go to sit against his wife and that he was forced into these actions by his father. He still loves Alice and from the highest source it was learned that he plans to make her a gift of $250,000 for her maintenance for the rest of her life, whether he loses or wins the trial.

Just three weeks before the trial began, Alice was visiting Emily at her home. A few close friends were there. Mrs. Rhinelander is said to have stated during the conversation, "Len will never leave me. He won't be able to face me in court and I know it. He still loves me and I love him. However, if things should turn for the worse, I'll never marry again."

Shortly after Rhinelander was yanked from his bride last fall by his father, he sent her a letter. According to Mrs. Rhinelander's attorney, the letter read in part as follows: "Honeybunch, Old Scout: I hope you will win this suit. Be sure to get the best lawyer obtainable at any cost. Much love, Signed, your loving husband."

Since the papers were filed starting the suit, Kip has been paying Alice a temporary alimony of $300 a month and thousands have been spent for counsel fees. Judging from the manner in which Alice's attorney tore down the flimsy fortification of Kip's attorneys, she did get the best lawyer and as far as his winning of the case is concerned in the language of the streets, "It's too bad, Jim."

ANONYMOUS

From Rhinelander Jury Reaches a Decision after Twelve Hours†

In Favor of Wife, According to Rumors, But Sealed Findings Are Locked in Safe. Will Be Announced Today. Loud Wrangling and Banging of Fists Heard in Jury Room during Deliberation. Juries Go to Their Homes. Told Not to Discuss Their Decision on 7 Issues on Which Court Will Base Verdict.

The jurors in the suit brought by Leonard Kip Rhinelander to annul his marriage to Alice Jones Rhinelander, daughter of a negro, reached an agreement shortly after 11:25 tonight, twelve hours after the case was placed in their hands.

The general impression about the court house was that when the jury's verdict is read tomorrow it will be found to be for the defendant. Reports from many quarters, the sources of which were difficult to ascertain, were that the jury's final decision was in favor of Alice Jones Rhinelander. From the very first ballot it was said that the jury had stood 10 to 2 in favor of the woman, and that a break came shortly after 11 o'clock.

Before any one in the court house but attendants knew that the agreement had been reached, the jurors handed their findings to Clerk of the Court Ellrodt in a sealed envelope, which he placed in a safe. The jurors immediately left the court house and went to their homes. They had been locked up at 6 P. M. with instructions from Justice Morschauser that if they were able unanimously to answer the seven questions involving the relations of Rhinelander and his wife they were to seal the findings, which would be received by the Justice tomorrow morning at 10 o'clock.

Although Justice Morschauser was staying at a hotel not far from the court house, he was not disturbed.

All Over, Says, Juror.

As the jurors filed from the court house past a group of newspaper men and a few others who had been patiently waiting, one reporter called out:

"Is it all over?"

"Yes, it's all over and sealed," called back one of the jurors, and he continued to the street with his companions.

The reaching of an agreement came as a surprise to almost every

† From *The New York Times*, December 5, 1925: 1,2. Copyright © 1925 by The New York Times Co. Reprinted with permission.

one in the court house except the jurors themselves. At 10 P. M. persons outside the jury room heard loud argument and the banging of fists on tables. Court attendants began to prepare for an all-night vigil. Half a dozen spectators in the court room sat back and dozed.

None of the principals in the suit was present. Rhinelander was at the Gramatan Inn, Bronxville, with his counsel of record, Leon R. Jacobs. Mrs. Rhinelander and the other members of her family were at the Jones home in New Rochelle. Lee Parsons Davis was at his home in New Rochelle.

Alvin Meland, assistant to Mr. Jacobs, and Richard Kehoe, aid to Mr. Davis, were the only attorneys connected with the case who remained at the court house.

Mr. Kehoe notified Mr. Davis by telephone, and Mr. Melund called the Gramatan Inn and told Mr. Jacobs, who it was supposed informed Rhinelander.

When Mrs. Rhinelander was told at the Jones home that the agreement had been reached and that most reports had it that the findings were in her favor, she said:

"I still have a great affection for Leonard Kip Rhinelander, my husband. If the agreement is in my favor, it will square me with the world. If it is true I am simply tickled to death."

A short time after the departure of the jurors, the court house was locked.

The nearest approach to a definite intimation of how some of the jurors felt came late in the afternoon when they asked to have some of the testimony read to them. Their request was interpreted as being favorable to Mrs. Rhinelander.

The reason for such deduction was this: When the jurors filed into court after the attorneys on both sides had been hurriedly summoned, they asked that Rhinelander's testimony relative to that given by Barbara Reynolds, a New Rochelle newspaper woman, be read to them. Mrs. Reynolds had testified that when she asked Rhinelander if he knew that he had married the daughter of a colored man he said that he did know it, but that his father did not know it, and that it would wreck his and his wife's happiness if his father learned of it.

*   *   *

ANONYMOUS

[Rhinelander Editorial]†

If anything more humiliating to the prestige of white America than the Rhinelander case has occurred recently it has escaped our attention. That high Nordic stream which produces super-men is here represented by a poor decadent descended from the best blood of white America. Here is a woman "accused" of Negro blood. Accused because out of slavery and house service, ignorance and poverty she has raised herself. Not far, God wot, but far enough at least for the Rhinelanders and others to receive her socially. This man begged to marry her and did. And what then? Did he care because she had black blood? Not a rap. But his family did not want other white folk to know it. When therefore the busy-body press discovered it and advertised it, he and his family ran like rabbits to cover and whined. Why could the press persecute, ridicule and strip naked, soul and body, this defenseless girl? Because so many white Americans have black blood which might come to light, they pounce and worry like wolves to prove their spotless family. What this poor girl wanted of this specimen of a man is more than we can fathom. But that is none of our business; she did want him and he wanted her. Where then is the shame in this mess, if shame there is?

It lies in the awful truth that if Rhinelander had used this girl as concubine or prostitute, white America would have raised no word of protest; white periodicals would have printed no headlines; white ministers would have said no single word. It is when he legally and decently marries the girl that Hell breaks loose and literally tears the pair apart. Magnificent Nordic morality!

It is a fine thing that contemptible appeals to race prejudice did not swerve the jury from the plain truth.

ANONYMOUS

Rhinelander Gets a Fair Deal††

Leonard Rhinelander must have expected the verdict that was returned by the jury in the case in which he was seeking an annulment of his marriage to an octoroon on the grounds that she deceived him as to her

† From *The Crisis* 31, no. 3 (January 1926): 112–13. W. W. Norton wishes to thank the Crisis Publishing Co., Inc., the publisher of the magazine of the National Association for the Advancement of Colored People, for use of *The Crisis Magazine* materials.

†† From *The Chicago Defender*, January 26, 1926: Section 2, p. 8. Used with permission of *The Chicago Defender*.

color when she became his wife. The evidence all favored the young woman. It was proven beyond all doubt that Rhinelander did not tell the truth when he sought to impress the jurors with his story that Miss Jones concealed the fact that she was part Negress from him while he was courting her. In fact, Rhinelander, it was shown at the trial, remarked that he did not care a rap whether she was of Colored blood or not while he was in the midst of his fervid courtship of the girl.

The jurors were all American citizens, judging by the comment they indulged in at the conclusion of the trial. Several of those who were interviewed by the newspapers stated that race prejudice was not allowed in their deliberation, but that Rhinelander was weighed as would have been any other citizen who had become involved in such an escapade. Miss Jones had not attempted to conceal her color, in the opinion of the members of the jury. She was flattered by the attention of a member of a socially prominent family and he seemed to be satisfied with her companionship, but had suddenly turned against her because of the objections of his family to such an alliance.

There is no question but that Rhinelander made a grievous error in marrying an octoroon, but since he became a party to the contract with both his eyes open, and while in possession of his normal faculties, fair minded citizens will be pleased with the verdict of the jury. Rhinelander now proposes to carry the case into the higher courts. If justice prevails in these proceedings the union will be allowed to stand. The young woman is the one who should proceed further in the courts, inasmuch as Rhinelander should be compelled to support her as long as he is legally wedded to her.

ANONYMOUS

Mrs. Rhinelander to Sail†

Says She is Going to England to See Mother's People, Not Her Husband.

Mrs. Alice Jones Rhinelander, the wife of Leonard Kip Rhinelander, who successfully fought his annulment suit last year, is booked to sail for Europe on the White Star liner Majestic tomorrow. Four staterooms have been reserved for her.

"I am going to meet my mother's people in England," said Mrs. Rhinelander yesterday. "I am not going to meet my husband, who is in Paris. As far as a reconciliation is concerned, you can see my lawyer about that. I have nothing to say except that there's nothing to it."

† From *The New York Times*, July 16, 1926: 2. Copyright © 1926 by The New York Times Co. Reprinted with permission.

About Nella Larsen

THELMA E. BERLACK

New Author Unearthed Right Here in Harlem†

In the heart of Harlem on West 135th street, to be exact, lives a new writer. But this person, 5 feet 2 inches in height and weighing 122 pounds, is not a native New Yorker. She was born in Chicago 35 years ago.

A high school education in Chicago, one year at Fisk University in Nashville, Tenn., and three years at the University of Copenhagen, Denmark, make up her general educational career.

"I have lived East only twelve years," she said as she seated herself comfortably on the long sofa in her spacious living room. (This room, by the way, has the air of a Greenwich Village studio with its multi-colored pillows, paintings, books and more books, flowers, large and small vases, and other furnishings.)

Twelve busy years these have been, for in this period she has done much specialized work. She was assistant superintendent of nurses at Lincoln Hospital for a year, did social services work for the Board of Health, worked as assistant children's librarian in the Seward Park branch of the Public Library and later as the children's librarian in the West 135th street branch.

For three years, however, this little woman has had trouble with her health. She no longer goes out to business.

Who discovered this writer? Carl Van Vechten—and in her living room is an autographed photograph of him. Five months in her head and six weeks on the typewriter is the time it took her to write her book. The publishers, Alfred A. Knopf, Inc., 730 Fifth avenue, have made her promise to do two more manuscripts for them—neither is to be of the propaganda type.

"Madame X," or whatever you want to call her, is a modern woman, for she smokes, wears her dresses short, does not believe in religion,

† From *The New York Amsterdam News,* May 23, 1928: n.p. Reprinted by permission of *The New York Amsterdam News.*

149

churches and the like, and feels that people of the artistic type have a definite chance to help solve the race problem.

Her hobbies are doing her own housework, and there is much to do to keep a five-room apartment so clean (and from the smell from the kitchen door she must be an excellent cook), sewing and playing bridge.

For nine years she has been married to a man who holds a Ph. D. degree in physics from the University of Michigan. He is employed downtown by an engineering company.

The only relatives she has in this country are her mother, who is white, and a half-sister. They live in California. Her father, a Danish West Indian, died before she was old enough to know much about him. All of his people live in Denmark.

By now you must know "the lady in question" is Nella Larsen, author of "Quicksand," a review of which appeared last week in The Amsterdam News.

MARY RENNELS

Behind the Backs of Books and Authors†

Nella Larsen ("Passing") has skin the color of maple syrup. Her costume of shading grays makes it seem lighter than it really is. When she was two her father, a West Indian negro, died. Her mother soon married one of her own race, a Dane. "I don't see my family much now," she says. "It might make it awkward for them, particularly my half-sister."

Nella Larsen has the uplift of the negro buried near her roots. "Propaganda isn't the way to accomplish it," she says.

Her years as a children's librarian in New York (she is in the Ghetto now) may be escape from her desire for the luxury of ten children. You would have to read the flap on her new book to know she had won the prize in literature and a bronze medal by the Harmon Foundation in its annual award for "distinguished achievement among the negroes." Also that she was head nurse of the hospital at Tuskegee Institute.

Her voice is like a muted violin. You have to listen for it. She is proud of her poise. She laughingly admits it is acquired. Underneath her satin surface Nordic and West Indian are struggling. It hurts one way and helps another. She doesn't mind being shooed up the employes' entrance in hotels, because her Nordic side waits for such a situation: her negro side understands it.

Nella Larsen's philosophy toward life is answered:—"I don't have any way of approaching life . . . it does things to me instead." She admits she is a fatalist if you point it out to her.

† From *The New York Telegram,* April 13, 1929: Section 2, pp. 1–2.

The "unforgivable sin" is being bored. She selects only amusing and natural people, not too intellectual. She would never pass because "with my economic status it's better to be negro. So many things are excused them. The chained and downtrodden negro is a picture that came out of the civil war."

Nella Larsen's husband is a research physicist . . . colors (green especially) and words have an emotional effect on her . . . she loves bridge . . . bad food annoys her . . . her favorite authors are Galsworthy and Carl Van Vechten, the latter "to some of us is a savior, to others a devil" . . . Roland Hayes and Robeson are the artistic leaders of her race . . . Countee Cullen is another Edna St. Vincent Millay "with something left out" . . . she says she is not quite sure what she wants to be spiritually . . . books, money and travel would satisfy her materially . . . her greatest weakness is dissatisfaction . . . she is convinced recognition and liberation will come to the negro only through individual effort . . . she would like to be twenty-five years younger. She wants things—beautiful and rich things.

[LETTER ABOUT NELLA LARSEN]

Jean Blackwell Hutson to Louise Fox
(August 1, 1969)†

SCHOMBURG COLLECTION
103 West 135th Street
New York, New York 10030
August 1, 1969

Miss Louise Fox
309 Ransom Street
Chapel Hill, N.C. 27514
Dear Miss Fox,

Nella Larsen is the most elusive of the authors whose biographies I have tried to trace. In a vertical file is a clipping from the *Forum* magazine of April, 1930 which contains her statement that the story on which she based "Sanctuary" "was told to me by an old Negro woman whom in my nursing days, was an inmate of Lincoln Hospital and Home, East 141st Street and Southern Boulevard, New York City."

I telephoned that Hospital and found that she graduated from the Nursing School formerly connected with it in 1915. From some of

† Reprinted by permission of the Schomburg Center for Research in Black Culture, The New York Public Library, Astor, Lenox and Tilden Foundations.

erstwhile friends I have learned that she was the wife of Dr. Elmer S. Imes, who is described on p. 711 of Woodson's *Negro in our History* as "Professor of Physics at Fisk University, engaged in research in molecuar physics and was regarded as one of the first to establish that the quantum theory could be expanded to include the rotational status of the molecule."

Nella Larsen was her maiden name, not a pseudonym, as you have inferred. Her father was Danish, according to the reminiscences of her former acquaintances in Harlem.

In her later years she lived down in Greenwich Village and did not come to the attention of Harlemites. Some people report that she was "passing" in the manner developed in her novel of that name. However, her complexion was not like that of a white person. Of course, in New York there are many dusky complexioned people from foreign countries that among them, perhaps, she might not have been identified as a Negro.

These informants said that she was found dead in Brooklyn, N.Y. several years ago, but the *New York Times* reported that there was no card for her in their morgue.

Sincerely yours,

(Mrs.) Jean Blackwell Hutson
Curator

AUTHOR'S STATEMENTS

[Nella Larsen Imes, Guggenheim Application]

Applications and accompanying documents should be sent by registered mail and must reach the Secretary of the Foundation not later than November 15, 1929. They are desired, for the convenience of the Committee of Selection, as early as possible.

In what field of learning, or of art, does your project lie?.........Creative writing
Concise statement of project .....Novel. Laid partly in the United States and partly in Europe. The theme will be the difference in intellectual and physical freedom for the Negro—and the effect on him—between Europe, especially the Latin countries Spain and France

PERSONAL HISTORY

Name in full.....................Nella Larsen Imes
Present address.................2588 Seventh Avenue, New York City.

A Permanent address..........2588 Seventh Avenue, New York City.......................

Present occupation ......Hack writing. Housework. Sewing.........................

Place of birth ....Chicago, Illinois, U.S.A. Date of birth...April, 13, 1893...

If not a native-born American citizen, date and place of naturalization.....................

Single, Married, Widowed, Divorced.........Married

Name of wife or husband ....Elmer S. Imes.........................

Address of wife or husband ....2588 Seventh Avenue, New York City

Name and address of nearest kin, if unmarried......................................

Age of children......None..

Have you any constitutional disorder or physical disability?.......No.:.................

With this application please submit a small recent photograph.

EDUCATION

1. Give a summary of your education in the following form:

	Name of Institution	Period of Study (*give dates*)	Degrees, Diplomas, Certificates (*give dates*)
Adademic: College			
University	Auditor at University of Copenhagen.	1910-12	None.
Technical			
Professional	Library School of the New York Public Library.	1922-23	Certificate.
Musical			
Artistic			
Special Study	Lincoln Hospital Training School for Nurses.	1912-15	Diploma

2. Give a list of the scholarships or fellowships you have previously held or now hold, stating in each case the places and periods of tenure, the studies pursued during your incumbency, and amounts of the stipends:

.... None. ....

....

....

....

3. State what foreign languages you have studied, and whether you are able to consult works on your subject in these languages. Estimate your proficiency in reading, writing and speaking each of them.

1. Danish. ....

.... Speaking—fairly fluent.   Reading—good ....

.... Writing—fair. ....

2. French. ....

.... Reading—fair ....

ACCOMPLISHMENTS:

1. Positions held (professional, teaching, scientific, administrative, business):

Name of Institution or Organization	Title of Position	Years of Tenure (give dates)	Compensation
Tuskegee Institute, Ala.	Head Nurse.	1915–16	$600 & maintaince
Lincoln Hopsital, N.Y.C.	Supervising Nurse.	1916–18	$800 " "
Department of Health. New York City.	District Nurse.	1918–21	$1600.
New York Public Library	Assistant	1921–22	$1000.
	Assistant Children's librarian.	1923–24	1300.
	Children's librarian.	1924–25	1500.
	General assistant.	Mar. 1929 to June 1929.	1620.

2. Of what learned, scientific or artistic societies are you a member?

.... None. ....

....

....

3. Submit a full account of the advanced work and research you have already done in this country or abroad, giving dates, subjects, and names of your principal teachers in these subjects. What are your present attainments in your proposed field of study?

3. 1926.   Began to work at fiction. Tried writing short stories. Two published by Young's Magazine.

    1927.   Wrote novel, 56000 words.

    1928.   Wrote novel, 45000 words.

    1929.   Writing short stories, reviews. Working on third novel when time is available.

4. Submit a *list* of your publication with exact titles, names of publishers, and dates and places of publication. (*Please do not submit copies of publications or manuscripts.*)

4. 1928   Quicksand, a novel published by Alfred A. Knopf, Inc.
           New York City. This novel was awarded the Bronze medal
           by the Harmon Foundation.

   1929.   Passing, a Novel published by Knopf. " " ".

PLANS FOR STUDY:

Submit a statement giving detailed plans for the study you would pursue during your tenure of a Fellowship. This statement should include, *later alla*; (1) a description of the project, including its character and scope, and the significance of its presumable contribution to knowledge, or to art; (2) the present state of the project, time of commencement, progress to date, and expectation as to completion; (3) the proposed foreign university, or institution of similar grade, or the place where the study would be carried on, and the foreign authorities, if any, with whom the work would be done; (4) your expectation as to publication of the results of your study; and (5) your ultimate purpose as a student. *This statement should be complete and carefully prepared.* (Please submit five copies.)

Novel.
The scene will be laid partly in the United States and partly in
Europe. The theme will be the difference in intellectual and physical for the Negro—and the effect on him—between Europe, especially the Latin countries, France and Spain. I have never been in
these countries and therefore feel that I am not prepared without
visiting them to judge attitudes and reactions of my here in a
foreign and favorable or more unfavorable environment. My plan is,
travel and residence in Europe, principally the South of France
and Spain, while completing the novel.

If awarded a Fellowship—
When would you wish to commence the study proposed. .... September 1930 ....
What is your estimate of its probable duration? .... One Year. ....

REFERENCES:

Submit a list of references from whom further confidential information may be obtained concerning your qualifications and from whom expert opinion may be obtained as to the value and practicability of your proposed studies.

Name of Reference	Position	Address
Mr. Carl Van Vechten	Author.	150 West 55th. Street. N.Y.C.
Mr. Walter F. White	Author.	409 Edgecombe Avenue. "
Mrs. Muriel Draper.	Writer.	24 East 40th. Street. "
Mrs. Alfred Knopf.	Publisher.	730 Fifth Avenue. "
Mr. James W. Johnson	Writer. Also secretary for the National Association for the Advancement of Colored People.	69 Fifth Avenue. "

If you have applied or expect to apply elsewhere for any fellowship or scholarship for the year 1930–31, note the facts regarding such applications:..........Have not applied........ ....Do not expect to.. ....

[In Defense of *Sanctuary*]†

To the Editor:

Having just finished reading Nella Larsen's story, "Sanctuary," published in the January issue of THE FORUM, I cannot help noting its striking resemblance to a story by Sheila Kaye-Smith entitled "Mrs. Adis," which was published in the *Century* for January, 1922. Aside from dialect and setting, the stories are almost identical. The structure, situation, characters, and plot are the same. One often finds in Miss Larsen's story the same words and expressions used by Sheila Kaye-Smith in "Mrs. Adis."

Marion Boyd

Oxford. O.

[EDITOR'S NOTE.—*Since receiving this letter and several others to the same effect, we have looked up Sheila Kaye-Smith's story and compared it with Nella Larsen's story. We, too, were impressed by the "striking resemblance" between them, and felt it our duty to call the matter to our author's attention, asking her, in fairness to* FORUM *readers, to explain how she came by her plot and the circumstances under which her story was written. She not only complied with this request, but also sent us four rough drafts of the story showing just how she worked it out from the plot stage to its final form in which we printed it. A careful examination of this material has convinced us that the story, "Sanctuary," was written by Nella Larsen in the manner she describes. The coincidence is, indeed, extraordinary, but there are many well authenticated cases of similar coincidences in history. For example, the incandescent lamp was invented almost simultaneously by Thomas Edison and an Englishman who had never heard of Edison. The "Encyclopaedia Britannica" also records how the theory of natural selection was worked out independently, and at precisely the same moment, by Charles Darwin and A. R. Wallace. Nella Larsen's letter of explanation follows in full.*]

---

† From "Nella Larsen's Story" and "The Author's Explanation," *Forum* Supplement 4, no. 83 (April 1930): 41–42.

THE AUTHOR'S EXPLANATION

To the Editor:

I have your letter with its astonishing enclosure this morning. I haven't as yet seen the *Century* story, but it seems to me that anyone who intended to lift a story would have avoided doing it as obviously as this appears to have been done—judging from the excerpts which you have sent me.

In justice to THE FORUM and to myself, I wish to explain exactly how I came by the material out of which I wrote "Sanctuary." The story is one that was told to me by an old Negro woman who, in my nursing days, was an inmate of Lincoln Hospital and Home, East 141st Street and Southern Boulevard, New York City. Her name was Christophe or Christopher. That was some time during the years from 1912 to 1913.

All the doctors and executives in this institution were white. All the nurses were Negroes. As in any other hospital, all infractions of rules and instances of neglect of duty were reported to and dealt with by the superintendent of nurses, who was white. It used to distress the old folks—Mrs. Christopher in particular—that we Negro nurses often had to tell things about each other to the white people. Her oft-repeated convictions were that if the Negro race would only stick together, we might get somewhere some day, and that what the white folks didn't know about us wouldn't hurt us.

All this used to amuse me until she told some of us about the death of her husband, who, she said, had been killed by a young Negro, and the killer had come to her for hiding without knowing whom he had killed. When the officers of the law arrived and she learned about her man, she still shielded the slayer, because, she told us, she intended to deal with him herself afterwards without any interference from "white folks."

For some fifteen years I believed this story absolutely and entertained a kind of admiring pity for the old woman. But lately, in talking it over with Negroes, I find that the tale is so old and so well known that it is almost folklore. It has many variations: sometimes it is the woman's brother, husband, son, lover, preacher, beloved master, or even her father, mother, sister, or daughter who is killed. A Negro sociologist tells me that there are literally hundreds of these stories. Anyone could have written it up at any time.

When I first thought of writing the story, my idea was to use Harlem with its peculiar tempo and atmosphere as a setting, as well as the Harlemese language. But that little old Negro countrywoman was so vivid before me that I wanted to get her down just as I remembered her. Had I had any idea that there was already a story with a similar plot in existence, I don't think I would have made use of the material at all; or, if I had, I should certainly have taken the city for background and would have told the story exactly as it was told to me, or much more differently than I have done.

Nella Larsen

New York City

LETTERS

To Carl Van Vechten†

Monday
Dear Carl,

This is a tardy "thank you", but for the past month it has seemed always to be tea time, as the immortal Alice remarked, with never time to wash the dishes between whiles.

What things there are to write, if one can only write them. Boiler menders, society ladies, children, acrobats, governesses, business men, countesses, flappers, Nile green bath rooms, beautifully filed, gay moods and shivering hesitations, all presented in an intensely restrained and civilized manner, and underneath the ironic survival of a much more primitive mood. Delicious.

It is nice to find some one writing as if he didn't absolutely despise the age in which he lives. And surely it is more interesting to belong to one's own time, to share its peculiar vision, catch that flying glimpse of the panorama which no subsequent generation can ever recover. I think "Firecrackers"[1] is really a very important book.

Nice too, to meet some old friends. Thanks for the peep at Edith Dale. I think you were *horrid* to the countess.

To Charles S. Johnson††

Mr. Charles S. Johnson
127 East Twenty-third Street
New York City

My dear Mr. Johnson:

I have before me Mr. Frank Horne's amazing review—in the July issue of Opportunity—of Mr. [Walter] White's latest novel, "Flight." I do not like this review. In fact so violently do I object to it that I am

---

† N.d. [1925]. From Carl Van Vechten Papers, Manuscripts and Archives Division, The New York Public Library, Astor, Lenox, and Tilden Foundations.
1. Van Vechten's 1925 novel.
†† N.d. [August 1926]. Walter White Correspondence. NAACP Papers, *Library of Congress*.

moved to put pen to paper to state my reasons for objecting. Surprise, that a reviewer apparently so erudite should have written such an unintelligent review. Anger, because such a book had been given to so understanding a person for review. Pity, because the reviewer had so entirely missed the chief idea of the book.

I pass over your reviewer's main reason for exasperation with "Flight," the fact that he had hoped some day to write a novel on this subject, because it is not at all pertinent to the review. A bit naive, of course, and usually "not done," but still unimportant, and certainly no business of your readers.

It is the blindness, not the abuse which annoys me. I doubt if ever Mr. Stuart Sherman or Mr. Carl Van Doren, supposing they had shared your reviewer's feelings, would have treated "Flight" so roughly. My quarrel with this very interesting piece of literary criticism is that seemingly your reviewer lacked the ability or the range of reading to understand the book which he attacked with so much assurance.

May I quote a little from the review as I go along?

"Mimi Daquin is a character worthy of a novel; she deserves a treatment of a kind to place her beside Maria Chandelaine; Mattie Frome and Salammbo." Just why, I wonder did your reviewer choose the passive French-Canadian girl, the trapped Mattie, and the Salammbo of ancient Carthage, with whom to disparage the rebellious, modern Mimi? Certainly, these are for their their own environments and times, excellent characters. But, so is Mimi for hers. And would not Galsworthy's unsurpassable Irene Forsyte, or Jacobsen's Maria Grubbe have been more effective for purposes of comparison as well as for disparagement? They, like Mimi Daquin, threw away material things for fulfillment of their spiritual destinies.

"There is in her travail the lonely vicissitudes of a lost race. . . ." Which "lost" race? It is here that your reviewer stumbles and falls. It is here that we detect his blindness. It is here that we become aware that he fails to realize that this is the heart of the whole tale. A lost race. Yes. But I suspect that he refers to the black race, while Mr. White obviously means that it is the white race which is lost, doomed to destruction by its own mechanical gods. How could your reviewer have missed this dominate note, this thing which permeates the whole book? It was this, that made Mimi turn from it. Surely, the thesis of "Flight" is "what shall it profit a man if he gain the whole world and lose his own soul?"

"Then too, we must conjecture that he leaves this girl at the most critical stage of her career." We do *not* conjecture anything of the kind. We know it. And we were meant to know it. Authors do not supply imaginations, they expect their readers to have their own, and, to use them. Judging by present day standards of fiction, the ending of

"Flight" is the perfect one, perfect in its aesthetic colouring, perfect in its subtle simplicity. For others of this type, I refer your reviewer to Sherwood Anderson's "Dark Laughter," to Carl Van Vechten's "Firecrackers," to Joseph Hergesheimer's "Tubal Cane."

"She leaves a white world with all of its advantages of body and spirit . . . to go back to 'her people' ". Here it is again, your reviewer's inability to grasp the fact that Mimi Daquin came to realize that, for her, there were no advantages of the spirit in the white world, and so, spiritual things being essential to her full existence she gave up voluntarily, the material advantages.

"How," asks your reviewer will she "adjust on a lower cramped scale a life that had become so full, how compensate for the intense freedom of being white?" Again, I point out that her life had *not* been full, it had, perhaps been novel, but not full. And I resent that word "lower", and in a lesser degree the word "cramped". I maintain that neither is applicable to Negro life, especially among people of Mimi's class. Inner peace compensated her for the "intense freedom of being white". Some people "feel" their race, (even some Negroes). [Crossed through line illegible.] Mr. White evidently does, and so, has given us Mimi Daquin. [Deleted line.] I come now to your reviewer's complaints about the author's style. He grumbles about "lack of clarity", "confusion of characters", "faulty sentence structure". These sins escaped me in my two readings, and even after they had been so publicly pointed out, I failed to find them. Even the opening sentence, so particularly cited, still seems to me all right. But then, I have been recently reading Huysmans, Conrad, Proust, and Thomas Mann. Naturally these things would not irritate me as they would an admirer of Louis Hemon and Mrs. Wharton. Too, there's Galsworthy, who opens his latest novel with a sentence of some thirty-odd words.

To my mind, warped as I have confessed by the Europeans and the American moderns, "Flight" is a far superior piece of work than "The Fire in the Flint". Less dramatic, it is more fastidious and required more understanding, keener insight. Actions and words count less and the poetic conception of the character, the psychology of the scene more, than in the earlier novel. "Flight" shows a more mature artistry.

It may be that your reviewer read the book hastily, superficially, and so missed both its meaning and its charm.

To Eddie Wasserman†

Home

Dear Eddie:

Are you going to the [Countee] Cullen-[Yolanda] DuBois wedding? I'm asking a few of the thousand and one invited guests to come by here for a cocktail before proceeding to the solemnities. Please come if you can. Come even if you are not expected at the wedding. It is at six o'clock on Monday the ninth. Any time between four and five-thirty you can wet your whistle at 236 West 135th Street.

We haven't seen you for years. Not since your grand birthday party. Do you still look the same?

Until Monday, then.

Nella Larsen Imes

Thursday

To Eddie Wasserman††

Home. Sunday

Dear Eddie:—

We were terribly disappointed that you didn't get here last week. And I was furious with myself for mentioning the damned wedding to you because it turned out that we didn't go. People kept coming in and then deciding not to go on to the wedding, so we were there until eight o'clock. Then we went out to dinner. It was very amusing too because the sandwiches kept getting fewer and fewer and I kept rescuing them from hungry guests and saying, firmly "You'll have to leave some for Eddie Wassermann and some one else." Then when you didn't appear they accused me of trying to save the food.

I do want to see your review. Will you save a copy? I'm too poor to subscribe to a clipping bureau. Besides, what's the use? It seems that your review will be the only notice I'll have. I would like to see that.

Elmer [Imes, Nella's husband] says hello.

Sincerely,

Nella Larsen Imes

† N.d. [April 3, 1928]. Nella Larsen Papers. The Schomburg Center for Research in Black Culture. From the Manuscripts, Archives, Rare Books Division, Schomburg Center for Research in Black Culture, The New York Public Library, Astor, Lenox, and Tilden Foundations.
†† N.d. [April 5, 1928]. Nella Larsen Papers. The Schomburg Center for Research in Black Culture. From the Manuscripts, Archives, Rare Books Division, Schomburg Center for Research in Black Culture, The New York Public Library, Astor, Lenox, and Tilden Foundations.

To Dorothy Peterson†

Saturday

Dear Dorothy:

I had your letter a week ago—or was it two?—and meant to acknowledge it at once, but I have been a busy woman.

I've been trying to get my book finished before giving up. Incidently I've been doing some work on Mirage.[2] I've never looked at it since we celebrated its departure to the U.S.A. in Paris. In May—or June, I gave it to Edward [Wasserman] to read. He said it was terrible. Early this month, I took a look at it, and I give you my word it was worse than that. It was appalling (2 L's?). The stuff was good. But the writing! So I've done it all over, except that chapter which made you so ill, and the last. And I've changed the name to Fall Fever. The one I'm doing now will probably be called "The Wingless Hour" from that verse of Swinburne:

> Can ye beat off one wave with prayer,
> Can ye move mountains? bid the flower
> Take flight and turn to a bird in the air?
> Can ye hold fast for shine or shower
> One wingless hour?

About the divorce—I've about come to the conclusion to get it here. It can be done discreetly in ten days for a hundred dollars or so. Can you imagine that! There are about eight grounds for divorce in Tennessee.—1. Adultery. 2. Desertion for two years. 3. Failure of wife to remove to the state if husband is living and working in Tennessee. (Note these last two. It explains a lot. especial [sic] why I am here still after coming for a mere visit). 4. Habitual drunkenness contracted after marriage. 5. Non-support. 6. Commission of a crime. 7 Bigamy. 8 Cruelty.

As I see it you pays your money and you takes your choice. And that's that. Much simpler, don't you think, to get it here quietly, quickly, and cheaply, and be done with it? No waiting around to establish residence. No hanging about to have the decree made final. A session with a good lawyer, a morning in court. And then finis!

Edward's and my novel is called Adrian and Eradne[?]. It's a perfectly silly thing, and there are two characters in the book who have these names. It went through Brandt and Brandt.

---

† N.d. The James Weldon Johnson Collection, Beinecke Library, Yale University. From the Dorothy Peterson Collection. Yale Collection of American Literature, Beinecke Rare Book and Manuscript Library.

2. Novel that Larsen was working on.

I think, perhaps, I'll send my two there though I did promise Harry Block a year or so ago to let him see them. I could of course send a letter with them asking Brandt and Brandt[3] to show them to him first.

I have never done anything with the thing I started in Malaga [Spain]. I had it out the other day and on going over it I thing it's mostly pretty good. We'll probably do it together. Edward the men and I the women. How do you like "The Gilded Palm Tree" for a title?

You will notice that I'm getting good on titles all of a sudden.

Margaret Reynolds is back with a rather handsome boyfriend. I wish I'd realized that she was coming back. I would have written you to come along, though it is as hot as hell here. Good writing weather.

My love to your father and Sidney

and Dorothy

Nella

To Dorothy Peterson†

Tuesday 19th

Dorothy Dear:—

Not yet have we heard from you. Sidney tells me he's had a cable— or your facts —but nothing more.

It has, as I informed you last week been as hot as hell here. A little better now though. And there is no news.

I saw Harry the other day—just a second—and am writing him a note, to thank him for $5.00 which he got from Knopf Inc. for me for reading a book in Danish.

Last night we went in to call on the Whites who are packing. They intend to look you up—and you have my <u>very</u> deepest sympathy.

Miller & Lyles show "Rang Tang" opened last Tuesday. It's pretty good they say. I didn't go. Was utterly prostrated by the heat. I haven't had on clothes for days—until last night of course.

There are no parties—to which I have been invited—Thank God! Though I'm asked to go in to Carl's to drink a cocktail on Friday afternoon. I don't know if it's in honor of the Whites' sailing or not.

<u>Your friend</u>, Mr. George C. B. is going to the whaty'mcall'm so fast that it's shocking. There are numerous little funny things to be told which I will save until your return. And some big ones. As Sidney says "I'm certainly glad he's not married to my sister." "Good God! Yes!" fervently agrees Elmer.

---

3. Literary agents.

† N.d. [July 19, 1927]. The James Weldon Johnson Collection, Beinecke Library, Yale University. From the Dorothy Peterson Collection. Yale Collection of American Literature, Beinecke Rare Book and Manuscript Library.

Countee Cullen's new book of poems is to be released this week. "Copper Sun" I think it's called. I've seen it. It's fair. Just that.

I know you will see Dorothy. She asked where you were and what you were going to do. I told her.

I do miss you very much and that is remarkable !! because I'm not in the habit of missing people. Elmer says I'm a selfish little beast. Etc. Etc.

I'm sending you a picture. If you haven't had my coat made, or cut, why I think I'd like this better. However it doesn't at all matter. I don't know what you've bought and I don't at all care as long as it's not yellow and purple, or something ungodly like that. Please don't forget to mention money when you write, so that I can send it if you need or want it.

I'm still looking for a place to move. Mrs. Beasely is looking too. It's really rather ridiculous I suppose but——. Right now when I look out into the Harlem streets I feel just like Helga Crane in my novel. Furious at being cornered[?] with all these niggers.

Our best love.

And behave yourself.

Nella.

Elmer says remember Katherine Mansfield.

To Dorothy Peterson†

Thursday 21st

Dorothy dear:—

You have both my letters by now—[ere][?] this. I have both of yours. Just disregard anything I said about the coat—unless you've done something about it. If so all right. Otherwise I won't have it. Let me know in reply to this. For I have my eye one one here.

I think I've told you all the news that's floating about these parts— and that's not much.

All Harlem is preparing to go to Hampton for the tennis tournaments. Not yours truly. I am still looking for a place to move.

I saw Alonzo yesterday. In the course of our conversation I mentioned that you had tried hard to write him [illegible word] but that he wasn't at his office or at his apartment. He said that he hopes you are having a pleasant time, that every year you send him a card, that

† N.d. [July 21, 1927]. The James Weldon Johnson Collection, Beinecke Library, Yale University. From the Dorothy Peterson Collection. Yale Collection of American Literature, Beinecke Rare Book and Manuscript Library.

he hopes this isn't an off year, and that he'll see more of you this winter than in winters past.

Rudolph Fisher has a fairish article in the *Mercury* about Harlem, called "The Caucasian Invasion ["The Caucasian Storms Harlem"]." It's mostly about cabarets.

I'm going to show Carl that "white" card after the sailing. It's very amusing because he's already given the young man a forty-three dollar cup from Tiffany, all engraved and everything. He made a special trip up to gaze upon the baby and present the cup. The other evening when I was there, Eddie was expected. He phoned, however, saying that something had tied him up downtown.

Walter Sr. came back from the telephone saying how disappointed Eddie was because "he is simply dying to see the baby." I haven't seen Eddie since, but when I do———

Dorothy, you'd better write some poetry, or something. I've met a man from Macmillan's who asked me to look out for any negro stuff and send them to him. (Rather mixed grammar but you get the implication)

I haven't seen your family recently. Sidney promised to call me up and come by this week.—Hasn't done so yet. Elmer is leaving tomorrow night for Oak Bluffs[4] to stay until Monday, so I think I'll run over to see your father Saturday or Sunday.

Elmer inquired for him at the office last Saturday—just too late. He'd left.

I have decided not to lead a social life next winter because I have to work like a nigger. I <u>must</u> make some money. Almost I've decided too to sell my house and spend a couple of years abroad. Elmer too, of course, Why don't you too?

Tonight we're going to the prize fight Dempsey-Sharky. It's at the polo grounds. Tickets 11.00 up. Elmer got two $27.50 from his chief. They had been given to him. I'm quite enthusiastic about it—the crowds they say are marvelous.

It will be good to see you back. Every one misses you. Colin asked especially to be remembered to you. And Carl, of course.
Our love, and take care of yourself.

Nella

---

4. See p. 16, n. 2.

To Dorothy Peterson†

Tuesday 2nd

Dorothy dear—

Yours truly has been ill. Better now.

I'm just realizing that you have been gone from here a month. Tempus fugit.

No news as usual.

Having been confined to 236 hasn't increased it any.

Sunday we had dinner with Carla and Fania. Carl's sister and niece,—not Diane—are here. Carl has been sick too. Saturday was his first day out as Sunday was mine. He sent oceans of love to you.

Vivienne came up about ten days ago. She brought Julian Langer, who is by way of being a <u>real</u> person. I'm sure you will like him. He's been everywhere and seen everything. Of which more anon—when you get back.

I feel <u>very</u> much ashamed to say that I have not seen your father since you left. And, Sidney tells Elmer, today he leaves for his vacation. He is well, so Sidney says—I shall write him though while he is away. And worst of all, I've got a book that I wanted to get to him before he got off. However, sending's better I guess.

Marion Beasely came to call on me about two weeks ago. I was out that time.

Zora [Neale] Hurston is married. Some doctor in Chicago. I don't know his name.

I saw Roland [Hayes?]—at a cabaret—recently. He seems to have fallen voluntarily in love with a very unsophisticated looking little girl of the Jewish persuasion—judging by appearance.

I think, quite seriously of moving downstairs, second floor back. There is one five-room apartment there. Not so many steps. Not so noisy—<u>but</u>—more accessible.

Wednesday—that is tomorrow night we are going to a midnight show, Miller and Lyles "Rang Tang." Party afterwards.

You <u>do</u> remember the tea for Ethel Waters—?—. Well, the *Pittsburgh Courier* says "Among those who have entertained Miss Waters are "Mr. and Mrs. Carl Van Vechten, at dinner. Mr. Edward Wasserman, millionaire banker, at a formal evening party. Mrs. Nella Larsen Imes <u>at tea</u>."

You know too that we've been around to Mr. Howe's bookshop. Had tea (very punk) there one afternoon, but did not meet Mr. Howe.

† [August 2, 1927]. James Weldon Johnson Collection, Beinecke Library, Yale University. From the Dorothy Peterson Collection. Yale Collection of American Literature, Beinecke Rare Book and Manuscript Library.

The *Chicago Defender* in speaking of the charm of Mr. Howe's book-shop and tea room says, "Miss Dorothy Petersen, Brooklyn Society matron, and Mrs. Elmer Imes, Harlem matron <u>and</u> <u>novelist</u>, find our lunches very superior." (To what)

I as well as Elmer, am now beginning to look forward to your return. I might just as well have gone over for all the work I've accomplished. Next time—

Our best love and take care of yourself.

Eddie sends love too. Colin says Hello.

Nella

To Langston Hughes†

2588 Seventh Avenue
New York City

My dear Langston,

Thanks for your letter. It cheered me very much. I fear the book is having a very hard time, and am therefore grateful for any kind words.

I had intended to send you a copy but put it off and put it off. Sheer laziness on my part. So all the copies I had went to people who came in and saw them and asked for them.

You will be interested to know that Floyd Calvin says that the only part of the book worth printing is the verse of your poetry.

Come in and see us when you are in town. We are moving to the address on the other side next Monday—in other words to "Uncle Tom's Cabin" as my husband calls the Rockefeller apartments.

Thanks again,

Sincerely

Nella Imes.

May first.

† N.d. From the Langston Hughes Papers, James Weldon Johnson Collection in the Yale Collection of American Literature, Beinecke Rare Book and Manuscript Library.

To Langston Hughes†

Tuesday 22nd.

Dear Langston,

I read [Langston Hughes's] *Not Without Laughter* some ten days ago and have been intending to get this letter off ever since. But it's been too hot to hold a pen. And I "seen" your picture in the papers Sunday.

You have done what I always contended impossible. Made middle class negroes interesting (or any other kind of middle class people). And your prose is lovely.

I hope you are going to have a good press and even a better sale. Any little thing—or big—that I can do please let me know.
Sincerely,
Nella Imes

To Carl Van Vechten††

Carl dear:—

I am so upset.

I'll never be interviewed again!

Walter called up yesterday to protest because Mary Rennels "said I said" that I didn't believe in propaganda.

Three Harlem Negroes have registered their protests (one very belligerently and indignantly) because I am reported to have stated that it's perfectly all right to send Negroes around to the back door.

Tonight when we got the damned paper Elmer rose in the air because he thinks I was "trying to pose as a silly uplifter of the race."

All these things are nothing.

But when I read that I had referred to you as a devil I almost had a stroke of paralysis. I do think the phrase is awfully clever —as she evidently did—But about you! That's really too thick.

I don't know at all what to do about it. I could die of rage and mortification. In fact I see no way out except suicide.

Please come to my party anyway.
My love to Fania and to you
Nella
Monday

---

† N.d. [1930]. From the Langston Hughes Papers, James Weldon Johnson Collection in the Yale Collection of American Literature, Beinecke Rare Book and Manuscript Library.
†† N.d. [April 15, 1929]. Carl Van Vechten Papers, The James Weldon Johnson Collection, Beinecke Library, Yale University. From the Yale Collection of American Literature, Beinecke Rare Book and Manuscript Library.

To Gertrude Stein†

Jose Villalonga 32
Terreno
Palma de Mallorca
Spain

Dear Miss Stein:

Every letter that comes to me from dear Carl Van Vechten speaks of you. But really he has no need to remind me to be sure to see you—if I may—when I go up to Paris, since it's one of my main reasons for going there.

I've been here since October and liking it well enough. It's fairly quiet and cheap and the climate is not too bad. I had thought that because it was a quiet place it would be a good place in which to get a lot of work done. It seems not. After this I shall know that live cities are the places in which to do live things—or is it living?—which is perhaps a good thing to find out as well as the fact that the less time one has the more one accomplishes.

I can quite understand why apart from his illness—Chopin and George Sand were so unhappy here. It's marvelously beautiful country—and brutal. And the people are so terribly placid, a resigned unhappy placidness. Even the children. Perhaps because they're so old and tired and everything has happened to them.

Or it maybe just that I've got a nostalgia, a yen to see the teeming streets of Harlem and hear some real laughter.

However, I shall be here until the end of April when I mean to go up to Paris by way of Marseille and Toulon.

Will you be at your Paris place in May? And may I call in to see you then?
Very sincerely yours,
Nella Larsen Imes
January 26, 1931

† The James Weldon Johnson Collection, Beinecke Library, Yale University. From the Gertrude Stein and Alice B. Toklas Papers, Yale Collection of American Literature, Beinecke Rare Book and Manuscript Library.

To Carl Van Vechten†

Friday

Carl dear:

Well here I am, and have been for a week. And it really is rather exciting, weather, people, and country.

You will be amused that I who have never tried this much discussed 'passing' stunt have waited until I reached the deep south to put it over. Grace Johnson and I drove about fifty miles south of here the other day and then walked into the best restaurant in a rather conservative town called Murfreesborough and demanded lunch and <u>got</u> it, plus all the service in the world, and an invitaiton to return. Everybody here seems to think that quite a stunt. Jim told me to be sure to tell you.

Their (the Johnsons') house is very lovely, and they seem to be quite happy here. Jim's class is interesting and very <u>much</u> alive. I visited twice and made a pretty bad speech on an occasion.

Elmer is looking very unwell, poor dear; but I don't know what I can do about it. Dr. Jones—the president seems to feel that I ought to come here to live for at least a poriton of the year and offers to build the kind of house I want, but I haven't made up my mind about it. There seems to be a lot of gossip floating about. But then, there's always gossip anywhere.

Roland Hayes did a very ironical thing when he was here. He went over to Georgia to see the man who owned his mother in the days before the war and found that he and his wife were both sick and poor and about to lose all that was left of the old plantation—the house in which they were living. So, like the heros in all the stories, he kept the mortgage from being foreclosed and did all the other proper things.

Grace Valentine's pictures are quite fascinating I think. So does everyone who has seen them—including Elmer.

All kinds of love to you both

Nella

† N.d. [May 14, 1932]. Carl Van Vechten Papers, The James Weldon Johnson Collection, Beinecke Library, Yale University. From the Yale Collection of American Literature, Beinecke Rare Book and Manuscript Library.

The Tragic Mulatto(a)

LYDIA MARIA CHILD

Lydia Maria Child (1802–1880) was an educator, editor, feminist, author, and abolitionist whose *An Appeal in Favor of That Class of Americans Called Africans* (1833) had widespread influence. "The Quadroons," published in *The Liberty Bell* in 1842, is often credited with inaugurating literary depictions of "the tragic mulatta": the mixed-race woman who cannot find happiness in either the black or white world and who represents the long line of women—both black and white—victimized by slavery.

The Quadroons†

"I promised thee a sister tale,
Of man's perfidious cruelty:
Come then and hear what cruel wrong
Befell the dark Ladie."

Coleridge

Not far from Augusta, Georgia, there is a pleasant place called Sand-Hills, appropriated almost exclusively to summer residences for the wealthy inhabitants of the neighbouring city. Among the beautiful cottages that adorn it was one far retired from the public roads, and almost hidden among the trees. It was a perfect model of rural beauty. The piazzas that surrounded it were wreathed with Clematis and Passion Flower. Magnificent Magnolias, and the superb Pride of India, threw shadows around it, and filled the air with fragrance. Flowers peeped out from every nook, and nodded to you in bye-places, with a most unexpected welcome. The tasteful hand of Art had not learned to *imitate* the lavish beauty and harmonious disorder of Nature, but they lived together in loving unity, and spoke in according tones. The gateway rose in a Gothic arch, with graceful tracery in iron-work, surmounted by a Cross, around which fluttered and played the Mountain Fringe, that lightest and most fragile of vines.

† From Werner Sollors, *An Anthology of Interracial Literature: Black-White Contacts in the Old World and the New* (New York: NYU Press, 2004, pp. 232–39; orig. publ. in *Fact and Fiction*, New York: S. Francis, 1846).

171

The inhabitants of this cottage remained in it all the year round, and peculiarly enjoyed the season that left them without neighbours. To one of the parties, indeed, the fashionable summer residents, that came and went with the butterflies, were merely neighbours-in-law. The edicts of society had built up a wall of separation between her and them; for she was a quadroon. Conventional laws could not be reversed in her favour, though she was the daughter of a wealthy merchant, was highly cultivated in mind and manners, graceful as an antelope, and beautiful as the evening star. She had early attracted the attention of a handsome and wealthy young Georgian; and as their acquaintance increased, the purity and bright intelligence of her mind, inspired him with far deeper interest than is ever excited by mere passion. It was genuine love; that mysterious union of soul and sense, in which the lowliest dew-drop reflects the image of the highest star.

The tenderness of Rosalie's conscience required an outward form of marriage; though she well knew that a union with her proscribed race was unrecognised by law, and therefore the ceremony gave her no legal hold on Edward's constancy. But her high poetic nature regarded the reality, rather than the semblance of things; and when he playfully asked how she could keep him if he wished to run away, she replied, "Let the church that my mother loved sanction our union, and my own soul will be satisfied, without the protection of the state. If your affections fall from me, I would not, if I could, hold you by a legal fetter."

It was a marriage sanctioned by Heaven, though unrecognised on earth. The picturesque cottage at Sand-Hills was built for the young bride under her own direction; and there they passed ten as happy years as ever blessed the heart of mortals. It was Edward's fancy to name their eldest child Xarifa; in commemoration of a quaint old Spanish ballad, which had first conveyed to his ears the sweet tones of her mother's voice. Her flexile form and nimble motions were in harmony with the breezy sound of the name; and its Moorish origin was most appropriate to one so emphatically "a child of the sun." Her complexion, of a still lighter brown than Rosalie's, was rich and glowing as an autumnal leaf. The iris of her large, dark eye had the melting, mezzotinto outline, which remains the last vestige of African ancestry, and gives that plaintive expression, so often observed, and so appropriate to that docile and injured race.

Xarifa learned no lessons of humility or shame, within her own happy home; for she grew up in the warm atmosphere of father's and mother's love, like a flower open to the sunshine, and sheltered from the winds. But in summer walks with her beautiful mother, her young cheek often mantled at the rude gaze of the young men, and her dark eye flashed fire, when some contemptuous epithet met her ear, as white ladies passed them by, in scornful pride and ill-concealed envy.

Happy as Rosalie was in Edward's love, and surrounded by an outward environment of beauty, so well adapted to her poetic spirit, she felt these incidents with inexpressible pain. For herself, she cared but little; for she had found a sheltered home in Edward's heart, which the world might ridicule, but had no power to profane. But when she looked at her beloved Xarifa, and reflected upon the unavoidable and dangerous position which the tyranny of society had awarded her, her soul was filled with anguish. The rare loveliness of the child increased daily, and was evidently ripening into most marvellous beauty. The father rejoiced in it with unmingled pride; but in the deep tenderness of the mother's eye there was an indwelling sadness, that spoke of anxious thoughts and fearful forebodings.

When Xarifa entered her ninth year, these uneasy feelings found utterance in earnest solicitations that Edward would remove to France, or England. This request excited but little opposition, and was so attractive to his imagination, that he might have overcome all intervening obstacles, had not "a change come o'er the spirit of his dream." He still loved Rosalie, but he was now twenty-eight years old, and, unconsciously to himself, ambition had for some time been slowly gaining an ascendency over his other feelings. The contagion of example had led him into the arena where so much American strength is wasted; he had thrown himself into political excitement, with all the honest fervour of youthful feeling. His motives had been unmixed with selfishness, nor could he ever define to himself when or how sincere patriotism took the form of personal ambition. But so it was, that at twenty-eight years old, he found himself an ambitious man, involved in movements which his frank nature would have once abhorred, and watching the doubtful game of mutual cunning with all the fierce excitement of a gambler.

Among those on whom his political success most depended, was a very popular and wealthy man, who had an only daughter. His visits to the house were at first of a purely political nature; but the young lady was pleasing, and he fancied he discovered in her a sort of timid preference for himself. This excited his vanity, and awakened thoughts of the great worldly advantages connected with a union. Reminiscences of his first love kept these vague ideas in check for several months; but Rosalie's image at last became an unwelcome intruder; for with it was associated the idea of restraint. Moreover Charlotte, though inferior in beauty, was yet a pretty contrast to her rival. Her light hair fell in silken profusion, her blue eyes were gentle, though inexpressive, and her delicate cheeks were like blush-rose-buds.

He had already become accustomed to the dangerous experiment of resisting his own inward convictions; and this new impulse to ambition, combined with the strong temptation of variety in love, met the ardent young man weakened in moral principle, and unfettered by laws of the land. The change wrought upon him was soon noticed by Rosalie.

> "In many ways does the full heart reveal
> The presence of the love it would conceal;
> But in far more the estranged heart lets know
> The absence of the love, which yet it fain would show."

At length the news of his approaching marriage met her ear. Her head grew dizzy, and her heart fainted within her; but, with a strong effort at composure, she inquired all the particulars; and her pure mind at once took its resolution. Edward came that evening, and though she would have fain met him as usual, her heart was too full not to throw a deep sadness over her looks and tones. She had never complained of his decreasing tenderness, or of her own lonely hours; but he felt that the mute appeal of her heart-broken looks was more terrible than words. He kissed the hand she offered, and with a countenance almost as sad as her own, led her to a window in the recess, shadowed by a luxuriant Passion Flower. It was the same seat where they had spent the first evening in this beautiful cottage, consecrated to their youthful loves. The same calm, clear moonlight looked in through the trellis. The vine then planted had now a luxuriant growth; and many a time had Edward fondly twined its sacred blossoms with the glossy ringlets of her raven hair. The rush of memory almost overpowered poor Rosalie; and Edward felt too much oppressed and ashamed to break the long, deep silence. At length, in words scarcely audible, Rosalie said, "Tell me, dear Edward, are you to be married next week?" He dropped her hand, as if a rifle-ball had struck him; and it was not until after long hesitation, that he began to make some reply about the necessity of circumstances. Mildly, but earnestly, the poor girl begged him to spare apologies. It was enough that he no longer loved her, and that they must bid farewell. Trusting to the yielding tenderness of her character, he ventured, in the most soothing accents, to suggest that as he still loved her better than all the world, she would ever be his real wife, and they might see each other frequently. He was not prepared for the storm of indignant emotion his words excited. Hers was a passion too absorbing to admit of partnership; and her spirit was too pure and kind to enter into a selfish league against the happiness of the innocent young bride.

At length this painful interview came to an end. They stood together by the Gothic gate, where they had so often met and parted in the moonlight. Old remembrances melted their souls. "Farewell, dearest Edward," said Rosalie. "Give me a parting kiss." Her voice was choked for utterance, and the tears flowed freely, as she bent her lips toward him. He folded her convulsively in his arms, and imprinted a long, impassioned kiss on that mouth, which had never spoken to him but in love and blessing.

With effort like a death-pang, she at length raised her head from his heaving bosom, and turning from him with bitter sobs, she said, "It is our *last*. God bless you. I would not have you so miserable as I am. Farewell. A *last* farewell." "The *last!*" exclaimed he, with a wild shriek. "Oh, Rosalie, do not say that!" and covering his face with his hands, he wept like a child.

Recovering from his emotion, he found himself alone. The moon looked down upon him mild, but very sorrowful; as the Madonna seems to gaze on her worshipping children, bowed down with consciousness of sin. At that moment he would have given worlds to have disengaged himself from Charlotte; but he had gone so far, that blame, disgrace, and duels with angry relatives, would now attend any effort to obtain his freedom. Oh, how the moonlight oppressed him with its friendly sadness! It was like the plaintive eye of his forsaken one; like the music of sorrow echoed from an unseen world.

Long and earnestly he gazed at that dwelling, where he had so long known earth's purest foretaste of heavenly bliss. Slowly he walked away; then turned again to look on that charmed spot, the nestling-place of his young affections. He caught a glimpse of Rosalie, weeping beside a magnolia, which commanded a long view of the path leading to the public road. He would have sprung toward her, but she darted from him, and entered the cottage. That graceful figure, weeping in the moonlight, haunted him for years. It stood before his closing eyes, and greeted him with the morning dawn.

Poor Charlotte! had she known all, what a dreary lot would hers have been; but fortunately, she could not miss the impassioned tenderness she had never experienced; and Edward was the more careful in his kindness, because he was deficient in love. Once or twice she heard him murmur, "dear Rosalie," in his sleep; but the playful charge she brought was playfully answered, and the incident gave her no real uneasiness. The summer after their marriage, she proposed a residence at Sand-Hills; little aware what a whirlwind of emotion she excited in her husband's heart. The reasons he gave for rejecting the proposition appeared satisfactory; but she could not quite understand why he was never willing that their afternoon drives should be in the direction of those pleasant rural residences, which she had heard him praise so much. One day, as their barouche rolled along a winding road that skirted Sand-Hills, her attention was suddenly attracted by two figures among the trees by the way-side; and touching Edward's arm, she exclaimed, "Do look at that beautiful child!"

He turned and saw Rosalie and Xarifa. His lips quivered, and his face became deadly pale. His young wife looked at him intently, but said nothing. There were points of resemblance in the child, that seemed to account for his sudden emotion. Suspicion was awakened, and she soon learned that the mother of that lovely girl bore the name of Rosalie; with this information came recollections of the "dear Rosalie," murmured in uneasy slumbers. From gossiping tongues she soon learned more than she wished to know. She wept, but not as poor Rosalie had done; for she never had loved, and been beloved, like her, and her nature was more proud. Henceforth a change came over her feelings and her manners; and Edward had no further occasion to assume a tenderness in return for hers. Changed as he was by ambition, he felt the wintry chill of her polite propriety, and sometimes in agony of heart, compared it with the gushing love of her who was indeed his wife.

But these, and all his emotions, were a sealed book to Rosalie, of which she could only guess the contents. With remittances for her and her child's support, there sometimes came earnest pleadings that she would consent to see him again; but these she never answered, though her heart yearned to do so. She pitied his fair young bride and would not be tempted to bring sorrow into their household by any fault of hers. Her earnest prayer was that she might never know of her existence. She had not looked on Edward since she watched him under the shadow of the magnolia, until his barouche passed her in her rambles some months after. She saw the deadly paleness of his countenance, and had he dared to look back, he would have seen her tottering with faintness. Xarifa brought water from a little rivulet, and sprinkled her face. When she revived, she clasped the beloved child to her heart with a vehemence that made her scream. Soothingly she kissed away her fears, and gazed into her beautiful eyes with a deep, deep sadness of expression, which Xarifa never forgot. Wild were the thoughts that pressed around her aching heart, and almost maddened her poor brain thoughts which had almost driven her to suicide the night of that last farewell. For her child's sake she conquered the fierce temptation then; and for her sake, she struggled with it now. But the gloomy atmosphere of their once happy home overclouded the morning of Xarifa's life.

> "She from her mother learnt the trick of grief,
> And sighed among her playthings."

Rosalie perceived this; and it gave her gentle heart unutterable pain. At last, the conflicts of her spirit proved too strong for the beautiful frame in which it dwelt. About a year after Edward's marriage, she was found dead in her bed, one bright autumnal morning. She had often expressed to her daughter a wish to be buried under a spreading oak, that shaded a rustic garden-chair, in which she and Edward had spent many happy evenings. And there she was buried; with a small white cross at her head, twined with the cypress vine. Edward came to the funeral, and wept long, very long, at the grave. Hours after midnight, he sat in the recess-window, with Xarifa folded to his heart. The poor child sobbed herself to sleep on his bosom; and the convicted murderer had small reason to envy that wretched man, as he gazed on the lovely countenance, which so strongly reminded him of his early and his only love.

From that time, Xarifa was the central point of all his warmest affections. He hired an excellent old negress to take charge of the cottage, from which he promised his darling child that she should never be removed. He employed a music master, and dancing master, to attend upon her; and a week never passed without a visit from him, and a present of books, pictures, or flowers. To hear her play upon the harp, or repeat some favourite poem in her mother's earnest accents and melodious tones, or to see her pliant figure float in the garland-dance, seemed to be the highest enjoyment of his life. Yet was the pleasure mixed with bitter thoughts. What would be the destiny of this fascinating young creature, so radiant with life and beauty? She belonged to a proscribed race; and though the brown colour on her soft cheek was scarcely deeper than the sunny side of a golden pear, yet was it sufficient to exclude her from virtuous society. He thought of Rosalie's wish to carry her to France: and he would have fulfilled it, had he been unmarried. As it was, he inwardly resolved to make some arrangement to effect it in a few years, even if it involved separation from his darling child.

But alas for the calculations of man! From the time of Rosalie's death, Edward had sought relief for his wretched feelings in the free use of wine. Xarifa was scarcely fifteen, when her father was found dead by the road-side; having fallen from his horse, on his way to visit her. He left no will; but his wife, with kindness of heart worthy of a happier domestic fate, expressed a decided reluctance to change any of the plans he had made for the beautiful child at Sand-Hills.

Xarifa mourned her indulgent father; but not as one utterly desolate. True, she had lived "like a flower deep hid in rocky cleft;" but the sunshine of love had already peeped in upon her. Her teacher on the harp was a handsome and agreeable young man of twenty, the only son of an English widow. Perhaps Edward had not been altogether unmindful of the result, when he first invited him to the flowery cottage. Certain it is, he had more than once thought what a pleasant thing it would be, if English freedom from prejudice should lead him to offer legal protection to his graceful and winning child. Being thus encouraged, rather than checked, in his admiration, George Elliot could not be otherwise than strongly attracted toward his beautiful pupil. The lonely and unprotected state in which her father's death left her, deepened this feeling into tenderness. And lucky was it for her enthusiastic and affectionate nature; for she could not live without an atmosphere of love. In her innocence, she knew nothing of the dangers in her path; and she trusted George with an undoubting simplicity, that rendered her sacred to his noble and generous soul. It seemed as if that flower-embosomed nest was consecrated by the Fates to Love. The French have well named it *La Belle Passion*; for without it life were "a year without spring, or a spring without roses." Except the loveliness of infancy, what does earth offer so much like Heaven, as the happiness of two young, pure, and beautiful beings, living in each other's hearts?

Xarifa inherited her mother's poetic and impassioned temperament; and to her above others, the first consciousness of these sweet emotions was like a golden sunrise on the sleeping flowers.

> "Thus stood she at the threshold of the scene
> Of busy life. . . .
> How fair it lay in solemn shade and sheen!
> And he beside her, like some angel, posted
> To lead her out of childhood's fairy land,
> On to life's glancing summit, hand in hand."

Alas, the tempest was brooding over their young heads. Rosalie, though she knew it not, had been the daughter of a slave, whose wealthy master, though he remained attached to her to the end of her days, yet carelessly omitted to have papers of manumission recorded. His heirs had lately failed, under circumstances which greatly exasperated their creditors; and in an unlucky hour, they discovered their claim on Angelique's grand-child.

The gentle girl, happy as the birds in spring-time, accustomed to the fondest indulgence, surrounded by all the refinements of life, timid as a fawn, and with a soul full of romance, was ruthlessly seized by a sheriff, and placed on the public auction-stand in Savannah. There she stood, trembling, blushing, and weeping; compelled to listen to the grossest language, and shrinking from the rude hands that examined the graceful proportions of her beautiful frame. "Stop that!" exclaimed a stern voice. "I bid two thousand dollars for her, without asking any of their d——d questions." The speaker was probably about forty years of age, with handsome features, but a fierce and proud expression. An older man, who stood behind him, bid two thousand five hundred. The first bid higher; then a third, a dashing young man, bid three thousand; and thus they went on, with the keen excitement of gamblers, until the first speaker obtained the prize, for the moderate sum of five thousand dollars.

And where was George, during this dreadful scene? He was absent on a visit to his mother, at Mobile. But, had he been at Sand-Hills, he could not have saved his beloved from the wealthy profligate, who was determined to obtain her at any price. A letter of agonized entreaty from her brought him home on the wings of the wind. But what could he do? How could he ever obtain a sight of her, locked up as she was in the princely mansion of her master? At last, by bribing one of the slaves, he conveyed a letter to her, and received one in return. As yet, her purchaser treated her with respectful gentleness, and sought to win her favour, by flattery and presents; but she dreaded every moment, lest the scene should change, and trembled at the sound of every footfall. A plan was laid for escape. The slave agreed to drug his master's wine; a ladder of ropes was prepared, and a swift boat was in readiness. But the slave, to obtain a double reward, was treacherous. Xarifa had scarcely given an answering signal to the low cautious whistle of her lover, when the sharp sound of a rifle was followed by a deep groan, and a heavy fall on the pavement of the court-yard. With frenzied eagerness she swung herself down by the ladder of ropes, and, by the glancing light of lanthorns, saw George, bleeding and lifeless at her feet. One wild shriek, that pierced the brains of those who heard it, and she fell senseless by his side.

For many days she had a confused consciousness of some great agony, but knew not where she was, or by whom she was surrounded. The slow recovery of her reason settled into the most intense melancholy, which moved the compassion even of her cruel purchaser. The beautiful eyes, always pensive in expression, were now so heart-piercing in their sadness, that he could not endure to look upon them. For some months, he sought to win her smiles by lavish presents, and delicate attentions. He bought glittering chains of gold, and costly bands of pearl. His victim scarcely glanced at them, and her attendant slave laid them away, unheeded and forgotten. He purchased the furniture of the cottage at Sand-Hills, and one morning Xarifa found her harp at the bedside, and the room filled with her own books, pictures, and flowers. She gazed upon them with a pang unutterable, and burst into an agony of tears; but she gave her master no thanks, and her gloom deepened.

At last his patience was exhausted. He grew weary of her obstinacy, as he was pleased to term it; and threats took the place of persuasion.

In a few months more, poor Xarifa was a raving maniac. That pure temple was desecrated; that loving heart was broken; and that beautiful head fractured against the wall in the frenzy of despair. Her master cursed the useless expense she had cost him; the slaves buried her; and no one wept at the grave of her who had been so carefully cherished, and so tenderly beloved.

FRANK J. WEBB

Little is known about Frank J. Webb (1828–1894), born a free black man in Philadelphia. One of the earliest novels in the African American tradition, *The Garies and Their Friends* focuses primarily on the Northern middle-class domestic lives of mixed couples and free blacks. In the excerpt that follows, Clarence, the passing son of the mixed-race Garies, discusses the difficulties of visiting his non-passing sister, Emily, his terror that his white fiancé, "Birdie," might learn of his racial heritage, and experiences the impossibility of telling her the truth. When his racial heritage is revealed by others and he is deprived of his intended, Clarence weakens and dies, and "Birdie" follows shortly and tragically thereafter.

From The Garies and Their Friends†

CHAPTER XXXI
THE THORN RANKLES

✳ ✳ ✳

On the whole, the town looked charmingly peaceful and attractive, and appeared just the quiet nook that a weary worker in cities would select as a place of retirement after a busy round of toils or pleasure.

There were little knots of idlers gathered about the railroad station, as there always is in quiet towns—not that they expect any one; but that the arrival and departure of the train is one of the events of the day, and those who have nothing else particular to accomplish feel constrained to be on hand to witness it. Every now and then one of them would look down the line and wonder why the cars were not in sight.

Amongst those seemingly the most impatient was Miss Ada Bell, who looked but little older than when she won the heart of the orphan Clarence, years before, by that kind kiss upon his childish brow. It was hers still—she bound it to her by long years of affectionate care, almost equalling in its sacrificing tenderness that which a mother would have bestowed upon her only child. Clarence, her adopted son, had written to her, that he was wretched, heart-sore, and ill, and longed to come to her, his almost mother, for sympathy, advice, and comfort: so she, with yearning heart, was there to meet him.

At last the faint scream of the steam-whistle was heard, and soon the lumbering locomotive came puffing and snorting on its iron path, dashing on as though it could never stop, and making the surrounding hills echo with the unearthly scream of its startling whistle, and

---

† From Frank J. Webb, *The Garies and Their Friends* (Baltimore: Hopkins UP, 1997, pp. 320–32; 380–92; orig. publ. London and New York: G. Routledge & Co., 1857).

arousing to desperation every dog in the quiet little town. At last it stopped, and stood giving short and impatient snorts and hisses, whilst the passengers were alighting.

Clarence stepped languidly out, and was soon in the embrace of Miss Ada.

"My dear boy, how thin and pale you look!" she exclaimed; "come, get into the carriage; never mind your baggage, George will look after that; your hands are hot—very hot, you must be feverish."

"Yes, Aunt Ada," for so he had insisted on his calling her

"I am ill—sick in heart, mind, and everything. Cut up the horses," said he, with slight impatience of manner,; "let us get home quickly. When I get in the old parlour, and let you bathe my head as you used to, I am sure I shall feel better. I am almost exhausted from fatigue and heat."

"Very well then, dear, don't talk now," she replied, not in the least noticing his impatience of manner; "when you are rested, and have had your tea, will be time enough."

They were soon in the old house, and Clarence looked round with a smile of pleasure on the room where he had spent so many happy hours. Good Aunt Ada would not let him talk, but compelled him to remain quiet until he had rested himself, and eaten his evening meal.

He had altered considerably in the lapse of years, there was but little left to remind one of the slight, melancholy-looking boy, that once stood a heavy-hearted little stranger in the same room, in days gone by. His face was without a particle of red to relieve its uniform paleness; his eyes, large, dark, and languishing, were half hidden by unusually long lashes; his forehead broad, and surmounted with clustering raven hair; a glossy moustache covered his lip, and softened down its fulness; on the whole, he was strikingly handsome, and none would pass him without a second look.

Tea over, Miss Ada insisted that he should lie down upon the sofa again, whilst she sat by and bathed his head. "Have you seen your sister lately?" she asked.

"No, Aunt Ada," he answered, hesitatingly, whilst a look of annoyance darkened his face for a moment; "I have not been to visit her since last fall—almost a year."

"Oh! Clarence, how can you remain so long away?" said she, reproachfully.

"Well, I can't go there with any comfort or pleasure," he answered, apologetically; "I can't go there; each year as I visit the place, their ways seem more strange and irksome to me. Whilst enjoying her company, I must of course come in familiar contact with those by whom she is surrounded. Sustaining the position that I do—passing as I am for a white man—I am obliged to be very circumspect, and have often been compelled to give her pain by avoiding many of her dearest friends when I have encountered them in public places, because of their complexion. I feel mean and cowardly whilst I'm doing it; but it is necessary—I can't be white and coloured at the same time; the two don't mingle, and I must consequently be one or the other. My education, habits, and ideas, all unfit me for associating with the latter; and I live in constant dread that something may occur to bring me out with the former. I don't avoid coloured people, because I esteem them my inferiors in refinement, education, or intelligence; but because they are subjected to degradations that I shall be compelled to share by too freely associating with them."

"It is a pity," continued he, with a sigh, "that I was not suffered to grow up with them, then I should have learnt to bear their burthens, and in the course of time might have walked over my path of life, bearing the load almost unconsciously. Now it would crush me, I know. It was a great mistake to place me in my present false position," concluded he, bitterly; "it has cursed me. Only a day ago I had a letter from Em, reproaching me for my coldness; yet, God help me! What am I to do!"

Miss Ada looked at him sorrowfully, and continued smoothing down his hair, and inundating his temples with Cologne; at last she ventured to inquire, "How do matters progress with you and Miss Bates? Clary, you have lost your heart there!"

"Too true," he replied, hurriedly; "and what is more—little Birdie (I call her little Birdie) has lost hers too. Aunt Ada, we are engaged!"

"With her parents' consent?" she asked.

"Yes, with her parents' consent; we are to be married in the coming winter."

"Then they know *all*, of course—they know you are coloured?" observed she.

"They know all!" cried he, starting up. "*Who* said they did—*who* told them?—tell me that, I say! Who has *dared* to tell them I am a coloured man?"

"Hush, Clarence, hush!" replied she, attempting to soothe him. "I do not know that any one has informed them; I only inferred so from your saying you were engaged. I thought *you* had informed them yourself. Don't you remember you wrote that you should?—and I took it for granted that you had."

"Oh! yes, yes; so I did! I fully intended to, but found myself too great a coward. *I dare not*—I cannot risk losing her. I am fearful that if she knew it she would throw me off for ever."

"Perhaps not, Clarence—if she loves you as she should; and even if she did, would it not be better that she should know it now, than have it discovered afterwards, and you both be rendered miserable for life."

"No, no, Aunt Ada—I cannot tell her! It must remain a secret until after our marriage; then, if they find it out, it will be to their interest to smooth the matter over, and keep quiet about it."

"Clary, Clary—that is *not* honourable!"

"I know it—but how can I help it? Once or twice I thought of telling her, but my heart always failed me at the critical moment. It would kill me to lose her. Oh! I love her, Aunt Ada," said he, passionately—"love her with all the energy and strength of my father's race, and all the doating tenderness of my mother's. I could have told her long ago, before my love had grown to its present towering strength, but craft set a seal upon my lips, and bid me be silent until her heart was fully mine, and then nothing could part us; yet now even, when sure of her affections, the dread that her love would not stand the test, compels me to shrink more than ever from the disclosure."

"But, Clarence, you are not acting generously; I know your conscience does not approve your actions."

"Don't I know that?" he answered, almost fiercely; "yet I dare not tell—I must shut this secret in my bosom, where it gnaws, gnaws, gnaws, until it has almost eaten my heart away. Oh, I've thought of that, time and again; it has kept me awake night after night, it haunts me at all hours; it is breaking down my health and strength—wearing my very life out of me; no escaped galley-slave ever felt more than I do, or lived in more constant fear of detection: and yet I must nourish this tormenting secret, and keep it growing in my breast until it has crowded out every honourable and manly feeling; and then, perhaps, after all my sufferings and sacrifice of candour and truth, out it will come at last, when I least expect or think of it."

Aunt Ada could not help weeping, and exclaimed, commiseratingly, "My poor, poor boy," as he strode up and down the room.

"The whole family, except her, seem to have the deepest contempt for coloured people; they are constantly making them a subject of bitter jests; they appear to have no more feeling or regard for them than if they were brutes—and I," continued he, "I, miserable, contemptible, false-hearted knave, as I am, I—I—yes, I join them in their heartless jests, and wonder all the while my mother does not rise from her grave and *curse* me as I speak!"

"Oh! Clarence, Clarence, my dear child!" cried the terrified Aunt Ada, "you talk deliriously; you have brooded over this until it has almost made you crazy. Come here—sit down." And seizing him by the arm, she drew him on the sofa beside her, and began to bathe his hot head with the Cologne again.

"Let me walk, Aunt Ada," said he after a few moments,—"let me walk, I feel better whilst I am moving; I can't bear to be quiet." And forthwith he commenced striding up and down the room again with nervous and hurried steps. After a few moments he burst out again—

"It seems as if fresh annoyances and complications beset me every day. Em writes me that she is engaged. I was in hopes, that, after I had married, I could persuade her to come and live with me, and so gradually break off her connection with coloured people; but that hope is extinguished now: she is engaged to a coloured man."

Aunt Ada could see no remedy for this new difficulty, and could only say, "Indeed!"

"I thought something of the kind would occur when I was last at home, and spoke to her on the subject, but she evaded giving me any definite answer; I think she was afraid to tell me—she has written, asking my consent."

"And will you give it?" asked Aunt Ada.

"It will matter but little if I don't; Em has a will of her own, and I have no means of coercing her; besides, I have no reasonable objection to urge: it would be folly in me to oppose it, simply because he is a coloured man—for, what am I myself? The only difference is, that his identity with coloured people is no secret, and he is not ashamed of it whilst I conceal my origin, and live in constant dread that some one may find it out." When Clarence had finished, he continued to walk up and down the room, looking very care worn and gloomy.

Miss Bell remained on the sofa, thoughtfully regarding him. At last, she rose up and took his hand in hers, as she used to when he was a boy, and walking beside him, saying, The more I reflect upon it, the more necessary I regard it that you should tell this girl and her parents your real position before you marry her. Throw away concealment, make a clean breast of it! you may not be rejected when they find her heart is so deeply interested. If you marry her with this secret hanging over you, it will embitter your life, make you reserved, suspicious, and consequently ill-tempered, and destroy all your domestic happiness. Let me persuade you, tell them ere it to be too late. Suppose it reached them through some other source, what would they then think of you?"

"Who else would tell them? Who else knows it? You, you," said he suspiciously—"*you* would not betray me. I thought you loved me, Aunt Ada."

"Clarence, my dear boy," she rejoined, apparently hurt by his hasty and accusing tone, "you *will* mistake me—I have no such intention. If they are never to learn it except through *me*, your secret is perfectly safe. Yet I must tell you that I feel and think that the true way to promote her happiness and your own, is for you to disclose to them your real position, and throw yourself upon their generosity for the result."

Clarence pondered for a long time over Miss Bell's advice, which she again and again repeated, placing it each time before him in a stronger light, until, at last, she extracted from him a promise that he would do it. "I know you are right, Aunt Ada," said he; "I am convinced of that—it is a question of courage with me. I know it would be more honourable for me to tell her now. I'll try to do it—I will make an effort, and summon up the courage necessary—God be my helper!"

"That's a dear boy!" she exclaimed, kissing him affectionately; "I know you will feel happier when it is all over; and even if she should break her engagement, you will be infinitely better off than if it was fulfilled and your secret subsequently discovered. Come, now," she concluded, "I am going to exert my old authority, and send you to bed; tomorrow, perhaps, you may see this in a more hopeful light."

Two days after this, Clarence was again in New York, amid the heat and dust of that crowded, bustling city. Soon after his arrival, he dressed himself, and started for the mansion of Mr. Bates, trembling as he went, for the result of the communication he was about to make.

Once on the way he paused, for the thought had occurred to him that he would write to them; then reproaching himself for his weakness and timidity, he started on again with renewed determination.

"I'll see her myself," he soliloquized. "I'll tell little Birdie all, and know my fate from her own lips. If I must give her up, I'll know the worst from her."

When Clarence was admitted, he would not permit himself to be announced, but walked tiptoe upstairs and gently opening the drawing-room door, entered the room.

Standing by the piano, turning over the leaves of some music, and merrily humming an air, was a young girl of extremely *petite* and delicate form. Her complexion was strikingly fair; and the rich curls of dark auburn that fell in clusters on her shoulders, made it still more dazzling by the contrast presented. Her eyes were grey, inclining to black; her features small, and not over-remarkable for their symmetry, yet by no means disproportionate. There was the sweetest of dimples on her small round chin, and her throat white and clear as the finest marble. The expression of her face was extremely childlike; she seemed more like a schoolgirl than a young woman of eighteen on the eve of marriage. There was something deliciously airy and fairylike in her motions, and as she slightly moved her feet in time to the music she was humming, her thin blue dress floated about her, and undulated in harmony with her graceful motions.

After gazing at her for a few moments, Clarence called gently, "Little Birdie." She gave a timid joyous little cry of surprise and pleasure, and fluttered into his arms.

"Oh, Clary, love, how you startled me! I did not dream there was any one in the room. It was so naughty in you," said she, childishly, as he pushed back the curls from her face and kissed her. "When did you arrive?"

"Only an hour ago," he answered.

"And you came here at once? Ah, that was so lover-like and kind," she rejoined, smiling.

"You look like a sylph to-night, Anne," said he, as she danced about him. "Ah," he continued, after regarding her for a few seconds with a look of intense admiration, "you want to rivet my chains the tighter,—you look most bewitching. Why are you so much dressed to-night?—jewels, sash, and satin slippers," he continued; "are you going out?"

"No, Clary," she answered. "I was to have gone to the theatre; but just at the last moment I decided not to. A singular desire to stay at home came over me suddenly. I had an instinctive feeling that I should lose some greater enjoyment if I went; so I remained at home; and here, love, are you. But what is the matter? you look sad and weary."

"I am a little fatigued," said he, seating himself and holding her hand in his: "a little weary; but that will soon wear off; and as for the sadness," concluded he, with a forced smile, "that *must* depart now that I am with you, Little Birdie."

"I feel relieved that you have returned safe and well," said she, looking up into his face from her seat beside him; "for, Clary, love, I had such a frightful dream, such a singular dream about you. I have endeavoured to shake it out of my foolish little head; but it won't go, Clary,—I can't get rid of it. It occurred after you left us at Saratoga. Oh, it was nothing though," said she, laughing and shaking her curls,—"nothing; and now you are safely returned, I shall not think of it again. Tell me what you have seen since you went away; and how is that dear Aunt Ada of yours you talk so much about?"

"Oh, she is quite well," answered he; "but tell, Anne, tell me about that dream. What was it, Birdie?—come tell me."

"I don't care to," she answered, with a slight shudder,—"I don't want to, love."

"Yes, yes,—do, sweet," importuned he; "I want to hear it."

"Then if I must," said she, "I will. I dreamed that you and I were walking on a road together, and 'twas such a beautiful road, with flowers and fruit, and lovely cottages on either side. I thought you held my hand; I felt it just as plain as I clasp yours now. Presently a rough ugly man overtook us, and bid you let me go; and that you refused, and held me all the tighter. Then he gave you a diabolical look, and touched you on the face, and you broke out in loathsome black spots, and screamed in such agony and frightened me so, that I awoke all in a shiver of terror, and did not get over it all the next day."

Clarence clutched her hand tighter as she finished, so tight indeed, that she gave a little scream of pain and looked frightened at him. "What is the matter?" she inquired "your hand is like ice, and you are paler than ever. You haven't let that trifling dream affect you so? It is nothing."

"I am superstitious in regard to dreams," said Clarence wiping the perspiration from his forehead. "Go," he asked faintly, "play me an air, love,—something quick and lively to dispel this. I wish you had not told me."

"But you begged me to," said she, pouting, as she took her seat at the instrument.

"How ominous," muttered he,—"became covered with black spots; that is a foreshadowing. How can I tell her," he thought. "It seems like wilfully destroying my own happiness." And he sat struggling with himself to obtain the necessary courage to fulfil the purpose of his visit, and became so deeply engrossed with his own reflections as to scarcely even hear the sound of the instrument.

"It is too bad," she cried, as she ceased playing: "here I have performed some of your favourite airs, and that too without eliciting a word of commendation. You are inexpressibly dull to-night; nothing seems to enliven you. What is the matter?"

"Oh," rejoined he, abstractedly, "am I? I was not aware of it."

"Yes, you are," said Little Birdie, pettishly; "nothing seems to engage your attention." And, skipping off to the table, she took up the newspaper, and exclaimed,—"Let me read you something very curious."

"No, no, Anne dear," interrupted he; "sit here by me. I want to say something serious to you—something of moment to us both."

"Then it's something very grave and dull, I know," she remarked; "for that is the way people always begin. Now I don't want to hear anything serious to-night; I want to be merry. You *look* serious enough; and if you begin to *talk* seriously you'll be perfectly unbearable. So you must hear what I am going to read to you first." And the little tyrant put her finger on his lip, and looked so bewitching, that he could not refuse her. And the important secret hung on his lips, but was not spoken.

"Listen," said she, spreading out the paper before her and running her tiny finger down the column. "Ah, I have it," she exclaimed at last, and began:—

" 'We learn from unimpeachable authority that the Hon.———, who represents a district of our city in the State legislature, was yesterday united to the Quateroon daughter of the late Gustave Almont. She is said to be possessed of a large fortune, inherited from her father; and they purpose going to France to reside,—a sensible determination; as, after such a *mésalliance*, the honourable gentleman can no longer expect to retain his former social position in our midst.— *New Orleans Watchman.*' "

"Isn't it singular," she remarked, "that a man in his position should make such a choice?"

"He loved her, no doubt," suggested Clarence; "and she was almost white."

"How could he love her?" asked she, wonderingly. "Love a coloured woman! I cannot conceive it possible," said she, with a look of disgust; "there is something strange and unnatural about it."

"No, no," he rejoined, hurriedly, "it was love, Anne,—pure love; it is not impossible. I—I——" "am coloured," he would have said; but he paused and looked full in her lovely face. He could not tell her,—the words slunk back into his coward heart unspoken.

She stared at him in wonder and perplexity, and exclaimed,—"Dear Clarence, how strangely you act! I am afraid you are not well. Your brow is hot," said she, laying her hand on his forehead; "you have been travelling too much for your strength."

"It is not that," he replied. "I feel a sense of suffocation, as if all the blood was rushing to my throat. Let me get the air." And he rose and walked to the window. Anne hastened and brought him a glass of water, of which he drank a little, and then declared himself better.

After this, he stood for a long time with her clasped in his arms; then giving her one or two passionate kisses, he strained her closer to him and abruptly left the house leaving Little Birdie startled and alarmed by his strange behaviour.

*　　*　　*

CHAPTER XXXVI
AND THE LAST

*　　*　　*

[Clarence] was now completely excluded from the society in which he had so long been accustomed to move; the secret of his birth had become widely known, and he was avoided by his former friends and sneered at as a "nigger." His large fortune kept some two or three whites about him, but he knew they were leeches seeking to bleed his purse, and he wisely avoided their society.

He was very wretched and lonely: he felt ashamed to seek the society of coloured men now that the whites despised and rejected him, so he lived apart from both classes of society, and grew moody and misanthropic.

*　　*　　*

He wrote often now to Emily and her husband, and seemed desirous to atone for his past neglect. Emily had written to him first; she had learned of his disappointment, and gave him a sister's sympathy in his loneliness and sorrow.

The chilly month of March had scarcely passed away when they received a letter from him informing them of his intention to return. He wrote, "I am no better, and my physician says that a longer residence here will not benefit me in the least—that I came *too late*. I cough, cough, cough, incessantly, and each day become more feeble. I am coming home, Emmy; coming home, I fear, to die. I am but a ghost of my former self. I write you this that you may not be alarmed when you see me. It is too late now to repine, but, oh! Em, if my lot had only been cast with yours—had we never been separated—I might have been to-day as happy as you are."

* * *

Emily tried to appear as though she did not notice the great change in his appearance, and talked cheerfully and encouragingly in his presence; but she wept bitterly, when alone, over the final separation which she foresaw was not far distant.

The next day Doctor Burdett called, and his grave manner and apparent disinclination to encourage any hope, confirmed the hopeless impression they already entertained.

Aunt Ada came from Sudbury at Emily's request; she knew her presence would give pleasure to Clarence, she accordingly wrote her to come, and she and Emily nursed by turns the failing sufferer.

Esther and her husband, Mrs. Ellis and Caddy, and even Kinch, were unremitting in their attentions, and did all in their power to amuse and comfort him.

Day by day he faded perceptibly, grew more and more feeble, until at last Doctor Burdett began to number days instead of weeks as his term of life. Clarence anticipated death with calmness—did not repine or murmur. Father Banks was often with him cheering him with hopes of a happier future beyond the grave.

One day he sent for his sister and desired her to write a letter for him. "Em," said he, "I am failing fast; these fiery spots on my cheek, this scorching in my palms, these hard-drawn, difficult breaths, warn me that the time is very near. Don't weep, Em!" continued he, kissing her—"there, don't weep—I shall be better off—happier—I am sure! Don't weep now—I want you to write to little Birdie for me. I have tried, but my hand trembles so that I cannot write legibly—I gave it up. Sit down beside me here, and write; here is the pen." Emily dried her eyes, and mechanically sat down to write as he desired. Motioning to him that she was ready, he dictated—

"MY DEAR LITTLE BIRDIE,—I once resolved never to write to you again, and partially promised your father that I would not; then I did not dream that I should be so soon compelled to break my resolution. Little Birdie, I am dying! My physician informs me that I have but a few more days to live. I have been trying to break away from earth's affairs and fix my thoughts on other and better things. I have given up all but you, and feel that I cannot relinquish you until I see you once again. So not refuse me, little Birdie! Show this to your father—he must consent to a request made by one on the brink of the grave."

"There, that will do; let me read it over," said he, extending his hand for the note. "Yes, I will sign it now—then do you add our address. Send it now, Emily—send it in time for to-night's mail."

"Clary, do you think she will come?" inquired his sister.

"Yes," replied he, confidently; "I am sure she will if the note reaches her." Emily said no more, but sealed and directed the note, which she immediately despatched to the post-office; and on the following day it reached little Birdie.

From the time when the secret of Clarence's birth had been discovered, until the day she had received his note, she never mentioned his name. At the demand of her father she produced his letters, miniature, and even the little presents he had given her from time to time, and laid them down before him without a murmur; after this, even when he cursed and denounced him, she only left the room, never uttering a word in his defence. She moved about like one who had received a stunning blow—she was dull, cold, apathetic. She would smile vacantly when her father smoothed her hair or kissed her cheek; but she never laughed, or sang and played, as in days gone by; she would recline for hours on the sofa in her room gazing vacantly in the air, and taking apparently no interest in anything about her. She bent her head when she walked, complained of coldness about her temples, and kept her hand constantly upon her heart.

Doctors were at last consulted; they pronounced her physically well, and thought that time would restore her wonted animation; but month after month she grew more dull and silent, until her father feared she would become idiotic, and grew hopeless and unhappy about her. For a week before the receipt of the note from Clarence, she had been particularly apathetic and indifferent, but it seemed to rouse her into life again. She started up after reading it, and rushed wildly through the hall into her father's library.

"See here!" exclaimed she, grasping his arm—"see there—I knew it! I've felt day after day that it was coming to that! You separated us, and now he is dying—dying!" cried she. "Read it—read it!"

Her father took the note, and after perusing it laid it on the table, and said coldly, "Well—"

"Well!" repeated she, with agitation—"Oh, father, it is not well! Father!" said she, hurriedly, "you bid me give him up—told me he was unworthy—pointed out to me fully and clearly why we could not marry: I was convinced we could not, for I knew you would never let it be. Yet I have never ceased to love him. I cannot control my heart, but I could my voice, and never since that day have I spoken his name. I gave him up—not that I would not have gladly married, knowing what he was—because you desired it—because I saw either your heart must break or mine. I let mine go to please you, and have suffered uncomplainingly, and will so suffer until the end; but I *must* see him once again. It will be a pleasure to him to see me once again in his dying hour, and I *must* go. If you love me," continued she, pleadingly, as her father made a gesture of dissent, "let us go. You see he is dying—begs you from the brink of the grave. Let me go, only to say good bye to him, and then, perhaps," concluded she, pressing her hand upon her heart, "I shall be better here."

Her father had not the heart to make any objection, and the next day they started for Philadelphia. They despatched a note to Clarence, saying they had arrived, which Emily received, and after opening it, went to gently break its contents to her brother.

"You must prepare yourself for visitors, Clary," said she, "no doubt some of our friends will call to-day, the weather is so very delightful."

"Do you know who is coming?" he inquired.

"Yes, dear," she answered, seating herself beside him, "I have received a note stating that a particular friend will call to-day—one that you desire to see."

"Ah!" he exclaimed, "it is little Birdie, is it not?"

"Yes," she replied, "they have arrived in town, and will be here to-day."

"Did not I tell you so?" said he, triumphantly. "I knew she would come. I knew it," continued he, joyfully. "Let me get up—I am strong enough—she is come—O! she has come."

Clarence insisted on being dressed with extraordinary care. His long fierce-looking beard was trimmed carefully, and he looked much better than he had done for weeks; he was wonderfully stronger, walked across the room, and chatted over his breakfast with unusual animation.

At noon they came, and were shown into the drawing-room, where Emily received them. Mr. Bates bowed politely, and expressed a hope that Mr. Garie was better. Emily held out her hand to little Birdie, who clasped it in both her own, and said, inquiringly: "You are his sister?"

"Yes," answered Emily. "You, I should have known from Clarence's description—you are his little Birdie?"

She did not reply—her lip quivered, and she pressed Emily's hand and kissed her. "He is impatient to see you," resumed Emily, "and if you are so disposed, we will go up immediately."

"I will remain here," observed Mr. Bates, "unless Mr. Garie partic- ularly desires to see me. My daughter will accompany you."

Emily took the hand of little Birdie in her own, and they walked together up the stairway. "You must not be frightened at his appear- ance," she remarked, tearfully, "he is greatly changed."

Little Birdie only shook her head—her heart seemed too full for speech—and she stepped on a little faster, keeping her hand pressed on her breast all the while.

When they reached the door, Emily was about to open it, but her companion stopped her, by saying: "Wait a moment—stop! How my heart beats—it almost suffocates me." They paused for a few moments to permit little Birdie to recover from her agitation, then throwing open the door they advanced into the room.

"Clarence!" said his sister. He did not answer; he was looking down into the garden. She approached nearer, and gently laying her hand on his shoulder, said, "Here is your little Birdie, Clarence." He neither moved nor spoke.

"Clarence!" cried she, louder. No answer. She touched his face—it was warm. "He's fainted!" exclaimed she; and, ringing the bell violently, she screamed for help. Her husband and the nurse rushed into the room; then came Aunt Ada and Mr. Bates. They bathed his temples, held strong salts to his nostrils—still he did not revive. Finally, the nurse opened his bosom and placed her hand upon his heart. *It was still—quite still:* CLARENCE WAS DEAD!

At first they could not believe it. "Let me speak to him," exclaimed little Birdie, distractedly; "he will hear my voice, and answer. Clarence! Clarence!" she cried. All in vain—all in vain. Clarence was dead!

They gently bore her away. That dull, cold look came back again upon her face, and left it never more in life. She walked about mournfully for a few years, pressing her hand upon her heart; and then passed away to join her lover, where distinctions in race or colour are unknown, and where the prejudices of earth cannot mar their happiness.

Our tale is now soon finished. They buried Clarence beside his parents; coloured people followed him to his last home, and wept over his grave. Of all the many whites that he had known, Aunt Ada and Mr. Balch were the only ones that mingled their tears with those who listened to the solemn words of Father Banks, "Ashes to ashes, dust to dust."

We, too, Clarence, cast a tear upon thy tomb—poor victim of prejudice to thy colour! and deem thee better off resting upon thy cold pillow of earth, than battling with that malignant sentiment that persecuted thee, and has crushed energy, hope, and life from many stronger hearts.

✳   ✳   ✳

WILLIAM WELLS BROWN

Born a slave in 1814, William Wells Brown (d. 1884) became a famous abolitionist, the author of one of the nation's most influential slave narratives, a novelist, a playwright, and an historian. *Clotel*, published in 1853, is the first novel published by an African American; Clotel's tragic story, an excerpt from which follows, is based on contemporary reports of Thomas Jefferson's mulatto daughter, abandoned and sold into slavery. The first chapter excerpted here draws particularly heavily on Childs's "The Quadroons."

From Clotel; or, The President's Daughter†

CHAPTER VIII
THE SEPARATION

"In many ways does the full heart reveal
The presence of the love it would conceal;
But in far more the estranged heart lets know
The absence of the love, which yet it fain would show."

At length the news of the approaching marriage of Horatio met the ear of Clotel. Her head grew dizzy, and her heart fainted within her; but, with a strong effort at composure, she inquired all the particulars, and her pure mind at once took its resolution. Horatio came that evening, and though she would fain have met him as usual, her heart was too full not to throw a deep sadness over her looks and tones. She had never complained of his decreasing tenderness, or of her own lonely hours; but he felt that the mute appeal of her heart-broken looks was more terrible than words. He kissed the hand she offered, and with a countenance almost as sad as her own, led her to a window in the recess shadowed by a luxuriant passion flower. It was the same seat where they had spent the first evening in this beautiful cottage, consecrated to their first loves. The same calm, clear moonlight looked in through the trellis. The vine then planted had now a luxuriant growth; and many a time had Horatio fondly twined its sacred blossoms with the glossy ringlets of her raven hair. The rush of memory almost overpowered poor Clotel; and Horatio felt too much oppressed and ashamed to break the long deep silence. At length, in words scarcely audible, Clotel said: "Tell me, dear Horatio, are you to be married next week?"

He dropped her hand as if a rifle ball had struck him; and it was not until after long hesitation, that he began to make some reply about the necessity of circumstances. Mildly but earnestly the poor girl begged him to spare apologies. It was enough that he no longer loved her, and that they must bid farewell. Trusting to the yielding tenderness of her character, he ventured, in the most soothing

† From William Wells Brown, *Clotel; or, The President's Daughter* (New York: Carol Publishing Group, 1995, pp. 111–15; 241–46; orig. publ. London: Partridge & Oakey, 1853).

accents, to suggest that as he still loved her better than all the world, she would ever be his real wife, and they might see each other frequently. He was not prepared for the storm of indignant emotion his words excited. True, she was his slave; her bones, and sinews had been purchased by his gold, yet she had the heart of a true woman, and hers was a passion too deep and absorbing to admit of partnership, and her spirit was too pure to form a selfish league with crime.

At length this painful interview came to an end. They stood together by the Gothic gate, where they had so often met and parted in the moonlight. Old remembrances melted their souls.

"Farewell, dearest Horatio," said Clotel. "Give me a parting kiss."

Her voice was choked for utterance, and the tears flowed freely, as she bent her lips toward him. He folded her convulsively in his arms, and imprinted a long impassioned kiss on that mouth, which had never spoken to him but in love and blessing. With efforts like a death-pang she at length raised her head from his heaving bosom, and turning from him with bitter sobs, "It is our last. To meet thus is henceforth crime. God bless you. I would not have you so miserable as I am. Farewell. A last farewell."

"The last?" exclaimed he, with a wild shriek. "Oh God, Clotel, do not say that"; and covering his face with his hands, he wept like a child. Recovering from his emotion, he found himself alone. The moon looked down upon him mild, but very sorrowfully; as the Madonna seems to gaze upon her worshipping children, bowed down with consciousness of sin. At that moment he would have given worlds to have disengaged himself from Gertrude, but he had gone so far, that blame, disgrace, and duels with angry relatives would now attend any effort to obtain his freedom. Oh, how the moonlight oppressed him with its friendly sadness! It was like the plaintive eye of his forsaken one, like the music of sorrow echoed from an unseen world. Long and earnestly he gazed at that cottage, where he had so long known earth's purest foretaste of heavenly bliss. Slowly he walked away; then turned again to look on that charmed spot, the nestling-place of his early affections. He caught a glimpse of Clotel, weeping beside a magnolia, which commanded a long view of the path leading to the public road. He would have sprung toward her but she darted from him, and entered the cottage. That graceful figure, weeping in the moonlight, haunted him for years. It stood before his closing eyes, and greeted him with the morning dawn. Poor Gertrude, had she known all, what a dreary lot would hers have been; but fortunately she could not miss the impassioned tenderness she never experienced; and Horatio was the more careful in his kindness, because he was deficient in love. After Clotel had been separated from her mother and sister, she turned her attention to the subject of Christianity, and received that consolation from her Bible that is never denied to the children of God. Although it was against the laws of Virginia, for a slave to be taught to read, Currer had employed an old free Negro, who lived near her, to teach her two daughters to read and write. She felt that the step she had taken in resolving never to meet Horatio again would no doubt expose her to his wrath, and probably cause her to be sold, yet her heart was too guileless for her to commit a crime, and therefore she had ten times rather have been sold as a slave than do wrong. Some months after the marriage of Horatio and Gertrude their barouche rolled along a winding road that skirted the forest near Clotel's cottage, when the attention of Gertrude was suddenly attracted by two figures among the trees by the wayside; and touching Horatio's arm, she exclaimed, "Do look at that beautiful child." He turned and saw Clotel and Mary. His lips quivered, and his face became deadly pale. His young wife looked at him intently, but said nothing. In returning home, he took another road; but his wife seeing this, expressed a wish to go back the way they had come. He objected, and suspicion was awakened in her heart, and she soon after learned that the mother of that lovely child bore the name of Clotel, a name which she had often heard Horatio murmur in uneasy slumbers. From gossiping tongues she soon learned more than she wished to know. She wept, but not as poor Clotel had done; for she never had loved, and been beloved like her, and her nature was more proud: henceforth a change came over her feelings and her manners, and Horatio had no further occasion to assume a tenderness in return for hers. Changed as he was by ambition, he felt the wintry chill of her polite propriety, and sometimes, in agony of heart, compared it with the gushing love of her who was indeed his wife. But these and all his emotions were a sealed book to Clotel, of which she could only guess the contents. With remittances for her and her child's support, there sometimes came earnest pleadings that she would consent to see him again; but these she never answered, though her heart yearned to do so. She pitied his young bride, and would not be tempted to bring sorrow into her household by any fault of hers. Her earnest prayer was, that she might not know of her existence. She had not looked on Horatio since she watched him under the shadow of the magnolia, until his barouche passed her in her rambles some months after. She saw the deadly paleness of his countenance, and had he dared to look back, he would have seen her tottering with faintness. Mary brought water from a rivulet, and sprinkled her face. When she revived, she clasped the beloved child to her heart with a vehemence that made her scream. Soothingly she kissed away her fears, and gazed into her beautiful eyes with a deep, deep sadness of expression, which poor Mary never forgot. Wild were the thoughts that passed round her aching heart, and almost maddened her poor brain; thoughts which had almost driven her to suicide the night of that last farewell. For her child's sake she had conquered the fierce temptation then; and for her sake, she struggled with it now. But the gloomy atmosphere of their once happy home overclouded the morning of Mary's life. Clotel perceived this, and it gave her unutterable pain.

> "Tis ever thus with woman's love,
>   True till life's storms have passed;
> And, like the vine around the tree,
>   It braves them to the last."

*   *   *

CHAPTER XXV
DEATH IS FREEDOM

> "I asked but freedom, and ye gave
> Chains, and the freedom of the grave."
>
>   —Snelling

There are, in the District of Columbia, several slave prisons, or "negro pens," as they are termed. These prisons are mostly occupied by persons to keep their slaves in, when collecting their gangs together for the New Orleans market. Some of them belong to the government, and one, in particular, is noted for having been the place where a number of free coloured persons have been incarcerated from time to time. In this district is situated the capital of the United States. Any free coloured persons visiting Washington, if not provided with papers asserting and proving their right to be free, may be arrested and placed in one of these dens. If they succeed in showing that they are free, they are set at liberty, provided they are able to pay the expenses of their arrest and imprisonment; if they cannot pay these expenses, they are sold out. Through this unjust and oppressive law, many persons born in the Free States have been consigned to a life of slavery on the cotton, sugar, or rice plantations of the Southern States. By order of her master, Clotel was removed from Richmond and placed in one of these prisons, to await the sailing of a vessel for New Orleans. The prison in which she was put stands midway between the capitol at Washington and the President's house. Here the fugitive saw nothing but slaves brought in and taken out, to be placed in ships and sent away to the same part of the country to which she herself would soon be compelled to go. She had seen or heard nothing of her daughter while in Richmond, and all hope of seeing her now had fled. If she was carried back to New Orleans, she could expect no mercy from her master.

At the dusk of the evening previous to the day when she was to be sent off, as the old prison was being closed for the night, she suddenly darted past her keeper, and ran for her life. It is not a great distance from the prison to the Long Bridge, which passes from the lower part of the city across the Potomac, to the extensive forests and woodlands of the celebrated Arlington Place, occupied by that distinguished relative and descendant of the immortal Washington, Mr. George W. Custis. Thither the poor fugitive directed her flight. So unexpected was her escape, that she had quite a number of rods the start before the keeper had secured the other prisoners, and rallied his assistants in pursuit. It was at an hour when, and in a part of the city where, horses could not be readily obtained for the chase; no bloodhounds were at hand to run down the flying woman; and for once it seemed as though there was to be a fair trial of speed and endurance between the slave and the slave-catchers. The keeper and his forces raised the hue and cry on her pathway close behind; but so rapid was the flight along the wide avenue, that the astonished citizens, as they poured forth from their dwellings to learn the cause of alarm, were only able to comprehend the nature of the case in time to fall in with the motley mass in pursuit, (as many a one did that night,) to raise an anxious prayer to heaven, as they refused to join in the pursuit, that the panting fugitive might escape, and the merciless soul dealer for once be disappointed of his prey. And now with the speed of an arrow—having passed the avenue—with the distance between her and her pursuers constantly increasing, this poor hunted female gained the *"Long Bridge,"* as it is called, where interruption seemed improbable, and already did her heart begin to beat high with the hope of success. She had only to pass three-fourths of a mile across the bridge, and she could bury herself in a vast forest, just at the time when the curtain of night would close around her, and protect her from the pursuit of her enemies.

But God by his Providence had otherwise determined. He had determined that an appalling tragedy should be enacted that night, within plain sight of the President's house and the capitol of the Union, which should be an evidence wherever it should be known, of the unconquerable love of liberty the heart may inherit; as well as a fresh admonition to the slave dealer, of the cruelty and enormity of his crimes. Just as the pursuers crossed the high draw for the passage of sloops, soon after entering upon the bridge, they beheld three men slowly approaching from the Virginia side. They immediately called to them to arrest the fugitive, whom they proclaimed a runaway slave. True to their Virginian instincts as she came near, they formed in line across the narrow bridge, and prepared to seize her. Seeing escape impossible in that quarter, she stopped suddenly, and turned upon her pursuers. On came the profane and ribald crew, faster than ever, already exulting in her capture, and threatening punishment for her flight. For a moment she looked wildly and anxiously around to see if there was no hope of escape. On either hand, far down below, rolled the deep foamy waters of the Potomac, and before and behind the rapidly approaching step and noisy voices of pursuers, showing how vain would be any further effort for freedom. Her resolution was taken. She clasped her *hands* convulsively, and raised *them*, as she at the same time raised her *eyes* towards heaven, and begged for that mercy and compassion *there*, which had been denied her on earth; and then, with a single bound, she vaulted over the railings of the bridge, and sunk for ever beneath the waves of the river!

Thus died Clotel, the daughter of Thomas Jefferson, a president of the United States; a man distinguished as the author of the Declaration of American Independence, and one of the first statesmen of that country.

Had Clotel escaped from oppression in any other land, in the disguise in which she fled from the Mississippi to Richmond, and reached the United States, no honour within the gift of the American people would have been too good to have been heaped upon the heroic woman. But she was a slave, and therefore out of the pale of their sympathy. They have tears to shed over Greece and Poland; they have an abundance of sympathy for "poor Ireland"; they can furnish a ship of war to convey the Hungarian refugees from a Turkish prison to the "land of the free and home of the brave." They boast that America is the "cradle of liberty;" if it is, I fear they have rocked the child to death. The body of Clotel was picked up from the bank of the river, where it had been washed by the strong current, a hole dug in the sand, and there deposited, without either inquest being held over it, or religious service being performed. Such was the life and such the death of a woman whose virtues and goodness of heart would have done honour to one in a higher station of life, and who, if she had been born in any other land but that of slavery, would have been honoured and loved. A few days after the death of Clotel, the following poem appeared in one of the newspapers:

"Now, rest for the wretched! the long day is past,
And night on yon prison descendeth at last.
Now lock up and bolt! Ha, jailor, look there!
Who flies like a wild bird escaped from the snare?
    A woman, a slave—up, out in pursuit,
        While linger some gleams of day!
        Let thy call ring out!—now a rabble rout
    Is at thy heels—speed away!

"A bold race for freedom!—On, fugitive, on!
Heaven help but the right, and thy freedom is won.
How eager she drinks the free air of the plains;
Every limb, every nerve, every fibre she strains;
    From Columbia's glorious capitol,
      Columbia's daughter flees
    To the sanctuary God has given—
      The sheltering forest trees.

"Now she treads the Long Bridge—joy lighteth her eye—
Beyond her the dense wood and darkening sky—
Wild hopes thrill her heart as she neareth the shore:
O, despair! there are *men* fast advancing before!
    Shame, shame on their manhood! they hear, they heed
      The cry, her flight to stay,
    And like demon forms with their outstretched arms,
      They wait to seize their prey!

"She pauses, she turns! Ah, will she flee back?
Like wolves, her pursuers howl loud on their track;
She lifteth to Heaven one look of despair—
Her anguish breaks forth in one hurried prayer—
    Hark! her jailor's yell! like a bloodhound's bay
      On the low night wind it sweeps!
    Now, death or the chain! to the stream she turns,
      And she leaps! O God, she leaps!

"The dark and the cold, yet merciful wave,
Receives to its bosom the form of the slave:
She rises—earth's scenes on her dim vision gleam,
Yet she struggleth not with the strong rushing stream:
    And low are the death-cries her woman's heart gives,
      As she floats adown the river,
    Faint and more faint grows the drowning voice,
      And her cries have ceased for ever!

"Now back, jailor, back to thy dungeons, again,
To swing the red lash and rivet the chain!
The form thou would'st fetter—returned to its God;
    The universe holdeth no realm of night
      More drear than her slavery—
    More merciless fiends than here stayed her flight—
      Joy! the hunted slave is free!

"That bond-woman's corse—let Potomac's proud wave
Go bear it along *by our Washington's grave*,
And heave it high up on that hallowed strand,
To tell of the freedom he won for our land.
    A weak woman's corse, by freemen chased down;

Hurrah for our country! hurrah!
To freedom she leaped, through drowning and death—
Hurrah for our country! hurrah!"

FRANCES E. W. HARPER

Frances E. W. Harper (1825–1911) was an activist, lecturer, poet, and writer. *Iola Leroy*, one of the first African American novels written by a woman, tells the sentimental story of Iola's discovery that her mother was her father's slave and that she is therefore black, not white; Iola is forced back into slavery but quickly gains her freedom and refuses to marry a white doctor and pass as a white woman, choosing instead a black husband, mulatto Dr. Latimer, and a life of service to the black race. Iola's brother, Harry, similarly marries within "his" race, choosing the college-educated teacher, Miss Delany.

From Iola Leroy; or, Shadows Uplifted†

CHAPTER XII
SCHOOL-GIRL NOTIONS

During Iola's stay in the North she found a strong tide of opposition against slavery. Arguments against the institution had entered the Church and made legislative halls the arenas of fierce debate. The subject had become part of the social converse of the fireside, and had enlisted the best brain and heart of the country. Anti-slavery discussions were pervading the strongest literature and claiming a place on the most popular platforms.

Iola, being a Southern girl and a slave-holder's daughter, always defended slavery when it was under discussion.

"Slavery can't be wrong," she would say, "for my father is a slave-holder, and my mother is as good to our servants as she can be. My father often tells her that she spoils them, and lets them run over her. I never saw my father strike one of them. I love my mammy as much as I do my own mother, and I believe she loves us just as if we were her own children. When we are sick I am sure that she could not do anything more for us than she does."

"But, Iola," responded one of her school friends, "after all, they are not free. Would you be satisfied to have the most beautiful home, the costliest jewels, or the most elegant wardrobe if you were a slave?"

---

† From Frances E. W. Harper, *Iola Leroy; or, Shadows Uplifted* (Boston: Beacon Press, 1987, pp. 97–109; orig. publ. Philadelphia: Garrigues Brothers, 1893).

"Oh, the cases are not parallel. Our slaves do not want their freedom. They would not take it if we gave it to them."

"That is not the case with them all. My father has seen men who have encountered almost incredible hardships to get their freedom. Iola, did you ever attend an anti-slavery meeting?"

"No; I don't think these Abolitionists have any right to meddle in our affairs. I believe they are prejudiced against us, and want to get our property. I read about them in the papers when I was at home. I don't want to hear my part of the country run down. My father says the slaves would be very well contented if no one put wrong notions in their heads."

"I don't know," was the response of her friend, "but I do not think that that slave mother who took her four children, crossed the Ohio River on the ice, killed one of the children and attempted the lives of the other two, was a contented slave. And that other one, who, running away and finding herself pursued, threw herself over the Long Bridge into the Potomac, was evidently not satisfied. I do not think the numbers who are coming North on the Underground Railroad can be very contented. It is not natural for people to run away from happiness, and if they are so happy and contented, why did Congress pass the Fugitive Slave Bill?"

"Well, I don't think," answered Iola, "any of our slaves would run away. I know mamma don't like slavery very much. I have often heard her say that she hoped the time would come when there would not be a slave in the land. My father does not think as she does. He thinks slavery is not wrong if you treat them well and don't sell them from their families. I intend, after I have graduated, to persuade pa to buy a house in New Orleans, and spend the winter there. You know this will be my first season out, and I hope that you will come and spend the winter with me. We will have such gay times, and you will so fall in love with our sunny South that you will never want to come back to shiver amid the snows and cold of the North. I think one winter in the South would cure you of your Abolitionism."

"Have you seen her yet?"

This question was asked by Louis Bastine, an attorney who had come North in the interests of Lorraine. The scene was the New England village where Mr. Galen's academy was located, and which Iola was attending. This question was addressed to Camille Lecroix, Bastine's intimate friend, who had lately come North. He was the son of a planter who lived near Leroy's plantation, and was familiar with Iola's family history. Since his arrival North, Bastine had met him and communicated to him his intentions.

"Yes; just caught a glimpse of her this morning as she was going down the street," was Camille's reply.

"She is a most beautiful creature," said Louis Bastine. "She has the proud poise of Leroy, the most splendid eyes I ever saw in a woman's head, lovely complexion, and a glorious wealth of hair. She would bring $2000 any day in a New Orleans market."

"I always feel sorry," said Camille, "when I see one of those Creole girls brought to the auction block. I have known fathers who were deeply devoted to their daughters, but who through some reverse of fortune were forced to part with them, and I always think the blow has been equally terrible on both sides. I had a friend who had two beautiful daughters whom he had educated in the North. They were cultured, and really belles in society. They were entirely ignorant of their lineage, but when their father died it was discovered that their mother had been a slave. It was a fearful blow. They would have faced poverty, but the knowledge of their tainted blood was more than they could bear."

"What became of them?"

"They both died, poor girls. I believe they were as much killed by the blow as if they had been shot. To tell you the truth, Bastine, I feel sorry for this girl. I don't believe she has the least idea of her negro blood."

"No, Leroy has been careful to conceal it from her," replied Bastine.

"Is that so?" queried Camille. "Then he has made a great mistake."

"I can't help that," said Bastine; "business is business."

"How can you get her away?" asked Camille. "You will have to be very cautious, because if these pesky Abolitionists get an inkling of what you're doing they will balk your game double quick. And when you come to look at it, isn't it a shame to attempt to reduce that girl to slavery? She is just as white as we are, as good as any girl in the land, and better educated than thousands of white girls. A girl with her apparent refinement and magnificent beauty, were it not for the cross in her blood, I would be proud to introduce to our set. She would be the sensation of the season. I believe to-day it would be easier for me to go to the slums and take a young girl from there, and have her introduced as my wife, than to have society condone the offense if I married that lovely girl. There is not a social circle in the South that would not take it as a gross insult to have her introduced into it."

"Well," said Bastine, "my plan is settled. Leroy has never allowed her to spend her vacations at home. I understand she is now very anxious to get home, and, as Lorraine's attorney, I have come on his account to take her home."

"How will you do it?"

"I shall tell her her father is dangerously ill, and desires her to come as quickly as possible."

"And what then?"

"Have her inventoried with the rest of the property."

"Don't she know that her father is dead?"

"I think not," said Bastine." "She is not in mourning, but appeared very light-hearted this morning, laughing and talking with two other girls. I was struck with her great beauty, and asked a gentleman who she was. He said, 'Miss Leroy, of Mississippi.' I think Lorraine has managed the affair so as to keep her in perfect ignorance of her father's death. I don't like the job, but I never let sentiment interfere with my work."

Poor Iola! When she said slavery was not a bad thing, little did she think that she was destined to drink to its bitter dregs the cup she was so ready to press to the lips of others.

"How do you think she will take to her situation?" asked Camille.

"O, I guess," said Bastine, "she will sulk and take it pretty hard at first; but if she is managed right she will soon get over it. Give her plenty of jewelry, fine clothes, and an easy time."

"All this business must be conducted with the utmost secrecy and speed. Her mother could not have written to her, for she has been suffering with brain fever and nervous prostration since Leroy's death, Lorraine knows her market value too well, and is too shrewd to let so much property pass out of his hands without making an effort to retain it."

"Has she any brothers or sisters?"

"Yes, a brother," replied Bastine; "but he is at another school, and I have no orders from Lorraine in reference to him. If I can get the girl I am willing to let well enough alone. I dread the interview with the principal more than anything else. I am afraid he will hem and haw, and have his doubts. Perhaps, when he sees my letters and hears my story, I can pull the wool over his eyes."

"But, Louis, this is a pitiful piece of business. I should hate to be engaged in it."

A deep flush of shame overspread for a moment the face of Lorraine's attorney, as he replied: "I don't like the job, but I have undertaken it, and must go through with it."

"I see no 'must' about it. Were I in your place I would wash my hands of the whole business."

"I can't afford it," was Bastine's hard, business-like reply. On the next morning after this conversation between these two young men, Louis Bastine presented himself to the principal of the academy, with the request that Iola be permitted to leave immediately to attend the sick-bed of her father, who was dangerously ill. The principal hesitated, but while he was deliberating, a telegram, purporting to come from Iola's mother, summoned Iola to her father's bedside without delay. The principal, set at rest in regard to the truthfulness of the dispatch, not only permitted but expedited her departure.

Iola and Bastine took the earliest train, and traveled without pausing until they reached a large hotel in a Southern city. There they were obliged to wait a few hours until they could resume their journey, the train having failed to make connection. Iola sat in a large, lonely parlor, waiting for the servant to show her to a private room. She had never known a great sorrow. Never before had the shadows of death mingled with the sunshine of her life.

Anxious, travel-worn, and heavy-hearted, she sat in an easy chair, with nothing to divert her from the grief and anxiety which rendered every delay a source of painful anxiety.

"Oh, I hope that he will be alive and growing better!" was the thought which kept constantly revolving in her mind, until she fell asleep. In her dreams she was at home, encircled in the warm clasp of her father's arms, feeling her mother's kisses lingering on her lips, and hearing the joyous greetings of the servants and Mammy Liza's glad welcome as she folded her to her heart. From this dream of bliss she was awakened by a burning kiss pressed on her lips, and a strong arm encircling her. Gazing around and taking in the whole situation, she sprang from her seat, her eyes flashing with rage and scorn, her face flushed to the roots of her hair, her voice shaken with excitement, and every nerve trembling with angry emotion.

"How dare you do such a thing! Don't you know if my father were here he would crush you to the earth?"

"Not so fast, my lovely tigress," said Bastine, "your father knew what he was doing when he placed you in my charge."

"My father made a great mistake, if he thought he had put me in charge of a gentleman."

"I am your guardian for the present," replied Bastine. "I am to see you safe home, and then my commission ends."

"I wish it were ended now," she exclaimed, trembling with anger and mortification. Her voice was choked by emotion, and broken by smothered sobs. Louis Bastine thought to himself, "she is a real spitfire, but beautiful even in her wrath."

During the rest of her journey Iola preserved a most freezing reserve towards Bastine. At length the journey was ended. Pale and anxious she rode up the avenue which led to her home.

A strange silence pervaded the place. The servants moved sadly from place to place, and spoke in subdued tones. The windows were heavily draped with crape, and a funeral air pervaded the house.

Mammy Liza met her at the door, and, with streaming eyes and convulsive sobs, folded her to her heart, as Iola exclaimed, in tones of hopeless anguish:——

"Oh, papa's dead!"

"Oh, my pore baby!" said mammy, "ain't you hearn tell 'bout it? Yore par's dead, an' your mar's bin drefful sick. She's better now."

Mam Liza stepped lightly into Mrs. Leroy's room, and gently apprised her of Iola's arrival. In a darkened room lay the stricken mother, almost distracted by her late bereavement.

"Oh, Iola," she exclaimed, as her daughter entered, "is this you? I am so sorry you came."

Then, burying her head in Iola's bosom, she wept convulsively. "Much as I love you," she continued, between her sobs, "and much as I longed to see you, I am sorry you came."

"Why, mother," replied Iola, astonished, "I received your telegram last Wednesday, and I took the earliest train I could get."

"My dear child, I never sent you a telegram. It was a trick to bring you down South and reduce you to slavery."

Iola eyed her mother curiously. What did she mean? Had grief dethroned her reason? Yet her eye was clear, her manner perfectly rational.

Marie saw the astounded look on Iola's face, and nerving herself to the task, said: "Iola, I must tell you what your father always enjoined me to be silent about. I did not think it was the wisest thing, but I yielded to his desires. I have negro blood in my veins. I was your father's slave before I married him. His relatives have set aside his will. The courts have declared our marriage null and void and my manumission illegal, and we are all to be remanded to slavery."

An expression of horror and anguish swept over Iola's face, and, turning deathly pale, she exclaimed, "Oh, mother, it can't be so! you must be dreaming!"

"No, my child; it is a terrible reality."

Almost wild with agony, Iola paced the floor, as the fearful truth broke in crushing anguish upon her mind.

Then bursting into a paroxysm of tears succeeded by peals of hysterical laughter, said:—

"I used to say that slavery is right. I didn't know what I was talking about." Then growing calmer, she said, "Mother, who is at the bottom of this downright robbery?"

"Alfred Lorraine; I have always dreaded that man, and what I feared has come to pass. Your father had faith in him; I never had."

"But, mother, could we not contest his claim. You have your marriage certificate and papa's will."

"Yes, my dear child, but Judge Starkins has decided that we have no standing in the court, and no testimony according to law."

"Oh, mother, what can I do?"

"Nothing, my child, unless you can escape to the North."

"And leave you?"

"Yes."

"Mother, I will never desert you in your hour of trial. But can nothing be done? Had father no friends who would assist us?"

"None that I know of. I do not think he had an acquaintance who approved of our marriage. The neighboring planters have stood so aloof from me that I do not know where to turn for either help or sympathy. I believe it was Lorraine who sent the telegram. I wrote to you as soon as I could after your father's death, but fainted just as I finished directing the letter. I do not think he knows where your brother is, and, if possible, he must not know. If you can by any means, *do* send a letter to Harry and warn him not to attempt to come home. I don't know how you will succeed, for Lorraine has us all under surveillance. But it is according to law."

"What law, mother?"

"The law of the strong against the weak."

"Oh, mother, it seems like a dreadful dream, a fearful nightmare! But I cannot shake it off. Where is Gracie?"

"The dear child has been running down ever since her papa's death. She clung to me night and day while I had the brain fever, and could not be persuaded to leave me. She hardly ate anything for more than a week. She has been dangerously ill for several days, and the doctor says she cannot live. The fever has exhausted all her rallying power, and yet, dear as she is to me, I would rather consign her to the deepest grave than see her forced to be a slave."

"So would I. I wish I could die myself."

"Oh, Iola, do not talk so. Strive to be a Christian, to have faith in the darkest hour. Were it not for my hope of heaven I couldn't stand all this trouble."

"Mother, are these people Christians who made these laws which are robbing us of our inheritance and reducing us to slavery? If this is Christianity I hate and despise it. Would the most cruel heathen do worse?"

"My dear child, I have not learned my Christianity from them. I have learned it at the foot of the cross, and from this book," she said, placing a New Testament in Iola's hands. "Some of the most beautiful lessons of faith and trust I have ever learned were from among our lowly people in their humble cabins."

"Mamma!" called a faint voice from the adjoining room. Marie immediately arose and went to the bedside of her sick child, where Mammy Liza was holding her faithful vigils. The child had just awakened from a fitful sleep.

"I thought," she said, "that I heard Iola's voice. Has she come?"

"Yes, darling; do you want to see her?"

"Oh, yes," she said, as a bright smile broke over her dying features.

Iola passed quickly into the room. Gracie reached out her thin, bloodless hand, clasped Iola's palm in hers, and said: "I am so glad you have come. Dear Iola, stand by mother. You and Harry are all she has. It is not hard to die. You and mother and Harry must meet me in heaven."

Swiftly the tidings went through the house that Gracie was dying. The servants gathered around her with tearful eyes, as she bade them all good-bye. When she had finished, and Mammy had lowered the pillow, an unwonted radiance lit up her eye, and an expression of ineffable gladness overspread her face, as she murmured: "It is beautiful, so beautiful!" Fainter and fainter grew her voice, until, without a struggle or sigh, she passed away beyond the power of oppression and prejudice.

* * *

WILLIAM DEAN HOWELLS

Journalist, autobiographer, essayist, travel writer, biographer, magazine editor, short-story writer, and prolific novelist, William Dean Howells (1837–1920) was often called the "Dean of American Realism" and the following excerpt from *An Imperative Duty,* which depicts Rhoda, the female character, in her attempt to reconcile herself to the new knowledge of her black race and its consequences for her domestic future, represents a dual attention to both social history and human psychology characteristic of Howells's work.

From An Imperative Duty†

* * *

I could never have married him—and that when he arrives we shall be gone, and he must never try to see me again. I've told you all that you could ask, Aunt Caroline, and now there is one thing I want you to answer me. Is there any one else who knows this?"

"No, indeed, child!" answered Mrs. Meredith instantly, and she thought for the instant that she was telling the truth. "Not another living soul. No one ever knew but your uncle—"

"Be careful, Aunt Caroline," said the girl, coming up to her sofa, and looking gloomily down upon her. "You had better always tell me the truth, now. Have you told no one else?"

"No one."

"Not Dr. Olney?"

It was too late, now that Mrs. Meredith perceived her error. She could not draw back from it, and say that she had forgotten; Rhoda would never believe that. She could only say, "No, not Dr. Olney."

† From William Dean Howells, *The Shadow of a Dream* and *An Imperative Duty* (Bloomington: Indiana University Press, 1970, pp. 56–63; orig. publ. New York: Harper & Brothers, Franklin Square, 1891).

"Tell me the truth, if you expect ever to see me again, in this world or the next. Is it the truth? Swear it!"

"It is the truth," said the poor woman, feeling this new and astonishing lie triply riveted upon her soul; and she sank down upon the pillow from which she had partly lifted herself, and lay there as if crushed under the burden suddenly rolled back upon her.

"Then I forgive you," said the girl, stooping down to kiss her.

The woman pushed her feebly away. "Oh, I don't want your forgiveness, now," she whimpered, and she began to cry.

Rhoda made no answer, but turned and went out of the room.

Mrs. Meredith lay exhausted. She was no longer hungry, but she was weak for want of food. After a while she slid from the sofa, and then on her hands and knees she crept to the table where the bottle that held Dr. Olney's sleeping medicine stood. She drank it all off. She felt the need of escaping from herself; she did not believe it would kill her; but she must escape at any risk. So men die who mean to take their lives; but it is not certain that death even is an escape from ourselves.

VIII

In the street where Rhoda found herself the gas was already palely burning in the shops, and the moony glare of an electric globe was invading the flush of the sunset whose after-glow still filled the summer air in the western perspective. She did not know where she was going, but she went that way, down the slope of the slightly curving thoroughfare. She had the letter which she meant to post in her hand, but she passed the boxes on the lamp-posts without putting it in. She no longer knew what she meant to do, in any sort, or what she desired; but out of the turmoil of horror, which she whirled round and round in, some purpose that seemed at first exterior to herself began to evolve. The street was one where she would hardly have met ladies of the sort she had always supposed herself of; gentility fled it long ago, and the houses that had once been middle-class houses had fallen in the social scale to the grade of mechanics' lodgings, and the shops, which had never been fashionable, were adapted strictly to the needs of a neighborhood of poor and humble people. They were largely provision stores, full of fruit, especially watermelons; there were some groceries, and some pharmacies of that professional neatness which pharmacies are of everywhere. The roadway was at this hour pretty well deserted by the express wagons and butcher carts that bang through it in the earlier day; and the horse-cars, coming and going on its incline and its final westward level, were in the unrestricted enjoyment of the company's monopoly of the best part of its space.

At the first corner Rhoda had to find her way through groups of intense-faced suburbans who were waiting for their respective cars, and who heaped themselves on board as these arrived, and hurried to find places, more from force of habit than from necessity, for the pressure of the evening travel was already over. When she had passed these groups she began to meet the proper life of the street—the women who had come out to cheapen the next day's provisions at the markets, the men, in the brief leisure that their day's work had left them before bedtime, lounging at the lattice doors of the drinking shops, or standing listlessly about on the curb-stones smoking. Numbers of young fellows, of the sort whose leisure is day-long, exchanged the comfort of a mutual support with the house walls, and stared at her as she hurried by; and then she began to encounter in greater and greater number the colored people who descended to this popular promenade from the uphill streets opening upon it. They politely made way for her, and at the first meeting that new agony of interest in them possessed her.

This was intensified by the deference they paid her as a young white lady, and the instant sense that she had no right to it in that quality. She could have borne better to have them rude and even insolent; there was something in the way they turned their black eyes in their large disks of white upon her, like dogs, with a mute animal appeal in them, that seemed to claim her and own her one of them, and to creep nearer and nearer and nearer and possess her in that late-found solidarity of race. She never knew before how hideous they were, with their flat wide-nostriled noses, their out-rolled thick lips, their mobile, bulging eyes set near together, their retreating chins and foreheads, and their smooth, shining skin; they seemed burlesques of humanity, worse than apes, because they were more like. But the men were not half so bad as the women, from the shrill-piped young girls, with their grotesque attempts at fashion, to the old grandmothers, wrinkled or obese, who came down the sloping sidewalks in their bare heads, out of the courts and alleys where they lived, to get the evening air. Impish black children swarmed on these uphill sidewalks, and played their games, with shrill cries racing back and forth, catching and escaping one another.

These colored folk were of all tints and types, from the comedy of the pure black to the closest tragical approach to white. She saw one girl, walking with a cloud of sable companions, who was as white as herself, and she wondered if she were of the same dilution of negro blood; she was laughing and chattering with the rest, and seemed to feel no difference, but to be pleased and flattered with the court paid her by the inky dandy who sauntered beside her.

"She has always known it; she has never felt it!" she thought, bitterly. "It is nothing; it is natural to her; I might have been like her."

She began to calculate how many generations would carry her back, or that girl back, in hue to the blackest of those loathsome old women. She knew what an octoroon was, and she thought, "I am like her, and my mother was darker, and my grandmother darker, and my great-grander like a mulatto, and then it was a horrible old negress, a savage stolen from Africa, where she had been a cannibal."

A vision of palm-tree roofs and grass huts, as she had seen them in pictures, with skulls grinning from the eaves, floated before her eyes; then a desert, with a long coffle of captives passing by, and one black naked woman, fallen out from weakness, kneeling, with manacled hands, and her head pulled back, and the Arab slaver's knife at her throat. She walked in a nightmare of these sights; all the horror of the wrong by which she came to be, poured itself round and over her.

She emerged from it at moments with a refusal to accept the loss of her former self: like that of the mutilated man who looks where his arm was, and cannot believe it gone. Like him, she had the full sense of what was lost, the unbroken consciousness of what was lopped away. At these moments, all her pride reasserted itself; she wished to punish her aunt for what she had made her suffer, to make her pay pang for pang. Then the tide of reality overwhelmed her again, and she grovelled in self-loathing and despair. From that she rose in a frenzy of longing to rid herself of this shame that was not hers; to tear out the stain; to spill it with the last drop of her blood upon the ground. By flamy impulses she thrilled towards the mastery of her misery through its open acknowledgment. She seemed to see herself and hear herself stopping some of these revolting creatures, the dreadfulest of them, and saying, "I am black, too. Take me home with you, and let me live with you, and be like you every way." She thought, "Perhaps I have relations among them. Yes, it must be. I will send to the hotel for my things, and I will live here in some dirty little back court, and try to find them out."

The emotions, densely pressing upon each other, the dramatizations that took place as simultaneously and unsuccessively as the events of a dream, gave her a new measure of time; she compassed the experience of years in the seconds these sensations outnumbered.

All the while she seemed to be walking swiftly, flying forward; but the ground was uneven: it rose before her, and then suddenly fell. She felt her heart beat in the middle of her throat. Her head felt light, like the blowball of a dandelion. She wished to laugh. There seemed two selves of her, one that had lived before that awful knowledge, and one that had lived as long since, and again a third that knew and pitied them both. She wondered at the same time if this were what people meant by saying one's brain was turned; and she recalled the longing with which her aunt said, "If I were *only* crazy!" But she knew that her own exaltation was not madness, and she did not wish for escape that way. "There must be some other," she said to herself; "if I can find the courage for it, I can find the way. It's like a ghost: if I keep going towards it, it won't hurt me; I mustn't be afraid of it. Now, let me see! What *ought* I to do? Yes, that is the key: *Duty*." Then her thought flew passionately off. "If *she* had done her duty all this might have been helped. But it was her cowardice that made her murder me. Yes, she has killed me!"

The tears gushed into her eyes, and all the bitterness of her trial returned upon her, with a pressure of lead on her brain.

In the double consciousness of trouble she was as fully aware of everything about her as she was of the world of misery within her; and she knew that this had so far shown itself without that some of the passers were noticing her. She stopped, fearful of their notice, at the corner of the street she had come to, and turned about to confront an old colored woman, yellow like saffron, with the mild, sad face we often see in mulattoes of that type, and something peculiarly pitiful in the straight underlip of her appealing mouth, and the cast of her gentle eyes. The expression might have been merely physical, or it might have been a hereditary look, and no part of her own personality, but Rhoda felt safe in it.

"What street is this?" she asked, thinking, suddenly, "She is the color of my grandmother; that is the way she looked," but though she thought this she did not realize it, and she kept an imperious attitude towards the old woman.

"Charles Street, lady."

"Oh, yes; Charles. Where are all the people going?"

"The colored folks, lady?"

"Yes."

"Well, lady, they's a kyind of an evenin' meetin' at ouah choach tonight. Some of 'em's goin' there, I reckon; some of 'em's just out fo' a walk."

"Will you let me go with you?" Rhoda asked.

"Why, certainly, lady," said the old woman. She glanced up at Rhoda's face as the girl turned again to accompany her. "But *I'm* a-goin' to choach."

"Yes, yes. That's what I mean. I want to go to your church with you. Are you from the South—Louisiana? She would be the color," she thought. "It might be my mother's own mother."

"No, lady: from Voginny. I was bawn a slave; and I lived there till after the wa'. Then I come Nawth."

"Oh," said Rhoda, disappointedly, for she had nerved herself to find this old woman her grandmother.

They walked on in silence for a while; then the old woman said, "I thought you wasn't very well, when I noticed you at the cawnah."

"I am well," Rhoda answered, feeling the tears start to her eyes again at the note of motherly kindness in the old woman's voice. "But I am in trouble; I am in trouble."

"Then you're gwine to the right place, lady," said the old woman, and she repeated solemnly these words of hope and promise which so many fainting hearts have stayed themselves upon: " 'Come unto me, all ye that labor and are heavy laden and I will give you rest unto your souls.' Them's the words, lady; the Lawd's own words. Glory be to God; glory be to God!" she added in a whisper.

"Yes, yes," said Rhoda, impatiently. "They are good words. But they are not for me. He can't make *my* burden light; He can't give *me* rest. If it were sin, He could; but it isn't sin; it's something worse than sin; more hopeless. If I were only a sinner, the vilest, the wickedest, how glad I should be!" Her heart uttered itself to this simple nature as freely as a child's to its mother.

"Why, sholy, lady," said the old woman, with a little shrinking from her as if she had blasphemed, "sholy you's a sinnah?"

"No, I am not!" said the girl, with nervous sharpness. "If I were a sinner, my sin could be forgiven me, and I could go free of my burden. But nothing can ever lift it from me."

"The Lawd kin do anything, the Bible says. He kin make the dead come to life. He done it oncet, too."

The girl turned abruptly on her. "Can He change your skin? Can He make black white?"

The old woman seemed daunted; she faltered. "I don't know as He ever tried, lady; the Bible don't tell." She added, more hopefully, "But I reckon He could do it if He wanted to."

"Then why doesn't He do it?" demanded the girl. "What does He leave you black for, when He could make you white?"

"I reckon He don't think it's worth while, if He can make me *willing to be black* so easy. Somebody's got to be black, and it might as well be me," said the old woman with a meek sigh.

"No, no one need be black!" said Rhoda, with a vehemence that this submissive sigh awakened in her. "If He cared for us, no one would be!"

" 'Sh!" said the old woman, gently.

They had reached the church porch, and Rhoda found herself in the tide of black worshippers who were drifting in. The faces of some were supernaturally solemn, and these rolled their large-whited eyes rebukingly on the young girls showing all their teeth in the smiles that gashed them from ear to ear, and carrying on subdued flirtations with the polite young fellows escorting them. It was no doubt the best colored society, and it was bearing itself with propriety and self-respect in the court of the temple. If their natural gayety and lightness of heart moved their youth to the betrayal of their pleasure in each other in the presence of their Maker, He was perhaps propitiated by the gloom of their elders.

" 'Tain't a regular evenin' meetin'," Rhoda's companion explained to her. "It's a kind o' lecture." She exchanged some stately courtesies of greeting with the old men and women as they pushed into the church; they called her sister, and they looked with at least as little surprise and offence at the beautiful young white lady with her as white Christians would have shown a colored girl come to worship with them. "De preacher's one o' the Southern students; I ain't hud him speak; but I reckon the Lawd's sent him, anyway."

Rhoda had no motive in being where she was except to confront herself as fully and closely with the trouble in her soul as she could. She thought, so far as such willing may be called thinking, that she could strengthen herself for what she had henceforth to bear, if she could concentrate and intensify the fact to her outward perception; she wished densely to surround herself with the blackness from which she had sprung, and to reconcile herself to it, by realizing and owning it with every sense.

✳ ✳ ✳

KATE CHOPIN

Kate Chopin (1851–1904) is the author of the feminist classic *The Awakening* (1899) as well as numerous novels and stories about gender, race, domesticity, and Creole society. "The Father of Désirée's Baby" was first published in *Vogue* Magazine, January 14, 1893: pp. 70ff.

The Father of Désirée's Baby†

As the day was pleasant, Madame Valmondé drove over to L'Abri to see Désirée and the baby.

It made her laugh to think of Désirée with a baby. Why, it seemed but yesterday that Désirée was little more than a baby herself; when Monsieur in riding through the gateway of Valmondé had found her lying asleep in the shadow of the big stone pillar.

The little one awoke in his arms and began to cry for "Dada." That was as much as she could do or say. Some people thought she might

---

† From Werner Sollors, *An Anthology of Interracial Literature: Black-White Contacts in the Old World and the New* (New York: NYU Press, 2004), pp. 431–35.

have strayed there of her own accord, for she was of the toddling age. The prevailing belief was that she had been purposely left by a party of Texans, whose canvas-covered wagon, late in the day, had crossed the ferry that Coton Maïs kept, just below the plantation. In time Madame Valmondé abandoned every speculation but the one that Désirée had been sent to her by a beneficent Providence to be the child of her affection, seeing that she was without child of the flesh. For the girl grew to be beautiful and gentle, affectionate and sincere,—the idol of Valmondé.

It was no wonder, when she stood one day against the stone pillar in whose shadow she had lain asleep, eighteen years before, that Armand Aubigny riding by and seeing her there, had fallen in love with her. That was the way all the Aubignys fell in love, as if struck by a pistol shot. The wonder was that he had not loved her before; for he had known her since his father brought him home from Paris, a boy of eight, after his mother died there. The passion that awoke in him that day, when he saw her at the gate, swept along like an avalanche, or like a prairie fire, or like anything that drives headlong over all obstacles.

Monsieur Valmondé grew practical and wanted things well considered: that is, the girl's obscure origin. Armand looked into her eyes and did not care. He was reminded that she was nameless. What did it matter about a name when he could give her one of the oldest and proudest in Louisiana? He ordered the *corbeille* from Paris, and contained himself with what patience he could until it arrived; then they were married.

Madame Valmondé had not seen Désirée and the baby for four weeks. When she reached L'Abri she shuddered at the first sight of it, as she always did. It was a sad looking place, which for many years had not known the gentle presence of a mistress, old Monsieur Aubigny having married and buried his wife in France, and she having loved her own land too well ever to leave it. The roof came down steep and black like a cowl, reaching out beyond the wide galleries that encircled the yellow stuccoed house. Big, solemn oaks grew close to it, and their thick-leaved, far-reaching branches shadowed it like a pall. Young Aubigny's rule was a strict one, too, and under it his negroes had forgotten how to be gay, as they had been during the old master's easygoing and indulgent lifetime.

The young mother was recovering slowly, and lay full length, in her soft white muslins and laces, upon a couch. The baby was beside her, upon her arm, where he had fallen asleep, at her breast. The yellow[1] nurse woman sat beside a window fanning herself.

Madame Valmondé bent her portly figure over Désirée and kissed

---

1. See p.118, n. 5.

her, holding her an instant tenderly in her arms. Then she turned to the child.

"This is not the baby!" she exclaimed, in startled tones. French was the language spoken at Valmondé in those days.

"I knew you would be astonished," laughed Désirée, "at the way he has grown. The little *cochon de lait!* Look at his legs, mamma, and his hands and fingernails,—real finger-nails. Zandrine had to cut them this morning. Isn't it true, Zandrine?"

The woman bowed her turbaned head majestically, "Mais si, Madame."

"And the way he cries," went on Désirée, "is deafening. Armand heard him the other day as far away as La Blanche's cabin."

Madame Valmondé had never removed her eyes from the child. She lifted it and walked with it over to the window that was lightest. She scanned the baby narrowly, then looked as searchingly at Zandrine, whose face was turned to gaze across the fields.

"Yes, the child has grown, has changed," said Madame Valmondé, slowly, as she replaced it beside its mother. "What does Armand say?"

Désirée's face became suffused with a glow that was happiness itself.

"Oh, Armand is the proudest father in the parish, I believe, chiefly because it is a boy, to bear his name; though he says not,—that he would have loved a girl as well. But I know it isn't true. I know he says that to please me. And mamma," she added, drawing Madame Valmondé's head down to her, and speaking in a whisper, "he hasn't punished one of them—not one of them—since baby is born. Even Négrillon, who pretended to have burnt his leg that he might rest from work—he only laughed, and said Négrillon was a great scamp. Oh, mamma, I'm so happy; it frightens me."

What Désirée said was true. Marriage, and later the birth of his son, had softened Armand Aubigny's imperious and exacting nature greatly. This was what made the gentle Désirée so happy, for she loved him desperately. When he frowned she trembled, but loved him. When he smiled, she asked no greater blessing of God. But Armand's dark, handsome face had not often been disfigured by frowns since the day he fell in love with her.

When the baby was about three months old, Désirée awoke one day to the conviction that there was something in the air menacing her peace. It was at first too subtle to grasp. It had only been a disquieting suggestion; an air of mystery among the blacks; unexpected visits from far-off neighbors who could hardly account for their coming. Then a strange, an awful change in her husband's manner, which she dared not ask him to explain. When he spoke to her, it was with averted eyes, from which the old love-light seemed to have gone out.

He absented himself from home; and when there, avoided her presence and that of her child, without excuse. And the very spirit of Satan seemed suddenly to take hold of him in his dealings with the slaves. Désirée was miserable enough to die.

She sat in her room, one hot afternoon, in her *peignoir*, listlessly drawing through her fingers the strands of her long, silky brown hair that hung about her shoulders. The baby, half naked, lay asleep upon her own great mahogany bed, that was like a sumptuous throne, with its satin-lined half-canopy. One of La Blanche's little quadroon boys—half naked too—stood fanning the child slowly with a fan of peacock feathers. Désirée's eyes had been fixed absently and sadly upon the baby, while she was striving to penetrate the threatening mist that she felt closing about her. She looked from her child to the boy who stood beside him, and back again; over and over. "Ah!" It was a cry that she could not help; which she was not conscious of having uttered. The blood turned like ice in her veins, and a clammy moisture gathered upon her face.

She tried to speak to the little quadroon boy; but no sound would come, at first. When he heard his name uttered, he looked up, and his mistress was pointing to the door. He laid aside the great, soft fan, and obediently stole away, over the polished floor, on his bare tiptoes.

She stayed motionless, with gaze riveted upon her child, and her face the picture of fright.

Presently her husband entered the room, and without noticing her, went to a table and began to search among some papers which covered it.

"Armand," she called to him, in a voice which must have stabbed him, if he was human. But he did not notice. "Armand," she said again. Then she rose and tottered towards him. "Armand," she panted once more, clutching his arm, "look at our child. What does it mean? tell me."

He coldly but gently loosened her fingers from about his arm and thrust the hand away from him. "Tell me what it means!" she cried despairingly.

"It means," he answered lightly, "that the child is not white; it means that you are not white."

A quick conception of all that this accusation meant for her nerved her with unwonted courage to deny it. "It is a lie; it is not true, I am white! Look at my hair, it is brown; and my eyes are gray, Armand, you know they are gray. And my skin is fair," seizing his wrist. "Look at my hand; whiter than yours, Armand," she laughed hysterically.

"As white as La Blanche's," he returned cruelly; and went away leaving her alone with their child.

When she could hold a pen in her hand, she sent a despairing letter to Madame Valmondé.

"My mother, they tell me I am not white. Armand has told me I am not white. For God's sake tell them it is not true. You must know it is not true. I shall die. I must die. I cannot be so unhappy, and live."

The answer that came was as brief:

"My own Désirée: Come home to Valmondé; back to your mother who loves you. Come with your child."

When the letter reached Désirée she went with it to her husband's study, and laid it open upon the desk before which he sat. She was like a stone image: silent, white, motionless after she placed it there.

In silence he ran his cold eyes over the written words. He said nothing. "Shall I go, Armand?" she asked in tones sharp with agonized suspense.

"Yes, go."

"Do you want me to go?"

"Yes, I want you to go."

He thought Almighty God had dealt cruelly and unjustly with him; and felt, somehow, that he was paying Him back in kind when he stabbed thus into his wife's soul. Moreover he no longer loved her, because of the unconscious injury she had brought upon his home and his name.

She turned away like one stunned by a blow, and walked slowly towards the door, hoping he would call her back.

"Good-by, Armand," she moaned.

He did not answer her. That was his last blow at fate.

Désirée went in search of her child. Zandrine was pacing the sombre gallery with it. She took the little one from the nurse's arms with no word of explanation, and descending the steps, walked away, under the live-oak branches.

It was an October afternoon; the sun was just sinking. Out in the still fields the negroes were picking cotton.

Désirée had not changed the thin white garment nor the slippers which she wore. Her hair was uncovered and the sun's rays brought a golden gleam from its brown meshes. She did not take the broad, beaten road which led to the far-off plantation of Valmondé. She walked across a deserted field, where the stubble bruised her tender feet, so delicately shod, and tore her thin gown to shreds.

She disappeared among the reeds and willows that grew thick along the banks of the deep, sluggish bayou; and she did not come back again.

Some weeks later there was a curious scene enacted at L'Abri. In the centre of the smoothly swept back yard was a great bonfire. Armand

Aubigny sat in the wide hallway that commanded a view of the spectacle; and it was he who dealt out to a half dozen negroes the material which kept this fire ablaze.

A graceful cradle of willow, with all its dainty furbishings, was laid upon the pyre, which had already been fed with the richness of a priceless *layette*. Then there were silk gowns, and velvet and satin ones added to these; laces, too, and embroideries; bonnets and gloves; for the *corbeille* had been of rare quality.

The last thing to go was a tiny bundle of letters; innocent little scribblings that Désirée had sent to him during the days of their espousal. There was the remnant of one back in the drawer from which he took them. But it was not Désirée's; it was part of an old letter from his mother to his father. He read it. She was thanking God for the blessing of her husband's love:—

"But, above all," she wrote, "night and day, I thank the good God for having so arranged our lives that our dear Armand will never know that his mother, who adores him, belongs to the race that is cursed with the brand of slavery."

MARK TWAIN

Twain's detective story about a mulatta slave who switches her black baby for her master's white one, was serialized in *The Century* magazine from December 1893 to June 1894 and enjoyed widespread popularity. In the following excerpt, the seemingly white man wrestles with sudden knowledge of his black heritage, knowledge which changes everything.

From Pudd'nhead Wilson and Those Extraordinary Twins†

CHAPTER 10

All say "How hard it is that we have to die"—a strange complaint to come from the mouths of people who have had to live.
                              —Pudd'nhead Wilson's Calendar

When angry, count four; when very angry, swear.
                              —Pudd'nhead Wilson's Calendar

Every now and then, after Tom went to bed, he had sudden wakings out of his sleep, and his first thought was, "O, joy, it was all a dream!"

---

† From Mark Twain, *Pudd'n head Wilson* and *Those Extraordinary Twins*, 2nd ed. Edited by Sidney E. Berger (New York: W. W. Norton, 2005), pp. 48–52.

Then he laid himself heavily down again, with a groan and the muttered words, "A nigger!—I am a nigger!—oh, I wish I was dead!"

He woke at dawn with one more repetition of this horror, and then he resolved to meddle no more with that treacherous sleep. He began to think. Sufficiently bitter thinkings they were. They wandered along something after this fashion:

"Why were niggers *and* whites made? What crime did the uncreated first nigger commit that the curse of birth was decreed for him? And why is this awful difference made between white and black?. . . . . . How hard the nigger's fate seems, this morning!—yet until last night such a thought never entered my head."

He sighed and groaned an hour or more away. Then "Chambers" came humbly in to say that breakfast was nearly ready. "Tom" blushed scarlet to see this aristocratic white youth cringe to him, a nigger, and call him "Young marster." He said, roughly—

"Get out of my sight!" and when the youth was gone, he muttered, "He has done me no harm, poor wretch, but he is an eyesore to me, now, for he is Driscoll the young gentleman, and I am a—oh, I wish I was dead!"

A gigantic irruption like that of Krakatoa a few years ago, with the accompanying earthquakes, tidal waves and clouds of volcanic dust, changes the face of the surrounding landscape beyong recognition, bringing down the high lands, elevating the low, making fair lakes where deserts had been, and deserts where green prairies had smiled before. The tremendous catastrophe which had befallen Tom had changed his moral landscape in much the same way. Some of his low places he found lifted to ideals, some of his ideals had sunk to the valleys, and lay there with the sackcloth and ashes of pumice stone and sulphur on their ruined heads.

For days he wandered in lonely places thinking, thinking, thinking—trying to get his bearings. It was new work. If he met a friend he found that the habit of a lifetime had in some mysterious way vanished—his arm hung limp instead of involuntarily extending the hand for a shake. It was the "nigger" in him asserting its humility, and he blushed and was abashed. And the "nigger" in him was surprised when the white friend put out his hand for a shake with him. He found the "nigger" in him involuntarily giving the road, on the sidewalk, to the white rowdy and loafer. When Rowena, the dearest thing his heart knew, the idol of his secret worship, invited him in, the "nigger" in him made an embarrassed excuse and was afraid to enter and sit with the dread white folks on equal terms. The "nigger" in him went shrinking and skulking here and there and yonder, and fancying it saw suspicion and maybe detection in all faces, tones and gestures. So strange and uncharacteristic was Tom's conduct that people noticed it and turned to look after him when he passed on; and when he glanced back—as he could not help doing, in spite of his best resistance—and caught that puzzled expression in a person's face, it gave him a sick feeling, and he took himself out of view as quickly as he could. He presently came to have a hunted sense and a hunted look, and then he fled away to the hill-tops and the solitudes. He said to himself that the curse of Ham was upon him.

He dreaded his meals; the "nigger" in him was ashamed to sit at the white folks' table, and feared discovery all the time; and once when Judge Driscoll said, "What's the matter with you?—you look as meek as a nigger," he felt as secret murderers are said to feel when the accuser says "Thou art the man!" Tom said he was not well, and left the table.

His ostensible "aunt's" solicitudes and endearments were become a terror to him, and he avoided them.

And all the time, hatred of his ostensible "uncle" was steadily growing in his heart; for he said to himself, "He is white; and I am his chattel, his property, his goods, and he can sell me, just as he could his dog."

For as much as a week after this, Tom imagined that his character had undergone a pretty radical change. But that was because he did not know himself.

In several ways his opinions were totally changed, and would never go back to what they were before, but the main structure of his character was not changed, and could not be changed. One or two very important features of it were altered, and in time effects would result from this, if opportunity offered; effects of a quite serious nature, too. Under the influence of a great mental and moral upheaval his character and habits had taken on the appearance of complete change, but after a while with the subsidence of the storm both began to settle toward their former places. He dropped gradually back into his old frivolous and easy-going ways, and conditions of feeling, and manner of speech, and no familiar of his could have detected anything in him that differentiated him from the weak and careless Tom of other days.

*   *   *

CHARLES WADDELL CHESTNUTT

Short story writer, essayist and novelist Charles Chesnutt (1858–1932) was one of the first African-American writers making serious use of folklore as well as writing extensively about both racial violence and the difficult experiences of mixed-race Americans. *The House Behind the Cedars* concerns Rowena Walden and her brother John, both passing for white under the name of Warwick. The following excerpt depicts Rowena's grief when her fiancé, George Tryon, a plantation-owning, wealthy white Southern gentleman, abandons her after learning that she is black. Heartbroken and weak, Rowena dies a tragic, painful death, just as Tryon is attempting to return to her, filled with remorse and with resolve to cross the color line.

From The House Behind the Cedars†

XIX

GOD MADE US ALL

Rena was convalescent from a two-weeks' illness when her brother came to see her. He arrived at Patesville by an early morning train before the town was awake, and walked unnoticed from the station to his mother's house. His meeting with his sister was not without emotion: he embraced her tenderly, and Rena became for a few minutes a very Niobe of grief.

"Oh, it was cruel, cruel!" she sobbed. "I shall never get over it."

"I know it, my dear," replied Warwick soothingly,—"I know it, and I'm to blame for it. If I had never taken you away from here, you would have escaped this painful experience. But do not despair; all is not lost. Tryon will not marry you, as I hoped he might, while I feared the contrary; but he is a gentleman, and will be silent. Come back and try again."

"No, John. I couldn't go through it a second time. I managed very well before, when I thought our secret was unknown; but now I could never be sure. It would be borne on every wind, for aught I knew, and every rustling leaf might whisper it. The law, you said, made us white; but not the law, nor even love, can conquer prejudice. *He* spoke of my beauty, my grace, my sweetness! I looked into his eyes and believed him. And yet he left me without a word! What would I do in Clarence now? I came away engaged to be married, with even the day set; I should go back forsaken and discredited; even the servants would pity me."

"Little Albert is pining for you," suggested Warwick. "We could make some explanation that would spare your feelings."

"Ah, do not tempt me, John! I love the child, and am grieved to leave him. I'm grateful, too, John, for what you have done for me. I am not sorry that I tried it. It opened my eyes, and I would rather die of knowledge than live in ignorance. But I could not go through

† From Charles Waddell Chesnutt, *The House Behind the Cedars* (New York: Modern Library, 2003, pp. 123–30. orig. publ. Boston and New York: Houghton, Mifflin and Co., 1900). Notes have been deleted.

it again, John; I am not strong enough. I could do you no good; I have made you trouble enough already. Get a mother for Albert—Mrs. Newberry would marry you, secret and all, and would be good to the child. Forget me, John, and take care of yourself. Your friend has found you out through me—he may have told a dozen people. You think he will be silent;—I thought he loved me, and he left me without a word, and with a look that told me how he hated and despised me. I would not have believed it—even of a white man."

"You do him an injustice," said her brother, producing Tryon's letter. "He did not get off unscathed. He sent you a message."

She turned her face away, but listened while he read the letter. "He did not love me," she cried angrily, when he had finished, "or he would not have cast me off—he would not have looked at me so. The law would have let him marry me. I seemed as white as he did. He might have gone anywhere with me, and no one would have stared at us curiously; no one need have known. The world is wide—there must be some place where a man could live happily with the woman he loved."

"Yes, Rena, there is; and the world is wide enough for you to get along without Tryon."

"For a day or two," she went on, "I hoped he might come back. But his expression in that awful moment grew upon me, haunted me day and night, until I shuddered at the thought that I might ever see him again. He looked at me as though I were not even a human being. I do not love him any longer, John; I would not marry him if I were white, or he were as I am. He did not love me—or he would have acted differently. He might have loved me and have left me—he could not have loved me and have looked at me so!"

She was weeping hysterically. There was little he could say to comfort her. Presently she dried her tears. Warwick was reluctant to leave her in Patesville. Her childish happiness had been that of ignorance; she could never be happy there again. She had flowered in the sunlight; she must not pine away in the shade.

"If you won't come back with me, Rena, I'll send you to some school at the North, where you can acquire a liberal education, and prepare yourself for some career of usefulness. You may marry a better man than even Tryon."

"No," she replied firmly, "I shall never marry any man, and I'll not leave mother again. God is against it; I'll stay with my own people."

"God has nothing to do with it," retorted Warwick. "God is too often a convenient stalking-horse for human selfishness. If there is anything to be done, so unjust, so despicable, so wicked that human reason revolts at it, there is always some smug hypocrite to exclaim, 'It is the will of God.' "

"God made us all," continued Rena dreamily, "and for some good purpose, though we may not always see it. He made some people white, and strong, and masterful, and—heartless. He made others black and homely, and poor and weak"—

"And a lot of others 'poor white' and shiftless," smiled Warwick.

"He made us, too," continued Rena, intent upon her own thought, "and He must have had a reason for it. Perhaps He meant us to bring the others together in his own good time. A man may make a new place for himself—a woman is born and bound to hers. God must have meant me to stay here, or He would not have sent me back. I shall accept things as they are. Why should I seek the society of people whose friendship—and love—one little word can turn to scorn? I was right, John; I ought to have told him. Suppose he had married me and then had found it out?"

To Rena's argument of divine foreordination Warwick attached no weight whatever. He had seen God's heel planted for four long years upon the land which had nourished slavery. Had God ordained the crime that the punishment might follow? It would have been easier for Omnipotence to prevent the crime. The experience of his sister had stirred up a certain bitterness against white people—a feeling which he had put aside years ago, with his dark blood, but which sprang anew into life when the fact of his own origin was brought home to him so forcibly through his sister's misfortune. His sworn friend and promised brother-in-law had thrown him over promptly, upon the discovery of the hidden drop of dark blood. How many others of his friends would do the same, if they but knew of it? He had begun to feel a little of the spiritual estrangement from his associates that he had noticed in Rena during her life at Clarence. The fact that several persons knew his secret had spoiled the fine flavor of perfect security hitherto marking his position. George Tryon was a man of honor among white men, and had deigned to extend the protection of his honor to Warwick as a man, though no longer as a friend; to Rena as a woman, but not as a wife. Tryon, however, was only human, and who could tell when their paths in life might cross again, or what future temptation Tryon might feel to use a damaging secret to their disadvantage? Warwick had cherished certain ambitions, but these he must now put behind him. In the obscurity of private life, his past would be of little moment; in the glare of a political career, one's antecedents are public property, and too great a reserve in regard to one's past is regarded as a confession of something discreditable. Frank, too, knew the secret—a good, faithful fellow, even where there was no obligation of fidelity; he ought to do something for

Frank to show their appreciation of his conduct. But what assurance was there that Frank would always be discreet about the affairs of others? Judge Straight knew the whole story, and old men are sometimes garrulous. Dr. Green suspected the secret; he had a wife and daughters. If old Judge Straight could have known Warwick's thoughts, he would have realized the fulfillment of his prophecy. Warwick, who had builded so well for himself, had weakened the structure of his own life by trying to share his good fortune with his sister.

"Listen, Rena," he said, with a sudden impulse, "we'll go to the North or West—I'll go with you—far away from the South and the Southern people, and start life over again. It will be easier for you, it will not be hard for me—I am young, and have means. There are no strong ties to bind me to the South. I would have a larger outlook elsewhere."

"And what about our mother?" asked Rena.

It would be necessary to leave her behind, they both perceived clearly enough, unless they were prepared to surrender the advantage of their whiteness and drop back to the lower rank. The mother bore the mark of the Ethiopian—not pronouncedly, but distinctly; neither would Mis' Molly, in all probability, care to leave home and friends and the graves of her loved ones. She had no mental resources to supply the place of these; she was, moreover, too old to be transplanted; she would not fit into Warwick's scheme for a new life.

"I left her once," said Rena, "and it brought pain and sorrow to all three of us. She is not strong, and I will not leave her here to die alone. This shall be my home while she lives, and if I leave it again, it shall be for only a short time, to go where I can write to her freely, and hear from her often. Don't worry about me, John,—I shall do very well."

Warwick sighed. He was sincerely sorry to leave his sister, and yet he saw that for the time being her resolution was not to be shaken. He must bide his time. Perhaps, in a few months, she would tire of the old life. His door would be always open to her, and he would charge himself with her future.

"Well, then," he said, concluding the argument, "we'll say no more about it for the present. I'll write to you later. I was afraid that you might not care to go back just now, and so I brought your trunk along with me."

He gave his mother the baggage-check. She took it across to Frank, who, during the day, brought the trunk from the depot. Mis' Molly offered to pay him for the service, but he would accept nothing.

"Lawd, no, Mis' Molly; I didn't hafter go out'n my way ter git dat trunk. I had a load er sperrit-bairls ter haul ter de still, an' de depot wuz right on my way back. It'd be robbin' you ter take pay fer a little thing lack dat."

"My son John's here," said Mis' Molly "an' he wants to see you. Come into the settin'-room. We don't want folks to know he's in town; but you know all our secrets, an' we can trust you like one er the family."

"I'm glad to see you again, Frank," said Warwick, extending his hand and clasping Frank's warmly. "You've grown up since I saw you last, but it seems you are still our good friend."

"Our very good friend," interjected Rena.

Frank threw her a grateful glance. "Yas, suh," he said, looking Warwick over with a friendly eye, "an' you is growed some, too. I seed you, you know, down dere where you live; but I didn't let on, fer you an' Mis' Rena wuz w'ite as anybody; an' eve'ybody said you wuz good ter cullud folks, an' he'ped 'em in deir lawsuits an' one way er 'nuther, an' I wuz jes' plum' glad ter see you gettin' 'long so fine, dat I wuz, certain sho', an' no mistake about it."

"Thank you, Frank, and I want you to understand how much I appreciate"—

"How much we all appreciate," corrected Rena.

"Yes, how much we all appreciate, and how grateful we all are for your kindness to mother for so many years. I know from her and from my sister how good you've been to them."

"Lawd, suh!" returned Frank deprecatingly, "you're makin' a mountain out'n a molehill. I ain't done nuthin' ter speak of—not half ez much ez I would 'a' done. I wuz glad ter do w'at little I could, fer frien'ship's sake."

"We value your friendship, Frank, and we'll not forget it."

"No, Frank," added Rena, "we will never forget it, and you shall always be our good friend."

Frank left the room and crossed the street with swelling heart. He would have given his life for Rena. A kind word was doubly sweet from her lips; no service would be too great to pay for her friendship.

When Frank went out to the stable next morning to feed his mule, his eyes opened wide with astonishment. In place of the decrepit, one-eyed army mule he had put up the night before, a fat, sleek specimen of vigorous mulehood greeted his arrival with the sonorous hehaw of lusty youth. Hanging on a peg near by was a set of fine new harness, and standing under the adjoining shed, as he perceived, a handsome new cart.

"Well, well!" exclaimed Frank; "ef I didn' mos' know whar dis mule, an' dis kyart, an' dis harness come from, I'd 'low dere'd be'n witchcraf' er cunjin' wukkin' here. But, oh my, dat is a fine mule!—I mos' wush I could keep 'im."

He crossed the road to the house behind the cedars, and found Mis' Molly in the kitchen. "Mis' Molly," he protested, "I ain't done nuthin' ter deserve dat mule. W'at little I done fer you wa'n't done fer pay. I'd ruther not keep dem things."

"Fer goodness' sake, Frank!" exclaimed his neighbor, with a well-simulated air of mystification, "what are you talkin' about?"

"You knows w'at I'm talkin' about, Mis' Molly; you knows well ernuff I'm talkin' about dat fine mule an' kyart an' harness over dere in my stable."

"How should I know anything about 'em?" she asked.

"Now, Mis' Molly! You folks is jes' tryin' ter fool me, an' make me take somethin' fer nuthin'. I lef' my ole mule an' kyart an' harness in de stable las' night, an' dis mawnin' dey're gone, an' new ones in deir place. Co'se you knows whar dey come from!"

"Well, now, Frank, sence you mention it, I did see a witch flyin' roun' here las' night on a broomstick, an' it 'peared ter me she lit on yo'r barn, an' I s'pose she turned yo'r old things into new ones. I wouldn't bother my mind about it if I was you, for she may turn 'em back any night, you know; an' you might as well have the use of 'em in the mean while."

"Dat's all foolishness, Mis' Molly, an' I'm gwine ter fetch dat mule right over here an' tell yo' son ter gimme my ole one back."

"My son's gone," she replied, "an' I don't know nothing' about yo'r old mule. And what would I do with a mule, anyhow? I ain't got no barn to put him in."

"I suspect you don't care much for us after all, Frank," said Rena reproachfully—she had come in while they were talking. "You meet with a piece of good luck, and you're afraid of it, lest it might have come from us."

"Now, Miss Rena, you oughtn't ter say dat," expostulated Frank, his reluctance yielding immediately. "I'll keep de mule an' de kyart an' de harness—fac', I'll have ter keep 'em, 'cause I ain't got no others. But dey're gwine ter be yo'n ez much ez mine. W'enever you wants anything hauled, er wants yo' lot ploughed, er anything—dat's yo' mule, an' I'm yo' man an' yo' mammy's."

So Frank went back to the stable, where he feasted his eyes on his new possessions, fed and watered the mule, and curried and brushed his coat until it shone like a looking-glass.

"Now dat," remarked Peter, at the breakfast-table, when informed of the transaction, "is somethin' lack rale w'ite folks."

No real white person had ever given Peter a mule or a cart. He had rendered one of them unpaid service for half a lifetime, and had paid for the other half; and some of them owed him substantial sums for work performed. But "to him that hath shall be given" Warwick paid for the mule, and the real white folks got most of the credit.

GEORGIA DOUGLAS JOHNSON

Georgia Douglas Johnson (1880?–1966) was one of the first African American poets to gain prominence during the Harlem Renaissance.

The Octoroon†

One drop of midnight in the dawn of life's pulsating stream
Marks her an alien from her kind, a shade amid its gleam;
Forevermore her step she bends insular, strange, apart—
And none can read the riddle of her wildly warring heart.

The stormy current of her blood beats like a mighty sea
Against the man-wrought iron of her captivity.
For refuge, succor, peace and rest, she seeks that humble fold
Whose every breath is kindliness, whose hearts are purest gold.

COUNTEE CULLEN

Countee Cullen (1903–1946) was one of the most prominent figures in the Harlem Renaissance whose books include *Color* (1925), *Copper Sun* (1927), the edited collection *Caroling Dusk* (1927), and others.

Near White††

Ambiguous of race they stand,
    By one disowned, scorned of another,
Not knowing where to stretch a hand,
    And cry, "My sister" or "My brother."

LANGSTON HUGHES

Langston Hughes (1902–1967) was one of the most recognized and brilliant writers of the Harlem Renaissance, the author of such works as *The*

---

† From Werner Sollors, *An Anthology of Interracial Literature: Black-White Contacts in the Old World and the New* (New York: NYU Press, 2004, p. 462; orig. publ. in G. D. Johnson, *Bronze: A Book of Verse* Boston: B. J. Brimmer, 1922).
†† From *Color* (New York: Harper & Brothers, 1925). Copyrights held by Amistad Research Center. Administered by Thompson and Thompson, New York, NY.

Weary Blues (1926), *Fine Clothes to the Jew* (1927), *Not Without Laughter* (1930), *Dear Lovely Death* (1931), *The Ways of White Folks* (1934), *The Big Sea* (1940), and many others. "Mulatto" was first published in 1927.

Mulatto†

I am your son, white man!

Georgia dusk
And the turpentine woods.
One of the pillars of the temple fell.

    You are my son!
    Like hell!

The moon over the turpentine woods.
The Southern night
Full of stars,
Great big yellow stars.
  What's a body but a toy?
    Juicy bodies
    Of nigger wenches
    Blue black
    Against black fences.
    O, you little bastard boy,
    What's a body but a toy?
The scent of pine wood stings the soft night air.
    What's the body of your mother?
Silver moonlight everywhere.
    What's the body of your mother?
Sharp pine scent in the evening air.
    A nigger night,
    A nigger joy,
    A little yellow
    Bastard boy.

    Naw, you ain't my brother.
    Niggers ain't my brother.
    Not ever.
    Niggers ain't my brother.

† From *The Collected Poems of Langston Hughes,* ed. Arnold Rampersad with David Roessel, associate editor (New York: Knopf, 1994), pp. 533–34. Copyright © 1994 by The Estate of Langston Hughes. Used by permission of Alfred A. Knopf, a division of Random House, Inc.

The Southern night is full of stars,
Great big yellow stars.
> O, sweet as earth,
> Dusk dark bodies
> Give sweet birth
To little yellow bastard boys.

> *Git on back there in the night,*
> *You ain't white.*

The bright stars scatter everywhere.
Pine wood scent in the evening air.
> A nigger night,
> A nigger joy.

> *I am your son, white man!*

> A little yellow
> Bastard boy.

FANNIE HURST

Fannie Hurst (1889–1968) was one of the most popular novelists of her day. A best seller in 1933, her novel *Imitation of Life* tells the story of white Bea Pullman and Delilah Johnston, her African American maid. These two single mothers raise their daughters Jessie and Peola together, until Peola decides to pass as white, breaking her mother's heart in the process, as the second excerpt which follows depicts.

From Imitation of Life†

CHAPTER 26

The more or less quiescent problem of Peola lifted its head the day that Jessie caused to explode off her lovely lips the "nigger."

✳ ✳ ✳

It came, bursting across the quiet like shrapnel, because immediately from the kitchen, as if part of it had struck out there, was Delilah on the scene, standing stunned and stockstill in the middle of a strange new silence.

---

† From Fannie Hurst, *Imitation of Life* (Durham: Duke University Press, 2004, pp. 147–50; 240–51; orig. publ. New York: Harper & Brothers, 1933).

"Nigger! No fair! You pushed! You're a little nigger and you've got no half-moons on your finger nails. Nig-nig-nig—ger!"

Nigger! How, how, had the word dawned into the tiny horizon of this household. Nigger.

"Jessie, how could you? Come here, my poor little Peola, to Miss Bea. . . ."

My poor little Peola, not at all! Something as agile and ready to leap as a leopard was out in Peola. Backed almost immediately by the enormous bulk of her mother, her hands flew together and clasped behind her back, so that her thin arms twisted like pulled twine, the small face settling into lines of a fury ridiculously too old for it. Actually, standing there in an anger ready to spring, she made a hissing sound.

"Honey-chile, your mammy's here. Take it standin'. You gotta learn to take it all your life that way. Nigger is a tame-cat word when we uses it ourselves ag'in' ourselves, and a wild-cat word when it comes jumpin' at us from the outside. Doan' let it git you."

"Jessie, apologize!"

"No, no, Miss Bea. 'Tain't no use makin' either one of dem make too much of dis. Peola's got to learn. What's happened is as nacheral as de tides. Dey been creepin' up on her since de day she was born, and now de first little wave is here, wettin' her feet. Jessie ain't to blame. God ain't, 'cause He had some good reason for makin' us black and white . . . and de sooner mah chile learns to agree wid Him the better. Oh, Miss Bea, doan' you remember 'way back when she was a baby, mah tellin' you de itch in her heart mah poor chile was born wid?"

Suddenly there turned upon her mother the small gripped fury of Peola. "You! You!" she screamed, the flanges of her nose whitening and spreading like wings as she beat small fists against the checkered apron frontage of Delilah. "You're so black! That's what makes me nigger."

"Peola, my child, how can you talk to your——"

"Hole a minute, Miss Bea. She doan' mean it no more'n her whitish pap used to mean it. Nobody can tell me dat white nigger married me 'cause he knew I'd slave for him. He could 'a' got plenty. He married me 'cause he knowed I jes' cain't help a-lovin'. Ain't nothin' gonna make me quit lovin' dis chile. She's got her pap's curse. Hating what he was. And it's a heap easier to be black when you're black lak I am, Miss Bea, dan it is to be white when you're black lak mah poor baby. Folks said I worked dese hands to de bone supportin' her pap 'cause I was proud he was white. Proud? De biggest curse what ever hit him or me was his whiteness. Oh, mah honey, cain't you see de Lord done had good reason for makin' you black? Oh, mah honey, cain't you see de glory in de Lawd's every move?"

Into the checkered fold of apron flowed the heat and bitter salt of her child, and finally into the thawing warmth of vasty bosom.

"Sh-h-h, mah baby-chile. Jessie didn' call you nigger wid her meanness. She called you dat wid her blood. Forgive dem 'cause dey know not what dey do is de Lawd's way for makin' it easy for us to bear our cross, as he bore hisn. Doan' cry, mah baby. If you let go of tears for every time you're gonna be called nigger, your tears will make a Red Sea big enough to drown us all in."

"Jessie, sweet, you don't know what a dreadful unkind word you just used to Peola."

"Peola is a nigger, Mother, isn't she? But I never meant to be bad."

"She is a negro, just as you are a white. Go over to her and tell her how naughty you have been to pick up a horrid street word without even knowing its meaning."

"No white chile cain't be comin' apologizin' to a black and puttin' ideas into her ahead. Stop dat tremblin', Peola, and walk over dar, and tell Jessie you're proud of bein' a nigger, 'cause it was de Lawd's work makin' you a nigger. . . ."

"I won't be a nigger! I won't be a nigger!"

"Got to, mah baby. The further 'long you go apin' whites and pleasurin' wid dem, de more you're letting yourself in for de misery. . . ."

"Won't! Won't!"

"Then brace your heart, mah baby, 'cause breakin's ahead for it. Brace your heart for de misery of tryin' to dye black blood white. Ain't no way to dye black white. God never even give a way to dye a black dress white, much less black blood. Never you mind, mah chile. Some day, on the white wings of a white hearse, wid white plumes and the trumpets of a heavenly host blowin' black and white welcome alike, we'll ride to glory to a land whar dar ain't no such heartbreakin' colors as black and white. Quit cryin' out your little heart. Sh-h-h-h. . . ."

"Delilah, stop her. She'll have a convulsion. Oh, Jessie, how could you!"

"I didn't mean nigger to be a mean word, Mother."

"Then don't dare to use it again! See now what you've done. Peola, you mustn't hold your breath!"

"I won't be nigger!"

"Yes, you will, baby, long as de Lawd is stronger dan you are."

"I won't! I won't!"

"Got to, mah baby. 'Tain't no tragedy unless you make it one. Dar is good black happiness in bein' black. Your maw's done found glory in de Lawd's way. She's gonna learn it to her baby. Remember, honey, some day on de wings of a white hearse—sh-h-h-h, mah little black baby will be carried to her heavenly host."

"She'll have a convulsion, Delilah, if you don't stop her."

"Better now dan when she's old enough to have grown-up ones. It ain't de bein' black, honey—it's bein' black in a white world you got to get your little hurtburn quiet about. . . ."

"I won't be black! I won't be nig——"

Off the small lips, which shuddered the word like a defective coupon out of a machine, spun foam.

"Delilah—the little thing—she's fainted . . . !"

She had. Quite stiffly and into a pallor that made her whiter than chalk.

⁎　⁎　⁎

CHAPTER 39

The night that, unannounced, Peola walked in, Bea, who had come into the apartment about ten o'clock after a monthly round-table dinner with her staff managers, was standing before her mirror in one of the new fluffy peignoirs that had lately replaced her cotton crêpe kimonos, braiding her hair into the two identical plaits she had worn to bed all of her adult life.

Through the open door of her father's room, she could hear his rumbling breathing, which was as definitely part of her night as the ticking of a clock. Once indeed, the night of his second stroke, both she and Delilah had darted from bed on no more alarm than the unwonted silence of his having skipped some of the breathings.

Whe-e-eze, it was going through the apartment the night that Peola turned unexpectedly up, as Bea stood in the immemorial attitude of a woman making a braid over one shoulder and binding it with a wisp of combing.

It was three and a half years since Peola had passed through New York for a two-day visit on her way from Washington, D.C., to Seattle, Washington, to accept the new position as librarian.

Her appearance, following a late ring at the door, answered by Delilah who had been moving about the kitchen at her nightly rite of peeling a cold red apple for Bea before she retired, had been the occasion of an instantaneous outcry and clatter of an apple bumping its way along the hallway.

"Praise be de Lawd Gawd Almighty for bein' in His heaven! It's mah chile come home to her waitin' and prayin' mammy! Lawd, you answered mah prayer. I knowed you would. Come out here, Missy Bea! Didn't I tell you mah chile would come home to her mammy?"

As a matter of fact, she had not told her. Bursting through the immense stress of this moment came the revelation of what must have lain crouching beneath the shell of Delilah's silence concerning this protracted absence of Peola.

Never a word out of her at all the delayed Christmas visits, procrastinations, postponements, except an apparently almost indifferent justification, difficult to ever have quite believed, yet so puzzlingly convincing.

"Mah chile ain't comin' home dis heah Christmas, after all. Sent her de money, but ah tole her to keep it and git herself something for to wear, her a-havin' de stylish jimjams lak all of 'em, includin' Miss Jessie, who ain't comin' home, neither. It's re-cat-a-log-in' time out dar whar she works. Is re-cat-a-log-in' something as fine as it sounds, Miss Bea?" Or: "If de chile didn't go git herself mumps so she cain't come home nohow, Easter time. We doan' want no mumps traipsin' in, gittin' cotched by mah chair-baby or Miss Jessie if she comes home from school. Well, ennyhow mumps is something easier on de mind dan re-cat-a-log-in'."

Not an intimation of that chronic ear-strain for the postman's footfall; of the long arid intervals between the neatly typed envelopes bearing the Seattle postmark. One to every ten or fifteen of Delilah's, as they went out in their cramped immature scrawl, bearing, in spite of every effort to convert her to a checking system, inclosures of bank notes pinned to the letter sheet.

And now here was Peola, straight as a blade, her banana-colored pallor standing out beneath the brim of the modish hat, walking into the routine of Delilah preparing to deliver the nightly polished apple on its nightly polished plate.

Flood gates went down, sweeping the one reticence known to Delilah, the secret inner hurts, turmoils, fears, and anguishes concerning this offspring of hers, along the surface of released tears.

"I knowed mah baby would come home to me. Every night, when I prayed to God, I knowed it. Dar's a knife jumped right out of mah heart when I opened dis door jes' now. Jumped plop out an' quit hurting when I laid eyes on mah chile. Gawd Almighty, praise be de Lawd, mah chile's come home. . . ."

The wide expanse of her face slashingly wet, the whites of her eyes seeming to pour rivulets down her face like rain against a window pane, her splayed lips dripping eaves of more tears, her throat even rained against, there was apparently no way that Delilah could capture the face of her child in an embrace. Rigid-eyed, it swung, the banana-colored mask, this way and that, away from the wetness. It eluded, it dipped, it came up dry and powdered with pallor, fastidiously untouched in the perfection of its maneuvers to escape the great wet crying surface that was after it.

"Mah baby. I knowed she'd come if I waited and prayed and prayed and waited. Mah baby, come home to her mammy, and nobody askin' it of her."

The dry inscrutable face, wrung and silent, stared across the vast shoulder of her mother; stared and stared at the figure of B. Pullman standing on the edge of that scene of the revelation of the pouring forth of this soul, this vast reticence of Delilah.

Here was the silence of a late evening suddenly strewn with the secret debris of all the released torments that during the years must have pressed against the infallible outward exuberance of Delilah. A crucifying kind of pity for it looked out from the face regarding Bea above the enormous mound of her mother's shoulder. Pity and a veritable nausea of revulsion. Peola was suffering that embrace, a demonstration against which her flesh and her staring eyes seemed to curl.

"Miss Jessie's letters comed oftener, but mah baby brunged herself instead of any letters. Look heah at mah honey-chile, Miss Bea. Miss Jessie never come home in no more style! Look at dat fur tibbet, will you! White wid black tails lak kings wear. Ain't she de fashionest-plate! Uh-uh, gimme dat valise! Doan' you spoil your pretty hands luggin' dat luggage. 'Gawd Almighty, mah chile's come home—an' will you look at dat tail to her walk. Struttin', I calls it, an' struttin' ain't none too good for her.—Gawd Almighty, mah chile's come home!"

It was obvious enough that what happened with such immediate sequence had not been planned by Peola at all, as she opened stiff lips to try and make manifest in the first few lines of her dreadful little preamble.

But somewhere her intentions, as revealed by her luggage and the late hour of her arrival, were failing her. The vast wet surface of a face that threatened to suck hers to it, the arms loaded with flesh that crowded and pressed her, the pronouncement that the small spare room off Delilah's which she had occupied on the rare occasions of visits to her mother was now preempted by the male nurse. Her intention to remain even overnight was failing her, failing her as she stood.

"Come right into your mammy's room, honey-chile, and take off your things and let your mammy feed and rest you. Ain't no place, wid mah chair-baby's nurse cluttering up de little room, for you to sleep tonight, exceptin' where you belongs, in your mammy's arms in your mammy's bed . . . something I wouldn't take ten million dollars for . . . mah baby wid her mammy in her bed. . . ."

"No. No. No. I mean, I couldn't. I can't. I mean, you see, it's better this way. Quickly. Let me talk it all, right here. In the hall. Standing. It will be better then for me to go. Please, Mrs. Pullman, you stay too. Please. You must. I've traveled three days and three nights to see you both this way together!"

"But, baby-chile—ain't you gonna let your mammy git you fixed and comfortable fust? You looks dead-beat, baby. Missy Bea and me will wait—not Mrs. Pullman, honey; dat ain't no way for to call—your best friend."

"Please! The sooner this is over the better for—everyone."

"Baby, you ain't in trouble?"

"Not unless you decide that I am."

"Lawdagawd——"

"Please! You—Mrs. Pullman—Missy Bea, tell her we must talk quietly and at once."

"But, Peola, your mother is happy and excited——"

"Jes' so happy, baby, I don't know where to turn fust."

"I know you are, dear. But I need so much to talk to you, now—at once—quietly——"

"I'll leave you and your mother alone, Peola."

"Oh no, no! No, no, please! Won't you please stay? You have to be here. That's why I've come. To see you both."

"Then come into my room. Don't bother with those heavy bags now, Delilah. Come."

"If it's because you got to sleep wid your ole mammy dat you don't want to stay tonight now dat you got your bags here, I kin roll mahself up on de floor."

"Delilah, you'll do nothing of the sort! Come into my room."

No sooner in, behind closed doors, than the daughter of Delilah, facing them, jerked off the small hat that revealed suddenly with startling distinctness the straight black hair and straight contrasting pallor of straight brow.

"Help me, you two!"

"Lordagawd! . . ."

"There is nobody but you two who can. Help me to pass!"

"Lordagawd!"

"I've been in Seattle four years now. I'm liked there. I've made good there. I've passed. You must have known that all along, Missy Bea."

"I've suspected it."

"There's nothing wrong in passing. The wrong is the world that makes it necessary."

Suddenly Delilah began to sway, throwing her apron up over her face and talking softly into it as her body rocked.

"Lordagawd, it's come! Give me strength. De white horses have cotched her. Lordagawd, give me strength."

"You'll never know," said Peola to Bea, as if trying to make herself heard above the noise of a crying child, "how I've dreaded all this. The wailing. The dreadful sounds—the awfulness. . . ."

"Lordagawd, forgive me for wailin', but after all dese years of mah prayin', you've seen fit, in your wisdom, for it to come this-away——"

"There is nothing wrong about this way. What the world does not know, will not hurt it. I'm not ungrateful. Please try and understand that. I know how good you are. Twenty thousand times too good for me. Twenty? Fifty! Fifty times fifty times! Everything you've given me has been more than I deserve, and you've given and given and given me since the day I was born. . . ."

"Oh, mah baby, a-givin' you has been the meanin' of livin'. A-givin' you, seein' you git fine and educated an' into what you are now, even if in de end it crucify me, is God's meanin' for puttin' breath of life into dis black hulk——"

"Then you do want me to be happy——?"

"I does, baby. . . . It hurts lak dis ole heart was a toothache, wantin' it."

"You do, you do, of course you do. And yet you know as well as I know, that with all you've given me over and above what I deserve, since the day I was born, I've been the most wretched . . ."

"Doan' say it, baby. It's de knife back in mah heart."

"I must say it in order to make you understand."

"Doan'. . . ."

"You at least can cry. I can't. You've got tears left. I haven't. I've cried myself dry. Cried myself out with self-loathing and self-pity and self-consciousness. I tell you I've prayed same as you, for the strength to be proud of being black under my white. I've tried to glory in my people. I've drenched myself in the life of Toussaint L'Ouverture, Booker Washington, and Frederick Douglass. I've tried to catch some of their spark. But I'm not that stuff. I haven't pride of race, or love of race. There's nothing grand or of-the-stuff-martyrs-are-made about me. I can't learn to endure being black in a white world. It might be easier if I was out-and-out-black like you. Then there wouldn't be any question. But I'm not. I'm light. No way of knowing how much white flows somewhere in my veins. I'm as white under my skin as I am on top. Sometimes I think if my pap were living he'd have things to tell me——"

"Peola!"

"Lord Gawd Almighty, it ain't mah chile talkin'—it's de horse in her neighin' out through her blood. . . ."

"Listen. You scarcely know me. I've gone my way, able to do so because you have been good and indulgent and generous. I haven't been a good daughter. I know that. I haven't been anything you deserved to have me be——"

"You're mah——"

"But as things go in this world, I have been a good girl, morally or whatever you want to call it. I've worked. I've studied. I've tried to make the best of myself. And all the time with the terrible odds against me of knowing I could never get anywhere I wanted to get!"

"Oh no, Peola!"

"Yes, Missy Bea! What do you know about the blight of not having the courage to face life in a black world? You've succeeded in a world that matters to you! Give me that same chance."

"What do you mean?"

"I've got on out there in Seattle. Librarian in the city's finest branch. I've been careful. I've watched my every step, made no false ones. I'm not black out there in Seattle. Nobody knows anything, except that I'm an orphaned girl out from the East earning a decent living. And now, and now—the test has come. Sooner or later it had to come. I've got to go on forever that way, or be thrown back into something I haven't the courage to face. You can help me. You two. Only you two and Jessie, who will, if you will. For God's sake make her stop those moaning sounds. I can't stand it. I wouldn't hurt a dog that way. Make her stop it. . . ."

"Delilah, you must give Peola the right to state her case. . . ."

"Lord Gawd Almighty, I'm breakin' in two! I cain't hear it no more. Lovin' de Lawd dat made me black, I bring mah baby-chile into a race dat I'm proud to be one of. A low-down, good-for-nothin' race of loafers, lots of 'em, but no worser dan loafers of any other color. Lovers of de Lawd and willin' servers is mah race, filled wid de blessin's of humility—a singin', happy, God-lovin', servin' race dat I loves an' is proud of, an' wants mah chile to love——"

"I can't! I've nothing against them, but I—I can't be what you want. I'm not the stuff. Not in a white world. If your skin is white like mine and your soul is white—like mine, there is no point to the needless suffering. I've got to be helped. You two can do it. And I need to terribly—now—now!—to pass completely."

"Lawd have—"

"Delilah, you must hear Peola out! What do you mean by 'now,' Peola?"

"It's the crisis that had to come sooner or later. You know what I mean. Oh, not what you're thinking. Not that. Just the ordinary inevitable crisis. . . ."

"Marriage?"

"Yes."

"White?"

"Yes."

"No, no, no! Gawd don't want His rivers to mix!"

"Please make her stop, Missy Bea!"

"Delilah, dear good Delilah, you're making it impossible for us to talk this thing out. Sit down here, next to me, and give me your hand—and hear Peola out."

"If mah hand ain't good enough for mah chile, if her runs away from sleepin' wid her ole black mammy, 'tain't good enough for to touch yours!"

"My dear, oh, my dear! Why, of course! Of course—my dear—" But what she attempted was apparently simply beyond Peola. Stepping around the small chintz chair that stood between them, she half described the gesture of taking her mother's hand and stood there locked in the midst of an effort that flooded her eyes, her face that would not flood with color, stamped with the tell-tale story of an aversion that was stronger than she was.

"Won't you please—won't you—release me—let me go—my way?"

"Let go what I 'ain't never had——"

"I need so terribly what it is in your power to grant me. I am safe except for you. He needs me so. Not even he realizes how much. Regardless of how much I love this boy, and I do, I do, I dare not risk letting him lose me by knowing. Neither dare I risk it for myself. I couldn't live. . . ."

"Black wimmin who pass, pass into damnation. . . ."

"O my God! What chance have I, Missy Bea, against her swamp and voodoo nonsense? . . ."

"Dat ain't swamp talk. Dat ain't voodoo. Dat's blood talk. Dat's de law-of-de-Lawd talk. You cain't go ag'in' de fallin' of de rain and de crackin' of de thunder. They're there. You're there. Black! You ain't lovin' nobody but yourself in dis here passin'. Your man will live to curse de day when your lie comes out in your chillun. . . ."

"I've taken care of that!"

"Peola!"

"I'm not ashamed. There are millions to populate the world besides me. There is no shame in being sterilized in the name of the happiness of another. He knows, without knowing why, that I can't have children. I want my happiness. I want my man. I want my life. I love him. I'll follow him to the ends of the earth. Which is practically what I propose to do."

"What end of the earth, Peola?"

"He's an engineer. We're going to Bolivia. I'll see to it that we stay there. His happiness will be the meaning of my life. I love him. He loves me. Knowing would blast his life and destroy mine. Nothing can happen to destroy us except if you . . . won't . . . help——"

"Lordagawd give me strength. . . ."

"Try, dear Miss Bea, to stop her. It's like a horror in a jungle—it's like—everything I'm trying to run away from. For God's sake—don't do that—stop swaying—stop praying——"

"Doan' leave me, baby. Doan' pass from me, baby. Even if I ain't never had you, doan' leave me. . . ."

"You're good. All my life I'll carry the memory of it locked up in my silence. But let me pass—Mammy——"

"Mammy! She called me Mammy—I's in her blood—she cain't help it.—Honey-chile, come to your mammy——"

"Don't you dare! You can't hold me. Blood can't, because there isn't enough of it between us. I don't care what you say. If my father had lived he might have had something to tell me that not even you know. Let me pass!"

"You cain't pass! You cain't! You cain't! God'll know it, even if nobody else does, and what you gonna do when you face him on his pearly throne. . . ."

"Let me take care of God! All that I want is your pledge. Both of yours. To let me pass, in silence. Give me your solemn oaths that so far as you are concerned, so far as ever entering my life with my husband is concerned, you do not know me, have never seen me, have never heard of me. It is that, for me, or nothing. It is life for me, or death. Promise me never to know me if you should meet me face to face in years to come. I'll see that you don't, but just to allow for the arm of coincidence, promise me!"

"O Lawd, was ever such words listened to——?"

"I know it sounds terrible. But, oh, my poor dear, it's in your power to give me my happiness! My freedom. Let me go. Let me pass. I need the promise. The oath. You've more than my happiness in your hands. You've my life."

They made a strange center, these three, to that conventional bedroom of taffeta, Circassian walnut, and unelaborate fixings of its unelaborate occupant. The furniture stood off at stiff angles from them as they held the formation of an unequal triangle, the rather cold remote light of a crystal chandelier packing them into a kind of pallor.

"You'll be well rid of me. I've been no good to you or for you."

"Lordagawd, you're a-askin' more of me dan to bury mah chile in her grave, but if dat's your will. . . ."

"I'm not worth your tears. I'm not worth a single one of them. I'm as vile in my own mind as I must be in yours. But somehow I'll make it up. I'll make it up to A.M. I'll make it up in trying to bring complete happiness to at least one human being. I'll make up for the rotten child I've been by making A.M. the best wife God ever made a man. He's just a darling, clean young boy, Mammy, a farmer kid who studied engineering when other fellows would have been hitting it high with his free time. He got to coming to the library evenings, after his mother died last March, leaving him without a tie in the world. Lonely kid. Darlingest clean fellow. Wonder if you know what it means, leading the lonely careful life I had to. All of sudden—all of a sudden the whole world bursting open, like a flower. I never dreamed—I never tried for him. It was just a case of a lonesome kid coming to the library evenings and the lonesomest girl in the world——"

"De makin's of misery—de makin's of misery——"

"I tell you no! He's gassed, to say nothing of half a hand he lost in Flanders. He's never yet shaken the hell of war out of his eyes. He needs change. We're going to make a fresh start. He's got this engineering chance in Bolivia. Thousands of miles from anyone who knows us. We'll get our roots down, there. What he doesn't know about me cannot ever hurt him. What he does know will bring him all the happiness there is. It's not a sin, Mammy, where there won't be children. It's all or nothing for me. You two have my life or my death in your hands."

"Oh, Peola, it isn't fair to put it that way to your mother."

"Don't you think I know that? Don't you think I've sweated agony before I took the train to come here? But it's all there is left. Life doesn't mean much to me, Missy Bea. Never has, until now. I couldn't go back to having it mean little again—and live on. Mammy's got you. You've got Jessie. I've found A.M. He loves me. I love him. I've done the—the right things—about the possibility of children. Never mind how. You couldn't believe how! It hasn't been easy. It's been terrible that—well, without him, I couldn't face a life that would be as sterile as I am."

"How have you dared!"

"One dares everything when there is nothing to lose and everything to gain. His mother died and he began studying on his evening engineering course at the library. He couldn't find the right lodgings. I got him a room where I was boarding. We got to sitting together on the stoop evenings, after library. Walking. Talking. He needed to be nursed out of a state of mind he'd gotten into about that half of hand. He's been so terribly gassed too. To show you the kind of boy he is, his mother never knew that, up to the day she died. Not a boy to go gadding around. Lonely. Me too. Self-conscious about his hand. I cured him of that. Mining engineers don't read much outside their work. I got him into the habit. We began to go rowing Sundays. With a book. A.M. is such a kid. Used to his mother——"

"Mah chile dat's gonna throw away her own mammy is a-lovin' him now for a-lovin' his mammy!"

"It's life, I tell you. Me clutching at life! You've got to let me pass into a new world. I haven't told him anything different than I've told everyone out there. Practically nothing except that I—I'm alone, too. They like me out there. He—loves me. He depends on me. He's out there now—waiting for me to come back before we set sail. He's got this South American job. It's a five-year one. A big chance. Most of it in jungle country. Once I get A.M. there—away—safely alone—mine—he need never know. Thousands have done it. He'll never know anything except how happy I can make him. And will. Oh, don't look at me like that, the two of you. What do you know of what I've been through? I know what I'm doing. It's all or nothing for me. For us. Oh, you two—please . . ."

"Lordagawd, help me—do for mah chile what she wants——"

"I want you to let me pass. I want your oath. Never so long as you live, if you meet me here or there—in the jungle or on the high seas, to recognize or own me. I leave you no name. No address. We'll have to live along on engineer's salary instead of your darling generosity. I'll have to learn to forget. You'll have to. If you have mercy, Mammy, and you have—let me pass."

"Dar's spikes through mah hands and dar's a spike through mah heart if ever dar was spikes in de hands and de heart of anybody besides our Lawd. . . ."

"Peola, you are asking of your mother something too terrible to be borne. . . ."

"As if everything she had to bear connected with me hasn't always been that. Let me go. Let her be free of me. There is nothing for either of us this way. Mammy, I beg—I beg—on my knees I beg. . . . I'll kiss your hands—I'll wash your feet. . . . Let me go——"

"No, no, no! Git up. Your mammy cain't bear dat. Git up for de love of Gawd. I got to let her go, Miss Bea. Lordagawd must help her from now on. Lordagawd and my prayers dat won't never leave her alone in de jungle. I got to let mah chile go, Miss Bea. Does you promise, too?"

"Yes,—Delilah——"

"Lordagawd, forgive mah chile, for she knows not what she does. Bless mah chile. Make happy mah chile. Strike me daid Lordagawd, if ever on dis earth I owns to bearin' her. . . ."

Seeing Delilah faint was the equivalent to beholding a great building slump to its side of earthquake.

Selections from Stories and Novels of Passing: "The Moment of Regret"

FRANCES E. W. HARPER

From Iola Leroy; or, Shadows Uplifted†

CHAPTER XXXII
WOOING AND WEDDING

Harry's vacation had been very pleasant. Miss Delany, with her fine conversational powers and ready wit, had added much to his enjoyment. Robert had given his mother the pleasantest room in the house, and in the evening the family would gather around her, tell her the news of the day, read to her from the Bible, join with her in thanksgiving for mercies received and in prayer for protection through the night. Harry was very grateful to Dr. Latimer for the kindly interest he had shown in accompanying Miss Delany and himself to places of interest and amusement. He was grateful, too, that in the city of P———doors were open to them which were barred against them in the South.

The bright, beautiful days of summer were gliding into autumn, with its glorious wealth of foliage, and the time was approaching for the departure of Harry and Miss Delany to their respective schools, when Dr. Latimer received several letters from North Carolina, urging him to come South, as physicians were greatly needed there. Although his practice was lucrative in the city of P———, he resolved he would go where his services were most needed.

A few evenings before he started he called at the house, and made an engagement to drive Iola to the park.

At the time appointed he drove up to the door in his fine equipage. Iola stepped gracefully in and sat quietly by his side to

---

† From Frances E. W. Harper, *Iola Leroy; or, Shadows Uplifted* (Boston: Beacon, 1987, pp. 267–74; orig. Philadelphia: Garrigues Brothers, 1893). See headnote, p. 200.

243

enjoy the loveliness of the scenery and the gorgeous grandeur of the setting sun.

"I expect to go South," said Dr. Latimer, as he drove slowly along.

"Ah, indeed," said Iola, assuming an air of interest, while a shadow flitted over her face. "Where do you expect to pitch your tent?"

"In the city of C———, North Carolina," he answered.

"Oh, I wish," she exclaimed, "that you were going to Georgia, where you could take care of that high-spirited brother of mine."

"I suppose if he were to hear you he would laugh, and say that he could take care of himself. But I know a better plan than that."

"What is it?" asked Iola, innocently.

"That you will commit yourself, instead of your brother, to my care."

"Oh, dear," replied Iola, drawing a long breath. "What would mamma say?"

"That she would willingly resign you, I hope."

"And what would grandma and Uncle Robert say?" again asked Iola.

"That they would cheerfully acquiesce. Now, what would I say if they all consent?"

"I don't know," modestly responded Iola.

"Well," replied Dr. Latimer, "I would say:—

"Could deeds my love discover,
   Could valor gain thy charms,
To prove myself thy lover
   I'd face a world in arms."

"And prove a good soldier," added Iola, smiling, "when there is no battle to fight."

"Iola, I am in earnest," said Dr. Latimer, passionately. "In the work to which I am devoted every burden will be lighter, every path smoother, if brightened and blessed with your companionship."

A sober expression swept over Iola's face, and, dropping her eyes, she said: "I must have time to think."

Quietly they rode along the river bank until Dr. Latimer broke the silence by saying:——

"Miss Iola, I think that you brood too much over the condition of our people."

"Perhaps I do," she replied, "but they never burn a man in the South that they do not kindle a fire around my soul."

"I am afraid," replied Dr. Latimer, "that you will grow morbid and nervous. Most of our people take life easily—why shouldn't you?"

"Because," she answered, "I can see breakers ahead which they do not."

"Oh, give yourself no uneasiness. They will catch the fret and fever of the nineteenth century soon enough. I have heard several of our ministers say that it is chiefly men of disreputable characters who are made the subjects of violence and lynch-law."

"Suppose it is so," responded Iola, feelingly. "If these men believe in eternal punishment they ought to feel a greater concern for the wretched sinner who is hurried out of time with all his sins upon his head, than for the godly man who passes through violence to endless rest."

"That is true; and I am not counseling you to be selfish; but, Miss Iola, had you not better look out for yourself?"

"Thank you, Doctor, I am feeling quite well."

"I know it, but your devotion to study and work is too intense," he replied.

"I am preparing to teach, and must spend my leisure time in study. Mr. Cloten is an excellent employer, and treats his employés as if they had hearts as well as hands. But to be an expert accountant is not the best use to which I can put my life."

"As a teacher you will need strong health and calm nerves. You had better let me prescribe for you. You need," he added, with a merry twinkle in his eyes, "change of air, change of scene, and change of name."

"Well, Doctor," said Iola, laughing, "that is the newest nostrum out. Had you not better apply for a patent?"

"Oh," replied Dr. Latimer, with affected gravity, "you know you must have unlimited faith in your physician."

"So you wish me to try the faith cure?" asked Iola, laughing.

"Yes, faith in me," responded Dr. Latimer, seriously.

"Oh, here we are at home!" exclaimed Iola. "This has been a glorious evening, Doctor. I am indebted to you for a great pleasure. I am extremely grateful."

"You are perfectly welcome," replied Dr. Latimer. "The pleasure has been mutual, I assure you."

"Will you not come in?" asked Iola.

Tying his horse, he accompanied Iola into the parlor. Seating himself near her, he poured into her ears words eloquent with love and tenderness.

"Iola," he said, "I am not an adept in courtly phrases. I am a plain man, who believes in love and truth. In asking you to share my lot, I am not inviting you to a life of ease and luxury, for year after year I may have to struggle to keep the wolf from the door, but your presence would make my home one of the brightest spots on earth, and one of the fairest types of heaven. Am I presumptuous in hoping that your love will become the crowning joy of my life?"

His words were more than a tender strain wooing her to love and happiness, they were a clarion call to a life of high and holy worth, a call which found a response in her heart. Her hand lay limp in his. She did not withdraw it, but, raising her lustrous eyes to his, she softly answered: "Frank, I love you."

After he had gone, Iola sat by the window, gazing at the splendid stars, her heart quietly throbbing with a delicious sense of joy and love. She had admired [white] Dr. Gresham and, had there been no barrier in her way, she might have learned to love him; but Dr. Latimer had grown irresistibly upon her heart. There were depths in her nature that Dr. Gresham had never fathomed; aspirations in her soul with which he had never mingled. But as the waves leap up to the strand, so her soul went out to Dr. Latimer. Between their lives were no impeding barriers, no inclination impelling one way and duty compelling another. Kindred hopes and tastes had knit their hearts; grand and noble purposes were lighting up their lives; and they esteemed it a blessed privilege to stand on the threshold of a new era and labor for those who had passed from the old oligarchy of slavery into the new commonwealth of freedom.

On the next evening, Dr. Latimer rang the bell and was answered by Harry, who ushered him into the parlor, and then came back to the sitting-room, saying, "Iola, Dr. Latimer has called to see you."

"Has he?" answered Iola, a glad light coming into her eyes. "Come, Lucille, let us go into the parlor."

"Oh, no," interposed Harry, shrugging his shoulders and catching Lucille's hand. "He didn't ask for you. When we went to the concert we were told three's a crowd. And I say one good turn deserves another."

"Oh, Harry, you are so full of nonsense. Let Lucille go!" said Iola.

"Indeed I will not. I want to have a good time as well as you," said Harry.

"Oh, you're the most nonsensical man I know," interposed Miss Delany. Yet she stayed with Harry.

"You're looking very bright and happy," said Dr. Latimer to Iola, as she entered.

"My ride in the park was so refreshing! I enjoyed it so much! The day was so lovely, the air delicious, the birds sang so sweetly, and the sunset was so magnificent."

"I am glad of it. Why, Iola, your home is so happy your heart should be as light as a school-girl's."

"Doctor," she replied, "I must be prematurely old. I have scarcely known what it is to be light-hearted since my father's death."

"I know it, darling," he answered, seating himself beside her, and drawing her to him. "You have been tried in the fire, but are you not better for the crucial test?"

"Doctor," she replied, "as we rode along yesterday, mingling with the sunshine of the present came the shadows of the past. I was thinking of the bright, joyous days of my girlhood, when I defended slavery, and of how the cup that I would have pressed to the lips of others was forced to my own. Yet, in looking over the mournful past, I would not change the Iola of then for the Iola of now."

"Yes," responded Dr. Latimer, musingly,

" 'Darkness shows us worlds of light
We never saw by day.' "

"Oh, Doctor, you cannot conceive what it must have been to be hurled from a home of love and light into the dark abyss of slavery; to be compelled to take your place among a people you have learned to look upon as inferiors and social outcasts; to be in the power of men whose presence would fill you with horror and loathing, and to know that there is no earthly power to protect you from the highest insults which brutal cowardice could shower upon you. I am so glad that no other woman of my race will suffer as I have done."

The flush deepened on her face, a mournful splendor beamed from her beautiful eyes, into which the tears had slowly gathered.

"Darling," he said, his voice vibrating with mingled feelings of tenderness and resentment, "you must forget the sad past. You are like a tender lamb snatched from the jaws of a hungry wolf, but who still needs protecting, loving care. But it must have been terrible," he added, in a painful tone.

"It was indeed! For awhile I was like one dazed. I tried to pray, but the heavens seemed brass over my head. I was wild with agony, and had I not been placed under conditions which roused all the resistance of my soul, I would have lost my reason."

"Was it not a mistake to have kept you ignorant of your colored blood?"

"It was the great mistake of my father's life, but dear papa knew something of the cruel, crushing power of caste; and he tried to shield us from it."

"Yes, yes," replied Dr. Latimer, thoughtfully, "in trying to shield you from pain he plunged you into deeper suffering."

"I never blame him, because I know he did it for the best. Had he lived he would have taken us to France, where I should have had a life of careless ease and pleasure. But now my life has a much grander significance than it would have had under such conditions. Fearful as the awakening was, it was better than to have slept through life."

"Best for you and best for me," said Dr. Latimer. "There are souls that never awaken; but if they miss the deepest pain they also lose the highest joy."

Dr. Latimer went South, after his engagement, and through his medical skill and agreeable manners became very successful in his practice. In the following summer, he built a cosy home for the reception of his bride, and came North, where, with Harry and Miss Delany as attendants, he was married to Iola, amid a pleasant gathering of friends, by Rev. Carmicle.

JAMES WELDON JOHNSON

When diplomat, editor, and writer James Weldon Johnson (1871–1938) first published his classic passing tale, *The Autobiography of an Ex-Colored Man* in 1912, he did so anonymously, leading many readers to believe that the novel was a true account. In the excerpt that follows, the novel's conclusion, the main characters conclude that passing may have been a mistake and that the white world was really a "mess of pottage," a judgment found in many black passing novels of the 1920s. The novel was reissued in the 1920s, under Johnson's own name and was one of the successful books of the Harlem Renaissance.

From The Autobiography of an Ex-Colored Man†

CHAPTER XI

I have now reached that part of my narrative where I must be brief, and touch only lightly on important facts; therefore, the reader must make up his mind to pardon skips and jumps and meager details.

When I reached New York I was completely lost. I could not have felt more a stranger had I been suddenly dropped into Constantinople. I knew not where to turn or how to strike out. I was so oppressed by a feeling of loneliness that the temptation to visit my old home in Connecticut was well nigh irresistible. I reasoned, however, that unless I found my old music teacher, I should be, after so many years of absence, as much of a stranger there as in New York; and, furthermore, that in view of the step which I had decided to take, such a visit would be injudicious. I remembered, too, that I had some property there in the shape of a piano and a few books, but decided that it would not be worth what it might cost me to take possession.

By reason of the fact that my living expenses in the South had been very small, I still had nearly four hundred dollars of my capital left. In contemplation of this, my natural and acquired Bohemian tastes asserted themselves, and I decided to have a couple of weeks' good time before worrying seriously about the future. I went to Coney Island and the other resorts, took in the pre-season shows along

† From James Weldon Johnson, *The Autobiography of an Ex-Colored Man* (New York: Dover, 1995, pp. 90–100; orig. publ. Boston: Sherman, French & Company, 1912).

Broadway, and ate at first class restaurants; but I shunned the old Sixth Avenue district as though it were pest infected. My few days of pleasure made appalling inroads upon what cash I had, and caused me to see that it required a good deal of money to live in New York as I wished to live, and that I should have to find, very soon, some more or less profitable employment. I was sure that unknown, without friends or prestige, it would be useless to try to establish myself as a teacher of music; so I gave that means of earning a livelihood scarcely any consideration. And even had I considered it possible to secure pupils, as I then felt, I should have hesitated about taking up a work in which the chances for any considerable financial success are necessarily so small. I had made up my mind that since I was not going to be a Negro, I would avail myself of every possible opportunity to make a white man's success; and that, if it can be summed up in any one word, means "money."

I watched the "want" columns in the newspapers and answered a number of advertisements; but in each case found the positions were such as I could not fill or did not want. I also spent several dollars for "ads" which brought me no replies. In this way I came to know the hopes and disappointments of a large and pitiable class of humanity in this great city, the people who look for work through the newspapers. After some days of this sort of experience, I concluded that the main difficulty with me was that I was not prepared for what I wanted to do. I then decided upon a course which, for an artist, showed an uncommon amount of practical sense and judgment. I made up my mind to enter a business college. I took a small room, ate at lunch counters, in order to economize, and pursued my studies with the zeal that I have always been able to put into any work upon which I set my heart. Yet, in spite of all my economy, when I had been at the school for several months, my funds gave out completely. I reached the point where I could not afford sufficient food for each day. In this plight, I was glad to get, through one of the teachers, a job as an ordinary clerk in a downtown wholesale house. I did my work faithfully, and received a raise of salary before I expected it. I even managed to save a little money out of my modest earnings. In fact, I began then to contract the money fever, which later took strong possession of me. I kept my eyes open, watching for a chance to better my condition. It finally came in the form of a position with a house which was at the time establishing a South American department. My knowledge of Spanish was, of course, the principal cause of my good luck; and it did more for me; it placed me where the other clerks were practically put out of competition with me. I was not slow in taking advantage of the opportunity to make myself indispensable to the firm.

What an interesting and absorbing game is money making! After each deposit at my savings-bank, I used to sit and figure out, all over again, my principal and interest, and make calculations on what the increase would be in such and such time. Out of this I derived a great deal of pleasure. I denied myself as much as possible in order to swell my savings. Even so much as I enjoyed smoking, I limited myself to an occasional cigar, and that was generally of a variety which in my old days at the "Club" was known as a "Henry Mud." Drinking I cut out altogether, but that was no great sacrifice.

The day on which I was able to figure up $1,000.00 marked an epoch in my life. And this was not because I had never before had money. In my gambling days and while I was with my "millionaire" I handled sums running high up into the hundreds; but they had come to me like fairy god-mother's gifts, and at a time when my conception of money was that it was made only to spend. Here, on the other hand, was a thousand dollars which I had earned by days of honest and patient work, a thousand dollars which I had carefully watched grow from the first dollar; and I experienced, in owning them, a pride and satisfaction which to me was an entirely new sensation. As my capital went over the thousand dollar mark, I was puzzled to know what to do with it, how to put it to the most advantageous use. I turned down first one scheme and then another, as though they had been devised for the sole purpose of gobbling up my money. I finally listened to a friend who advised me to put all I had in New York real estate; and under his guidance I took equity in a piece of property on which stood a rickety old tenement-house. I did not regret following this friend's advice, for in something like six months I disposed of my equity for more than double my investment. From that time on I devoted myself to the study of New York real estate, and watched for opportunities to make similar investments. In spite of two or three speculations which did not turn out well, I have been remarkably successful. To-day I am the owner and part-owner of several flat-houses. I have changed my place of employment four times since returning to New York, and each change has been a decided advancement. Concerning the position which I now hold, I shall say nothing except that it pays extremely well.

As my outlook on the world grew brighter, I began to mingle in the social circles of the men with whom I came in contact; and gradually, by a process of elimination, I reached a grade of society of no small degree of culture. My appearance was always good and my ability to play on the piano, especially ragtime, which was then at the height of its vogue, made me a welcome guest. The anomaly of my social position often appealed strongly to my sense of humor. I frequently smiled inwardly at some remark not altogether complimentary to people of color; and more than once I felt like declaiming, "I am a colored man. Do I not disprove the theory that one drop of Negro blood renders a man unfit?" Many a night when I returned to my room after an enjoyable evening, I laughed heartily over what struck me as the capital joke I was playing.

Then I met her, and what I had regarded as a joke was gradually changed into the most serious question of my life. I first saw her at a musical which was given one evening at a house to which I was frequently invited. I did not notice her among the other guests before she came forward and sang two sad little songs. When she began I was out in the hallway where many of the men were gathered; but with the first few notes I crowded with others into the doorway to see who the singer was. When I saw the girl, the surprise which I had felt at the first sound of her voice was heightened; she was almost tall and quite slender, with lustrous yellow hair and eyes so blue as to appear almost black. She was as white as a lily, and she was dressed in white. Indeed, she seemed to me the most dazzlingly white thing I had ever seen. But it was not her delicate beauty which attracted me most; it was her voice, a voice which made one wonder how tones of such passionate color could come from so fragile a body.

I determined that when the programme was over I would seek an introduction to her; but at the moment, instead of being the easy man of the world, I became again the bashful boy of fourteen, and my courage failed me. I contented myself with hovering as near her as politeness would permit; near enough to hear her voice, which in conversation was low, yet thrilling, like the deeper middle tones of a flute. I watched the men gather around her talking and laughing in an easy manner, and wondered how it was possible for them to do it. But destiny, my special destiny, was at work. I was standing near, talking with affected gayety to several young ladies, who, however, must have remarked my preoccupation; for my second sense of hearing was alert to what was being said by the group of which the girl in white was the center, when I heard her say, "I think his playing of Chopin is exquisite." And one of my friends in the group replied, "You haven't met him? Allow me—" then turning to me, "Old man, when you have a moment I wish you to meet Miss———." I don't know what she said to me or what I said to her. I can remember that I tried to be clever, and experienced a growing conviction that I was making myself appear more and more idiotic. I am certain, too, that, in spite of my Italian-like complexion, I was as red as a beet.

Instead of taking the car I walked home. I needed the air and exercise as a sort of sedative. I am not sure whether my troubled condition of mind was due to the fact that I had been struck by love or to the feeling that I had made a bad impression upon her.

As the weeks went by, and when I had met her several more times, I came to know that I was seriously in love; and then began for me days of worry, for I had more than the usual doubts and fears of a young man in love to contend with.

Up to this time I had assumed and played my rôle as a white man with a certain degree of nonchalance, a carelessness as to the outcome, which made the whole thing more amusing to me than serious; but now I ceased to regard "being a white man" as a sort of practical joke. My acting had called for mere external effects. Now I began to doubt my ability to play the part. I watched her to see if she was scrutinizing me, to see if she was looking for anything in me which made me differ from the other men she knew. In place of an old inward feeling of superiority over many of my friends, I began to doubt myself. I began even to wonder if I really was like the men I associated with; if there was not, after all, an indefinable something which marked a difference.

But, in spite of my doubts and timidity, my affair progressed; and I finally felt sufficiently encouraged to decide to ask her to marry me. Then began the hardest struggle of my life, whether to ask her to marry me under false colors or to tell her the whole truth. My sense of what was exigent made me feel there was no necessity of saying anything; but my inborn sense of honor rebelled at even indirect deception in this case. But however much I moralized on the question, I found it more and more difficult to reach the point of confession. The dread that I might lose her took possession of me each time I sought to speak, and rendered it impossible for me to do so. That moral courage requires more than physical courage is no mere poetic fancy. I am sure I would have found it easier to take the place of a gladiator, no matter how fierce the Numidian lion, than to tell that slender girl that I had Negro blood in my veins. The fact which I had at times wished to cry out, I now wished to hide forever.

During this time we were drawn together a great deal by the mutual bond of music. She loved to hear me play Chopin, and was herself far from being a poor performer of his compositions. I think I carried her every new song that was published which I thought suitable to her voice, and played the accompaniment for her. Over these songs we were like two innocent children with new toys. She had never been anything but innocent; but my innocence was a transformation wrought by my love for her, love which melted away my cynicism and whitened my sullied soul and gave me back the wholesome dreams of my boyhood. There is nothing better in all the world that a man can do for his moral welfare than to love a good woman.

My artistic temperament also underwent an awakening. I spent many hours at my piano, playing over old and new composers. I also wrote several little pieces in a more or less Chopinesque style, which I dedicated to her. And so the weeks and months went by. Often words of love trembled on my lips, but I dared not utter them, because I knew they would have to be followed by other words which I had not the courage to frame. There might have been some other woman in my set with whom I could have fallen in love and asked to marry me without a word of explanation; but the more I knew this girl, the less could I find it in my heart to deceive her. And yet, in spite of this specter that was constantly looming up before me, I could never have believed that life held such happiness as was contained in those dream days of love.

One Saturday afternoon, in early June, I was coming up Fifth Avenue, and at the corner of Twenty-third Street I met her. She had been shopping. We stopped to chat for a moment, and I suggested that we spend half an hour at the Eden Musée. We were standing leaning on the rail in front of a group of figures, more interested in what we had to say to each other than in the group, when my attention became fixed upon a man who stood at my side studying his catalogue. It took me only an instant to recognize in him my old friend "Shiny." My first impulse was to change my position at once. As quick as a flash I considered all the risks I might run in speaking to him, and most especially the delicate question of introducing him to her. I must confess that in my embarrassment and confusion I felt small and mean. But before I could decide what to do he looked around at me and, after an instant, said, "Pardon me; but isn't this————?" The nobler part in me responded to the sound of his voice, and I took his hand in a hearty clasp. Whatever fears I had felt were quickly banished, for he seemed, at a glance, to divine my situation, and let drop no word that would have aroused suspicion as to the truth. With a slight misgiving I presented him to her, and was again relieved of fear. She received the introduction in her usual gracious manner, and without the least hesitancy or embarrassment joined in the conversation. An amusing part about the introduction was that I was upon the point of introducing him as "Shiny," and stammered a second or two before I could recall his name. We chatted for some fifteen minutes. He was spending his vacation North, with the intention of doing four or six weeks' work in one of the summer schools; he was also going to take a bride back with him in the fall. He asked me about myself, but in so diplomatic a way that I found no difficulty in answering him. The polish of his language and the unpedantic manner in which he revealed his culture greatly impressed her; and after we had left the Musée she showed it by questioning me about him. I was surprised at the amount of interest a refined black man could arouse. Even after changes in the conversation she reverted several times to the subject of "Shiny." Whether it was more than mere curiosity I could not tell; but I was convinced that she herself knew very little about prejudice.

Just why it should have done so I do not know; but somehow the "Shiny" incident gave me encouragement and confidence to cast the die of my fate; but I reasoned that since I wanted to marry her only, and since it concerned her alone, I would divulge my secret to no one else, not even her parents.

One evening, a few days afterwards, at her home, we were going over some new songs and compositions, when she asked me, as she often did, to play the "13th Nocturne." When I began she drew a chair near to my right, and sat leaning with her elbow on the end of the piano, her chin resting on her hand, and her eyes reflecting the emotions which the music awoke in her. An impulse which I could not control rushed over me, a wave of exaltation, the music under my fingers sank almost to a whisper, and calling her for the first time by her Christian name, but without daring to look at her, I said, "I love you, I love you, I love you." My fingers were trembling, so that I ceased playing. I felt her hand creep to mine, and when I looked at her her eyes were glistening with tears. I understood, and could scarcely resist the longing to take her in my arms; but I remembered, remembered that which has been the sacrificial altar of so much happiness—Duty; and bending over her hand in mind, I said, "Yes, I love you; but there is something more, too, that I must tell you." Then I told her, in what words I do not know, the truth. I felt her hand grow cold, and when I looked up she was gazing at me with a wild, fixed stare as though I was some object she had never seen. Under the strange light in her eyes I felt that I was growing black and thick-featured and crimp-haired. She appeared not to have comprehended what I had said. Her lips trembled and she attempted to say something to me; but the words stuck in her throat. Then dropping her head on the piano she began to weep with great sobs that shook her frail body. I tried to console her, and blurted out incoherent words of love; but this seemed only to increase her distress, and when I left her she was still weeping.

When I got into the street I felt very much as I did the night after meeting my father and sister at the opera in Paris, even a similar desperate inclination to get drunk; but my self-control was stronger. This was the only time in my life that I ever felt absolute regret at being colored, that I cursed the drops of African blood in my veins, and wished that I were really white. When I reached my rooms I sat and smoked several cigars while I tried to think out the significance of what had occurred. I reviewed the whole history of our acquaintance, recalled each smile she had given me, each word she had said to me that nourished my hope. I went over the scene we had just gone through, trying to draw from it what was in my favor and what was against me. I was rewarded by feeling confident that she loved me, but I could not estimate what was the effect upon her of my confession. At last, nervous and unhappy, I wrote her a letter, which I dropped into the mailbox before going to bed, in which I said:

"I understand, understand even better than you, and so I suffer even more than you. But why should either of us suffer for what neither of us is to blame? If there is any blame, it belongs to me, and I can only make the old, yet strongest plea that can be offered, I love you; and I know that my love, my great love, infinitely overbalances that blame, and blots it out. What is it that stands in the way of our happiness? It is not what you feel or what I feel; it is not what you are or what I am. It is what others feel and are. But, oh! is that a fair price? In all the endeavors and struggles of life, in all our strivings and longings there is only one thing worth seeking, only one thing worth winning, and that is love. It is not always found; but when it is, there is nothing in all the world for which it can be profitably exchanged."

The second morning after, I received a note from her which stated briefly that she was going up in New Hampshire to spend the summer with relatives there. She made no reference to what had passed between us; nor did she say exactly when she would leave the city. The note contained no single word that gave me any clue to her feelings. I could only gather hope from the fact that she had written at all. On the same evening, with a degree of trepidation which rendered me almost frightened, I went to her house.

I met her mother, who told me that she had left for the country that very afternoon. Her mother treated me in her usual pleasant manner, which fact greatly reassured me; and I left the house with a vague sense of hope stirring in my breast, which sprang from the conviction that she had not yet divulged my secret. But that hope did not remain with me long. I waited one, two, three weeks, nervously examining my mail every day, looking for some word from her. All of the letters received by me seemed so insignificant, so worthless, because there was none from her. The slight buoyancy of spirit which I had felt gradually dissolved into gloomy heartsickness. I became preoccupied, I lost appetite, lost sleep, and lost ambition. Several of my friends intimated to me that perhaps I was working too hard.

She stayed away the whole summer. I did not go to the house, but saw her father at various times, and he was as friendly as ever. Even after I knew that she was back in town I did not go to see her. I determined to wait for some word or sign. I had finally taken refuge and comfort in my pride, pride which, I suppose, I came by naturally enough.

The first time I saw her after her return was one night at the theater. She and her mother sat in company with a young man whom I knew slightly, not many seats away from me. Never did she appear more beautiful; and yet, it may have been my fancy, she seemed a trifle paler and there was a suggestion of haggardness in her countenance. But that only heightened her beauty; the very delicacy of her charm melted down the strength of my pride. My situation made me feel weak and powerless, like a man trying with his bare hands to break the iron bars of his prison cell. When the performance was over I hurried out and placed myself where, unobserved, I could see her as she passed out. The haughtiness of spirit in which I had sought relief was all gone; and I was willing and ready to undergo any humiliation.

Shortly afterward we met at a progressive card party, and during the evening we were thrown together at one of the tables as partners. This was really our first meeting since the eventful night at her house. Strangely enough, in spite of our mutual nervousness, we won every trick of the game, and one of our opponents jokingly quoted the old saw, "Lucky at cards, unlucky in love." Our eyes met, and I am sure that in the momentary glance my whole soul went out to her in one great plea. She lowered her eyes and uttered a nervous little laugh. During the rest of the game I fully merited the unexpressed and expressed abuse of my various partners; for my eyes followed her wherever she was, and I played whatever card my fingers happened to touch.

Later in the evening she went to the piano and began to play very softly, as to herself, the opening bars of the 13th Nocturne. I felt that the psychic moment of my life had come, a moment which if lost could never be called back; and, in as careless a manner as I could assume, I sauntered over to the piano and stood almost bending over her. She continued playing; but, in a voice that was almost a whisper, she called me by my Christian name and said, "I love you, I love you, I love you." I took her place at the piano and played the Nocturne in a manner that silenced the chatter of the company both in and out of the room; involuntarily closing it with the major triad.

We were married the following spring, and went to Europe for several months. It was a double joy for me to be in France again under such conditions.

First there came to us a little girl, with hair and eyes dark like mine, but who is growing to have ways like her mother. Two years later there came a boy, who has my temperament, but is fair like his mother, a little golden-headed god, a face and head that would have delighted the heart of an old Italian master. And this boy, with his mother's eyes and features, occupies an inner sanctuary of my heart; for it was for him that she gave all; and that is the second sacred sorrow of my life.

The few years of our married life were supremely happy, and, perhaps she was even happier than I; for after our marriage, in spite of all the wealth of her love which she lavished upon me, there came a new dread to haunt me, a dread which I cannot explain and which was unfounded, but one that never left me. I was in constant fear that she would discover in me some shortcoming which she would unconsciously attribute to my blood rather than to a failing of human nature. But no cloud ever came to mar our life together; her loss to me is irreparable. My children need a mother's care, but I shall never marry again. It is to my children that I have devoted my life. I no longer have the same fear for myself of my secret being found out; for since my wife's death I have gradually dropped out of social life; but there is nothing I would not suffer to keep the "brand" from being placed upon them.

It is difficult for me to analyze my feelings concerning my present position in the world. Sometimes it seems to me that I have never really been a Negro, that I have been only a privileged spectator of their inner life; at other times I feel that I have been a coward, a deserter, and I am possessed by a strange longing for my mother's people.

Several years ago I attended a great meeting in the interest of Hampton Institute at Carnegie Hall. The Hampton students sang the old songs and awoke memories that left me sad. Among the speakers were R. C. Ogden, Ex-Ambassador Choate, and Mark Twain; but the greatest interest of the audience was centered in Booker T. Washington; and not because he so much surpassed the others in eloquence, but because of what he represented with so much earnestness and faith. And it is this that all of that small but gallant band of colored men who are publicly fighting the cause of their race have behind them. Even those who oppose them know that these men have the eternal principles of right on their side, and they will be victors even though they should go down in defeat. Beside them I feel small and selfish. I am an ordinarily successful white man who has made a little money. They are men who are making history and a race. I, too, might have taken part in a work so glorious.

My love for my children makes me glad that I am what I am, and keeps me from desiring to be otherwise; and yet, when I sometimes open a little box in which I still keep my fast yellowing manuscripts, the only tangible remnants of a vanished dream, a dead ambition, a sacrificed talent, I cannot repress the thought, that, afte all, I have chosen the lesser part, that I have sold my birthright for a mess of pottage.

WALTER WHITE

Civil rights leader Walter White (1893–1955) worked in various capacities with the NAACP for over thirty years and served as its Executive Secretary from 1931 until his death, leading anti-lynching crusades and the struggle for integration. Blond and blue-eyed, White was noted for his refusal to pass as white. His other books included *The Fire in the Flint, Rope and Faggot: A Biography of Judge Lynch* and *A Man Called White*. In *Flight*, White's heroine Mimi passes for white for many years until, as the following excerpt depicts, she comes to see something deeper in black culture than exists in her white world and decides, at last, to return to being black.

From Flight†

✳ ✳ ✳

The next night she slipped from the house after an early dinner and with the spirit of high adventure hurried through the melting snow towards the West Side subway station. She came to the surface again in Harlem and there she wandered through the streets. She wondered why in the days when restlessness had gripped her after a hard day at Francine's she had never come to Harlem as she had walked through the streets where French and Italian and Gipsy and Jewish people lived,—wondered even as she knew why she had not come to Negro Harlem.

It was a new Harlem she now saw, or rather, though she did not realize it, it was a new Mimi through whose eyes she saw it. Gone were the morose, the worried, the unhappy, the untranquil faces she had been seeing down town for years. Here there was light and spontaneous laughter, here there was real joyfulness in voices and eyes. Here was leisureliness, none of the hectic dashing after material things which brought little happiness when gained. She lingered near a crowd that chatted with frequent outbursts of spontaneous laughter. A wizened little Negro was being bantered by another as the first one sought to prove his non-existent prowess as a fighter.

"I hit him three or four times and he only hit me once," he boasted loudly.

"Go on, Mushmouth, that's all David hit Goliath," his tormentor cheerfully answered. A third man who had seen the fight completed the boastful one's rout when he described pungently the expression on the face of the defeated one: "He made a face like a nigger tasting his first olive!" . . .

As Mimi sat in the roaring subway on her way home, she felt within her a renewing of her old eagerness towards life. Here was something real that the unknowing and unseeing had called "native humour" and "Negro comedy." But, somewhat vaguely, she felt the thing went deeper than that. She speculated as to the lasting value of machines

---

† From Walter White, *Flight* (Baton Rouge: Louisiana State University Press, 1998, pp. 294–300; orig. publ. New York: Knopf, 1926).

and all that they brought—whether a radio over which came "Yes, We Have No Bananas" added measurably to the sum total of happiness. She was wondering yet when sleep overcame her. . . .

In the days that followed there came to her out of the tangled maze of her thoughts a clearer conception of the causes underlying her discontent. She loved the comforts of her home, from the shiny brass knocker on the snowy white front door to the full-length mirrors in which she loved to gaze at her rounded form after her morning bath in the big blue-and-white porcelain tub. But she wondered if the sombre, cynical companions she met in her home and in other places were worth the price she was paying for these luxuries. People who were playing at enjoying life but whose unhappiness shone through all they did or said. She wondered. . . .

CHAPTER XXIV

Carnegie Hall was surrounded by streams of people, white and black, that were swallowed up in the vast building. Their car finally edged its way towards the curb close enough for them to alight. Inside, Mimi noted that every seat seemed to be taken as she followed Jimmie down the aisle in the wake of the grey-clad usher. The tiers of seats on the platform too were rapidly filling. The rumble of voices hushed. Out of a door on one side of the platform came a short dark figure followed by a taller one whose skin was brown. A salvo of applause welled up and swept over the bowing figure as he faced the shifting panorama of upturned faces.

Silence. The pianist leaned low over his instrument, and long brown fingers lightly touched ivory keys, prodding them gently in light, gentle touches. A chord. The immobile figure of the singer galvanized into tense attentiveness. Back went the head on which crisply curled hair hung close. Eyes shut, gleaming teeth were revealed as a thin pure note poured from parted lips. The harsh guttural tones of the German were transmuted into a finespun sound as pure and delicate as a silken thread. Out it poured.

> If thou art near me,
> I will go with joy to death and rest;
> Ah, how happy were my end,
> with the pressure of thy fair hands and
> the glance of thy true eyes.

Through songs by Bach and Schubert, by Brahms and Franck, by Quilter and Jensen, the singer made his way. And then he sang the songs of his own people. Not a sound disturbed the spell he had woven, the auditors dared hardly breathe. "Nobody Knows de

Trouble I See," he sang, a strange, wistful sadness pervading the music.

As from a fountain of bronze, tiny jets of gold and silver sound were flung in a pellucid stream high above the heads of the silent throng. It broke against the ceiling, the iridescent bubbles bursting in radiant glory, dissolving into myriad little drops of sound, each perfect and complete in itself. Down they were wafted in gentle benediction upon the heads of the listeners. Soothing, comforting, they brought peace and rest and happiness. Before them fled all worries, all cares, all lines of sex and class and race melting the heterogeneous throng into a perfect unity.

Upon Mimi the music served as magic metal keys which opened before her eyes mystic rooms, some of them long closed, some of them never opened for her before, all of them musty through long dark days and longer nights of disuse.

> "Nobody knows the trouble I see,
> Nobody knows but Jesus. . . ."

Ghostly figures moved shadowily across the rooms—figures with eyes sad with the tragedies of a thousand years, eyes bright with the faith which is born of strength in trial. Figures which by some strange legerdemain began as she watched them to lose their unearthly diaphanousness and, like Galatea,[1] to become flesh and blood. The transformation did not startle nor alarm her—instead, held fast in the spell woven by the black singer, the re-creation of life in the figures before her seemed the most natural thing in the world.

A vast impenetrable tangle of huge trees appeared, their pithy bulk rising in ebon beauty to prodigious heights. As she gazed, half afraid of the wild stillness, the trees became less and less blackly solid, shading off into ever lighter greys. Then the trees were white, then there were none at all. In their stead an immense circular clearing in which moved at first slowly, then with increasing speed, a ring of graceful, rounded, lithe women and stalwart, magnificently muscled men, all with skins of midnight blackness. To music of barbaric sweetness and rhythm they danced with sinuous grace and abandon. Soft little gurgling cries punctuated the music, cries which came more sharply, like little darting arrows, as the ecstatic surrender of the figures to the dance increased.

A loud cry of alarm and of warning came from afar. The dance stopped, the dancers poised in wonder and indecision. Another cry, nearer, more intelligible. The black men seized their spears and short swords. The women were huddled in the middle of the living ring. From the murky darkness of the trees there burst weird creatures

1. In the Pygmalion story, the female statue Aphrodite brings to life is sometimes called Galatea.

shouting. Weird, for their faces were not black as all men's faces were, but obviously covered with some white substance to make them more terrible, their hair not curly and black but straight and yellow. The fight was on. Gorily it went on and on. Back the ebon fighters were swept before the strange, diabolic weapons like black reeds which spurted lead and flame. Back they were swept treading on the bodies of their dead and dying comrades. Soon but a few were left. The invaders seized these, overpowering them through numbers. The women too were seized and hurried away to huge, stinking hulks of ships, vessels a hundred times as huge as the craft hewn from great trees of the black warriors. . . .

"Sometimes I'm up,
Sometimes I'm down,
Oh, yes, Lord;
Sometimes I'm almost to the ground. . . ."

Another door was opened for Mimi. This time she saw a ship wallowing in the trough of immense waves. Aboard there strode up and down unshaven, deep-eyed, fierce-looking sailors who sought with oath and blow and kick to still the clamorous outcries of their black passengers. These were close packed in ill-smelling, inadequate quarters where each day stalked the spectre whose visit meant one mouth less to feed. Black bodies were tossed carelessly overboard. No sooner did one of them touch the water than came sinister streaks of grey and white which seized the body long before the wails from the ship had died in the distance.

Under the spell of the music other doors opened one by one. This time it was an expansive field covered with white blossoms brilliant against the dusty green foliage of the cotton plants. Black figures bent low while near them stood with watchful eye and ready whip an overseer.

Another time it was at "the big house"; another, at muscle-wearying and spirit-crushing toil of another kind. But from them all there came these same weirdly sweet notes which now were being voiced by the slender dark figure on the platform yonder. A world of motion and of labour was caught up and held immobile in the tenuous, reluctant notes. Over them hovered that overtone of hope too great for extinction by whatever hardship or sorrow which might come to the singers. It was the personification of faith, a faith strong and immovable, a faith unshakable, a faith which made a people great. Against that faith, Mimi felt, contumely, brutality, oppression, scorn could do naught but dash and break like angry waves against huge granite cliffs.

To her sitting there in the semi-darkness came a vision of her own people which made her blood run fast. Whatever other faults they might possess, her own people had not been deadened and dehumanized by bitter hatred of their fellow men. The venom born of oppression practiced upon others weaker than themselves had not entered their souls. These songs were of peace and hope and faith, and in them she felt and knew the peace which so long she had been seeking and which so long had cluded her grasp.

Tears crept unnoticed to Mimi's eyes and made little cascades down her cheeks. A line of verse sprang to her mind with poignant appropriateness: "The music yearning like a God in pain." She knew she had found the answer to the riddle which had puzzled her. She looked at Jimmie as he gruffly cleared his throat, ashamed of the emotion which too had seized him. He seemed alien, a total stranger. She marvelled that she had married this man, had lived with him, he whom she did not know. Silently they drove home through the quiet emptiness of lower Fifth Avenue. Mimi without speaking went to her room and closed the door. Calm peace filled her. She knew now why she had been ill at ease, restless, dissatisfied with the life which at first had seemed so happy a one.

She knew too that Jimmie would not, could not understand. Should she try to tell him? No, she decided. It were better to leave his dreams and illusions undisturbed—he had little enough real happiness as it was. And his convictions, his prejudices were too deeply rooted, she was sure, to enable him to comprehend without pain and suffering. He had done all he could—it was not wholly his fault. . . .

A brilliant but cold sun was creeping over the housetops out of the East as she softly closed the door behind her and stood upon the topmost step. Another book in her life was being closed with the shutting of the door. Mimi raised her eyes to the cross on the church across the Square. Her head went up and her shoulders straightened. She joyously drew into her lungs deep draughts of the cold air.

"Free! Free! Free!" she whispered exultantly as with firm tread she went down the steps. "*Petit* Jean—my own people—and happiness!" was the song in her heart as she happily strode through the dawn, the rays of the morning sun dancing lightly upon the more brilliant gold of her hair. . . .

JESSIE REDMON FAUSET

Writer Jessie Redmon Fauset (1882–1961) published *There Is Confusion*, *The Chinaberry Tree*, and *Comedy, American Style*, as well as essays, poems, and short stories. Her writing is often considered a counterpart to Larsen's. In her roles as literary and contributing editor to *The Crisis*, she was an influential advocate for other black writers. In Fauset's passing novel *Plum Bun*, two passers discover the risks of masking their black identities when they fall in love with each other and, as the excerpt that follows reveals, one reveals his true identity before the other has also done so.

From Plum Bun†

CHAPTER V

All the next day and the next she dwelt on Anthony's story; she tried to put herself in his place, to force herself into a dim realization of the dark chamber of torture in which his mind and thoughts had dwelt for so many years. And she had added her modicum of pain, had been so unsympathetic, so unyielding; in the midst of the dull suffering, the sickness of life to which perhaps his nerves had become accustomed she had managed to inject an extra pinprick of poignancy. Oh, she would reward him for that; she would brim his loveless, cheated existence with joy and sweetness; she would cajole him into forgetting that terrible past. Some day he should say to her: "You have brought me not merely new life, but life itself." Those former years should mean no more to him than its pre-natal existence means to a baby.

Her fancy dwelt on, toyed with all the sweet offices of love; the delicate bondage that could knit together two persons absolutely *en rapport*. At the cost of every ambition which she had ever known she would make him happy. After the manner of most men his work would probably be the greatest thing in the world to him. And he should be the greatest thing in the world to her. He should be her task, her "job," the fulfilment of her ambition. A phrase from the writings of Anatole France came drifting into her mind. "There is a technique of love." She would discover it, employ it, not go drifting haphazardly, carelessly into this relationship. And suddenly she saw her affair with Roger in a new light; she could forgive him, she could forgive herself for that hitherto unpardonable union if through it she had come one iota nearer to the understanding and the need of Anthony.

His silence—for although the middle of the week had passed she had received no letter,—worried her not one whit. In the course of time he would come to her, remembering her perfect sympathy of the Sunday before and thinking that this woman was the atonement for what he considered her race. And then she would surprise him, she would tell him the truth, she would make herself inexpressibly dearer

---

† From Jessie Redmon Fauset, *Plum Bun: A Novel without a Moral* (London: Pandora, 1985, pp. 293–306; orig. publ. New York: Frederick A. Stokes, 1929).

and nearer to him when he came to know that her sympathy and her tenderness were real, fixed and lasting, because they were based and rooted in the same blood, the same experiences, the same comprehension of this far-reaching, stupid, terrible race problem. How inexpressibly happy, relieved and overwhelmed he would be! She would live with him in Harlem, in Africa, anywhere, any place. She would label herself, if he asked it; she would tell every member of her little coterie of white friends about her mixed blood; she would help him keep his vow and would glory in that keeping. No sacrifice of the comforts which came to her from "passing," of the assurance, even of the safety which the mere physical fact of whiteness in America brings, would be too great for her. She would withdraw where he withdrew, hate where he hated.

His letter which came on Thursday interrupted her thoughts, her fine dreams of self-immolation which women so adore. It was brief and stern, and read:

> "Angèle, don't think for one moment that I do not thank you for Sunday. . . . My heart is at your feet for what you revealed to me then. But you and I have nothing in common, have never had, and now can never have. More than race divides us. I think I shall go away. Meanwhile you are to forget me; amuse yourself, beautiful, charming, magnetic Angel with the men of your own race and leave me to my own.
>
> "ANTHONY."

It was such a strange letter; its coldness and finality struck a chill to her heart. She looked at the lonely signature, "Anthony,"—just that, no word of love or affection. And the phrase: "More than race divides us." Its hidden significance held a menace.

The letter was awaiting her on her return from work. She had come in all glowing with the promise of the future as she conceived it. And then here were these cold words killing her high hopes as an icy blast kills the too trusting blossoms of early spring. . . . Holding the letter she let her supper go untasted, unregarded, while she evolved some plan whereby she could see Anthony, talk to him. The tone of his letter did not sound as though he would yield to ordinary persuasion. And again in the midst of her bewilderment and suffering she was struck afresh with the difficulties inherent in womanhood in conducting the most ordinary and most vital affairs of life. She was still a little bruised in spirit that she had taken it upon herself to go to Anthony's rooms Sunday; it was a step she felt conventionally, whose justification lay only in its success. As long as she had considered it successful, she had been able to relegate it to the uttermost limbo of her self-consciousness. But now that it seemed to avail nothing it loomed up before her in all its social significance. She was that creature whom men, in their selfish fear, have contrived to paint as the least attractive of human kind,—"a girl who runs after men." It seemed to her that she could not stand the application of the phrase, no matter how unjustly, how inaptly used in her own case.

Looking for a word of encouragement she reread the note. The expression "My heart is at your feet" brought some reassurance; she remembered, too, his very real emotion of Sunday, only a few days before. Men, real men, men like Anthony, do not change. No, she could not let him go without one last effort. She would go to Harlem once more to his house, she would see him, reassure him, allay his fears, quench his silly apprehensions of non-compatability. As soon as he knew that they were both coloured, he'd succumb. Now he was overwrought. It had never occurred to her before that she might be glad to be coloured. . . . She put on her hat, walked slowly out the door, said to herself with a strange foreboding: "When I see this room again, I'll either be very happy, or very, very sad. . . ." Her courage rose, braced her, but she was sick of being courageous, she wanted to be a beloved woman, dependent, fragile, sought for, feminine; after this last ordeal she would be "womanly" to the point of ineptitude. . . .

During the long ride her spirits rose a little. After all, his attitude was almost inevitable. He thought she belonged to a race which to him stood for treachery and cruelty; he had seen her with Roger, Roger, the rich, the gay; he saw her as caring only for wealth and pleasure. Of course in his eyes she was separated from him by race and by more than race.

For long years she was unable to reconstruct that scene; her mind was always too tired, too sore to re-enact it.

As in a dream she saw Anthony's set, stern face, heard his firm, stern voice: "Angel-girl,—Angèle I told you not to come back. I told you it was all impossible."

She found herself clutching at his arm, blurting out the truth, forgetting all her elaborate plans, her carefully pre-concerted drama. "But, Anthony, Anthony, listen, everything's all right. I'm coloured; I've suffered too; nothing has to come between us."

For a moment off his guard he wavered. "Angèle, I didn't think you'd lie to me."

She was in tears, desperate. "I'm not lying, Anthony. It's perfectly true."

"I saw that picture of your mother, a white woman if I ever saw one,——"

"Yes, but a white coloured woman. My father was black, perfectly black and I have a sister, she's brown. My mother and I used to 'pass' sometimes just for the fun of it; she didn't mind being coloured. But I minded it terribly,—until very recently. So I left my home,—in

Philadelphia,—and came here to live,—oh, going for white makes life so much easier. You know it, Anthony." His face wan and terrible frightened her. "It doesn't make you angry, does it? You've passed yourself, you told me you had. Oh Anthony, Anthony, don't look at me like that! What is it?"

She caught at his hand, following him as he withdrew to the shiny couch where they both sat breathless for a moment. "God!" he said suddenly; he raised his arms, beating the void like a madman. "You in your foolishness, I in my carelessness, 'passing, passing' and life sitting back laughing, splitting her sides at the joke of it. Oh, it was all right for you,—but I didn't care whether people thought I was white or coloured,—if we'd only known,——"

"What on earth are you talking about? It's all right now."

"It isn't all right; it's worse than ever." He caught her wrist. "Angel, you're sure you're not fooling me?"

"Of course I'm not. I have proof, I've a sister right here in New York; she's away just now. But when she comes back, I'll have you meet her. She is brown and lovely,—you'll want to paint her . . . don't you believe me, Anthony?"

"Oh yes, I believe you," he raised his arms again in a beautiful, fluid gesture, let them fall. "Oh, damn life, damn it, I say . . . isn't there any end to pain!"

Frightened, she got on her knees beside him. "Anthony, what's the matter? Everything's going to be all right; we're going to be happy."

"You may be. I'll never be happy. You were the woman I wanted,—I thought you were white. For my father's sake I couldn't marry a white girl. So I gave you up."

"And I wouldn't stay given up. See, here I am back again. You'll never be able to send me away." Laughing but shamefaced, she tried to thrust herself into his arms.

"No, Angel, no! You don't understand. There's, there's somebody else——"

She couldn't take it in. "Somebody else. You mean,—you're married? Oh Anthony, you don't mean you're married!"

"No, of course not, of course not! But I'm engaged."

"Engaged, engaged and not to me,—to another girl? And you kissed me, went around with me? I knew other men did that, but I never thought that of you! I thought you were like my father!" And she began to cry like a little girl.

Shamefaced, he looked on, jamming his hands tightly into his pockets. "I never meant to harm you; I never thought until that day in the park that you would care. And I cared so terribly! Think, I had given you up, Angèle,—I suppose that isn't your name really, is it?—and all of a sudden, you came walking back into my life and I said, 'I'll have the laugh on this damned mess after all. I'll spend a few days with her, love her a little, just a little. She'll never know, and I'll have a golden memory!' Oh, I had it coming to me, Angel! But the minute I saw you were beginning to care I broke off short."

A line from an old text was running through her head, rendering her speechless, inattentive. She was a little girl back in the church again in Philadelphia; the minister was intoning "All we like sheep have gone astray." He used to put the emphasis on the first word and Jinny and she would look at each other and exchange meaning smiles; he was a West Indian and West Indians had a way of misplacing the emphasis. The line sounded so funny: "*All* we like sheep,——" but perhaps it wasn't so funny after all; perhaps he had read it like that not because he was a West Indian but because he knew life and human nature. Certainly *she* had gone astray,—with Roger. And now here was Anthony, Anthony who had always loved her so well. Yet in his background there was a girl and he was engaged.

This brought her to a consideration of the unknown fiancée,—her rival. Deliberately she chose the word, for she was not through yet. This unknown, unguessed at woman who had stolen in like a thief in the night. . . .

"Have you known her long?" she asked him sharply.

"Who? Oh my,—my friend. No, not as long as I've known you."

A newcomer, an upstart. Well at least she, Angela, had the advantage of precedence.

"She's coloured, of course?"

"Of course."

They sat in a weary silence. Suddenly he caught her in his arms and buried his head in her neck. A quick pang penetrated to the very core of her being. He must have been an adorable baby. . . . Anthony and babies!

"Now God, Life, whatever it is that has power, this time you must help me!" cried her heart. She spoke to him gently.

"Anthony, you know I love you. Do you still love me?"

"Always, always, Angel."

"Do you—Oh, Anthony, I don't deserve it, but do you by any chance worship me?"

"Yes, that's it, that's just it, I worship you. I adore you. You are God to me. Oh, Angèle, if you'd only let me know. But it's too late now."

"No, no don't say that, perhaps it isn't too late. It all depends on this. Do you worship *her*, Anthony?" He lifted his haggard face.

"No—but she worships *me*. I'm God to *her*, do you see? If I fail her she won't say anything, she'll just fall back like a little weak kitten, like a lost sheep, like a baby. She'll die." He said as though unaware of his listener. "She's such a little thing. And sweet."

Angela said gently: "Tell me about her. Isn't it all very sudden? You said you hadn't known her long."

He began obediently. "It was not long after I—I lost you. She came to me out of nowhere, came walking to me into my room by mistake; she didn't see me. And she put her head down on her hands and began to cry terribly. I had been crying too—in my heart, you understand,—and for a moment I thought she might be the echo of that cry, might be the cry itself. You see, I'd been drinking a little,—you were so far removed, white and all that sort of thing. I couldn't marry a white woman, you know, not a white American. I owed that to my father.

"But at last I saw it was a girl, a real girl and I went over to her and put my hand on her shoulder and said: 'Little girl, what's the matter?'

"And she lifted her head, still hidden in the crook of her arm, you know the way a child does and said: 'I've lost my sister.' At first I thought she meant lost in the street and I said 'Well, come with me to the police station, I'll go with you, we'll give them a description and you'll find her again. People don't stay lost in this day and time.' I got her head on my shoulder, I almost took her on my knee, Angèle, she was so simple and forlorn. And presently she said: 'No, I don't mean lost that way; I mean she's left me, she doesn't want me any more. She wants other people.' And I've never been able to get anything else out of her. The next morning I called her up and somehow I got to seeing her, for her sake, you know. But afterwards when she grew happier,— she was so blithe, so lovely, so healing and blessed like the sun or a flower,—then I saw she was getting fond of me and I stayed away.

"Well, I ran across you and that Fielding fellow that night at the Van Meier lecture. And you were so happy and radiant, and Fielding so possessive,—damn him!—damn him!—he—you didn't let him hurt you, Angèle?"

As though anything that had ever happened in her life could hurt her like this! She had never known what pain was before. White-lipped, she shook her head. "No, he didn't hurt me."

"Well, I went to see her the next day. She came into the room like a shadow,—I realized she was getting thin. She was kind and sweet and far-off; impalpable, tenuous and yet there. I could see she was dying for me. And all of a sudden it came to me how wonderful it would be to have someone care like that. I went to her; I took her in my arms and I said: 'Child, child, I'm not bringing you a whole heart but could you love me?' You see I couldn't let her go after that."

"No," Angela's voice was dull, lifeless. "You couldn't. She'd die."

"Yes, that's it; that's just it. And I know you won't die, Angel."

"No, you're quite right. I won't die."

An icy hand was on her heart. At his first words: "She came walking into my room,——" an icy echo stirred a memory deep, deep within her inner consciousness. She heard Jinny saying: "I went walking into his room,——"

Something stricken, mortally stricken in her face fixed his attention. "Don't look like that, my girl, my dear Angel. . . . There are three of us in this terrible plight,—if I had only known. . . . I don't deserve the love of either of you but if one of you two must suffer it might as well be she as you. Come, we'll go away; even unhappiness, even remorse will mean something to us as long as we're together."

She shook her head. "No, that's impossible,—if it were someone else, I don't know, perhaps—I'm so sick of unhappiness,—maybe I'd take a chance. But in her case it's impossible."

He looked at her curiously. "What do you mean 'in her case'?"

"Isn't her name Virginia Murray?"

"Yes, yes! How did you guess it? Do you know her?"

"She's my sister. Angèle Mory,—Angela Murray, don't you see. It's the same name. And it's all my fault. I pushed her, sent her deliberately into your arms."

He could only stare.

"I'm the unkind sister who didn't want her. Oh, can't you understand? That night she came walking into your room by mistake it was because I had gone to the station to meet her and Roger Fielding came along. I didn't want him to know that I was coloured and I,—I didn't acknowledge her, I cut her."

"Oh," he said surprised and inadequate. "I don't see how you could have done that to a little girl like Virginia. Did she know New York?"

"No." She drooped visibly. Even the loss of him was nothing compared to this rebuke. There seemed nothing further to be said.

Presently he put his arm about her. "Poor Angèle. As though you could foresee! It's what life does to us, leads us into pitfalls apparently so shallow, so harmless and when we turn around there we are, caught, fettered,——"

Her miserable eyes sought his. "I was sorry right away, Anthony. I tried my best to get in touch with her that very evening. But I couldn't find her,—already you see, life was getting even with me, she had strayed into your room."

He nodded. "Yes, I remember it all so plainly. I was getting ready to go out, was all prepared as a matter of fact. Indeed I moved that very night. But I loitered on and on, thinking of you.

"The worst of it is I'll always be thinking of you. Oh Angèle, what does it matter, what does anything matter if we just have each other? This damned business of colour, is it going to ruin all chances of happiness? I've known trouble, pain, terrible devastating pain all my life. You've suffered too. Together perhaps we could find peace. We'd go to your sister and explain. She is kind and sweet; surely she'd understand."

He put his arms about her and the two clung to each other, solemnly, desperately, like children.

"I'm sick of pain, too, Anthony, sick of longing and loneliness. You can't imagine how I've suffered from loneliness."

"Yes, yes I can. I guessed it. I used to watch you. I thought you were probably lonely inside, you were so different from Miss Lister and Mrs. Starr. Come away with me and we'll share our loneliness together, somewhere where we'll forget,——"

And Virginia? You said yourself she'd die,——"

"She's so young, she—she could get over it." But his tone was doubtful, wavering.

She tore herself from him. "No, I took her sister away from her; I won't take her lover. Kiss me good-bye, Anthony."

They sat on the hard sofa. "To think we should find one another only to lose each other! To think that everything, every single thing was all right for us but that we were kept apart by the stupidity of fate. I'd almost rather we'd never learned the truth. Put your dear arms about me closer, Angel, Angel. I want the warmth, the sweetness of you to penetrate into my heart. I want to keep it there forever. Darling, how can I let you go?"

She clung to him weeping, weeping with the heart-broken abandonment of a child.

A bell shrilled four times.

He jumped up. "It's Sanchez, he's forgotten his key; thank God he did forget it. My darling, you must go. But wait for me. I'll meet you,—we'll go to your house, we'll find a way. We can't part like this!" His breath was coming in short gasps; she could see little white lines deepening about his mouth, his nostrils. Fearfully she caught at her hat.

"God bless you; good-bye Anthony. I won't see you again."

Halfway down the black staircase she met the heedless Sanchez, tall, sallow, thin, glancing at her curiously with a slightly amused smile. Politely he stood aside to let her pass, one hand resting lightly against his hip. Something in his attitude made her think of her unfinished sketch of Life. Hysterical, beside herself, she rushed down the remaining steps afraid to look around lest she should see the thin dark figure in pursuit, lest her ears should catch the expansion of that faint meaning smile into a guffaw, uproarious, menacing.

GEORGE S. SCHUYLER

Controversial journalist, satirist, and novelist George Samuel Schuyler (1895–1977) worked in a number of different genres, from essays to science-fiction. His bi-racial marriage to Texas heiress Josephine Cogdell became famous as a racial experiment. *Black No More* lampoons racial attitudes on both sides of the color line. In the excerpt that follows, a black male passer, now living as white, finds a white woman who had spurned him in Harlem and, later in the novel, marries her and joins forces with her racist father.

From Black No More†

This book is dedicated
to all Caucasians in the great republic
who can trace their ancestry
back ten generations
and confidently assert that there are no
Black leaves, twigs, limbs or branches on
their family trees.

FOUR

Matthew Fisher, alias Max Disher, joined the Easter Sunday crowds, twirling his malacca stick and ogling the pretty flappers who passed giggling in their spring finery. For nearly three months he had idled around the Georgia capital hoping to catch a glimpse of the beautiful girl who on New Year's Eve had told him "I never dance with niggers." He had searched diligently in almost every stratum of Atlanta society, but he had failed to find her. There were hundreds of tall, beautiful, blonde maidens in the city; to seek a particular one whose name one did not know was somewhat akin to hunting for a Russian Jew in the Bronx or a particular Italian gun-man in Chicago.

For three months he had dreamed of this girl, carefully perused the society columns of the local newspapers on the chance that her picture might appear in them. He was like most men who have been repulsed by a pretty girl, his desire for her grew stronger and stronger.

He was not finding life as a white man the rosy existence he had anticipated. He was forced to conclude that it was pretty dull and that he was bored. As a boy he had been taught to look up to white folks as just a little less than gods; now he found them little different from the Negroes, except that they were uniformly less courteous and less interesting.

Often when the desire for the happy-go-lucky, jovial good-fellowship of the Negroes came upon him strongly, he would go down

† From George S. Schuyler, *Black No More: being an account of the strange and wonderful workings of science in the land of the free, A.D. 1933–1940* (Boston: Northeastern University Press, 1989, pp. 62–79; orig. publ. New York: Macaulay Company, 1931).

to Auburn Avenue and stroll around the vicinity, looking at the dark folk and listening to their conversation and banter. But no one down there wanted him around. He was a white man and thus suspect. Only the black women who ran the "Call Houses" on the hill wanted his company. There was nothing left for him except the hard, materialistic, grasping, inbred society of the whites. Sometimes a slight feeling of regret that he had left his people forever would cross his mind, but it fled before the painful memories of past experiences in this, his home town.

The unreasoning and illogical color prejudice of most of the people with whom he was forced to associate infuriated him. He often laughed cynically when some coarse, ignorant white man voiced his opinion concerning the inferior mentality and morality of the Negroes. He was moving in white society now and he could compare it with the society he had known as a Negro in Atlanta and Harlem. What a let-down it was from the good breeding, sophistication, refinement and gentle cynicism to which he had become accustomed as a popular young man about town in New York's Black Belt. He was not able to articulate this feeling but he was conscious of the reaction nevertheless.

For a week, now, he had been thinking seriously of going to work. His thousand dollars had dwindled to less than a hundred. He would have to find some source of income and yet the young white men with whom he talked about work all complained that it was very scarce. Being white, he finally concluded, was no Open Sesame to employment for he sought work in banks and insurance offices without success.

During his period of idleness and soft living, he had followed the news and opinion in the local daily press and confessed himself surprised at the antagonistic attitude of the newspapers toward Black-No-More, Incorporated. From the vantage point of having formerly been a Negro, he was able to see how the newspapers were fanning the color prejudice of the white people. Business men, he found were also bitterly opposed to Dr. Crookman and his efforts to bring about chromatic democracy in the nation.

The attitude of these people puzzled him. Was not Black-No-More getting rid of the Negroes upon whom all of the blame was placed for the backwardness of the South? Then he recalled what a Negro street speaker had said one night on the corner of 138th Street and Seventh Avenue in New York: that unorganized labor meant cheap labor; that the guarantee of cheap labor was an effective means of luring new industries into the South; that so long as the ignorant white masses could be kept thinking of the menace of the Negro to Caucasian race purity and political control, they would give little thought to labor organization. It suddenly dawned upon Matthew

Fisher that this Black-No-More treatment was more of a menace to white business than to white labor. And not long afterward he became aware of the money-making possibilities involved in the present situation.

How could he work it? He was not known and he belonged to no organization. Here was a veritable gold mine but how could he reach the ore? He scratched his head over the problem but could think of no solution. Who would be interested in it that he could trust?

He was pondering this question the Monday after Easter while breakfasting in an armchair restaurant when he noticed an advertisement in a newspaper lying in the next chair. He read it and then re-read it.

THE KNIGHTS OF NORDICA
Want 10,000 Atlanta White Men and Women to
Join in the Fight for White Race Integrity.

Imperial Klonklave Tonight

The racial integrity of the Caucasian Race is being
threatened by the activities of a scientific
black Beelzebub in New York
Let us Unite Now Before It Is

TOO LATE!

Come to Nordica Hall Tonight
Admission Free.

Rev. Henry Givens,
Imperial Grand Wizard

Here, Matthew figured, was just what he had been looking for. Probably he could get in with this fellow Givens. He finished his cup of coffee, lit a cigar and paying his check, strolled out into the sunshine of Peachtree Street.

He took the trolley out to Nordica Hall. It was a big, unpainted barn-like edifice, with a suite of offices in front and a huge auditorium in the rear. A new oil cloth sign reading "THE KNIGHTS OF NORDICA" was stretched across the front of the building.

Matthew paused for a moment and sized up the edifice. Givens must have some money, he thought, to keep up such a large place. Might not be a bad idea to get a little dope on him before going inside.

"This fellow Givens is a pretty big guy around here, ain't he?" he asked the young man at the soda fountain across the street.

"Yessah, he's one o' th' bigges' men in this heah town. Used to be a big somethin' or other in th' old Ku Klux Klan 'fore it died. Now he's stahtin' this heah Knights o' Nordica."

"He must have pretty good jack," suggested Matthew.

"He oughtta have," answered the soda jerker. "My paw tells me he was close to th' money when he was in th' Klan."

Here, thought Matthew, was just the place for him. He paid for his soda and walked across the street to the door marked "Office." He felt a slight tremor of uneasiness as he turned the knob and entered. Despite his white skin he still possessed the fear of the Klan and kindred organizations possessed by most Negroes.

A rather pretty young stenographer asked him his business as he walked into the ante room. Better be bold, he thought. This was probably the best chance he would have to keep from working, and his funds were getting lower and lower.

"Please tell Rev. Givens, the Imperial Grand Wizard, that Mr. Matthew Fisher of the New York Anthropological Society is very anxious to have about a half-hour's conversation with him relative to his new venture." Matthew spoke in an impressive, businesslike manner, rocked back on his heels and looked profound.

"Yassah," almost whispered the awed young lady, "I'll tell him." She withdrew into an inner office and Matthew chuckled softly to himself. He wondered if he could impress this old fakir as easily as he had the girl.

Rev. Henry Givens, Imperial Grand Wizard of the Knights of Nordica, was a short, wizened, almost-bald, bull-voiced, ignorant ex-evangelist, who had come originally from the hilly country north of Atlanta. He had helped in the organization of the Ku Klux Klan following the Great War and had worked with a zeal only equalled by his thankfulness to God for escaping from the precarious existence of an itinerant saver of souls.

Not only had the Rev. Givens toiled diligently to increase the prestige, power and membership of the defunct Ku Klux Klan, but he had also been a very hard worker in withdrawing as much money from its treasury as possible. He convinced himself, as did the other officers, that this stealing was not stealing at all but merely appropriation of rightful reward for his valuable services. When the morons finally tired of supporting the show and the stream of ten-dollar memberships declined to a trickle, Givens had been able to retire gracefully and live on the interest of his money.

Then, when the newspapers began to recount the activities of Black-No-More, Incorporated, he saw a vision of work to be done, and founded the Knights of Nordica. So far there were only a hundred members but he had high hopes for the future. Tonight, he felt would tell the story. The prospect of a full treasury to dip into again made his little gray eyes twinkle and the palms of his skinny hands itch.

The stenographer interrupted him to announce the newcomer.

"Hum-n!" said Givens, half to himself. "New York Anthropological

Society, eh? This feller must know somethin'. Might be able to use him in this business. . . . All right, show him in!"

The two men shook hands and swiftly appraised each other. Givens waved Matthew to a chair.

"How can I serve you, Mr. Fisher?" he began in sepulchral tone dripping with unction.

"It is rather," countered Matthew in his best salesman's croon, "how I can serve you and your valuable organization. As an anthropologist, I have, of course, been long interested in the work with which you have been identified. It has always seemed to me that there was no question in American life more important than that of preserving the integrity of the white race. We all know what has been the fate of those nations that have permitted their blood to be polluted with that of inferior breeds." (He had read some argument like that in a Sunday supplement not long before, which was the extent of his knowledge of anthropology.) "This latest menace of Black-No-More is the most formidable the white people of America have had to face since the founding of the Republic. As a resident of New York City, I am aware, of course, of the extent of the activities of this Negro Crookman and his two associates. Already thousands of blacks have passed over into the white race. Not satisfied with operating in New York City, they have opened their sanitariums in twenty other cities from Coast to Coast. They open a new one almost every day. In their literature and advertisements in the darky newspapers they boast that they are now turning four thousand Negroes white every day." He knitted his blond eyebrows. "You see how great the menace is? At this rate there will not be a Negro in the country in ten years, for you must remember that the rate is increasing every day as new sanitariums are opened. Don't you see that something must be done about this immediately? Don't you see that Congress must be aroused; that these places must be closed?" The young man glared with belligerent indignation.

Rev. Givens saw. He nodded his head as Matthew, now glorying in his newly-discovered eloquence made point after point, and concluded that this pale, dapper young fellow, with his ready tongue, his sincerity, his scientific training and knowledge of the situation ought to prove a valuable asset to the Knights of Nordica.

"I tried to interest some agencies in New York," Matthew continued, "but they are all blind to this menace and to their duty. Then someone told me of you and your valuable work, and I decided to come down here and have a talk with you. I had intended to suggest the organization of some such militant secret order as you have started, but since you've already seen the necessity for it, I want to hasten to offer my services as a scientific man and one familiar with the facts and able to present them to your members."

"I should be very glad," boomed Givens, "very happy, indeed, Brother Fisher, to have you join us. We need you. I believe you can help us a great deal. Would you, er—ah, be interested in coming out to the mass meeting this evening? It would help us tremendously to get members if you would be willing to get up and tell the audience what you have just related about the progress of this iniquitous nigger corporation in New York."

Matthew pretended to think over the matter for a moment or two and then agreed. If he made a hit at the initial meeting, he would be sure to get on the staff. Once there he could go after the larger game. Unlike Givens, he had no belief in the racial integrity nonsense nor any confidence in the white masses whom he thought were destined to flock to the Knights of Nordica. On the contrary he despised and hated them. He had the average Negro's justifiable fear of the poor whites and only planned to use them as a stepladder to the real money.

When Matthew left, Givens congratulated himself upon the fact that he had been able to attract such talent to the organization in its very infancy. His ideas must be sound, he concluded, if scientists from New York were impressed by them. He reached over, pulled the dictionary stand toward him and opened the big book at A.

"Lemme see, now," he muttered aloud. "Anthropology. Better git that word straight 'fore I go talkin' too much about it. . . . Humn! Humn! . . . That boy must know a hull lot." He read over the definition of the word twice without understanding it, and then cutting off a large chew of tobacco from his plug, he leaned back in his swivel chair to rest after the unaccustomed mental exertion.

Matthew went gaily back to his hotel. "Man alive!" he chortled to himself. "What a lucky break! Can't keep old Max down long. . . . Will I speak to 'em? Well, I won't stay quiet!" He felt so delighted over the prospect of getting close to some real money that he treated himself to an expensive dinner and a twenty-five-cent cigar. Afterward he inquired further about old man Givens from the house detective, a native Atlantan.

"Oh, he's well heeled—the old crook!" remarked the detective. "Damnify could ever understand how such ignorant people get a-hold of th' money; but there y'are. Owns as pretty a home as you can find around these parts an' damn 'f he ain't stahtin' a new racket."

"Do you think he'll make anything out of it?" inquired Matthew, innocently.

"Say, Brother, you mus' be a stranger in these parts. These damn, ignorant crackers will fall fer anything fer a while. They ain't had no Klan here fer goin' on three years. Leastwise it ain't been functionin'." The old fellow chuckled and spat a stream of tobacco juice into a nearby cuspidor. Matthew sauntered away. Yes, the pickings ought to be good.

Equally enthusiastic was the Imperial Grand Wizard when he came home to dinner that night. He entered the house humming one of his favorite hymns and his wife looked up from the evening paper with surprise on her face. The Rev. Givens was usually something of a grouch but tonight he was as happy as a pickpocket at a country fair.

"What's th' mattah with you?" she inquired, sniffing suspiciously.

"Oh, Honey," he gurgled, "I think this here Knights of Nordica is going over big; going over big! My fame is spreading. Only today I had a long talk with a famous anthropologist from New York and he's going to address our mass meeting tonight."

"Whut's an anthropologist?" asked Mrs. Givens, wrinkling her seamy brow.

"Oh-er, well, he's one of these here scientists what knows all about this here business what's going on up there in New York where them niggers is turning each other white," explained Rev. Givens hastily but firmly. "He's a mighty smaht feller and I want you and Helen to come out and hear him."

"B'lieve Ah will," declared Mrs. Givens, "if this heah rheumatism'll le' me foh a while. Doan know 'bout Helen, though. Evah since that gal went away tuh school she ain't bin int'rested in nuthin' upliftin' "

Mrs. Givens spoke in a grieved tone and heaved her narrow chest in a deep sigh. She didn't like all this newfangled foolishness of these young folks. They were getting away from God, that's what they were, and she didn't like it. Mrs. Givens was a Christian. There was no doubt about it because she freely admitted it to everybody, with or without provocation. Of course she often took the name of the Creator in vain when she got to quarreling with Henry; she had the reputation among her friends of not always stating the exact truth; she hated Negroes; her spouse had made bitter and profane comment concerning her virginity on their wedding night; and as head of the ladies' auxiliary of the defunct Klan she had copied her husband's financial methods; but that she was a devout Christion no one doubted. She believed the Bible from cover to cover, except what it said about people with money, and she read it every evening aloud, greatly to the annoyance of the Imperial Grand Wizard and his modern and comely daughter.

Mrs. Givens had probably once been beautiful but the wear and tear of a long life as the better half of an itinerant evangelist was apparent. Her once flaming red hair was turning gray and roan-like, her hatchet face was a criss-cross of wrinkles and lines, she was round-shouldered, hollow-chested, walked with a stoop and her long, bony, white hands looked like claws. She alternately dipped snuff and smoked an evil-smelling clay pipe, except when there was company at the house. At such times Helen would insist her mother "act like civilized people."

Helen was twenty and quite confident that she herself was civilized. Whether she was or not, she was certainly beautiful. Indeed, she was such a beauty that many of the friends of the family insisted that she must have been adopted. Taller than either of her parents, she was stately, erect, well proportioned, slender, vivid and knew how to wear her clothes. In only one way did she resemble her parents and that was in things intellectual. Any form of mental effort, she complained, made her head ache, and so her parents had always let her have her way about studying.

At the age of eleven she had been taken from the third grade in public school and sent to an exclusive seminary for the double purpose of gaining social prestige and concealing her mental incapacity. At sixteen when her instructors had about despaired of her, they were overjoyed by the decision of her father to send the girl to a "finishing school" in the North. The "finishing school" about finished what intelligence Helen possessed; but she came forth, four years later, more beautiful, with a better knowledge of how to dress and how to act in exclusive society, enough superficialties to enable her to get by in the "best" circles and a great deal of that shallow facetiousness that passes for sophistication in American upper-class life. A winter in Manhattan had rounded out her education. Now she was back home, thoroughly ashamed of her grotesque parents, and, like the other girls of her set, anxious to get a husband who at the same time was handsome, intelligent, educated, refined and rolling in wealth. As she was ignorant of the fact that no such man existed, she looked confidently forward into the future.

"I don't care to go down there among all those gross people," she informed her father at the dinner table when he broached the subject of the meeting. "They're so crude and elemental, don't you know," she explained, arching her narrow eyebrows.

"The common people are the salt of the earth," boomed Rev. Givens. "If it hadn't been for the common people we wouldn't have been able to get this home and send you off to school. You make me sick with all your modern ideas. You'd do a lot better if you'd try to be more like your Ma."

Both Mrs. Givens and Helen looked quickly at him to see if he was smiling. He wasn't.

"Why don'tcha go, Helen?" pleaded Mrs. Givens. "Yo fathah sez this heah man f'm N'Yawk is uh—uh scientist or somethin' an' knows a whole lot about things. Yuh might l'arn somethin'. Ah'd go mys'f if 'twasn't fo mah rheumatism." She sighed in self-pity and finished gnawing a drumstick.

Helen's curiosity was aroused and although she didn't like the idea of sitting among a lot of mill hands, she was anxious to see and hear this reputedly brilliant young man from the great metropolis where not long before she had lost both her provincialism and chastity.

"Oh, all right," she assented with mock reluctance. "I'll go."

The Knights of Nordica's flag-draped auditorium slowly filled. It was a bare, cavernous structure, with sawdust on the floor, a big platform at one end, row after row of folding wooden chairs and illuminated by large, white lights hanging from the rafters. On the platform was a row of five chairs, the center one being high-backed and gilded. On the lectern downstage was a bulky Bible. A huge American flag was stretched across the rear wall.

The audience was composed of the lower stratum of white working people: hard-faced, lantern-jawed, dull-eyed adult children, seeking like all humanity for something permanent in the eternal flux of life. The young girls in their cheap finery with circus makeup on their faces; the young men, aged before their time by child labor and a violent environment; the middle-aged folk with their shiny, shabby garb and beaten countenances; all ready and eager to be organized for any purpose except improvement of their intellects and standard of living.

Rev. Givens opened the meeting with a prayer "for the success, O God, of this thy work, to protect the sisters and wives and daughters of these, thy people, from the filthy pollution of an alien race."

A choir of assorted types of individuals sang "Onward Christian Soldiers" earnestly, vociferously and badly.

They were about to file off the platform when the song leader, a big, beefy, jovial mountain of a man, leaped upon the stage and restrained them.

"Wait a minute, folks, wait a minute," he commanded. Then turning to the assemblage: "Now people let's put some pep into this. We wanna all be happy and get in th' right spirit for this heah meetin'. Ah'm gonna ask the choir to sing th' first and last verses ovah ag'in, and when they come to th' chorus, Ah wantcha to all join in. Doan be 'fraid. Jesus wouldn't be 'fraid to sing 'Onward Christian Soldiers,' now would he? Come on, then. All right, choir, you staht; an' when Ah wave mah han' you'll join in on that theah chorus."

They obediently followed his directions while he marched up and down the platform, red-faced and roaring and waving his arms in time. When the last note had died away, he dismissed the choir and stepping to the edge of the stage he leaned far out over the audience and barked at them again.

"Come on, now, folks! Yuh caint slow up on Jesus now. He won't be satisfied with jus' one ole measly song. Yuh gotta let 'im know that yuh love 'im; that y're happy an' contented; that yuh ain't got no troubles an' ain't gonna have any. Come on, now. Le's sing that ole favorite what yo'all like so well: 'Pack Up Your Troubles in Your Old Kit Bag and Smile, Smile, Smile.'" He bellowed and they followed him. Again the vast hall shook with sound. He made them rise and grasp each other by the hand until the song ended.

Matthew, who sat on the platform alongside old man Givens viewed the spectacle with amusement mingled with amazement. He was amused because of the similarity of this meeting to the religious orgies of the more ignorant Negroes and amazed that earlier in the evening he should have felt any qualms about lecturing to these folks on anthropology, a subject with which neither he nor his hearers were acquainted. He quickly saw that these people would believe anything that was shouted at them loudly and convincingly enough. He knew what would fetch their applause and bring in their memberships and he intended to repeat it over and over.

The Imperial Grand Wizard spent a half-hour introducing the speaker of the evening, dwelt upon his supposed scholastic attainments, but took pains to inform them that, despite Matthew's vast knowledge, he still believed in the Word of God, the sanctity of womanhood and the purity of the white race.

For an hour Matthew told them at the top of his voice what they believed: i.e., that a white skin was a sure indication of the possession of superior intellectual and moral qualities; that all Negroes were inferior to them; that God had intended for the United States to be a white man's country and that with His help they could keep it so; that their sons and brothers might inadvertently marry Negresses or, worse, their sisters and daughters might marry Negroes, if Black-No-More, Incorporated, was permitted to continue its dangerous activities.

For an hour he spoke, interrupted at intervals by enthusiastic gales of applause, and as he spoke his eye wandered over the females in the audience, noting the comeliest ones. As he wound up with a spirited appeal for eager soldiers to join the Knights of Nordica at five dollars per head and the half-dozen "planted" emissaries led the march of suckers to the platform, he noted for the first time a girl who sat in the front row and gazed up at him raptly.

She was a titian blonde, well-dressed, beautiful and strangely familiar. As he retired amid thunderous applause to make way for Rev. Givens and the money collectors, he wondered where he had seen her before. He studied her from his seat.

Suddenly he knew. It was she! The girl who had spurned him; the girl he had sought so long; the girl he wanted more than anything in the world! Strange that she should be here. He had always thought of her as a refined, educated and wealthy lady, far above associating with such people as these. He was in a fever to meet her, some way, before she got out of his sight again, and yet he felt just a little disappointed to find her here.

He could hardly wait until Givens seated himself again before questioning him as to the girl's identity. As the beefy song leader led the roaring of the popular closing hymn, he leaned toward the Imperial Grand Wizard and shouted: "Who is that tall golden-haired girl sitting in the front row? Do you know her?"

Rev. Givens looked out over the audience, craning his skinny neck and blinking his eyes. Then he saw the girl, sitting within twenty feet of him.

"You mean that girl sitting right in front, there?" he asked, pointing.

"Yes, that one," said Matthew, impatiently.

"Heh! Heh! Heh!" chuckled the Wizard, rubbing his stubbly chin. "Why that there's my daughter, Helen. Like to meet her?"

Matthew could hardly believe his ears. Givens's daughter! Incredible! What a coincidence! What luck! Would he like to meet her? He leaned over and shouted "Yes."

LANGSTON HUGHES

Passing†

Chicago,
Sunday, Oct. 10.

DEAR MA,

I felt like a dog, passing you downtown last night and not speaking to you. You were great, though. Didn't give a sign that you even knew me, let alone I was your son. If I hadn't had the girl with me, Ma, we might have talked. I'm not as scared as I used to be about somebody taking me for colored any more just because I'm seen talking on the street to a Negro. I guess in looks I'm sort of suspect-proof, anyway. You remember what a hard time I used to have in school trying to convince teachers I was really colored. Sometimes, even after they met you, my mother, they wouldn't believe it. They just thought I had a mulatto mammy, I guess. Since I've begun to pass for white, nobody has ever doubted that I am a white man. Where I work, the boss is a Southerner and is always cussing out Negroes in my presence, not dreaming I'm one. It is to laugh!

Funny thing, though, Ma, how some white people certainly don't like colored people, do they? (If they did, then I wouldn't have to be

† From *The Ways of White Folks*, by Langston Hughes (New York: Vintage Books, 1990), pp. 51–54. Copyright 1934 and renewed 1962 by Langston Hughes. Used by permission of Alfred A. Knopf, a division of Random House, Inc. See headnote, p. 227.

passing to keep my good job.) They go out of their way sometimes to say bad things about colored folks, putting it out that all of us are thieves and liars, or else diseased—consumption and syphilis, and the like. No wonder it's hard for a black man to get a good job with that kind of false propaganda going around. I never knew they made a practice of saying such terrible things about us until I started passing and heard their conversations and lived their life.

But I don't mind being "white", Ma, and it was mighty generous of you to urge me to go ahead and make use of my light skin and good hair. It got me this job, Ma, where I still get $65 a week in spite of the depression. And I'm in line for promotion to the chief office secretary, if Mr. Weeks goes to Washington. When I look at the colored boy porter who sweeps out the office, I think that that's what I might be doing if I wasn't light-skinned enough to get by. No matter how smart that boy'd get to be, they wouldn't hire him for a clerk in the office, not if they knew it. Only for a porter. That's why I sometimes get a kick out of putting something over on the boss, who never dreams he's got a colored secretary.

But, Ma, I felt mighty bad about last night. The first time we'd met in public that way. That's the kind of thing that makes passing hard, having to deny your own family when you see them. Of course, I know you and I both realize it is all for the best, but anyhow it's terrible. I love you, Ma, and hate to do it, even if you say you don't mind.

But what did you think of the girl with me, Ma? She's the kid I'm going to marry. Pretty good looking, isn't she? Nice disposition. The parents are well fixed. Her folks are German-Americans and don't have much prejudice about them, either. I took her to see a colored revue last week and she thought it was great. She said, "Darkies are so graceful and gay." I wonder what she would have said if I'd told her I was colored, or half-colored—that my old man was white, but you weren't? But I guess I won't go into that. Since I've made up my mind to live in the white world, and have found my place in it (a good place), why think about race any more? I'm glad I don't have to, I know that much.

I hope Charlie and Gladys don't feel bad about me. It's funny I was the only one of the kids light enough to pass. Charlie's darker than you, even, Ma. I know he sort of resented it in school when the teachers used to take me for white, before they knew we were brothers. I used to feel bad about it, too, then. But now I'm glad you backed me up, and told me to go ahead and get all I could out of life. That's what I'm going to do, Ma. I'm going to marry white and live white, and if any of my kids are born dark I'll swear they aren't mine. I won't get caught in the mire of color again. Not me. I'm free, Ma, free!

I'd be glad, though, if I could get away from Chicago, transferred to the New York office, or the San Francisco branch of the firm— somewhere where what happened last night couldn't ever occur again. It was awful passing *you* and not speaking. And if Gladys or Charlie were to meet me in the street, they might not be as tactful as you were—because they don't seem to be very happy about my passing for white. I don't see why, though. I'm not hurting them any, and I send you money every week and help out just as much as they do, if not more. Tell them not to queer me, Ma, if they should ever run into me and the girl friend any place. Maybe it would have been better if you and they had stayed in Cincinnati and I'd come away alone when we decided to move after the old man died. Or at least, we should have gone to different towns, shouldn't we?

Gee, Ma, when I think of how papa left everything to his white family, and you couldn't legally do anything for us kids, my blood boils. You wouldn't have a chance in a Kentucky court, I know, but maybe if you'd tried anyway, his white children would have paid you something to shut up. Maybe they wouldn't want it known in the papers that they had colored brothers. But you was too proud, wasn't you, Ma? I wouldn't have been so proud.

Well, he did buy you a house and send all us kids through school. I'm glad I finished college in Pittsburgh before he died. It was too bad about Charlie and Glad having to drop out, but I hope Charlie gets something better to do than working in a garage. And from what you told me in your last letter about Gladys, I don't blame you for being worried about her—wanting to go in the chorus of one of those South Side cabarets. Lord! But I know it's really tough for girls to get any kind of a job during this depression, especially for colored girls, even if Gladys is high yellow [mulatto], and smart. But I hope you can keep her home, and out of those South Side dumps. They're no place for a good girl.

Well, Ma, I will close because I promised to take my weakness to the movies this evening. Isn't she sweet to look at, all blonde and blue-eyed? We're making plans about our house when we get married. We're going to take a little apartment on the North Side, in a good neighborhood, out on one of those nice quiet side streets where there are trees. I will take a box at the Post Office for your mail. Anyhow, I'm glad there's nothing to stop letters from crossing the color-line. Even if we can't meet often, we can write, can't we, Ma?

With love from your son,
JACK.

Selected Writings from the Harlem Renaissance

JOSEPH SEAMON COTTER, JR.

Journalist and poet Joseph Seamon Cotter, Jr. (1895–1919) was the author, most famously, of *The Band of Gideon*, written one year before he died.

The Mulatto to His Critics†

Ashamed of my race?
And of what race am I?
I am many in one.
Through my veins there flows the blood
Of Red Man, Black Man, Briton, Celt and Scot,
In warring clash and tumultuous riot.
I welcome all,
But love the blood of the kindly race
That swarthes my skin, crinkles my hair,
And puts sweet music into my soul.

JESSIE REDMON FAUSET

The Sleeper Wakes††

Amy recognized the incident as the beginning of one of her phases. Always from a child she had been able to tell when "something was going to happen." She had been standing in Marshall's store, her young, eager gaze intent on the lovely little sample dress which was not from Paris, but quite as dainty as anything that Paris could pro-

---

† From Werner Sollors, ed., *An Anthology of Interracial Literature: Black-White Contacts in the Old World and the New* (NY: NYU Press, 2004), p. 461.
†† From *The Crisis* (August 1920): 168–73; (September 1920): 226–29; (October 1920); 267–74. See headnote, p. 262.

285

duce. It was not the lines or even the texture that fascinated Amy so much, it was the grouping of colors—of shades. She knew the combination was just right for her.

"Let me slip it on, Miss," said the saleswoman suddenly. She had nothing to do just then, and the girl was so evidently charmed and so pretty—it was a pleasure to wait on her.

"Oh, no," Amy had stammered. "I haven't time." She had already wasted two hours at the movies, and she knew at home they were waiting for her.

The saleswoman slipped the dress over the girl's pink blouse, and tucked the linen collar under so as to bring the edge of the dress next to her pretty neck. The dress was apricot-color shading into a shell pink and the shell pink shaded off again into the pearl and pink whiteness of Amy's skin. The saleswoman beamed as Amy, entranced, surveyed herself naively in the tall looking-glass.

Then it was that the incident befell. Two men walking idly through the dress-salon stopped and looked—she made an unbelievably pretty picture. One of them with a short, soft brown beard,—"fuzzy" Amy thought to herself as she caught his glance in the mirror—spoke to his companion.

"Jove, how I'd like to paint her!" But it was the look on the other man's face that caught her and thrilled her. "My God! Can't a girl be beautiful!" he said half to himself. The pair passed on.

Amy stepped out of the dress and thanked the saleswoman half absently. She wanted to get home and think, think to herself about that look. She had seen it before in men's eyes, it had been in the eyes of the men in the moving-picture which she had seen that afternoon. But she had not thought *she* could cause it. Shut up in her little room she pondered over it. Her beauty,—she was really good-looking then—she could stir people—men! A girl of seventeen has no psychology, she does not go beneath the surface, she accepts. But she knew she was entering on one of her phases.

She was always living in some sort of story. She had started it when as a child of five she had driven with the tall, proud, white woman to Mrs. Boldin's home. Mrs. Boldin was a bride of one year's standing then. She was slender and very, very comely, with her rich brown skin and her hair that crinkled thick and soft above a low forehead. The house was still redolent of new furniture; Mr. Boldin was spick and span—he, unlike the furniture, remained so for that matter. The white woman had told Amy that this henceforth was to be her home.

Amy was curious, fond of adventure; she did not cry. She did not, of course, realize that she was to stay here indefinitely, but if she had, even at that age she would hardly have shed tears, she was always too eager, too curious to know, to taste what was going to happen next. Still since she had had almost no dealings with colored people and she knew absolutely none of the class to which Mrs. Boldin belonged, she did venture one question.

"Am I going to be colored now?"

The tall white woman had flushed and paled. "You—" she began, but the words choked her. "Yes, you are going to be colored now," she ended finally. She was a proud woman, in a moment she had recovered her usual poise. Amy carried with her for many years the memory of that proud head. She never saw her again.

When she was sixteen she asked Mrs. Boldin the question which in the light of that memory had puzzled her always. "Mrs. Boldin, tell me—am I white or colored?"

And Mrs. Boldin had told her and told her truly that she did not know.

"A—a—mee!" Mrs. Boldin's voice mounted on the last syllable in a shrill crescendo. Amy rose and went downstairs.

Down the comfortable, but rather shabby dining-room which the Boldins used after meals to sit in, Mr. Boldin, a tall black man, with aristocratic features, sat practicing on a cornet, and Mrs. Boldin sat rocking. In all of their eyes was the manifestation of the light that Amy loved, but how truly she loved it, she was not to guess till years later.

"Amy," Mrs. Boldin paused in her rocking, "did you get the braid?" Of course she had not, though that was the thing she had gone to Marshall's for. Amy always forgot essentials. If she went on an errand, and she always went willingly, it was for the pure joy of going. Who knew what angels might meet one unawares? Not that Amy thought in biblical or in literary phrases. She was in the High School it is true, but she was simply passing through, "getting by" she would have said carelessly. The only reading that had ever made any impression on her had been fairy tales read to her in those long remote days when she had lived with the tall proud woman; and descriptions in novels or histories of beautiful, stately palaces tenanted by beautiful, stately women. She could pore over such pages for hours, her face flushed, her eyes eager.

At present she cast about for an excuse. She had so meant to get the braid. "There was a dress—" she began lamely, she was never deliberately dishonest.

Mr. Boldin cleared his throat and nervously fingered his paper. Cornelius ceased his awful playing and blinked at her short-sightedly through his thick glasses. Both of these, the man and the little boy, loved the beautiful, inconsequent creature with her airy, irresponsible ways. But Mrs. Boldin loved her too, and because she loved her she could not scold.

"Of course you forgot," she began chidingly. Then she smiled. "There was a dress that you looked at *perhaps*. But confess, didn't you go to the movies first?"

Yes, Amy confessed she had done just that. "And oh, Mrs. Boldin, it was the most wonderful picture—a girl—such a pretty one—and she was poor, awfully. And somehow she met the most wonderful people and they were so kind to her. And she married a man who was just tremendously rich and he gave her everything. I did so want Cornelius to see it."

"Huh!" said Cornelius who had been listening not because he was interested, but because he wanted to call Amy's attention to his playing as soon as possible. "Huh! I don't want to look at no pretty girl. Did they have anybody looping the loop in an airship?"

"You'd better stop seeing pretty girl pictures, Amy," said Mr. Boldin kindly. "They're not always true to life. Besides, I know where you can see all the pretty girls you want without bothering to pay twenty-five cents for it."

Amy smiled at the implied compliment and went on happily studying her lessons. They were all happy in their own way. Amy because she was sure of their love and admiration, Mr. and Mrs. Boldin because of her beauty and innocence and Cornelius because he knew he had in his foster-sister a listener whom his terrible practicing could never bore. He played brokenly a piece he had found in an old music-book. "*There's an aching void in every heart, brother.*"

"Where do you pick up those old things, Neely?" said his mother fretfully. But Amy could not have her favorite's feelings injured.

"I think it's lovely," she announced defensively. "Cornelius, I'll ask Sadie Murray to lend me her brother's book. He's learning the cornet, too, and you can get some new pieces. Oh, isn't it awful to have to go to bed? Good-night, everybody." She smiled her charming, ever ready smile, the mere reflex of youth and beauty and content.

"You do spoil her, Mattie," said Mr. Boldin after she had left the room. "She's only seventeen—here, Cornelius, you go to bed—but it seems to me she ought to be more dependable about errands. Though she is splendid about some things," he defended her. "Look how willingly she goes off to bed. She'll be asleep before she knows it when most girls of her age would want to be up in the street."

But upstairs Amy was far from asleep. She lit one gas-jet and pulled down the shades. Then she stuffed tissue paper in the keyhole and under the doors, and lit the remaining gas-jets. The light thus thrown on the mirror of the ugly oak dresser was perfect. She slipped off the pink blouse and found two scarfs, a soft yellow and a soft pink,—she had had them in a scarf-dance for a school entertainment. She wound them and draped them about her pretty shoulders and loosened her hair. In the mirror she apostrophized the beautiful, glowing vision of herself.

"There," she said, "I'm like the girl in the picture. She had nothing but her beautiful face—and she did so want to be happy." She sat down on the side of the rather lumpy bed and stretched out her arms. "I want to be happy, too." She intoned it earnestly, almost like an incantation. "I want wonderful clothes, and people around me, men adoring me, and the world before me. I want—everything! It will come, it will all come because I want it so." She sat frowning intently as she was apt to do when very much engrossed. "And we'd all be so happy. I'd give Mr. and Mrs. Boldin money! And Cornelius—he'd go to college and learn all about his old airships. Oh, if I only knew how to begin!"

Smiling, she turned off the lights and crept to bed.

II

Quite suddenly she knew she was going to run away. That was in October. By December she had accomplished her purpose. Not that she was the least bit unhappy but because she must get out in the world,—she felt caged, imprisoned. "Trenton is stifling me," she would have told you, in her unconsciously adopted "movie" diction. New York she knew was the place for her. She had her plans all made. She had sewed steadily after school for two months—as she frequently did when she wanted to buy her season's wardrobe, so besides her carfare she had $25. She went immediately to a white Y.W.C.A., stayed there two nights, found and answered an advertisement for clerk and waitress in a small confectionery and bakery-shop, was accepted and there she was launched.

Perhaps it was because of her early experience when as a tiny child she was taken from that so different home and left at Mrs. Boldin's, perhaps it was some fault in her own disposition, concentrated and egotistic as she was, but certainly she felt no pangs of separation, no fear of her future. She was cold too,—unfired though so to speak rather than icy,—and fastidious. This last quality kept her safe where morality or religion, of neither of which had she any conscious endowment, would have availed her nothing. Unbelievably then she lived two years in New York, unspoiled, untouched, going to work on the edge of Greenwich Village early and coming back late, knowing almost no one and yet altogether happy in the expectation of something wonderful, which she knew some day must happen.

It was at the end of the second year that she met Zora Harrison. Zora used to come into lunch with a group of habitués of the place— all of them artists and writers Amy gathered. Mrs. Harrison (for she was married as Amy later learned) appealed to the girl because she knew so well how to afford the contrast to her blonde, golden beauty. Purple, dark and regal, enveloped in velvets and heavy silks, and strange marine blues she wore, and thus made Amy absolutely happy. Singularly enough, the girl, intent as she was on her own life and experiences, had felt up to this time no yearning to know these strange, happy beings who surrounded her. She did miss Cornelius, but otherwise she was never lonely, or if she was she hardly knew it, for she had always lived an inner life to herself. But Mrs. Harrison magnetized her—she could not keep her eyes from her face, from her wonderful clothes. She made conjectures about her.

The wonderful lady came in late one afternoon—an unusual thing for her. She smiled at Amy invitingly, asked some banal questions and their first conversation began. The acquaintance once struck up progressed rapidly—after a few weeks Mrs. Harrison invited the girl to come to see her. Amy accepted quietly, unaware that anything extraordinary was happening. Zora noticed this and liked it. She had an apartment in 12th Street in a house inhabited only by artists—she was by no means one herself. Amy was fascinated by the new world into which she found herself ushered; Zora's surroundings were very beautiful and Zora herself was a study. She opened to the girl's amazed vision fields of thought and conjecture, phases of whose existence Amy, who was a builder of phases, had never dreamed. Zora had been a poor girl of good family. She had wanted to study art, she had deliberately married a rich man and as deliberately obtained in the course of four years a divorce, and she was now living in New York studying by means of her alimony and enjoying to its fullest the life she loved. She took Amy on a footing with herself—the girl's refinement, her beauty, her interest in colors (though this in Amy at that time was purely sporadic, never consciously encouraged), all this gave Zora a figure about which to plan and build a romance. Amy had told her the truth, but not all about her coming to New York. She had grown tired of Trenton—her people were all dead—the folks with whom she lived were kind and good but not "inspiring" (she had borrowed the term from Zora and it was true, the Boldins, when one came to think of it, were not "inspiring"), so she had run away.

Zora had gone into raptures. "What an adventure! My dear, the world is yours. Why, with your looks and your birth, for I suppose you really belong to the Kildares who used to live in Philadelphia, I think there was a son who ran off and married an actress or someone—they disowned him I remember,—you can reach any height. You must marry a wealthy man—perhaps someone who is interested in art and who will let you pursue your studies." She insisted always that Amy had run away in order to study art. "But luck like that comes to few," she sighed, remembering her own plight, for Mr. Harrison had been decidedly unwilling to let her pursue her studies, at least to the extent she wished. "Anyway you must marry wealth,—one can always get a divorce," she ended sagely.

Amy—she came to Zora's every night now—used to listen dazedly at first. She had accepted willingly enough Zora's conjecture about her birth, came to believe it in fact—but she drew back somewhat at such wholesale exploitation of people to suit one's own convenience, still she did not probe too far into this thought—nor did she grasp at all the infamy of exploitation of self. She ventured one or two objections however, but Zora brushed everything aside.

"Everybody is looking out for himself," she said fairly. "I am interested in you, for instance, not for philanthropy's sake, but because I am lonely, and you are charming and pretty and don't get tired of hearing me talk. You'd better come and live with me awhile, my dear, six months or a year. It doesn't cost any more for two than for one, and you can always leave when we get tired of each other. A girl like you can always get a job. If you are worried about being dependent you can pose for me and design my frocks, and oversee Julienne"—her maid-of-all-work—"I'm sure she's a stupendous robber."

Amy came, not at all overwhelmed by the good luck of it—good luck was around the corner more or less for everyone, she supposed. Moreover, she was beginning to absorb some of Zora's doctrine—she, too, must look out for herself. Zora *was* lonely, she *did* need companionship, Julienne *was* careless about change and old blouses and left-over dainties. Amy had her own sense of honor. She carried out faithfully her share of the bargain, cut down waste, renovated Zora's clothes, posed for her, listened to her endlessly and bore with her fitfulness. Zora was truly grateful for this last. She was temperamental but Amy had good nerves and her strong natural inclination to let people do as they wanted stood her in good stead. She was a little stolid, a little unfeeling under her lovely exterior. Her looks at this time belied her—her perfect ivory-pink face, her deep luminous eyes,—very brown they were with purple depths that made one think of pansies—her charming, rather wide mouth, her whole face set in a frame of very soft, very live, brown hair which grew in wisps and tendrils and curls and waves back from her smooth, young forehead. All this made one look for softness and ingenuousness. The ingenuousness was there, but not the softness—except of her fresh, vibrant loveliness.

On the whole then she progressed famously with Zora. Sometimes the latter's callousness shocked her, as when they would go strolling through the streets south of Washington Square. The children, the people all foreign, all dirty, often very artistic, always immensely human, disgusted Zora except for "local color"—she really could reproduce them wonderfully. But she almost hated them for being what they were.

"Br-r-r, dirty little brats!" she would say to Amy. "Don't let them touch me." She was frequently amazed at her protégée's utter indifference to their appearance, for Amy herself was the pink of daintiness. They were turning from MacDougall into Bleecker Street one day and Amy had patted a child—dirty, but lovely—on the head.

"They are all people just like anybody else, just like you and me, Zora," she said in answer to her friend's protest.

"You *are* the true democrat," Zora returned with a shrug. But Amy did not understand her.

Not the least of Amy's services was to come between Zora and the too pressing attention of the men who thronged about her.

"Oh, go and talk to Amy," Zora would say, standing slim and gorgeous in some wonderful evening gown. She was an extraordinarily attractive creature, very white and pink, with great ropes of dazzling gold hair, and that look of no-age which only American women possess. As a matter of fact she was thirty-nine, immensely sophisticated and selfish, even, Amy thought, a little cruel. Her present mode of living just suited her; she could not stand any condition that bound her, anything at all *exigeant*. It was useless for anyone to try to influence her. If she did not want to talk, she would not.

The men used to obey her orders and seek Amy sulkily at first, but afterwards with considerably more interest. She was so lovely to look at. But they really, as Zora knew, preferred to talk to the older woman, for while with Zora indifference was a role, second nature now but still a role—with Amy it was natural and she was also a trifle shallow. She had the admiration she craved, she was comfortable, she asked no more. Moreover she thought the men, with the exception of Stuart James Wynne, rather uninteresting—they were faddists for the most part, crazy not about art or music, but merely about some phase such as cubism or syncopation.

Wynne, who was much older than the other half-dozen men who weekly paid Zora homage—impressed her by his suggestion of power. He was a retired broker, immensely wealthy (Zora, who had known him since childhood, informed her), very set and purposeful and polished. He was perhaps fifty-five, widely traveled, of medium height, very white skin and clear, frosty blue eyes, with sharp, proud features. He liked Amy from the beginning, her childishness touched him. In particular he admired her pliability—not knowing it was really indifference. He had been married twice; one wife had divorced him, the other had died. Both marriages were unsuccessful owing to his dominant, rather unsympathetic nature. But he had softened considerably with years, though he still had decided views, was glad to see that Amy, in spite of Zora's influence, neither smoked nor drank. He liked her shallowness—she fascinated him.

Zora had told him much—just the kind of romantic story to appeal to the rich, powerful man. Here was beauty forlorn, penniless, of splendid birth,—for Zora once having connected Amy with the Philadelphia Kildares never swerved from that belief. Amy seemed to Wynne everything a girl should be—she was so unspoiled, so untouched. He asked her to marry him. If she had tried she could not have acted more perfectly. She looked at him with her wonderful eyes.

"But I am poor, ignorant—a nobody," she stammered. "I'm afraid I don't love you either," she went on in her pretty troubled voice, "though I do like you very, very much."

He liked her honesty and her self-depreciation, even her coldness. The fact that she was not flattered seemed to him an extra proof of her native superiority. He, himself, was a representative of one of the South's oldest families, though he had lived abroad lately.

"I have money and influence," he told her gravely, "but I count them nothing without you." And as for love—he would teach her that, he ended, his voice shaking a little. Underneath all his chilly, polished exterior he really cared.

"It seems an unworthy thing to say," he told her wistfully, for she seemed very young beside his experienced fifty-five years, "but anything you wanted in this world could be yours. I could give it to you,—clothes, houses and jewels."

"Don't be an idiot," Zora had said when Amy told her. "Of course, marry him. He'll give you a beautiful home and position. He's probably no harder to get along with than anybody else, and if he is, there is always the divorce court."

It seemed to Amy somehow that she was driving a bargain—how infamous a one she could not suspect. But Zora's teachings had sunk deep. Wynne loved her, and he could secure for her what she wanted. "And after all," she said to herself once, "it really is my dream coming true."

She resolved to marry him. There were two weeks of delirious, blissful shopping. Zora was very generous. It seemed to Amy that the whole world was contributing largely to her happiness. She was to have just what she wanted and as her taste was perfect she afforded almost as much pleasure to the people from whom she bought as to herself. In particular she brought rapture to an exclusive modiste in Forty-second Street who exclaimed at her "so perfect taste."

"Mademoiselle is of a marvelous, of an absolute correctness," she said. Everything whirled by. After the shopping there was the small, impressive wedding. Amy stumbled somehow through the service, struck by its awful solemnity. Then later there was the journey and the big house waiting them in the small town, fifty miles south of Richmond. Wynne was originally from Georgia, but business and social interests had made it necessary for him to be nearer Washington and New York.

Amy was absolute mistress of himself and his home, he said, his voice losing its coldness. "Ah, my dear, you'll never realize what you mean to me—I don't envy any other man in this world. You are so beautiful, so sweet, so different!"

III

From the very beginning *he* was different from what she had supposed. To start with he was far, far wealthier, and he had, too, a tradition, a family-pride which to Amy was inexplicable. Still more inexplicably he had a race-pride. To his wife this was not only strange but foolish. She was as Zora had once suggested, the true democrat. Not that she preferred the company of her maids, though the reason for this did not lie *per se* in the fact that they were maids. There was simply no common ground. But she was uniformly kind, a trait which had she been older would have irritated her husband. As it was, he saw in it only an additional indication of her freshness, her lack of worldliness which seemed to him the attributes of an inherent refinement and goodness untouched by experience.

He, himself, was intolerant of all people of inferior birth or standing and looked with contempt on foreigners, except the French and English. All the rest were variously "guineys," "niggers," and "wops," and all of them he genuinely despised and hated, and talked of them with the huge intolerant carelessness characteristic of occidental civilization. Amy was never able to understand it. People were always first and last, just people to her. Growing up as the average colored American girl does grow up, surrounded by types of every hue, color and facial configuration she had had no absolute ideal. She was not even aware that there was one. Wynne, who in his grim way had a keen sense of humor, used to be vastly amused at the artlessness with which she let him know that she did not consider him to be good-looking. She never wanted him to wear anything but dark blue, or sombre mixtures always.

"They take away from that awful whiteness of your skin," she used to tell him, "and deepen the blue of your eyes."

In the main she made no attempt to understand him, as indeed she made no attempt to understand anything. The result, of course, was that such ideas as seeped into her mind stayed there, took growth and later bore fruit. But just at this period she was like a well-cared for, sleek, house-pet, delicately nurtured, velvety, content to let her days pass by. She thought almost nothing of her art just now except as her sensibilities were jarred by an occasional disharmony. Likewise, even to herself, she never criticized Wynne, except when some act or attitude of his stung. She could never understand why he, so fastidious, so versed in elegance of word and speech, so careful in his surroundings, even down to the last detail of glass and napery, should take such evident pleasure in literature of a certain prulient [sic] type. He fairly revelled in the realistic novels which to her depicted sheer badness. He would get her to read to him, partly because he liked to be read to, mostly because he enjoyed the realism and in a slighter degree because he enjoyed seeing her shocked. Her point of view amused him.

"What funny people," she would say naively, "to do such things." She could not understand the liaisons and intrigues of women in the society novels, such infamy was stupid and silly. If one starved, it was conceivable that one might steal; if one were intentionally injured, one might hit back, even murder; but deliberate nastiness she could not envisage. The stories, after she had read them to him, passed out of her mind as completely as though they had never existed.

Picture the two of them spending three years together with practically no friction. To his dominance and intolerance she opposed a soft and unobtrusive indifference. What she wanted she had, ease, wealth, adoration, love, too, passionate and imperious, but she had never known any other kind. She was growing cleverer also, her knowledge of French was increasing, she was acquiring a knowledge of politics, of commerce and of the big social questions, for Wynne's interests were exhaustive and she did most of his reading for him. Another woman might have yearned for a more youthful companion, but her native coldness kept her content. She did not love him, she had never really loved anybody, but little Cornelius Boldin—he had been such an enchanting, such a darling baby, she remembered,— her heart contracted painfully when she thought as she did very often of his warm softness.

"He must be a big boy now," she would think almost maternally, wondering—once she had been so sure!—if she would ever see him again. But she was very fond of Wynne, and he was crazy over her just as Zora had predicted. He loaded her with gifts, dresses, flowers, jewels—she amused him because none but colored stones appealed to her.

"Diamonds are so hard, so cold, and pearls are dead," she told him. Nothing ever came between them, but his ugliness, his hatefulness to dependents. It hurt her so, for she was naturally kind in her careless, uncomprehending way. True, she had left Mrs. Boldin without a word, but she did not guess how completely Mrs. Boldin loved her. She would have been aghast had she realized how stricken her flight had left them. At twenty-two, Amy was still as good, as unspoiled, as pure as a child. Of course with all this she was too unquestioning, too selfish, too vain, but they were all faults of her lovely, lovely flesh. Wynne's intolerance finally got on her nerves. She used to blush for his unkindness. All the servants were colored, but she had long since ceased to think that perhaps she, too, was colored, except when he, by insult toward an employee, overt, always at least implied, made her realize his contemptuous dislike and disregard for a dark skin or Negro blood.

"Stuart, how can you say such things?" she would expostulate. "You can't expect a man to stand such language as that." And Wynne would sneer, "A man—you don't consider a nigger a man, do you? Oh, Amy, don't be such a fool. You've got to keep them in their places."

Some innate sense of the fitness of things kept her from condoling outspokenly with the servants, but they knew she was ashamed of her husband's ways. Of course, they left—it seemed to Amy that Peter, the butler, was always getting new "help,"—but most of the upper servants stayed, for Wynne paid handsomely and although his orders were meticulous and insistent the retinue of employees was so large that the individual's work was light.

Most of the servants who did stay on in spite of Wynne's occasional insults had a purpose in view. Callie, the cook, Amy found out, had two children at Howard University—of course she never came in contact with Wynne, the chauffeur had a crippled sister. Rose, Amy's maid and purveyor of much outside information, was the chief support of the family. About Peter, Amy knew nothing: he was a striking, taciturn man, very competent, who had left the Wynnes' service years before and had returned in Amy's third year. Wynne treated him with comparative respect. But Stephen, the new valet, met with entirely different treatment. Amy's heart yearned toward him, he was like Cornelius, with short-sighted, patient eyes, always willing, a little over-eager. Amy recognized him for what he was: a boy of respectable, ambitious parentage, striving for the means for an education; naturally far above his present calling, yet willing to pass through all this as a means to an end. She questioned Rosa about him.

"Oh, Stephen," Rosa told her, "yes'm, he's workin' for fair. He's got a brother at the Howard's and a sister at the Smith's. Yes'm, it do seem a little hard on him, but Stephen, he say, they're both goin' to turn roun' and help him when they get through. That blue silk has a rip in it, Miss Amy, if you was thinkin' of wearin' that. Yes'm, somehow I don't think Steve's very strong, kinda worries like. I guess he's sorta nervous."

Amy told Wynne. "He's such a nice boy, Stuart," she pleaded, "it hurts me to have you so cross with him. Anyway don't call him names." She was both surprised and frightened at the feeling in her that prompted her to interfere. She had held so aloof from other people's interests all these years.

"I *am* colored," she told herself that night. "I feel it inside of me. I must be or I couldn't care so about Stephen. Poor boy, I suppose Cornelius is just like him. I wish Stuart would let him alone. I wonder if all white people are like that. Zora was hard, too, on unfortunate people." She pondered over it a bit. "I wonder what Stuart would say if he knew I was colored?" She lay perfectly still, her smooth brow knitted, thinking hard. "But he loves me," she said to herself still silently. "He'll always love my looks," and she fell to thinking that all the wonderful happenings in her sheltered, pampered life had come to her through her beauty. She reached out an exquisite arm, switched on a light, and picking up a hand-mirror from a dressing-table, fell to studying her face. She was right. It was her chiefest asset. She forgot Stephen and fell asleep.

But in the morning her husband's voice issuing from his dressing-room across the hall, awakened her. She listened drowsily. Stephen, leaving the house the day before, had been met by a boy with a telegram. He had taken it, slipped it into his pocket, (he was just going to the mailbox) and had forgotten to deliver it until now, nearly twenty-four hours later. She could hear Stuart's storm of abuse—it was terrible, made up as it was of oaths and insults to the boy's ancestry. There was a moment's lull. Then she heard him again.

"If your brains are a fair sample of that black wench of a sister of yours—"

She sprang up then thrusting her arms as she ran into her pink dressing-gown. She got there just in time. Stephen, his face quivering, was standing looking straight into Wynne's smoldering eyes. In spite of herself, Amy was glad to see the boy's bearing. But he did not notice her.

"You devil!" he was saying. "You white-faced devil! I'll make you pay for that!" He raised his arm. Wynne did not blench.

With a scream she was between them. "Go, Stephen, go,—get out of the house. Where do you think you are? Don't you know you'll be hanged, lynched, tortured?" Her voice shrilled at him.

Wynne tried to thrust aside her arms that clung and twisted. But she held fast till the door slammed behind the fleeing boy.

"God, let me by, Amy!" As suddenly as she had clasped him she let him go, ran to the door, fastened it and threw the key out the window.

He took her by the arm and shook her. "Are you mad? Didn't you hear him threaten me, me,—a nigger threaten me?" His voice broke with nigger, "And you're letting him get away! Why, I'll get him. I'll set bloodhounds on him, I'll have every white man in this town after him! He'll be hanging so high by midnight—" he made for the other door, cursing, half-insane.

How, *how* could she keep him back! She hated her weak arms with their futile beauty! She sprang toward him. "Stuart, wait," she was breathless and sobbing. She said the first thing that came into her head. "Wait, Stuart, you cannot do this thing." She thought of Cornelius—suppose it had been he—"Stephen,—that boy,—he is my brother."

He turned on her. "What!" he said fiercely, then laughed a short laugh of disdain. "You are crazy," he said roughly, "My God, Amy! How can you even in jest associate yourself with these people? Don't you suppose I know a white girl when I see one? There's no use in telling a lie like that."

Well, there was no help for it. There was only one way. He had turned back for a moment, but she must keep him many moments—an hour. Stephen must get out of town.

She caught his arm again. "Yes," she told him, "I did lie. Stephen is not my brother, I never saw him before." The light of relief that crept into his eyes did not escape her, it only nerved her. "But I *am* colored," she ended.

Before he could stop her she had told him all about the tall white woman. "She took me to Mrs. Boldin's and gave me to her to keep. She would never have taken me to her if I had been white. If you lynch this boy, I'll let the world, your world, know that your wife is a colored woman."

He sat down like a man suddenly stricken old, his face ashen. "Tell me about it again," he commanded. And she obeyed, going mercilessly into every damning detail.

IV

Amazingly her beauty availed her nothing. If she had been an older woman, if she had had Zora's age and experience, she would have been able to gauge exactly her influence over Wynne. Though even then in similar circumstances she would have taken the risk and acted in just the same manner. But she was a little bewildered at her utter miscalculation. She had thought he might not want his friends—his world by which he set such store—to know that she was colored, but she had not dreamed it could make any real difference to him. He had chosen her, poor and ignorant, out of a host of women, and had told her countless times of his love. To herself Amy Wynne was in comparison with Zora for instance, stupid and uninteresting. But his constant, unsolicited iterations had made her accept his idea.

She was just the same woman she told herself, she had not changed, she was still beautiful, still charming, still "different." Perhaps, that very difference had its being in the fact of her mixed blood. She had been his wife—there were memories—she could not see how he could give her up. The suddenness of the divorce carried her off her feet. Dazedly she left him—though almost without a pang for she had only liked him. She had been perfectly honest about this, and he, although consumed by the fierceness of his emotion toward her, had gradually forced himself to be content, for at least she had never made him jealous.

She was to live in a small house of his in New York, up town in the 80's. Peter was in charge and there was a new maid and a cook. The servants, of course, knew of the separation, but nobody guessed why. She was living on a much smaller basis than the one to which she had become so accustomed in the last three years. But she was very comfortable. She felt, at any rate she manifested, no qualms at receiving alimony from Wynne. That was the way things happened, she supposed when she thought of it at all. Moreover, it seemed to her perfectly in keeping with Wynne's former attitude toward her; she did not see how he could do less. She expected people to be consistent. That was why she was so amazed that he in spite of his oft iterated love, could let her go. If she had felt half the love for him which he had professed for her, she would not have sent him away if he had been a leper.

"Why I'd stay with him," she told herself, "if he were one, even as I feel now."

She was lonely in New York. Perhaps it was the first time in her life that she had felt so. Zora had gone to Paris the first year of her marriage and had not come back.

The days dragged on emptily. One thing helped her. She had gone one day to the modiste from whom she had bought her trousseau. The woman remembered her perfectly—"The lady with the exquisite taste for colors—ah, madame, but you have the rare gift." Amy was grateful to be taken out of her thoughts. She bought one or two daring but altogether lovely creations and let fall a few suggestions:

"That brown frock, Madame,—you say it has been on your hands a long time? Yes? But no wonder. See, instead of that dead white you should have a shade of ivory, that white cheapens it." Deftly she caught up a bit of ivory satin and worked out her idea. Madame was ravished.

"But yes, Madame Ween is correct,—as always. Oh, what a pity that the Madame is so wealthy. If she were only a poor girl—Mlle. Antoine with the best eye for color in the place has just left, gone back to France to nurse her brother—this World War is of such a horror! If someone like Madame, now, could be found, to take the little Antoine's place!"

Some obscure impulse drove Amy to accept the half proposal: "Oh! I don't know, I have nothing to do just now. My husband is abroad." Wynne had left her with that impression. "I could contribute the money to the Red Cross or to charity."

The work was the best thing in the world for her. It kept her from becoming too introspective, though even then she did more serious, connected thinking than she had done in all the years of her varied life.

She missed Wynne definitely, chiefly as a guiding influence for she had rarely planned even her own amusements. Her dependence on him had been absolute. She used to picture him to herself as he was before the trouble—and his changing expressions as he looked at her, of amusement, interest, pride, a certain little teasing quality that used to come into his eyes, which always made her adopt her "spoiled child air," as he used to call it. It was the way he liked her best. Then last, there was that look he had given her the morning she had told him she was colored—it had depicted so many emotions, various and yet distinct. There were dismay, disbelief, coldness, a final aloofness.

There was another expression, too, that she thought of sometimes—the look on the face of Mr. Packard, Wynne's lawyer. She, herself, had attempted no defense.

"For God's sake why did you tell him, Mrs. Wynne?" Packard asked her. His curiosity got the better of him. "You couldn't have been in love with that yellow rascal," he blurted out. "She's too cold really, to love anybody," he told himself. "If you didn't care about the boy why should you have told?"

She defended herself feebly. "He looked so like little Cornelius Boldin," she replied vaguely, "and he couldn't help being colored." A clerk came in then and Packard said no more. But into his eyes had crept a certain reluctant respect. She remembered the look, but could not define it.

She was so sorry about the trouble now, she wished it had never happened. Still if she had it to repeat she would act in the same way again. "There was nothing else for me to do," she used to tell herself.

But she missed Wynne unbelievably.

If it had not been for Peter, her life would have been almost that of a nun. But Peter, who read the papers and kept abreast of times, constantly called her attention, with all due respect, to the meetings, the plays, the sights which she ought to attend or see. She was truly grateful to him. She was very kind to all three of the servants. They had the easiest "places" in New York, the maids used to tell their friends. As she never entertained, and frequently dined out, they had a great deal of time off.

She had been separated from Wynne for ten months before she began to make any definite plans for her future. Of course, she could not go on like this always. It came to her suddenly that probably she would go to Paris and live there—why or how she did not know. Only Zora was there and lately she had begun to think that her life was to be like Zora's. They had been amazingly parallel up to this time. Of course she would have to wait until after the war.

She sat musing about it one day in the big sitting-room which she had had fitted over into a luxurious studio. There was a sewing-room off to the side from which Peter used to wheel into the room waxen figures of all colorings and contours so that she could drape the various fabrics about them to be sure of the best results. But today she was working out a scheme for one of Madame's customers, who was of her own color and size and she was her own lay-figure. She sat in front of the huge pier glass, a wonderful soft yellow silk draped about her radiant loveliness.

"I could do some serious work in Paris," she said half aloud to herself. "I suppose if I really wanted to, I could be very successful along this line."

Somewhere downstairs an electric bell buzzed, at first softly, then after a slight pause, louder, and more insistently.

"If Madame sends me that lace today," she was thinking, idly, "I could finish this and start on the pink. I wonder why Peter doesn't answer the bell."

She remembered then that Peter had gone to New Rochelle on business and she had sent Ellen to Altman's to find a certain rare velvet and had allowed Mary to go with her. She would dine out, she told them, so they need not hurry. Evidently she was alone in the house.

Well she could answer the bell. She had done it often enough in the old days at Mrs. Boldin's. Of course it was the lace. She smiled a bit as she went downstairs thinking how surprised the delivery-boy would be to see her arrayed thus early in the afternoon. She hoped he wouldn't go. She could see him through the long, thick panels of glass in the vestibule and front door. He was just turning about as she opened the door.

This was no delivery-boy, this man whose gaze fell on her hungry and avid. This was Wynne. She stood for a second leaning against the doorjamb, a strange figure surely in the sharp November weather. Some leaves—brown, skeleton shapes—rose and swirled unnoticed about her head. A passing letter-carrier looked at them curiously.

"What are you doing answering the door?" Wynne asked her roughly. "Where is Peter? Go in, you'll catch cold."

She was glad to see him. She took him into the drawing room—a wonderful study in browns—and looked at him and looked at him.

"Well," he asked her, his voice eager in spite of the commonplace words, "are you glad to see me? Tell me what you do with yourself."

She could not talk fast enough, her eyes clinging to his face. Once it struck her that he had changed in some indefinable way. Was it a slight coarsening of that refined aristocratic aspect? Even in her subconsciousness she denied it.

He had come back to her.

"So I design for Madame when I feel like it, and send the money to the Red Cross and wonder when you are coming back to me." For the first time in their acquaintanceship she was conscious deliberately of trying to attract, to hold him. She put on her spoiled child air which had once been so successful.

"It took you long enough to get here," she pouted. She was certain of him now. His mere presence assured her.

They sat silent a moment, the late November sun bathing her head in an austere glow of chilly gold. As she sat there in the big brown chair she was, in her yellow dress, like some mysterious emanation, some wraith-like aura developed from the tone of her surroundings.

He rose and came toward her, still silent. She grew nervous, and talked incessantly with sudden unusual gestures. "Oh, Stuart, let me give you tea. It's right there in the pantry off the dining-room. I can wheel the table in." She rose, a lovely creature in her yellow robe. He watched her intently.

"Wait," he bade her.

She paused almost on tiptoe, a dainty golden butterfly.

"You are coming back to live with me?" he asked her hoarsely.

For the first time in her life she loved him.

"Of course I am coming back," she told him softly. "Aren't you glad? Haven't you missed me? I didn't see how you *could* stay away. Oh! Stuart, what a wonderful ring!"

For he had slipped on her finger a heavy dull gold band, with an immense sapphire in an oval setting—a beautiful thing of Italian workmanship.

"It is so like you to remember," she told him gratefully. "I love colored stones." She admired it, turning it around and around on her slender finger.

How silent he was, standing there watching her with his sombre yet eager gaze. It made her troubled, uneasy. She cast about for something to say.

"You can't think how I've improved since I saw you, Stuart. I've read all sorts of books—Oh! I'm learned," she smiled at him. "And Stuart," she went a little closer to him, twisting the button on his perfect coat, "I'm so sorry about it all,—about Stephen, that boy, you know. I just couldn't help interfering. But when we're married again, if you'll just remember how it hurts me to have you so cross—"

He interrupted her. "I wasn't aware that I spoke of our marrying again," he told her, his voice steady, his blue eyes cold.

She thought he was teasing. "Why you just asked me to. You said 'aren't you coming back to live with me—' "

Still she didn't comprehend. "But what do you mean?" she asked bewildered.

"What do you suppose a man means?" he returned deliberately, "when he asks a woman to live with him but not to marry him?"

She sat down heavily in the brown chair, all glowing ivory and yellow against its sombre depths.

"Like the women in those awful novels?" she whispered. "Not like those women!—Oh Stuart! you don't mean it!" Her very heart was numb.

"But you must care a little—" she was amazed at her own depth of feeling. "Why I care—there are all those memories back of us—you must want me really—"

"I do want you," he told her tensely. "I want you damnably. But— well—I might as well out with it—A white man like me simply doesn't marry a colored woman. After all what difference need it make to you? We'll live abroad—you'll travel, have all the things you love. Many a white woman would envy you." He stretched out an eager hand.

She evaded it, holding herself aloof as though his touch were contaminating. Her movement angered him.

"Oh, hell!" he snarled at her roughly. "Why don't you stop posing? What do you think you are anyway? Do you suppose I'd take you for my wife—what do you think can happen to you? What man of your own race could give you what you want? You don't suppose I am going to support you this way forever, do you? The court imposed no alimony. You've got to come to it sooner or later—you're bound to fall to some white man. What's the matter—I'm not rich enough?"

Her face flamed at that—"As though it were *that* that mattered!"

He gave her a deadly look. "Well, isn't it? Ah, my girl, you forget you told me you didn't love me when you married me. You sold yourself to me then. Haven't I reason to suppose you are waiting for a higher bidder?"

At these words something in her died forever, her youth, her illusions, her happy, happy blindness. She saw life leering mercilessly in her face. It seemed to her that she would give all her future to stamp out, to kill the contempt in his frosty insolent eyes. In a sudden rush of savagery she struck him, struck him across his hateful sneering mouth with the hand which wore his ring.

As *she* fell, reeling under the fearful impact of his brutal but involuntary blow, her mind caught at, registered two things. A little thin stream of blood was trickling across his chin. She had cut him with the ring, she realized with a certain savage satisfaction. And there was something else which she must remember, which she *would* remember if only she could fight her way out of this dreadful clinging blackness, which was bearing down upon her—closing her in.

When she came to she sat up holding her bruised, aching head in her palms, trying to recall what it was that had impressed her so.

Oh yes, her very mind ached with the realization. She lay back again on the floor, prone, anything to relieve that intolerable pain. But her memory, her thoughts went on.

"Nigger," he had called her as she fell, "nigger, nigger," and again, "nigger."

"He despised me absolutely," she said to herself wonderingly, "because I was colored. And yet he wanted me."

V

Somehow she reached her room. Long after the servants had come in, she lay face downward across her bed, thinking. How she hated Wynne, how she hated herself! And for ten months she had been living off his money although in no way had she a claim on him. Her whole body burned with the shame of it.

In the morning she rang for Peter. She faced him, white and haggard, but if the man noticed her condition, he made no sign. He was, if possible, more imperturbable than ever.

"Peter," she told him, her eyes and voice very steady, "I am leaving this house today and shall never come back."

"Yes, Miss."

"And, Peter, I am very poor now and shall have no money besides what I can make for myself."

"Yes, Miss."

Would nothing surprise him, she wondered dully. She went on "I don't know whether you knew it or not, Peter, but I am colored, and hereafter I mean to live among my own people. Do you think you could find a little house or little cottage not too far from New York?"

He had a little place in New Rochelle, he told her, his manner altering not one whit, or better yet his sister had a four-room house in Orange, with a garden, if he remembered correctly. Yes, he was sure there was a garden. It would be just the thing for Mrs. Wynne.

She had four hundred dollars of her very own which she had earned by designing for Madame. She paid the maids a month in advance—they were to stay as long as Peter needed them. She, herself, went to a small hotel in Twenty-eighth Street, and here Peter came for her at the end of ten days, with the acknowledgement of the keys and receipts from Mr. Packard. Then he accompanied her to Orange and installed her in her new home.

"I wish I could afford to keep you, Peter," she said a little wistfully, "but I am very poor. I am heavily in debt and I must get that off my shoulders at once."

Mrs. Wynne was very kind, he was sure; he could think of no one with whom he would prefer to work. Furthermore, he often ran down from New Rochelle to see his sister; he would come in from time to time, and in the spring would plant the garden if she wished.

She hated to see him go, but she did not dwell long on that. Her only thought was to work and work and work and save until she could pay Wynne back. She had not lived very extravagantly during those ten months and Peter was a perfect manager—in spite of her remonstrances he had given her every month and account of his expenses. She had made arrangements with Madame to be her regular designer. The French woman guessing that more than whim was behind this move drove a very shrewd bargain, but even then the pay was excellent. With care, she told herself, she could be free within two years, three at most.

She lived a dull enough existence now, going to work steadily every morning and getting home late at night. Almost it was like those early days when she had first left Mrs. Boldin, except that now she had no high sense of adventure, no expectation of great things to come, which might buoy her up. She no longer thought of phases and the proper setting for her beauty. Once indeed catching sight of her face late one night in the mirror in her tiny work-room in Orange, she stopped and scanned herself, loathing what she saw there.

"You *thing!*" she said to the image in the glass, "if you hadn't been so vain, so shallow!" And she had struck herself violently again and again across the face until her head ached.

But such fits of passion were rare. She had a curious sense of freedom in these days, a feeling that at last her brain, her senses were liberated from some hateful clinging thralldom. Her thoughts were always busy. She used to go over that last scene with Wynne again and again trying to probe the inscrutable mystery which she felt was at the bottom of the affair. She groped her way toward a solution, but always something stopped her. Her impulse to strike, she realized, and his brutal rejoinder had been actuated by something more than mere sex antagonism, there was *race* antagonism there—two elements clashing. That much she could fathom. But that he despising her, hating her for not being white should yet desire her! It seemed to her that his attitude toward her—hate and yet desire, was the attitude in microcosm of the whole white world toward her own, toward that world to which those few possible strains of black blood so tenuously and yet so tenaciously linked her.

Once she got hold of a big thought. Perhaps there *was* some root, some racial distinction woven in with the stuff of which she was formed which made her persistently kind and unexacting. And perhaps in the same way this difference, helplessly, inevitably operated in making Wynne and his kind, cruel or at best indifferent. Her reading for Wynne reacted to her thought—she remembered the grating insolence of white exploiters in foreign lands, the wrecking of African villages, the destruction of homes in Tasmania. She couldn't imagine where Tasmania was, but wherever it was, it had been the realest thing in the world to its crude inhabitants.

Gradually she reached a decision. There were two divisions of people in the world—on the one hand insatiable desire for power; keenness, mentality; a vast and cruel pride. On the other there was ambition, it is true, but modified, a certain humble sweetness, too much inclination to trust, an unthinking, unswerving loyalty. All the advantages in the world accrued to the first division. But without bitterness she chose the second. She wanted to be colored, she hoped, she was colored. She wished even that she did not have to take advantage of her appearance to earn a living. But that was to meet an end. After all she had contracted her debt with a white man, she would pay him with a white man's money.

The years slipped by—four of them. One day a letter came from Mr. Packard. Mrs. Wynne had sent him the last penny of the sum received from Mr. Wynne from February to November, 1914. Mr. Wynne had refused to touch the money, it was and would be indefinitely at Mrs. Wynne's disposal.

She never even answered the letter. Instead she dismissed the whole incident,—Wynne and all,—from her mind and began to plan for her future. She was free, free! She had paid back her sorry debt with labor, money and anguish. From now on she could do as she pleased. Almost she caught herself saying "something is going to happen." But she checked herself, she hated her old attitude.

But something *was* happening. Insensibly from the moment she knew of her deliverance, her thoughts turned back to a stifled hidden longing, which had lain, it seemed to her, an eternity in her heart. Those days with Mrs. Boldin! At night,—on her way to New York,—in the work-rooms,—her mind was busy with little intimate pictures of that happy, wholesome, unpretentious life. She could see Mrs. Boldin, clean and portly, in a lilac chambray dress, upbraiding her for some trifling, yet exasperating fault. And Mr. Boldin, immaculate and slender, with his noticeably polished air—how kind he had always been, she remembered. And lastly, Cornelius: Cornelius in a thousand attitudes and engaged in a thousand occupations, brown and near-sighted and sweet—devoted to his pretty sister, as he used to call her; Cornelius, who used to come to her as a baby as willingly as to his mother; Cornelius spelling out colored letters on his blocks, pointing to them stickily with a brown, perfect finger; Cornelius singing like an angel in his breathy, sexless voice and later murdering everything possible on his terrible cornet. How had she ever been able to leave them all and the "dear shabbiness of that home!" Nothing, she realized, in all these years had touched her inmost being, had penetrated to the core of her cold heart like the memories of those early, misty scenes.

One day she wrote a letter to Mrs. Boldin. She, the writer, Madame A. Wynne, had come across a young woman, Amy Kildare, who said that as a girl she had run away from home and now she would like to come back. But she was ashamed to write. Madame Wynne had questioned the girl closely and she was quite sure that this Miss Kildare had in no way incurred shame or disgrace. It had been some time since Madame Wynne had seen the girl but if Mrs. Boldin wished, she would try to find her again—perhaps Mrs. Boldin would like to get in touch with her. The letter ended on a tentative note.

The answer came at once.

My dear Madame Wynne:
    My mother told me to write you this letter. She says even if Amy Kildare had done something terrible, she would want her

to come home again. My father says so too. My mother says, please find her as soon as you can and tell her to come back. She still misses her. We all miss her. I was a little boy when she left, but though I am in the High School now and play in the school orchestra, I would rather see her than do anything I know. If you see her, be sure to tell her to come right away. My mother says thank you.

Yours respectfully,
CORNELIUS BOLDIN

The letter came to the modiste's establishment in New York. Amy read it and went with it to Madame. "I must go away immediately. I can't come back—you may have these last two weeks for nothing." Madame, who had surmised long since the separation, looked curiously at the girl's flushed cheeks, and decided that "Monsieur Ween" had returned. She gave her fatalistic shrug. All Americans were crazy.

"But, yes, Madame, if you must go, absolument."

When she reached the ferry, Amy looked about her searchingly. "I hope I'm seeing you for the last time. I'm going home, home!" Oh, the unbelievable kindness! She had left them without a word and they still wanted her back!

Eventually she got to Orange and to the little house. She sent a message to Peter's sister and set about her packing. But first she sat down in the little house and looked about her. She would go home, home—how she loved the word, she would stay there a while, but always there was life, still beckoning. It would beckon forever she realized to her adventurousness. Afterwards she would set up an establishment of her own,—she reviewed possibilities—in a rich suburb, where white women would pay for her expertness, caring nothing for realities, only for externals.

"As I myself used to care," she sighed. Her thoughts flashed on. "Then some day I'll work and help with colored people—the only ones who have really cared for and wanted me." Her eyes blurred.

She would never make any attempt to find out who or what she was. If she were white, there would always be people urging her to keep up the silliness of racial prestige. How she hated it all!

"Citizen of the world, that's what I'll be. And now I'll go home."

Peter's sister's little girl came over to be with the pretty lady whom she adored.

"You sit here, Angel, and watch me pack," Amy said, placing her in a little arm-chair. And the baby sat there in silent observation, one tiny leg crossed over the other, surely the quaintest, gravest bit of bronze, Amy thought, that ever lived.

"Miss Amy cried," the child told her mother afterwards.

Perhaps Amy did cry, but if so she was unaware. Certainly she laughed more happily, more spontaneously than she had done for years. Once she got down on her knees in front of the little arm-chair and buried her face in the baby's tiny bosom.

"Oh Angel, Angel," she whispered, "do you suppose Cornelius still plays on that cornet?"

COUNTEE CULLEN

Heritage†

(For Harold Jackman)[1]

What is Africa to me:
Copper sun or scarlet sea,
Jungle star or jungle track,
Strong bronzed men, or regal black
Women from whose loins I sprang
When the birds of Eden sang?
One three centuries removed
From the scenes his fathers loved,
Spicy grove, cinnamon tree,
What is Africa to me?

So I lie, who all day long
Want no sound except the song
Sung by wild barbaric birds
Goading massive jungle herds,
Juggernauts of flesh that pass
Trampling tall defiant grass
Where young forest lovers lie.
Plighting troth beneath the sky.
So I lie, who always hear,
Though I cram against my ear
Both my thumbs, and keep them there,
Great drums throbbing through the air.
So I lie, whose fount of pride,
Dear distress, and joy allied,
Is my somber flesh and skin,
With the dark blood dammed within
Like great pulsing tides of wine

† From Henry Louis Gates Jr. and Nellie Y. McKay, eds., *The Norton Anthology of African American Literature*, 2nd. ed. (New York: W. W. Norton, 2004), pp. 1347–50. Copyrights held by Amistad Research Center. Administered by Thompson and Thompson, New York NY. Notes have been deleted. See headnote, p. 227.
1. Harlem teacher and Cullen's intimate.

That, I fear, must burst the fine
Channels of the chafing net
Where they surge and foam and fret.

Africa? A book one thumbs
Listlessly, till slumber comes.
Unremembered are her bats
Circling through the night, her cats
Crouching in the river reeds,
Stalking gentle flesh that feeds
By the river brink; no more
Does the bugle-throated roar
Cry that monarch claws have leapt
From the scabbards where they slept.
Silver snakes that once a year
Doff the lovely coats you wear,
Seek no covert in your fear
Lest a mortal eye should see;
What's your nakedness to me?
Here no leprous flowers rear
Fierce corollas in the air;
Here no bodies sleek and wet,
Dripping mingled rain and sweat,
Tread the savage measures of
Jungle boys and girls in love.
What is last year's snow to me,
Last year's anything? The tree
Budding yearly must forget
How its past arose or set—
Bough and blossom, flower, fruit,
Even what shy bird with mute
Wonder at her travail there,
Meekly labored in its hair.
One three centuries removed
From the scenes his fathers loved,
Spicy grove, cinnamon tree,
What is Africa to me?

So I lie, who find no peace
Night or day, no slight release
From the unremittant beat
Made by cruel padded feet
Walking through my body's street.
Up and down they go, and back,
Treading out a jungle track.
So I lie, who never quite

Safely sleep from rain at night—
I can never rest at all
When the rain begins to fall;
Like a soul gone mad with pain
I must match its weird refrain;
Ever must I twist and squirm,
Writhing like a baited worm,
While its primal measures drip
Through my body, crying, "Strip!
Doff this new exuberance.
Come and dance the Lover's Dance!"
In an old remembered way
Rain works on me night and day.

Quaint, outlandish heathen gods
Black men fashion out of rods,
Clay, and brittle bits of stone,
In a likeness like their own,
My conversion came high-priced;
I belong to Jesus Christ,
Preacher of humility;
Heathen gods are naught to me.

Father, Son, and Holy Ghost,
So I make an idle boast;
Jesus of the twice-turned cheek,
Lamb of God, although I speak
With my mouth thus, in my heart
Do I play a double part.
Ever at Thy glowing altar
Must my heart grow sick and falter,
Wishing He I served were black,
Thinking then it would not lack
Precedent of pain to guide it,
Let who would or might deride it;
Surely then this flesh would know
Yours had borne a kindred woe.
Lord, I fashion dark gods, too,
Daring even to give You
Dark despairing features where,
Crowned with dark rebellious hair,
Patience wavers just so much as
Mortal grief compels, while touches
Quick and hot, of anger, rise
To smitten cheek and weary eyes.
Lord, forgive me if my need
Sometimes shapes a human creed.

All day long and all night through,
One thing only must I do:
Quench my pride and cool my blood,
Lest I perish in the flood.
Lest a hidden ember set
Timber that I thought was wet
Burning like the dryest flax,
Melting like the merest wax,
Lest the grave restore its dead.
Not yet has my heart or head
In the least way realized
They and I are civilized.

COUNTEE CULLEN

Two Who Crossed a Line†

(She Crosses)

From where she stood the air she craved
    Smote with the smell of pine;
It was too much to bear; she braved
    Her gods and crossed the line.

And we were hurt to see her go,
    With her fair face and hair,
And veins too thin and blue to show
    What mingled blood flowed there.

We envied her a while, who still
    Pursued the hated track;
Then we forgot her name, until
    One day her shade came back.

Calm as a wave without a crest,
    Sorrow-proud and sorrow-wise,
With trouble sucking at her breast,
    With tear-disdainful eyes,

She slipped into her ancient place,
    And, no word asked, gave none;

† From Werner Sollors, *An Anthology of Interracial Literature: Black-White Contacts in the Old World and the New* (New York: NYU Press, 2004), pp. 530–31. Copyrights held by Amistad Research Center. Administered by Thompson and Thompson, New York NY. See headnote, p. 227.

Only the silence in her face
    Said seats were dear in the sun.

(He Crosses)

He rode across like a cavalier,
    Spurs clicking hard and loud;
And where he tarried dropped his tear
    On heads he left low-bowed.

But, "Even Stephen," he cried, and struck
    His steed an urgent blow;
He swore by youth he was a buck
    With savage oats to sow.

To even up some standing scores,
    From every flower bed
He passed, he plucked by threes and fours
    Till wheels whirled in his head.

But long before the drug could tell,
    He took his anodyne;
With scornful grace, he bowed farewell
    And retraversed the line.

                                                    1925

W. E. B. DU BOIS

Sociologist, scholar, pacifist, activist, anti-imperialist, historian, editor and writer W. E. B. Du Bois (1868–1963) was one of the leading intellectuals of the twentieth century and one of the most influential senior figures of the Harlem Renaissance.

Criteria of Negro Art†

I do not doubt but there are some in this audience who are a little disturbed at the subject of this meeting, and particularly at the subject I have chosen. Such people are thinking something like this: "How is

---

† From *W. E. B. Du Bois: Writings* (New York: Library of America, 1986), pp. 993–1002. This essay was originally published in *The Crisis* (October 1926). W. W. Norton wishes to thank the Crisis Publishing Co., Inc., the publisher of the magazine of the National Association for the Advancement of Colored People, for use of *The Crisis Magazine* materials.

it that an organization like this, a group of radicals trying to bring new things into the world, a fighting organization which has come up out of the blood and dust of battle, struggling for the right of black men to be ordinary human beings—how is it that an organization of this kind can turn aside to talk about Art? After all, what have we who are slaves and black to do with Art?"

Or perhaps there are others who feel a certain relief and are saying, "After all it is rather satisfactory after all this talk about rights and fighting to sit and dream of something which leaves a nice taste in the mouth".

Let me tell you that neither of these groups is right. The thing we are talking about tonight is part of the great fight we are carrying on and it represents a forward and an upward look—a pushing onward. You and I have been breasting hills; we have been climbing upward; there has been progress and we can see it day by day looking back along blood-filled paths. But as you go through the valleys and over the foothills, so long as you are climbing, the direction,—north, south, east or west,—is of less importance. But when gradually the vista widens and you begin to see the world at your feet and the far horizon, then it is time to know more precisely whither you are going and what you really want.

What do we want? What is the thing we are after? As it was phrased last night it had a certain truth: We want to be Americans, full-fledged Americans, with all the rights of other American citizens. But is that all? Do we want simply to be Americans? Once in a while through all of us there flashes some clairvoyance, some clear idea, of what America really is. We who are dark can see America in a way that white Americans can not. And seeing our country thus, are we satisfied with its present goals and ideals?

In the high school where I studied we learned most of Scott's "Lady of the Lake" by heart. In after life once it was my privilege to see the lake. It was Sunday. It was quiet. You could glimpse the deer wandering in unbroken forests; you could hear the soft ripple of romance on the waters. Around me fell the cadence of that poetry of my youth. I fell asleep full of the enchantment of the Scottish border. A new day broke and with it came a sudden rush of excursionists. They were mostly Americans and they were loud and strident. They poured upon the little pleasure boat,—men with their hats a little on one side and drooping cigars in the wet corners of their mouths; women who shared their conversation with the world. They all tried to get everywhere first. They pushed other people out of the way. They made all sorts of incoherent noises and gestures so that the quiet home folk and the visitors from other lands silently and half-wonderingly gave way before them. They struck a note not evil but wrong. They carried, perhaps, a sense of strength and accomplishment, but their hearts had no conception of the beauty which pervaded this holy place.

If you tonight suddenly should become full-fledged Americans; if your color faded, or the color line here in Chicago was miraculously forgotten; suppose, too, you became at the same time rich and powerful;—what is it that you would want? What would you immediately seek? Would you buy the most powerful of motor cars and outrace Cook County? Would you buy the most elaborate estate on the North Shore? Would you be a Rotarian or a Lion or a What-not of the very last degree? Would you wear the most striking clothes, give the richest dinners and buy the longest press notices?

Even as you visualize such ideals you know in your hearts that these are not the things you really want. You realize this sooner than the average white American because, pushed aside as we have been in America, there has come to us not only a certain distaste for the tawdry and flamboyant but a vision of what the world could be if it were really a beautiful world; if we had the true spirit; if we had the Seeing Eye, the Cunning Hand, the Feeling Heart; if we had, to be sure, not perfect happiness, but plenty of good hard work, the inevitable suffering that always comes with life; sacrifice and waiting, all that—but, nevertheless, lived in a world where men know, where men create, where they realize themselves and where they enjoy life. It is that sort of a world we want to create for ourselves and for all America.

After all, who shall describe Beauty? What is it? I remember tonight four beautiful things: The Cathedral at Cologne, a forest in stone, set in light and changing shadow, echoing with sunlight and solemn song; a village of the Veys in West Africa, a little thing of mauve and purple, quiet, lying content and shining in the sun; a black and velvet room where on a throne rests, in old and yellowing marble, the broken curves of the Venus of Milo; a single phrase of music in the Southern South—utter melody, haunting and appealing, suddenly arising out of night and eternity, beneath the moon.

Such is Beauty. Its variety is infinite, its possibility is endless. In normal life all may have it and have it yet again. The world is full of it; and yet today the mass of human beings are choked away from it, and their lives distorted and made ugly. This is not only wrong, it is silly. Who shall right this well-nigh universal failing? Who shall let this world be beautiful? Who shall restore to men the glory of sunsets and the peace of quiet sleep?

We black folk may help for we have within us as a race new stirrings; stirrings of the beginning of a new appreciation of joy, of a new desire to create, of a new will to be; as though in this morning of group life we had awakened from some sleep that at once dimly mourns the past and dreams a splendid future; and there has come the conviction that the Youth that is here today, the Negro Youth, is a different kind of Youth, because in some new way it bears this mighty prophecy on its breast, with a new realization of itself, with new determination for all mankind.

What has this Beauty to do with the world? What has Beauty to do with Truth and Goodness—with the facts of the world and the right actions of men? "Nothing", the artists rush to answer. They may be right. I am but an humble disciple of art and cannot presume to say. I am one who tells the truth and exposes evil and seeks with Beauty and for Beauty to set the world right. That somehow, somewhere eternal and perfect Beauty sits above Truth and Right I can conceive, but here and now and in the world in which I work they are for me unseparated and inseparable.

This is brought to us peculiarly when as artists we face our own past as a people. There has come to us—and it has come especially through the man we are going to honor tonight[1]—a realization of that past, of which for long years we have been ashamed, for which we have apologized. We thought nothing could come out of that past which we wanted to remember; which we wanted to hand down to our children. Suddenly, this same past is taking on form, color and reality, and in a half shamefaced way we are beginning to be proud of it. We are remembering that the romance of the world did not die and lie forgotten in the Middle Age; that if you want romance to deal with you must have it here and now and in your own hands.

I once knew a man and woman. They had two children, a daughter who was white and a daughter who was brown; the daughter who was white married a white man; and when her wedding was preparing the daughter who was brown prepared to go and celebrate. But the mother said, "No!" and the brown daughter went into her room and turned on the gas and died. Do you want Greek tragedy swifter than that?

Or again, here is a little Southern town and you are in the public square. On one side of the square is the office of a colored lawyer and on all the other sides are men who do not like colored lawyers. A white woman goes into the black man's office and points to the white-filled square and says, "I want five hundred dollars now and if I do not get it I am going to scream."

Have you heard the story of the conquest of German East Africa? Listen to the untold tale: There were 40,000 black men and 4,000 white men who talked German. There were 20,000 black men and 12,000 white men who talked English. There were 10,000 black men and 400 white men who talked French. In Africa then where the Mountains of the Moon raised their white and snow-capped heads

1. Carter G. Woodson.

into the mouth of the tropic sun, where Nile and Congo rise and the Great Lakes swim, these men fought; they struggled on mountain, hill and valley, in river, lake and swamp, until in masses they sickened, crawled and died; until the 4,000 white Germans had become mostly bleached bones; until nearly all the 12,000 white Englishmen had returned to South Africa, and the 400 Frenchmen to Belgium and Heaven; all except a mere handful of the white men died; but thousands of black men from East, West and South Africa, from Nigeria and the Valley of the Nile, and from the West Indies still struggled, fought and died. For four years they fought and won and lost German East Africa; and all you hear about it is that England and Belgium conquered German Africa for the allies!

Such is the true and stirring stuff of which Romance is born and from this stuff come the stirrings of men who are beginning to remember that this kind of material is theirs; and this vital life of their own kind is beckoning them on.

The question comes next as to the interpretation of these new stirrings, of this new spirit: Of what is the colored artist capable? We have had on the part of both colored and white people singular unanimity of judgment in the past. Colored people have said: "This work must be inferior because it comes from colored people." White people have said: "It is inferior because it is done by colored people." But today there is coming to both the realization that the work of the black man is not always inferior. Interesting stories come to us. A professor in the University of Chicago read to a class that had studied literature a passage of poetry and asked them to guess the author. They guessed a goodly company from Shelley and Robert Browning down to Tennyson and Masefield. The author was Countée Cullen. Or again the English critic John Drinkwater went down to a Southern seminary, one of the sort which "finishes" young white women of the South. The students sat with their wooden faces while he tried to get some response out of them. Finally he said, "Name me some of your Southern poets". They hesitated. He said finally, "I'll start out with your best: Paul Laurence Dunbar"!

With the growing recognition of Negro artists in spite of the severe handicaps, one comforting thing is occurring to both white and black. They are whispering, "Here is a way out. Here is the real solution of the color problem. The recognition accorded Cullen, Hughes, Fauset, White and others shows there is no real color line. Keep quiet! Don't complain! Work! All will be well!"

I will not say that already this chorus amounts to a conspiracy. Perhaps I am naturally too suspicious. But I will say that there are today a surprising number of white people who are getting great satisfaction out of these younger Negro writers because they think it is going to stop agitation of the Negro question. They say, "What is the use of your fighting and complaining; do the great thing and the reward is there". And many colored people are all too eager to follow this advice; especially those who are weary of the eternal struggle along the color line, who are afraid to fight and to whom the money of philanthropists and the alluring publicity are subtle and deadly bribes. They say, "What is the use of fighting? Why not show simply what we deserve and let the reward come to us?"

And it is right here that the National Association for the Advancement of Colored People comes upon the field, comes with its great call to a new battle, a new fight and new things to fight before the old things are wholly won; and to say that the Beauty of Truth and Freedom which shall some day be our heritage and the heritage of all civilized men is not in our hands yet and that we ourselves must not fail to realize.

There is in New York tonight a black woman molding clay by herself in a little bare room, because there is not a single school of sculpture in New York where she is welcome. Surely there are doors she might burst through, but when God makes a sculptor He does not always make the pushing sort of person who beats his way through doors thrust in his face. This girl is working her hands off to get out of this country so that she can get some sort of training.

There was Richard Brown. If he had been white he would have been alive today instead of dead of neglect. Many helped him when he asked but he was not the kind of boy that always asks. He was simply one who made colors sing.

There is a colored woman in Chicago who is a great musician. She thought she would like to study at Fontainebleau this summer where Walter Damrosch and a score of leaders of Art have an American school of music. But the application blank of this school says: "I am a white American and I apply for admission to the school."

We can go on the stage; we can be just as funny as white Americans wish us to be; we can play all the sordid parts that America likes to assign to Negroes; but for any thing else there is still small place for us.

And so I might go on. But let me sum up with this: Suppose the only Negro who survived some centuries hence was the Negro painted by white Americans in the novels and essays they have written. What would people in a hundred years say of black Americans? Now turn it around. Suppose you were to write a story and put in it the kind of people you know and like and imagine. You might get it published and you might not. And the "might not" is still far bigger than the "might". The white publishers catering to white folk would say, "It is not interesting"—to white folk, naturally not. They want Uncle Toms, Topsies, good "darkies" and clowns. I have in my office a story with all the earmarks of truth. A young man says that he started out to write and had his stories accepted. Then he began to write about the things he knew best about, that is, about his own people. He submitted a story to a magazine which said, "We are sorry, but we cannot take it". "I sat down and revised my story, changing the color of the characters and the locale and sent it under an assumed name with a change of address and it was accepted by the same magazine that had refused it, the editor promising to take anything else I might send in providing it was good enough."

We have, to be sure, a few recognized and successful Negro artists; but they are not all those fit to survive or even a good minority. They are but the remnants of that ability and genius among us whom the accidents of education and opportunity have raised on the tidal waves of chance. We black folk are not altogether peculiar in this. After all, in the world at large, it is only the accident, the remnant, that gets the chance to make the most of itself; but if this is true of the white world it is infinitely more true of the colored world. It is not simply the great clear tenor of Roland Hayes that opened the ears of America. We have had many voices of all kinds as fine as his and America was and is as deaf as she was for years to him. Then a foreign land heard Hayes and put its imprint on him and immediately America with all its imitative snobbery woke up. We approved Hayes because London, Paris and Berlin approved him and not simply because he was a great singer.

Thus it is the bounden duty of black America to begin this great work of the creation of Beauty, of the preservation of Beauty, of the realization of Beauty, and we must use in this work all the methods that men have used before. And what have been the tools of the artist in times gone by? First of all, he has used the Truth—not for the sake of truth, not as a scientist seeking truth, but as one upon whom Truth eternally thrusts itself as the highest handmaid of imagination, as the one great vehicle of universal understanding. Again artists have used Goodness—goodness in all its aspects of justice, honor and right—not for sake of an ethical sanction but as the one true method of gaining sympathy and human interest.

The apostle of Beauty thus becomes the apostle of Truth and Right not by choice but by inner and outer compulsion. Free he is but his freedom is ever bounded by Truth and Justice; and slavery only dogs him when he is denied the right to tell the Truth or recognize an ideal of Justice.

Thus all Art is propaganda and ever must be, despite the wailing of the purists. I stand in utter shamelessness and say that whatever art I have for writing has been used always for propaganda for gaining the right of black folk to love and enjoy. I do not care a damn for any art that is not used for propaganda. But I do care when propaganda is confined to one side while the other is stripped and silent.

In New York we have two plays: "White Cargo" and "Congo". In "White Cargo" there is a fallen woman. She is black. In "Congo" the fallen woman is white. In "White Cargo" the black woman goes down further and further and in "Congo" the white woman begins with degradation but in the end is one of the angels of the Lord.

You know the current magazine story: A young white man goes down to Central America and the most beautiful colored woman there falls in love with him. She crawls across the whole isthmus to get to him. The white man says nobly, "No". He goes back to his white sweetheart in New York.

In such cases, it is not the positive propaganda of people who believe white blood divine, infallible and holy to which I object. It is the denial of a similar right of propaganda to those who believe black blood human, lovable and inspired with new ideals for the world. White artists themselves suffer from this narrowing of their field. They cry for freedom in dealing with Negroes because they have so little freedom in dealing with whites. DuBose Heywood writes "Porgy" and writes beautifully of the black Charleston underworld. But why does he do this? Because he cannot do a similar thing for the white people of Charleston, or they would drum him out of town. The only chance he had to tell the truth of pitiful human degradation was to tell it of colored people. I should not be surprised if Octavius Roy Cohen had approached the *Saturday Evening Post* and asked permission to write about a different kind of colored folk than the monstrosities he has created; but if he has, the *Post* has replied, "No. You are getting paid to write about the kind of colored people you are writing about."

In other words, the white public today demands from its artists, literary and pictorial, racial pre-judgment which deliberately distorts Truth and Justice, as far as colored races are concerned, and it will pay for no other.

On the other hand, the young and slowly growing black public still wants its prophets almost equally unfree. We are bound by all sorts of customs that have come down as second-hand soul clothes of white patrons. We are ashamed of sex and we lower our eyes when people will talk of it. Our religion holds us in superstition. Our worst side has been so shamelessly emphasized that we are denying we have or ever had a worst side. In all sorts of ways we are hemmed in and our new young artists have got to fight their way to freedom.

The ultimate judge has got to be you and you have got to build yourselves up into that wide judgment, that catholicity of temper which is going to enable the artist to have his widest chance for freedom. We can afford the Truth. White folk today cannot. As it is now we are handing everything over to a white jury. If a colored man wants to publish a book, he has got to get a white publisher and a white newspaper to say it is great; and then you and I say so. We must come to the place where the work of art when it appears is reviewed and acclaimed by our own free and unfettered judgment. And we are going to have a real and valuable and eternal judgment only as we make ourselves free of mind, proud of body and just of soul to all men.

And then do you know what will be said? It is already saying. Just as soon as true Art emerges; just as soon as the black artist appears, someone touches the race on the shoulder and says, "He did that because he was an American, not because he was a Negro; he was born here; he was trained here; he is not a Negro—what is a Negro anyhow? He is just human; it is the kind of thing you ought to expect".

I do not doubt that the ultimate art coming from black folk is going to be just as beautiful, and beautiful largely in the same ways, as the art that comes from white folk, or yellow or red; but the point today is that until the art of the black folk compels recognition they will not be rated as human. And when through art they compell recognition then let the world discover if it will that their art is as new as it is old and as old as new.

I had a classmate once who did three beautiful things and died. One of them was a story of a folk who found fire and then went wandering in the gloom of night seeking again the stars they had once known and lost; suddenly out of blackness they looked up and there loomed the heavens; and what was it that they said? They raised a mighty cry: "It is the stars, it is the ancient stars, it is the young and everlasting stars!"

NELLA LARSEN

Freedom†

He wondered, as he walked deftly through the impassioned traffic on the Avenue, how she would adjust her life if he were to withdraw from it. . . . How peaceful it would be to have no woman in one's life! These months away took on the appearance of a liberation, a temporary recess from a hateful existence in which he lived in intimacy with someone he did not know and would not now have chosen. . . . He began, again, to speculate on the pattern her life would take without him. Abruptly, it flashed upon him that the vague irritation of many weeks was a feeling of smoldering resentment against her.

The displeasure that this realization caused him increased his ill humor and distaste. He began to dissect her with an acrimomy that astonished himself. Her unanimated beauty seemed now only a thin

† From [Pseud. Allen Semi], *Young's Realistic Stories Magazine* 51 (1926): 241–43.

disguise for an inert mind, and not for the serene beauty of soul which he had attributed to her. He suspected, too, a touch of depravity, perhaps only physical, but more likely mental as well. Reflection convinced him that her appeal for him was bounded by the senses, for witness his disgust and clarity of vision, now that they were separated. How could he have been so blinded? Why, for him she had been the universe; a universe personal and unheedful of outside persons or things. He had adored her in a slavish fashion. He groaned inwardly at his own mental caricature of himself, sitting dumb, staring at her in fatuous worship. What an ass he had been!

His work here was done, but what was there to prevent him from staying away for six months—a year—forever? . . . Never to see her again! . . . He stopped, irresolute. What would she do? He tried to construct a representation of her future without him. In his present new hatred, she became a creature irresistibly given to pleasure at no matter what cost. A sybarite! A parasite too!

He was prayerfully thankful that appreciation of his danger had come before she had sapped from him all physical and spiritual vitality. But her future troubled him even while he assured himself that he knew its road, and laughed ruefully at the picture of her flitting from mate to mate.

A feverish impatience gripped him. Somehow, he must contrive to get himself out of the slough into which his amorous folly had precipitated him. . . . Three years. Good God! At the moment, those three years seemed the most precious of his life. And he had foolishly thrown them away. He had drifted pleasantly, peacefully, without landmarks; would be drifting yet but for the death of a friend whose final affairs had brought him away. . . .

He started. Death! Perhaps she would die. How that would simplify matters for him. But no; she would not die. He laughed without amusement. She would not die; she would outlast him, damn her! . . . An angry resentment, sharp and painful as a whiplash, struck him. Its passing left him calm and determined. . . .

He braced himself and continued to walk. He had decided; he would stay. With this decision, he seemed to be reborn. He felt cool, refreshed, as if he had stepped out from a warm, scented place into a cold, brisk breeze. He was happy. The world had turned to silver and gold, and life again became a magical adventure. Even the placards in the shops shone with the light of paradise upon them. One caught and held his eye. Travel . . . Yes, he would travel; lose himself in India, China, the South Seas . . . Radiance from the most battered vehicle and the meanest pedestrian. Gladness flooded him. He was free.

A year, thick with various adventures, had slid by since that spring day on which he had wrenched himself free. He had lived, been happy, and with no woman in his life. The break had been simple: a telegram hinting at prolonged business and indefinite return. There had been no reply. This had annoyed him, but he told himself it was what he had expected. He would not admit that, perhaps, he had missed her letter in his wanderings. He had persuaded himself to believe what he wanted to believe—that she had not cared. Actually, there had been confusion in his mind, a complex of thoughts which made it difficult to know what he really had thought. He had imagined that he shuddered at the idea that she had accepted the most generous offer. He pitied her. There was, too, a touch of sadness, a sense of something lost, which he irritably explained on the score of her beauty. Beauty of any kind always stirred him. . . . Too bad a woman like that couldn't be decent. He was well rid of her.

But what had she done? How had he taken it? His contemptuous mood visualized her at times, laughing merrily at some jest made by his successor, or again sitting silent, staring into the fire. He would be conscious of every detail of her appearance: her hair simply arranged, her soft dark eyes, her delicate chin propped on hands rivaling the perfection of La Gioconda's. Sometimes there would be a reversion to the emotions which had ensnared him, when he ached with yearning, when he longed for her again. Such moments were rare. Another year passed, during which his life had widened, risen, and then crashed. . . .

Dead? How could she be dead? Dead in childbirth, they had told him, both his mistress and the child she had borne him. She had been dead on that spring day when, resentful and angry at her influence in his life, he had reached out toward freedom—to find only a mirage; for he saw quite plainly that now he would never be free. It was she who had escaped him. Each time he had cursed and wondered, it had been a dead woman whom he had cursed and about whom he had wondered. . . . He shivered; he seemed always to be cold now. . . .

Well rid of her! How well he had not known, nor how easily. She was dead. And he had cursed her. But one didn't curse the dead. . . . Didn't one? Damn her! Why couldn't she have lived, or why hadn't she died sooner? For long months he had wondered how she had arranged her life, and all the while she had done nothing but to complete it by dying.

The futility of all his speculations exasperated him. His old resentment returned. She *had* spoiled his life; first by living and then by dying. He hated the fact that she had finished with him, rather than he with her. He could not forgive her. . . . Forgive her? She was dead. He felt somehow that, after all, the dead did not care if you forgave them or not.

Gradually, his mind became puppet to a disturbing tension which drove it back and forth between two thoughts: he had left her; she was dead. These two facts became lodged in his mind like burrs pricking at his breaking faculties. As he recalled the manner of his leaving her, it seemed increasingly brutal. She had died loving him, bearing him a child, and he had left her. He tried to shake off the heavy mental dejection which weighed him down, but his former will and determination deserted him. The vitality of the past, forever dragging him down into black depression, frightened him. The mental fog, thick as soot, into which the news of her death had trapped him, appalled him. He must get himself out. A wild anger seized him. He began to think of his own death, self-inflicted, with feeling that defied analysis. His zest for life became swallowed up in the rising tide of sorrow and mental chaos which was engulfing him.

As autumn approached, with faint notice on his part, his anger and resentment retreated, leaving in their wake a gentle stir of regret and remorse. Imperceptibly, he grew physically weary; a strange sensation of loneliness and isolation enveloped him. A species of timidity came upon him; he felt an unhappy remoteness from people, and began to edge away from life.

His deepening sense of isolation drove him more and more back upon his memories. Sunk in his armchair before the fire, he passed the days and sometimes the nights, for he had lost count of these, merged as they were into one another.

His increasing mental haziness had rejected the fact of her death; often she was there with him, just beyond the firelight or the candlelight. She talked and laughed with him. Sometimes, at night, he woke to see her standing over him or sitting in his chair before the dying fire. By some mysterious process, the glory of first love flamed again in him. He forgot that they had ever parted. His twisted memories visioned her with him in places where she had never been. He had forgotten all but the past, and that was brightly distorted.

He sat waiting for her. He seemed to remember that she had promised to come. Outside, the street was quiet. She was late. Why didn't she come? Childish tears fell over his cold cheeks. He sat weeping in front of the sinking fire.

A nameless dread seized him; she would not come! In the agony of his disappointment, he did not see that the fire had died and the candles had sputtered out. He sat wrapped in immeasurable sadness. He knew that she would not come.

Something in this thought fired his disintegrating brain. She would not come; then he must go to her.

He rose, shaking with cold, and groped toward the door. Yes, he would go to her.

The gleam of a streetlight through a French window caught his attention. He stumbled toward it. His cold fingers fumbled a moment with the catch, but he tore it open with a spark of his old determination and power, and stepped out—and down to the pavement a hundred feet below.

GEORGE S. SCHUYLER

From The Negro-Art Hokum†

Negro art "made in America" is as non-existent as the widely advertised profundity of Cal Coolidge, the "seven years of progress" of Mayor Hylan, or the reported sophistication of New Yorkers. Negro art there has been, is, and will be among the numerous black nations of Africa; but to suggest the possibility of any such development among the ten million colored people in this republic is self-evident foolishness. Eager apostles from Greenwich Village, Harlem, and environs proclaimed a great renaissance of Negro art just around the corner waiting to be ushered on the scene by those whose hobby is taking races, nations, peoples, and movements under their wing. New art forms expressing the "peculiar" psychology of the Negro were about to flood the market. In short, the art of Homo Africanus was about to electrify the waiting world. Skeptics patiently waited. They still wait.

True, from dark-skinned sources have come those slave songs based on Protestant hymns and Biblical texts known as the spirituals, work songs and secular songs of sorrow and tough luck known as the blues, that outgrowth of rag-time known as jazz (in the development of which whites have assisted), and the Charleston, an eccentric dance invented by the gamins around the public market-place in Charleston, S.C. No one can or does deny this. But these are contributions of a caste in a certain section of the country. They are foreign to Northern Negroes, West Indian Negroes, and African Negroes. They are no more expressive or characteristic of the Negro race than the music and dancing of the Appalachian highlanders or the Dalmatian peasantry are expressive or characteristic of the Caucasian race. If one wishes to speak of the musical contributions of the peasantry of the South, very well. Any group under similar circumstances would have produced something similar. It is merely a coincidence that this peasant class happens to be of a darker hue than the other inhabitants of the land. One recalls the remarkable likeness of the minor strains of the Russian mujiks[1] to those of the Southern Negro.

† From David Levering Lewis, ed., *The Portable Harlem Renaissance Reader* (New York: Penguin, 1994); pp. 96–99. Reprinted with permission from the June 16, 1926 issue of *The Nation*. See headnote, p. 270.
1. Free Russian peasants, pre-1917.

As for the literature, painting, and sculpture of Aframericans—such as there is—it is identical in kind with the literature, painting, and sculpture of white Americans: that is, it shows more or less evidence of European influence. In the field of drama little of any merit has been written by and about Negroes that could not have been written by whites. The dean of the Aframerican literati is W. E. B. Du Bois, a product of Harvard and German universities; the foremost Aframerican sculptor is Meta Warwick Fuller, a graduate of leading American art schools and former student of Rodin; while the most noted Aframerican painter, Henry Ossawa Tanner, is dean of American painters in Paris and has been decorated by the French Government. Now the work of these artists is no more "expressive of the Negro soul"—as the gushers put it—than are the scribblings of Octavus Cohen[2] or Hugh Wiley.[3]

This, of course, is easily understood if one stops to realize that the Aframerican is merely a lampblacked Anglo-Saxon. If the European immigrant after two or three generations of exposure to our schools, politics, advertising, moral crusades, and restaurants becomes indistinguishable from the mass of Americans of the older stock (despite the influence of the foreign-language press), how much truer must it be of the sons of Ham who have been subjected to what the uplifters call Americanism for the last three hundred years. Aside from his color, which ranges from very dark brown to pink, your American Negro is just plain American. Negroes and whites from the same localities in this country talk, think, and act about the same. Because a few writers with a paucity of themes have seized upon imbecilities of the Negro rustics and clowns and palmed them off as authentic and characteristic Aframerican behavior, the common notion that the black American is so "different" from his white neighbor has gained wide currency. The mere mention of the word "Negro" conjures up in the average white American's mind a composite stereotype of Bert Williams, Aunt Jemima, Uncle Tom, Jack Johnson, Florian Slappey, and the various monstrosities scrawled by the cartoonists. Your average Aframerican no more resembles this stereotype than the average American resembles a composite of Andy Gump, Jim Jeffries, and a cartoon by Rube Goldberg.

*　*　*

2. Southern Jewish writer known for comic portrayals of African-Americans.
3. Midwestern writer known for both comic portrayals of African-Americans and for creating the "Chinese detective," James Lee Wong.

CARL VAN VECHTEN

Born in Cedar Rapids, Iowa, Carl Van Vechten (1880–1964) became a consummate urban sophisticate and brought many other white artists and intellectuals to Harlem. A photographer, writer, and influential patron of black artists, Van Vechten became especially controversial upon publication of *Nigger Heaven*, which scandalized even some of his friends. In the portion of that novel excerpted here, Byron, an aspiring black writer, has lost his job and finds himself turning away from his upright girlfriend towards Lasca Sartoris, a much wilder denizen of Harlem's nightlife.

From Nigger Heaven†

Three

* * *

Sooner or later his thoughts obstinately reverted to Lasca. *She* had understanding. She, he felt certain, would give him sympathy. She was a real man's woman. He telephoned her more than once, but invariably received the message that she was still out of town and it was not known when she would return.

* * *

In his present mood he had no desire to return to his sordid hole in the wall. Finding a couple of dollars in his pocket, he determined to visit the Black Venus. He wanted to be cheered up and at this cabaret there was always excitement of some kind. Perhaps Irwin would be there, or Lucas Garfield. Perhaps a new golden-brown girl. He felt he wanted to be unfaithful to Mary, to degrade her ideal. He wanted to throw mud at everything she stood for. He'd like to tell her about it afterwards.

Preparing to descend the stairs that led to the cabaret, he was violently pushed aside. Two waiters were forcing a man out into the street. As they brushed past him Byron turned to see them deliver a final kick in the fellow's buttocks. Landing with a thud in the muddy gutter, the victim lay inert, apparently insensible. Byron felt sick. Life was so cruel. For the moment he experienced a pang of compassion for this stranger. I might be that man, he said to himself with a gush of self-pity.

In the dance hall his mood changed perceptibly. The room was crowded; all the tables were occupied with gay men and women,

† From *Nigger Heaven* (Urbana: University of Illinois Press, 2000; orig. publ. New York: Knopf, 1926) pp. 200–15. Used with permission of the Carl Van Vechten Trust. Notes are by the Editor of this Norton Critical Edition.

laughing, drinking. A yellow girl in red with a megaphone was making the rounds of the tables. As he stood, hesitating by the doorway, wondering if he could find a place, she shouted her song in his ear:

> She did me dirty,
> She did me wrong,
> She kept me fooled all along.
> But I've been so lonesome
> Since she went away
> That if she'll come home
> I'll let her stay . . .

I'll be three times God damned if I will! Byron gritted his teeth as he surrendered his coat to the girl in the check-room.

Dawggone, ef that ain't the cat's kanittans! a fat, cheerful-looking black man near him exclaimed.

Bardacious![1] agreed his companion.

Byron heard his name called: Dick was advancing towards him.

Hello, old chap!

Hello yourself! cried Byron, grasping his friend's hand. What in the world are you doing here?

Slumming. Brought some friends up with me. Come and sit with us. We've got plenty of gin.

I'd be glad to. I was wondering where I would sit. He hesitated before he inquired, Are you white or coloured tonight?

Buckra,[2] of course. And so are my friends, but they'll be delighted to meet you. They've heard about the New Negro! Dick grinned.

Well, Byron replied, I don't feel very new tonight. I feel more like Old Black Joe. However, I'll do the best I can for your patronizing friends.

Dick was more sober at once. I didn't mean that, he assured Byron. They're not a bit that sort. They honestly, seriously want to meet some people, and I didn't know a soul in the place before you came.

Look at duh spagingy-spagade[3] talkin' wid duh fagingy-fagade,[4] Byron heard a voice behind him say.

Out fo' a little hootchie-pap,[5] Ah pre-sume, another voice commented.

Well, evidently they don't see behind the mask even here, Byron said. He was in a better humour.

Of course not, Dick replied as he took his friend's arm and led him to the table. His companions turned out to be Rusk Baldwin, the

1. Bold, excellent, outrageous.
2. White.
3. Pig Latin: Spade (black).
4. Pig Latin: fay (white).
5. Sex.

well-known columnist, and Roy McKain, the novelist. Byron recognized both names at once.

I can't see, McKain averred to Byron, after a few trivial remarks had passed back and forth, how fellows like you find anybody to talk to up here. Just look around! I'll bet you're the only college man in the place.

Oh, Byron knows a few, Dick remarked with a wink.

Well, it's wonderful up here, Baldwin exclaimed. I had no idea it would be like this. It's as wild as a jungle. Look at that waiter dancing the Charleston up the floor.

I don't see how he holds that tray of glasses, the novelist said. He doesn't spill a drop.

This remark reminded Dick that he had forgotten as yet to fill his friend's glass. He supplied his omission.

Can you Charleston, Mr. Kasson? Baldwin inquired.

Not very well, Byron responded.

McKain regarded him with unfeigned amazement. Why, he asserted, I thought all coloured people could dance the Charleston, didn't you, Dick?

I don't know much about it, was Dick's answer.

McKain poured out half a glass of gin and filled the receptacle to the brim with ginger ale. His enthusiasm mounted, soared.

I think you are a wonderful people, he announced, a perfectly wonderful people! Such verve and vivacity! Such dancing! Such singing! And I've always thought coloured people were lazy! I suppose, he added reflectively, that it's because you're all so happy. That's it, Rusk, he cried, they're all so happy!

Do you know the poems of a young coloured fellow named Langston Hughes? Baldwin demanded of Byron.

Yes, I do.

Well, I thought they were good before I came up here, but he's just a bus-boy or something like that, and he doesn't understand his race. Listen to this:

> My hands!
> My dark hands!
> Break through the wall!
> Find my dream!
> Help me to shatter this darkness,
> To smash this night,
> To break this shadow
> Into a thousand lights of sun,
> Into a thousand whirling dreams
> Of sun!

Well, I thought that was good, Baldwin repeated laughing, but now I see it's only bus-boy bunk. He don't understand his race.

I should say not, McKain agreed.

I took the trouble to learn it too, Baldwin continued. I thought it was good. Let's see, how does it go on?

> I lie down in the shadow.
> No longer the light of my dream before me,
> Above me.
> Only the thick wall.
> Only the shadow.

Bunk, echoed McKain. Bunk. It isn't a bit like that.

The entertainer had at last arrived at their table. Swaying back and forth, her eyes obliquely surveying the room, her mind apparently a vacuum, she howled through her megaphone:

> Did me dirty . . . did me wrong . . .

Pleasing sentiment, Baldwin remarked. How much shall I give her? he demanded of Byron.

Oh, half a dollar. A quarter. It doesn't matter.

McKain took out his purse and extracted a dollar bill.

Roy! some one across the room hailed him.

Why, there's Dana Paton, McKain cried. He's calling us over. He dragged Baldwin away with him.

They mean all right, Byron, Dick assured his friend apologetically.

I suppose they do, Byron replied, but I've had a hell of a day and I guess I'm more nervous than usual. They're not bad . . . for ofays,[6] he added.

His friend gave him a close scrutiny. You'd pass for Spanish or Portuguese, he assured him. Why don't you come over? There's no good bucking the game. It isn't worth it.

Byron's lip curled. I couldn't, he responded. I just couldn't. I don't blame you, or any one else who does, but I couldn't. I guess I haven't got the guts.

What you're doing requires more guts.

Don't let's talk about it, Byron urged impatiently.

As the music stopped, the laughter rose and fell. An atmosphere of fate hovered over the place, as if something were going to happen that nobody could prevent. Behind them a man sang softly to his companion:

> Firs' gal Ah love, she gi' me her right han',
> She's quit me in duh wrong for annuder man:
> Learn me to let all women alone.

6. Whites.

Ha! Ha!

Did you ever see yo' sweetie when her good man ain' aroun',
Did you ever see yo' sweetie when her good man ain' aroun',
Gits up in duh mawnin', turns duh feather bed upside down?

Now an amber searchlight shot across the room. The jazz band vomited, neighed, barked, and snorted and the barbaric ceremony began.

Dick pointed to a sinewy figure, fantastically garbed, making his way from the entrance across the floor. Look! he exclaimed. That's the Scarlet Creeper!

Who's he? Byron inquired.

Haven't you heard of the famous Creeper? Why he's the most celebrated character along Lenox Avenue. Lives off women, a true Eastman. He's the sheik of the dives, Anatole Longfellow by name.

As the Creeper eased past the dancers—so slinking and catlike was his gait that walking would scarcely describe it—they edged away from him, although there was a whispered recognition from nearly every couple in the hall. It was apparent that his entrance had caused a sensation and it was also quite evident that he was very contented with his reception. People might not speak to him, but they spoke about him. The Creeper was accompanied by a sinister, hunchback dwarf with a wizened, wrinkled, black face like a monkey's, the chin discoloured by a tetter, the head glowing with bushy, laniferous, silver hair. As the pair seated themselves at a recently deserted table adjoining that occupied by Byron and Dick three waiters immediately Charlestoned up.

This obviously explains the origin of the phrase "dancing attendance," Dick remarked.

The Creeper gave his orders in a consequential manner and the waiters hastened away to execute his commands. Byron and Dick were in a position where they might observe the fellow without seeming to do so. Apparently, he was making some faint effort to control his tone, but in order to make himself heard over the tipsy dignity of the jazz band, he was obliged to raise his voice which, moreover, was placed so excellently forward in his mouth that its resonance was double that of the ordinary organ.

Dat Nigger ain' got long ter live, the Creeper was announcing.

The hunchback cringed in mock dismay, as he rubbed his hands together and smiled his approval. Then, making a significant gesture with his right middle finger around his throat, he croaked, Ah bet you cut him every way but loose.

Carvin's too good fo' an achin' pain lak him. Ah'll git him wid a gun.

The hunchback rolled his eyes until only the whites were visible, the while he licked his thick, black lips with his fat, red tongue.

No man steal mah gal an' live, the Creeper went on. Dey'll soon be throwin' dirt in his face.

Dat Ruby's one God damn fool, the leering dwarf contributed. One God damn fool! he repeated, wagging his head savagely from side to side. He was almost in ecstasy.

The waiter returned with the drinks which he deposited on the table. The Creeper, having filled his own glass, contemptuously bestowed a few drops in that of his companion.

Well, whispered Byron, it looks bad for somebody.

Nothing but cheap boasting, Dick retorted. These shines[7] that live off women are all cowards. He won't do a damn thing.

The Creeper had swirled into a dance with a handsome mulatto. His palms were flat across her shoulders, his slender fingers spread apart. There was an ancient impiety about the sensual grace of their united movement.

Take your eyes off the golden-brown, Dick warned, laughing.

You know my type!

It wouldn't take long to learn that.

Byron turned to his companion and looked at him earnestly. Dick, I want to ask you something, he said. Now . . . now . . . that you've gone white, do you really want . . . pinks for boody?[8]

Dick averted his eyes. That's the worst of it, he groaned. I just don't. Give me blues every time.

Baldwin and McKain rejoined them.

Talking to a fellow who's making drawings, the novelist explained. God, but this place is great! I could live up here. Is all Harlem like this?

The question awakened a swarm of perverse, dancing images in Byron's brain. They crowded about each other, all the incongruities, the savage inconsistencies, the peculiar discrepancies, of this cruel, segregated life.

Yes, he replied, I suppose it is.

7. Blacks.
8. Sex.

LANGSTON HUGHES

Passing for White, Passing for Colored, Passing for Negroes Plus†

In the current issue of OUR WORLD, there is a brilliantly written and stunningly illustrated article on Hawaii called "Revolt In Paradise." It contains some saddening revelations, particularly concerning mainland Negroes passing for Japanese, Chinese, Hawaiian—or anything but what they are. Some, light enough, of course, pass for white. But others are passing for colored. Not Negro colored, any kind of colored but COLORED colored. Just as some folks I know who are as Negro as I am insist that they are Indians.

In my travels about the world, I have occasionally come across American Negroes passing for some other colored nationality. Even in Paris, where there seemed little need to me to attempt to pass for anything, I met a young lady from Georgia passing for Javanese. On the boat coming home to New York, I met a quite brownskin woman from the Middle West passing as an Argentinian on a very meager knowledge of Spanish. And in Hollywood I met a cute little colored girl who looked no more East Indian than Dinah Washington, with a caste mark on her forehead pretending to be from Bombay. I admired her nerve.

It is true that in the United States there are some advantages in being or pretending to be, any kind of colored person but an American Negro. That is the reason, so Harlem teaches me, many brownskin Puerto Ricans make little haste to learn English. They feel that if they speak English well, they will be taken for American Negroes—which is about the last thing, apparently, anybody want to be. Woe is us, and woe is me! I, however, have never felt that way. It has always seemed to me more fun being frankly colored, AMERICAN NEGRO COLORED, than pretending to be anything else. But I do not condemn people who, for financial reasons, find it advantageous to be something else, at least not in the USA.

But it does seem to me a little silly to attempt to pass for something else in countries where color makes little, if any, difference. A friend of mine last year on a pilgrimage to Rome, told me that she met a member of our race from her home town who never passed for white at home, passing so determinedly in Italy that she would not even speak to a colored person Now, that made no sense at all in Rome, as far as I can see for there the Italians like colored Americans better

† From *The Chicago Defender*, Schomburg Center for Research in Black Culture, New York, Clipping file, "Passing." Used with permission of *The Chicago Defender*. See headnote, p. 227.

than they do white Americans. In fact, from all I can hear today, it is an advantage to be colored in many parts of Europe rather than white, if you are from this country.

Some Negroes take full advantage of this, and are going in for being what one might call 100 percent colored, Negroes plus, even pretending to be more Negro than they naturally are. I have even heard recently of some American WHITES in Europe claiming to be colored when they discovered that Negroness might get them a better public reception than whiteness. Speaking of Negroes who use race to popularity, when I was last in Europe, I remember Negro musicians who, at home, oiled and conked their hair down, letting it go entirely natural abroad when they discovered that the European women loved the feel of natural Negro hair—so alive and springy. I have heard Negroes sing spirtiuals abroad who would not think of singing one at home—when they learned how much Enropeans love and respect our folk songs,

But to get back to passing for colored—but not American colored. Even in Mexico, which is a brownskin country, some Negroes pass for Indians or Mexicans. There is little need for this, as far as I could tell when I lived there. No one Jim Crows[1] or segregates anybody as a rule and some Mexicans are dark as Joe Black. So why go to all the trouble of passing?" Why Negroes who do not try to pass for anything at home should suddenly want to pass for something else abroad has always puzzled me. The foreigners are seldom fooled. White American tourists may be taken in, but not the natives. And white American tourists are about the last people it would seem to me worthwhile impressing if, by passing, one can get a better job, I say: "Go to it." But to pass in a foreign country for social or other non-lucrative reason, seems to me sort of silly.

Maybe my race pride gets the better or me, but I think it is much more fun being one's self as were two anonymous Negroes in this world I love. Their names I never knew, but I will not forget them, because they were so colored. One was all dressed up like a Tauk in baggy trousers and a red fez serving Turkish coffee in the Haus Vaterland in Berlin. But when he saw us come in, a party of colored folks from home he yelled, "Hey now! What gives in Harlem?"

And when I first got off the boat in Shanghai and got into a rickshaw and went riding down the Band toward the hotel, whom should I pass in another rickshaw going the opposite way, but a very colored boy. As soon as we spied each other through the traffic in the busy street, he half rose and I half rose, and both of us helled, "Hy!" The rickshaw went on. I never saw him again in the whole time I was in China. I never knew his name. But race had greeted race across

1. See p. 49, n. 8.

space. And I remember his grin much more clearly than I remember the features of any of the face of any of the heads turned away by persons passing for something other than Negro with such ardor that they wanted to fool even me in a foreign land. Read how some colored folks in Honolulu would not let OUR WORLD take their pictuires for a colored magazine!

CRITICISM

MARY MABEL YOUMAN

Nella Larsen's *Passing*: A Study in Irony†

The critics have generally adjudged Nella Larsen's second novel, *Passing*, inferior to her first *Quicksand*. I would not quarrel with the overall judgment, but it seems to me that the evaluations are based on an erroneous perception of the theme of the novel. The critics feel that the novel is Clare Kendry's story, and it is about the problems of a Black "passing for white" and then desiring to return to a Black world.[1] *Passing*, in my opinion, is a novel which shows that Backs can and do lose the spiritual values of Blackness though they remain in a black world. Thus, Irene Redfield, the true protagonist, who could (but rarely does) "pass for white" has more truly lost her heritage than Clare who literally removes herself from Black life and lives as a white among whites. The title *Passing* is thus ironic, for it is Irene who "passes." The theme of the novel develops this irony.

The action of the novel is quickly told. Irene Redfield remeets a childhood friend, Clare Kendry, who has been "passing" for the last twelve years. Clare has become tired of her sterile, restricted white life; so she make surreptitious trips to Harlem to nurture her now reawakened spiritual needs. She then considers abandoning the material advantages she possesses as a white to remain permanently. Part of the attraction is Irene's husband, Brian. Distraught because her own life is becoming a shambles, Irene pushes Clare from a sixth story window to her death.

Stated baldy, the plot seems melodramatic, and the irony is not immediately apparent. One must also consider the style of the novel. It is Irene who tells the story, not Clare. And it is Irene's values that are rejected by the author. Irene's major concerns in life are security, middle-class morality, and middle-class standing. Anything that threatens these values must be destroyed. In turn, Irene has lost her Black heritage of spontaneity, freedom from convention, and zest for life. She is uneasily aware that her life lacks the highest goals, but she rejects changes—in effect she has "passed" into the conventional-

---

† From Mary Mabel Youman, "Nella Larsen's *Passing*: A Study in Irony," *College Language Association Journal* 18 (1974): 235–41. Reprinted by permission of the College Language Association.
1. See Robert A. Bone, *The Negro Novel in America*, rev. ed. (New Haven: Yale University Press, 1966), p. 102; Sterling Brown, *The Negro in American Fiction* (Washington: Associates in Negro Folk Education, 1937; rpt. New York, 1969); p. 143; Hugh M. Gloster, *Negro Voices in American Fiction* (Chapel Hill: University of North Carolina Press, 1948), pp. 144–146; Saunders Redding, *To Make a Poet Black* (Chapel Hill: University of North Carolina Press, 1939), pp. 117–118.

ized, mechanized, non-humane white world. This despite her assertions that she is a strong race woman and that Clare "cared nothing for the race."[2]

That Larsen believed the Black heritage to be more important than middle-class security and restrictions is supported by her comments on two other literary works. About Walter White's novel *Flight* (also about "passing" and the Black heritage), she writes: "Mr. White obviously means that it is the white race which is lost, doomed to destruction by its own mechanical gods. . . . It was this that made Mimi turn from it. Surely, the thesis of 'Flight' is what shall it profit a man if he gain the whole world and lose his own soul?"[3] Note also Larsen's statement in a letter to Gertrude Stein. Larsen's reflecting on "Melanctha," a short story which indicates that freedom, spontaneity, and lack of conventional restrictions are innate in Blacks. "I never cease to wonder how you came to write it and just why you and not some one of us should so accurately have caught the spirit of this race of mine."[4] *Passing* develops the theme of a lost Black heritage; Irene has sold her birthright for a mess of pottage.

Having indicated why it is unlikely that Larsen would approve of a protagonist who negates the Black heritage, let us examine Irene Redfield. The opening paragraph indicates Irene's character. She has just received a letter from Clare. "After her other ordinary and clearly directed letters the long envelope of thin Italian paper with its almost illegible scrawl seemed out at place and alien. And there was, too, something mysterious and slightly furtive about it. A thin sly thing which bore no return address to betray the sender. . . . Furtive, but yet in some peculiar, determined way a little flaunting. Purple ink. Foreign paper of extraordinary size" (p. 3) [5]. At first glance the letter may be considered poor taste, but more thought will make the reader aware that this writer has a zest for life and means to flaunt the conventions that might restrict her. For Irene, events are to be orderly, not mysterious; open, not furtive: conventional, not flaunting. Clare's vitality is disturbing; and even more disturbing is Irene's subconscious realization that she could easily respond to this force.

Consciously, Irene has her life ordered to her satisfaction. Her husband is a physician, thus giving her both economic security and secure social standing. Her activities are restricted to her own class and include teas, shopping expeditions, parties and helping the poor.

---

2. Nella Larsen, *Passing* (New York: Alfred A. Knopf, 1920), p. 90. Other quotations from *Passing* will be taken from this [Knopf] edition and will be indicated by parentheses in the text. Bracketed page numbers refer to this Norton Critical Edition.
3. Nella Larsen, "Correspondence," A response to Frank Horne's review of *Flight Opportunity*, IV (September, 1926), 295.
4. Quoted in Seon Manley and Susan Belcher, *O, Those Extraordinary Women on the joys of literary lib* (New York, 1972), p. 185.

This last, however, is not a personal effort based on humanitarian feelings, but a solidifying of her own middle-class position. She belongs to the Negro Welfare League because it is expected of one of her class. She does help organize and attend the League's annual dance. But she obviously considers it a social event rather than a fund raiser for less prosperous Blacks. She does not want nor expect to meet the objects of her charity; true all classes can and do attend the dance, but the social stratas do not mix. Irene's real attitude toward the lower-class is revealed in her relations with her servants. Clare, visiting the Redfields, frequently talks with the maid and cook, savoring the Black spirit. This, to Irene, is "an exasperating childlike lack of perception" (pp. 144–145) [57]. One is not supposed to be friendly with the hired help. It is class, not race, that motivates Irene. In Chicago, she has tea with Clara and Gertrude, another former friend. But Gertrude has married a butcher and is thus, to Irene, more an object than a participant in the tea.

Irene wants her middle-class life to remain intact with no disturbing currents or eddies from the outside world—class or race. This is an impossibility, especially from the racial standpoint. Her husband is agonizingly aware of the pressures of being Black; Irene willfully ignores them. She has tried keep her sons from learning the world "nigger" and its connotations, but inevitably they learn the epithet. Brian, dissatisfied with his lack of opportunities, has yearned for years to migrate to South America where race relations are better. Irene has bluntly refused to even consider such a possibility. Her refusal is based partially on a consideration of what she feels is best for her sons, but the primary reason is her personal security. The recollection of the fierce quarrels on the subject angers, frightens, and bewilders her. Why would anyone want to give up this known security for an uncertain unknown?

Irene's middle-class life is also threatened by lack of adherence to her Puritanical morality. To her sexuality is not an inherent human quality, but a definite indication of one's social class. She wants to remove her son from his present school because the boys are talking about sex. Irene finds it distasteful to even speak of the subject to her husband. Note her circumlocutions: "I'm terribly afraid he's [her son] picked up some queer ideas about things—some things—from the older boys, you know" (p. 104) [42]. Brian disciphers this correctly to mean sex. Irene feels that if she can place her son in a better (i.e. middle-class) school, this part of his education can be halted.

Irene in her attitudes toward sexuality reflects the middle-class position. There is both distaste and avid curiosity involved. After Clare leaves the Black world of South Chicago, she is occasionally seen in company with rich white men. In the discussions which follow, "the girls would always look knowingly at one another and then with little excited giggles, draw away their shining eyes and say with lurking undertones of regret or disbelief some such thing as: 'Oh, well, maybe she's got a job or something,' or 'After all, it mayn't have been Clare,' or 'You can't believe all you hear' " (p. 26) [13].

This fascination and rejection continue for Irene when Clare re-emerges in Harlem. Though she disowns the fascination, there is also a sub-conscious recognition that Clare has a humane quality that Irene is lacking. Clare is "capable of heights and depths of feeling that she, Irene Redfield, had never known." Irene immediately adds, "Indeed, never cared to know" (p. 118) [47]; but she suspects that her life is incomplete. Later she admits, "she couldn't now be sure that she had ever truly known love. Not even for Brian. He was her husband and the father of her sons. But was he anything more? Had she ever wanted or tried for more? In that hour she thought not." (p. 201) [77].

In accordance with her philosophy, Irene decides that her loss of feeling is not as important as her gain—security. To keep her world safe she is even able to overlook infidelity, as long as no one else knows. Brian has responded to Clare's passionate love of life. Irene discovering this is shocked, but her reaction is to safeguard her position. She goes on with her normal social life; no one must suspect. She comforts herself that Clare plans to leave Harlem soon, and until then Irene intends "to hold fast to the outer shell of her marriage, to keep her life fixed, certain" (p. 201) [77]. But she almost succumbs to despair, for what if Clare does not leave? Irene is well aware that a secure economic position is of little value to Clare. Thus when Clare's husband, John Bellew, discovers her at a Black party (he is violently prejudiced and will certainly divorce her), Irene must act. "She couldn't have Clare Kendry cast aside by Bellew. She couldn't have her free" (p. 209) [79]. She pushes Clare out the window to her death. In preserving her ultimate value—security, Irene has committed the ultimate inhumanity—murder.

Irene's adherence to a sterile middle-class lifestyle leads inevitably to the need to destroy the passionate, life-giving Clare. Irene fears being discovered, but she is not sorry for her action; it was necessary. She has "passed" from human to monster, a movement concomitant with losing her Black spiritual heritage and accepting middle-class security as the goal of life. The fact that she lives and Clare dies is Larsen's indictment of American values. Murdering the life-giving force is a prelude to a spiritual wasteland.

That Larsen rejects Irene and her values is evident; the difficulty of the novel lies in the vagueness of the desirable Black spirit. Clare makes two comments on her desire to return to the Black world: "I am lonely, so lonely . . . cannot help longing to be with you again, as I have never longed for anything before; and I once wanted many things in my life . . . You can't know how in this pale life of mine I am all the time seeing the bright pictures of that other that I often thought I was glad to be free of. . . . It's like an ache, a pain that never ceases . . . [ellipsis Larsen's] (p. 8) [7]; and "You don't know, you can't realize how I want to see Negroes to be with them again, and to talk with them, to hear them laugh" (p. 129) [51]. Clare, of course, does return; and she finds the experience so necessary to her spiritual welfare that she will give up her white existence. (One feels that even without the love between her and Brian she would have made this decision.) The theme of spiritual renewal at the roots is clear enough, but problem lies in its development. Clare's return is mostly to the middle-class Black world that envelopes Irene, not to the people who have preserved their spiritual heritage. While Clare may be drinking deeply of her heritage, the actual teas and dances are reflections of the same sort of occasions in her white world.

Still Blacks are supposed to be different, and better. In discussing "passing" with white Hugh Wentworth, Irene says that Blacks can always recognize race. "There are ways. But they're not definite or tangible. . . . It's easy for a Negro to 'pass' for white. But I don't think it would be simple for a white person to 'pass' for coloured [*sic*]" (pp. 141–142) [56]. The reader is aware, vaguely, that the intangibles of the Black heritage are the aforementioned spontaneity, freedom from conventional restraints, zest for life, and laughter. However, none of these attributes are dramatized in the picture given of Irene's world. A party at Felise's, a Black friend, is supposed to represent the epitome of Black life and is supposedly a source of renewal for Clare. The general description promises much: "Dave Freeland was at his best, brilliant, crystal clear and sparkling. Felise, too, was amusing, and not so sarcastic as usual, because she liked the dozen or so guests that dotted the long, untidy living-room. Brian was witty, though, Irene noted, his remarks were somewhat more barbed than was customary even with him. And there was Ralph Hazelton, throwing nonsensical shining things into the pool of talk, which to others, even Clare, picked up and flung back with fresh adornment" (p. 205) [78]. However, the actual conversation reported is far from "sparkling," and the "brilliant" Dave Freeland even remarks, "you're as sober as a judge" (p. 205) [78].

Clearly there is an insolvable conflict in asserting that Clare is renewed by the Black heritage while allowing her to see only this pallid middle-class society. This difficulty is inherent in the choice of technique for the novel. Irene is the narrator, but she rejects the Black heritage. Since she is Clare's sponsor (albeit unwillingly) to the return to Black life, she can only introduce her to her own class. Thus the novel shows clearly what is to be rejected, but remains disconcertingly vague on what should be joyously embraced.

However, the novel is clear that Blacks do have a humane, spiritual birthright. It is also clear that merely belonging to the race does not guarantee that one will enjoy the benefits of the legacy. Though Clare is the literal "passer," she returns to her birthright; Irene who remains "Black" has sold her soul and "passed" into white inhumanity.

CLAUDIA TATE

Nella Larsen's *Passing*: A Problem of Interpretation†

Nella Larsen's *Passing* (1929) has been frequently described as a novel depicting the tragic plight of the mulatto.[1] In fact, the passage on the cover of the 1971 Collier edition refers to the work as "the tragic story of a beautiful light-skinned mulatto passing for white in high society."[2] It further states that *Passing* is a "searing novel of racial conflict. . . ."[3] Though *Passing* does indeed relate the tragic fate of a mulatto who passes for white, it also centers on jealousy, psychological ambiguity and intrigue. By focusing on the latter elements, *Passing* is transformed from an anachronistic, melodramatic novel into a skillfully executed and enduring work of art.

Set in a romanticized region of Harlem's Sugar Hill in 1927, where beautiful Black socialites swirl about in designer gowns, sip tea from antique china cups and jaunt between home and resort, the world of *Passing* is, as Hoyt Fuller says in the Introduction to the 1971 edition, as unreal, "artificial and ultimately as lifeless as a glamorous stage set" (p. 19). Fuller's assessment is certainly accurate enough. We must assume, however, that Larsen was equally aware of the novel's obvious artificiality, and therefore could not have intended to pass off this fantasy land as a fictive replica of external reality. I suggest that *Passing*'s social pretentiousness is not, as critics have frequently said,[4]

† From Claudia Tate, "Nella Larsen's *Passing*: A Problem of Interpretation." Reprinted from *Black American Literature Forum* 14, no. 4 (Winter 1980): 142–46.

1. Robert A. Bone, *The Negro Novel in America*, rev. ed. (New Haven: Yale University Press, 1966), p. 102; Sterling Brown, *The Negro in American Fiction*, rev. ed. (New York: Atheneum, 1969), p. 143; Nick A. Ford, *The Contemporary Negro Novel: A Study in Race Relations* (Boston: Meador, 1936), pp. 50–51; Hugh M. Gloster, *Negro Voices in American Fiction* (Chapel Hill: The University of North Carolina Press, 1948), pp. 146–47; Saunders Redding, *To Make a Poet Black* (Chapel Hill: The University of North Carolina Press, 1939), pp. 117–18; Amritjit Singh, *The Novels of the Harlem Renaissance* (University Park: The Pennsylvania State University Press, 1976), pp. 98–100; Mary Mabel Youman, "Nella Larsen's *Passing*: A Study in Irony," *C.L.A. Journal*, XVIII, No. 2 (1974), 235–41 [reprinted in this edition, p. 337].
2. Hoyt Fuller, cover remarks, *Passing* by Nella Larsen (New York: Collier, 1971). Future references to the text of *Passing* will appear parenthetically in the text. Bracketed page numbers refer to this Norton Critical Edition.
3. Fuller, cover remarks.
4. Bone et al.

a deficiency of Larsen's artistic vision but an intentional stylistic device.

The story is told from the point of view of the principal character, Irene Redfield, whose observations and interpretations account for every detail of the unfolding narrative. The story begins with Irene recalling the events surrounding her renewed friendship with a childhood acquaintance, Clare Kendry. During their chance meeting, Irene recalls the events of the past twelve years in flashbacks. The recollection of past events presents a rather comprehensive picture of the two women, both of whom are light-skinned enough to be mistaken for white. Irene is a socialite, married to a successful Black physician, Brian Redfield, and they live in a fashionable section of Harlem. Clare is married to a wealthy white man, John Bellew, who is unaware of her racial identity. Although Clare's domestic life is comfortable, she grows increasingly weary of its monotony, and as a result she seeks excitement by socializing with Irene and her Harlem friends without Bellew's knowledge. Clare's frequent association with Irene makes Irene envious of Clare's extraordinary beauty. In fact, she becomes obsessed with envy once she suspects that Brian and Clare are romantically involved. The climax occurs when Bellew follows Clare to a social gathering at the residence of a Black couple, where he surmises that she too is Black. During his angry outburst and the resulting confusion, Clare mysteriously falls to her death through an open window, bringing the story to its tragic conclusion.

Ostensibly, *Passing* conforms to the stereotype of the tragic mulatto. However, many factors make such an interpretation inadequate. The conventional tragic mulatto is a character who "passes" and reveals pangs of anguish resulting from forsaking his or her Black identity. Clare reveals no such feelings; in fact, her psychology is inscrutable. Moreover, Clare does not seem to be seeking out Blacks in order to regain a sense of racial pride and solidarity. She is merely looking for excitement, and Irene's active social life provides her with precisely that. An equally important reason for expanding the racial interpretation is that alone it tends to inhibit the appreciation of Larsen's craft. Larsen gave great care to portraying the characters; therefore, the manner of their portrayal must be important and ultimately indispensable to interpreting *Passing*'s meaning. Thus, the "tragic mulatto" interpretation not only is unsuited to the book's factual content, but also disregards the intricately woven narrative.

An understanding of *Passing* must be deduced not merely from its surface content but also from its vivid imagery, subtle metaphors, and carefully balanced psychological ambiguity. For example, although the story has a realistic setting, it is not concerned with the ordinary course of human experience. The story develops from a highly artificial imitation of social relationships which reflect Irene's spiritual adventures.

These characteristics are more compatible with the romance than with the tragedy. But for the purposes of this study *Passing* is treated as a romance of psychological intrigue in which race is more a device to sustain suspense than merely a compelling social issue.

The work's central conflict develops from Irene's jealousy of Clare and not from racial issues which are at best peripheral to the story. The only time Irene is aware that race even remotely impinges on her world occurs when the impending exposure of Clare's racial identity threatens to hasten the disruption of Irene's domestic security. Race, therefore, is not the novel's foremost concern, but is merely a mechanism for setting the story in motion, sustaining the suspense, and bringing about the external circumstances for the story's conclusion. The real impetus for the story is Irene's emotional turbulence, which is entirely responsible for the course that the story takes and ultimately accountable for the narrative ambiguity. The problem of interpreting *Passing* can, therefore, be simplified by defining Irene's role in the story and determining the extent to which she is reliable as the sole reporter and interpreter of events. We must determine whether she accurately portrays Clare, or whether her portrait is subject to, and in fact affected by, her own growing jealousy and insecurity. In this regard, it is essential to ascertain precisely who is the tragic heroine—Irene who is on the verge of total mental disintegration or Clare whose desire for excitement brings about her sudden death.

Initially, *Passing* seems to be about Clare Kendry, inasmuch as most of the incidents plot out Clare's encounters with Irene and Black society. Furthermore, Irene sketches in detail Clare's physical appearance down to "[her] slim golden feet" (p. 127) [53] Yet, she is unable to perceive the intangible aspects of Clare's character, and Larsen uses Irene's failure as a means of revealing disturbing aspects of her own psychological character.

Irene tells us that Clare is a "lovely creature" (p. 42) [12] in fact she is "just a shade too good-looking" (p. 120) [50]. Irene is fascinated by Clare's eyes, which she says are "strange[ly] languorous" (p. 120) [50], provocative and magnificent. Her frequent references to Clare's eyes do not refer merely to a physical feature, but become a symbolic statement of Clare's total mystery. More important to the story, though, than Clare's beauty (which we must remember is related entirely through Irene's sensibilities) is its emotional effect on Irene. Clare makes Irene "[feel] dowdy and commonplace" (p. 128) [53], thus making her constantly aware that she is comparatively mediocre in the light of Clare's sheer loveliness, which is "absolute and beyond challenge" (p. 60) [21]. As a result, Irene becomes more insecure, and she tries to mitigate her growing discontent with suspicions about Clare's fidelity.

Long before we encounter Clare Kendry, Larsen creates a dense psychological atmosphere for her eventual appearance. In the very first paragraph of the narrative, Larsen describes Clare's letter from Irene's point of view:

> It was the last letter in Irene Redfield's little pile of morning mail. After her other ordinary and clearly directed letters the long envelope of thin Italian paper with its almost illegible scrawl seemed out of place and alien. And there was, too, something mysterious and slightly furtive about it. A thin sly thing which bore no return address to betray the sender. Not that she hadn't immediately known who its sender was. Some two years ago she had one very like it in outward appearance. Furtive, but yet in some peculiar, determined way a little flaunting. Purple ink. Foreign paper of extraordinary size (p. 29). [5]

Larsen uses ambiguous and emotional terminology to refer to Clare's letter: "alien," "mysterious," "slightly furtive," "sly," "furtive," "peculiar," "extraordinary." Repeated references to the letter's beguiling unobtrusiveness and its enthralling evasiveness heighten the mystery which enshrouds both the almost illegible handwriting and its author. The letter itself is animated with feline cunning—"a thin sly thing." From one perspective the letter is insubstantial; from another, it possesses "extraordinary size." The letter rejects every effort of precise description. Provocative, bewitching, vividly conspicuous and yet elusive, the letter resembles the extraordinary physical appearance of Clare Kendry as she is later described, sitting in Irene's parlor:

> Clare, exquisite, golden, fragrant, flaunting, in a stately gown of shining black taffeta, whose long full skirt lay in graceful folds . . . her glistening hair drawn smoothly back . . . her eyes sparking like dark jewels. . . . Irene regretted that she hadn't counselled Clare to wear something ordinary and inconspicuous (pp. 127–28) [53].

In the next paragraph of the introductory section there are numerous references made to danger which incite a sense of impending disaster. The suspense is associated first with the letter and then with Clare. The letter is, to use T. S. Eliot's term, "an objective correlative," in that it objectifies abstract aspects of Clare's character, and its very presence reflects her daring defiance of unwritten codes of social propriety. Like Clare herself, the letter excites "a little feeling of apprehension" (p. 32) [6], which grows in intensity to "a dim premonition of some impending disaster" (p. 115) [47], and foreshadows the story's tragic ending.

The letter, therefore, is a vivid though subtle narrative device. It foreshadows Clare's actual arrival and characterizes her extraordinary beauty. It also suggests abstract elements of Clare's enigmatic character which evolve into a comprehensive, though ambiguous portrait.

Furthermore, it generates the psychological atmosphere which cloaks Clare's character, rendering her indiscernible and mysterious.

Irene is literally obsessed with Clare's beauty, a beauty of such magnitude that she seems alien, impervious, indeed inscrutable. Upon meeting Clare in Chicago, "Irene [felt that] . . . about the woman was some quality, an intangible something, too vague to define, too remote to seize" (p. 43) [12]. On one occasion we are told that "Irene turned an oblique look on Clare and encountered her peculiar eyes fixed on her with an expression so dark and deep and unfathomable that she had for a short moment the sensation of gazing into the eyes of some creature utterly strange and apart" (p. 77) [29]. On another occasion, Irene puzzles "over that look on Clare's incredibly beautiful face. . . . It was unfathomable, utterly beyond any experience or comprehension of hers" (pp. 84–85) [33]. Irene repeatedly describes Clare in hyperbole—"too vague," "too remote," "so dark and deep and unfathomable," "utterly strange," "incredibly beautiful," "utterly beyond any experience. . . ." These hyperbolic expressions are ambiguous. They create the impression that Clare is definitely, though indescribably, different from and superior to Irene and other ordinary people.

Irene's physical appearance, on the other hand, is drawn sketchily. We know that she has "warm olive skin" (p. 95) [37] and curly black hair (p. 40) [70]. Though Irene is not referred to as a beauty, given her confidence and social grace, we are inclined to believe that she is attractive. Despite the fact that little attention is given to Irene's physical portrayal, her encounter with Clare provides the occasion for the subtle revelation of her psychological character. Hence, the two portraits are polarized and mutually complementary—one is purely external, while the other is intensely internal.

Irene is characterized as keenly intelligent, articulate and clever. In this regard, the social gatherings seem to be more occasions for her to display a gift for witty conversation than actual events. Whether in the midst of a social gathering or alone, Irene often falls prey to self-dramatization, which is half egoism and half ironic undercutting for the evolving story. She also never cares to know emotional rapture, but prefers instead "only to be tranquil . . . [and] unmolested . . ." (p. 178) [76]. Hence, her personal feelings are confined to an outer shell of superficial awareness. Although she is further portrayed as possessing an acute awareness of discernment, she tends to direct this ability entirely toward others and employ hyperbole rather than exact language for its expression. Her perceptions, therefore, initially seem generally accurate enough, until she becomes obsessed with jealousy.

As the story unfolds, Irene becomes more and more impulsive, nervous and insecure, indeed irrational. She tends to jump to conclusions which discredit her credibility as a reliable source of information. For example, on several occasions Irene assumes that Clare questions her racial loyalty (pp. 63, 93 and 108). On another occasion, she assumes that Clare is involved with the man who escorted her to the Drayton Hotel dining room (p. 74). And eventually, she concludes that Clare and Brian are having an affair (pp. 149 and 173). Each of her assumptions may indeed be correct, but we observe no tangible evidence of their support; consequently, we cannot know with any certainty whether or not Irene's suspicions are true.

Although we only know the external details of Clare's life, we observe the total essence of Irene's psychology. We have also noted that thematic information is seldom communicated directly, but implied through dramatic scenes. Hence, Irene's character, like Clare's, achieves cohesion from the suggestive language Irene employs (especially when describing Clare), the psychological atmosphere permeating her encounters with Clare, and the subtle nuances in characterization. The realistic impact of incidents in and of themselves neither fully characterizes Irene nor conveys the novel's meaning. Meaning in *Passing*, therefore, must be pieced together like a complicated puzzle from allusion and suggestions. Irene gives form to Clare, but we are left with the task of fashioning Irene from her reflections of Clare's extraordinary beauty.

The ambiguous ending of *Passing* is another piece of the puzzle. The circumstances surrounding Clare's death support several interpretations. The most obvious interpretation is that Irene in a moment of temporary insanity pushed Clare out of the window. This interpretation has received widest acceptance, although the manner in which Larsen dramatizes Irene's alleged complicity receives no serious attention at all. Critics take her involvement in Clare's death for granted as merely a detail of the plot.[5] A close examination of the events surrounding Clare's death, however, reveals that the evidence against her, no matter how convincing, is purely circumstantial. No one actually observes Irene push Clare, and Irene never admits whether she is guilty, not even to herself. We are told only that

> [Irene] ran across the room, her terror tinged with ferocity, and laid a hand on Clare's bare arm. One thought possessed her. She couldn't have Clare Kendry cast aside by Bellew. She couldn't have her free.
>
> Before them stood John Bellew, speechless now in his hurt and anger. Beyond them the little huddle of other people, and Brian stepping out from among them.

5. Bone, et al.

What happened next, Irene Redfield never afterwards allowed herself to remember. Never clearly. (p. 184) [79].

At this moment Clare falls through the open window, and Irene responds by saying that "she wasn't sorry. [That she] was amazed, incredulous almost" (p. 185) [80]. Larsen provides no clarification for Irene's remark or its emotional underpinning. We do not know whether she is simply glad that Clare is permanently out of her life by means of a quirk of fate, whether she does not regret killing her, or whether she has suffered momentary amnesia and therefore does not know her role in Clare's death. In fact, Larsen seems to have deliberately avoided narrative clarity by weaving ambiguity into Irene's every thought and expression. For example, shortly after Clare's fall, Irene wonders what the other people at the party may be thinking about the circumstances surrounding Clare's death. Her speculations further cloud the narrative with other possible explanations for Clare's death. Irene wonders, "What would the others think? That Clare had fallen? That she had deliberately leaned backward? Certainly one or the other. Not . . ." (p. 185) [80]. A literal interpretation of this passage suggests that Clare may have accidentally fallen through the open window, or that she may have committed suicide. The passage can also be interpreted to mean that Irene hopes that the guests will mistakenly assume her innocence in their effort to arrive at a more agreeable explanation than murder. Of course, the passage may merely reflect Irene's genuine attempt to deduce what the others would necessarily conclude in light of her innocence. A few moments later, Irene fiercely mutters to herself that "it was an accident, a terrible accident" (p. 186) [80]. This expression may be merely her futile effort at denying involvement in murder. Or, it may be her insistence that she is indeed innocent, though she suspects that no one will believe her. Or, she could be uncertain of her involvement and struggling to convince herself that she is innocent. In all cases we must be mindful that there is still no tangible proof to support one interpretation over another. Although we may be inclined to accept the conventional interpretation, we must remember that all evidence is circumstantial, and we cannot determine Irene's guilt beyond a reasonable doubt.

In reference to other explanations for Clare's death mentioned above, we note that the possibility of accidental death is the least satisfying interpretation. Consequently, we disregard it, despite its being a plausible assumption as well as the conclusion which the authorities reach.

The last alternative—suicide—tends to be inadvertently neglected altogether, inasmuch as Clare's motives are not discernible. Nothing is left behind, neither note nor explaining discourse, to reveal her motives. However, this interpretation does deserve consideration, since it enhances the ambiguous conclusion and draws heavily on Larsen's narrative techniques of allusion and suggestion.

Early in the text we are given the circumstances surrounding the death of Clare's father. When his body was brought before her, she stood and stared silently for some time. Then after a brief emotional outburst, "[s]he glanced quickly about the bare room, taking everyone in, even the two policemen, in a sharp look of flashing scorn. And, in the next instance, she . . . turned and vanished through the door [never to return]" (p. 31) [6]. The last scene in the story bears a striking resemblance to this, and the motives for Clare's behavior in the early scene suggest a possible motive for her suicide. "Clare stood at the window, as composed as if everyone were not staring at her in curiosity and wonder. . . . One moment Clare had been there . . . the next she was gone" (pp. 184–85) [79]. In both instances Clare surveys the fragments of her life, and in both she vanishes, leaving behind a painful situation which she cannot alter. In the latter, she is utterly alone, and suicide is the ultimate escape from the humiliation that awaits her.

Passing's conclusion defies simple solution. I cannot resolve this problem by accepting a single explanation, since Larsen, on one hand, deliberately withheld crucial information that would enable me to arrive at a definite conclusion, and on the other, she counterbalanced each possible interpretation with another of equal credibility. Although I am unable to determine Irene's complicity in Clare's death, this dilemma is neither a deterrent to appreciating Larsen's meticulous narrative control nor an evasion of my critical responsibility. To the contrary, my admission of uncertainty is my honest response to the work, given only after serious consideration of my position as a literary critic. In fact, my inability to arrive at a conclusion in and of itself attests to Larsen's consummate skill in dramatizing psychological ambiguity. I realize that this critical posture is not a popular one. Of course, I could insist, as many critics have done, that Irene pushed Clare out of that window.[6] To build a case for this interpretation would not be difficult. But to do so would be forcing the work to fit the demands of critical expectations rather than allowing the work to engender meaningful critical response. This approach would be of no service to the work and ultimately discredit the criticism itself. What I am certain of, though, is that *Passing* is not the conventional tragic mulatto story at all. It is an intriguing romance in which Irene Redfield is the

6. Bone, et al.

unreliable center of consciousness, and she and not Clare Kendry is the heroine.

Larsen's focus on a mulatto character, the plagiarism scandal surrounding her short story, "Sanctuary," published in 1939,[7] and aspects of her personal life probably account for the sparsity of serious, critical attention given to her work. Critics, of course, hastily comment on Larsen's skill as they either celebrate other Harlem Renaissance writers or look ahead to the socially conscious writers of the '30s. Few address the psychological dimension of Larsen's work.[8] They see instead a writer who chose to escape the American racial climate in order to depict trite melodramas about egocentric black women passing for white. This critical viewpoint has obscured Larsen's talent and relegated *Passing* to the status of a minor novel of the Harlem Renaissance. But Larsen's craft deserves more attention than this position attracts. *Passing* demands that we recognize its rightful place among important works of literary subtlety and psychological ambiguity.

MARY HELEN WASHINGTON

Nella Larsen: Mystery Woman of the Harlem Renaissance†

> There are two "colored" movies—innumerable parties—and cards. Cards played so intensely that it fascinates and repulses at once. Movies worthy and worthless—but not even a low-caste spoken stage.
>
> Parties, plentiful. Music and much that is wit and color and gaiety. But they are like the richest chocolate; stuffed costly chocolate that makes the taste go stale if you have too many of them. That makes plain whole bread taste like ashes.
>
> "On Being Young—a Woman—and Colored"

Marita O. Bonner wrote this essay on being a young, black, middle-class woman in the 1920s, and won the 1925 essay contest sponsored by the NAACP's *Crisis* magazine, edited by W.E.B. DuBois. Three years after Bonner's essay won the *Crisis* prize, Nella Larsen published the first of her two novels, *Quicksand* and *Passing*, which dealt

---

7. See: Adelaide Cromwell Hill, Introduction to Nella Larsen's *Quicksand* (New York: Collier, 1971), p. 16.
8. Amritjit Singh in *The Novels of the Harlem Renaissance* discusses the manic-depressive behavior of Helga Crane, the heroine of Larsen's *Quicksand*, (pp. 102–103) but psychological analysis is not employed in his discussion of *Passing* (pp. 99–100).
† From Mary Helen Washington, "Nella Larsen: Mystery Woman of the Harlem Renaissance, *Ms. Magazine* (December 1980): 44–50. Reprinted by permission of the author. Notes are by the Editor of this Norton Critical Edition.

with this same problem: the marginal black woman of the middle class, who was both unwilling to conform to a circumscribed existence in the black world and unable to move freely in the white world. We may perhaps think this is a strange dilemma for a black woman to experience or certainly an atypical one, for most black women then, as now, were struggling against much more naked and brutal realities and would be contemptuous of so esoteric a problem as feeling uncomfortable among black people. Is there anything relevant in the lives of women who arrogantly expected to live in Harlem in the middle-class enclave of Sugar Hill, to summer at resorts like Idlewild[1] in Michigan, to join exclusive black clubs and sororities? Weren't the interests that preoccupied Larsen in her work just the spoiled tantrums of "little yellow[2] dream children" grown up?

But during the 1920s, Larsen's novels enjoyed some popularity as "uplift novels" that presented proof that blacks were intelligent, refined, and morally equal to whites. The novel about the fair-skinned woman who challenged color lines to improve her social situation was viewed as a kind of protest against a rigid caste system. Even militants like DuBois appreciated the struggles of the educated black elite he called the "Talented Tenth."

Fifty years after the heyday of her very brief literary career, Larsen is for the most part unknown, unread, and dismissed—both by black critics and their white counterparts—even though her perceptive inquiries speak clearly to the predicament of the middle-class black woman of our own generation.

Her preoccupation with the theme of marginality was the first venture into an ocean that blacks would navigate in somewhat larger numbers as the Afro-American experience is modified for some of us by greater access to education, economic resources, and social mobility. One subtle effect of this change has been the loosening of the more obvious ties of commonality between the privileged few and the majority of the black community—ties that may have had a clearer purpose when racial barriers were more stark.

There were many reasons for Larsen to choose, in the 1920s, the theme of the black woman as outsider. There were the contradictions of her own life: Larsen's mother was a white woman from Denmark; her father, a black West Indian. Widowed when Larsen was a young girl, her mother remarried, this time to "one of her own kind." In the new all-white family—father, mother, and second daughter—Larsen's blackness was an embarrassment. In a 1929 newspaper interview Larsen confirms a painful isolation from them: "I don't see

1. See p. 16, n. 2.
2. See p. 118, n. 5.

my family much now. It might make it awkward for them, particularly my half-sister."

Larsen was constantly negotiating the chasm between black and white. For a while she studied at Fisk, the black university in Nashville. Then she enrolled for three years at the University of Copenhagen in Denmark, where her white relatives lived. Little is known about the three-year period of her life in Europe, though the autobiographical character Helga Crane, the mulatto outcast in *Quicksand*, suggests some possible scenarios. Perhaps, like Helga, she was received warmly by her Danish relatives, and treated as something of a curiosity, her dark skin standing out in vivid relief against so many pale blonds. Helga also grows discontented playing the role of exotic freak and finds herself longing desperately to be surrounded by brown laughing faces and to be immersed in the warm spontaneity of black Harlem life.

Larsen returned to the States and enrolled in another black school, Lincoln Training School for Nurses, from which she graduated in 1915. She went to another black setting, Tuskegee Institute in Alabama, where she worked as a nurse. She was 22 years old when she abruptly left Tuskegee after only one year—the exact age of Helga Crane when she too left her job at a Southern black college, disgusted with its hostility to individuality and innovation. It was a society with a pretentious, formal code of behavior, perhaps even more complicated and rigid than the highest upper-class white society. Helga finds it intolerable among blacks who preach racial solidarity and yet value cream-colored skin and hate the softly blurred speech of their own race.

A similar experience probably accounts for Larsen's abrupt departure from Tuskegee for New York. There she worked as a children's librarian for eight years, during which she wrote the only two books she would ever publish.

Nella Larsen won a Guggenheim in 1930, the first black woman to win a creative writing award from that foundation, and she traveled to Spain to work on a third novel. It was never completed. Instead Nella Larsen entered into a 30-year silence. She worked as a supervising nurse at Bethel Hospital in Brooklyn, neither passing for white nor identifying with blacks. She died in obscurity in Brooklyn in 1963.

There are a few clues about why Nella Larsen fell silent as a literary voice. In 1930 she was accused of plagiarizing a story that was published in *Forum* magazine. Though she was supported by her editor, who had seen several drafts of the story, she was nonetheless devastated by the criticism. Then in 1933 she was divorced from her husband, Dr. Elmer Innes [sic], a physicist at Fisk University. The divorce was crudely sensationalized by one widely read black newspaper. The

Baltimore *Afro-American* reported "rumors" that Professor Innes [sic] was involved with a white woman and that Larsen's frequent trips to Europe had helped to cause the breakup and added that the speculation at Fisk was that Larsen had tried to kill herself by jumping out of a window.

These two events of public shame, plus a fragile and vulnerable personality, a sense of oddness that made her seem strange even to her friends, and a deep-seated ambivalence about her racial status combined to reinforce her sense of herself as the Outsider and may finally have pushed her into a life of obscurity.

Always there is the ambivalence: in her personal correspondence Larsen is detached and aloof speaking about "the Negroes" as though she were observing a comic opera, and yet there is the unmistakable race pride as she observes the style and coping power of poor blacks in the South. She once wrote in a letter to Carl Van Vechten, a white novelist and critic of the Harlem Renaissance period, that she found poor Southern blacks quaint and amusing: "I've never seen anything quite so true to what's expected. Mostly black and good-natured and apparently quite shiftless, frightfully clean and decked out in the most appalling colors, but somehow just right. Terribly poor." Then she hastens to add that the poor whites by comparison are tragic and depressing.

What happens to a writer who is legally black but internally identifies with both blacks and whites, who is supposed to be content as a member of the black elite, but feels suffocated by its narrowness, who is emotionally rooted in the black experience and yet wants to live in the whole world not confined to a few square blocks and the mentality that make up Sugar Hill?

Her two novels give no indication that Nella Larsen ever solved this problem of duality. All of Larsen's women characters choose self-destruction, and yet her novels sensitively explore the consciousness of the marginal black woman. Larsen's characters—Helga Crane, Irene Redfield, and Clare Kendry—are black women out of step with their time, as middle-class black women in the 1920s. Like strange projectiles, or plants trying to sustain themselves without roots or nourishment, they are detached and isolated from the black community. Helga Crane feels claustrophobic in the black Southern college and in black Harlem where she is forced to observe taboos and conventions that constrict her spirit. The proscription against wearing bright colors (because bright colors supposedly emphasize a dark-skinned woman's blackness) amuses her, for example, but she sees it as one of the innumerable internal controls people already under severe restraints must submit to. Even more intolerable for Helga is the absolute law against any kind of interracial mixing, which Helga's Harlem friends consider an act of disloyalty to the race. One woman in *Quicksand* is ostracized because she is seen dancing publicly with white men. Helga is never able to completely deny her blackness, so she lives with resentment and rancor, having to "ghettoize" her own life.

In Larsen's second novel, *Passing*, one can see most clearly how she failed to resolve the dilemma of the marginal woman. The central character, Clare Kendry, is married to a white man and has been passing for white all of her married life. Passionate and daring, the mysterious Clare lives in both the black and white worlds, feeling no permanent allegiance to either, nor any of the classic anguish of the tragic mulatto. This golden and graceful woman is simply determined to escape the poverty of her childhood and to have whatever she wants in life regardless of the price or the danger.

Passing becomes, in Larsen's terms, a metaphor for the risk-taking experience, the life lived without the supports other black women clung to in order to survive in a white-dominated, male-dominated society. One clear indication of Clare's striving for autonomy is that she is never called by her married name, Mrs. Bellew. She is only and always Clare Kendry, a woman of such passion and vitality that she mocks the shallowness of her childhood friend, the pretentious and proper Irene Redfield.

Why does Clare pass for white? Because it enables her to marry a man of means. Because she, like most other black women of the 1920s, if she achieved middle-class status, did it by virtue of a man's presence in her life, by virtue of his status—a grandfather who owned an undertaking business, a father who became a doctor, a husband elected to public office.

Larsen's failure in dealing with this problem of marginality is implicit in the very choice of "passing" as a symbol or metaphor of deliverance for her women. It is an obscene form of salvation. The woman who passes is required to deny everything about her past—her girlhood, her family, places with memories, folk customs, folk rhymes, her language, the entire long line of people who have gone before her. She lives in terror of discovery—what if she has a child with a dark complexion, what if she runs into an old school friend, how does she listen placidly to racial slurs? And more, where does the woman who passes find the equanimity to live by the privileged status that is based on the oppression of her own people?

Larsen's heroines are all finally destroyed somewhere down the paths they choose. Helga Crane loses herself in a loveless marriage to an old black preacher by whom she has five children in as many years. She finally retreats into illness and silence, eventually admitting to herself a suppressed hatred for her husband. *Passing*'s Irene Redfield suspects an affair between her friend Clare (recently surfaced from the white world) and her black physician husband. This threatens her material and psychological security. In the novel's melodramatic ending, she pushes Clare off the balcony of a seventeenth-floor apartment and sinks into unconsciousness when she is questioned about Clare's death.

And Nella Larsen, who created Helga and Irene, chose oblivion for herself. From the little we know of the last 30 years of her life, she handled the problem of marginality by default, living entirely without any racial or cultural identity. Her exile was so complete that one of her biographers couldn't find an obituary for her: "I couldn't even bury Nella Larsen," she said.

But unlike the women in her novels, Larsen did not die from her marginality. She lived 70 years, was an active part of the high-stepping Harlem Renaissance, traveled abroad, and worked as a nurse for 40 years. She was an unconventional woman by 1920s standards: she wore her dresses short, smoked cigarettes, rejected religion, and lived in defiance of the rules that most black women of her education and means were bound by. She lived through the conflicts of the marginal woman and felt them passionately. Why didn't she leave us the greater legacy of the mature model, the perceptions of a woman who confronts the pain, alienation, isolation, and grapples with these conundrums until new insight has been forged from the struggle? Why didn't she continue to write after 1929?

If there are any answers to these questions, we have to look again in the two novels to find them. Both novels end with images of numbness, suffocation, blunted perceptions, loss of consciousness, invisibility. It is a world even more restricted than that in Ralph Ellison's *The Invisible Man,* another novel about marginality and the Afro-American experience. The "invisible man" at least has the choice of a range of work options, mobility, and political activism. Who can imagine a black woman character replicating the intense activities of a black man who—in literature and life—is at least sometimes physically free to hop a freight North or to highball it down the track from coast to coast as a Pullman porter, to organize and lead political movements without apology, to wield the tools of an occupation other than personal service and earn a living by sheer physical skill? And the characters in the literature of white women move through a variety of places and experiences with relative ease when compared to black women. They can be artists in Europe or illustrators in New York or farmers in Iowa or retirees in Florida without suffering the permanent absence of community. In their insistence that black women are estranged from the right to aspire and achieve in the wide world of thought and action, *Quicksand* and *Passing* are brilliant witnesses to the position of a colored woman in a white, male world.

She did not solve her own problems, but Larsen made us understand as no one did before her that the image of the middle-class black woman as a coldly self-centered snob, chattering irrelevantly at bridge club and sorority meetings, was as much a mask as a grin on the face of Stepin

Fetchit. The women in her novels, like Larsen, are driven to emotional and psychological extremes in their attempts to handle ambivalence, marginality, racism, and sexism. She has shown us that behind the carefully manicured exterior, behind the appearance of security is a woman who hears the beating of her wings against a walled prison.

As black women move further into areas that were once the private reserve of whites, those few of us—those fortunate few whose lives are not stunted and dreamless—are finding ourselves facing the tensions that Nella Larsen knew, and it is for us to do something about them, to take what she started further than she was able to go.

The sweet music of the Black Bottom is receding into the background while a new chorus of possibilities is playing insistently and captivatingly. Like Paule Marshall's Reena, Alice Walker's Sarah Davis, and Nella Larsen's driven heroines, we are condemned to a new freedom. We will not be able to define ourselves exclusively by the parameters of the black community, but we must not become unhinged from the gifts and insights inherent in our tradition; otherwise, like Larsen's rootless women, we will have to live out the absurdities of a racist and sexist society. There will still be achievement conflicts and symptoms of marginality and struggles to avoid cheap status-seeking and also trips to the symphony which may not be understood. But there will also be what Nella Larsen was never to know: bold strides into new worlds, work not thwarted nor diminished by petty and unreal restrictions, and, ultimately, some triumph.

CHERYL A. WALL

From Passing for What? Aspects of Identity in Nella Larsen's Novels†

True, she was attractive, unusual, in an exotic, almost savage way, but she wasn't one of them.

Quicksand (124)

". . . I was determined . . . to be a person and not a charity or a problem, or even a daughter of the indiscreet Ham. Then, too, I wanted things. I knew I wasn't bad-looking and that I could 'pass.' "

Passing (56) [19][1]

At the height of the Harlem Renaissance, Nella Larsen published two novels, *Quicksand* (1928) and *Passing* (1929). They were widely and

† From Cheryl A. Wall, "Passing for What? Aspects of Identity in Nella Larsen's Novels." Reprinted from *Black American Literature Forum* 20, no. 1/2 (Spring-Summer 1986): 99–111.
1. Bracketed page numbers refer to this Norton Critical Edition.

favorably reviewed. Applauded by the critics, Larsen was heralded as a rising star in the black artistic firmament. In 1930 she became the first Afro-American woman to receive a Guggenheim Fellowship for Creative Writing. Her star then faded as quickly as it had risen, and by 1934 Nella Larsen had disappeared from Harlem and from literature.[2] The novels she left behind prove that at least some of her promise was realized. Among the best written of the time, her books comment incisively on issues of marginality and cultural dualism that engaged Larsen's contemporaries, such as Jean Toomer and Claude McKay, but the bourgeois ethos of her novels has unfortunately obscured the similarities. However, Larsen's most striking insights are into psychic dilemmas confronting certain black women. To dramatize these, Larsen draws characters who are, by virtue of their appearance, education, and social class, atypical in the extreme. Swiftly viewed, they resemble the tragic mulattoes of literary convention. On closer examination, they become the means through which the author demonstrates the psychological costs of racism and sexism.

For Larsen, the tragic mulatto was the only formulation historically available to portray educated middle-class black women in fiction.[3] But her protagonists subvert the convention consistently. They are neither noble nor long-suffering; their plights are not used to symbolize the oppression of blacks, the irrationality of prejudice, or the absurdity of concepts of race generally. Larsen's deviations from these traditional strategies signal that her concerns lie elsewhere, but only in the past decade have critics begun to decode her major themes. Both *Quicksand* and *Passing* contemplate the inextricability of the racism and sexism which confront the black woman in her quest for a wholly integrated identity. As they navigate between racial and cultural polarities, Larsen's protagonists attempt to fashion a sense of self free of both suffocating restrictions of ladyhood and fantasies of the exotic female Other. They fail. The tragedy for these mulattoes is the impossibility of self-definition. Larsen's protagonists assume false identities that ensure social survival but result in psychological suicide. In one way or another, they all "pass." Passing for white, Larsen's novels remind us, is only one way this game is played.

❉   ❉   ❉

2. Biographical material may be found in my entry on Larsen in *American Women Writers*; in Adelaide Cromwell Hill's "Introduction" to *Quicksand*; and in Mary Helen Washington's "Nella Larsen: Mystery Woman of the Harlem Renaissance."
3. For a full discussion of the tragic mulatto convention in novels by black women, see Barbara Christian's *Black Women Novelists* (35–61).

Response to Larsen's second novel, *Passing*, has been less favorable [than to *Quicksand*]. From one perspective, critics argue that *Passing* fails to exploit fully the drama of racial passing and declines instead into a treatment of sexual jealousy. If, from another perspective, the novel is the best treatment of its subject in Afro-American literature, then the topic of blacks passing for white is dated and trivial.[4] In Larsen's novel, however, "passing" does not refer only to the socio-logical phenomenon of blacks crossing the color line. It represents instead both the loss of racial identity and the denial of self required of women who conform to restrictive gender roles. Like "quicksand," "passing" is a metaphor of death and desperation, and both central metaphors are supported by images of asphyxiation, suffocation, and claustrophobia. Unlike "quicksand," "passing" provokes definite asso-ciations and expectations that Larsen is finally unable to transcend. Looking beyond these associations, one sees that *Passing* explores the same themes as its predecessor. Though less fully developed than [*Quicksand*'s] Helga Crane, the main characters of this novel likewise demonstrate the price black women pay for their acquiescence and, ultimately, the high cost of rebellion.

Two characters, Irene Redfield and Clare Kendry, dominate the novel: Both are attractive, affluent, and able to "pass." Irene identifies with blacks, choosing to "pass" only for occasional convenience, while Clare has moved completely into the white world. Each assumes a role Helga Crane rejects: Irene is the perfect lady, and Clare, the exotic Other. A chance meeting in the tearoom of an exclusive Chicago hotel, on an occasion when both women are "passing," introduces the action of the novel. Clare recognizes the childhood friend she has not seen in twelve years, and she is eager to renew the acquaintance. Irene, assured and complacent in her life as the wife of a Harlem physician, is more cautious. Reluctantly, she accepts Clare's invitation to tea, where they are joined by another school friend, Gertrude, who is married to a white man, and by Clare's husband Jack Bellew. Bellew proves to be a rabid racist, and Irene vows never to see Clare again. Two years later, her resolve is shaken. While visiting New York, and partly in response to her husband's bigotry, Clare longs for the company of blacks. She presents herself at Irene's home uninvited and, over Irene's objections, makes increasingly frequent jaunts to Harlem. Distressed by the unsettling effect produced by Clare's presence, Irene begins to suspect that Clare is having an affair with Dr. Redfield. But before Irene can act on her suspicions, Bellew follows Clare to Harlem and confirms his. Clare Kendry falls through a sixth-story window to her death.

4. These conclusions reflect the views, respectively, of Amaritjit Singh in *The Novels of the Harlem Renaissance* (99), of Robert Bone in *The Negro Novel in America* (102), and of Hoyt Fuller in his "Introduction" to *Passing* (14).

Although her death is typical of the tragic mulatto's fate, the Clare Kendry character breaks the mold in every other respect.[5] Her motives for "passing" are ambiguous. Though she seeks the freedom to define herself, she also wants the material comforts the white world offers. As she explains, " ' . . . I was determined to get away, to be a person and not a charity or a problem, or even a daughter of the indiscreet Ham. Then, too, I wanted things. I knew I wasn't bad-looking and that I could "pass" ' " (56) [19]. The psychic rewards are few, but at first Clare is sure the money is worth its price. Bellew is an international banking agent, apparently as rich as Croesus, who indulges his wife's love of luxury. Clare can chat glibly of travels to pre-War Paris and post-War Budapest. She can also refer to herself as a " 'deserter,' " yet Irene looks in vain for traces of pain, fear, or grief on her countenance. Even when Clare begins to doubt the wisdom of her choice, she claims no noble purpose, merely loneliness and a vague yearning for " 'my own people.' " In fact, her trips to Harlem involve more pleasure-seeking than homecoming. At one point, she confesses to Irene: " 'Why, to get the things I want badly enough, I'd do anything, hurt anybody, throw anything away. Really, 'Rene, I'm not safe' " (139) [58] In drawing such an unsympathetic character, Larsen seems initially merely to flout the tragic-mulatto convention.

Rather than emphasize the pathos of the "passing" situation, Larsen stresses its attractive veneer. Clare Kendry always looks exquisite, whether wearing a "superlatively simple cinnamon-brown frock" with a "little golden bowl of a hat" or a stately black taffeta gown. Clothes, furnishings, notepaper—all the accoutrements of Clare's life are painstakingly described. At times Larsen's intentions seem definitely satirical, as when on one occasion Clare chooses a dress whose shade not only suits her but sets off her hotel room's decor! But at other points Larsen seems to solicit the reader's admiration for the graceful, elegant Clare.

Annis Pratt's analysis of patterns in women's fiction offers a tenable explanation for such inconsistency: "It is as if the branch of women's fiction that deals most specifically with society were incapable of either fully rejecting it or fully accommodating to it, the result being the disjunction of narrative structure, ambivalence of tone, and inconclusive characterizations typical of this category"

---

5. Most commentators have read *Passing* as a tragic-mulatto story, but two critics offer sharply different views. Mary Mabel Youmans argues in "Nella Larsen's *Passing*: A Study in Irony" [reprinted in this edition, p. 337] that Irene is the one who actually "passes" because she gives up her racial heritage for middle-class security. And in "Nella Larsen's *Passing*: A Problem of Interpretation" [reprinted in this edition, p. 342], Claudia Tate argues that *Passing* is an intriguing romance in which Irene Redfield is the heroine and the unreliable center of consciousness.

(168). *Passing* displays all of these features with its abrupt and unearned ending, its often arch and stilted dialogue, and the author's wavering response to her characters. To be sure, Larsen's own social world was mirrored in her novel, and she evidently found it difficult to reject it out of hand. Nevertheless, what seems at first an annoying preoccupation with "minutiae" (to borrow Hoyt Fuller's apt term) becomes instead a statement on the condition of women in the book.

Clare's survival depends literally on her abiltity to keep up appearances. She must look like the white society matron she pretends to be. But her looks, clothes, and facile conversation are the envy of the other female characters. They too spend an inordinate amount of time shopping and preening. In their lives, maintaining the social niceties is an obligation, and pouring tea is, in the words of one, " 'an occupation.' " Each of these characters, like Clare, relies on a husband for material possessions, security, identity. Each reflects and is a reflection of her husband's class status. Clare's is merely an extreme version of a situation all share.

An analysis of the Irene Redfield character supports this reading. The novel is told from her point of view, and she consistently calls attention to the differences between herself and Clare. More often than not, Nella Larsen minimizes these differences to great effect. For example, Irene craves stability and abhors the risks Clare thrives on; she is a devoted mother, whereas Clare professes little interest in the welfare of her daughter, and she prides herself on her loyalty to the race. However, Irene's world is barely more secure than that of her friend, and when it is threatened, she is every bit as dangerous. The parallels are established in the first encounter described above, when, because both are "passing," they are playing the same false role. Indeed it is Irene who fears detection; her alarmed, defensive reaction contrasts ironically with the cool demeanor assumed by Clare, whose only concern is recognizing an old friend. In the subsequent meeting with Bellew, Irene is horrified that Clare, whom he jokingly calls "Nig," tolerates her husband's bigotry; but Irene herself listens to his insults. She even imagines that "under other conditions" she could like the man. Her attempt to excuse her cowardice by claiming to have acted out of loyalty to race and to Clare as a member of the race is entirely specious. Although Irene does volunteer work for the "Negro Welfare League," the race is important to her only insofar as it gives the appearance of depth to a shallow life.

What Irene does value is her marriage, not out of any deep love for her husband Brian, but because it is her source of security and permanence. Much like Anne Grey's in *Quicksand*, the Redfields' marriage is passionless; the couple sleep in separate bedrooms, and Brian argues that the sooner their children learn that sex is " 'a grand joke,' " the better off they will be. The Redfields' life is one Irene has "arranged." She has dissuaded Brian from pursuing his dream of a new life in Brazil. She has spun a cocoon around her sons, forbidding discussion of racism and of sex as too disagreeable, and she plans someday to send the boys to European boarding schools (like the one Clare's daughter attends in Switzerland). Nothing is allowed to encroach upon the sanctuary of home and family.

When Clare enters this safe harbor, she upsets the order Irene cherishes. She visits unannounced, plays with the children, and chats with the servants. She poses other threats as well. Typically, Irene bolsters her self-image by defining herself in relation to her "inferiors": Her comments on women whose husbands are less successful than hers evidence this snobbery. When, for example, Gertrude expresses her anger at Bellew's racism—a deeper anger than Irene can muster—Irene dismisses her. After all, Gertrude looks like the butcher's wife she is; her feelings could not matter. Clare is too clearly Irene's equal, in many respects her superior, to be neutralized in this way. Compared to Clare, Irene feels at times "dowdy and commonplace" (128) [53]. Partly in self-defense and partly because Clare invites the role, Irene begins to view her friend as an exotic Other. Watching her, she has the sensation of "gazing into the eyes of some creature utterly strange and apart" (77) [29]. Then again, Clare's look was "unfathomable, utterly beyond any comprehension" of Irene's (85) [33]. Irene invents for Clare a complex inner life. But she is not responding to the person before her so much as to her own notions of Otherness. Clare's "Negro eyes" symbolize the unconscious, the unknowable, the erotic, and the passive. In other words, they symbolize those aspects of the psyche Irene denies within herself. Her confused sense of race becomes at last an evasion by which she avoids confronting her deepest feelings.

Clare's repeated assertions of her own dangerousness reinforce Irene's fears and allow her to objectify Clare completely. When her suspicions grow that Clare is interested in Brian, Clare becomes a menace she must eliminate; for without Brian, Irene believes she is nothing. Her opportunity comes during the confusion surrounding Bellew's unexpected appearance at a Harlem party. Although the evidence is all circumstantial, Larsen strongly implies that Irene pushes Clare through the window,[6] She is certainly capable of it for by the end of the novel Irene is indeed Clare's double, willing to " 'do anything, hurt anybody, throw anything away' " to get what she wants. A psychological suicide, if not a murderer, she too has played the game of "passing" and lost.

---

6. Tate insists that the evidence is adequate to determine Irene's guilt or innocence (145).

Passing, like *Quicksand*, demonstrates Larsen's ability to explore the psychology of her characters. She exposes the sham that is middle-class security, especially for women whose total dependence is morally debilitating. The absence of meaningful work and community condemn them to the "walled prison" of their own thoughts. In this cramped enclosure, neurosis and fantasy breed. She exposes as well the fears and self-contempt experienced by those, like Helga, who seek to escape the constrictions of middle-class life. Helga is an admirable character because she recognizes early on that "passing" is not worth the price. Her integrity earns her no victory; her rebellion is as ineffectual as the dishonorable Clare's. As these characters deviate from the norm, they are defined—indeed too often define themselves—as Other. They thereby cede control of their lives. But, in truth, the worlds these characters inhabit offer them no possibility of autonomy or fulfillment.

Nathan Huggins has observed that of the Harlem Renaissance writers "Nella Larsen came as close as any to treating human motivation with complexity and sophistication. But she could not wrestle free of the mulatto condition that her main characters had been given" (236). I would argue that Larsen achieves a good measure of complexity and sophistication, yet Huggins' point has merit, especially in regard to *Passing*. Much more than *Quicksand*, this novel adheres to the pattern: the victim caught forever betwixt and between until she finds in death the only freedom she can know. The inevitable melodrama weakens the credibility of the narrative and diverts attention from the author's real concerns. Still, the plot reveals something of the predicament of the middle-class black woman, and the book itself illuminates problems facing the black woman novelist.

Among the images of black women presented in fiction before the Harlem Renaissance, the tragic mulatto character was the least degrading and the most attractive, which partly explains its prominence in Jessie Fauset's novels and in those of her predecessors, dating back to Harriet Wilson and Frances Watkins Harper. Nella Larsen's personal history doubtless increased the character's appeal for her, as the reality behind the image was her own story. Besides, depicting the tragic mulatto was the surest way for a black woman fiction writer to gain a hearing. It was also an effective mask. In a sense Nella Larsen chose to "pass" as a novelist; not surprisingly, readers who knew what they were seeing—that is, reading—missed the point.

Works Cited

Bone, Robert. *The Negro Novel in America*. Rev. ed. New Haven: Yale UP, 1965.

Christian, Barbara. *Black Women Novelist: The Development of a Tradition, 1892–1976*. Westport: Greenwood, 1980.

Fuller, Hoyt. "Introduction." *Passing*. By Nella Larsen. New York: Collier. [97] 11–24.

Hill, Adelaide Cromwell. "Introduction." *Quicksand*. By Nella Larsen. New York, Collier, 1971. 9–17.

Huggins, Nathan I. *Harlem Renaissance*. New York: Oxford UP, 1971.

Larsen, Nella. *Passing*. 1929. New York: Collier, 1971.

———. *Quicksand*. 1928. New York: Collier, 1971.

Pratt, Annis. *Archetypal Patterns in Women's Fiction*. Bloomington: Indiana UP, 1981.

Singh, Amaritjit. *The Novels of the Harlem Renaissance: Twelve Black Writers*. 1923–1933. University Park: Pennsylvania State UP, 1976.

Tate, Claudia. "Nella Larsen's *Passing*: A Problem of Interpretation." *Black American Literature Forum* 14 (1980): 142–46.

Wall, Cheryl. "Nella Larsen." *American Women Writers: A Critical Reference Guide from Colonial Times to the Present*. Ed. Lina Mainero. New York: Frederick Ungar, 1980. 2: 507–09.

Washington, Mary Helen. "Nella Larsen: Mystery Woman of the Harlem Renaissance." *MS*. Dec. 1980: 44–50.

Youmans, Mary Mabel. "Nella Larsen's *Passing*: A Study in Irony." *CLA Journal* 18 (1974): 235–41.

DEBORAH E. MCDOWELL

From [Black Female Sexuality in *Passing*]†

Until the early 1970s when previously "lost" work by women writers began to be recovered and reprinted, Nella Larsen was one of several women writers of the Harlem Renaissance relegated to the back pages of that movement's literary history, a curious fate since her career had such an auspicious beginning. Touted as a promising writer by blacks and whites alike, Larsen was encouraged by some of the most influential names on the 1920s arts scene. Walter White, onetime director of the NAACP, read drafts of *Quicksand* and urged Larsen along to its completion. Carl Van Vechten, popularly credited

† From Introduction to Nella Larsen, *Quicksand* and *Passing*. Edited by Deborah E. McDowell. Copyright © 1986 by Rutgers, the State University. Reprinted by permission of Rutgers University Press, pp. ix–xvi, xxiii–xxxv.

with promoting many Harlem Renaissance writers, introduced the novel to his publisher, Knopf. These efforts paid off. Larsen won second prize in literature in 1928 for *Quicksand* from the Harmon Foundation which awarded outstanding achievement by Negroes. *Quicksand* was also well received by the critics. In his review of the novel W. E. B. DuBois, for example, praised it as the "best piece of fiction that Negro America has produced since the heyday of Chesnutt."[1] *Passing* was equally well received. One reviewer gave the novel high marks for capturing, as did no other novel of the genre, the psychology of racial passing with "consummate art."[2] Due largely to the success of these first two novels, Larsen won a Guggenheim in 1930—the first black female creative writer to be so honored—to do research on a third novel in Spain and France. That novel was never published.

After the publication of *Passing*, Larsen published her last piece, a story entitled "Sanctuary." The subject of much controversy, many speculate that the scandal it created helped to send Larsen into obscurity. Following the publication of the story in 1930 Larsen was accused of plagiarism. One reader wrote to the editor of the magazine about the striking resemblance of Larsen's story to one by Sheila Kaye-Smith, entitled, "Mrs. Adis," published in the January 1922 issue of *Century* magazine. The editor of *The Forum* conducted an investigation and was finally convinced that the resemblance between the stories was an extraordinary coincidence. In compliance with the editor's request, Larsen wrote a detailed explanation of the way in which she came by the germ for her story, trying to vindicate herself. Despite her editor's support, Larsen never recovered from the shock of the charge.[3] She disappeared from the literary scene and returned to nursing at Bethel Hospital in Brooklyn where she remained until her retirement. She died in Brooklyn in 1964, practically in obscurity.

Why a career with such auspicious beginnings had such an inauspicious ending has continued to perplex students of the Harlem Renaissance. Many search for answers in the scattered fragments of Larsen's biography, which reveal a delicate and unstable person. Though there is precious little information about Larsen, some pieces of her life's puzzle are fairly widely known.[4] Born in Chicago

1. W. E. B. DuBois, *Voices of a Black Nation: Political Journalism in the Harlem Renaissance*, ed. Theodore G. Vincent, reviews of *Home to Harlem*, and *Quicksand* (San Francisco: Ramparts, 1973), p. 359.
2. "The Browsing Reader," *The Crisis* 36 (July 1929): 234.
3. For the full accusation and the explanations that Larsen and her editor provided, see "Our Rostrum," in *The Forum* 83 (1930): 41.
4. For additional biographical information, see Mary Helen Washington, "Nella Larsen: Mystery Woman of the Harlem Renaissance," *Ms.*, December 1980, pp. 44–50 [reprinted in this edition, p. 350]; Adelaide Cromwell Hill's introduction to *Quicksand* (New York: Collier-Macmillan, 1971); and the definitive biography of Nella Larsen by Thadious Davis forthcoming from LSU Press [published 1994]. I would like to thank Thadious Davis and Charles Larson for new information about Larsen that allowed me to correct errors in this fourth printing.

in 1891, she was the daughter of a Danish mother and a black West Indian father who died when Larsen was a young girl. Larsen's mother remarried, this time to a white man who treated his step-daughter with some disfavor. Never feeling connected to this newly configured family, Larsen searched vainly for the sense of belonging it could not provide. Fickle and unsettled, Larsen roamed from place to place, searching for some undefined and undefinable "something." She studied science for a year at Fisk University in Tennessee, during her rocky marriage to physicist Elmer S. Imes, a professor there. She left Fisk to travel to Denmark where she audited classes at the University of Copenhagen. Returning to the states, she studied nursing at Lincoln Hospital Training School for Nurses in New York, graduating in 1915.

For a brief time after her nurse's training, she was superintendent of nurses at Tuskegee Institute in Alabama. Unable to tolerate its stifling atmosphere, she left after only a year and returned to New York. There she worked as a nurse, between 1916 and 1918 at the hospital where she was trained; and, between 1918 and 1921, for New York City's Department of Health. Dissatisfied with this career, she began work in 1921 at the children's division of the New York Public Library, enrolling in its training program. During her employment as a librarian, she began to write.

Since the beginning of Larsen's career, critics have praised her as a "gifted writer,"[5] commending her skill at the craft of fiction—most notably, successful characterization, narrative unity, and economy. However, they have consistently criticized the endings of her novels *Quicksand* (1928) and *Passing* (1929), which reveal her difficulty with rounding off stories convincingly. Larsen shared this problem of unconvincing endings with her black female contemporaries, Jessie Fauset and Zora Neale Hurston. Fauset's *There Is Confusion* (1924), for example, ends with the heroine's renunciation of her successful stage career to marry, accepting "as a matter of course" that her husband "was the arbiter of her own and her child's destiny."[6] Or there is the example of Missy May in Zora Neale Hurston's story, "The Gilded Six Bits" (1933), who proudly boasts to her husband, "if you burn me, you won't get a thing but wife ashes." At the story's end, weak from bearing her husband a "lil boy chile," she crawls to pick up the silver dollars that he is throwing through the door.[7] Or, finally,

---

5. See for example, Hiroko Sato, "Under the Harlem Shadows: A Study of Jessie Fauset and Nella Larsen," in *The Harlem Renaissance Remembered*, ed. Arna Bontemps (New York: Dodd, Mead, 1972), p. 84, and Amritjit Singh, *The Novels of the Harlem Renaissance* (University Park and London: Pennsylvania State University Press, 1976).
6. Jessie Fauset, *There Is Confusion* (1924; rpt. New York: AMS Press, 1974), p. 292.
7. "The Gilded Six Bits" in *Spunk: The Selected Short Stories of Zora Neale Hurston* (Berkeley: Turtle Island Foundation, 1985, pp. 54–68.

there is the case of Arvay Henson in Hurston's last novel, *Seraph on the Suwanee* (1948), who retreats from the brink of independence and self-realization and returns to her verbally abusive husband, resolved that "he was her man and her care" and "[h]er job was mothering. What more could any woman want and need? . . . Yes, she was serving and meant to serve. She made the sun welcome to come on in, then snuggled down again beside her husband."[8]

These unearned and unsettling endings sacrifice strong and emerging independent female identities to the most acceptable demands of literary and social history. But these endings seem far less unsettling when compared to those of *Quicksand* and *Passing*. Though both novels feature daring and unconventional heroines, in the end, they sacrifice these heroines to the most conventional fates of narrative history: marriage and death, respectively. In *Quicksand*, the cultured and refined Helga Crane marries a rural southern preacher and follows him to his backwoods church to "uplift" his parishioners. At the end of the novel, she is in a state of emotional and physical collapse from having too many children. In *Passing*, the defiant and adventurous Clare, who flouts all the social rules of the black bourgeoisie, falls to her death under melodramatic and ambiguous circumstances.

Critics of Larsen have been rightly perplexed by these abrupt and contradictory endings. But if examined through the prism of black female sexuality, not only do they make more sense, they also illuminate the peculiar pressures on Larsen as a woman writer during the male-dominated Harlem Renaissance. They show her grappling with the conflicting demands of her racial and sexual identities and the contradictions of a black and feminine aesthetic. Moreover, while these endings appear to be concessions to the dominant ideology of romance—marriage and motherhood—viewed from a feminist perspective, they become much more radical and original efforts to acknowledge a female sexual experience, most often repressed in both literary and social realms.

I

Since the very beginning of their history running over roughly 130 years, black women novelists have treated sexuality with caution and reticence, a pattern clearly linked to the network of social and literary myths perpetuated throughout history about black women's libidinousness. It is well known that during slavery the white slave master constructed an image of black female sexuality which shifted responsibility for his own sexual passions onto his female slaves. They, not

---

8. Zora Neale Hurston, *Seraph on the Suwanee* (1948; rpt. New York: AMS Press, 1974), pp. 310, 311.

he, had wanton, insatiable desires that he was powerless to resist. The image did not end with emancipation. So persistent was it that black club women devoted part of their first national conference in July 1895 to addressing it.[9] Though myths about black women's lasciviousness were not new to the era, a letter from one J. W. Jacks, a white male editor of a Missouri newspaper, made them a matter of urgent concern to black club women. Forwarded to Josephine S. Pierre Ruffin, editor of *The Woman's Era*,[1] the letter attacked black women's virtue, supplying "evidence" from other black women. According to Jacks, when a certain negro woman was asked to identify a newcomer to the community, she responded, "the negroes will have nothing to do with 'dat nigger,' she won't let any man, except her husband sleep with her, and we don't 'sociate with her."[2] Mrs. Ruffin circulated the letter widely to prominent black women and to heads of other women's clubs around the country, calling for a conference to discuss this and other social concerns of black women.

Given this context, it is not surprising that a pattern of reticence about black female sexuality dominated novels by black women in the nineteenth and early twentieth centuries. They responded to the myth of the black woman's sexual licentiousness by insisting fiercely on her chastity. Fighting to overcome their heritage of rape and concubinage, and following the movement by black club women of the era, they imitated the "purity," the sexual morality of the Victorian bourgeoisie. In such works as Emma Dunham Kelley's *Megda* (1891), Frances E. W. Harper's *Iola Leroy* (1892), and Pauline Hopkins's *Contending Forces* (1900),[3] black heroines struggle to defend and preserve the priceless gem of virginity.

Even in Larsen's day, the Freudian 1920s, the Jazz Age of sexual abandon and "free love"—when female sexuality, in general, was acknowledged and commercialized in the advertising, beauty, and fashion industries—black women's novels preserve their reticence

9. During the nineteenth century, black women formed a network of clubs throughout the country, in which politically minded black women were committed to racial uplift (or Negro improvement). The clubs were largely unaffiliated until they convened in Boston in 1895 for their first national conference and became the National Association of Colored Women (NACW) in 1896. Predating both the NAACP and the Urban League, the NACW was the first national black organization with a commitment to racial struggles. For a detailed description of the activities of the organization see "Black Feminism versus Peasant Values" in Wilson J. Moses, *The Golden Age of Black Nationalism* (Hamden, Conn.: Archon Books, 1978), 103–31.
1. Founded and edited by Mrs. Ruffin, a social activist, *The Woman's Era* was the first magazine in the United States to be owned, published, and managed exclusively by black women.
2. Quoted in Moses, *Golden Age*, p. 115.
3. Though Harriet Wilson's recently discovered novel, *Our Nig* (1859), predates these novels influenced by the efforts of the club movement, the emphasis on the priceless gem of virginity is still strong. See the Vintage edition of the novel edited and with an introduction by Henry Louis Gates, Jr., New York, 1983.

about sexuality. Larsen and Jessie Fauset, among the most prolific novelists of the decade, lacked the daring of their contemporaries, the black female blues singers such as Bessie, Mamie, and Clara Smith (all unrelated), Gertrude "Ma" Rainey, and Victoria Spivey. These women sang openly and seductively about sex and celebrated the female body and female desire as seen, for example, in a stanza from Ma Rainey's, "It's Tight like That": "See that spider crawling up the wall . . . going to get his ashes hauled. / Oh it's tight like that." Or Clara Smith's "Whip It to a Jelly": "There's a new game, that can't be beat / You move most everything 'cept your feet / Called whip it to a jelly, stir it in a bowl / You just whip it to a jelly, if you like good jelly roll."[4]

Jessie Fauset and Nella Larsen could only hint at the idea of black women as sexual subjects behind the safe and protective covers of traditional narrative subjects and conventions. Though their heroines are not the paragons of chastity that their nineteenth-century predecessors created, we cannot imagine them singing a Bessie Smith lyric such as "I'm wild about that thing" or "You've got to get it, bring it, and put it right here." Rather, they strain to honor the same ethics of sexual conduct called for by a respondent to a 1920s symposium titled "Negro Womanhood's Greatest Needs." Conducted by some of the same leading Negro club women who had organized around Jacks' libelous attack on black women's virtue, the symposium ran for several issues in *The Messenger*, one of the black "little magazines" of the period. The writer lamented what she called the "speed and disgust" of the Jazz Age which created women "less discreet and less cautious than [their] sisters in years gone by." These "new" women, she continued, were "rebelling against the laws of God and man." Thus, she concluded that the greatest need of Negro womanhood was to return to the "timidity and modesty peculiar to pure womanhood of yesterday."[5]

The blues lyrics and the club women's symposium capture, respectively, the dialectic of desire and fear, pleasure and danger that defines women's sexual experiences in male-dominated societies. As Carole Vance maintains, "Sexuality is simultaneously a domain of restriction, repression, and danger as well as a domain of exploration, pleasure, and agency."[6] For women, and especially for black women,

---

4. For a discussion of black women blues singers see Michele Russel's "Slave Codes and Liner Notes," in *But Some of Us Are Brave*, ed. Gloria Hull, Patricia Bell Scott, and Barbara Smith (Old Westbury: The Feminist Press, 1982), pp. 129–40.
5. *The Messenger*, 9 (September 1927), p. 150.
6. Carole Vance, "Pleasure and Danger: Toward a Politics of Sexuality," in *Pleasure and Danger: Exploring Female Sexuality*, ed. Carole S. Vance (Boston: Routledge and Kegan Paul, 1984), p. 1. For an excellent discussion in Vance's anthology, of the sexuality of black women, see Hortense Spillers, "Interstices: A Small Drama of Words," pp. 73–100. See also Rennie Simson, "The Afro-American Female: The Historical Context of the Construction of Sexual Identity," and Barbara Omolade, "Hearts of Darkness," both in *Powers of Desire: The Politics of Sexuality*, ed. Ann Snitow *et. al* (New York: Monthly Review Press, 1983).

sexual pleasure leads to the dangers of domination in marriage, repeated pregnancy, or exploitation and loss of status.

Both *Quicksand* and *Passing* wrestle simultaneously with this dialectic between pleasure and danger. In their reticence about sexuality, they look back to their nineteenth-century predecessors, but in their simultaneous flirtation with female sexual desire, they are solidly grounded in the liberation of the 1920s. Their ideological ambivalences are rooted in the artistic politics of the Harlem Renaissance, regarding the representation of black sexuality, especially black female sexuality.

II

The issue of representing black sexuality was highly controversial during the movement. As many have argued, Carl Van Vechten's novel *Nigger Heaven* (1926)[7] set the pattern that would dominate the literary treatment of black sexuality in the decade. Amritjit Singh suggests, for example, that the novel "had a crippling effect on the self-expression of many black writers by either making it easier to gain success riding the bandwagon of primitivism, or by making it difficult to publish novels that did not fit the profile of the commercial success formula adopted by most publishers for black writers."[8]

Such novels as Claude McKay's infamous *Home to Harlem* (1928) and Arna Bontemps's *God Sends Sunday* (1931) are said to follow the Van Vechten script. In them black women are mainly "primitive exotic" sex objects, many of them prostitutes, an image which Nathan Huggins correctly identifies as a "male fantasy." It is difficult, he adds rightly, "to draw sympathetic females whose whole existence is their bodies and instinct." Besides, he concludes, "Perhaps women, whose freedom has natural limitations—they have babies—are essentially conservative."[9] Helga Crane's outcome poignantly demonstrates this connection between sexuality and reproduction.

There were those—Jessie Fauset, Nella Larsen, W. E. B. DuBois, among them—who found the primitive/exotic stereotype associated with Van Vechten limited, at best. DuBois voiced his objections vehemently on the pages of the *Crisis,* virtually waging a one man, morality-minded campaign against the "nastiness" he saw embodied in novels that seemed to follow the Van Vechten lead. DuBois was committed to the struggle of "racial uplift" and social equality, a struggle best waged, in his opinion, by the "talented tenth," the elite

7. Excerpt from *Nigger Heaven* is reprinted in this edition, p. 326 [*Editor*].
8. Singh, *Novels of the Harlem Renaissance*, p. 25.
9. Nathan Huggins, *Harlem Renaissance* (New York: Oxford University Press, 1971), pp. 188–89.

group of black intellectuals and artists. In that struggle, art had a vital, and necessarily propagandistic role to play.[1]

DuBois reviewed Claude McKay's *Home to Harlem* and Larsen's *Quicksand* together for the *Crisis*, praising Larsen's novel as "a fine, thoughtful and courageous piece of work," while criticizing McKay's as so "nauseating" in its emphasis on "drunkenness, fighting, and sexual promiscuity" that it made him "feel . . . like taking a bath."[2]

In this context, Larsen was indeed caught between the proverbial rock and hard place. On the one side, Carl Van Vechten, roundly excoriated along with his "followers" by many members of the black middle-class intelligentsia, was her friend. He was responsible for introducing *Quicksand* to Knopf, and perhaps Larsen showed her gratitude by dedicating *Passing* to him and his wife Fania Marinoff. On the other side, Larsen was a member of the black intelligentsia whose attitudes about art Van Vechten had criticized in *Nigger Heaven*, using Russett Durwood as mouthpiece. Durwood advises Byron Kasson, the would-be black writer, to abandon the old cliches and formulas and write about what he knows—black life in the raw. Harlem is "overrun with fresh, unused material," he tells Kasson. "Nobody has yet written a good gambling story; nobody has touched the outskirts of cabaret life; nobody has gone into the curious subject of the diverse tribes of the region." He concludes with the prediction that if the "young Negro intellectuals don't get busy, a new crop of Nordics is going to spring up . . . and . . . exploit this material before the Negro gets around to it."[3] Van Vechten was one such Nordic.

In her criticism of such black bourgeois intellectuals as Robert Anderson and James Vayle in *Quicksand*, Larsen would seem to share some of Van Vechten's opinions of that class. But as much as she could poke fun at their devotion to "racial uplift," she belonged, blood and breath, to that class, and must have found it extremely difficult to cut her ties with it.

To be writing about black female sexuality within this conflicted context, then, posed peculiar problems for Larsen. The questions confronting her might well be formulated: How to write about black female sexuality in a literary era that often sensationalized it and pandered to the stereotype of the primitive exotic? How to give a black

---

1. In a statement well known to students of The Harlem Renaissance, DuBois argued, "All art is propaganda and ever must be, despite the wailing of the purists." ("Criteria of Negro Art," in *W. E. B. DuBois: The Crisis Writings*, ed. Daniel Walden [Greenwich, Conn.: Fawcett, 1972], p. 288 [reprinted in this edition, p. 312]). In a section of this essay which has interesting implications for Larsen's treatment of black female sexuality, DuBois describes two plays, "White Cargo" and "Congo." In the first, "there is a fallen woman. She is black. In 'Congo' the fallen woman is white. In 'White Cargo' the black woman goes down further and further and in 'Congo' the white woman begins with degradation but in the end is one of the angels of the Lord" (p. 288).
2. Reviews of *Home to Harlem* and *Quicksand* in *Voices of a Black Nation*, p. 359.
3. Carl Van Vechten, *Nigger Heaven* (New York: Knopf, 1926), pp. 222–23.

female character the right to healthy sexual expression and pleasure without offending the proprieties established by the spokespersons of the black middle class? The answers to these questions for Larsen lay in attempting to hold these two virtually contradictory impulses in the same novel. We might say that Larsen wanted to tell the story of the black woman with sexual desires, but was constrained by a competing desire to establish black women as respectable in black middle-class terms. The latter desire committed her to exploring black female sexuality obliquely and, inevitably, to permitting it only within the context of marriage, despite the strangling effects of that choice both on her characters and on her narratives.

* * *

III

Irene . . . was trying to understand the look on Clare's face as she had said goodbye. Partly mocking, it had seemed, and partly menacing. *And something else for which she could find no name.* [Emphasis added]

—*Passing*

She wished to find out about this hazardous business of 'passing,' this breaking away from all that was familiar and friendly to take one's a chance in another environment.

—*Passing*

Larsen reopens the question of female sexuality in *Passing* with much bolder suggestions [than in *Quicksand*]. While in *Quicksand* she explores these questions within the "safe" and "legitimate" parameters of marriage, in *Passing*, she takes many more risks. Although Clare and Irene—the novel's dual protagonists—are married, theirs are sexless marriages. In Clare's case, the frequent travels of her financier husband and her fear of producing a dark child, explain this situation. In Irene's case, the narrative strongly indicates, her own sexual repression is at fault. It is significant that Irene and her husband sleep in separate bedrooms (he considers sex a joke) and that she tries to protect her sons from schoolyard discussions about sex. Having established the absence of sex from the marriages of these two women, Larsen can flirt, if only by suggestion, with the idea of a lesbian relationship between them.

It is no accident that critics have failed to take into account the novel's flirtation with this idea, for many are misled, as with *Quicksand*, by the epigraph.[4] Focusing on racial identity or racial ambiguity and

---

4. See, for example, Hugh Gloster, *Negro Voices in American Fiction* (New York: Russell and Russell, 1948); J. Saun[d]ers Redding, *To Make a Poet Black* (Chapel Hill: University of North Carolina Press, 1945); Hiroko Sato, "Under the Harlem Shadows . . ."; and Robert Bone, *Negro Novel*.

cultural history, the book invites the reader to place race at the center of any critical interpretation. Interestingly, Larsen uses the almost romantic refrain of Countée Cullen's poem "Heritage" as the novel's epigraph—"One three centuries removed / From the scenes his fathers loves, / Spicy grove, cinnamon tree, / What is Africa to me?"—foregoing the more dramatic and more appropriate possibilities of the poem's ending:

> All day long and all night through,
> One thing only must I do:
> Quench my pride and cool my blood,
> Lest I perish in the flood.
> Lest a hidden ember set
> Timber that I thought was wet
> Burning like the dryest flax,
> Melting like the merest wax,
> Lest the grave restore its dead.

Not only does the epigraph mislead the reader, but Irene, the central consciousness of the narrative, does as well. It is largely through her eyes, described appropriately as "unseeing," that most of the narrative's events are filtered, significantly, in retrospect and necessarily blurred. The classic unreliable narrator, Irene is confused and deluded about herself, her motivations, and much that she experiences. It is important, therefore, to see the duplicity at the heart of her story. As Beatrice Royster rightly observes,

> Irene is an ideal choice as narrator of a tale with double meanings. She tells the story as the injured wife, betrayed by friend and husband; she tells it as a confession to clear her conscience of any guilt in Clare's death.[5]

Irene paints herself as the perfect, nurturing, self-sacrificing wife and mother, the altruistic "race woman," and Clare as her diametrical opposite. In Clare, there was "nothing sacrificial." She had "no allegiance beyond her own immediate desire. She was selfish, and cold and hard," Irene reports. Clare had the "ability to secure the thing that she wanted in the face of any opposition, and in utter disregard of the convenience and desires of others. About her there was some quality, hard and persistent, with the strength and endurance of rock, that would not be beaten or ignored." Irene describes Clare as "catlike," suggesting that she is given to deception, to furtive, clandestine activity. On the basis of her observations of Clare, Irene concludes, with an attitude

5. Beatrice Royster, "The Ironic Vision of Four Black Women Novelists: A Study of the Novels of Jessie Fauset, Nella Larsen, Zora Neale Hurston, and Ann Petry" Ph.D. dissertation, Emory University, 1975), p. 86.

of smug self-satisfaction, that she and Clare are not only "strangers . . . in their racial consciousness," but also "strangers in their ways and means of living. Strangers in their desires and ambitions."

As is often typical of an unreliable narrator, Irene is, by turns, hypocritical and obtuse, not always fully aware of the import of what she reveals to the reader. Ironically, detail for detail, she manifests the same faults of which she so harshly accuses Clare. Despite her protestations to the contrary, Irene, with a cold, hard, exploitative, and manipulative determination, tries to protect her most cherished attainment: security, which she equates with marriage to a man in a prestigious profession, the accouterments of middle-class existence—children, material comfort, and social respectability. Moreover, Irene resorts to wily and feline tactics to insure that illusion of security. After persuading her husband to abandon his dream of leaving racist Harlem to practice medicine in Brazil, Irene rationalizes that she had done this, "not for her—she had never really considered herself—but for him and the boys."

Even Irene's work with racial uplift programs, such as the Negro Welfare League, reveal her true value orientation. Although she deludes herself that this work is a barometer of her racial consciousness, it is actually self-serving, not undertaken for the good of the race. The social functions that Irene arranges, supposedly designed to aid the unfortunate black masses and to give them a sense of belonging, are so heavily attended by prominent whites that her husband, Brian, fears, " 'Pretty soon the colored people won't be allowed in at all, or will have to sit in Jim Crowed sections.' " Thus, the narrative betrays Irene at every turn, as she comes to evince all that she abominates in Clare.

Not only does Larsen undercut Irene's credibility as narrator, but she also satirizes and parodies the manners and morals of the black middle class that Irene so faithfully represents. That parody comes through in the density of specificity in the novel, as seen in the description of a typically run morning in Irene's household:

> They went into the dining-room. [Brian] drew back her chair and she sat down behind the fat-bellied German coffeepot, which sent out its morning fragrance mingled with the smell of crisp toast and savoury bacon, in the distance. With his long, nervous fingers he picked up the morning paper from his own chair and sat.
>
> Zulena, a small mahogany-coloured creature, brought in the grapefruit.
>
> They took up their spoons.

The descriptions of the endless tea and cocktail parties and charity balls capture the sterility and banality of the bourgeoisie, likewise emphasizing Larsen's satire.

There were the familiar little tinkling sounds of spoons striking against frail cups, the soft running sounds of inconsequential talk, punctuated now and then with laughter. In irregular small groups, disintegrating, coalescing, striking just the right note of disharmony, disorder in the big room, which Irene had furnished with a sparingness that was almost chaste, moved the guests with that slight familiarity that makes a party a success.

Although Irene is clearly deluded about her motives, her racial loyalty, her class, and her distinctness from Clare, the narrative suggests that her most glaring delusion concerns her feelings for Clare. Though, superficially, Irene's is an account of Clare's passing for white and related issues of racial identity and loyalty, underneath the safety of that surface is the more dangerous story—though not named explicitly—of Irene's awakening sexual desire for Clare. The narrative traces this developing eroticism in spatial terms. It begins on the roof of the Drayton hotel (with all the suggestions of the sexually illicit), intensifies at Clare's tea party, and, getting proverbially "close to home," explodes in Irene's own bedroom. Preoccupied with appearances, social respectability, and safety, however, Irene tries to force these emerging feelings underground. The narrative dramatizes that repression effectively in images of concealment and burial. Significantly, the novel's opening image is an envelope (a metaphoric vagina) which Irene hesitates to open, fearing its "contents would reveal" an "attitude toward danger." Irene's fears are well founded, given the sexual overtones of Clare's letter:

> "for I am lonely, so lonely . . . cannot help longing to be with you again, as I have never longed for anything before; and I have wanted many things in my life. . . . It's like an ache, a pain that never ceases. . . . and it's your fault, 'Rene dear. At least partly. For I wouldn't now, perhaps, have this terrible, this wild desire if I hadn't seen you that time in Chicago."

Irene tries to preserve "a hardness from feeling" about the letter, though "brilliant red patches flamed" in her cheeks. Unable to explain her feelings for Clare, "for which she could find no name," Irene dismisses them as "Just somebody walking over [her] grave." The narrative suggests pointedly that Clare is the body walking over the grave of Irene's buried sexual feelings.

Lest the reader miss this eroticism, Larsen employs fire imagery— the conventional representation of sexual desire—introducing and instituting this imagery in the novel's opening pages. Irene begins her retrospective account of her reunion with Clare, remembering that the day was "hot," the sun "brutal" and "staring," its rays "like molten rain." Significantly, Irene, feeling "sticky and soiled from contact with so many sweating bodies," escapes to the roof of the Drayton Hotel where she is reunited with Clare, after a lapse of many years. (Irene is, ironically, "escaping" to the very thing she wants to avoid.)

From the very beginning of their reencounter, Irene is drawn to Clare like a moth to a flame. (Suggestively, Clare is frequently dressed in red). The "lovely creature" "had for her a fascination, strange and compelling." Because so many critics have missed the significance of the erotic attraction between Irene and Clare, it is useful to trace this theme by quoting from the novel in substantial detail.

When the two are reunited, Irene first notices Clare's "tempting mouth"; her lips, "painted a brilliant geranium-red, were sweet and sensitive and a little obstinate." Into Clare's "arresting eyes" "there came a smile and over Irene the sense of being petted and caressed." At the end of this chance encounter, "standing there under the appeal, the caress, of [Clare's] eyes, Irene had the desire, the hope, that this parting wouldn't be the last."

When Irene has tea at Clare's house, she notices that Clare "turned on . . . her seductive caressing smile." Afterwards, a "slight shiver [runs] over [Irene]" when she remembers the mysterious look on Clare's "incredibly beautiful face." "She couldn't, however, come to any conclusion about its meaning. . . . It was unfathomable, utterly beyond any experience or comprehension of hers."

The awakening of Irene's erotic feelings for Clare coincides with Irene's imagination of an affair between Clare and Brian. Given her tendency to project her disowned traits, motives, and desires onto others, it is reasonable to argue that Irene is projecting her own developing passion for Clare onto Brian, although in "all their married life she had had no slightest cause to suspect [him] of any infidelity, of any serious flirtation even." The more the feelings develop, the more she fights them, for they threaten the placid surface of her middle-class existence as a doctor's wife. "Safety and security," Irene's watchwords, crop up repeatedly in the novel, after Clare arrives, and explain Irene's struggle to avoid her.

Not deterred, however, Clare visits Irene's house unannounced, coming first to the bedroom where she "drop[s] a kiss on [Irene's] dark curls," arousing in Irene "a sudden inexplicable onrush of affectionate feeling. Reaching out, she grasped Clare's two hands in her own and cried with something like awe in her voice: 'Dear God! But aren't you lovely, Clare!' " Their conversation in this scene has a sexual double edge, heightened by Irene's habitual gesture of lighting cigarettes.

Clare scolds Irene for not responding to her letter, describing her repeated trips to the post office. "I'm sure they were all beginning to think that I'd been carrying on an illicit love-affair and that the man had thrown me over." Irene assures Clare that she is concerned simply about the dangers of Clare's passing for white in Harlem, the risks she runs of being discovered by "knowing Negroes." Clare's immediate response is "You mean you don't want me, 'Rene?" Irene replies, "It's terribly foolish, and not just the right thing." It's "dangerous," she continues, "to run such silly risks." "It's not safe. Not safe at all." But "as if in contrition for that flashing thought," "Irene touched [Clare's] arm caressingly."

Irene's protestations about race are noticeably extreme and disproportionate to the situation, especially since she passes occasionally herself. Further, they function in the same way that Helga's response to Axel Olsen functions [in *Quicksand*]: as a mask for the deeper, more unsettling issues of sexuality. Irene tries to defuse the feelings by absorbing herself in the ritual of empty tea parties, but "It was as if in a house long dim, a match had been struck, showing ghastly shapes where had been only blurred shadows."

At one such party, near the narrative's end, Clare is, in typical fashion, an intruding presence, both at the party and in Irene's thoughts. "Irene couldn't remember ever having seen [Clare] look better." Watching "the fire roar" in the room, Irene thinks of Clare's "beautiful and caressing" face.

In the final section of the novel, Clare comes to Irene's house before they go to the fateful Christmas party. Coming again into Irene's room, "Clare kisse[s] her bare shoulder, seeming not to notice a slight shrinking." As they walk to the party, Clare at Brian's side, Irene describes a "live thing pressing against her." That "live thing," represented clearly as full-blown sexual desire, must be contained, and it takes Clare's death to contain it. Significantly, in Irene's description of the death, all of the erotic images used to describe Clare throughout the novel converge.

> Gone! The soft white face, the bright hair, the disturbing scarlet mouth, the dreaming eyes, the caressing smile, the whole tortured loveliness that had been Clare Kendry. That beauty that had torn at Irene's placid life. Gone! The mocking daring, the gallantry of her pose, the ringing bells of her laughter.

Although the ending is ambiguous and the evidence circumstantial, I agree with Cheryl Wall that, "Larsen strongly implies that Irene pushes Clare through the window," and, in effect, becomes "a psychological suicide, if not a murderer."[6] To suggest the extent to which Clare's death represents the death of Irene's sexual feelings for Clare, Larsen uses a clever objective correlative: Irene's pattern of lighting cig-

---

6. Cheryl Wall, "Passing for What? Aspects of Identity in Nella Larsen's Novels," *Black American Literature Forum*, in press. Quoted with author's permission. [Wall's essay is reprinted in this edition, p. 356.]

arettes and snuffing them out. Minutes before Clare falls from the window to her death, "Irene finished her cigarette and threw it out, watching the tiny spark drop slowly down to the white ground below." Clearly attempting a symbolic parallel, Clare is described as "a vital glowing thing, like a flame of red and gold" who falls from (or is thrown out of) the window as well. Because Clare is a reminder of that repressed and disowned part of Irene's self, Clare must be banished, for, more unacceptable than the feelings themselves is the fact that they find an object of expression in Clare. In other words, Clare is both the embodiment and the object of the sexual feelings that Irene banishes.

Larsen's becomes, in effect, a banishing act as well. Or put another way, the idea of bringing a sexual attraction between two women to full narrative expression is, likewise, too dangerous a move, which helps to explain why critics have missed this aspect of the novel. Larsen's clever narrative strategies almost conceal it. In *Passing* she uses a technique found commonly in narratives by Afro-American and women novelists with a "dangerous" story to tell: "safe" themes, plots, and conventions are used as the protective cover underneath which lie more dangerous subplots. Larsen envelops the subplot of Irene's developing if unnamed and unacknowledged desire for Clare in the safe and familiar plot of racial passing.[7] Put another way, the novel's clever strategy derives from its surface theme and central metaphor—passing. It takes the form of the act it describes. Implying false, forged, and mistaken identities, the title functions on multiple levels: thematically, in terms of the racial and sexual plots; and strategically, in terms of the narrative's disguise.

The structure of the novel complements and reinforces this disguise. Neat and symmetrical, *Passing* is composed of three sections, with four chapters each. The order and control which that tight organization suggests are a clever cover for the unconventional subplot in the novel's hiding places.

The novel performs a double burial: the erotic subplot is hidden beneath its safe and orderly cover and the radical implications of that plot are put away by the disposal of Clare. Although she is the novel's center of vitality and passion, that vitality and passion, which the narrative seems to affirm, are significantly contained by the narrative's end. And Clare becomes a kind of sacrificial lamb on the altar of social and literary convention.

Clare suffers the fate that many a female character has suffered when she has what Rachel Blau DuPlessis terms, "an appropriate

---

7. In her novel *Plum Bun*, published the same year as *Passing*, Jessie Fauset, another black female novelist of the period, used fairy tale conventions to deflect her critique of the romance and the role its underlying ideology plays in disempowering women. See the recent edition of Fauset's novel, with an introduction by Deborah E. McDowell (London: Routledge and Kegan Paul, 1985).

relationship to the 'social script.'" Death results, she continues, when "energies of selfhood, often represented by sexuality . . . are expended outside the 'couvert' of marriage or valid [generally spelled heterosexual] romance."[8] While Larsen criticizes the cover of marriage, as well as other social scripts for women, she is unable in the end to extend that critique to its furthest reaches.

In ending the novel with Clare's death, Larsen repeats the narrative choice which *Quicksand* makes: to punish the very values the novel implicitly affirms, to honor the very value system the text implicitly satirizes. The ending, when hidden racial identities are disclosed, functions on the ideological as well as the narrative level. Larsen performs an act of narrative "dis"-closure, undoing or doing the opposite of what she has promised. Or, to borrow from *Quicksand*, Larsen closes *Passing* "without exploring to the end that unfamiliar path into which she had strayed."

IV

Both *Quicksand* and *Passing* are poised between the tensions and conflicts that are Western culture's stock ambivalences about female sexuality: lady Jezebel or virgin/whore. Larsen sees and indicts the sources of this ambivalence: the network of social institutions—education, marriage, and religion, among the most prominent—all interacting with each other to strangle and control the sexual expression of women. But, like her heroine Helga, Larsen could "neither conform nor be happy in her nonconformity."

Considering the focus of both her novels on black female sexuality, one naturally wonders if Nella Larsen would have taken still more risks had her short, but accomplished, literary career been extended. However oblique and ambivalent Larsen's treatment of black female sexuality, because she gave her characters sexual feelings at all, she has to be regarded as something of a pioneer, a trailblazer in the Afro-American female literary tradition. To be sure, her novels only flirt with the idea of a female sexual passion. We might say that they represent the desire, the expectation, the preparation of eroticism that contemporary black women's novels are attempting to bring to franker and fuller expression. In such novels as Ann Allen Shockley's *Loving Her* (1974), Gayl Jones's *Corrigedora* (1975) and *Eva's Man* (1976), Toni Morrison's *Sula* (1976), Alice Walker's *The Color Purple* (1982), Ntozake Shange's *Sassafrass, Cypress, and Indigo* (1982), Gloria Naylor's *The Women of Brewster Place* (1982), among others, black women are naming what at least one stream of Larsen's imag-

---

8. Rachel Blau DuPlessis, *Writing beyond the Ending: Narrative Strategies of Twentieth-Century Women Writers* (Bloomington: Indiana University Press, 1985), p. 15.

ination and her literary milieu found a "nameless," "shameful impulse."

THADIOUS M. DAVIS

Nella Larsen's Harlem Aesthetic†

"I do so want to be famous," Nella Larsen wrote to Henry Allen Moe of the Guggenheim Foundation. She was in Spain for the completion of her year as the foundation's first black woman to receive a fellowship in creative writing: "The work goes fairly well. But I like it. Of course, that means nothing because I really can't tell if it's good or not. But the way I hope and pray that it is [is] like a physical pain. I do . . . want to be famous."[1] The statement in context is innocent enough, but it is an indication of the attitudes and values Larsen held throughout the 1920s and early 1930s when she was writing fiction.

At thirty-seven, Larsen had published her first novel, *Quicksand*, brought out by Knopf, but which she had considered submitting to Albert and Charles Boni, for as she said: "It would be nice to get a thousand dollars . . . and publicity."[2] *Quicksand's* reception in 1928 fueled her determination to be a famous novelist. She promptly decided that she "was asking for the Harmon Award," because as she assessed her chances, "Looking back on the year's output of Negro literature I don't see why I shouldn't have a book in. There's only Claude McKay besides.—Rudolph [Fisher] is just too late—. . . .[3] She immediately sought out recommendations from James Weldon Johnson, W.E.B. DuBois, and Lillian Alexander when she discovered that one had to be *nominated* for the Harmon Award.

Larsen had already shaved two years off her age in order to comply with the image of youth promoted during the Renaissance. The daughter of an interracial union, Larsen had come a long way by the end of the 1920s when she no longer admitted to being from a working-class background on Chicago's South Side. However, it was not simply upward mobility that she sought during the Renaissance; by then, she had already been married to a physicist since May 1919.

† From Thadious M. Davis, "Nella Larsen's Harlem Aesthetic," in *The Harlem Renaissance: Reevaluations*, ed. Amritjit Singh, William S. Shiver, and Stanley Brodwin (New York: Garland, 1989), pp. 245–56. Copyright © 1989. Reproduced by permission of Routledge/Taylor and Francis Group, LLC.
1. Letter to Henry Allen Moe, 11 January 1931, in the John Simon Guggenheim Foundation Files. Hereafter referred to as GFF.
2. Letter to Carl Van Vechten, 1 July 1926, in the James Weldon Johnson Collection, Beinecke Rare Book and Manuscript Library, Yale University, New Haven, Connecticut. Hereafter referred to as JWJC.
3. Letter to Carl Van Vechten, n.d., circa 3 September 1928, JWJC.

She was seeking instead to become someone important in her own right.

Nella Larsen, novelist, emerged from a particular cultural configuration—Harlem of the New Negro Renaissance; perhaps no other could have produced her. While her art was dependent upon a number of factors, it was obviously linked to her historical situation. With an influx of 87,417 blacks during the 1920s, the 25-block area above 125th Street was, as James Weldon Johnson declared, "the greatest Negro city in the world."[4] Harlem provided a place for black life, in Alain Locke's view, to seize "its first chances for group expression and self-determination. . . . There is a fresh spiritual and cultural focusing. We have, as the heralding sign, an unusual outburst of creative expression."[5] This "unusual outburst of creative expression" was possible in a particular environment not only conducive to black creativity, but also to inspire participation in that creativity.

In April 1927, when Nella Larsen and her husband Elmer Imes moved from Jersey City to an apartment in Harlem's 135th Street, they arrived seeking proximity to the "cultural Capital." Larsen especially welcomed the move as the convergence of her social and literary interests. Her initial aim was imitative; she wanted to join herself through writing to a particular phenomenon. The creative activity, whether a Zora Neal[e] Hurston telling stories, an Aaron Douglas drawing illustrations, a Countee Cullen or Langston Hughes writing poetry, inspired confidence in artistic potential and promised rewards for involvement.

For Larsen, the activity was like a whirlwind. As she stated: "It has seemed always to be tea time, as the immortal Alice remarked, with never time to wash the dishes between while."[6] Her actions were controlled by her conscious desire to achieve recognition and were perhaps controlled too by her unconscious hope to belong. While for some the stirrings in Harlem may have been racial and aesthetic, for Larsen they were primarily practical. Her objective was to use art to protract her identity onto a larger social landscape as emphatically as possible.

Larsen had made her decision to become part of the growing number of "New Negro" writers in 1925 when, as Arna Bontemps recalled, "It did not take long to discover . . . the sighs of wonder, amazement and sometimes admiration . . . that here was one of the 'New Negroes.' "[7] The reception accorded young artists motivated

4. James Weldon Johnson, "The Making of Harlem," in *Survey Graphic*, 6 (March 1925), 635.
5. Alain Locke, "Foreword," in *The New Negro* (New York: Albert & Charles Boni, 1925), p. xvii.
6. Letter to Carl Van Vechten, Monday [1925], Carl Van Vechten Collection, New York Public Library, New York. Hereafter, CVVC. [Letter reprinted in this edition, p. 168].
7. Arna Bontemps, *Personals* (London: Paul Bremen, 1963), p. 4.

Larsen to turn to writing, at first stories, which early in 1926 she sold to a ladies magazine. These stories, and especially her first novel, *Quicksand* (1928), were part of her attempt to "cash in" on the cultural awakening, to stake her own claim for the recognition and development of identity that other authors were accorded. Basically, it was not enough to write; it was *essential* to publish.

The writer during the Renaissance was just as often *made* as born. Walter White had written *The Fire in the Flint* (1924) in response to a wave of white interest in race material. And others had answered the call by publishers for "Negro" works by producing poetry, fiction, and drama. In that milieu it was possible to become a writer with an announcement to "friends" that a project was under way or through a notice that a publisher was searching for "Negro" materials. In 1927, for example, Larsen wrote to her friend Dorothy Peterson, "You'd better write some poetry, or something. I've met a man from Macmillan's who's asked me to look out for any Negro stuff and send them to him."⁸ She would and did believe that any and all of her intelligent, lively friends could and would want to produce "poetry, or something" in order to take advantage of the opportunities for recognition and prestige that publishing, particularly with a white firm, would bring. Talent or inclination or aptitude or inspiration had little to do with it.

Larsen herself had become known as a budding writer even before an audience had seen her fiction; rumor had it as early as the start of 1926 that she was writing a novel. "How do these things get about?" she asked Van Vechten, and added, "It is the awful Truth. But, who knows if I'll get through with the damned thing. Certainly not I."⁹

The two prongs of inspiration for Larsen were public acclaim and social activity, both intricately tied to the climate for publishing things "Negro." In this she may have been similar to others; there were, however, writers who wrote out of a different set of aesthetic values, such as Georgia Douglas Johnson, who revealed in 1927:

> I wrote because I love to write. . . . If I might ask of some fairy godmother special favors, one would sure to be for a clearing space, elbow room in which to think and write and live beyond the reach of the wolf's fingers.¹

Nella Larsen, however, functioned in what Gilbert Osofsky called the "myth world of the twenties."² Described in 1929 as having a

---

8. Letter to Dorothy Peterson, Thursday 21st [1927], JWJC. [Letter reprinted in this edition, p. 164].
9. Letter to Carl Van Vechten, 1 July 1926, JWJC.
1. Georgia Douglas Johnson, "The Contest Spotlight," *Opportunity* (July 1927), p. 204.
2. Gilbert Osofsky, *Harlem: The Making of a Ghetto, Negro New York, 1890–1930* (1965; rpt. New York: Harper & Row, 1968).

"satin surface,"[3] she revealed her ritual for reading a good book: "a Houbigant scented bath, the donning of my best green crepe de chine pyjamas, fresh flowers on the bedside table, piles of freshly covered pillows and my nicest bed covers."[4] Her pretentious description portrays not merely a sense of aesthetic pleasure, but also the degree to which she was removed from ordinary black life.

Drawn to the class of blacks and of whites who could ignore the poverty that Harlem bred, along with the possibilities for its residents, Larsen responded to a world of glitter and potential that distanced itself from the teeming masses. In the process, she created precarious boundaries for her work and life: "I'm still looking for a place to move. . . . Right now when I look out into the Harlem streets I feel just like Helga Crane in my novel. Furious at being connected with all these niggers."[5] Being ensconced in a five-room apartment was not enough to make her forget that she was trapped among lower-class blacks whom she once described as "mostly black . . . quite shiftless, frightfully clean and decked out in appalling colours."[6] When she found a better apartment on Seventh Avenue, which she called "Uncle Tom's Cabin,"[7] she would more readily admit "that she would never pass" because, as she told a reporter, "with my economic status it's better to be a Negro [sic]."[8] She might have added—especially if she could be labeled one of the "talented tenth" of the race and associate with people accustomed to prestige, position, and comfort.

But, as Langston Hughes pointed out in *The Big Sea* (1940): "All of us knew that the gay sparkling life of the so-called Renaissance . . . was not so gay and sparkling beneath the surface. . . . I thought it wouldn't last long. . . . for how could a large and enthusiastic number of people be crazy about Negroes forever?"[9] Whereas Hughes's assessment is familiar, Alain Locke's is not. In 1936, eleven years after his confident pronouncements in *The New Negro*, and after the Harlem riots of March 1935, Locke wrote another Harlem essay for *Survey Graphic*, "Harlem: Dark Weather Vane," in which he broke what he called a "placid silence and Pollyanna complacency" about "the actual predicament of the mass of life in Harlem": "For no cultural advance is safe without some sound economic underpinning . . . and no emerging elite—artistic, professional or mercantile—can suspend itself in thin air over the abyss of

3. Mary Rennels, *The New York Telegram,* 13 April 1929. [Reprinted in this edition, p. 85].
4. Letter to Carl Van Vechten, Friday sixth. [1926], JWJC.
5. Letter to Dorothy Peterson, Tuesday 19th [1927], JWJC. [Letter reprinted in this edition, p. 163].
6. Letter to Fania Marinoff and Carl Van Vechten, 22 May 1930, JWJC.
7. Letter to Carl Van Vechten, 1 May 1928, JWJC.
8. Mary Rennels, *New York Telegram,* 13 April 1929.
9. Langston Hughes, *The Big Sea: An Autobiography* (New York: Knopf, 1940), pp. 227–228.

a mass of unemployed [people] stranded in an over-expensive, disease-and crime-ridden slum . . . for there is no cure or saving magic in poetry and art, an emerging generation of talent, or international prestige and interracial recognition, for unemployment, . . . for high rents, high mortality rates, civic neglect, capitalistic exploitation."[1] Locke includes the two elements that were key components of Nella Larsen's Harlem aesthetic; the two are "international prestige" and "interracial recognition."

Partly because she was a black person in a predominantly white world in Chicago and a nobody in the primarily bourgeois world of elite blacks in New York, Larsen sought a career in writing as a way to become somebody. The single claim that she could and did make about being special was that she was a mulatto, daughter of "a Danish lady and a Negro from the Virgin Islands," as she wrote in her 1927 author's publicity sketch for Knopf; later, once *Quicksand* had been published, she could point out that she had not worked outside her home for three years, inflate her educational background and previous employment, and emphasize that her husband had a Ph.D. in physics and worked *downtown* for an engineering firm.

Larsen had married well, but the marriage did not guarantee her acceptance or prominence or make her comfortable within the black elite. She had neither college credentials to call upon, nor a prominent family to smooth her way. What she had was ambition and drive and intelligence. The ambivalences in her fiction and ultimately in her life result perhaps more from her attempts to enter into a class that never knew her for the person she had been in her early life—the child of a working-class immigrant family; it is the background that Larsen could never reveal once she had transformed herself from *Nellie* to *Nella*, member of a black society that was not only race conscious, but class conscious as well.

Larsen wanted her own life to become a kind of fairy tale, "like a princess out of a modern fairy tale," as she observed of Fania Marinoff, Van Vechten's wife.[2] But discontented with life in the limelight of her prince, she desired her *own* spotlight, as is indicated by her transition from calling herself Nella *Imes* to Nella Larsen, or Nella Larsen Imes when necessary, after she had finished her first novel. She confessed in 1929 that she "would like to be twenty-five years younger [and that] she want[ed] things—beautiful and rich things."[3]

Nella Larsen as a novelist was driven not by an inner need to write, but by a craving for what she called "fame" and what Locke described as prestige or recognition. Larsen, however, was not the

1. Alain Locke, "Harlem: Dark Weather-Vane," *Survey Graphic,* 25 (August 1936), 457–462, 493–495.
2. Letter to Carl Van Vechten, Wednesday [1926], CVVC.
3. Rennels, *New York Telegram,* 13 April 1929.

only one whose values emphasized prestige and recognition: others such as Richard Bruce Nugent, Wallace Thurman, Albert Rice, Walter White, or Gwendolyn Bennett also wanted the fame that was almost assured by being part of the New Negro movement. I would not criticize the effort that such individuals put into their writing or dismiss the fact that the writing itself functioned as a means of insight.

I do not question Nella Larsen's effort or seriousness of purpose. Her hard work is a persistent refrain in her letters: "I have been working like a coloured person," she stressed repeatedly, and she would also, as she said, "sweat blood over her work, and console herself with Van Vechten's maxim: 'Easy writing makes bad reading.' "[4] Moreover, she saw herself as a serious novelist, despite being one who would underline the appositive "novelist" after her name in news items noting her attendance at social functions before sending the clippings to her friends. She never gave her occupation as anything other than "writer," and never referred to herself except as "novelist." My doubts about her work lie, therefore, in the somewhat inexplicable area of motivation and intention. I believe that Larsen's commitment to writing may have been inextricably linked to tangible social rewards. She seems to have valued social popularity on the same level as her writing, and it may well be that the publicity she received as one of the two black women *novelists* in the 1920s forced her to take the production of work seriously so that she could sustain her new identity.

Larsen "worked" privately on her writing and publicly on her social standing. She promoted herself on the stage that encouraged her transformation. Because she was bound by the larger expectations of the Renaissance and her own internal pressure to achieve, the measure she set for herself was public acknowledgment of her work and productivity. One result was the intensification of a split between her work as a creative process and her work as a source of public recognition—the standard by which she, like Locke and others, measured achievement. Because one of her objectives remained constant—reaping the benefits of social prominence—she was forced to set unreasonably short deadlines for her finished work and that self-imposed restriction ultimately frustrated her.

The tension between individual work and social interaction was exacerbated by her own underlying conception of writing, her Harlem aesthetic: writing was a "product," which could, upon reception, confirm self-identity as well as very self-worth. Larsen had in the Renaissance a formidable model for understanding writing in the contexts of upward mobility, status, and achievement, not in the private creative process but in the public end result. The result validates

4. Letter to Carl Van Vechten, 7 April 1931, JWJC.

the power of the black writer to define the self in the larger world, yet validates as well the power of the larger world to determine and arbitrate the conditions of that validation.

Though Hughes had warned in 1926 that the "present vogue in things Negro . . . may do as much harm as good for the budding colored artist," and that the "Negro artist works against an undertow of sharp criticism and misunderstanding from his own group and unintentional bribes from the whites,"[5] his message was not heard distinctly. Tangible production was the most viable means of asserting the existence of the "New Negro" and measuring achievement. Locke's 1925 announcement of "outbursts of creative expression"— that is to say, published works—as a "heralding sign" established the stage in a way that he may not have fully intended. Achievement for Larsen and other racially defined writers was thus seemingly construed as public acknowledgment without which the creative act was incomplete. Achievement consisted of both publication and reception by an audience, preferably a white one.

Considered in this context, Walter White's letter to Claude McKay on 20 May 1925 is revealing:

> Things are certainly moving with rapidity . . . so far as the Negro artist is concerned. Countee Cullen has had a book of verse accepted by Harper . . . and . . . Knopf accepted a volume by Langston Hughes. Rudolph Fisher . . . has had two excellent short stories in *The Atlantic Monthly*. . . . James Weldon Johnson is at work on a book of Negro spirituals. . . .
>
> The Negro artist is really in the ascendancy. . . . There is unlimited opportunity . . . you will be amazed at the eagerness of magazine editors and book publishers to get hold of promising writers.
>
> Let me as a friend urge you to get your novel ready for publication as soon as possible.[6]

The trap here is evident. The black individual generally has an internal barometer that measures, accurately or not, his or her own selfhood in a society whose locus of meaning has little to do with the meaning of blackness. However, the black individual, who for whatever reasons wants and needs a validation of the self in the external world, may well resort to what that world has accepted as worthy of measurement.

This awareness is one that McKay had formulated when he responded to White's letter: "I am so happy about the increased

5. Langston Hughes, "The Negro Artist and the Racial Mountain," *The Nation*, 23 June 1926, pp. 692–694; reprinted in *Voices from the Harlem Renaissance*, ed. Nathan Irvin Huggins (New York: Oxford University Press, 1976), p. 307.
6. In NAACP Papers, Library of Congress, Washington, D.C.

interest in the creative life of the Negro. It is for Negro aspirants to the creative life themselves to make the best of it—to discipline themselves and do work that will hold ground firmly [to] the very highest white standards. Nothing less will help Negro art forward; a boom is a splendid thing but if the masses are not up to standard people turn aside from them after the novelty has worn off."[7] McKay shifts his focus away from White's emphasis on quantity and publication to "the creative life" and quality; albeit he too leaves "white standards" as the aesthetic measure.

For Larsen, too, in the sparkling social world of the Renaissance with its interracial conclaves and its hope for uplift, the printed product evidenced the New Negro's reality. Each group of published works was carefully added to the list of verifiable products, of achievement of oneself and the race; each writer's productivity was dutifully proclaimed in the records for the year. It is not surprising, then, that this tally-sheet approach could not last, that most writers did not endure, so that in a retrospective view of the Renaissance, one can marvel not at the lists of works produced during a relatively brief period, but instead take note of the casualties—those black writers who, for whatever conjunction of personal factors and external causes, simply did not make it into the next decade, or if into it, then not out of it. By 1936 Locke himself was to observe, "indeed, [we] find it hard to believe that the rosy enthusiasms and hope of 1925 were more than bright illusions or a cruelly deceptive mirage. Yet after all there was a renaissance, with its poetic spurt of cultural and spiritual advance, vital and significant but uneven accomplishments. . . ."[8]

Few would quarrel with Locke here, and few would challenge his interpretation of the accomplishments as being "vital and significant but uneven." Too few have, however, asked why the accomplishments were so uneven. One answer to that question might pose as well an answer to the questions of why the Renaissance ended so abruptly— a question that is more frequently answered, but in such a way as to link not aesthetics but economics to the decline of the movement. Perhaps another answer to the question may lie in the particular and personal motivations of individual writers, in the impetus for their will to create. Their aesthetics thus emphasized both the product and the status that came with it, these two being more important to them than either artistic creativity or economic gain.

For a brief time, one of these authors, Nella Larsen, captured the spirit of a unique time for modern black writers. She praised the activity as "writing as if [one] didn't absolutely despise the age in which [one] lives. . . . Surely it is more interesting to belong to one's own time, to share its peculiar vision, catch that flying glimpse of the panorama which no subsequent generation can ever recover."[9] In her own words, in her own "flying glimpse of the panorama," Larsen saw a world of middle-class blacks that became the basis for her fictional vision, but she saw, too, the complexities of personal identification with that world. While it cannot be claimed that she saw either steadily or whole, it is evident that the angle and the scope of her vision resulted from her particular involvement with her time. Perhaps then, like others such as Thurman, Larsen was more acutely a victim of the New Negro Renaissance than has been assumed. Had she completed her three novels in progress, she might have emerged from her age with a more substantial canon, and with more of the fame that she so wanted. Yet that canon, in all probability, would not have altered the estimation of her relationship to her age, even though she had the individual talent to transcend "hack work," as she herself once labeled her early stories.[1] Larsen was a writer inspired to write by the confluence of activities in the Harlem of the Renaissance, and limited as well by that very inspiration.

MARK J. MADIGAN

From Miscegenation and "The Dicta of Race and Class": The Rhinelander Case and Nella Larsen's *Passing*†

* * *

The title of Larsen's novel refers to the capability of light-skinned African-Americans to cross, or "pass," the color line undetected. In writing of racial passing, Larsen worked within a well-established tradition: William Wells Brown, Charles W. Chesnutt, Kate Chopin, and James Weldon Johnson were only a few of the writers who had dealt with this topic before her. *Passing,* however, is distinguished by its deft presentation of the subject from the perspectives of two mulatto women of the 1920s: Clare Kendry and Irene Redfield. The novel begins in an expensive Chicago restaurant where both women are passing. There, Clare recognizes Irene as a childhood friend and invites her to tea at her home. Irene, the wife

9. Letter to Carl Van Vechten, Monday [1925], CVVC. [Letter reprinted in this edition, p. 158].
1. Guggenheim Application, 14 November 1929, CFF. [Reprinted in this edition, p. 152].
† From Mark Madigan, "Miscegenation and 'The Dicta of Race and Class.'" *Modern Fiction Studies,* 36, no. 4 (Winter 1990): 524–28. © Purdue Research Foundation. Reprinted with permission of the Johns Hopkins University Press. Bracketed page numbers refer to this Norton Critical Edition.

of a successful Harlem doctor, keeps the date, but when she meets Clare's racist white husband—who does not know his wife's true race—vows never to see her old friend again. The two do meet again, however, when Clare pays a visit to New York City two years later. Despite Irene's reluctance to rekindle the friendship, Clare makes frequent visits to the Redfields' apartment, and the plot is complicated when Irene begins to suspect that her husband is having an affair with Clare. Clare's husband further complicates matters when he learns by chance that his wife is actually a mulatto. Irene then fears that her own husband will leave her if Clare is divorced. The Rhinelander case is mentioned at this crucial point in the narrative, as Irene wonders whether racial deception could be grounds for Clare's divorce:

> What if Bellew should divorce Clare? Could he? There was the Rhinelander case. But in France, in Paris, such things were easy. If he divorced her—If Clare were free—But of all the things that could happen, that was the one she did not want. She must get her mind away from that possibility. She must. (228) [71–72]

Larsen's offhand manner of referring to the Rhinelander case assumes a familiarity on the part of her readers, but what was once common knowledge now demands some explanation. The case centered on the marriage of Leonard Kip Rhinelander, a member of one of New York's oldest and wealthiest families, and Alice B. Jones, a mulatto chambermaid, on 14 October, 1924—just one week after the twenty-two year-old Rhinelander had received a share of his family's fortune in cash, jewels, real estate, and stocks. The improbable love-affair between the young aristocrat and the chambermaid was short-lived, however, as Leonard filed suit for annulment after just one month of marriage on the grounds that his wife had deceived him about her true racial identity. He charged that the marriage "was obtained by fraud" and that she had tricked him into believing her dark-skinned father was Cuban, not African-American. In their initial complaint, Rhinelander's lawyers portrayed their client as a naïve young man who had been duped by a woman concerned only with his money ("Rhinelander Sues to Annul Marriage").

What on the surface may have seemed a private affair actually became a long, emotionally-charged trial held before packed courtrooms. It was a year-long event marked by several bizarre developments, including rumors of bribery and extortion, the public reading of Leonard's love-letters, the partial disrobing of the defendant so that jurors could examine her skin, and testimony from such well-known persons as Irving Berlin and Al Jolson. Attorneys for the defense initially claimed Alice Rhinelander was caucasian, but then admitted she was a quadroon mulatto and sought to prove that Leonard knew of her race before the marriage and enticed her to be his mistress and later his wife nevertheless. Alice further contended that her new husband and she would have lived happily together had it not been for Leonard's father who had coerced his son into seeking the divorce ("Rhinelander's Wife Now Planning Suit").

The press exploited the sensational nature of the case, publishing the prosecution's virulent, often racist attempts to discredit Alice Rhinelander, as well as Leonard's letters and other courtroom testimony on the intimate details of the love-affair. In 1924 and 1925, a total of eighty-eight articles on the Rhinelander case appeared in the *New York Times*, nearly a quarter of them on the front page. The *New York Herald Tribune* also followed the trial closely under headlines such as "Kip Rhinelander is 'Brain Tied' Counsel Pleads." "Rhinelander's Bride Admits Negro Blood," and "Kip Rhinelander Admits Ardent Pursuit of Wife." As the trial progressed, it became obvious that Leonard had indeed known his wife was a mulatto before he married her but had since been convinced by his father—perhaps under the threat of being disinherited—not to introduce African-American ancestry into the Huguenot family bloodline. The defense badly embarrassed the new husband during cross-examination in which he repeatedly contradicted his earlier statements, and the newspapers reported the unravelling of his case in painstaking detail. The *New York Times*, for example, was unsparing in its description of Leonard during cross-examination, reporting on 18 November 1925:

> A sadly confused young man stuttered his way through the intimate confessions of his courtship today. . . . He squirmed and drank huge quantities of water. He stammered more than ever, and at times just refused to answer and stared, dumb and abashed, at the rail before him. ("Rhinelander Says He Pursued Girl")

The *Boston Globe* reported on its front page the same day:

> The astonished gasps with which the first of his admissions were heard by the crowd of spectators whose struggles to get into the courtroom had become a small riot, changed to amazed stares as confession followed confession from his halting tongue. ("Rhinelander Admits Pursuit")

The case received substantial coverage in African-American news publications as well. The focus of that coverage was less sensationalistic, and more critical of the social forces which destroyed the Rhinelanders' marriage. *Opportunity: A Journal of Negro Life* offered the opinion that "the fierce fires of love had blinded both to the dicta of race and class" ("Rhinelander's Suit"), while *The Messenger: World's Greatest Negro Monthly* lamented in its December issue: "We are not sufficiently civilized yet to accord to two sane individuals the right to determine their own destiny, and we won't be so long as our minds are fastened by the incrusted dogma of race, creed, nationality, politics, or economics" ("The Rhinelander Case"). W. E. B. Du Bois, meanwhile, took a harsher editorial position in *The Crisis*:

> . . . if Rhinelander had used this girl as concubine or prostitute, white America would have raised no word of protest; white periodicals would have printed no headlines; white ministers would have said no single word. It is when he legally and decently tries to marry the girl that Hell breaks loose and literally tears the pair apart. Magnificent Nordic morality! ("Rhinelander" 113)

Du Bois was particularly critical of the white press's handling of the story, asking how they could "persecute, ridicule and strip naked, soul and body, this defenseless girl" ("Rhinelander"). Among the most pernicious statements, however, were those spoken in the courtroom itself. For instance, both white and African-American publications reported this closing appeal by Judge Isaac Mills of the prosecution:

> There isn't a father among you—and remember I sought to get fathers on this jury—there isn't a father among you who would not rather see his own son in his casket than to see him wedded to a mulatto woman. . . . There is not a mother among your wives who would not rather see her daughter with her white hands crossed in her shroud than see her locked in the embrace of a mulatto husband. ("Rhinelander's Suit" 4)

On 5 December 1925, the New York State Supreme Court jury which heard the trial ruled that Alice Rhinelander had not deceived her husband. The foreman said the case had been decided fairly:

> Race prejudice didn't enter into the case at all, and neither did the unsavory details in the letters. We decided it merely as a case between a man and a woman, and in reaching our verdict considered Rhinelander as a normal man with normal sense of perception. We didn't consider what the future might hold for them, as that was not up to us for decision. ("Rhinelander Loses; No Fraud is Found")

The verdict culminated the first of a series of defeats Leonard would suffer in the courts as whatever love he once felt for his wife was lost amidst a welter of legal proceedings. By April 1926, after an unsuccessful attempt to appeal the decision, he had spent over $50,000 in legal fees alone. A year and a half later, the press reported that his whereabouts were unknown ("Alice Rhinelander Seek Separation").

Alice Rhinelander, meanwhile, filed her own suit for separation in 1927 on the grounds that she had been abandoned and that publicity from the annulment trial amounted to "cruel and inhumane treatment" ("Alice Rhinelander Seek Separation"). The claim was supported by the fact that her life had been threatened by the Ku Klux Klan, which openly searched for her in Florida where she had gone soon after the New York court decision. Alice Rhinelander later brought a $500,000 suit against her father-in-law for alienation of her husband's affections ("Philip Rhinelander Sued By Son's Wife"). The vitriolic charges and counter-charges of the Rhinelander case remained in the newspaper headlines throughout 1928 and 1929, while Larsen and other Harlem Renaissance novelists, including Jessie Fauset. Rudolph Fisher, and Walter White, were writing of crossing the color line in their fiction.[1] Although I have not found specific reference to the Rhinelanders in these works, it seems most likely—given the publicity and location of the trial in the nearby suburb of White Plains—that the case would have informed their treatments of passing as it informed Larsen's.[2]

By the end of the decade, it was well known that Alice Rhinelander had succeeded in obtaining a substantial "voluntary" monthly payment from her husband and was pressing for an even larger amount; it was reported that she even rejected an outright cash settlement of $100,000 during the Great Depression ("Mrs. Rhinelander Rejects Peace Offer"). When Leonard Rhinelander was finally granted a Las Vegas divorce in 1930, his wife received a cash payment of $31,500 and an annuity of $3,600 payable quarterly for the rest of her life. For her part, Alice was required to drop all pending lawsuits, waive dower rights, and relinquish use of the Rhinelander name ("Rhinelander Case Closed"). The final strange chapter of the story, however, was not closed until six years later when Leonard died of pneumonia at the age of thirty-four.

Although the Rhinelanders' divorce was not settled until after the publication of *Passing*, Nella Larsen made use of the initial court decision in her novel. In the specific context of the paragraph in *Passing*, Irene Redfield's hopes are at first buoyed by the fact that the Rhinelander annulment was denied, and then dashed by the prospect

---

1. See, for example. Walter White's *Flight* (1926). Rudolph Fisher's *The Walls of Jericho* (1926) and Jessie Fauset's *Plum Bun* (1929) and *Comedy American Style* (1933).
2. Some thirty years later, the makers of the film *Night of the Quarter Moon* (1959) also seem to have been aware of the Rhinelander case. The film, which was directed by Hugo Haas and starred Julie London and John Drew Barrymore, tells the story of a wealthy young man who meets and marries a quadroon woman in Mexico. Under pressure from his aristocrat family, the new husband later, claims he did not know of his wife's race when he married her and she is ordered to disrobe at the annulment proceedings. *Night of the Quarter Moon* (later retitled *Flesh and Flame*) dillers from the Rhinelander case in other respects, particularly the happy ending in which the young lovers are reunited, but the similarities are nonetheless striking. Critics panned the film for being melodramatic and poorly directed. The Rhinelander case may also have been a source for Faulkner's '*Absalom Absalom*', a connection I am currently investigating.

of a Paris divorce. (Ironically, her faith in the Rhinelander decision seems misplaced, for the jury ruled that there had been no racial deception, not that passing should be precluded as grounds for divorce.) The scene in the novel ends with Irene's inner turmoil unresolved. From the subject of divorce and the Rhinelander case her thoughts shift to how much easier her life would be if Clare were dead, and then recoil in guilt to memories of her courtship and marriage. That Larsen has the case enter Irene's mind so quickly, however, testifies to the Rhinelanders' importance to discussions of miscegenation, the law, and racial passing during the period of the Harlem Renaissance.

In a broader context, the Rhinelander case is a metaphor for the central concerns of Larsen's book: *Passing*, above all else, portrays a world in which its protagonists, like the Rhinelanders, are bound by what *Opportunity* referred to as "the dicta of race and class." For Clare, escape is realized only in death as she falls through a sixth-story window when confronted by her husband about her true racial identity. Although she did not suffer comparable physical violence, there can be little argument that Alice Rhinelander also led a life circumscribed by the issue of race. Acquitted of racial deception by law, Alice was persecuted nonetheless as her marriage was ruined and she was forced to endure a long, humiliating annulment trial.

Nella Larsen's mention of the Rhinelander case is, then, a brief but important part of *Passing*. In this book about marriage and racial passing, the historical reference calls attention to the era's most celebrated legal case concerned with that very issue. Moreover, Larsen's casual manner of reference makes clear that the Rhinelander case provided a ready context for the discussion of similar cases. In all of its legal, economic, social, and racial entanglements, the marriage of Leonard Kip Rhinelander and Alice B. Jones was but one example of how complex the issue of passing could be during the period of the Harlem Renaissance.

Works Cited

"Alice Rhinelander Seeks Separation." *New York Times* 30 Dec. 1927: 9.

Faus[e]t, Jessie. *Comedy American Style*. New York: Stokes, 1933.

——. *Plum Bun*. New York: Stokes, 1929.

"Kip Rhinelander Admits Ardent Pursuit of Wife." *New York Herald Tribune* 11 Nov. 1925: 21.

"Kip Rhinelander is 'Brain Tied' Counsel Pleads." *New York Herald Tribune* Nov. 1925: 14.

Larsen, Nella. *Quicksand and Passing*. 1928, 1929. Ed. Deborah E. McDowell. New Brunswick: Rutgers UP, 1986.

"Mrs. Rhinelander Rejects Peace Offer." *New York Times* 4 June 1930.

"Philip Rhinelander Sued By Son's Wife." *New York Times* 14 July 1929.

"Rhinelander." Editorial. *The Crisis* Jan. 1926: 112–113.

"Rhinelander Admits Pursuit." *Boston Globe* 18 Nov. 1925: 1.

"Rhinelander's Bride Admits Negro Blood." *New York Herald Tribune*. 11 Nov. 1925: 10.

"The Rhinelander Case." Editorial. *The Messenger: World's Greatest Negro Monthly* Dec. 1925: 388.

"Rhinelander Case Closed." *New York Times* 6 Sept. 1930: 17.

"Rhinelander Loses; No Fraud is Found." *New York Times* 6 Dec. 1925: 27.

"Rhinelander Says He Pursued Girl." *New York Times* 18 Nov. 1925: 4.

"Rhinelander Sues to Annul Marriage." *New York Times* 27 Nov. 1924: 1.

"Rhinelander's Suit." Editorial. *Opportunity: A Journal of Negro Life* Jan. 1926: 4.

"Rhinelander's Wife Now Planning Suit." *New York Times* 23 Nov. 1925: 23.

White, Walter. *Flight*. New York: Knopf, 1926.

JENNIFER DEVERE BRODY

Clare Kendry's "True" Colors: Race and Class Conflict in Nella Larsen's *Passing*†

Interpretations of Nella Larsen's *Passing* (1929) often have failed to explain the complex symbolism of the narrative. Indeed, dismissive or tendentious criticisms of the text have caused it to be eclipsed by Larsen's "earlier and more intriguing" book, *Quicksand* (1928).[1] This essay reexamines *Passing* as a work concerned with the simultaneous representation and construction of race and especially class, within a circumscribed community. As such, my paper contributes to debates within Black feminist criticism about the value of these aspects of identity in relation to the production of black female subjectivities. I contend that the novel's main characters are neither

---

† From Jennifer DeVere Brody, "Clare Kendry's 'True' Colors: Race and Class Conflict in Nella Larsen's *Passing*," *Callaloo* 15, no. 4 (Fall 1992): 1053–65. © Charles H. Rowell. Reprinted with permission of the Johns Hopkins University Press.

1. See Claudia Tate, "Nella Larsen's Passing: A Problem of Interpretation," *Black American Literature Forum* 14 (Winter 1980): 180–246 [sic; reprinted in this edition, p. 342]; and Deborah McDowell's "Introduction," *Quicksand and Passing* (New Brunswick, NJ: Rutgers University Press, 1988), ix–xxxvii. [Reprinted in this edition, p. 363].

purely "psychological" beings, as Claudia Tate asserts, nor are they essentially "sexual" creatures, as Deborah McDowell argues. Rather, I read Irene Redfield and Clare Kendry as representatives of different ideologies locked in struggle for dominance.

In her introduction to *Passing* Deborah McDowell, one of the most astute critics of Larsen's work, states that "many critics have been misled by the novel's epigraph . . . [since] it invites the reader to place race at the center of any critical interpretation."[2] It would appear that McDowell herself has been misled by *Passing*'s obviously unreliable narrator. So too, McDowell seems to agree with Claudia Tate's belief that, "Race is peripheral to *Passing*. It is more a device to sustain the suspense than a compelling social issue."[3] I disagree with these assertions because it seems to me that the text is "all about race" or rather, the mediation of race in relation to sexuality and class.[4]

McDowell recognizes certain tropes employed by Larsen and, like many other critics, she maintains that Irene Redfield is the primary referent of the novel's title. Ultimately, however, McDowell is unable to give a full explication of the text's meaning since she tries to read/uce the text as a tale of latent sexual passion without discussing the key issues of race and class. Thus, while her discussion is certainly valuable, one might also say that it reifies sexuality at the risk of not exploring how sexuality is connected inextricably with other historically produced phenomena such as race and class. In order to sustain her ingenious reading of *Passing* as a tale that "passes for straight" and sublimates lesbian desire, McDowell misses the more intricate implications addressed by Larsen's work. The iconography McDowell reads as sexual is simultaneously racial: it also expresses class positionality. For example, the objective correlative envelope used in the first paragraph of the novel signifies not only the "sexual" (McDowell reads it as a "metaphorical vagina") but also the sender's race (alien) and class (elite). Thus, my reading emends McDowell's by insisting on the importance of race and class in *Passing*.

If race as well as class conflict must occupy a primary position in any discussion of *Passing*, what is the significance of the first words in the narrative? The epigraph from Countee Cullen's poem, "Heritage" (1925), reads as follows:

2. See Deborah McDowell, ed., "Introduction," *Quicksand and Passing by Nella Larsen* (New Brunswick, NJ: Rutgers University Press, 1986). Subsequent references to this edition are noted in the text. Bracketed page numbers refer to this Norton Critical Edition.
3. Tate, 144. Even the most recent critic, Charles Lawson [sic], claims "the primary theme is not race . . . but marital stability" (xv): See his "Introduction," *Intimations of Things Distant: The Collected Fiction of Nella Larsen* (New York: Doubleday Books, 1992).
4. Although she gives little critical attention to *Passing*, Hazel Carby summarizes her discussion of Larsen's novels by stating that "Larsen's representations of both race and class are structured through a prism of black female sexuality" in *Reconstructing Womanhood: The Emergence of the Afro-American Woman Novelist* (New York: Oxford University Press, 1987), 174.

> One three centuries removed,
> From the scenes his fathers loved,
> Spicey grove, cinnamon tree,
> What is Africa to me?

This well-known quatrain (repeated twice in Cullen's work) has been used by many African-American authors to interrogate the "race concept" in the Americas. Indeed, it is *a* if not *the* most problematic question for all African-Americans who must negotiate the hyphenated divide. In *Passing*, these couplets become the subconscious refrain of each of the main characters in the text. However, the question, "What is Africa to me," is never answered explicitly. Larsen's ambiguity in this matter, as in the ending of the text, invite the reader to speculate about the meaning of these "privileged" lines. If "Heritage" is the narrative of one who "tries to define his [sic] relationship to some white, ontological being and finds that a Black impulse ceaselessly draws him [sic] back,"[5] it would seem to describe Clare Kendry rather than Irene Redfield, although it could refer to both. Any interpretation would depend upon one's definition of a "Black" impulse. Indeed, this is the problem Larsen's complex narrative addresses.

In my reading of *Passing*, "Africa," as a romanticized Harlem Renaissance construction, represents liberation for Clare Kendry who ironically comes to represent key aspects of this "Africa" in the text, and denigration for Irene Redfield. Thus, again, I argue that readings of race or more accurately, definitions of Blackness are indeed central to *Passing*. Ironically, it is Irene Redfield's story; one might even say that, "in a strange transference of conditions, Irene inherits Clare's life of duplicity and isolation."[6] This is ironic because Irene remains at least superficially a part of the Black world, whereas Clare supposedly leaves this world when she marries a white man.

Irene describes the difference between herself and Clare Kendry in the following manner:

> Since childhood their lives had never really touched. Actually, they were strangers. Strangers in their desires and ambitions. Strangers even in their racial consciousness. Between them the barrier was just as high, just as broad, and just as firm as if in Clare did not run that strain of black blood. In truth, it was higher, broader, and firmer; because for her there were perils, not known or imagined, by those others who had no such secrets to alarm or endanger them. (192)[44]

Irene correctly delineates the difference between herself and Clare: the two figures are ideological strangers. However, the readers must

---

5. Houston A. Baker, Jr., *The Many-Colored Coat of Dreams: The Poetry of Countee Cullen* (Detroit: Broadside Press, 1974), 34.
6. Lawson [sic], xv.

guard against believing Irene's discourse. The key to deciphering the second part of this passage lies in its diction and in the iconography established in the text. Who builds barriers between herself and her racial heritage? Who is it who describes herself as being in a perpetual state of alarm, always in danger? Certainly not Clare Kendry: thus, the latter half of this quotation does not refer to Clare Kendry. This passage is a confession—Irene's confession. It is she who harbors a secret desire to be white and not Clare.[7]

Irene believes that,

> She belongs in [the] world of rising towers. She [is] American . . . Race [is that] thing that binds and suffocates her . . . enough to suffer as a woman and an individual, on one's own account, without having to suffer for the race as well. It [is] a brutality, and undeserved. Surely, [there are] no other people so cursed as Ham's dark children. (225) [69]

This quotation, an interior monologue, expresses some of the most important aspects of Irene Redfield's ideology. She expresses and embodies numerous stereotypical middle-class values. So much so, in fact, that she sounds exactly like Clare Kendry's white, Christian, spinster aunts who tell Clare that Noah "had cursed Ham and his sons for all time" (159) [00]. Clare's aunts view Negroes as either "charities or problems" (159) [00]. Irene also is guilty of treating African-Americans, not as individuals but as objects of her own ability to serve and have power over them. Like the protagonist in Andrea Lee's 1985 novel, *Sarah Phillips*, Irene "locates herself within rather than outside of the normative community . . . Her very presence within . . . exclusionary communities suggests that the circumstances of race and gender alone protect no one from the seductions of reading her own experience as normative and fetishing the experience of the other."[8] In *Passing*, Irene consistently aligns herself with conservative and bourgeois elements in American society and views her friend Clare as an "exotic other."

She persistently fights to preserve her "security" and the status quo. "Fixity," "stasis," and above all "security" are her watchwords.

---

7. Lauren Berlant's brief analysis of *Passing* does account for the complexity of the class, race, and gender of Larsen's characters and I agree with her assertion that "what Irene wants is relief from the body she has: her intense class identification with the discipline of the bourgeois body is only one tactic for producing the corporeal 'fog' in which she walks" (112). However, I disagree with Berlant's conclusion that Irene's desire is "not to pass as a white woman—but to move unconsciously and unobstructed through the public sphere" (111). It seems to me that this reading contradicts itself because, as I argue later, to move "unconsciously through the public sphere" is a right reserved only for unmarked, transcendent bodies—not for bodies such as the one Irene inhabits. See Lauren Berlant, "National Brands/National Bodies: *Imitation of Life,*" *Comparative American Identities: Race, Sex and Nationality in the Modern Text*, ed. Hortense Spillers (New York: Routledge, 1991).

8. For a more detailed explication of this problem see Valerie Smith's discussion of *Sarah Phillips* in "Black Feminist Theory," *Changing Our Own Words*, ed. Cheryl Wall (New Brunswick, NJ: Rutgers University Press, 1989), 38–57.

Irene's constant attempts to avoid conflict and confrontation—in short to steer clear of Clare Kendry and the radical elements Clare represents, including, according to McDowell's reading, lesbian sexuality—are not successful. In this, as in so many things, Irene mimics middle-class culture which often tries to isolate itself from poverty and perversion by situating itself in a relationship above and beyond the lower-class.[9] Irene Redfield desperately desires to be free of the burden of race-consciousness and to join those who reside in the rising towers of capitalist American society.

Clare Kendry is simultaneously complicit with and subversive to such middle-class values. The terror that she incites is "like a scarlet spear . . . leaping at [its] heart" (217) [62]. Clare threatens Irene throughout the novel. Indeed, much of the novel's dramatic tension is derived from Irene's attempts to "discipline" Clare in the Foucauldian sense of "arresting and regulating her movements; clearing up confusion; and dissipating [those like Clare who] wander about the country in unpredictable ways."[1] In other words, Clare's profound contradictions, seen only by Irene who knows Clare's "true colors," drive the latter to destruction.

Although Clare looks white and is married to someone white, she oddly maintains a stronger sense of "double-consciousness" than does Irene.[2] She remains perpetually aware of her own racial origin and her duplicitous positionality. This is in contrast to Irene who has many moments in which she sees herself simply and purely as "an American." Both puritanical and anti-theatrical, Irene is threatened by Clare's ability to simultaneously imitate and denounce white society. She accuses Clare of having a tendency toward "theatrical heroics" (144) [6]. Throughout the text, Clare plays the part of the trickster and wears her "ivory mask" (157) [17] that "grins and smiles" in the face of hateful whites (and Irene). Her laugh is "the very essence of mockery . . . and [she] *knows* [about Negro culture] as if she'd been there and heard" (154) [15] all along. That is to say that although Clare has been passing for a number of years, she has managed to keep abreast of Negro culture. She appropriates white power and uses it to her advantage.

Interestingly, the first image of Clare shows her "sitting on a ragged blue sofa, sewing pieces of bright red cloth together, while her drunken father [a janitor] . . . raged . . . up and down the shabby room, bellowing curses" (143–44) [5]. This brief description provides

9. For a fuller explication of this dynamic see Peter Stallybrass and Allon White, *The Politics and Poetics of Transgression* (Ithaca: Cornell University Press, 1986).
1. See Michel Foucault's discussion of panopticism in *Discipline and Punish*, trans. Alan Sheridan (New York: Vintage Books, 1979), 195–228.
2. Dubois uses this phrase in *The Souls of Black Folk* to describe the sensation of "looking at one's self through the eyes of others." See W.E.B. Dubois, *The Souls of Black Folk* in *Three Negro Classics* (New York: Avon Books, 1965), 215.

the reader with much information about Clare's background and class. She was poor and until her marriage she worked as a domestic for weekly wages at the home of her white aunts. "In spite of certain unpleasantness and possible danger, she *takes* money" (144) [6] [italics mine] in order to sew herself a dress to wear to a Church picnic. Later, she "steals [time] from her endless domestic tasks" (152) [13] and by implication, from her white aunts. She tells Irene, "You had all the things I wanted and never had . . . I used to almost hate you for it . . . but it also made me more determined to get them and more" (159) [19]. Thus, ironically, we see that one of the prime motivations for Clare's "passing" is her desire for Irene's appreciation: for approval from her bourgeois neighbors.

Clare is not a member of the rising Black bourgeoisie nor was she ever a member of the aspiring middle-classes. She rose rapidly, readily "passed" and in so doing surpassed Irene in terms of class and material wealth. Yet in shifting her class status, Clare maintains a clear sense of her prior identity. Her Gatsbyesque ascendance to the upper-echelons of white society is undercut by her patriotic (not patronizing) racial sympathies. She occupies an extremely precarious position.

Throughout the pages of *Passing*, Clare sounds alarms—her laugh is "a trill . . . like the ringing of bells" (151) [50; 80], she incites outrage, she telephones. Like a revolution, Clare is not polite. She does not "draw back or turn aside; certainly not because of any alarms or feeling of outrage on the part of others" (143) [5]. She attacks from below. She is dangerous, mysterious, furtive and seductive. Clare has the power to reduce Irene to reaction. Thus, the narrative plays out a racial, sexual, and class war between these characters.

The spatial and ideological positions held by Clare and Irene are revealed in several scenes in which they interact. These scenes occur in the most "civilized" of places—tea rooms, parlors, boudoirs and ballrooms—but, as in Virginia Woolf's novels, these genteel settings turn out to be the arenas of the most brutal and biting behavior. The irony in these scenes, indeed in the book as a whole, is subtle and sophisticated.[3]

For example, Chapter Two of the first section, entitled "Encounter," begins ominously with

> buildings shudder[ing] as if in protest of the heat . . . Quivering
> lines [springing] up from baked pavements . . . automobiles . . .
> were a dancing blaze, and the glass of the shop windows threw

---

3. I have chosen two key scenes to discuss in detail. The metaphors that support my reading of the novel are ubiquitous. Unfortunately, it is beyond the scope of this essay to elucidate each of the important moments in the book.

> out a blinding radiance. Sharp particles of dust rose from the burning sidewalks, stinging the seared or dripping skins of wilting pedestrians. What small breeze there was seemed like the breath of a flame fanned by slow bellows. (146) [7]

In this description of a scorching summer day in Chicago, Larsen's language is violent. Things shuddering in protest, dancing blazes, blinding radiances, rising particles, burning sidewalks—these images suggest a city under siege. The passage brings to mind the tumultuous race riots of the "Red Summer" of 1919. Paralleling the plot of Larsen's story, the "outright conflict [of the race riots against white Americans] was a course pointing to almost certain doom."[4] And indeed, this scene marks the beginning of Clare Kendry's ultimately doomed attack upon Irene Redfield.[5]

Irene Redfield is among the crowds who are fighting the Chicago heat. Characteristically, she is shopping for "things" to bring back from her visit—the inevitable material possessions which are the necessary symbols of wealth. Irene makes her way about the Chicago streets in the land in which "mechanical aeroplanes are readily available" but "drawing books are more difficult to acquire" (146) when suddenly a man collapses in front of her. At this moment, Irene "edges her way out of the increasing crowd feeling disagreeably damp and sticky from contact with so many sweating bodies" (147) [8]. Irene's desire to distance herself from the "sweating masses" is evidence of her distaste for the working-classes. She feels a "need for immediate safety" and, feeling faint herself, she hails a taxi.

A remarkable exchange occurs in the blank margin and moment between Irene's statement to the taxi driver that she "might benefit from some tea" and his suggestion that she go to the Drayton Hotel. In this moment, Irene passes; and yet, neither the omniscient narrator nor Irene comment upon this transgression. The entire event merely occurs in the blank margin of the page. It is so natural for Irene to pass that she is not even conscious that she is doing so. Astonishingly, during the cab ride she simply "makes some small attempts to repair the damage that the heat and crowds had done to her appearance" (147) [8]—had her hair started to "go back"?—and then, blissfully enters the Drayton Hotel. Irene's omission in the scene suggests that she is comfortable with such transgressions.

Irene feels "like [she is] being wafted upwards on a magic carpet to another world, pleasant, quiet and strangely remote from the sizzling one that she had left below" (147) [8]. Safely sequestered on the roof-top of an ivory tower, Irene surveys the "specks of cars and

---

4. David Levering Lewis, *When Harlem Was in Vogue* (New York: Alfred A. Knopf, 1984), 24.
5. It should be noted that Clare's married name is Bellew, which is similar to "bellow," the source of *seeming* relief in the scene above.

people creeping about in the streets below [and thinks] how silly they look" (148) [9]. Although Clare Kendry occupies this same space in the text, she *never* looks askance at "those below." Again, the text reveals that this distancing—this constant need to move "away from" and "above" is characteristic of Irene and those things associated with her.

The pleasant quiet of the Drayton turns out to be, like all restricted, "white only" islands in the white hegemony, only a temporary sanctuary. The "rank" air is broken by motion, commotion, fluidity and ferocity—by the form of Clare Kendry. Clare continually collapses the distance between Irene and "the masses" as well as the distance between Irene's African heritage and her desire to be "white." Much of the novel is devoted to realizing Irene's desire not to "be the link between [Clare] and her poorer dark brethren" (185) [39] since such a position would interfere with Irene's view of herself as a private American citizen. Clare's ability to accomplish this feat is dependent on her unique position as a black woman who can wear the mask of mimicry (quite literally she looks like a beautiful white woman) and at the same time, unmask the performative nature of such dominant identities. Clare does pass; but with an altogether different sensibility than does Irene. As in Jessie Fauset's passing novel, *Plum Bun* (1928), a clear distinction is drawn between passing as "play-acting" and "passing where a principle is involved."[6] In both *Plum Bun* and *Passing*, "play passing" is acceptable but principled passing is not. The problem comes in distinguishing between these two modes. In reading Clare as the "playful passer" and Irene as the "principled passer" I hope to deconstruct the tensions between these modes.

Clare uses her "ivory mask" as a decoy to distract her adversaries and to allow her to infiltrate hostile territories. She is never completely comfortable in white society, as Irene seems to be. Irene, not recognizing Clare as her childhood acquaintance, admires Clare's appearance—her mastery of the "proper" form. Clare's physical features, for the most part, conform to a fixed standard of beauty that Irene idealizes or affirms as do those in the Black community who label "straight hair" "good hair." It is only later in the text that Irene sees Clare's "heritage" clearly. Clare had

> always had that pale gold hair . . . the ivory skin had a peculiar soft lustre. And the eyes were magnificent! dark, sometimes absolutely black, always luminous . . . arresting eyes, slow and mesmeric, and with all their warmth, something withdrawn and

---

6. Jessie Fauset, *Plum Bun: A Novel without a Moral* (London: Pandora Press, 1985), 19. There is a definite difference between Mattie's "play" passing and her daughter Angela's attempts to pass "on principle."

secret about them . . . Ah! Surely! They were Negro eyes! mysterious and concealing. And set in that ivory face under that bright hair, there was about them something exotic. (161) [21]

Even before Irene solves the mystery of Clare's identity, Irene notices that there is something disturbing about the "attractive [white] woman in the green dress." She has an "odd sort of smile . . . which Irene would have *classed* as too provocative for a waiter" (149) [9] [italics mine]. I assume that the waiter in this scene is Black and that Clare Kendry's smile is a gesture of identification and/or mutual understanding. Needless to say, such an action is deemed "too provocative" by Irene. An analogous situation occurs later in the book when Irene bristles at the sight of "Clare descending to the kitchen, and with—to Irene—an exasperating childlike lack of perception, spending her visit in talk with Zulena and Sadie [Irene's chocolate-colored maids]" (208, [brackets are Brody's]) [57].

The ensuing scene between Clare and Irene demonstrates further the manner in which these two figures struggle to attain and/or maintain power over each other in the text. The battle begins with a stare from Clare. This action immediately puts Irene on the defensive: suddenly, she is conscious of her race and the fact that she is passing when she ought not to be. She claims that "she is not ashamed of being Negro . . . but it is the idea of being ejected from any place . . . that disturbs her" (150) [11]. The difficulty with this position especially in America of the 1920s is that to be a "negro" is to be perpetually in the position of being ejected from one's "place" (should one be so fortunate to have a place); or, more commonly, to be put back into a place which one might not necessarily wish to occupy.

It is significant that it is Clare's knowing look that incites Irene's insecurities about her racial, sexual and class status and not, as we might expect, the scrutiny of any of the white characters in the book. This too is proof that Irene wishes to distance herself from her background while Clare wishes to collapse the distance between her own appearance and her current chosen position.

When Clare rises and approaches Irene's table, Irene fears that her status will change—that she will be "found out." Despite Irene's protestations to the contrary (she is after all a myopic and unreliable narrator) Irene *does* fear that her race will be discovered. In Irene's view of American society, she feels she is forced to value class over race. Race is that element which, to her mind, hinders one's pursuit of wealth and happiness. Ironically, race or rather her ability to simulate a racial stereotype, empowers Clare.

Clare has the advantage at this moment and Irene is forced to "look-up" to her. The latter decides to "surrender" to Clare's disarming smile—believing all the while that Clare is white. When Irene discovers Clare's "true" identity (she recognizes Clare's "ringing" laugh), she immediately "starts to rise" (151) [11], but Clare "commands" her to remain seated. I cite this seemingly innocuous introduction of "old acquaintances" to emphasize the shifts in power that reveal Clare's desire for parity with her bourgeois friends and Irene's equally ironic desire for ascendancy and "white" security. The omnipresent military metaphors express the seriousness of the racial, sexual and class conflicts that drive the narrative. Clare has control in this section of the text and the dynamics of her movement symbolize this fact.

It is in this scene at the Drayton that the reader learns of Irene's thoroughly middle-class upbringing. Irene went to college, is a member of the Y.W.C.A. committee and the Negro Welfare League. Even her maiden name, Westover, may be read as a sign of her status in the book. She values Western traditions over any "African" influences. Irene has tried to destroy parts of her heritage by insisting that a "rising tower" (the letter 'I' itself) remain in her name—in short, by calling herself Irene. In her segregated youth, her Negro friends knew her simply as 'Rene. As she tells Clare, "nobody calls me 'Rene anymore" (151) [11]. Irene is aware that she often feels "outnumbered, a sense of aloneness in her adherence to her own class and kind; not merely in the great thing of marriage but in the whole pattern of her life" (166) [25]. These details suggest that Clare ironically infiltrates a particular segment of dominant American society whereas Irene yearns for assimilation or absorption into that same world.

As the two women "fill in the gap of twelve years with talk" (155) [00]. Clare remains in control of the situation. Actually it is Irene who "pours tea" while Clare "drinks in" (155) all her mundane gossip. Irene realizes that time is passing and that she must be going. She realizes also that "she has not asked Clare about her own life and has a very definite reluctance to do so" (155) [16]. Like Clare's aunts, Irene assumes that Clare is "living in sin" as a "kept woman."

As if reading Irene's mind Clare states, " 'Rene dear, now that I've found you [and found you out?] I mean to see lots and lots of you. We're here for a month . . . Jack, that's my husband, is here on business" (156) [16]. This statement actually is a biting retort to Irene's unvoiced thoughts. Not only does Clare insist upon calling Irene, 'Rene, her old "Negro" name, but she also subverts Irene's assumptions about her marital status. Furthermore, to add insult to injury, Clare gives Irene "a curious little sidelong glance and a sly, ironical smile . . . as if she had been in the secret of the other's thoughts and was mocking her" (156) [16].

Clare tells Irene how she managed to pass and marry a wealthy white man. She is surprised that Irene "never 'passed' over [since] it's such a frightfully easy thing to do. If one's the type, all that's needed is a little nerve" (158) [18]. Irene is falsely fascinated by this "hazardous business of 'passing,' this breaking away from all that was familiar and friendly to take one's chances in another environment" (157) [17]. If one looks closely at Irene's statement and thinks back to the beginning of this chapter when she describes her relief at being "wafted upward . . . to another world" (146) [8] it becomes clear that Irene already knows about passing—that she is already quite comfortable doing so. Her desire to hear Clare's story is self-indulgent. She hangs on the other's words as if to say, "if only I could . . . completely." She is upset to hear that Clare's aunts are white since she has no white relatives. As for Clare, she 'passes' to acquire the economic advantages she never had and perhaps, ironically, to move closer to the Black middle-class that once rejected her for being part of the "poorer brethren." Certainly, one might read Clare as the embodiment of Irene's bourgeois fantasies.

Irene tries to convince herself, as she will do over and over in the text, that she is "through with Clare Kendry" (163) [23]; but Irene (like the white hegemony) does not have absolute control of the arena and Clare Kendry is not through with her. Clare continues her assault in Chapter Two of the next section of the book, entitled "Re-Encounter." In this scene, Clare accosts Irene in her own bedroom. It is during this encounter that Irene begins to plot Clare's murder. Irene throws a letter from Clare into the trash and thinks

> The thing, the discontent which had exploded into words would surely die, flicker out, at last . . . conscious that she had been merely deceiving herself . . . and that it still lived. But it *would die*. Of that she was certain . . . In the meantime, while it was still living and still had the power to flare up and alarm her . . . it had to be smothered. (188) [41]

The "it" mentioned above is Clare as the phrase, "living things that had the power to flare up and alarm" Irene, suggests.

Clare slyly invades Irene's space, and "tossing aside" (193) Irene's expressions of awe, "seats herself slantwise in Irene's favorite chair" (193) [46]. She demands to know why Irene refused to respond to her gestures. Irene "lit a cigarette, blew out the match, and dropped it . . . She was trying to collect her arguments, for some sixth sense warned her" (194) [46] that Clare Kendry was a formidable adversary. Indeed, Clare, with her clarity of vision, sees through Irene's feeble excuses about "running the risk of knowing Negroes . . . and doing the right thing" (194) [46]:

> The tinkle of Clare's laugh rang out . . . Oh 'Rene, . . . the right thing! Leaning forward [up in her face], Clare looked into Irene's disapproving brown eyes. . . . (195) [46]

This affront brings Irene to "her feet before she even realized that she had risen" (195) [46]. She tries to retort with more of her bland bourgeois rhetoric about "safety"; Clare flings this back at her as if to say "Safe! Damn being safe!" (195) [47] to Irene "for whom safety, security, were all-important" (195) [47]. Irene is forced to "sit down" (195). As in the scene at the Drayton, "Clare's deep voice broke the small silence" of Irene. Clare has taken control.

The issue of class enters into the discussion when Irene tells Clare that she cannot come to the Negro Welfare League dance unescorted since, "It's a public thing. All sorts of people go, anybody who can pay a dollar, even ladies of easy virtue looking for trade . . . you might be mistaken for one" (199) [50]. To Irene's surprise, Clare does not object to this possibility. Clare claims "her dollar is as good as anyone's" (199) [51], thus hinting at her knowledge of herself as sexual commodity. This view contrasts sharply with Irene's iterations of her sentimental sacrifices in the name of "wife and mother." This scene may be read simultaneously as a scene of suppressed sexual desire, racial conflict and improper class sympathies. That Clare understands selling one's perceived identity for profit should not surprise us; nor should Irene's prudish revulsion at the mention of mercenary, market tactics seem a contradiction in her character.

Like Sula and Nel in Toni Morrison's *Sula* (1973), Clare and Irene are childhood friends who grow to evince different and conflicting racial, sexual, and class values. In *Sula*, Morrison discusses the consequence of what she calls "the free fall." In many ways, the enunciation of the free fall clarifies the fundamental difference between not only Nel and Sula but between their ideological counterparts, Irene and Clare (who, like Nel and Sula, may be caught in an adulterous triangle). In *Sula*, Morrison describes Nel's reaction following her discovery of Sula, her best friend, fornicating with Nel's husband. The passage reads:

> Now Nel was one of *them*. One of the spiders whose only thought was the next rung of the web, who dangled in dark dry places suspended by their own spittle, more terrified of the free fall than the snake's breath below. Their eyes so intent on the wayward stranger who trips into their net, they were blind to the cobalt on their own backs, . . . they were merely victims and knew how to behave in that role (just as Nel knew how to behave as the wronged wife.) But the free fall, . . . that demanded inven-

tion: a thing to do with wings . . . a full surrender to downward flight if they wished to stay alive.[7]

I quote this passage at length because I feel that it illuminates important aspects of the intricate relationship between Irene and Clare. Irene, like Nel, concerns herself with getting methodically to the next rung on the pre-defined ladder of success; so, too, she is terrified of "falling"—of losing her secure status. She even knows, as we shall see, how to behave as the wronged wife. Clare, on the other hand, resembles Sula not only in her attraction to her friend's husband, but more importantly, in her ability to invent herself and to surrender to an oxymoronic "downward flight."

For Clare, a fall from her achieved position as upper-class "white" wife would be a desired fall back into her past life as lower-class black Clare Kendry. As Irene notes, "Clare Kendry had remained almost what she had always been" (202) [52] determined lower-class Black girl. Irene, on the other hand, has completely passed over to the other side as her defense of John Bellew, Clare's white husband, demonstrates. In the tea party scene (Chapter 3) Irene had been disgusted by Clare's husband's racist remarks. However, in this later scene, she defends "his side of the thing" (200). Irene begs Clare "to be reasonable" when the latter threatens to kill John.

At this point in the text, unorthodox alliances are drawn between the characters. Suddenly, Irene begins to side with Clare's white husband, John Bellew. If one believes that Clare and Brian Redfield are having an affair, then Irene's sympathy for John might be the result of their similar position as cuckolds. McDowell might read Irene's desire to spare John's life as a symptom of Irene's need for security and the "cover" of heterosexual marriage. However, in my reading, Irene also sympathizes with John's position because she sees Clare's as he does—as "Nig."

Irene's ability to murder Clare depends in part upon her ability to objectify her in this manner—to read her disturbingly as the embodiment of her fantasies and of her worst nightmare. Irene begins to frame Clare (literally and figuratively) when she mentions that "Eighteenth-century France would have been a marvelous setting for Clare" (216) [61]. Here, Irene hints at the fact that Clare has revolutionary tendencies at the same time she marks Clare as an historicized Other—as the bearer of a cruel material history. This view of Clare prepares the way for Irene's decision to destroy that "thing" which has terrorized her with thoughts of Past and Passing throughout the text.

7. Toni Morrison, *Sula* (New York: New American Library, 1973), 120.

In perhaps the most blatant incident that prefigures Clare's murder, Irene sees "Clare's ivory face . . . what it always was, beautiful and caressing. Or maybe today a little masked. Unrevealing. Unaltered and undisturbed by any emotion within or without" (220) [65]. Irene is looking at Clare during yet another tea party. Suddenly, "Rage boils up in [Irene] . . . there is a slight crash. On the floor at her feet lays a shattered cup. Dark stains dot the bright rug [and] spread" (221) [66]. Irene has dropped a cup on purpose or so she tells Hugh Wentworth. She explains that the cup was

> the ugliest thing that your [white] ancestors, the charming confederates ever owned. I have forgotten how many thousands of years ago it was that Brian's great-great granduncle owned it. But it has, or had, a good hoary history. It was brought north by way of the . . . underground . . . I've never figured out a way of getting rid of it until about five minutes ago. I had an inspiration. I had only to break it, and I was rid of it forever. So simple! (222) [67]

The cup, like Clare, is an ugly material reminder of Irene's heritage which she can no longer bear. It is a relic of the Civil War and as a broken vessel it is analogous not only to the broken body of the Nation, but it also foreshadows Clare's own broken body at the end of the novel. In this deluded moment, Irene figures out a way to rid her stable life of Clare Kendry and her "menace of impermanence" (229) [72]. The scene ends with Irene saying, "Goodbye . . . Goodbye" (222) not only to her departing tea-guests but to Clare Kendry as well. Thus, Irene Redfield, like a good upstanding citizen, elects to fight for *her* country. Irene follows her instinct to preserve her property and her place in the world of rising towers. She will do her duty and defend her territory, her position, her ideology.

The closing scene in the Finale begins by stating that "the year was getting on towards its end"—so too the narrative and more significantly, Clare's life. Symbolically, the last battle between Irene and Clare takes place at the end of December. Clare, who looks "radiant in her shining red gown" (223) [74], arrives at Irene's house ready to attend what is most likely the last party of the season. Before Clare's arrival, Irene has had one of her frequent arguments with her husband, Brian Redfield. The fact that Irene is most often referred to by her married name, Mrs. Redfield, is somewhat of a red herring; for Brian Redfield is ideologically and iconographically allied with Clare Kendry. Again, we see that Irene occupies a similar position to Clare's white husband: both she and John Bellew are married to that which, ideologically, they most despise.

Irene detests Brian because he refuses to conform to her vision of their marriage as exemplifying the status quo. Brian, who hates

America, does not want to be the stereotypical Black bourgeois doctor with a light-skinned wife and two sons. He would like to practice medicine in Brazil—to go beyond the bounds of conventional expectations; but of course, Irene for whom status is everything finds this problematic. In this last chapter, Irene argues with Brian about a dinner-table topic that Irene believes is "inappropriate." It is an argument over ideology.

Irene believes that the topic of "why only Blacks are lynched" is something that should be ignored. No doubt she believes this because lynching as an American phenomenon is intertwined with the history of race, sexuality, and class conflict. Irene follows her prudish sensibilities and demands that the discussion end; but not before Brian explains to his sons that Blacks are killed because they are the most hated (194) [73]. The subtext in this conversation is clear/Clare. Irene kills Clare in part because Clare is Black and "most hated." Irene

> Sees with perfect clearness that dark truth which she had from that first October afternoon felt about Clare Kendry and of which Clare herself had once warned her—that she got the things she wanted because she met the great conditions of conquest, sacrifice . . . If Clare was freed, anything might happen. (236) [77]

As Irene, Brian and Clare walk toward the party, Brian asks Clare about "nigger-power."[8] Not only does Clare instantly get the joke, but she unabashedly tells about her father being a janitor in the "good ole days" (236) [77] and of frequently having to walk up long flights of stairs. Again, we see Clare allied, at least metaphorically, with her poorer Black past.

The scene describes Clare Kendry's only explicit ascent in the novel. Unlike Irene's consistent upwardly mobile ascents, this scene prepares Clare to take her "free fall." As she climbs, Clare looks down and notices a "lovely garden with undisturbed snow" (236) [00]. Slowly, she makes her way to the Freeland's top-floor apartment which is, for her, the "freeland" (i.e., heaven) so often evoked in Negro spirituals.

Moments before her death, Clare is the epitome of composure. This last vision of Clare suggests that she went to her death knowingly and perhaps proudly as a Black woman. Thus Clare does not die a "sacrificial lamb on the altar of social and literary convention"[9] rather, "she seemed unaware of any danger . . . There was even a faint smile on her full, red lips and in her shining eyes" (238–39)

8. It is interesting to note that "nigger-power" is self-power; it relies upon self-empowerment and is not dependent upon technology.
9. McDowell, xxx.

[79]. This reading, of course, does not leave out the possibility of Clare's suicide. I believe that Irene misses and misreads the subtlety of Clare's behavior in this final moment. As I have shown, Clare has never been afraid of being "found out"—that is Irene's fear. Indeed, Clare might have looked forward to the moment when Bellew would realize that he had been duped by his wife. Such is the natural culmination of Clare's tea in Chicago (Chapter Three, Section I); but Irene never understood that event fully nor is she able to grasp Clare's role as a triumphant trickster. Irene is much too myopic, too literal, too far removed from a certain class of her race to comprehend.

Clare's smile finally maddens Irene so that "she runs across the room, her terror tinged with ferocity, and" (239) [79] the next instant, Clare's body is seen smashed on the pavement below. While recognizing that the text is not explicit in its ending (we do not know if Clare commits suicide, is killed by Bellew, or pushed out the window by Irene); it seems to me that my reading points to Irene as the murderer. Irene eulogizes Clare and reveals her own fraught fixation for her former friend. She reports:

> One moment Clare had been there, a vital glowing thing, like a flame of red and gold. The next she was gone . . . Gone! The soft white face, the bright hair, the disturbing scarlet mouth, the dreaming eyes, the caressing smile, the whole torturing loveliness that had been Clare Kendry. That beauty that had torn at Irene's placid life. Gone! The mocking daring, the gallantry of her pose, and the ringing bells of laughter. (239) [80]

Although McDowell reads this passage as one "in which all the erotic images used to describe Clare throughout the novel converge" (xxix), it also inscribes Clare's racial and class identities which have been represented similarly (e.g., a scarlet spear, the subversive smile that grins, her Negro eyes, her alarming laugh, etc.). *Passing* closes as Irene "sinks down under a great heaviness" (242) [82] which turns everything "dark" (242) [82]. In this final scene, *Passing* reads as a biting critique of Black bourgeoisie ideologies. Although Irene Westover succeeds in squelching the revolutionary possibilities inherent in Clare's character, Clare Kendry remains an intriguingly problematized and formidable "Black" adversary in Irene's world of rising towers, conventional romance, and stable class structure. One wonders if "beating against the walled prison of Irene's thoughts was the shunned fancy that, though absent, Clare Kendry was still present, . . . close" (224) [68].

HELENA MICHIE

From Sororophobia†

* * *

If *Quicksand* links the exploration of race to sexuality through a series of sororophobic contrasts, *Passing* intensifies the relationship between racial and sexual identity by focusing the story more closely on a single pair of women. *Passing*, even more than *Quicksand*, explores the constructedness and the relationality of race and sexuality. Both are contingent terms; race and sexuality find their meaning only through a series of binary oppositions that get embodied as characterological and positional differences between the two main female characters, Irene Redfield and Clare Bellew. The relationality that characterizes the novel's sense of racial and sexual identity gets embodied as a complicated, ambivalent, and important relationship in which the two women act out, sometimes simultaneously, the positions of childhood friends, sexual rivals, potential lovers, and, finally—according to most readings of the novel—murderer and victim.

Passing begins with the construction of self through difference. In one of the novel's first scenes, where Irene and Clare meet again after many years, both are "passing" for white, but they are passing differently. Irene is passing, as she says later, "only for convenience," only publicly and only temporarily; she is taking advantage of her light skin to drink an iced tea at an exclusive restaurant. For Clare passing is a way of life: her husband, an unabashed racist, thinks she is white. The scene of their encounter in the rooftop restaurant of Chicago's Drayton Hotel is a marvelous encounter of loyalties, allegiances, and duplicities, in which Irene, from whose point of view the novel unfolds, struggles to come to terms with the degree and kind of Clare's otherness to herself.

The scene opens with an interchange of gazes as Irene watches Clare watching her. The clash of gazes is a battle both for control and identity, as Irene finally turns Clare's [gaze?] toward herself to wonder if Clare has seen through her attempt to pass. The visual economy set up by this exchange of looks complicates feminist notions of the heterosexual gaze, as the two women negotiate their differences and their power through looking and turning away. Irene begins with a casual appraisal of the other woman's face and clothing: "An

---

† From Helena Michie, *Sororophobia: Differences among Women in Literature and Culture* (New York: Oxford University Press, 1992), pp. 147–54. Reprinted by permission of Oxford University Press. Bracketed page numbers refer to this Norton Critical Edition. Footnotes have been omitted.

attractive-looking woman, was Irene's opinion, with those dark, almost black, eyes and that wide mouth like a scarlet flower against the ivory of her skin. Nice clothes too, just right for the weather, thin and cool without being mussy, as summer things are so apt to be." Irene's evaluative glance objectifies the other woman; "that mouth" and "those eyes" suggest a distance appropriate to this almost instinctive judgment of one woman by another. For a brief moment, the more general allusion to the propensity of summer clothes to be "mussy" marks an identification of Irene with the unknown woman, a sense of a common feminine problem, an inhabitation, however brief, of the body of the other woman. Irene's gaze, with its familiar attention to the contrast between skin and clothing, mimics that of Larsen's narrator in both *Quicksand* and *Passing*; again, it suggests a female self constructed out of difference and opposition that takes the form of a subtle dialogue between colors.

Irene's summary glance judges not only the other woman's beauty, but her sexuality as well. Irene takes in and tries to evaluate the smile Clare bestows on the waiter: "it was an odd sort of smile. Irene couldn't quite define it, but she was sure that she would have classed it, coming from another woman, as being just a shade too provocative for a waiter." (149) [10] Before Irene recognizes Clare, the smile is mysterious, hard to categorize: nonetheless Irene's categories, inescapably sexual, remain in place. The hypothetical "other woman" ironically foreshadows Clare's identity and the part she will play in Irene's life. After their mutual recognition, Clare smiles at the waiter again, and this time "Irene was sure that it was too provocative for a waiter." (152) [12] Irene's judgment depends on a careful calibration of race and class; she is able to "class" Clare's smile only when she knows the background of the other woman. The smile, "a shade too provocative for a waiter," must be calculated not only in terms of color, but in terms of the slight shades of color that make up the racial and psychological grammar of this novel. It is no accident that Irene's final judgment is articulated in sexual terms, for eroticism is the lexicon into which all differences are finally translated.

If Irene conventionally, almost automatically, "sizes up" the other woman, she also, out of convention, turns away. Clare's returning gaze cuts across the visual etiquette of the glance:

> The dress decided, (Irene's) thoughts had gone back to the snag of Ted's book, her unseeing eyes far away on the lake, when by some sixth sense she was acutely aware that someone was watching her. . . . Very slowly she looked around, and into the dark eyes of the woman in the green frock at the next table. But she evidently failed to realized (sic) that such an intense interest as she was showing might be embarrassing, and continued to

> stare. Her demeanor was that of one who with utmost singleness of mind and purpose was determined to impress firmly and accurately each detail of Irene's features upon her memory for all time, nor (sic) showed the slightest trace of disconcertment at having been detected in her steady scrutiny. (149) [10]

Clare's power throughout the novel will lie in her ability to cut through convention, her ability not to turn other people's opinions, assumptions, glances, back upon herself. Her eyes are magnetic, seductive; Irene turns *into* them as if she is drawn not only to but inside Clare. Clare, on the other hand, cannot, will not internalize; she draws people in without allowing them to change her.

The battle of the gazes is over, not so much when Irene establishes Clare's reason for gazing, as when Irene turns her own gaze toward herself, first superficially—"had she, in her haste in the taxi put her hat on backwards? . . . Something wrong with her dress?"—and then more deeply: "Did that woman, could that woman, somehow know that here before her very eyes on the roof of the Drayton sat a Negro?" (149–50) [10] The ironies here are manifold: that Clare, whose "passing" is so much more dangerous, so much more problematic than Irene's, should cause Irene to question her own safety; that Clare, who refuses, at least as the narrative itself presents it, any self-reflection, should produce such reflection, such reflexiveness, in another woman; that Irene should at this point calibrate her racial identity against Clare's supposed whiteness when later she will calibrate it against the always unquantifiable sense of her blackness.

The scene sets up the axes of difference between the women—whiteness and blackness, proper and improper sexuality—that will remain the constant structuring principles of the novel while the position of the two women on these axes will shift from situation to situation, from moment to moment. The movement of the novel is always in the direction of the complication and the eroticization of difference: as the novel progresses, the stakes of difference also get higher, its price more painful and its negotiation more violent and destructive.

McDowell sees *Passing* as a novel in code, where racial difference provides a cover for questions of sexuality, where racial "passing" becomes an oblique way of talking about the covert operation of lesbian desire between Irene and Clare:

> In *Passing* (Larsen) uses a technique found commonly in narratives by Afro-American and woman novelists with a "dangerous" story to tell: "safe" themes, plots, and conventions are used as the protective cover underneath which lie more dangerous subplots. Larsen envelops the subplot of Irene's developing if

> unnamed and unacknowledged desire for Clare in the safe and familiar plot of racial passing. (McDowell, p. xxx)[1]

While I have no trouble with a lesbian reading of the relationship between Irene and Clare, I do think the hierarchization of the two plots is unnecessary and untrue to the complex and contradictory gestures toward the presentation of selfhood that this novel attempts. While on a narrative level racial passing is a relatively "safe" topic that cozily establishes Larsen in the literary tradition of the tragic mulatto, passing—on the level of story—is fraught with danger. Clare continually risks her husband's violence if she is ever found out; his hatred of "niggers" and "black devils" is made abundantly clear in the wonderfully complex tea party scene in which he openly avows his racism as he is surrounded, unknown to him, by three black women who represent various degrees of passing.

It is true that as the novel progresses, racial passing is continually eroticized, both by Clare's presumed affair with Irene's husband and by Irene's conflicted desire for Clare. In the end, of course, it is not John Bellow who pushes Clare out the window, but Irene, the other woman, in whose murderous impulse questions of race and sexuality come fatally together. Racial passing and sexuality are inextricable; both are brought painfully to bear, for instance, on Irene's decision not to betray Clare to her husband: Irene keeps quiet, as we shall see, because of a curious mixture of racial loyalty and sexual self-preservation. No matter how self-deluded or hypocritical we find Irene, the truth is that she is herself torn between racial and sexual alliances; McDowell's privileging of sexuality, her sense that race is merely a "cover," makes Irene too scheming, too sure of herself in a novel in which, as in *Quicksand*, the category of self is constantly under investigation. The privileging of one category over the other also disrupts the almost obsessively neat balance of race and sex in the novel—a balance and an obsessiveness that McDowell would probably see as itself an indication of the novel's need to provide a tidy framework for a disruptive "subplot." Nonetheless, Irene's relations to everyone in the story are mediated equally by sexual and racial concerns; this is clear with Clare, but also in her half-glimpsed relations with her children: Irene has two arguments with her husband about Brian junior—one in which she asks Brian not to encourage his son to talk about sex and one in which she tells him not to tell Brian junior too much about the "race problem." Both problems are unspeakable for Irene, both are spoken through her by the structure of the novel.

Both race and sex get explored through female difference in this novel as in *Quicksand*. *Passing*, however, complicates an already

---

1. For an excerpted version of this essay, see pp. 363–79 in this Norton Critical Edition.

eroticized notion of female difference by simultaneously making Clare and Irene rivals for Brian's affections and by making more explicit than in *Quicksand* their desire for each other. Again, this does not seem to me an "either or" situation; just as in the dance scene in *Quicksand* Helga feels desire for and through Audrey Denney, so Irene oscillates between—to the extent that they can be separated at all—desire for Clare and identification with her.

Both kinds of erotics work through sororophobic contrast, a contrast that simultaneously links *Passing* to *Quicksand* and suggests that *Passing* somehow moves beyond its predecessor. Clare acts in this novel as Helga does in *Quicksand*; it is as if *Passing* is an attempt to tell *Quicksand* from Anne's point of view; Irene even has a moment of introspection almost identical to Anne's when she acknowledges the ability of the other woman to feel more, and more deeply, than she can:

> Her voice was brittle. For into (Irene's) mind had come a thought, strange and irrelevant, a suspicion, that had surprised and shocked her and driven her to her feet. It was that in spite of her determined selfishness the woman before her was yet capable of heights and depths of feeling that she Irene Redfield, had never know. Indeed, never cared to know. (195) [47]

Like many passages in *Passing*, this one takes advantage of pronominal confusion to make a point. The "she" here as elsewhere is constantly shifting, and we need the "Irene Redfield" of the penultimate sentence to make sense of the paragraph. The explanatory phrase simultaneously suggests the stability of a self we could call Irene Redfield, and works as a defensive gesture that exposes the relationality of self-making. The reassuring contrasts Irene is constantly invoking between herself and Clare are undermined both by their similarities and Irene's inexplicable, to her, desire *for* Clare.

Like Helga, who, in the dance scene in *Quicksand*, simultaneously identifies with and desires Audrey Denney, Irene feels at the same time a desire for and a desire to be Clare. Irene's senses of self and sexuality come tenuously together in Clare's presence, over Clare's body, in response to Clare's beauty; as we have seen, that sense of self is itself divided and shifting, but it shifts primarily in response to Clare.

At the end of the first half of the novel, Irene thinks, for the second time, that she has exorcised Clare from her life. After the humiliating scene at Clare's tea party in which she was forced to pass in front of John Bellew, she has no desire to see or to hear from Clare again. Clare reenters Irene's life and the narrative through the mail; her letter, on "foreign" paper, directed in purple ink, lies at the bottom of Irene's "little pile of mail," looking "out of place and alien." It is the only letter without a return address. (143) [5] This letter scene represents an attempt on Irene's part to construe Clare as "foreign," to persuade herself that she and Clare live in different worlds. The lack of return address suggests, besides secrecy, Clare's continual denigration of the universe she inhabits with her husband, her insistence that, despite her decision to pass, Harlem is somehow the pertinent address: that it is still, in fact, her home.

Canonically, mysterious letters suggest love affairs, and it is precisely as an affair that Clare's return to Harlem is structured. Not only must Clare hide her visits to Harlem from her husband as she would an extramarital relationship, but her rhetoric about Harlem and its inhabitants is explicitly erotic. When she complains that Irene has not returned her letter, Clare claims that she has taken to haunting the post office for a reply: "every day I went to that nasty little post-office place. I'm sure they were all beginning to think that I'd been carrying on an illicit love-affair." (194) [46] The suggestion of adultery points simultaneously at Clare's future relationship with Brian and at her feelings for Irene; it also suggests what might be called an erotics of passing; both Irene and Brian speak at times of the excitement and danger both passing and "going back" entail.

Irene's response to Clare's sudden appearance in her bedroom is—to her—completely unexpected. She is shocked out of her disapproval and composure by Clare's beauty: "Looking at the woman before her, Irene Redfield had a sudden inexplicable onrush of affectionate feeling. Reaching out, she grasped Clare's two hands with her own and cried with something like awe in her voice: 'Dear God! But aren't you lovely, Clare!' " (194) [46] This is only the first of several scenes in Irene's bedroom where Irene works out her complicated relationships with her husband and her friend: alone with Clare in her own bedroom, Irene seems capable of admiring Clare without resentment or envy; it is only when the two move downstairs and into the gaze first of Brian and then of the Harlem community, that Irene sees Clare's beauty as a threat to herself. When Irene first descends the stairs to meet Clare and take her to her first Harlem dance, she makes a "choked little exclamation of admiration at Clare's beauty." It is Brian's presence that constructs an opposition between Clare and Irene. Under Brian's gaze, Clare, "exquisite, golden, fragrant, flaunting, in a stately gown of shining black taffeta," makes "Irene, with her new rose-colored chiffon frock ending at the knees, and her cropped curls, (feel) dowdy and commonplace." (203) [53] Alone, the two women have their differences; in public, with Brian, these differences are frozen into canonical forms.

Clare's body takes on a different value, a difference valence, under Irene's private gaze and under a more public, heterosexual one. To Brian, they appear as conventional rivals; he even refers to Irene's assessment of Clare's intelligence as "feline"; to a casual observer, a conventional gaze, Irene is simply being "catty." And indeed, Brian is, in this novel, a stock figure, a sign of a conventionally rivalrous plot, a plot that in some sense, for all the pain it causes her, Irene seems desperate to enter. It is important to note that Irene has no real evidence that Brian and Clare have actually embarked on a sexual relationship; it is simply the easiest and most plausible solution of racial and sexual identity infinitely more painful than "infidelity" as it is usually construed.

Significantly, the scene where Irene "discovers" Brian's infidelity takes place in their bedroom as Irene makes up her face for one of her endless series of tea parties. Brian has invited Clare in spite of Irene's reluctance; it is this conflict that sets up the discovery. After Irene explains why she did not invite Clare, Brian is silent: "He continued to stand beside the bed, seeming to look at nothing in particular. Certainly not at her. True, his gaze was on her, but in it there was some quality that made her feel that at that moment she was no more to him than a pane of glass through which he stared." (216) [61] Once again, Irene is the subject of the gaze; this one unmakes her, renders her invisible. Unlike Clare's more overtly dangerous gaze on the roof of the Drayton, this does not take into account her face, her features, or her past. Irene both challenges and submits to the authority of this gaze by continuing, as Brian stares at and through her, to make up her face in the mirror, "complet(ing) the bright red arch of her full lips." Brian's gaze is a challenge to her self-making, her making up; despite the bright red mouth she creates, she is invisible.

It is in the mirror that Irene first sees what she reads as signs that her husband has been unfaithful:

> Brian's head came round with a jerk. His brows lifted in an odd surprise. Her voice, she realized, *had* gone queer. But she had an instinctive feeling that it hadn't been the whole cause of his attitude. And that little straightening motion of the shoulders. Hadn't it been like that of a man drawing himself up to receive a blow? Her fright was like a scarlet spear of terror leaping at her heart. Clare Kendry! So that was it! Impossible. It couldn't be. In the mirror before her she saw that he was still regarding her with that air of slight amazement. She dropped her eyes to the jars and bottles on the table and began to fumble among them with hands whose fingers shook slightly. "Of course," she said carefully. "I'm glad you did (invite Clare). And in spite of my recent remarks, Clare does add to any party. She's so easy on the eyes." (217) [62]

It is tempting to argue that the adulterer Irene sees in the mirror is not her husband but herself, that this is a scene in which she realizes her own desires and projects them onto a tired story of sexual betrayal. Whatever the explicitly erotic relationship between Irene and Clare, however, this is still a scene about self-making, the production of public and private self through sexuality and color. The red spear of anger mimics the red arch of Irene's lips as her public persona becomes internalized, private, and vulnerable. Irene's contention that Clare is "easy on the eyes" is both a joking pretense of alignment with a male desiring gaze and an appropriation of that gaze in self-assertion and self-defense. Clare is "easy on the eyes" both because she is beautiful and because she allows Irene access to a desiring and inquiring exchange of gazes which Brian does not. Again, in one sentence, Irene moves between identification and distancing as she articulates in the most deliberately offhand and hackneyed terms the convolutions of sororophobic looking.

Again, it is not because Clare takes her husband away from her— whether she wants to do this in the first place is completely unclear— that Clare is dangerous. It is because, in this exchange of gazes as in the one on the rooftop, she forces Irene to look at herself and the constructedness of her marriage, her sexuality, and her racial position. Clare challenges Irene through the idiom of displacement: from the beginning of the novel, Irene is desperate to defend her social, racial, and geographical position against all "foreign" challenges whether they be Brian's desire to move to Brazil or Clare's entry into her life. It is as a challenge to self-making that Clare menaces Irene; she can neither keep Clare in the place of difference nor in the place of sameness. Clare is other, but at the same time someone with whom Irene must at moments identify.

Clare's unmaking, her undoing of Irene, must ultimately be challenged by a final and instinctive displacement; Irene's murderous dislodging of Clare from her life, from Harlem, and from the windowsill on which she is leaning while she confronts the intrusion of her husband John Bellew into her "other" life in Harlem. The instinctive violence of Irene's gesture dramatizes in a single instant the intensity of the sexual and racial conflict between the two women. Irene takes her revenge on the body that has both tantalized and infuriated her; when she mourns, she mourns her friend's "glorious body mutilated." Even in death, Clare is not exorcised; neither, significantly, is the entanglement of Irene's body with Clare's. The novel's final paragraph describes Irene's swoon into unconsciousness as her body mimics—again with a difference—the trajectory of Clare's: "Her quaking knees gave way under her. She moaned and sank down, moaned again. Through the great heaviness that submerged and drowned her she was dimly conscious of strong arms lifting her up. Then everything was dark." (42) [82] Irene, unlike Clare, will rise again in life; the "strong arms"—perhaps John's—hold out that promise. She must first, however, travel through a darkness that is both her own and Clare's, a darkness whose completeness suggests a welcoming back into the world of Harlem, into a simpler and more comprehensive notion of race and community.

* * *

JUDITH BUTLER

Passing, Queering: Nella Larsen's Psychoanalytic Challenge†

Can identity be viewed other than as a by-product of a manhandling of life, one that, in fact, refers no more to a consistent pattern of sameness than to an inconsequential process of otherness?
—Trinh T. Minh-ha

A number of theoretical questions have been raised by the effort to think the relationship between feminism, psychoanalysis, and race studies. For the most part, psychoanalysis has been used by feminist theorists to theorize sexual difference as a distinct and fundamental set of linguistic and cultural relations. The philosopher Luce Irigaray has claimed that the question of sexual difference is *the* question for our time.[1] This privileging of sexual difference implies not only that sexual difference should be understood as more fundamental than other forms of difference, but that other forms of difference might be *derived* from sexual difference. This view also presumes that sexual difference constitutes an autonomous sphere of relations or disjunctions, and is not to be understood as articulated through or *as* other vectors of power.

What would it mean, on the other hand, to consider the assumption of sexual positions, the disjunctive ordering of the human as "masculine" or "feminine" as taking place not only through a heterosexualizing symbolic with its taboo on homosexuality, but through a complex set of racial injunctions which operate in part through the taboo on miscegenation. Further, how might we understand homosexuality and miscegenation to converge at and as the constitutive outside of a normative heterosexuality that is at once the regulation of a racially pure reproduction? To coin Marx, then, let us remember that the reproduction of the species will be articulated as the reproduction *of* rela-

† From Judith Butler, "Passing, Queering: Nella Larsen's Psychoanalytic Challenge." Copyright © 1993 from *Bodies That Matter: On the Discursive Limits of "Sex"* (New York: Routledge, 1993), pp. 167–85, 274–77. Reproduced by permission of Routledge/Taylor and Francis Group LLC. Bracketed page numbers refer to this Norton Critical Edition.
1. See Luce Irigaray, *Éthique de la différence sexuelle* (Paris: Minuit, 1984), p. 13.

tions of reproduction, that is, as the cathected site of a racialized version of the species in pursuit of hegemony through perpetuity, that requires and produces a normative heterosexuality in its service.[2] Conversely, the reproduction of heterosexuality will take different forms depending on how race and the reproduction of race are understood. And though there are clearly good historical reasons for keeping "race" and "sexuality" and "sexual difference" as separate analytic spheres, there are also quite pressing and significant historical reasons for asking how and where we might read not only their convergence, but the sites at which the one cannot be constituted save through the other. This is something other than juxtaposing distinct spheres of power, subordination, agency, historicity, and something other than a list of attributes separated by those proverbial commas (gender, sexuality, race, class), that usually mean that we have not yet figured out how to think the relations we seek to mark. Is there a way, then, to read Nella Larsen's text as engaging psychoanalytic assumptions not to affirm the primacy of sexual difference, but to articulate the convergent modalities of power by which sexual difference is articulated and assumed?

Consider, if you will, the following scene from Nella Larsen's *Passing*[3] in which Irene descends the stairs of her home to find Clare, in her desirable way, standing in the living room. At the moment Irene lights upon Clare, Brian, Irene's husband, appears to have found Clare as well. Irene thus finds Clare, finds her beautiful, but at the same time finds Brian finding Clare beautiful as well. The doubling will prove to be important. The narrative voice is sympathetic to Irene, but exceeds her perspective on those occasions on which Irene finds speaking to be impossible.

> She remembered her own little choked exclamation of admiration, when, on coming downstairs a few minutes later than she had intended, she had rushed into the living room where Brian was waiting and had found Clare there too. Clare, exquisite, golden, fragrant, flaunting, in a stately gown of shining black taffeta, whose long, full skirt lay in graceful folds about her slim golden feet; her glistening hair drawn smoothly back into a small twist at the nape of her neck; her eyes sparkling like dark jewels (233) [53].

Irene's exclamation of admiration is never voiced, choked back it seems, retained, preserved as a kind of seeing that does not make its way into speech. She would have spoken, but the choking appears to

---

2. Freud. *Totem and Taboo* attests to the inseparability of the discourse of species reproduction and the discourse of race. In that text, one might consider the twin uses of "development" as (a) the movement toward an advanced state of culture and (b) the "achievement" of genital sexuality within monogamous heterosexuality.

3. *Passing*, in *An Intimation of Things Distant: The Collected Fiction of Nella Larsen*, Charles Larson, ed., forward by Marita Golden (New York: Anchor Books, 1992), pp. 163–276.

stifle her voice; what she finds is Brian waiting, Brian finding Clare as well, and Clare herself. The grammar of the description fails to settle the question of who desires whom: "she had rushed into the living room where Brian was waiting and had found Clare there too": is it Irene who finds Clare, or Brian, or do they find her together? And what is it that they find in her, such that they no longer find each other, but mirror each other's desire as each turns toward Clare. Irene will stifle the words which would convey her admiration. Indeed, the exclamation is choked, deprived of air; the exclamation fills the throat and thwarts her speaking. The narrator emerges to speak the words Irene might have spoken: "exquisite, golden, fragrant, flaunting." The narrator thus states what remains caught in Irene's throat, which suggests that Larsen's narrator serves the function of exposing more than Irene herself can risk. In most cases where Irene finds herself unable to speak, the narrator supplies the words. But when it comes to explaining exactly how Clare dies at the end of the novel, the narrator proves as speechless as Irene.

The question of what can and cannot be spoken, what can and cannot be publicly exposed, is raised throughout the text, and it is linked with the larger question of the dangers of public exposure of both color and desire. Significantly, it is precisely what Irene describes as Clare's flaunting that Irene admires, even as Irene knows that Clare, who passes as white, not only flaunts but hides—indeed, is always hiding *in* that very flaunting. Clare's disavowal of her color compels Irene to take her distance from Clare, to refuse to respond to her letters, to try to close her out of her life. And though Irene voices a moral objection to Clare's passing as white, it is clear that Irene engages many of the same social conventions of passing as Clare. Indeed, when they both meet after a long separation, they are both in a rooftop cafe passing as white. And yet, according to Irene, Clare goes too far, passes as white not merely on occasion, but in her life, and in her marriage. Clare embodies a certain kind of sexual daring that Irene defends herself against, for the marriage cannot hold Clare, and Irene finds herself drawn by Clare, wanting to be her, but also wanting her. It is this risk-taking, articulated at once as a racial crossing and sexual infidelity, that alternately entrances Irene and fuels her moral condemnation of Clare with renewed ferocity.

After Irene convinces herself that Brian and Clare are having an affair, Irene watches Clare work her seduction and betrayal on an otherwise unremarkable Dave Freeland at a party. The seduction works through putting into question both the sanctity of marriage and the clarity of racial demarcations:

> Scraps of their conversation, in Clare's husky voice, floated over to her; ". . . always admired you . . . so much about you long

ago . . . everybody says so . . . no one but you . . ." And more of the same. The man hung rapt on her words, though he was the husband of Felise Freeland, and the author of novels that revealed a man of perception and a devastating irony. And he fell for such pishposh! And all because Clare had a trick of sliding down ivory lids over astonishing black eyes and then lifting them suddenly and turning on a caressing smile (254) [66].

Here it is the trick of passing itself that appears to eroticize Clare, the covering over of astonishing black by ivory, the sudden concession of the secret, the magical transformation of a smile into a caress. It is the changeability itself, the dream of a metamorphosis, where that changeableness signifies a certain freedom, a class mobility afforded by whiteness that constitutes the power of that seduction. This time Irene's own vision of Clare is followed not only by a choking of speech, but by a rage that leads to the shattering of her tea cup, and the interruption of chatter. The tea spreads on the carpet like rage, like blood, figured as dark color itself suddenly uncontained by the strictures of whiteness: "Rage boiled up in her. / There was a slight crash. On the floor at her feet lay the shattered cup. Dark stains dotted the bright rug. Spread. The chatter stopped. Went on. Before her. Zulena gathered up the white fragments" (254) [66].

This shattering prefigures the violence that ends the story, in which Clare is discovered by Bellew, her white racist husband, in the company of African-Americans, her color "outed," which initiates her swift and quite literal demise: with Irene ambiguously positioned next to Clare with a hand on her arm, Clare falls from the window, and dies on the street below. Whether she jumped or was pushed remains ambiguous: "What happened next, Irene Redfield never afterwards allowed herself to remember. Never clearly. One moment Clare had been there, a vital glowing thing, like a flame of red and gold. The next she was gone" (271) [79].

Prior to this moment, Bellew climbs the stairs to the Harlem apartment where the salon is taking place, and discovers Clare there; her being there is sufficient to convince him that she is black. Blackness is not primarily a visual mark in Larsen's story, not only because Irene and Clare are both light-skinned, but because what can be seen, what qualifies as a visible marking, is a matter of being able to read a marked body in relation to unmarked bodies, where unmarked bodies constitute the currency of normative whiteness. Clare passes not only because she is light-skinned, but because she refuses to introduce her blackness into conversation, and so withholds the conversational marker which would counter the hegemonic presumption that she is white. Irene herself appears to "pass" insofar as she enters conversations which presume whiteness as the norm without contesting that assumption. This dissociation from blackness that she performs through silence is reversed at the end of the story in which she is exposed to Bellew's white gaze in clear association with African-Americans. It is only on the condition of an association that conditions a naming that her color becomes legible. He cannot "see" her as black before that association, and he claims to her face with unrestrained racism that he would never associate with blacks. If he associates with her, she cannot be black. But if she associates with blacks, she becomes black, where the sign of blackness is contracted, as it were, through proximity, where "race" itself is figured as a contagion transmissable through proximity. The added presumption is that if he were to associate with blacks, the boundaries of his own whiteness, and surely that of his children, would no longer be easily fixed. Paradoxically, his own racist passion *requires* that association; he cannot be white without blacks and without the constant disavowal of his relation to them. It is only through that disavowal that his whiteness is constituted, and through the institutionalization of that disavowal that his whiteness is perpetually—but anxiously—reconstituted.[4]

Bellew's speech is overdetermined by this anxiety over racial boundaries. Before he knows that Clare is black, he regularly calls her "Nig," and it seems that this term of degradation and disavowal is passed between them as a kind of love toy. She allows herself to be eroticized by it, takes it on, acting as if it were the most impossible appellation for her. That he calls her "Nig" suggests that he knows or that there is a kind of knowingness in the language he speaks. And yet, if he can call her that and remain her husband, he cannot know. In this sense, she defines the fetish, an object of desire about which one says, "I know very well that this cannot be, but I desire this all the same," a formulation which implies its equivalence: "Precisely because this cannot be, I desire it all the more." And yet Clare is a fetish that holds in place both the rendering of Clare's blackness as an exotic source of excitation and the denial of her blackness altogether. Here the "naming" is riddled with the knowledge that he claims not to have; he notes that she is becoming darker all the time; the term of degradation permits him to see and not to see at the same time. The term sustains her desire as a kind of disavowal, one which structures not only the ambivalence in his desire for Clare, but the erotic ambivalence by which he constitutes the fragile boundaries of his own racial identity. To reformulate an earlier claim, then: although he claims that he would never associate with African-

---

4. This suggests one sense in which "race" might be construed as performative. Bellew produces his whiteness through a ritualized production of its sexual barriers. This anxious repetition accumulates the force of the material effect of a circumscribed whiteness, but its boundary concedes its tenuous status precisely because it requires the "blackness" that it excludes. In this sense, a dominant "race" is constructed (in the sense of *materialized*) through reiteration and exclusion.

Americans, he requires the association and its disavowal for an erotic satisfaction that is indistinguishable from his desire to display his own racial purity.

In fact, it appears that the uncertain border between black and white is precisely what he eroticizes, what he needs in order to make Clare into the exotic object to be dominated.[5] His name, Bellew, like bellow, is itself a howl, the long howl of white male anxiety in the face of the racially ambiguous woman whom he idealizes and loathes. She represents the spectre of a racial ambiguity that must be conquered. But "Bellew" is also the instrument that fans the flame, the illumination that Clare, literally "light," in some sense *is*. Her luminescence is dependent on the life he breathes into her; her evanescence is equally a function of that power. "One moment Clare had been there, a vital glowing thing, like a flame of red and gold. The next she was gone. / There was a grasp of horror, and above it a sound not quite human, like a beast in agony. 'Nig! My God! Nig!' " Bellew bellows, and at that moment Clare vanishes from the window (271) [79]. His speech vacillates between degradation and deification, but opens and closes on a note of degradation. The force of that vacillation illuminated inflames Clare, but also works to extinguish her, to blow her out. Clare exploits Bellew's need to see only what he wants to see, working not so much the appearance of whiteness, but the vacillation between black and white as a kind of erotic lure. His final naming closes down that vacillation, but functions also as a fatal condemnation—or so it seems.

For it is, after all, Irene's hand which is last seen on Clare's arm, and the narrator, who is usually able to say what Irene cannot, appears drawn into Irene's nonnarrativizable trauma, blanking out, withdrawing at the crucial moment when we expect to learn whose agency it was that catapulted Clare from the window and to her death below. That Irene feels guilt over Clare's death is not quite reason enough to believe that Irene pushed her, since one can easily feel guilty about a death one merely wished would happen even when one knows that one's wish could not be the proximate cause of the death. The gap in the narrative leaves open whether Clare jumped, Irene pushed, or the force of Bellew's words literally bellowed her out the window. It is, I would suggest, this consequential gap, and the triangulation that surrounds it, that occasions a rethinking of psychoanalysis, in particular, of the social and psychic status of "killing judgments." How are we to explain the chain that leads from judgment to exposure to death, as it operates through the interwoven vectors of sexuality and race?

5. This is like the colonized subject who must resemble the colonizer to a certain degree, but who is prohibited from resembling the colonizer too well. For a fuller description of this dynamic, see Homi Bhabha, "Of Mimicry and Man," p. 126.

Clare's fall: is this a joint effort, or is it at least an action whose causes must remain not fully knowable, not fully traceable? This is an action ambiguously executed, in which the agency of Irene and Clare is significantly confused, and this confusion of agency takes place in relation to the violating speech of the white man. We can read this "finale," as Larsen calls it, as rage boiling up, shattering, leaving shards of whiteness, shattering the veneer of whiteness. Even as it appears that Clare's veneer of whiteness is shattered, it is Bellew's as well; indeed, it is the veneer by which the white project of racial purity is sustained. For Bellew thinks that he would never associate with blacks, but he cannot be white without his "Nig," without the lure of an association that he must resist, without the spectre of a racial ambiguity that he must subordinate and deny. Indeed, he reproduces that racial line by which he seeks to secure his whiteness through producing black women as the necessary and impossible object of desire, as the fetish in relation to which his own whiteness is anxiously and persistently secured.

There are clearly risks in trying to think in psychoanalytic terms about Larsen's story, which, after all, published in 1929, belongs to the tradition of the Harlem Renaissance, and ought properly to be read in the context of that cultural and social world. Whereas many critics have read the text as a tragic story of the social position of the mulatto, others have insisted that the story's brilliance is to be found in its psychological complexity. It seems to me that perhaps one need not choose between the historical and social specificity of the novel, as it has been brought to light by Barbara Christian, Gloria Hull, Hazel Carby, Amritjit Singh, and Mary Helen Washington, on the one hand, and the psychological complexity of cross-identification and jealousy in the text as it has been discussed by Claudia Tate, Cheryl Wall, Mary Mabel Youmans, and Deborah McDowell.[6] Both Tate and

6. Where references in the text are made to the following authors, they are to the following studies unless otherwise indicated: Houston A. Baker, Jr., *Modernism and the Harlem Renaissance* (Chicago: Chicago University Press, 1987); Robert Bone, *The Negro Novel in America* (New Haven: Yale University Press, 1958); Hazel Carby, *Reconstructing Womanhood: The Emergence of the Afro-American Woman Novelist* (London and New York: Oxford University Press, 1987); Barbara Christian, *Black Women Novelists: The Development of a Tradition 1892–1976* (Westport, Ct.: Greenwood Press, 1980) and "Trajectories of Self-Definition: Placing Contemporary Afro-American Women's Fiction," in Marjórie Pryse and Hortense J. Spillers, eds., *Conjuring: Black Women, Fiction, and Literary Tradition* (Bloomington: Indiana University Press, 1985), pp. 233–48; Henry Louis Gates, Jr., *Figures in Black: Words, Signs, and the "Racial" Self* (New York and London: Oxford University Press, 1987); Nathan Huggins, *Harlem Renaissance* (New York and London: Oxford University Press, 1971); Gloria Hull, *Color, Sex, and Poetry: Three Women Writers of the Harlem Renaissance* (Bloomington: Indiana University Press, 1987); Deborah E. McDowell, "Introduction" in *Quicksand and Passing* (New Brunswick: Rutgers University Press, 1986) [reprinted in this edition, p. 363]; Jacquelyn Y. McLendon, "Self-Representation as Art in the Novels of Nella Larsen," in Janice Morgan and Colette T. Hall, eds., *Redefining Autobiography in Twentieth-Century Fiction* (New York: Garland, 1991); Hiroko Sato, "Under the Harlem Shadow: A Study of Jessie Faucet and Nella Larsen," in Arno [sic] Bontemps, ed., *The Harlem Renaissance Remembered* (New York: Dodd, 1972), pp. 63–89; Amritjit

McDowell suggest that critics have split over whether this story ought to be read as a story about race and, in particular, as part of the tragic genre of the mulatto, or whether it ought to be read as psychologically complex and, as both McDowell and Carby insist, an allegory of the difficulty of representing black women's sexuality precisely when that sexuality has been exoticized or rendered as an icon of primitivism. Indeed, Larsen herself appears to be caught in that very dilemma, withholding a representation black women's sexuality precisely in order to avert the consequence of it becoming exoticized. It is this withholding that one might read in *Quicksand*, a novella published the year before *Passing*, where Helga's abstinence is directly related to the fear of being depicted as belonging to "the jungle." McDowell writes, "since the beginning of their 130-year history, black women novelists have treated sexuality with caution and reticence. This is clearly linked to the network of social and literary myths perpetuated throughout history about black women's libidinousness."[7]

The conflict between Irene and Clare, one which spans identification desire, jealousy, and rage, calls to be contextualized within the historically specific constraints of sexuality and race which produced this text in 1929. And though I can only do that in a very crude way here, I would like briefly to sketch a direction for such an analysis. For I would agree with both McDowell and Carby not only that is it unnecessary to choose whether this novella is "about" race or "about" sexuality and sexual conflict, but that the two domains are inextricably linked, such that the text offers a way to read the racialization of sexual conflict.

Claudia Tate argues that "race . . . is not the novel's foremost concern" and that "the real impetus for the story is Irene's emotional turbulence" (142) and the psychological ambiguity that surrounds Clare's death. Tate distinguishes her own psychological account from those who reduce the novel to a "trite melodrama" (146) of black women passing for white. By underscoring the ambiguity of Clare's death, Tate brings into relief the narrative and psychic complexity of the novella. Following Tate, Cheryl Wall refuses to separate the psychological ambiguity of the story from its racial significance.

Singh, *The Novels of the Harlem Renaissance* (State College: Pennsylvania State University Press, 1976); Claudia Tate, "Nella Larsen's *Passing*. A Problem of Interpretation," *Black American Literature Forum* 14:4 (1980): pp. 142–46 [reprinted in this edition, p. 342]; Hortense Thornton, "Sexism as Quagmire: Nella Larsen's *Quicksand*," *CLA Journal* 16 (1973): pp. 285–301; Cheryl Wall, "Passing for What? Aspects of Identity in Nella Larsen's Novels," *Black American Literature Forum*, vol. 20, nos. 1–2 (1986), pp. 97–111 [reprinted in this edition, p. 356]; Mary Helen Washington, *Invented Lives: Narratives of Black Women 1860–1960* (New York: Anchor-Doubleday, 1987).

7. Deborah E. McDowell, " 'That nameless . . . shameful impulse': Sexuality in Nella Larsen's *Quicksand* and *Passing*," in Joel Weixlmann and Houston A. Baker, Jr., eds., *Black Feminist Criticism and Critical Theory: Studies in Black American Literature*, vol. 3 (Greenwood, Fla.: Penkevill Publishing Company, 1988), p. 141. Reprinted in part as "Introduction" to *Quicksand and Passing*. All further citations to McDowell in the text are to this essay.

Agreeing that "Larsen's most striking insights are into psychic dilemmas confronting certain black women," she argues that what appear to be "the tragic mulattoes of literary convention" are also "the means through which the author demonstrates the psychological costs of racism and sexism." For Wall, the figure of Clare never fully exists apart from Irene's own projections of "otherness" (108). Indeed, according to Wall, Irene's erotic relation to Clare participates in a kind of exoticism that is not fully different from Bellew's. Irene sees in Clare's seductive eyes "the unconscious, the unknowable, the erotic, and the passive," where, according to Wall, "[these] symbolize those aspects of the psyche Irene denies within herself" (108–109). Deborah McDowell specifies this account of psychological complexity and projection by underscoring the conflicted homoeroticism between Clare and Irene. McDowell writes, "though, superficially, Irene's is an account of Clare's passing for white and related issues of racial identity and loyalty, underneath the safety of that surface is the more dangerous story—though not named explicitly—of Irene's awakening sexual desire for Clare" (xxvi). Further, McDowell argues that Irene effectively displaces her own desire for Clare in her "imagination of an affair between Clare and Brian" (xxviii), and that in the final scene "Clare's death represents the death of Irene's sexual feelings, for Clare" (xxix).

To understand the muted status of homosexuality within this text—and hence the displacement, jealousy, and murderous wish that follow—it is crucial to situate this repression in terms of the specific social constraints on the depiction of black female sexuality mentioned above. In her essay, "The Quicksands of Representation," Hazel Carby writes,

> Larsen's representation of both race and class are structured through the prism of black female sexuality. Larsen recognized that the repression of the sensual in Afro-American fiction in response to the long history of the exploitation of black sexuality led to the repression of passion and the repression or denial of female sexuality and desire. But, of course, the representation of black female sexuality meant risking its definition as primitive and exotic within a racist society . . . Racist sexual ideologies proclaimed the black woman to be a rampant sexual being, and in response black women writers either focused on defending their morality or displaced sexuality onto another terrain [174].

McDowell, on the other hand, sees Larsen as resisting the sexual explicitness found in black female blues singers such as Bessie Smith and Ma Rainey (xiii), but nevertheless wrestling with the problem of rendering public a sexuality which thereby became available to an exoticizing exploitation.[8] In a sense, the conflict of lesbian desire in the story can be read in what is almost spoken, in what is withheld from speech, but which always threatens to stop or disrupt speech. And in this sense the muteness of homosexuality converges in the story with the illegibility of Clare's blackness.

To specify this convergence let me turn first to the periodic use of the term "queering" in the story itself, where queering is linked to the eruption of anger into speech such that speech is stifled and broken, and then to the scene in which Clare and Irene first exchange their glances, a reciprocal seeing that verges on threatening absorption. Conversations in *Passing* appear to constitute the painful, if not repressive, surface of social relations. It is what Clare withholds in conversation that permits her to "pass" and when Irene's conversation falters, the narrator refers to the sudden gap in the surface of language as "queer" or as "queering." At the time, it seems, "queer" did not yet mean homosexual, but it did encompass an array of meanings associated with the deviation from normalcy which might well include the sexual. Its meanings include: of obscure origin, the state of feeling ill or bad, not straight, obscure, perverse, eccentric. As a verb-form, "to queer" has a history of meaning: to quiz or ridicule, to puzzle, but also to swindle and to cheat. In Larsen's text, the aunts who raise Clare as white forbid her to mention her race; they are described as "queer" (189) [19]. When Gertrude, another passing black woman, hears a racial slur against blacks Larsen writes, "from Gertrude's direction came a queer little suppressed sound, a snort or a giggle" (202) [30]—something queer, something short of proper conversation, passable prose. Brian's longing to travel to Brazil is described as an "old, queer, unhappy restlessness" (208) [00], suggesting a longing to be freed of propriety.

That Larsen links queerness with a potentially problematic eruption of sexuality seems clear: Irene worries about her sons picking up ideas about sex at school; Junior, she remarks, " 'picked up some queer ideas about things—some things—from the older boys.' 'Queer ideas?' [Brian] repeated. 'D'you mean ideas about sex, Irene?" Yes-es. Not quite nice ones, dreadful jokes, and things like that' " (219–220) [42]. Sometimes conversation becomes "queer" when anger interrupts the social surface of conversation. Upon becoming convinced that Brian and Clare are having an affair, Irene is described by Larsen this way: "Irene cried out: 'But Brian, I—' and stopped, amazed at the fierce anger that had blazed up in her./ Brian's head came round with a jerk. His brows lifted in an odd surprise./ Her voice, she realized *had*

---

8. Jewelle Gomez suggests that black lesbian sexuality very often thrived behind the church pew. See Jewelle Gomez, "A Cultural Legacy Denied and Discovered: Black Lesbians in Fiction by Women," *Home Girls: A Black Feminist Anthology* (Latham, NY: Kitchen Table Press, 1983), pp. 120–21.

gone queer" (249) [62]. As a term for betraying what ought to remain concealed, "queering" works as the exposure within language—an exposure that disrupts the repressive surface of language—of both sexuality and race. After meeting Clare's husband on the street with her black friend Felise, Irene confesses that she has previously "passed" in front of him. Larsen writes, "Felise drawled: 'Aha! Been 'passing' have you? Well, I've queered that' " (259) [70].

In the last instance, queering is what upsets and exposes passing; it is the act by which the racially and sexually repressive surface of conversation is exploded, by rage, by sexuality, by the insistence on color.

Irene and Clare first meet up after years apart in a café where they are both passing as white. And the process by which each comes to recognize the other, and recognize her as black is at once the process of their erotic absorption each into the other's eyes. The narrator reports that Irene found Clare to be "an attractive-looking woman . . . with those dark, almost black, eyes and that wide mouth like a scarlet flower against the ivory of her skin . . . a shade too provocative" (177) [9]. Irene feels herself stared at by Clare, and clearly stares back, for she notes that Clare "showed [not] the slightest trace of disconcert-ment at having been detected in her steady scrutiny." Irene then "feel(s) her color heighten under the continued inspection, [and] slid her eyes down. What she wondered could be the reason for such per-sistent attention? Had she, in her haste in the taxi, put her hat on backwards?" From the start, then, Irene takes Clare's stare to be a kind of inspection, a threat of exposure which she returns first as scrutiny and distrust only then to find herself thoroughly seduced: "She stole another glance. Still looking. What strange languorous eyes she had!" Irene resists being watched, but then falls into the gaze, averts the recognition at the same time that she "surrenders" to the charm of the smile.

The ambivalence wracks the motion of the narrative. Irene subse-quently tries to move Clare out of her life, refuses to answer her let-ters, vows not to invite her anywhere, but finds herself caught up by Clare's seduction. Is it that Irene cannot bear the identification with Clare, or is it that she cannot bear her desire for Clare; is it that she identifies with Clare's passing but needs to disavow it not only because she seeks to uphold the "race" that Clare betrays but because her desire for Clare will betray the family that works as the bulwark for that uplifted race? Indeed, this is a moral version of the family which opposes any sign of passion even within the marriage, even any passionate attachment to the children. Irene comes to hate Clare not only because Clare lies, passes, and betrays her race, but because Clare's lying secures a tentative sexual freedom for Clare, and reflects back to Irene the passion that Irene denies herself. She hates Clare not only because Clare has such passion, but because Clare awakens such passion in Irene, indeed, a passion *for* Clare: "In the look Clare gave Irene, there was something groping, and hopeless, and yet so absolutely determined that it was like an image of the futile searching and firm resolution in Irene's own soul, and increased the feeling of doubt and compunction that had been growing within her about Clare Kendry." She distrusts Clare as she distrusts herself, but this groping is also what draws her in. The next line reads: "She gave in" (231) [51].

When Irene can resist Clare, she does it in the name of "race," where "race" is tied to the DuBoisian notion of uplift and denotes an idea of "progress" that is not only masculinist but which, in Larsen's story, becomes construed as upward class mobility. This moral notion of "race" which, by the way, is often contested by the celebratory rhetoric of "color" in the text, also requires the idealization of bourgeois family life in which women retain their place in the family. The institution of the family also protects black women from a public exposure of sexuality that would be rendered vulnerable to a racist construction and exploitation. The sexuality that might queer the family becomes a kind of danger: Brian's desire to travel, the boys' jokes, all must be unilaterally subdued, kept out of public speech, not merely in the name of race, but in the name of a notion of racial progress that has become linked with class mobility, masculine uplift, and the bourgeois family. Ironically, Du Bois himself came to praise Larsen's *Quicksand* precisely for elevating black fiction beyond the kind of sexual exoticization that patrons such as Carl Van Vechten sought to promote.[9] Without recognizing that Larsen was struggling with the conflict produced, on the one hand, by such exotic and racist renderings and, on the other hand, by the moral injunctions typified by Du Bois, Du Bois himself praises her writings as an example of uplift itself.[1] And yet, one might argue that *Passing* exemplifies precisely the cost of uplift for black women as an ambiguous death/suicide, whereas *Quicksand* exemplifies that cost as a kind of death in marriage, where both stories resolve on the impossibility of sexual freedom for black women.[2]

9. For an analysis of the racist implications of such patronage, see Bruce Kellner, " 'Refined Racism': White Patronage in the Harlem Renaissance," in *The Harlem Renaissance Reconsidered*, pp. 93–106.

1. McDowell writes, "Reviewing Claude McKay's *Home to Harlem* and Larsen's *Quicksand* together for *The Crisis*, for example, Du Bois praised Larsen's novel as 'a fine, thoughtful and courageous piece of work,' but criticized McKay's as so 'nauseating' in its emphasis on 'drunkenness, fighting, and sexual promiscuity' that it made him feel . . . like taking a bath." She cites "Rpt. in *Voices of a Black Nation: Political Journalism in the Harlem Renaissance*, Theodore G. Vincent, ed., (San Francisco: Ramparts Press, 1973), p. 359," in McDowell, p. 164.

2. Indeed, it is the ways in which Helga Crane consistently uses the language of the "primitive" and the "jungle" to describe sexual feeling that places her in a tragic alliance with Du Bois.

What becomes psychically repressed in *Passing* is linked to the specificity of the social constraints on black women's sexuality that inform Larsen's text. If, as Carby insists, the prospect of black women's sexual freedom at the time of Larsen's writing rendered them vulnerable to public violations, including rape, because their bodies continued to be sites of conquest within white racism, then the psychic resistance to homosexuality and to a sexual life outside the parameters of the family must be read in part as a resistance to an endangering public exposure.

To the extent that Irene desires Clare, she desires the trespass that Clare performs, and hates her for the disloyalty that that trespass entails. To the extent that Irene herself eroticizes Clare's racial trespass and Clare's clear lack of loyalty for family and its institutions of monogamy, Irene herself is in a double bind: caught between the prospect of becoming free from an ideology of "race" uncritical in its own masculinism and classism, on the one hand, and the violations of white racism that attend the deprivatization of black women's sexuality, on the other. Irene's psychic ambivalence toward Clare, then, needs to be situated in this historical double-bind.[3] At the same time, we can see mapped within Larsen's text the incipient possibility of a solidarity among black women. The identification between Clare and Irene might be read as the unlived political promise of a solidarity yet to come.

McDowell points out that Irene imagines that Brian is with Clare, and that this imagining coincides with the intensification of Irene's desire *for* Clare. Irene passes her desire for Clare through Brian; he becomes the phantasmatic occasion for Irene to consummate her desire for Clare, but also to deflect from the recognition that it is *her* desire which is being articulated through Brian. Brian carries that repudiated homosexuality, and Irene's jealousy, then, can be understood not only as a rivalry with him for Clare, but the painful consequence of a sacrifice of passion that she repeatedly makes, a sacrifice that entails the displacement or rerouting of her desire through Brian. That Brian appears to act on Irene's desire (although this, importantly, is never confirmed and, so, may be nothing other than an imaginary conviction on Irene's part), suggests that part of that jealousy is anger that he occupies a legitimated sexual position from which he can carry out the desire which she invested in him, that he dares to act the desire which she relegated to him to act on. This is not to discount the possibility that Irene also desires Brian, but there

---

3. For an effort to reconcile psychoanalytic conflict and the problematic of incest and the specific history of the African-American family post-slavery, see Hortense J. Spillers, " 'The Permanent Obliquity of the In(pha)llibly Straight': In the Time of the Daughters and the Fathers," in Cheryl Wall, ed., *Changing Our Own Words* (New Brunswick: Rutgers, 1989), pp. 127–149.

is very little evidence of a passionate attachment to him in the text. Indeed, it is against his passion, and in favor of preserving bourgeois ideals that she clamors to keep him. Her jealousy may well be routed along a conventional heterosexual narrative, but * * * that is not to foreclose the interpretation that a lesbian passion runs that course.

Freud writes on a certain kind of "jealousy" which appears at first to be the desire to have the heterosexual partner whose attention has wandered, but is motivated by a desire to occupy the place of that wandering partner in order to consummate a foreclosed homosexuality. He calls this a "delusional jealousy . . . what is left of a homosexuality that has run its course, and it rightly takes its position among the classical forms of paranoia. As an attempt at defence against an unduly strong homosexual impulse it may, in a man, be described in the formula: "*I* do not love him, *she* loves him!' "[4] And, in a woman and in *Passing*, the following formula might apply: "I, Irene, do not love her, Clare: he, Brian, does!"

It is precisely here, in accounting for the sacrifice, that one reformulation of psychoanalysis in terms of race becomes necessary. In his essay on narcissism, Freud argues that a boy child begins to love through sacrificing some portion of his own narcissism, that the idealization of the mother is nothing other than that narcissism transferred outward, that the mother stands for that lost narcissism, promises the return of that narcissism, and never delivers on that promise. For as long as she remains the idealized object of love, she carries his narcissism, she is his displaced narcissism, and, insofar as *she carries it*, she is perceived to *withhold it from him*. Idealization, then, is always at the expense of the ego who idealizes. The ego-ideal is produced as a consequence of being severed from the ego, where the ego is understood to sacrifice some part of its narcissism in the formation and externalization of this ideal.

The love of the ideal will thus always be ambivalent, for the ideal deprecates the ego as it compels its love. For the moment, I would like to detach the logic of this explanation from the drama between boy child and mother which is Freud's focus (not to discount that focus, but to bring into relief other possible foci), and underscore the consequence of ambivalence in the process of idealization. The one I idealize is the one who carries for me the self-love that I myself have invested in that one. And accordingly, I hate that one, for he/she has taken my place even as I yielded my place to him/her, and yet I require that one, for he/she represents the promise of the return of my own self-love. Self-love, self-esteem is thus preserved and vanquished at the site of the ideal.

4. Sigmund Freud, "Some Neurotic Mechanisms in Jealousy, Paranoia and Homosexuality," S[tandard]E[dition], Vol. 18, 1922, p. 225.

How can this analysis be related to the questions concerning the racialization of sexuality I have tried to pose? The ego-ideal and its derivative, the super-ego, are regulatory mechanisms by which social ideals are psychically sustained. In this way, the social regulation of the psyche can be read as the juncture of racial and gendered prohibitions and regulations and their forced psychic appropriations. Freud argues speculatively that this ego-ideal lays the groundwork for the super-ego, and that the super-ego is lived as the psychic activity of "watching" and, from the perspective that is the ego, the experience of "being watched": "it (the super-ego) constantly watches the real ego and measures it by that (ego-) ideal." Hence, the super-ego stands for the measure, the law, the norm, one which is embodied by a fabrication, a figure of a being whose sole feature it is to watch, to watch in order to judge, as a kind of persistent scrutiny, detection, effort to expose, that hounds the ego and reminds it of its failures. The ego thus designates the psychic experience of being seen, and the super-ego, that of seeing, watching, exposing the ego. Now, this watching agency is not the same as the idealization which is the ego-ideal; it stands back both from the ego-ideal and the ego, and measures the latter against the former and always, always finds it wanting. The super-ego is not only the measure of the ego, the interiorized judge, but the activity of prohibition, the psychic agency of regulation, what Freud calls *conscience*.[5]

For Freud, this superego represents a norm, a standard, an ideal which is in part socially received; it is the psychic agency by which social regulation proceeds. But it is not just any norm; it is the set of norms by which the sexes are differentiated and installed. The super-ego thus first arises, says Freud, as a prohibition that regulates sexuality in the service of producing socially ideal "men" and "women." This is the point at which Lacan intervened in order to develop his notion of the symbolic, the set of laws conveyed by language itself which compel conformity to notions of "masculinity" and "femininity."

---

5. Significantly, Freud argues that conscience is the sublimation of homosexual libido, that the homosexual desires which are prohibited are not thoroughly destroyed; they are satisfied by the prohibition itself. In this way, the pangs of conscience are nothing other than the displaced satisfactions of homosexual desire. The guilt about such desire is, oddly, the very way in which that desire is preserved.

This consideration of guilt as a way of locking up or safeguarding desire may well have implications for the theme of white guilt. For the question there is whether white guilt is itself the satisfaction of racist passion, whether the reliving of racism that white guilt constantly performs is not itself the very satisfaction of racism that white guilt ostensibly abhors. For white guilt—when it is not lost to self-pity—produces a paralytic moralizing that *requires* racism to sustain its own sanctimonious posturing; precisely because white moralizing is itself nourished by racist passions, it can never be the basis on which to build and affirm a community across difference; rooted in the desire to be exempted from white racism, to produce oneself as the exemption, this strategy virtually requires that the white community remain mired in racism; hatred is merely transferred outward, and thereby preserved, but it is not overcome.

And many psychoanalytic feminists have taken this claim as a point of departure for their own work. They have claimed in various ways that sexual difference is as primary as language, that there is no speaking, no writing, without the presupposition of sexual difference. And this has led to a second claim which I want to contest, namely, that sexual difference is more primary or more fundamental than other kinds of differences, including racial difference. It is this asser- tion of the priority of sexual difference over racial difference that has marked so much psychoanalytic feminism as white, for the assump- tion here is not only that sexual difference is more fundamental, but that there is a relationship called "sexual difference" that is itself unmarked by race. That whiteness is not understood by such a per- spective as a racial category is clear; it is yet another power that need not speak its name. Hence, to claim that sexual difference is more fundamental than racial difference is effectively to assume that sex- ual difference is white sexual difference, and that whiteness is not a form of racial difference.

Within Lacanian terms, the ideals or norms that are conveyed in language are the ideals or norms that govern sexual difference, and that go under the name of the symbolic. But what requires radical rethinking is what social relations compose this domain of the sym- bolic, what convergent set of historical formations of racialized gen- der, of gendered race, of the sexualization of racial ideals, or the racialization of gender norms, makes up both the social regulation of sexuality and its psychic articulations. If, as Norma Alarcón has insisted, women of color are "multiply interpellated," called by many names, constituted in and by that multiple calling, then this implies that the symbolic domain, the domain of socially instituted norms, is composed of *racializing norms*, and that they exist not merely along- side gender norms, but are articulated through one another.[6] Hence, it is no longer possible to make sexual difference prior to racial dif- ference or, for that matter, to make them into fully separable axes of social regulation and power.

In some ways, this is precisely the challenge to psychoanalysis that Nella Larsen offers in *Passing*. And here is where I would follow Bar- bara Christian's advice to consider literary narrative as a place where theory takes place,[7] and would simply add that I take Larsen's *Pass- ing* to be in part a theorization of desire, displacement, and jealous rage that has significant implications for rewriting psychoanalytic theory in ways that explicitly come to terms with race. If the watch-

6. Norma Alarcón, "The Theoretical Subject(s) of *This Bridge Called My Back* and Anglo-American Feminism," in Gloria Anzaldúa, ed., *Making Face, Making Soul: Haciendo Caras* (San Francisco: Aunt Lute, 1990), pp. 356–69.
7. Barbara Christian, "The Race for Theory" in *The Nature and Context of Minority Discourse* (New York: Oxford University Press, 1990), pp. 37–49.

ing agency described by Freud is figured as a watching judge, a judge who embodies a set of ideals, and if those ideals are to some large degree socially instituted and maintained, then this watching agency is the means by which social norms sear the psyche, expose it to a condemnation that can lead to suicide. Indeed, Freud remarked that the superego, if left fully unrestrained, will fully deprive the ego of its desire, a deprivation which is psychic death, and which Freud claims leads to suicide. If we rethink Freud's "super-ego" as the psychic force of social regulation, and we rethink social regulation in terms which include vectors of power such as gender and race, then it should be possible to articulate the psyche politically in ways which have consequences for social survival.

For Clare, it seems, cannot survive, and her death marks the success of a certain symbolic ordering of gender, sexuality and race, as it marks as well the sites of potential resistance. It may be that as Zulena, Irene's black servant, picks up the shattered whiteness of the broken tea cup, she opens the question of what will be made of such shards. We might read a text such as Toni Morrison's *Sula* as the piecing together of the shattered whiteness that composes the remains of both Clare and Irene in Nella Larsen's text, rewriting Clare as Sula, and Irene as Nel, refiguring that lethal identification between them as the promise of connection in Nel's final call: "girl, girl, girlgirlgirl."[8]

At the close of Larsen's *Passing*, it is Bellew who climbs the stairs and "sees" Clare, takes the measure of her blackness against the ideal of whiteness and finds her wanting. Although Clare has said that she longs for the exposure in order to become free of him, she is also attached to him and his norm for her economic well-being, and it is no accident—even if it is figured as one—that the exposure of her color leads straightway to her death, the literalization of a "social death." Irene, as well, does not want Clare free, not only because Irene might lose Brian, but because she must halt Clare's sexual freedom to halt her own. Claudia Tate argues that the final action is importantly ambiguous, that it constitutes a "psychological death" for Irene just as it literalizes death for Clare. Irene appears to offer a helping hand to Clare who somehow passes out the window to her death. Here, as Henry Louis Gates, Jr. suggests, passing carries the double meaning of crossing the color line and crossing over into death: passing as a kind of passing on.[9]

If Irene turns on Clare to contain Clare's sexuality, as she has turned on and extinguished her own passion, she does this under the eyes of the bellowing white man; his speech, his exposure, his watching divides them against each other. In this sense, Bellew speaks the

8. Toni Morrison, *Sula* (New York: Knopf, 1973), p. 174.
9. Henry Louis Gates, Jr., *Figures*, p. 202.

force of the regulatory norm of whiteness, but Irene identifies with that condemnatory judgment. Clare is the promise of freedom at too high a price, both to Irene and to herself. It is not precisely Clare's race that is "exposed," but blackness itself is produced as marked and marred, a public sign of particularity in the service of the dissimulated universality of whiteness. If Clare betrays Bellew, it is in part because she turns the power of dissimulation against her white husband, and her betrayal of him, at once a sexual betrayal, undermines the reproductive aspirations of white racial purity, exposing the tenuous borders that that purity requires. If Bellew anxiously reproduces white racial purity, he produces the prohibition against miscegenation by which that purity is guaranteed, a prohibition that requires strictures of heterosexuality, sexual fidelity, and monogamy. And if Irene seeks to sustain the black family at the expense of passion and in the name of uplift, she does it in part to avert the position for black women outside the family, that of being sexually degraded and endangered by the very terms of white masculinism that Bellew represents (for instance, she tells Clare not to come to the dance for the Negro Welfare Fund alone, that she'll be taken as a prostitute). Bellew's watching, the power of exposure that he wields, is a historically entrenched social power of the white male gaze, but one whose masculinity is enacted and guaranteed through heterosexuality as a ritual of racial purification. His masculinity cannot be secured except through a consecration of his whiteness. And whereas Bellew requires the spectre of the black woman as an object of desire, he must destroy this spectre to avoid the kind of association that might destabilize the territorial boundaries of his own whiteness. This ritualistic expulsion is dramatized quite clearly at the end of *Passing* when Bellew's exposing and endangering gaze and Clare's fall to death are simultaneous with Irene's offer of an apparently helping hand. Fearing the loss of her husband and fearing her own desire, Irene is positioned at the social site of contradiction: both options threaten to jettison her into a public sphere in which she might become subject, as it were, to the same bad winds. But Irene fails to realize that Clare is as constrained as she is, that Clare's freedom could not be acquired at the expense of Irene, that they do not ultimately enslave each other, but that they are both caught in the vacillating breath of that symbolic bellowing:"Nig! My God! Nig!"

If Bellew's bellowing can be read as a symbolic racialization, a way in which both Irene and Clare are interpellated by a set of symbolic norms governing black female sexuality, then the symbolic is not merely organized by "phallic power," but by a "phallicism" that is centrally sustained by racial anxiety and sexualized rituals of racial purification. Irene's self-sacrifice might be understood then as an effort to avoid becoming the object of that kind of sexual violence, as one that makes her cling to an arid family life and destroy whatever emergence of passion might call that safety into question. Her jealousy must then be read as a psychic event orchestrated within and by this social map of power. Her passion for Clare had to be destroyed only because she could not find a viable place for her own sexuality to live. Trapped by a promise of safety through class mobility, Irene accepted the terms of power which threatened her, becoming its instrument in the end. More troubling than a scene in which the white man finds and scorns his "Other" in the black women, this drama displays in all its painfulness the ways in which the interpellation of the white norm is reiterated and executed by those whom it would—and does—vanquish. This is a performative enactment of "race" that mobilizes every character in its sweep.

And yet, the story reoccupies symbolic power to expose that symbolic force in return, and in the course of that exposure began to further a powerful tradition of words, one which promised to sustain the lives and passions of precisely those who could not survive within the story itself. Tragically, the logic of "passing" and "exposure" came to afflict and, indeed, to end Nella Larsen's own authorial career, for when she published a short story, "Sanctuary," in 1930, she was accused of plagiarism, that is, exposed as "passing" as the true originator of the work.[1] Her response to this condemning exposure was to recede into an anonymity from which she did not emerge. Irene slipped into such a living death, as did Helga in *Quicksand*. Perhaps the alternative would have meant a turning of that queering rage no longer against herself or Clare, but against the regulatory norms that force such a turn: against both the passionless promise of that bourgeois family and the bellowing of racism in its social and psychic reverberations, most especially, in the deathly rituals it engages.

ANN DUCILLE

From *Passing* Fancies†

* * *

However concerned with authenticity, ideology, sexuality, and the social contradictions of the day *There Is Confusion, Quicksand, The Chinaberry Tree*, and *Plum Bun* may be, perhaps no novel of the era attends to the iconography of the black female body and the dialec-

---

1. I am thankful to Barbara Christian for pointing out to me the link between the theme of "passing" and the accusation of plagiarism against Larsen.

† From Ann duCille, "*Passing* Fancies," in *The Coupling Convention: Sex, Text, and Tradition in Black Women's Fiction* (New York: Oxford University Press, 1993), pp. 103–09. Reprinted by permission of Oxford University Press.

tics of desire more dramatically than Nella Larsen's second novel, *Passing* (1929). In fact, in *Passing* the degree of notice Irene Redfield takes of her friend Clare Kendry's draped-down body has led Deborah McDowell to argue that Larsen establishes (if only by implication) the possibility of a sexual attraction between the two women characters. To support her claim, McDowell reads carefully the body language of the text. Steeped as it is in double entendres, red dresses, bare shoulders, and fire imagery, the novel indeed presents a plethora of erotic figures to be read. Irene is ever aware of Clare's "tempting mouth," her "seductive caressing smile," her "arresting eyes," her "incredibly beautiful face," which sends a "slight shiver" over the spectator. As seen through Irene's eyes, Clare is "a lovely creature," "really almost too good-looking," whose gaze leaves her feeling "petted and caressed."

McDowell takes as additional evidence of an erotic attraction between the two women the text's opening image: an envelope containing a letter from the long-lost Clare, who has been passing for white. McDowell views this envelope as a metaphorical vagina and argues that Irene, to whom the envelope is addressed, is justified in her reluctance to open it, given the sexual overtones of the letter it contains:

> For I am lonely . . . cannot help longing to be with you again, as I have never longed for anything before; and I have wanted many things in my life. . . . It's like an ache, a pain that never ceases . . . and it's your fault, 'Rene dear. At least partly. For I wouldn't now, perhaps, have this terrible, this wild desire if I hadn't seen you that time in Chicago [7].[1]

The letter leaves Irene with flaming cheeks and a rush of feeling for which she can find no name. The eroticism of this and other sexually loaded passages is textually confirmed, according to McDowell, by Larsen's use of fire imagery, "the conventional representation of sexual desire" (xxvii).

McDowell's reading is an enabling one. It redirects our long-diverted critical attention to the treatment of female sexuality not only in Larsen's work but in that of her contemporaries as well, and it raises important questions about the homoerotic undertones and overtones of this and other texts. Who owns the gaze? Is the gaze inherently masculine or essentially sexual? What happens when women gaze upon each other? Is the very act of gazing upon the female body an appropriation of the masculine and an invocation of the erotic? Is there a grammar of the female gaze? These are among

---

1. Deborah E. McDowell, introduction to *Quicksand* and *Passing*, xxvi–xxvii [reprinted in this edition, p. 363]. This is as quoted by McDowell; I will return to the actual letter a little later. [Bracketed page numbers refer to this Norton Critical Edition.]

the questions occasioned by McDowell's reading of a lesbian subtext in *Passing*. I am not certain, however, that this provocative interpretation, despite its attention to the figurative language of the text, ultimately supports its own thesis or answers its own questions about what McDowell describes tentatively as Larsen's flirtation with the suggestion of the idea of a lesbian relationship between Irene and Clare (xxiii).

To express my skepticism more directly: I am not convinced that the metaphors in *Passing* always hold the erotic meanings McDowell assigns to them. I am not convinced, for example, that the envelope containing Clare's letter is the metaphorical vagina McDowell constructs it to be. With its "extraordinary size," "thin Italian paper," and purple ink, the mysterious missive, and Irene's reaction to it, might as readily be taken to symbolize the enveloped self afraid to confront its absent (repressed, denied, buried) other—a calling card from the grave of buried feelings, as it were.

What happens if we historicize Larsen's grammar, placing it within the blues/bohemian/bourgeois moment? Does such a placement give the text's linguistic figures a different face value altogether? Viewed in historical perspective, the looking, touching, and caressing that McDowell reads as signs of lesbian attraction may have more to do with homosociability than with either homo- or heterosexuality, with the nature of both women's culture and social and linguistic conventions at the time. That is to say, the interaction between Clare and Irene may reflect the moment's preoccupation with the "always already sexual" black female body, or it may suggest a not necessarily sexual way of being women together, which the spread of Freudian thought recoded and perhaps destroyed. It may also reflect a woman's way of talking through the body—of expressing material or experiential desire in bodily terms. As Lauren Berlant has argued, "there may be a difference between wanting someone sexually and wanting someone's body." What Irene wants, Berlant suggests, is not to make love to Clare, but "to occupy, to experience the privileges of Clare's body . . . to wear [Clare's] way of wearing her body, like a prosthesis, or a fetish."[2] "Fetish" seems to me very much the right trope: a figuring of the black female body as fetishized commodity that Larsen earlier critiqued in *Quicksand*. But if Irene wants to wear the experiences of Clare's fetishized body, Clare wants to don Irene's as well, including, perhaps, Irene's husband, Dr. Brian Redfield.

Here I think we come to the crux of Larsen's complex social and psychosexual critique. Clare and Irene—the exotic and the elite—may represent the dialectics of the Harlem Renaissance moment

---

2. Lauren Berlant, "National Brands/National Body: *Imitation of Life*," in *Comparative American Identities: Race, Sex, and Nationality in the Modern Text*, ed. Hortense Spillers (New York: Routledge, 1991), p. 111.

itself. Written as part vamp, part flapper, and part femme fatale, Clare reflects the bohemian fascination with sexuality, the Greenwich Village high life, the glamorous, the risqué, the foreign, and the forbidden. Irene, on the other hand, with her race work, literary salons, and house parties, signifies the propriety, the manners, the social and racial uplift, and especially the security with which the black bourgeoisie of the 1920s was preoccupied. For Irene, after all, "security was the most important and desired thing in life." Not for "happiness, love, or some wild ecstacy that she had never known would she exchange her security" (235) [76]. Viewed in this light, the text's actual sexual preference may be for the autoerotic: Clare and Irene may be read as body doubles or, perhaps more precisely, as halved selves through whom Larsen explores a host of dialectics, not the least of which are desire and danger, woman-proud promiscuity and repression, freedom and confinement.

At the risk of mixing my own bourgeois blues metaphor, I might even suggest that Larsen has rescored "The Love Song of J. Alfred Prufrock," creating a "you and I" who represent opposing sides of a divided self. But "The Love Song of Irene Redfield" is sung without the touch of levity or the conscious self-consciousness of Eliot's poem. Irene issues no wake-up call to "you and I"; she invites no engagement with her alter ego. She is bent instead on denying the other, on preserving the status quo of her comfortable, secure middle-class existence.

Larsen has given us something more than just another simple doubling or dividing, however, for Clare is less Irene's alter ego than her alter libido, the buried, long-denied sexual self whose absence in his wife has led Irene's husband, Brian, to conclude, with some bitterness, that sex (with Irene?) is a joke. To Irene's concerns that their older son is picking up "some queer ideas about things—some things—from older boys," Brian responds scornfully: "D'you mean ideas about sex, Irene? . . . Well, what of it? . . . The sooner and the more he learns about sex, the better for him. And most certainly if he learns that it's a grand joke, the greatest in the world. It'll keep him from lots of disappointments later on" (188–89) [42]. The fact that Irene cannot bring herself to say the word sex, even to her husband, suggests that she may be the source of Brian's own sexual disappointments. The Redfields' marriage, we know, is largely passionless. The couple sleep in separate bedrooms, and there is a general chill in the air between them, which warms up only in the presence of the decidedly sensual Clare, who Irene suspects is "capable of heights and depths of feeling that she, Irene Redfield, had never known. Indeed, never cared to know" (195) [47]. This "suspicion" (Larsen's word) will later be linked to another: that Brian and Clare are having an affair, that Brian has found in Clare Kendry the heights and depths of feeling missing in his wife.

But if Clare is Irene's alter libido, Irene is Clare's as well, a connection to the "primitive" Negro past, gone but too instinctual to be forgotten. This instinctive need to rejoin—the need of the exotic sexual other (Clare) to reconnect with its equally (but differently) exotic racial self (Irene, though perhaps more what Irene represents than with what she is)—may be the source of the longing, the ache, the unceasing pain, and the wild desire Clare writes of in her letter to Irene. A closer look at the letter, with the phrases McDowell omits, lends support to this possible interpretation. (Italics indicate the omitted phrases; except for the closing set, the ellipses are Larsen's.)

> ". . . For I am lonely, so lonely . . . cannot help longing to be with you again, as I have never longed for anything before; and I have wanted many things in my life. . . . *You can't know how in this pale life of mine I am all the time seeing the bright pictures of that other that I once thought I was glad to be free of.* . . . It's like an ache, a pain that never ceases. . . ." *Sheets upon thin sheets of it. And ending with,* "and it's your fault. . . ." (145) [7]

While McDowell's edited version of the letter situates Irene as the absolute object of Clare's desire, the actual letter directs the bulk of that "wild desire" to the *other* Negro life Irene represents: the black life Clare shed like a dead skin some time ago and now wants to reclaim, it seems, by appropriating the experiences of Irene's skin, a bit like any other primitivist. Clare, in fact, can be read as a comment on primitivists who enjoy the privileges of white skin by day but flock to Harlem by night to enjoy the pleasures they associate with black flesh. Irene suggests as much herself when she tells Clare at one point that white people come to Harlem for the same reason Clare has started coming: "[T]o see Negroes . . . to get material to turn into shekels . . . to gaze on the great and near great while they gaze on the Negroes" (198) [50]. The threat to Irene in this configuration is the threat of the displaced other attempting to reclaim its racial self through the absorption of its alternate subjectivity. Put another way, the object of desire for both Irene and Clare is a total subjectivity, a whole self—coded in both racial and sexual terms, repressed in Irene and expressed in Clare. The problem is that two halves make only one whole; therefore, the completeness Clare is so intent on pursuing can be attained only at the expense of Irene's subjectivity. In such a reading, the danger Irene senses but cannot name is a fear of a loss of self, and the attraction—the "inexplicable onrush of affectionate feeling"—is love for lost self.

This reading of possible autoerotic signification in *Passing* is by no means a denial of McDowell's homoerotic theory, however, but a possible expansion of it. For there is no essential sexual self; homosexuality is often encoded textually as self-love or narcissism. Through her "unseeing eyes," Irene comes to view Clare as the intruding, insinuating other she loves to hate, but Clare may actually be the threatening, disruptive, daring, sexual self—with "a having way"—that Irene hates to love. Hates enough and fears enough perhaps to kill.

But this interplay of self and other can be read on a variety of levels: the failure, even betrayal, of female friendship, for example, a failure with tragic consequences. "Unseeing" as her eyes may be, Irene recognizes a kind of duplicity in Clare's sudden friendship. She has the sense at times that Clare is acting, and views her friend's "catlike" ways as a threat to her own stability. "The trouble with Clare," she concludes, "was, not only that she wanted to have her cake and eat it too, but that she wanted to nibble at the cake of other folk as well" (182) [35]. Irene begins to suspect that the particular cake Clare has been nibbling at is the "devil's food" of Dr. Brian Redfield.

For McDowell, an affair between friend and husband exists only in Irene's imagination, as a projection "of her own developing passion for Clare onto Brian" (xxviii). The novel itself, however, leaves wonderfully ambiguous the question of an affair between Brian and Clare, even as it drops a number of clues that would seem to confirm Irene's suspicions. If we read Clare as a departed daughter desperate to return to the racial fold, an affair between her and Brian becomes almost a narrative necessity. For just as marriage to a white man confirmed Clare as white, coupling with a black man is an alchemy that may turn her black again.

Even in a more conservative reading, however, Irene is not irrationally out of line to be suspicious of a friend who warns: "I haven't any proper morals or sense of duty, as you have, that makes me act as I do. . . . Can't you realize that I'm not like you a bit? Why, to get the things I want badly enough, I'd do anything, hurt anybody, throw anything away. Really, 'Rene, I'm not safe" (210) [58]. This revelation of self is followed by a fit of uncontrollable and inconsolable crying. Irene will later remember this tearful warning and link it directly to what she reads as Clare's willingness to sacrifice the respectability and security of marriage (what Irene holds most dear about her own marriage), to hurt friends and break up families, even to give up her child, if Brian and the black world he is a part of are what she wants. The text turns in part, however, on the fact that Irene is as determined to keep what she has as Clare is to get what she wants.

While it is again a detail that can be read on a variety of levels, it is interesting to note that Irene's eyes cease to be described as "unseeing" at the precise moment she becomes aware of the affair between Clare and Brian—real or imagined. "She closed her unseeing eyes and clenched her fists," we are told, in what I believe is the last reference to Irene's myopia. After a generous flow of "hot tears of rage and shame," she says to her face in the mirror: "I do think . . .

that you've been something—oh, very much—of a damned fool" (218) [63]. While critics have generally read the repeated reference to Irene's "unseeing eyes" as an indication of the distorted vision that makes her an untrustworthy narrator, the description may also mean that Irene is the proverbial "last one to know" wife who has been blind to a friend's play for her husband.

As her own internally stagnant but externally proper marriage withers even more, Irene becomes increasingly convinced that Brian is having an affair with Clare. Her fears for her own marriage or, rather, the outward appearance of her marriage, mount when she meets Clare's husband, John Bellew, on the street as she is walking arm in arm with an "unmistakably colored" woman friend. She knows that it is a short step from Bellew's realizing that his wife's white-skinned childhood friend, Irene, is colored to his realizing that his white-skinned wife is colored, too. Irene is afraid that nigger-hating Bellew will divorce Clare, leaving her free for Brian. She keeps her fears and her suspicions to herself, however, and begins to think: "If Clare should die! Then—Oh, it was vile! To think, yes, to wish that!" But while they make her feel faint and sick, thoughts of Clare's death continue to dance in her head.

With the stage thus set and the key players thus primed, the curtain opens on a Harlem apartment party, where an outraged John Bellew suddenly bursts in and confronts his wife with the truth of her racial identity: "So you're a nigger, a damned dirty nigger!" Clare, standing serene by an open window, is unperturbed, smiling that famous faint smile that so maddens Irene. With a "terror tinged with ferocity," the text tells us, Irene rushes across the room and lays her hand on Clare's bare arm. "She couldn't have Clare Kendry cast aside by Bellew. She couldn't have her free" (239) [79]. In the confusion that follows and with Irene by her side, Clare falls, throws herself, or is pushed out the window and plummets six stories to her death.

Many critics read Clare's death at the end of the novel as yet another unfortunate "concession to convention." Once again, a high-spirited, defiant heroine is confined to either the deathbed of marriage or the graveyard. For Cheryl Wall, Clare's death is merely the typical fate of the mulatta heroine.[3] For Robert Bone, however, Clare's "passing" is the text's tragic flaw—"a false and shoddy denoue-ment [that] prevents the novel from rising above mediocrity."[4] For Deborah McDowell, Larsen's ending seems to "punish the very values the novel implicitly affirms, to honor the very value system the text implicitly satirizes" (xxx–xxxi). And while Margaret Perry acknowledges that Larsen may have wanted the ending to leave the

---

3. Wall, "Passing for What?" 106. [Wall's essay reprinted in this edition, p. 356].
4. Bone, *The Negro Novel in America*, 102.

reader perpetually perplexed, she maintains that the ambiguity of the circumstances of Clare's death "does not give the book any artistic complexity that might intrigue the imagination."[5]

I would argue, however, that in its purposeful ambiguity, *Passing* ultimately affirms neither Irene's values nor Clare's; rather, it holds both up to scrutiny, if not ridicule, as signs of the times. But as Thadious Davis, Claudia Tate, and others have pointed out, how one views the ending of *Passing* may depend on who one holds to be the novel's central figure. As my own reading no doubt reveals, *Passing* seems to me to be very much Irene's story. Clare, however central to the unraveling of the plot, is a foil against whom Irene's middle-class consciousness develops or, more correctly, deteriorates in demonic degrees. When Irene instead of Clare is taken to be the central figure and when murder rather than suicide or accident is viewed as the cause of Clare's death, the text's heroine ceases to be a typical, passive, conventional tragic mulatta who pales beside the powerful image of woman-proud blues performers. She becomes instead a protector of the precious domestic realm—defender of middle-class marriage, bourgeois home, family, fidelity, and, above all, security. She gives new meaning to the term "home protection." As a wife, betrayed by friend and husband alike, fighting for her marriage, Irene gains what Houston Baker might call "blues force" as a heroine. She becomes, in such a reading, at once an active agent in the ordering of her own life and a grotesque, which may be precisely the point.

The infinite possibilities of Larsen's fictive invention, in my view, make *Passing* artistically complex beyond the limits of any particular reading or any single rhythm. Perhaps this is why I want not to discredit Deborah McDowell's inspired and empowering interpretation but to disrupt the fixity of the reading—to wrest it from the assumption that Larsen's sexual signifying *necessarily* suggests lesbian attraction, particularly where no "definition" is offered for "lesbian." Ironically, while she has elsewhere chided Barbara Smith for her "vague and imprecise" definition of lesbianism,[6] McDowell offers no clarification of her own usage of the term. She appears to take "lesbian relationship" to mean a necessarily *physical* attraction of female

5. Margaret Perry, *Silence to the Drums: A Survey of the Literature of the Harlem Renaissance* (Westport, CT: Greenwood, 1976).
6. Deborah McDowell, "New Directions for Black Feminist Criticism," in *The New Feminist Criticism: Essays on Women, Literature, and Theory*, ed. Elaine Showalter (New York: Pantheon, 1985), 190. In "Toward a Black Feminist Criticism," Barbara Smith suggests that "if in a woman writer's work a sentence refuses to do what it is supposed to do, if there are strong images of women and if there is a refusal to be linear, the result is innately lesbian literature" (175). Smith takes Toni Morrison's *Sula* (1973) as a case in point, arguing that *Sula* works as a lesbian text "because of Morrison's consistently critical stance toward the heterosexual institutions of male-female relationships, marriage, and the family." McDowell criticizes this definition, arguing that Smith has "simultaneously oversimplified and obscured the issue of lesbianism." See Barbara Smith, "Toward a Black Feminist Criticism," 168.

body to female body for seizure of erotic pleasure and sexual satisfaction. *Passing* seems to me, however, to transcend such limited definitions. What is most engaging about the text is the multiplicity of meanings inspired by Larsen's brilliant use of the body and her clever manipulation of both metaphor and materiality. Larsen accomplishes in *Passing* that "surplus of signifiers"—the superabundance of interpretability—which, according to Frank Kermode, makes a work a classic.[7] In both *Quicksand* and *Passing,* Larsen creates that unreal estate * * *, a fantastic realm we as critics seem to need to ground in a particular objective reality. McDowell's reading opens windows into the text, to be sure, but it also seems to me to hinge precisely what Larsen, in splendid ambiguity, has so cleverly unhinged.

The heroines of Jessie Fauset and Nella Larsen are by no means spayed, passionless decorations, adorning the pristine pages of immaculately conceived lace-curtain romances. They are, on the contrary, implicitly sexual beings, finely tuned to both the power and the vulnerability of their own female bodies. At a moment when black female sexuality was either completely unwritten to avoid endorsing sexual stereotypes or sensationally overwritten to both defy and exploit those stereotypes, Fauset and Larsen edged the discourse into another realm: a realm precariously balanced on the cusp of the respectable and the risqué; a realm that is at times *neutral,* perhaps, but never *neuter;* a realm in which they, too, participate in reclaiming the black body and in defining African American expressive culture.

* * *

---

7. Frank Kermode, *The Classic: Literary Images of Permanence and Change* (New York: Viking, 1975), 140.

GEORGE HUTCHINSON

Nella Larsen and the Veil of Race†

People see what they want to see, and then they'll claim you. Not claim you, but label you. Because it's not really about claiming you. The white people don't want you around. You're not really white . . . And for Blacks—and it's not for all Blacks—there's sort of this feeling that, yeah, she is black and yes, we'll call her black, but she's not black like we are. . . . I was recognized by the black community as an outstanding black student, of course. That used to upset me, that they would claim me because I did well academically, but I wasn't a part of their world.

—Heidi Durrow, daughter of Danish mother and African-American father, quoted in Lise Funderburg, *Black, White, Other*

While studies of cultural syncretism, transnationalism, and "hybridity" have lately become all the rage, there is one area in which claims of racially "hybrid" identity are still subtly resisted, quietly repressed, or openly mocked. The child of both black and white parents encounters various forms of incomprehension in a society for which "blackness" and "whiteness" seem to constitute two mutually exclusive and antagonistic forms of identity. Moreover, the shift to terms presumably marking ethnic or cultural descent—"European" and "African"—has done little to clarify the situation of those "black" subjects who are at the same time, say, German, or, as in the case of the young woman quoted above, Danish-American.

For more than a decade, the strongest Nella Larsen scholarship has been motivated by a reaction against earlier approaches to her fiction that stressed the importance of biracial subjectivity, connected to fiction of the "tragic mulatto." The best recent criticism tends to focus on other issues, particularly feminist themes.[1] Often the difficulties of Larsen's mulatto characters are treated as metaphors for supposedly more important issues, such as black and/or female identity generally. Even when issues of race take center stage, unexamined assumptions about the relations between biracial and black

---

† From George Hutchinson, "Nella Larsen and the Veil of Race," *American Literary History* 9, no. 2 (Summer 1997): 329–49. Reprinted by permission of Oxford University Press.

1. See, for example, Butler (167–85); Wall; McDowell; Blackmore; McLendon (71–111); Hostetler; Dearborn (59–60); Tate; Thornton; and du Cille (73–79). [Butler, Wall, McDowell, Tate, and duCille are reprinted in this edition; see Table of Contents for page numbers].

identity obscure Larsen's antagonistic relation to (black *and* white) American racial mores.

When Larsen's—or her fictional characters'—feelings of ethnic difference from most middle-class black women have not been shunted aside, they have been viewed as neurotic effects of internalized racism and/or an inability to merge "reality" and self-image. Such charges, matching popular perceptions of self-identified biracial persons, have now received an enormous transfusion from biographies by Charles R. Larson (*Invisible Darkness*) and Thadious Davis [*Nella Larsen, Novelist of the Harlem Renaissance: A Woman's Life Unveiled*], which purport to show that Larsen had little connection with her Danish mother and fantasized her relationship to Danish culture to distinguish herself from other blacks, to gain prestige, and to hide the trauma of her childhood.

Each of these biographies—but particularly Davis's, upon which my critique will focus—ends up buttressing the American racial ideology that renders biracial subjectivity invisible, untenable, or fraudulent. Indeed, it seems that this ideology, at least in Davis's case, has determined which aspects of Larsen's life and environment receive the most notice, the most careful investigation, the most meticulous research; which episodes are suspected as fictitious; which relationships count as most significant and how those relationships are interpreted; which aspects of her work reveal most clearly her own psychological makeup; and which aspects are irrelevant or nonautobiographical. The result, despite Davis and Larson's immense and often invaluable labor, is to further obscure crucial aspects of their subject's life and achievement.

1

Larsen's stories of her development from childhood to maturity are not always consistent in their details, but the basic narrative goes like this: She was born of the union of a female white immigrant from Denmark and a man of color from the Danish West Indies. The father soon died or abandoned the family, and the mother later married a white Danish immigrant and gave birth to a second daughter. Nella was unwanted by the stepfather and half-sister. Nella and her mother apparently went to Denmark at some point in her childhood, and Nella's formal education began in a private school for children of immigrants at age eight. Around college age, Larsen attended Fisk University briefly, then visited Denmark for three years, staying with her mother's people and auditing classes at the University of Copenhagen. Eventually, however, she returned to the US and studied nursing, then worked as a nurse in New York and as a head nurse and teacher at Tuskegee. Disappointed with Tuskegee, she returned to

New York, studied library science, and worked as a librarian, in the meantime marrying a rising black physicist, Elmer S. Imes. Her contact with her family had effectively ceased by this time because of the difficulties it might cause them, particularly her white half-sister.

Though they disagree on a number of points, Larson and Davis claim that the most crucial of these biographical details are wrong. In *Invisible Darkness* (which also treats Jean Toomer), Larson characterizes Larsen's stories of her early life as glamorous fictions motivated by a need to conceal the trauma of childhood rejection by her mother (184–92). Close on the heels of Larson's book came Davis's *Nella Larsen, Novelist of the Harlem Renaissance: A Woman's Life Unveiled*. In a recent work on women's biography, Linda Wagner-Martin calls Davis's book one of the best biographies ever written about a woman, and in a review for *American Literature* says Davis has found "the key to [her] subject's being" (*Telling*; Rev. of *Nella Larsen* 60). *Booklist*'s starred review, quoted on the paperback edition's back cover, calls *Nella Larsen* "an astute, rigorous, and deeply compassionate biography . . . and an invaluable chapter in the history of African Americans." In *American Quarterly*, Shelley Fisher Fishkin hailed "Davis's superb and painstakingly researched biography," noting that it "will undoubtedly fuel attentive interest in Larsen in the future" (Fishkin 149). Davis, too, purports to disprove virtually all we thought we knew about Larsen—which is to say, virtually all that Larsen said about her life. A hefty volume with the appearance of a "definitive" biography, the book is already having a powerful impact on Larsen scholarship.

Davis suggests that Larsen's natural father, Peter Walker, may have decided to "pass" and thus became the "white" Peter Larsen; too dark to pass, Nella found herself gradually pushed out of the family.[2] But Larsen's deepest trauma, Davis contends, derived from the fact that her mother, Mary/Marie, emotionally abandoned her daughter early on, and Peter took primary responsibility for her; allegedly, Larsen hardly knew her mother, who may have forced her placement in an "Erring Woman's Refuge" when Larsen was very young. Her mother's racism and abandonment caused Larsen's ambivalence toward African-Americans, "confusion" about race, and competitiveness toward other

---

2. I lack space here to demonstrate the weakness of Davis's argument that Peter Larsen was "passing" (although I would not rule out the possibility). However, both Larson and Davis may have misidentified the wedding of Larsen's mother and stepfather; the ages of both spouses on the 1894 marriage license cited by Davis and Larson (which gives the groom's home as Harlan, Iowa) are off by several years according to other records of Larsen's family, but happen to match the ages of *another* Peter Larsen and Marie Hansen who married in Chicago in 1894 and moved back to Ute, Iowa, near the husband's former home in Harlan, according to a descendant of this latter Peter Larsen and a local historian in Harlan (License no. 1030237; Braun; Petersen).

women. To cope with her trauma, she invented compensatory fictions of a loving mother, a trip to Denmark in her teens, and an exotic story of her family background intended to win status in the black elite.

Davis's argument fits into a common pattern of thinking about persons who, while fully aware of their social designation, feel a measure of alienation from the black community because of those aspects of the self, marked as "white," that do not fit in that community. Personal history and familial bonds collide with definitions of "the race" as family in which whites do not belong. If "mixed-race" persons have often found themselves cast out of families reconstituted as white, they have also found themselves expected to repudiate, hide, or at least avoid identifying with their white kin to achieve identity as resolutely African American.

The situation produces, in Larsen's fiction, a critical perspective on American racial ideologies, both "black" and "white," which further problematizes the character's sense of blackness by putting her into a subversive relationship to its rituals of incorporation and exclusion. The result is a contradiction of normative American racial subjectivities. In Larsen's fiction and in her life this contradiction expresses itself in disruptions of critics' and biographers' narrative expectations. The drama of biracial subjectivity is forced to fit within more easily recognized patterns or is explained on the grounds of normative assumptions that serve a dualistic disciplinary system of race.

Both Davis and Larson conclude that Larsen never lived in Denmark partly because when she applied in 1929 for a passport to visit Spain and France, she attested that this was her first passport application. One might wonder whether the daughter of Danish immigrants would have needed a passport to visit Denmark near the turn of the century, but the truth is even simpler. Sources on travel between the US and Denmark at the time show that no Americans needed passports to visit Scandinavia (Baedeker xi).

Indeed, the records of travel to the US from Denmark reveal that Marie Larsen took her daughters to her native country when Nella was six or younger and returned when Nella was seven on the Scandinavian-American Line, the line mentioned in Larsen's novel *Quicksand*. Peter Larsen was not with them (Direct-emigration lists 326).[3] On the passenger list filled out when they arrived in New York en route to Chicago, an officer wrote across the entire line of the form an explanation of the trip, apparently in Marie's words: "return-

3. "Mary Larsen" is listed as age 29, originally of Denmark but now from the US; "Nelly Larsen" born in the US is listed as 7; and "Any Larsen," also born in the US, is listed as 5. All used ticket number 335, the mother's. The ages match those of Marie, Nelly, and Anna Larsen on 19 April 1898.

ing from a visit in Denmarc; 12 years stay in U.S.A.; going back to my haūsband" (List or Manifest, S. S. *Norge*, 6 May 1898). In the space for "read/write," Marie answered "no" for both children. I will return to the significance of this in a moment.

This trip proves that Larsen was considerably closer to her mother and her mother's Danish kin than either Larson or Davis believe. It undermines Davis's assumption that Nella's mother emotionally abandoned her at a young age and that Peter was her "primary" parent, an assumption that is foundational for Davis's book.

What are the bases of Davis's judgment on this issue? A census form of 1910 (when Larsen was 19, perhaps no longer living in Chicago) states that Marie Larsen had only one daughter. Davis, like Larson, concludes that Marie "denied giving birth" to Nella: "Marie Larsen . . . informed the census taker that she had given birth to one child and that she had one child surviving. Since Anna is the daughter recorded as living in the household, she is the child to whom Marie Larsen refers" (Davis 27). Marie's "denial in 1910 of giving birth to Nella Larsen" (47) becomes an unsubstantiated refrain in Davis's biography. However, *nothing* on the census form indicates who spoke with the census officer. We know that Larsen's white half-sister, who at age 17 was the only daughter living at home at the time of the census, later denied knowing of Nella's existence and that Larsen said the chief strain in the family was between herself and her stepfather and half-sister, to whom her existence was an embarrassment. Moreover, the census shows that an unrelated boarder, who may not have known about Nella, was living in the home. We also know, thanks to Larson, that Marie spoke several times about Nella to a white friend after 1910, identifying her father as an African American (Larson 187)— evidence that conflicts with Davis's assertion of Marie's attempt to completely bury the memory of her daughter's existence.

Davis also makes much of a school registration form of 1903 that lists Peter in the space for "father" (suggesting to Davis that he was not just a stepfather) and an "X" in the spaces for "mother" and "guardian." On such evidence Davis builds her argument that Marie wanted nothing to do with Nella from early on, and that Peter, possibly her actual "black" father, was the parent who primarily cared for her. However, the school registers do not support Davis's assertions. The majority of the registration cards on file for the period are filled out exactly like Larsen's, with the father's name provided and X's in the spaces for "mother" and "guardian." Mother's names appear so rarely as to suggest that they were included mainly on forms for children with single mothers; guardians almost never appear (Elementary School Register Records).[4] Considering the incidence of step-parenting at the time, it

4. Incidentally, the card for Nellie Larson was missing when I checked the files in July 1996, apparently having been misplaced.

is reasonable to suppose that stepfathers were commonly named in the "father" category.

Neither the school registration form nor the 1910 census tells us anything definite about the relationship between Larsen and her mother. We can be sure, however, that this relationship prompted chronic public (and perhaps private) abuse of Marie Larsen. This may have something to do with Larsen's lifelong feelings of loyalty to and identification with her mother, feelings Davis implies are pathological. Indeed, the dangers of being a white mother of a "mulatto" daughter on the near-South side of Chicago were considerable in the early 1900s. Sources that Davis cites in other contexts about black life in Chicago point out that miscegenation was the flashpoint of race relations in the city when Larsen was reaching puberty. Whites and blacks known to have married across the color line often lost their jobs. To avoid suspicion, white spouses even "passed" as black. Police would not allow saloons to serve a "mixed" clientele. White mothers of biracial children faced the most intense hostility of all and were generally assumed to be prostitutes (Drake and Cayton 1: 116–20, 130, 137; Spear 40, 44). For all we know, Marie may have done everything she could to help Nella short of divorcing her husband— which would have deprived both mother and daughter of financial support. As the narrator of *Quicksand* points out, "Even foolish, despised women must have food and clothing; even unloved little Negro girls must be somehow provided for" (23). The wonder is that Peter Larsen married Nella's mother; perhaps he was prompted to marry her because she had already given birth to their daughter, Anna.

The information on the passenger list of 1898 explains Larsen's late entrance into school. Davis charges that Larsen lied about her early schooling. She informed Knopf's publicity department in 1926 that "Her formal education started at the age of eight. She and her half-sister . . . attended a small private school, whose pupils were mostly the children of German or Scandinavian parents" (qtd. in Davis 22).[5] Because the only school record for her—a form for the Zeno Colman school of 1903—says Larsen had entered *that* school at age nine and a half and was beginning seventh grade in fall 1903, Davis concludes that Larsen did not even start school until she was nearly ten. Yet the Colman school records do not tell us when Larsen's formal schooling began; like the forms for many of her schoolmates, they tell us only when she started *at Colman*.

To further discredit Larsen's testimony, Davis writes, "Contrary to Nella Larsen's later claim, the Colman School has no history as a private school" (23). But Larsen never said the Colman school was

5. A similar statement appeared on the dust jacket for *Passing* (qtd. in Larson, *Invisible* 185).

private. She said only that she went to a private school at the age of eight. Normally, Larsen would have started first grade at age six or seven, but we now know that she was in Denmark for at least part of that school year and returned unable to read or write. If she started school in fall 1898, she would have been seven and a half years old and turned eight in the course of the academic year. It is therefore easy to believe that, having missed the first grade, Larsen went to a small private school catering mainly to German and Scandinavian immigrants; at the turn of the century this was hardly unusual. This would also help explain how Larsen managed to be ready for seventh grade in fall 1903. Had she received her first formal schooling only at age nine and a half, as Davis asserts, then how could she have been prepared for seventh grade only three years later?

Another sensational aspect of Davis's account of Larsen's early youth is her hypothesis that Marie Larsen forced her placement in Chicago's "Erring Woman's Refuge for Reform" sometime before the census of 1900, from which Peter, Davis speculates, later "saved" her (29–30). The census of 1900 shows a "Nellie Larson" living in this institution as of 1 June 1900. But Davis neglects to mention that the census lists her date of birth as July 1892, her father and mother as unknown, and her race as "white" (Twelfth Census, sheet 21). We have Davis and Larson to thank for establishing that Larsen was born 13 April 1891—also the date given on her school register of 1903 (Elementary School Registers). Although, beginning in the late 1920s, Larsen fibbed about the year (listing it as 1893), she consistently gave her birthdate as April 13. Moreover, it is difficult to believe that an American official of 1900 would identify the Nella Larsen we know as white. Indeed, the fact that the girl of unknown parentage in the Erring Woman's Refuge was considered "white" by those who responded to the census contradicts Davis's surmise that Larsen's parents placed her there because she, unlike the rest of the family, was too dark to "pass." As several Nellie Larsons/Larsens lived in Chicago at the turn of the century, we have little reason to believe that the seven-year-old white girl in the Erring Woman's Refuge for Reform was the nine-year-old "colored" girl who would later become a Harlem Renaissance novelist. This is, rather, a piece of speculative "evidence" that fits a particular narrative trajectory the biographer is trying hard to justify—featuring a sympathetic "black" father who "passes" being unable to protect his daughter from the "white" mother's insistence on getting rid of her.

This hypothesis eventually becomes a basis of Davis's readings of *Quicksand* and *Passing* as discharges of violence against Marie Larsen, with much more sympathetic characters standing in for Peter Larsen. Thus, about *Passing* Davis writes:

> If Clare is read as parent and if the maternal/paternal roles are reversed, as Larsen frequently reversed roles and names, then Clare becomes a representation of Peter Larsen with the racist Bellew as spouse standing in for Marie/Mary Larsen, the mother who resented the presence of her own black daughter in her reconfigured family. . . . The situation is much the same in *Quicksand* when Peter Nilssen's unnamed wife rejects all claims of kinship for herself and her husband with his black niece. In *Passing*, Clare's remarkable strength of will, and her equally apparent weakness of character, becomes a way of understanding Peter Larsen, his inability to protect his daughter, and his crossing the color line. (327)

And again, "The child Margery [in *Passing*], like a young version of Larsen herself, is isolated from parents, committed to an institutional life in a boarding school, and is the least of her mother's or her father's concerns" (328).

We can see that, by this central point in Davis's narrative, the unsubstantiated hypotheses that Peter Walker "passed" to become Peter Larsen and that Nella Larsen, rejected by her mother, was placed in the Erring Woman's Refuge at her mother's insistence have taken on the functions of facts which ground the literary analysis. Contrary to Davis's convoluted analysis, *Quicksand* represents the mother as genuinely caring for Helga in childhood (though gradually coming to hate black people) but feeling compelled to marry and to remain married—fighting against the rest of the family's resentment of the "colored" daughter all the while—in order to provide for her girl at least until she reached adulthood and could fend for herself. Larsen's stories of her life are consistent with her first novel (which she told Carl Van Vechten expressed "the awful truth" [qtd. in Davis 9]) in implying that her stepfather and half-sister were chiefly responsible for her estrangement from the family, however strained the relationship with her mother may have been. Such representations should be trusted until far more conclusive evidence to the contrary surfaces.

The Larsens sent Nella off to Fisk in fall 1907—a decision Davis attributes, without evidence, to Peter's concern for her. But in March 1908, Davis points out, her mother visited her for a few days. Larsen dropped out of Fisk at the end of the semester, later claiming that she visited her mother's family in Denmark for three years after this. Davis, discounting the story and implying that it fantasizes a relationship with her mother and her mother's kin, speculates that Marie told Nella the family could or would no longer support her, that she would have to shift for herself.

Davis speculates that instead of visiting Denmark, Larsen "may have married shortly after leaving Fisk and spent at least a year in a small southern community. . . . Females who became pregnant while attending Fisk were expelled, and a woman could not marry and remain a student, even if no pregnancy were involved. A liaison with a male student could well have led Larsen to a premature marriage from which she later extricated herself" (67–68). Thus Larsen becomes a possibly pregnant black teenager, possibly married to an African-American in the rural South, and not the lonely and socially suspect "mulatto" at Fisk who, following her white mother's advice, went to stay with her European relatives.

Larsen did go to Denmark after leaving Fisk. She boarded for her return from Copenhagen on the ship *C. F. Tietgen* 14 January 1909 (Filipsen). When she disembarked two weeks later, an officer listed her nationality as American, her "race or people" as "Scandinavian" (List or Manifest, S. S. *C. F. Tietgen*).[6] She was going home to her parents, Mr. and Mrs. Peter Larsen, at "143 W. 70th Str. Chicago, Ill."—the address Larson first identified as that of her family. Larsen was not exactly "passing." In contemporary Danish sailors' terms, she was not a "Negro."[7] Nor would she have been able to "pass" as Scandinavian on the basis of her appearance, which clearly revealed her mixed ancestry. The family identification—particularly her mother's "race"—and Danish custom would seem to be the defining factors here.

The passenger list does not explain what Larsen did until 1912, when she reappears in reliable American records; but we have no reason to doubt that, as she claimed, she stayed while in Copenhagen with relatives on her mother's side. Notably, at age 17, Marie Hansen (Larsen) herself had left her family in Denmark to start a new life as an American; at practically the same age, no doubt with her mother's support, Larsen (who had by now adopted "Marie" as a middle name) would start a "new life" in Denmark, though one that did not last.

Although Davis does not entirely dismiss the possibility that Larsen

6. The racial identification is particularly striking in that a ship's surgeon had to sign for the veracity of the identification of all passengers, and the forms explicitly state that "any alien whose appearance indicates an admixture of Negro blood" should be classified as "African (black)" ("Instructions for Filling Alien Manifests"). Certainly Larsen's "Negro blood" was apparent. However, since Larsen was not an "alien," the "Scandinavian" label did not violate the letter of the rules.
7. A striking lacuna in Davis's biography is the lack of research into racial formation in the Danish Virgin Islands, which differed dramatically from that of the US. Indeed, Larsen's natural father probably never considered himself a "Negro," since this designation applied only to lower-class and so-called full-blooded Negroes in his native country. Furthermore, Virgin Islanders identified strongly with Denmark and were proud of their Danish citizenship (until the United States' purchase of the islands in 1917). Had Larsen's parents assimilated American concepts of race and nationality, she probably would never have been born. On racial designations in the Danish Virgin Islands, see Lewis (29, 248) and Harman (147–48).

went to Denmark, important aspects of her subsequent interpretations of Larsen's life and novels depend on the assumption that the
Denmark episode was a fabrication. Davis casts doubt on Larsen's
statements even in ways that contradict Davis's own evidence: "While
it is possible that Larsen could have spent some time with her
father's or her mother's 'Scandinavian' relatives, . . . throughout her
public life she displayed little intimate or firsthand knowledge of that
country, even though she could speak and read Danish" (68–69). Let
us remember that Larsen's first two publications presented several
riddles and games she said she learned in Denmark as a child—interpreted by Davis as misleading attempts to raise her status by placing
her childhood self in a "white, foreign country" (140–41). Larsen's
first novel, *Quicksand*, dramatizes striking contrasts between the
racial ideologies of Danes and Americans. It also conveys many
details about Copenhagen (some of which, incidentally, pertain to
the city of 1908 but not of 1920) that no American could have picked
up without experience. I do not have space to go into these details
here; suffice it to say that the chapters set in Denmark are an impressive if compressed comparative study of Danish and American cul-
tures from the perspective of a young woman who identifies in part
with (and against) both of them. Larsen's experience in Denmark,
including exposure to the art and literature of Scandinavia's "Modern Breakthrough" (which centered in Copenhagen), probably had
much to do with her early authorial ambitions. This suggests a context for Larsen's fiction that deserves considerable further scrutiny.

Discussing Larsen's use of her mother's name as her own middle
name at Fisk and when she entered the Lincoln Hospital School for
Nurses (two events bracketing the Denmark visit), Davis states that
"the family that Nellie Larson had known for a brief seven years was
moving more exclusively into a white world, while she had been consigned to a black one" (47). The claim that Larsen, at age 16, had
known the family for just seven years makes sense only if one
assumes that she spent the years before 1900 in the Erring Woman's
Refuge for Reform. Earlier Davis presented this as a mere hypothesis (which does not hold up, as we have seen); here it functions as a
proven fact to make her identification with her mother seem all the
more misguided and pathetic.

To cast further doubt on Larsen's claims of "Danishness" and to
distance her from her mother, Davis elsewhere informs us that, "In a
private conversation in the 1930s . . . [Larsen] revealed that her
mother was German, though born in Denmark" (46). Davis then
points out that Larsen received an "F" in German at the Fisk Normal
School, adding, "The F in German is noteworthy because Larsen
later claimed German was her mother's first language" (50). But
Davis has never demonstrated that Larsen claimed German was her

mother's first language. Once again, Davis casts doubt on Larsen's remarks about her mother to widen the apparent gap between them, suggesting Nella barely knew Marie Larsen. However, the ethnic identification of Marie Larsen is easily explained. Many Danes originally from the southern part of the country were of German descent, the border having shifted over time. Marie's parents may well have been "German" Danes. Alternatively, they may have been Danish although their ancestral homes were in Germany.[8] In short, Larsen evidently had a fairly clear sense of her mother's antecedents, and explanations for her description of her mother's ethnic descent are not hard to find in light of Danish regional and ethnic history.

2

The effect of discounting Larsen's Danish experience and Danish background and her connection to her mother is to subordinate her mature story of her life to a story that cannot accommodate the possibility of someone being both African American and Danish American, reinforcing Davis's general attack on Larsen's "delusion about her whiteness" (16). Davis also accuses Larsen of "assimilationism" and "social climbing" for taking "more pride in her inclusion in interracial gatherings than . . . all-black ones" (232). Larsen's correspondence reveals chiefly that she *enjoyed* and was *invited* to more interracial gatherings than all-black ones. Those blacks who avoided or disdained interracial social affairs were not her friends. This would include—understandably—many middle-class black Americans of the time. As Drake and Cayton would later point out, middle-class backs had "scant interest in the world of white society, and little tolerance for those who ha[d]"[8] (139). Larsen's attitudes toward interracial friendships invited pariah status. Her own fiction stresses repeatedly that this was a typical problem for designated "Negroes" whose connections with white people were deemed too intimate.

Leaving aside Larsen's extended visits to Denmark, what does it mean to say that a woman raised by a Danish mother and stepfather in an immigrant neighborhood is an "assimilationist" because she prefers interracial social occasions and informs people of her Danish background? What is being demanded here is apparently that she

---

8. It is also possible that Davis's source, speaking in an interview five decades after her conversation with Larsen, incorrectly remembered and that Marie was Danish although born in Germany. In either case, the background to this personal history is the protracted struggle between Denmark and Germany for control over the border territories of Schleswig and Holstein. This pivotal series of events in modern Danish history set off a massive migration from Schleswig to Denmark and to the US; many of the emigrants called Denmark their country of origin, though their homes were in Germany (Connery 96; Jones 34–42, 61–62; Hvidt 155–57; Christensen, 13–14, 24, 73, 81, 89).

forget or *suppress* a central aspect of her identity and her personal history.

Davis uses skeptical tones when narrating Larsen's representations of verifiable facts about her biracial background. To her in-laws, "She presented herself as the daughter of an interracial couple and as having been raised in an all-white circle, and begged off identifying her relatives, suggesting that race separated her from them. Her self-representation was determined by an effort to retain a certain glamour about her unusual background" (Davis 5). Yet we know that Larsen's "self-representation" in these respects was entirely accurate. Davis continues: "In labelling herself a mulatto, [Larsen] appropriated language less prevalent among African Americans but popular among West Indians, who used the term to distinguish themselves from the black masses and to evoke a class officially situated between whites and blacks in their native lands. Larsen projected both Danish and West Indian origins as a mark of uniqueness" (5). *Projected?* Davis herself believes that Larsen's father was a man of color from the West Indies and that her mother had immigrated from Denmark. Why is Larsen's attestation to these facts judged to be misleading?

The fact that people from the Caribbean thought of "mulattoes" as "*a class* officially situated between whites and blacks" does not explain Larsen's usage. People in that position did not *also* refer to themselves as Negro, as Larsen usually did. Larsen's occasional reference to herself as "mulatto" (a term she seems actually to have avoided) derives from the desire to specify that she has a black and a white parent and is unwilling to deny either of them. This is a very common desire among children from interracial families.

Davis repeatedly evaluates Larsen's claims to interracial and Danish parentage cynically: "In emphasizing a mixed-racial and ethnic background, Larsen Imes was not underscoring marginality. Rather, as a mulatto, Larsen Imes was stressing her place within a particular group of African Americans for whom such backgrounds inferred class position and social prominence" (141). On the contrary, by Larsen's day, claiming a white mother was no route to social acceptance among the light-skinned African-American elite. To claim a white parent was to invite suspicions of illegitimacy that fit stereotypes about "mulatto" women. Miscegenation was something that purportedly happened only out of wedlock—and, indeed, was illegal in most of the United States and therefore "illegitimate" by definition.

As Larsen's fiction itself stresses, by the early twentieth century it had become distinctly disadvantageous to be perceived as the immediate "colored" offspring of a white person, although being a light-skinned Negro continued to have relative advantages. Yet Davis writes that "Alleging the death of a black West Indian father and the alienation from a white mother remarried to a white man provided

Nella Larsen with unusual social mobility. . . . African Americans would comprehend the racial imperatives that would separate a white mother from her black daughter, and without questioning, they would form a personal bond with the daughter based on a shared understanding of racism" (48). *Quicksand* tells us the opposite; as Helga Crane tearfully tells the "race woman," Mrs. Hayes-Rore, a story much like the one Larsen told of her own life, Hayes-Rore turns away from her, feeling that "The story, dealing as it did with race intermingling and possibly adultery, was beyond definite discussion. For among black people, as among white people, it is tacitly understood that these things are not mentioned—and therefore they do not exist" (41). She then advises Helga not to tell anyone in Harlem about her background: "Colored people won't understand it" (41). Helga thanks her for the advice and reaches out to take her "slightly soiled hand."

The *only way* Larsen could avoid the sort of charge Davis levels against her for "projecting" the Danish origins of her mother is by keeping her Danish background under wraps, by "passing" as the daughter of two Negro parents. This is precisely what Mrs. Hayes-Rore tells Helga Crane to do before introducing her to African-American society. The result, for Helga, is a feeling of suffocation and deep shame for betraying her mother—and herself.

According to research on the subject (even in sources Davis uses to flesh out the situation of African Americans in Chicago), black response to interracial unions and the people born of them was just as Larsen presented it—and remains so to this day in some quarters. In the minds of middle-class Negroes, light mulattoes between 1890 and 1920 became "associated with sin and degradation." It was assumed that "mixing" occurred only among the "lowest" of the "low." Black families had, according to one so-called mixed-race researcher, "an artificially exaggerated animus against interracial unions" (qtd. in Williamson 116; F. James; Davis 57; Drake and Cayton 144–45; Williamson 116–18).

Davis's resistance to Larsen's sense of identity, as well as to Larsen's interracial background and adult social preferences, effectively matches attitudes of the black elite that caused Larsen deep pain throughout her life and that partly inspired her fiction.

3

At times Davis comes much closer to sympathizing with Larsen's position: "Her interracial heritage, though ambiguous was part of her self that she could neither deny nor obscure, not even for position within an elite African-American group after which she patterned her mature, sophisticated self" (13). But by terming her interracial heritage "ambiguous" and implying that Larsen really longed for the sort of identity elite African Americans modeled, this evaluation takes away more than it gives in understanding.

Indeed, when the evidence shows Larsen's desire to differentiate herself from the African-American elite, Davis can only interpret this desire negatively—despite the fact that elsewhere Davis recognizes that elite African Americans would *not* accept someone of Larsen's background as their social equal. Although Larsen most often identified herself as "Negro," she ran "the risk of elevating her alliances with whites and emphasizing her difference from African Americans" (Davis 13). Davis predictably ascribes Larsen's negative responses to particular black women—notably Jessie Fauset, whom Davis regards as Larsen's role model—to "envy" and "psychological disintegration," while significant ideological and ethnic differences are ignored.

Indeed, Davis goes on for several pages about Fauset in attempting to show (with purely hypothetical scenarios of Larsen's thought processes) what a good role model she was for Larsen. "Fauset's background, credentials, achievement, and style impressed Nella Larsen Imes, who saw in Fauset a reflection of the accomplished woman that she herself wanted, and intended, to be" (144). As the delegate of a black women's sorority to the second Pan-African Congress of 1921, Davis informs us, Fauset spoke on women's rights and "colored" women's professional progress.

> Such sentiments particularly endeared her [Fauset] to Larsen Imes, who was at a transitional point at which a new vocation and a rewriting of her self were possible. For Larsen Imes, Fauset functioned as a mirror reflecting a different female image, and her own potential. Fauset's image is in the background of Larsen Imes's transformation of self in the 1920s, and it would reappear as psychological transference in her disintegration during the 1930s. (144).

At no point does Davis provide evidence of Larsen's admiration for Fauset. Not a single footnote directs us to a letter, a conversation, or any other form of support for the idea that Fauset was Larsen's crucial role model as she became an artist. Indeed, many of Fauset's attributes match those of women Larsen attacks in her fiction.

One role of Fauset in Larsen's literary career may have been to serve as an ideological antagonist—someone whose vision of racial identity, especially for mulattoes, Larsen consciously rejected and may have written her fiction to refute. In Fauset's novels, mulatto characters overcome their weaknesses by repudiating their links to white people, being welcomed into the black bourgeoisie, and becoming whole-hearted "race" men and women, committed to uplifting the race. No doubt at considerable cost, including a certain amount of ostracism, Larsen rejected this option in both her writing and her life.

Yet Davis blames Larsen's marginality in the Harlem Renaissance in part on the fading of Fauset's role in the movement: "Estrangement from Fauset would leave Larsen Imes in relative isolation. . . . Eventually she had left only the white male Van Vechten, who though generous in spirit and unfailingly interested in African Americans, never fully comprehended Nella Larsen Imes as a woman of color" (160–61).

There is plenty of evidence in the correspondence between Van Vechten and Larsen, some of it quoted by Davis, that Van Vechten understood this woman better, and cared more about her, than Fauset. (This is not to insist that he understood her all that well.) Whereas we have little evidence of Larsen's feelings toward Fauset, we have plenty of evidence that she was an intimate friend and admirer of Carl Van Vechten—that, along with Dorothy Peterson, he was one of her closest and most loyal friends, even after she had forever given up on writing. Of all her acquaintances, he alone publicly defended her against the plagiarism charges that mortally wounded her literary career, and he hosted birthday parties for her well into the 1930s. But we bring an entirely different set of assumptions to our judgments about interracial relationships than to interacial ones (if such terms apply to Larsen's relationships), and insist on our theories about them regardless of the evidence. If Van Vechten was one of Larsen's best friends, then, according to the obligatory rhetoric, this can only be bad news.

Larsen expected her work to meet the sort of hostility from the black bourgeoisie that Van Vechten's had encountered. Indeed, Larsen and her husband expected "uplifters" at the NAACP to take umbrage at *Quicksand* (see Imes, correspondence to Van Vechten, 7 March 1927). Both Larsen and her husband were astonished by the positive black response to her novel. "On May thirteenth [1928], Sunday, The *Woman's Auxillairy* [sic] of the N.A.A.C.P *is going to give a tea for me!!!*" she informed Van Vechten—with double underscoring for "Woman's Auxillairy" and quintuple for "me." She continued, "The good God only knows why. I hope you will get an invitation because this will be a time when I will need all of my friends." She worried about her husband's reaction to the news, and "wanted very much to have the pleasure of refusing . . . I hope I did the wise thing to accept" (Imes, Correspondence to Van Vechten, 1 May 1928). Larsen's trepidation is not surprising. The NAACP women's auxiliary included the sort of people she had satirized in her novel.

Larsen's closest white friends were people Fauset held in contempt:

the publication of *Nigger Heaven* (1926) was one of the incidents that inspired her and W. E. B. Du Bois to conduct their poll for *The Crisis*, "The Negro in Art: How Shall He Be Portrayed?" (1926–27). Larsen, on the other hand, wrote Van Vechten with sympathetic tongue-in-check that he was "the best thing that ever happened to the Negro race" (Imes, 7 May 1927). To Davis, this is simply more evidence of snobbishness and racial self-hatred on Larsen's part.

Larsen's second novel, *Passing*, was dedicated to Van Vechten and his wife Fania Marinoff; she was thumbing her nose at the black uplifters who had pilloried *Nigger Heaven*.[9] Like *Quicksand*, *Passing* was in part a satire of black and white obsessions with "racial integrity"—through this critique has yet to be recognized in the scholarship surrounding the novel. This is not to suggest that Larsen categorically disdained the black bourgeoisie, nor that she ignored the pervasiveness of white racism, but those members of the black elite whom she did befriend, and who befriended her, all enjoyed strong interracial friendships. Larsen apparently preferred neither all-white nor all-black social circles; she liked to be part of a "mixed" group, even at the end of her life, when (as Larson and Davis show) her two closest acquaintances were a black woman and a white woman.

All the evidence suggests that Larsen's mother remained a part of her self that was permanent, undeniable, and racially coded. This is not a pathology to be diagnosed. The feelings many blacks had toward interracial intimacy (however reasonable their motivation) were not just feelings Larsen could not share; they made her feel partly excluded, "different," even defiant—for understandable reasons. She is so emphatic on this point in *Quicksand*, especially, that one has to be struck by Davis's tendencies to sweep it under the rug, or to dismiss Larsen's views as "simplistic" and blind to the "realities" of racism.

Larsen's ideas about race were anything but simplistic, and her awareness of the reality of racism was more intimate and multifaceted than that of any other American author of her generation, for reasons that have everything to do with her personal history. Yet current studies of her fiction firmly discount the significance of biracial and Danish-American identity to *Quicksand*, or else interpret biracial subjectivity as merely a metaphor for more "important" concerns—black and/or female identity, in particular.

Davis, at the end of her biography, widens her scope to show the coherence of the narrative she has imposed on Larsen's life with a

9. After taking the manuscript of *Quicksand* in to Knopf, she had written her friend, "Heaven forbid that I should ever be bitten by the desire to write another novel! Except, perhaps, one to dedicate to you. For, why should Langston Hughes be the only one to enjoy notoriety for the sake of his convictions?" (Imes to Van Vechten, 7 March 1927). Hughes had dedicated his just-published *Fine Clothes to the Jew* (1927) to Van Vechten, and had been roasted for the book in the mainstream black press.

narrative of black women's emergence in American literature and acad-eme. Larsen, we are informed, only found her "longed for 'place'" posthumously when African Americans of the post-1960s forged "famil-ial ties" with her in their "effort to establish kinship and heritage . . . lay-ing claim to Nella Larsen as one of their own" (455). Larsen has indeed been rescued from obscurity thanks chiefly to black feminist critics, especially Davis—and by Charles Larson, as well. However, one can only conclude that the process by which Davis has made Larsen fit into the kinship system and cultural identity here modeled has done strange violence to the story of her life, subordinating it to assumptions about race and identity she knowingly, persistently rejected.

Despite the many valuable facts the biographers have managed to recover, the stories they tell are fundamentally flawed, reproducing the bipolar structure of American black/white racial culture at the expense of the interracial subject. In the final analysis, Davis's work particularly follows the perennial American tendency to scapegoat or repress interracial communion, a tendency that blighted Larsen's life and that she resisted to her very death—for all we know, as eloquently in her long and productive nursing career as in her novels. Never embracing Jean Toomer's idea of a "new race," Larsen rather exposed the violence of racialization as such—the force that had divided her from her mother—in the attempt to make it ethically insupportable, an affront to humanity. This is not a project that those who value the possibilities of democratic culture in a multiracial state can afford to dismiss, although we may feel forced to work within racialized parameters, as Larsen did. If we have found the life of Larsen so hard to understand, her self-representations so hard to believe, then in what corresponding ways have we directed ourselves away from the most original and important truths of her fictions?

Works Cited

Baedeker, Karl. *Norway, Sweden, and Denmark, with Excursions to Iceland and Spitzbergen: Handbook for Travelers*. New York: Scrib-ner's, 1912.

Blackmore, David L. "'That Unreasonable Restless Feeling': The Homosexual Subtexts of Nella Larsen's *Passing." African American Review* 26 (1992): 475–84.

Braun, Patricia Galster. Letter to the author. 11 July 1996.

Butler, Judith. *Bodies That Matter: On the Discursive Limits of "Sex."* New York: Routledge, 1993.

Christensen, Thomas Peter. *A History of the Danes in Iowa*. 1952. New York: Arno, 1979.

Connery, Donald S. *The Scandinavians*. New York: Simon, 1966.

Davis, F. James. *Who Is Black? One Nation's Definition*. University Park: Pennsylvania State UP, 1991.

Davis, Thadious. *Nella Larsen, Novelist of the Harlem Renaissance: A Woman's Life Unveiled*. Baton Rouge: Louisiana State UP, 1994.

Dearborn, Mary V. *Pocahontas's Daughters: Gender and Ethnicity in American Culture*. New York: Oxford Up, 1986.

Direct-emigration lists, 1897–1901. Landsarkivet for Sjaelland, Copenhagen.

Drake, St. Clair, and Horace Cayton. *Black Metropolis*. Vol. 1. New York: Harper, 1962. 2 vols.

Du Cille, Ann. *The Coupling Convention: Sex, Text, and Tradition in Black Women's Fiction*. New York: Oxford UP, 1993.

Elementary School Register Records (card file). Colman School, 1880s–1920s. Bureau of Former Student Records, Chicago Board of Education.

Elementary School Registers (microfilm). Colman School, reel 44. Bureau of Former Student Records, Chicago Board of Education.

Filipsen, Vibeke. Letter to the author. 9 Feb. 1995.

Fishkin, Shelley Fisher. "Essentialism and Its Discontents." *American Quarterly* 48 (1996): 142–52.

Funderburg, Lise. *Black, White, Other: Biracial Americans Talk About Race and Identity*. New York: Morrow, 1994.

Harman, Jeanne Perkins. *The Virgins: Magic Islands*. New York: Appleton, 1961.

Hostetler, Ann E. "The Aesthetics of Race and Gender in Nella Larsen's *Quicksand*." *PMLA* 105 (1990): 35–46.

Hvidt, Kristian. *Danes Go West*. Copenhagen: Rebild National Park Society, 1976.

Imes, Nella Larsen. Correspondence with Carl Van Vechten. Carl Van Vechten Papers. American Literature Collection. Beinecke Rare Book and Manuscript Library, Yale University, New Haven.

"Instructions for Filling Alien Manifests." Passenger and Crew Lists of New York, 1897–1924. U.S. Immigration and Naturalization Service. National Archives, Washington, DC.

Jones, W. Glyn. *Denmark: A Modern History*. London: Croom, 1986.

Larsen, Nella. *Quicksand. "Quicksand" and "Passing."* Ed. Deborah E. McDowell. New Brunswick: Rutgers UP, 1986.

Larson, Charles R. "Introduction." *An Intimation of Things Distant: The Collected Fiction of Nella Larsen*. Ed. Charles R. Larson. New York: Anchor, 1992. ix–xxxv.

———. *Invisible Darkness: Jean Toomer and Nella Larsen*. Iowa City: U of Iowa P, 1993.

Lewis, Gordon K. *The Virgin Islands: A Caribbean Lilliput*. Evanston: Northwestern UP, 1972.

License no. 1030237. Cook County Vital Records, Marriage Licenses, 1871–1920. Cook County Records, Chicago.

"List or Manifest of Alien Immigrants for the Commissioner of Immigration." S. S. *Norge*, 6 May 1898. Included in "New York Passenger Arrivals, May 6, 1898." U.S. Immigration and Naturalization Service. Washington: National Archives.

"List or Manifest of Alien Passengers for the United States." S. S. *C.F. Tietgen*, 29 January 1909. In "New York Passenger Arrivals, January 29, 1909." U.S. Immigration and Naturalization Service. Washington: National Archives.

McDowell, Deborah E. "Introduction." *"Quicksand" and "Passing."* By Nella Larsen. Ed. Deborah E. McDowell. New Brunswick: Rutgers UP, 1986. ix–xxxv.

McLendon, Jacquelyn Y. *The Politics of Color in the Fiction of Jessie Fauset and Nella Larsen*. Charlottesville: UP of Virginia, 1995.

Petersen, Mae. Letter to the author. 9 May 1996.

Spear, Allan H. *Black Chicago*. Chicago: U of Chicago P, 1967.

Tate, Claudia. "Nella Larsen's *Passing*: A Problem of Interpretation." *Black American Literature Forum* 14 (1980): 142–46.

Thornton, Hortense E. "Sexism as Quagmire: Nella Larsen's *Quicksand*." *CLA Journal* 16 (1973): 285–301.

Twelfth Census, 1900: Cook County, Illinois. Enumeration District 1029. Microfilm reel 1240286 in Genealogical Society Archives, Salt Lake City.

Wagner-Martin, Linda. Rev. of *Nella Larsen, Novelist of the Harlem Renaissance: A Woman's Life Unveiled*, by Thadious Davis. *American Literature* 67 (1995): 159–160.

———. *Telling Women's Lives: The New Biography*. New Brunswick: Rutgers UP, 1994.

Wall, Cheryl A. "Passing for What? Aspects of Identity in Nella Larsen's Novels." *Black American Literature Forum* 20 (1986): 97–111.

Williamson, Joel. *New People: Miscegenation and Mulattoes in the United States*. New York, Free, 1980.

KATE BALDWIN

From The Recurring Conditions of Nella Larsen's *Passing*†

"Border Line"
I used to wonder
About living and dying—
I think the difference lies
Between tears and crying

I used to wonder
About here and there—
I think the distance
Is nowhere
—Langston Hughes[1]

And though no perfect likeness they can trace,
Yet each pretends to know the copied face.
These, with false glosses feed their own ill nature,
And turn to libel, what was meant a satire.[2]

Part I Untimely Endings

It was not until the end of March 1964 that someone at New York's Metropolitan Hospital noticed that Nella Larsen Imes had been absent from her nursing duties for at least a week. Because in the previous months Larsen had intentionally fallen out of touch with her few remaining friends, no one but her colleagues at the hospital might have suspected some misadventure, something amiss. In fact, Larsen had died, without fanfare or mishap, while reading in bed. Just as thirty years earlier she had done her best to disentangle herself from her peers in what has come to be known as the "Harlem Renaissance,"[3] towards the end of her life Larsen

---

† From Kate Baldwin, "The Recurring Conditions of Nella Larsen's *Passing*," *Theory@Buffalo* 4 (1998): pp. 50–90. Reprinted by permission of the author. Bracketed page numbers refer to this Norton Critical Edition.
1. Langston Hughes, *Selected Poems of Langston Hughes* (New York: Random House, 1990), 81.
2. Taken from a letter from Larsen to Carl Van Vechten (October 6, 1926). Larsen ascribes the passage to Osbert Sitwell's Triple Figure, in which she had found this Congreve poem. The letter is from the James Weldon Johnson Collection, Beinecke Rare Book and Manuscript Library, Yale University. Hereafter JWJC.
3. For a discussion of the potentially misleading implications of this designation, see Hazel Carby, "The Quicksands of Representation," *Reconstructing Womanhood: The Emergence of the Afro-American Woman Novelist* (New York: Oxford University Press, 1987). 163–167.

purposefully disassociated herself from social ties. And yet despite the outpouring of acquaintances from her later life who appeared at her memorial service, Larsen somehow seemed to remain elusive of their grasp, to retain, in a sense, artistic control over the indeterminancy with which, in the end, she would be read. This partiality for the impartial is nowhere better reflected than in the eulogy, read by Alice Carper, that closed with the following sentiment, "Her passing is a great loss, and she will be missed by her coworkers and many friends."[4] These seemingly mundane funereal words magnetize, however unwittingly, the contingencies of Larsen's death and of her life by bringing the two together under the rubric of an idea that had haunted Larsen throughout her life, and as Carper's words attest, through her ritual removal from it: "passing."[5]

Necessarily situated at the center of theoretical debates between proponents of identity politics and social constructionists, the notion of racial "passing" disrupts both sides' attempts to assert a coherent racial self. Demonstrating on the one hand how employing blood as a metaphor for corporeal difference makes uncomfortable allies out of advocates of identity politics and advocates of the so-called "One Drop Rule" propounded by Plessy v. Ferguson in 1896, and on the other hand, how in place of physiological difference "race" has come to be understood as more than fact, that is, a manifestation or affect which cannot be reduced, passing consistently causes cognitive gaps. A novel such as Larsen's *Passing*, which supplies its own theories about race and representation, puts this discussion into the context of narrative structure by foregrounding the parallel strategies of "passing" as a social act and *Passing* as a narrative one. In fact, *Passing* uses "passing" to further its own cause: as an enabling fiction, based on a misreading, in which the body proves to be an unreliable source for the revelation of identity. In so doing *Passing* provokes narrative tensions between the status of "the feminine" and "the abject" in relation to the racialized body.[6]

These tensions contribute to the protagonist's inability to remember, an inability which, by foregrounding the protagonist's difficulty

4. Alice L. Carper, Eulogy for Nella Larsen Imes, April 6, 1964, as cited in Thadious Davis, *Nella Larsen: Novelist of the Harlem Renaissance* (Baton Rouge: Louisiana State University Press, 1994). 453.
5. Like that of her death, the exact circumstances of Larsen's birth, including the racial identities of her parents, are unclear. She was, however, raised as "white" for a few years in Chicago prior to being sent to school to be readied for her role as a proper black middle class woman. Larsen's sister, Anna Larsen Gardner, a successfully "white" woman, repeatedly denied her relation to Nella, who was somewhat darker, and feigned surprise when she was awarded a large sum upon Nella's death. See Davis, especially 441–455.
6. "Abjection" as a theoretical term has been most fully elaborated by Julia Kristeva in *Powers of Horror: An Essay on Abjection*, trans. Leon Roudiez (New York: Columbia University Press, 1982). * * *

in locating her place within the passing narrative, allows the reader to examine the space between an identifiably "real" racial self and an idealized one. Passing is an act that implicity interrogates its own end, and so, too, does *Passing* rely upon successive re-readings of its closing pages. * * * Passing persistently reminds the subject of the inescapability of the body—Project[ing] an unnameable boundary between identity and idealization that the social order must sublimate in order to maintain the illusion of identity as stable, coherent, and infinitely achieved. * * * Passing faces its own impossibility, that is, the possibility that it cannot exist without some prior ascription to either (racial) essentialism or (social) constructionism both of which, as *Passing* demonstrates, insist on understanding the self without examining the structures of the symbolic (or "white" superiority) in which these discourses are embedded. Both essentialism and constructionism read through the body—either as visible or as necessarily invisible—so that all the corresponding attributes of the racial self become ways of seeing the "it" in which one's consummate racial "identity" is lodged. Rather than simply subverting racial "difference," passing disrupts the neatness of such a coherent "choice." In interrogating the tendency to use the term "passing" as necessarily indicative of a subversive act, passing works to uphold the very categories it would seek to sever, not simply those of "black" and "white," but of the very confines of identity as anything but impartial. In place of subversion, *Passing* asks us to read the "error" of identity, to acknowledge that when talking about passing we are also talking about the story that passing enables us to tell, the story of identity as necessarily always displaced.

In the eulogy read by Alice Carper, the very substitution of "passing" for "death" suggests a synechdochal relation in which "passing" stands in for "death" to create an illusion of identicalness. "Passing," in this sense, "passes" for "death" with "reading" serving as the unspoken agent of their connectedness. "Passing," that is to say "death," names itself within the very act of reading. But in naming itself, "passing" also names its own failure, that is its non-identicalness which never can be "read" entirely. "Passing" as *active* participle—i.e., racial passing—maps out a kind of life in death by continually signifying its own failure to find "meaning" in a face, the "truth" of which is necessarily found elsewhere.[7] Larsen's wish to disengage from previous attachments reflects

---

7. As Henry Louis Gates, Jr. has argued racial passing can imply simultaneously difference and death as in the phrase "passing on." See Henry Louis Gates, Jr. *Figures in Black: Words, Signs and the "Racial Self"* (New York: Oxford University Press, 1987), 202. Also cited in Judith Butler's "Passing, Queering: Nella Larsen's Psychoanalytic Challenge," *Bodies That Matter: On the Discursive Limits of "Sex"* (New York: Routledge, 1993), 167–185 [reprinted in this edition, p. 417]. For a variety of recent analyses of passing see *Passing and the Fictions of Identity*, ed. Elaine K. Ginsberg (Durham: Duke University Press, 1996).

a certain disinterestedness in endings, a desire to defer specificity, and an unwillingness on some level, finally, to "pass." But at the same time the circumstances of Larsen's death also suggest the opposite: Larsen's acceptance of her own passing or at least an understanding of her passing" as an act intimately related to, if not entirely subsumed by, the very *act* of reading. How fitting then Larsen's death by reading (in bed).

Larsen's fullest attempt to trace out the social and psychic dilemmas of "passing" can be found in her novel *Passing*, the story of an uneasy friendship between two light-skinned black women. Perhaps appropriately Larsen's *Passing* remains imbricated in some confusion as to the accuracy of endings and their relationship to reading. While it is fairly well known that there were two published endings to the novel—both published by Knopf, the first in 1929, and the second in 1930—the implications of these two, quite different, endings have not be investigated.[8] Both versions are currently in circulation: one published in 1989 by Rutgers, and the other published by Doubleday's Anchor Books in 1992 and by Penguin in 1997. Rutgers' *Passing* reprints the 1929 edition:

> Her quaking knees gave way under her. She moaned and sank down, moaned again. Through the great heaviness that submerged and drowned her she was dimly conscious of strong arms lifting her up. Then everything was dark.[9]

A footnote refers to the deletion of two additional sentences. The Anchor and Penguin editions of *Passing* closes [sic] with these additional lines, lines that appeared in the second and third editions published by Knopf:

> Centuries after, she heard the strange man saying: "Death by misadventure, I'm inclined to believe. Let's go up and have another look at that window."[1]

In the Anchor and Penguin editions, there is no mention of the original ending.[2]

The fact that there are two different endings currently in circulation highlights the problematics involved in reading passing. Just as

8. A bibliographic reference to the disparity between the two endings can be found in Mark J. Madigan, " 'Then everything was dark'?: The Two Endings of Nella Larsen's Passing," *Papers of the Bibliographical Society of America* 83, no. 4 (December 1990): 591–593.
9. Nella Larsen, "Passing," *Quicksand and Passing*, ed. Deborah E. McDowell (New Brunswick: Rutgers University Press, 1986). 242. [Reprinted in this edition, p. 363].
1. Nella Larsen, "Passing," An Intimation of Things Distant: The Collected Fiction of Nella Larsen, ed. Charles Larson (New York: Anchor Books, 1992), 276; and Larsen, *Passing* (New York: Penguin, 1997). 114. [In the Penguin edition, these variant endings are discussed both in Thadious M. Davis's Introduction and in her "A Note on the Text"—*Editor*].
2. I will proceed to use the labels "first" and "second" ending only as a way to delineate, with no intention of assigning priority or importance to one or the other. However, for the sake of clarity, all quotes henceforth will be taken from, paginated, and cited in the main text in accordance with the 1989 Rutgers edition.

it is difficult to make a decisive reading of *Passing,* passing as a topic necessarily invokes questions of identity and self which are hardly teleological. When talking about racial passing, there is an assumption that deception is taking place on the level of the visible, that if the passer were true to her race, then she would be visibly recognizable as accountable to it. In excavating the truth of race as never self-coincident, passing provides a story for which the vocabulary of race proves insufficient. Moments of passing which disrupt the smooth functioning of taxonomic systems can be witnessed in locutionary moments of arrest, that is, in a certain rupture in the narrative code to which characters ascribe and are ascribed. In much the same way that *Passing* leaves us uncertain as to the real closure of the text, passing continues to spin us into the realm of the "imaginary," that is, outside the realm of the symbolic, to its underside where we find abjection. In generating its own failure to recuperate proper meaning, passing defers finality. In this way the dilemma of *Passing*'s ending reflects the structure of passing as necessarily partial, as both narrative and performative decoy, as a figure for cultural authority caught in the act of composing its own image.

At issue in the closing of the pages of *Passing* is the very question of causality as it relates specifically to the spectacle of death. Some discussions of *Passing* have concurred that Irene Redfield, the protagonist of the novella, is guilty of Clare Kendry's (Irene's nemesis) death, going so far as to say that Clare embodies a symbolic black world of earthy bodiliness that Irene, as the opposite image of Clare, has to suppress. They argue that the novella's denouement, in which Clare plunges to her death, can be read as an intentional act executed by Irene: By pushing Clare off the porch, Irene succeeds in silencing both the color and, implicitly, the sexuality represented by the Harlem Renaissance and encapsulated in the body of Clare Kendry.[3] In her book, *Black Looks: Race and Representation,* the critic bell hooks writes,

> The course I teach on black women writers is a consistent favorite among students. The last semester that I taught this course we had the usual passionate discussion of Nella Larson's [sic] novel *Passing* . . . I suggested to the class that Clare, the black woman who has passed for white all her adult life and married a wealthy white businessman with whom she has a child, is

---

3. I am referring here to two articles, one by Jacquelyn Y. McLendon titled "Self-Representation as Art in the Novels of Nella Larsen," *Gender & Genre in Literature,* ed. Janice Morgan (New York: Garland Publishing, Inc. 1991); the other by Jennifer Devere Brody titled "Clare Kendry's 'True' Colors: Race and Class Conflict in Nella Larsen's *Passing,*" *Callaloo* 15 (Fall 1992): 1053–1065 [reprinted in this edition, p. 393]; as well as a talk by Corinne E. Blackmer titled "Mask or Veil: Lesbianism and Race in Nella Larsen's *Passing,*" presented at the 1992 *Modern Language Association Conference,* New York, New York.

the only character in the novel who truly desires 'blackness' and that it is this desire that leads to her murder . . . [4]

Figuring the entire black *race* into one *passing* body proves quite a burden for a single body to bear, but hooks does not broach the question of whether Clare's passing problematizes her status as a "black woman." In order to support her assumption that Clare is undoubtedly a black woman, the only character who "truly desires blackness," hooks argues that the death of Clare is a murder with intent to kill, or "racial annihilation." Why is it that desire becomes the measure of one's racial authenticity? According to hooks it is because the position of "loving blackness" in "a white supremacist culture" is so taboo that one black and white formulation of truth proceeds from another. If hooks were to interrogate the function of Clare as a passing figure, her reading of Clare's death would need to depend less upon fixed racial formulae, thereby allowing for the partial, if not contradictory, "natures" of racial and sexual identities as they come to be socially represented.

The use of the phrase "death by misadventure" (in the "second" ending to *Passing*) to describe Clare's death suggests not only ambiguity about the nature of Clare's death, but *Passing*'s insistence on interrogating its own narrative authority. According to the O.E.D. "misadventure" comes from the French *mesavenir*—to chance badly—and means "ill-luck, bad fortune, a mishap or misfortune."[5] This word has a more specific definition in its legal usage: "an accident that causes serious injury or death to a human being and that does not involve negligence, wrongful purpose, or unlawful conduct."[6] Certainly the "second" ending allows us to ascertain that Clare's death was not a murder in any intentional sense. Rather the uncertainty of Clare's death symbolizes a challenge to the very self-enclosed and group identity affirming narrative that passing, as a ritual tale of elimination in the name of racial difference, recounts. In its use, then, of borrowed language, *Passing*'s invocation of "death by misadventure" turns to literary precedent, the Hades chapter of James Joyce's *Ulysses*, first published in 1922. The phrase, "death by misadventure" arises when Bloom learns of his father's suicide.[7]

4. bell hooks, *Black Looks: Race and Representation* (Boston: South End Press, 1992). 9.
5. *The Oxford English Dictionary*, Second Edition (Oxford: Clarendon Press, 1989), IX:844.
6. *Black's Law Dictionary* goes to even greater lengths to exonerate those involved in "misadventure." The definition therein reads: "mischance or accident; a casualty caused by the act of one person inflicting injury upon another. Homicide by 'misadventure' occurs where a man, doing a lawful act, without any intention of hurt, unfortunately kills another." *Black's Law Dictionary Fifth Edition* (St. Paul: West Publishing Co., 1979).
7. Because there has been recent debate as to the accuracy of various editions of *Ulysses*, it is with critical attention that I have chosen the 1993 Oxford edition, which most closely resembles the edition Larsen would have read.

That afternoon of the inquest. The redlabelled bottle on the table. The room in the hotel with hunting pictures. Stuffy it was. Sunlight through the slats of the Venetian blind. The coroner's ears, big and hairy. Boots giving evidence. Thought he was asleep first. Then saw like yellow streaks on his face. Had slipped down to the foot of the bed. Verdict: overdose. Death by misadventure. The letter. For my son Leopold.

No more pain. Wake no more. Nobody owns.[8]

Despite the scandal surrounding *Ulysses*, and the difficulties that Egoist Press had in distributing the text, Larsen was able to attain the novel through her friend, Dorothy Peterson, in 1927.[9] It is more than likely that Larsen, a librarian at the time, had read *Ulysses* by the time she began working on *Passing* in 1928, and a juxtaposition of the two death scenes reveals similarities. Both occur in a room foreign to the protagonist. Both uses of the phrase "death by misadventure" appear in the police report, suggesting that if we believe the official report we can infer that the legal usage of the phrase is the appropriate one. However, Joyce's use of "death by misadventure" contradicts this conclusion.[1] Bloom's father's death is an "overdose," and Bloom understands the phrase to mean that his father has committed suicide. Is it possible to interpret Clare's death as a suicide of specific "overdose" proportions?[2] The three phrases that close Bloom's memory of his father's death are "No more pain. Wake no more. Nobody owns"— three phrases which could well be applied to Clare as the woman seeking escape from the waking pain of functioning, in the passing narrative, as the very site from which meaning is derived. In other words, as the liminal character for which *Passing* cannot locate an appropriate name, Clare defines the terms of community in which she circulates. The perpetuity of this community as coherent nuclei of racial difference depends upon the threatening of closed borders in order to reaffirm the terms of racial difference. Making herself absent, refusing to operate as the arbiter of difference, Clare disowns a community in which she had no claim to ownership, no authority. Clare

---

8. James Joyce, *Ulysses*: "The 1922 Text" (Rpt. Oxford: Oxford University Press, 1993). 93.
9. As Thadious Davis records, "Occasionally, she asked that friends traveling abroad bring her particular books, such as James Joyce's *Ulysses*, which she requested from Dorothy Peterson in 1927." Davis, 164.
1. The phrase "death by misadventure" is commonly found in 1920s mystery novels, a fact that could either corroborate the ubiquity of *Passing's* veiled determinism or contradict it.
2. The closest criticism has come to such an interpretation can be found in the work of Cheryl Wall, who talks about Clare's death as "psychological murder." See her article, "Passing for What? Aspects of Identity in Nella Larsen's Novels," *Black American Literature Forum* 20, no. 1–2 (1986): 97–112 [reprinted in this edition, p. 356]. Judith Butler provides a compelling psychoanalytic reading of death as "shattering the veneer of whiteness," but she, too, does not explore the possibility that Clare's death could also represent an "overdose." See her essay, "Passing, Queering: Nella Larsen's Psychoanalytic Challenge," *Bodies That Matter: On the Discursive Limits of "Sex."* [Reprinted in this edition, p. 417].

lacked authority because the narrative of passing preceded her. Her self-sacrifice is a refusal of the terms which bind her, while at the same time the very idea of choice—did she have a choice?—is thrown into question. What Clare leaves behind, and the means *Passing* offers us to interpret what remains repeatedly reframes this question be returning us as readers to the site of *Passing*'s end. In place of an ending, howerver, we find refusal. In fact, *Passing* requires that we read across the threshold of its narrative boundaries. *Passing*, in a sense, refuses the recurrence of cultural self-identification, and in its place offers recurring doubt—elements of a story which resist completion.

No doubt Larsen's own exchange at the hands of those around her during the 1920s had some impact on her own ambivalent relationship to endings. In fact, Larsen's "ending" as a novelist testifies to the persistence of this ambivalent rapport. Her decision to fall out from the artistic circle of which she was a vital member came about in part as a response to an accusation of plagiarism following the publication of her short story, "Sanctuary," in 1930. Although Larsen was acquitted of the charge, her career never recovered from the scandal; Larsen's subsequent equivocation elaborates on her own relationship to Passing. In May of 1932 she wrote to her close friend Carl Van Vechten that she had passed only once: "You will be amused to know that I who have never tried this much discussed 'passing' stunt have waited until I reached the deep south to put it over."[3] Larsen's reference to passing as a "stunt" offers a reading of Clare's death as a stunt turned sour: an incident which turned on the act of getting too close to an edge—whether of the color line or a sixth story window—and at the last minute transformed Clare from daredevil to tragic figure. And while Larsen claimed not to have passed until 1932, being the first black woman to receive a Guggenheim Fellowship (in 1930) must have felt like a kind of passing. To be sure, Larsen's inclusion in the small literary set led by Van Vechten and his wife Fania Marinoff afforded her all kinds of luxuries not usually available to the most black woman of the time. We can only imagine Larsen's disgust and disappointment at being publicly branded a plagiarist by the white publishing world, a label akin to "caught passing."[4]

In abandoning the literary world Larsen also stepped away from the door leading to the wealthy, white social circles in which she once traveled; both Van Vechten and Dorothy Peterson, long time correspondents with Larsen, were dropped from her life. Yet the influence Van

3. Letter to Carl Van Vechten, May 14, 1932, JWJC. [Letter reprinted in this edition, p. 170].
4. Judith Butler makes a similar point which she credits to Barbara Christian. Butler writes, "Tragically, the logic of 'passing' and 'exposure' came to afflict and, indeed, to end Nella Larsen's own authorial career, for when she published a short story, 'Sanctuary,' in 1930, she was accused of plagiarism, that is, exposed as 'passing' as the true originator of the work" (185).

Vechten exerted upon Larsen prior to her public humiliation cannot be underestimated. During the 1920s Van Vechten provided both monetary and social support to several "fledgling" New Negroes. His connection to Knopf was direct and powerful—both *Quicksand* (Larsen's first novel) and *Passing* were accepted for publication by Knopf with the Van Vechten stamp of approval. Larsen dedicated *Passing* to Van Vechten, whom she called as "the grandest friend I've ever had, and I hope I will never do anything to merit the withdrawal of your friendship."[5] In spite of a deeply divided reaction to Van Vechten's own novel, *Nigger Heaven*, on the part of a growing African-American literary set, Van Vechten continued to act as arbiter of black representation throughout the late twenties and into the early thirties. Unlike other African-American notables, Larsen celebrated *Nigger Heaven*'s spontaneity of prose: "the first time I tore through it breathlessly. The second time I read it ever so carefully, tasting the full savor of its fastidious styles and subtleties," and credited the author with having caught what she called "the spirit inherent" in African-Americans, "the mixedness of things, the savagery under the sophistication."[6] Larsen's comments only reconfirm that the "black experience" can be rendered in "racialized" terms that appeal both to "blacks" and "whites."[7]

Larsen dealt with the task of "race" placed upon her by people like Van Vechten, who sought the construction of a particular race aesthetics, by abandoning the project with which she had hoped to combat this burden. Larsen withdrew from the literary spotlight into relative obscurity; her uncatalogued correspondence ends in 1933.[8] As a novelist who proclaimed herself ardently materialistic, Larsen had seen the path of author as a means to an end: "Her dream did not carry with it a place for herself in a bohemian world of artists; rather, it was an updated version of the dream of a middle-class woman to achieve status, position, and money within the upper social echelons."[9] Whereas Larsen did not feel comfortable among "the masses of black people, especially the lower, working-class folk,"[1] her experience as one conscripted by racial ontology into "the masses" caused her to eschew the prominent position of novelist and return to a working-class existence. Her voice as active participant in the cultural production of blackness was thereby delimited until the recent

5. Letter to Carl Van Vechten, 18 February, 1928, JWJC.
6. Letter to Carl Van Vechten, 12 August, 1926; and Wednesday 6 [1926].
7. For more information about this period, and the scandal surrounding *Nigger Heaven*, see David Levering Lewis's incisive account in *When Harlem Was in Vogue* (New York: Oxford, 1979), in particular 180–191. Larsen's response to Van Vechten's *Nigger Heaven* is strikingly similar to Richard Wright's equally unpopular response to Gertrude Stein's Melanctha.
8. The Beinecke collection of her letters is the only existing compilation of her correspondence.
9. Davis, 217.
1. Davis, 189.

recovery of her work by contemporary critics of African-American history and literature. As we have seen, Larsen's multi-layered relationship to passing shapes her into a figure that, like other passing characters, requires her silencing, an arrest that forces readers of *Passing* into the uneasy position of attempting to interpret the ambivalences mandated by that silence.

Part II Lettering Memory

Passing's narrative, however, provides pieces of interpretive scaffolding with which we can begin to address these ambivalences. To begin with, *Passing* is told through the memory of Irene. If it is Irene who, as we witnessed above, proceeds to pass out at the end of the story, then it follows that the story is over—we can no longer be privy to a narrative that came to us from a character who is no longer conscious. Or can we? The second ending goes beyond the limits of the narrative as it has been told to us. If we see that the second ending is indeed in excess of its frame, then we also can see that the overstepping of narrative boundaries questions the power and reliability of Irene's memory, or the narrative itself. For if the ending requires movement across the threshold of Irene's consciousness, then perhaps *Passing* requires such a movement. In other words, I propose that the story that *Passing* enables, the story that *Passing* "pushes off," is precisely the story found in the tension between Irene's selective memory and her unconscious forgetting.

We can see how an anxiety over the real, much like that evinced by the uncertainty over the true ending, gets set up in terms of construction and containment through the letter which introduces us to Clare Kendry. Part One of *Passing* works as a series of Irene's recollections triggered by a letter from Clare. The novel begins:

> It was the last letter in Irene Redfield's little pile of morning mail. After her other ordinary and clearly directed letters the long envelope of thin Italian paper with its almost illegible scrawl seemed out of place and alien. And there was, too, something mysterious and slightly furtive about it. A thin sly thing which bore no return address to betray the sender. Not that she hadn't immediately known who its sender was. Some two years ago she had one very like it in outward appearance. Furtive, but yet in some peculiar, determined way a little flaunting. Purple ink. Foreign paper of extraordinary size (143). [5]

The passage sets up Clare, not yet named, as an exotic other, "out of place and alien," "mysterious," "peculiar," and "foreign." The language works through a tension between the "readable" and the "unreadable;" whereas Irene knows just by looking who the sender is,

she can barely make out the "almost illegible" scrawl. Clare is immediately depicted in terms of appearances which entice yet remain
inscrutable, terms which indicate Irene's epistemological praxis of
displacement. Framing Clare so as to identify her within the bounds
of what Irene claims is her "true self" only marks the shell of a prior
history, the public signifiers through which Clare has passed. The letter's framing reconfirms connections between narrative and performative structures of passing—connections which are further
strengthened by Irene's inability to fully comprehend the gaps in her
response to the letter/Clare. If the letter figures Clare, then Clare,
too, is "language," the condition of the speaking subject. "Passing" in
this sense becomes a process of signification.

How is this done? Clare's letter jostles Irene's memory so that Irene
generates a series of recollections which place Clare within "all that
she [Irene] remembered" about Clare in her youth up to the time that
Clare literally "passed" out of Irene's life. If our access to the truth of
the story is limited to "all that Irene remembered," then we must ask
where are the gaps, the untruths, according to Irene's memory?
Larsen shows Irene attempting a break from the position of merely
being observed to being a manipulator of the situation by allowing the
reader to "see" Clare's history through the eyes of Irene, or only
through that which Irene recollects. The first thing we learn about
Clare in this manner is that she was a "selfish, material, and deceitful
little girl" (144). Already Larsen portrays Irene's projection of herself
onto Clare, for we have learned that Irene is prone to similar man-
nerisms herself. Larsen's use of the third-person consciousness moves
the reader to Irene's "delusional" opinion: her manipulative and self-
deceptive interpretations display Irene's own unwillingness to remember clearly. Moreover, Clare's letter remains to some extent off-limits
to the reader—it is full of ellipses inserted by Irene, pieces of the letter which Irene finds unreadable.

Irene's reactions to the letter provide the terms of her ambivalence.
"She was wholly unable to comprehend such an attitude towards
danger as she was sure the letter's contents would reveal . . . This was
of a piece with all that she knew of Clare Kendry. Stepping always on
the edge of danger" (143) [5]. As the first in a series of signs of "feminine" sexual anxiety, the "illegible scrawl" with "no return address"
to "betray" the sender, is written in "purple ink" on "foreign paper,"
"peculiar" and a "little flaunting." If Irene's sense of danger is in part
a fear of "real" sexual desire, then this fear expresses itself in terms
of "real" racial uneasiness. Clare is a passer. And like Clare, Irene,
too, has the appearance of one who could pass. Rescue from "real"
danger by means of framing Clare as a fantasy signals what will continue as a mode by which Irene's concerns about Clare summon a
Lacanian paradigm: As Slavoj Zizek rephrases it, "Lacan's thesis that

'there is no sexual relationship' means precisely that the structure of the 'real' sexual act (of the act with a flesh-and-blood partner) is already inherently phantasmatic—the 'real' body of the other serves only as a support" for a phantasmatic projection.[2]

The ways in which Irene's racializing account of Clare's body makes manifest its phantasmatic underpinings, reappears at the end of Part One, when we are returned again to the only other letter Clare wrote to Irene. Like the first, this letter comes couched in terms of the alien, yet again Irene "had, at first glance, instinctively known [it] came from Clare Kendry" (177) [33]. But if Clare is figured by "language," Irene represents a resistance to representation, to "being read." Irene's dilemma can be pictured as one that comes into focus as a struggle between the material and the immaterial, the social and the semiotic. Clare comes to be represented in writing, creating an existence in writing that, according to Irene, threatens to unleash Clare's "actual" body. Irene repeatedly confuses material and body, the immaterial and the bodiless. Irene's response to Clare's letter is that it is simply too much, but in destroying the letter, Irene learns that "Clare" cannot be destroyed. "Clare" is the "Clare" Irene has conjured through her own phantasm[a]tic projections and necessarily failed to grasp, a dilemma which prompts the question: If the physical body, like a letter, can be destroyed, when it is killed, does the body continue to live on in language? This is a question with which Irene appears to do battle as she remembers Clare and in so doing consistently brings her into a narrative life that appears to have very "real" effects on Irene's own passing story.

Part III Going Native

> "Observation means observing the tacit rules of different scopic regimes. . . . We see through eyes not with them."
> —Martin Jay, *Downcast Eyes*

We learn the lesson of passing when Irene recollects her first encounter with Clare, at the for-whites-only-Drayton hotel. Because it is Clare (although Irene does not at first recognize her as such) who presents the threat of exposing Irene, or reading her as someone who is passing, the moment at which race comes alive is the moment at which passing appears. Suddenly race holds consequences of particular importance to Irene, consequences such as public humiliation or "losing face." Because Irene relies upon the idea of race as visible, she falls into the trap of employing racial categories that can be visu-

---

2. Slavoj Zizek, "The Spectre of Ideology," *Mapping Ideology*, ed. Slavoj Zizek, London: Verso, 1994.

ally demarcated, while at the same time exposing an elision of these fields of vision.[3] A partnership between the fixity of race and passing as mutually dependent concepts is emphasized in this scene by emerging on at least two fronts: Both Irene and Clare are passing. But how does the text signify passing across these two very different faces? A brief crossing over carried out only in times of utmost necessity and convenience comprises Irene's conception of passing, whereas for Clare passing finds its fullest definition in death, i.e., the total renunciation and/or erasure of "blackness." Or perhaps not. As the text demonstrates at this critical juncture—the meeting of two passing bodies—passing can sustain neither definition, that passing is repeatedly shaped and reproduced precisely through these types of conflicts over and between space and race.

The upward mobility of Irene's entrance to the Drayton indicates not only a switch in racial identity, but a calculated alteration of class as well. It is at this precise moment, when Irene and Clare meet in conjugal passing that race emerges as a material entity. But what does it mean that Irene doesn't recognize Clare? We are told that something about Clare's smile at the waiter disturbs Irene, "she was sure she could have classed it, coming from another woman, as being just a shade too provocative for a waiter. About this one, however, there was something that made her hesitate to name it" (149) [10]. Clare is coded as white, but she also embodies the (hidden) trait of black bodiliness, a trait which only Irene can detect. In recognizing Clare by not recognizing her as Clare, Irene performs the same act on Clare that she did on a more general level on the street. She "classes" Clare as a wealthy woman which is to say that she sees race as *visible*, but she also maintains that race is cultural, that is, an "essence" she can see by not seeing. Clare is thus "raced" through class and "eroticized" by virtue of her passing and not by the color of her skin. Because of her liminality, Clare is recognizable but not properly namable. As in several instances, Clare's face is "unfathomable," "something for which she had no name" (206) [55], a face by which Irene, whose memory "plays a trick on her," "remembers"

3. It is clear that Irene does not "know" Clare is black when she first encounters her on the roof of the Drayton; it is only when Clare fulfills requirements of Irene's definition of blackness as an essential quality that can be detected by non-visual elements which then inform visual ones that Irene comes to label Clare as "black." Butler also argues that in *Passing* "blackness is not primarily a visual mark," p. 170. As Walter Benn Michaels writes, "The very idea of passing—whether it takes the form of looking like you belong to a different race or of acting like you belong to a different race—requires an understanding of race as something separate from the way you look and the way you act. If race really were nothing but culture, that is, if race really were nothing but a distinctive array of beliefs and practices, then, of course, there could be no passing, since to believe and practice what the members of any race believed and practiced would, by definition, make you a member of that race." See his essay "The No Drop Rule," *Critical Inquiry* 20 (Summer 1994), 768.

Clare. And because it is such scenes of non-recognition which repeatedly call up Clare, we as readers become wise to just the kinds of tricks Irene's memory is wont to play.

If Irene's processes of recollection depend upon calculated displacements, how do these gaps called "forgetfulness" emerge? One way is in Irene's constant refusal to name names. Just as Clare's ability to pass successfully from one side of the race barrier to the other problematizes Irene's notion of race and racial remembering, race in the novel comes to be constituted through the disruptions of identity it creates—without ritual threat, there is no name for racial difference. In order to distinguish her random acts of passing from those of Clare, Irene recalls herself as a "Negro" tied to her race by fixed commodities such as community, roots, and family— by background and accountability. These attributes remind her of her self-identicalness as a black woman and thus Irene knows that she is black. Because Irene reads Clare as a "haver" marked by "that having way of hers," Irene's interest in passing works with the presupposition that passing is not a state of being, that, instead, passing is a kind of having, precisely the kind of having of which Clare has so much.[4] Therefore, even though she occasionally passes, Irene is still in the position of being, whereas Clare *is* not, because Clare *is passing*. Irene recalls Clare with a "having" way emphasized as Clare both comes to have "it" and to use "it" as an expenditure: "it" does not define who she is because it can never mark Clare in the same way it marks Irene. Clare asks, "Tell me honestly, haven't you ever thought of 'passing'?" "No. Why should I?" Irene responds, "You see, Clare, I *[ha]ve* everything I want." In fact, Irene claims that as her "understanding was rapidly increasing" about Clare, so too did her "pity and contempt. Clare was so daring, so lovely, and so *'having'* " (174) [31]. By having so much, then, Clare is in *excess* of being. And yet, Irene neither concedes to Clare a position of "being" black or "having" race, that is, Irene interpolates Clare's *excess* into a simultaneous *lack*.

Part IV Grave Walking

Larsen's framing device, "this is what Irene Redfield remembered," begs the question, "what did Irene Redfield forget?" Asking this question allows us to conjecture about the imaginary levels of negotiation

---

4. According to Irene, the difference between "being" and "having" is precisely the difference between being racialized—being other than white—and having the possessions that one could only really have as a white person in the 1920's. Which is to say that in spite of what the she "remembers," Irene's understanding of race doesn't extend to class, for clearly if whiteness is defined as "having" then if one is designated as "having" whiteness, one has undergone a process of racialization that relies upon material markers which are no less "race" determining than skin color.

in which Irene remembers Clare. For example, recalling Clare, Irene sighs, "she's really almost too good looking" (156) [16]. The danger of Irene's being subsumed by Clare as well as of Clare being in excess of herself looms—what, we are prompted to ask, would "too good looking" look like? Instead of pursuing such questions, Irene ascribes to Clare a bit of the uncanny. Irene is consistently able to "intuit" (a process which implies an essential truth, rather than the production of a truth) Clare's presence as one which lurks "on the edge of danger," an experience Irene records as "somebody walking over my grave." The logic generated by the text of Irene's memory makes explicit connections between the unreadable, passing and death. Irene's interpretation of Clare's presence as an "intangible something, too vague to define, too remote to seize, but which was very familiar" (151) [12] suggests that these linkages can be mapped through a particular "passing" that in *Passing* figures itself as a death within life or abjection.

According to Julia Kristeva the abject signifies a liminal status by demarcating a position which cannot be ascribed as either inside or out. We understand that passing invokes imaginary levels of negotiation that rest upon kinds of "lived" raciality—what I will provisionally call a "phenomenality" of passing. And it is at this point, on the level of the experiential as charted in *Passing*, that passing is like abjection.

* * *

Clare comes to us coded as abject in various ways. We hear numerous references to Clare's appeal from the viewpoint of Irene, a perspective which gauges its desire in measures of detail: Irene recalls Clare's "fluttering dress of green chiffon," a "mingled pattern of narcissuses, jonquils and hyacinths," "dark, almost black eyes," "wide mouth like a scarlet flower against the ivory of her skin" (148) [9]. Irene notices how Clare "spread her napkin, and saw the silver spoon in the white hand split the dull gold of the melon" (149) [10]. As well as attesting to the strength of Irene's memory, these details attest to Irene's ability to dissect, delect and take pleasure in the woman before her. The recollection of these details, however, also coincides with the moment of nonrecognition—for despite the fact that she tabulates the minutiae of Clare's appearance, Irene apparently cannot piece together Clare as a "person."

It is, in fact, only when Irene comes to be unsettled by a "small inner disturbance, odious and hatefully familiar" (150) [10] that Irene begins to see Clare as an entirety. Sitting at separate tables above the heat of a mid-summer Chicago street, Clare and Irene enjoy a moment of passing on the rooftop of the elite Drayton Hotel. As an "inner" and "familiar" disturbance prompts Irene to suture Clare's disparate parts, Clare becomes not just a person, but a white woman. The "inner," "familiar" "disturbance" can be read as Irene's fear of being caught passing or yet another attempt on Irene's part to locate race inside as opposed to on the surface: she "sees" Clare as white while claiming "to know" that Clare is black. Both possibilities find simultaneous support as Irene projects her own fear of being revealed as passing onto Clare and in so doing ascribes to Clare the process of racialization to which she believes all whites subscribe. "Absurd! Impossible! White people were so stupid about such things for all that they usually asserted that they were able to tell; and by the most ridiculous means, finger-nails, palms of hands, shapes of ears, teeth, and other equally silly rot" (150) [11]. Irene tells us that the way white people go about recognizing race is by means of abject details, the bodily debris of a person, who in the course of this process becomes not a person but a corpse. Ironically, it is this self-same process of "racialization," or "objectification" that "white people" do, that Clare "does," with which Irene "racializes," "abjects," and "recognizes" Clare. In so doing Irene claims her concern is not that she is "ashamed of being a Negro," but that the "idea of being ejected from any place," causes her to feel "anger, scorn, and fear" (150) [11]. In other words, Irene is afraid of having her liminal status, as a black woman who is passing in a for-whites-only space, revealed, of being ab-jected (literally "thrown out") herself. Moreover Irene's taxonomy of race by process of elimination reveals that "whiteness" is no more achieved "identity" than "blackness," that the odiousness lies at the site of identity as absolute.

* * *

One short passage provides a vivid illustration of simultaneous desires and identifications between Irene and Clare. After a brief and unpleasant exchange with Brian in which Irene amazes herself with her own anger, "her voice, she realized *had* gone queer," Irene sits at her dressing table in anticipation of an evening with Clare. "The face in the mirror vanished from her sight, blotted out by this thing which so suddenly flashed across her groping mind. Impossible for her to put it immediately into words or give it outline, for, prompted by some impulse of self-protection, she recoiled from exact expression" (217–218) [63]. Instead of seeing her own reflection in the mirror, Irene sees a vision of Clare, and the moment of overlap creates an unspeakable sight: Irene sees her own displacement. Irene's only recourse is to "close her unseeing eyes and clench her fists." The slips in Irene's memory, like her tendencies to recoil from exact expression, indicate spaces which cannot be put in precise terms, but which nonetheless receive a kind of continual rearticulation through representations of Clare as abject—unaccountable, unfathomable, and unspeakable. The danger of an articulated black female sexuality presents itself as nostalgia, which appears to Irene not as a simple memory but as a recollection reinterpreted by contemporary fictional constructs (she fantasizes that Brian and Clare are having an affair) projected back into her preconsciousness to function not only as screens against the present pain of cultural repression of a same-sex drive, but against the even more unthinkable, a racially ambiguous, "same-sex coupling".[5] In order to keep such memories at bay, so that (what Irene experiences as) "reality" can emerge, Irene inserts into the space of conscious desire an ideal of the Family adopted from what she envisions as the urban white upper-middle class.[6] In this particular scene, that part of reality that remains for Irene non-symbolized returns in spectral apparitions which are warded off by redirecting their unspeakability through the hetero-conduit of Brian.[7]

Beneath the lingering radiance of Clare's gaze, the chapter closes as the scene closes. Irene leaves the apartment struck, yet again, by Clare's "look."

> Partly mocking, it had seemed, and partly menacing. And something for which she could find no name. For an instant a recrudescence of that sensation of fear which she had while looking into Clare's eyes that afternoon touched her. A slight shiver ran over her.

5. Diana Fuss makes a similar argument in her article, "Fashion and the Homospectatorial Look," *Critical Inquiry* 18 (Summer 1992): 713–737. However, I have purposefully put quotation marks around the phrase "same-sex" because I do not believe that Fuss fully problematizes the difficulty of asserting any essential "sex" as "the same;" a question which needs to be asked, in the same way that I am asking about "black" and "white" with regard to Clare and Irene, is who is the "woman" who would constitute, or is being produced as the "same" in a sexual coupling? For more information about the "dangers of black female sexuality" see: Barbara Christian, "The Highs and Lows of Black Feminist Criticism," *Reading Black/Reading Feminist*, ed. Henry Louis Gates, Jr. (New York: Oxford University Press, 1987). 44–52; Michele Wallace, *Black Macho and the Myth of the Superwoman* (London: Verso, 1990); Hazel Carby, *Reconstructing Womanhood: The Emergence of the Afro-American Female Novelist* (New York: Oxford University Press, 1987); Gloria Hull, *Color, Sex and Poetry: Three Women Writers of the Harlem Renaissance* (Bloomington: Indiana University Press, 1987); Deborah E. McDowell, "Introduction," in *Quicksand and Passing* (Rutgers edition); Hortense Thornton, "Sexism as Quagmire: Nella Larsen's *Quicksand*," *CLA Journal* 16 (1973), 285–301.
6. Irene can only "see" whiteness as that which would enable upward social mobility. Likewise, she believes the "white upper-middle class" Family to be superior to her own; it is an ideal to which she can aspire while in the act of producing it.
7. See Zizek, "The Spectre of Ideology," in particular 21, where he writes, "To put it simply, reality is never directly 'itself', it presents itself only via its incomplete-failed symbolization, and spectral apparitions emerge in this very gap that forever separates reality from the real, and on account of which reality has the character of a (symbolic) fiction: the spectre gives body to that which escapes (the symbolically structured) reality . . . what the spectre conceals is not reality but its 'primordially repressed', the irrepresentable X on whose 'repression' reality itself is founded." A useful way of linking the psychoanalytic frame here to the Marxist notion of class struggle is to propose, as Zizek does, that "there is no class struggle 'in reality': 'class struggle' designates the very antagonism that prevents the objective (social) reality from constituting itself as a self-enclosed whole." Irene's unspoken aspirations to a white "middle" class social standing represents just such an "absence" of class struggle, the absence or which provides a revelation of how the struggle functions.

It's nothing, she said, 'just somebody walking over my grave, as the children say.'

. . . late that night, she stood frowning and puzzling over that look on Clare's incredibly beautiful face. She couldn't, however, come to any conclusion about its meaning, try as she might. It was unfathomable, utterly beyond any experience or comprehension of hers. (176) [33]

Reinvoking Clare's image, Irene finds herself face to face with the spectre of an image of herself. Irene's [sic] summons Clare's haunting image in order to reject it as different from herself, as abject. Just as Irene can keep her psychic borders straight by forgetting that she is passing, she can at once elicit and suppress the disturbing uncertainty which Clare's image provokes within those borders. If it is true that the success of "heterosexuality" depends upon a calling up and subsequent suppression of the homoerotic, then it also true that the success of passing sustains itself through a similar, but perhaps less deeply imbedded, psychic mechanism which forces one to know and simultaneously forget. The danger of not forgetting, in both cases, is that passing will be exposed. We see this demonstrated in the figure of Clare, who presents us with the danger of the failure to recollect as one which bespeaks the possibility of literally *passing away*.

According to Irene, the obvious threat that Clare poses is a disruption of family/race. In this mission she becomes partners with Brian, to whom the conversation then turns. In this section, slips in Irene's memory re-emerge so that a past tense becomes again present. Again by using the third person consciousness limited to Irene, Larsen's text prompts the reader to question not only the reliability of Irene's memory but, by highlighting Irene's stalwart refusal to question her notion of race, the text also encourages the reader to read against Irene and question any idea of identity as a stable construct. Irene's frantic efforts not to think about the implications of passing because such thoughts disrupt her entire career/goal/ideal of racial uplift and family happiness, encourage us, as readers, to do just that.

Part V Where the Nuts Come From

The threat that Brian poses to Irene's stable notion of family is similar to that of Clare's: both suggest transience of one kind or another. Irene strives to keep these threats separate by framing one in terms of the family—Brian wants to move to Brazil—and the other, as we have seen, in terms of race. In Brian's case, this threat presents itself in terms of a literal disruption and re-placement of the Redfield family. But Brian's wishes to migrate, like Clare's racial aspirations, can also be read as encoded in sexual terms. Both plots carry a sexual sub-text which finds an indirect vocabulary with which to express itself through a proliferation of the word "queer."

* * *

Hence when Irene intuits that Brian and Clare are having an affair, we witness a triangulation of "desire" which works oddly, nei-ther captured in Girardian terms or illuminated by those of Eve Kosofsky Sedgwick.[8] Irene, Clare and Brian create a triangle "between women" as it were, but one in which each of the positions can be interpreted in various ways in which gender is not necessar-ily the underlying determinant. In the preceding section, I specu-lated about various ways that desire works between Irene and Clare before Brian comes on the scene. Brian becomes a factor in this con-figuration as soon as Irene decides that he and Clare are having an affair. In order to occupy the space between both and control them Irene uses the same strategies of manipulation, deception and coy-ness that she uses to convince herself that Clare and Brian are sex-ually involved.

While one could read Irene's conviction as a simple projection of her own desire for Clare onto Brian—a valid and viable interpreta-tion—I would venture to propose an alternative approach. I think it is not without reason that Brian comes to us coded as queer. Once Brian has been relegated as queer, that is, outside "normalcy," not only has he joined the realm of Irene and Clare, but his autonomy has been circumscribed. If Irene filters desire for Clare through Brian, Brian then becomes an enabler, a conduit for Irene's desire. At once central to the plot and bracketed on the sidelines, Brian's peripheral presence creates a fundamental double motion. But, supposing Irene does indeed use Brian as a conduit for her desire, then what purpose does projection serve? Irene can talk about "the having way of Clare's" so that Clare becomes the "it" girl. But if Clare has "it" then the following passage suggests that Brian does too:

> The thing, this discontent which had exploded into words, would surely die, flicker out, at last. True, she had in the past often been tempted to believe that *it* had died, only to become conscious, in some instinctive, subtle way, that she had been merely deceiving herself for a while and that it still lived. But *it* would die. Of that she was certain. She had only to direct and guide her man [. . .] Yes, *it* would die, as long ago she had made

---

8. Here I refer to two texts which deal with the triangulation of desire: Rene Girard's *Deceit, Desire and the Novel* (Baltimore: Johns Hopkins University Press, 1965) and Eve Kosofsky Sedgwick's *Between Men: English Literature and Male Homosexual Desire* (New York: Columbia University Press, 1985).

up her mind that *it* should. But in the meantime, while *it* was still living and still had the power to flare up and alarm her, *it* would have to be banked, smothered . . . (187, [41] Emphases added)

As in the tea scene at Clare's, "it" can be interpreted as referring to nothing explicitly, leaving open speculation as to just what or who it is. Most striking, however, is the way the "it" here, linked as it is to Brian's peregrinations, at the same time bespeaks Irene's attitude towards Clare. In talking about "it" as a threat that "still had the power to flare up and alarm her," that "would have to be banked," that "would die," Irene alludes simultaneously to Clare and it. The end of Clare also becomes the end of "it"—for Irene has not only projected her own desire for Clare onto Brian, but she has also projected her fears about Brian onto Clare. The two, in Irene's mind, become accomplices in a plot that threatens more than just her sense of stability, but her physical and psychic well-being, her life. The solution she articulates is to "direct and guide her man," to keep him on a straight line. Brian is used by Irene as a stable representative of the black race with its ties to community and family. The paradox is that precisely those things which Irene needs Brian to signify would prove "false" if he leaves his home. In his spoken desire to move to Brazil we hear the "threat" of homosexuality. While Brian is typically read as supporting Irene and Clare and their passings, Brian is not simply a conduit, and the triangle is far from fixed. This can be read as yet another instance of Irene's forgetfulness—that Brian is the real threat to her image of family, home, community, whereas Clare is only mirroring Irene's always already present threat to herself. Which is not to say that Irene is not conscious of Brian as a problem, but instead of worrying about the possibility of being a single mother— and perhaps being forced into an economic position in which "passing" would become a necessity—Irene would rather convince herself that Brian and Clare are having an affair than imagine that she, herself, might be "passing" too.

Part VI Distance Nowhere

> On close inspection, all literature is probably a version of the apocalypse that seems to me rooted on the fragile border where identities do not exist or only barely so—double, fuzzy, heterogeneous, animal, metamorphosed, altered, abject.
>
> —Julia Kristeva

In my opening section I discussed the denouement of the novella in which Clare falls to her death from a sixth story window. This "ending" brings together several of the strands with which I have been piecing together my argument. To begin with, we see a foreshadowing of Clare's death at least twice before her actual fall. The first instance occurs when Irene shreds Clare's letters into tiny pieces.

> With an unusual methodicalness she tore the offending letter into tiny ragged squares that fluttered down and made a small heap in her black crepe de Chine lap. The destruction completed, she gathered them up, rose, and moved to the train's end. Standing there, she dropped them over the railing and watched them scatter, on tracks, on cinders, on forlorn grass, in rills of dirty water. (178) [34]

Like the second letter which gets "torn across and flung into the scrap-basket," this letter consigns Clare to a site of abjection. "Cinders," "forlorn grass" and "dirty water" set the mood as Irene destroys Clare's final letter. However, as Irene consoles herself, "and that was that," we realize that it is precisely such abjected bits of Irene's memory which constantly resurface, refusing to let her forget a lifetime of passing intimately linked to abjection. Irene's "memories" reflect the remnant pieces of a fabricated collective memory of abjection which here takes psychic shape through an exchange between women. Is it merely a coincidence that Clare's shredded letter rests in Irene's lap? Irene's attempts to do away with Clare, to keep her apart and "refuse her recognition" return Irene not only to Clare but also to her "feminine" self. Despite attempts to "drop Clare out of her mind and turn her thoughts to her own affairs. To home, to the boys, to Brian" (178), Irene and her conscious need to forget Clare allow Clare to be constantly reinvoked as a threat to her family. And it is precisely the degree to which Irene simultaneously reads and refuses to read Brian as queer that permits her to misremember her desire to be like Clare, that is, to pass. Irene, like Clare, "is passing," that is, she confounds these boundaries herself. Because we have access to Clare's gestures only by way of Irene, Clare's devices on the Redfields may also be a projection of Irene's own devices on Clare. Both want to inhabit the space of the other. In either or both cases, identity becomes a violent fulfillment of desire. In the end Clare dies, but Irene is left to a fate of always returning to that end as a site of recurring loss.

The second foreshadowing of Clare's fate occurs at a tea-party. Irene overhears "scraps" of Clare's conversation, "scraps" emphasized by the use of ellipses which splice Clare's phrases into telegraphic bursts. Clare's inscrutability thereby underlined, Irene's "mental and physical languor receded. Brian. What did it mean? How would it affect her and the boys? The boys! She had a surge of relief. It ebbed, vanished. A feeling of absolute unimportance followed. Actually, she didn't count. She was to him, only the mother of his sons. That was all. Alone she was nothing. Worse. An obstacle. Rage boiled up in her" (221) [66]. Again, Irene uses gaps and spaces, "languor" to conjoin Clare and Brian. In so doing Irene again allows herself and Clare to overlap, so that the "obstacle" Irene presents to Brian and Clare becomes the "obstacle" Clare presents to Irene and "the boys". Irene's inconsequence, her "absolute unimportance" quickly becomes Clare's. "There was a slight crash. On the floor at her feet lay the shattered cup. Dark stains on the bright rug. Spread (221) [66]. The symbolism needs little explanation: the white tea-cup "slips" from Irene's hands, much like Clare is soon to slip from Irene's arms. The two scenarios are further paralleled by the appearance of Hugh Wentworth who rushes to Irene's side to declare, "Must have pushed you. Clumsy of me. Don't tell me it's priceless and irreplaceable" (221) [66]. Hugh immediately assumes responsibility for a "crime" he didn't commit by claiming to have "pushed" Irene.

Pushing is precisely the question at issue in Clare's death—everyone wants to know, did Irene push her? Irene responds, "Oh, no, you didn't push me. Cross your heart, hope to die, and I'll tell you how it happened." Irene then goes on to call the cup the "ugliest thing that your ancestors, the charming Confederates ever owned [. . .] It was brought North by way of the subway. . . . call it the underground" (222) [66]. This narrative inserts the present passing tale into foundational stories from the past, not with the intention of transcending the past, but rather with the intention of protecting 'now' from uncertain fate by reactivating the already known terms of 'then.' The white cup represents the transportation via the underground railway of a history of racial miscegenation, the kind which produces passing characters. In allowing the cup to shatter, then, Irene also encourages, symbolically, the degradation of the "passing" strand of African-American history. "I've never figured out a way of getting rid of it until just about five minutes ago. I had an inspiration. I had only to break it, and I was rid of it forever. So simple! And I'd never thought of it before!" (222) [67] Again, Irene is forgetful. As we well know, destruction is not a new tactic for Irene's—it is the self-same one she deployed when she shredded Clare's letters. In getting rid of "it" forever, though, Irene runs the risk of ("hope to die") losing herself. What Irene forgets is that as representative "passer" Clare actually supports, for Irene, the narrative of racial difference in which Irene has placed the legitimacy of her own existence.

What happened next, Irene Redfield never afterwards allowed herself to remember. Never clearly. One moment Clare had been there, a vital, glowing thing, like a flame of red and gold. The next she was gone . . . Irene wasn't sorry. But she mustn't, she warned herself, think of that. She was too tired, and too shocked. And, indeed, both were true. She was utterly weary, and she was violently staggered. But her thoughts reeled on. If only she could be as free of mental as she was of bodily vigor; could only put from her memory the vision of her hand on Clare's arm. (239) [79–80]

Irene "never allowed" herself to remember exactly what happened, as if the threat or risk of remembering is too great, or would somehow carry her over the passing line, would somehow cause her, like Clare, to die. The danger of remembering Clare's death, like the danger of contemplating her own acts of passing, presents itself as a dilemma of a trauma which cannot be fully articulated. Irene cannot remember what happened because she claims to have forgotten the language with which to describe the event. The event itself is "queer." It produces a gap in comprehension that Irene cannot fill because her language is inadequate to narrate Clare's death. We have access to the story of passing's "trauma" through the fragmented pieces of the story which Irene's memory allows us to know. Therefore, *Passing* takes shape through what could be termed a recurrence of abjection, through the inability to "properly remember," to become a proper tale to pass on. *Passing* necessitates a turning away from totalization, the reification of racial difference, the reinvigoration of the social order. Like the two endings which present equally legitimate claims as the official, authentic close of *Passing*, within the structure of *Passing* itself we find a similar dual legitimacy—a double motion which brings the story to a brink of remembering, but at the same time forces a horizon further from view. In a sense, *Passing* refuses the predominant terms and nominal relations of passing. When Irene contemplates what she senses to be Brian's waywardness, she hopes that "at bottom it was just Brazil." Ironically, what we learn from Irene's half-hearted attempt to get to the bottom of the problem is that a return to the bottom—the site of passing/abjection—often projects us forward. Recounting the passing tale ensures the permanence and legitimacy of the world of racial difference, reaffirmed through the telling of this story. However, in encouraging its readers to go back and read the end as a site of production, *Passing* launches a narrative which resists such containment; *Passing* pushes the reader into the distance lying between here and there.

GAYLE WALD

Passing and Domestic Tragedy†

* * *

Of the three literary texts this chapter analyzes [James Weldon Johnson's *Autobiography of An Ex-Colored Man*, Jessie Fauset's "The Sleeper Wakes," and Nella Larsen's *Passing*] Larsen's *Passing*, published in the waning years of the New Negro Renaissance, is arguably the most pessimistic about the possibilities for constructing "positive" middle-class black subjects within the terms of the passing narrative. Their satire notwithstanding, Johnson's *Autobiography* and Fauset's "The Sleeper Wakes" are also marked in their optimism, both about the project of racial uplift and the appropriation of passing as a source of negative instruction to their protagonists (as well as, perhaps, to their readers). However ambiguously they may signify, both the ex-colored man's regretful references to Booker T. Washington and Amy Kildare's eager anticipation of beginning her work for the "race" allude positively to racial uplift values of racial solidarity, economic self-help, class assimilation, and service to the masses. Larsen's novella does not reject these values, but neither does it manage to portray the same confidence either in them or in its middle-class black protagonists as the arbiters of "race" progress. This shift in outlook is signposted through her text's very different representation of raced and gendered violence. By ending her book with Irene Redfield's likely murder of her "friend" Clare Kendry, Larsen primarily emphasizes the lack of solidarity between her two protagonists, only one of whom (Clare) is passing for white within her marriage. Insofar as we can assume that Irene pushes Clare out of an apartment window (such a move being foreshadowed in the meeting of the two protagonists on the roof of the Drayton Hotel), then it is possible to conclude that Irene quite literally extinguishes the agency of the passing plot in the narrative. Yet it is hardly clear that this act resolves any of the dilemmas (real or imagined) Irene faces, or for that matter any of the many questions—about the stability of race and gender identities, the construction of national citizenship, and the nature of "race" loyalty—that *Passing* raises.

In narrative terms, two elements distinguish Larsen's text from the earlier works of Johnson and Fauset (or even from Fauset's novel *Plum Bun*, also published in 1929). The first is *Passing*'s representa-

† From Gayle Wald, *"Passing* and Domestic Tragedy," in *Crossing the Line: Racial Passing in Twentieth-Century U.S. Literature and Culture* (Durham: Duke University Press, 2000), pp. 46–50. Copyright © 2000 Duke University Press. All rights reserved. Used by permission of the author. Bracketed page numbers refer to this Norton Critical Edition.

tion of Clare's desire for racial "homecoming"—rather than her desire to pass—as a primary source of narrative strife and dissonance. Unlike "The Sleeper Wakes," which ultimately demands Amy's homecoming as a means of bringing anticipated closure to the passing plot, *Passing* renders the status of such homecoming a primary site of interrogation. Accordingly, Larsen initiates the narrative proper with Irene's receipt of Clare's letter announcing Clare's desire to reinitiate contact with "Negro" society (a beginning that renders it necessary for the reader to go back in time through Irene's memory of their first reunion in Chicago). As a result, the focus of Larsen's text is not the development of an individual subjectivity through an act that ultimately must be repudiated, but the very status of racial "community."

The notion of community tacitly alludes to the other distinguishing characteristic of *Passing:* namely, its ingenious triangulation of the passing plot. Unlike both Johnson's and Fauset's texts, Larsen's novella explores the volatile relationship between two female protagonists, both of whom pass for white and both of whom see class privilege as a key to their survival as women within a patriarchal society. Primarily such a strategy of triangulation enables Larsen to filter her narrative through the watchful eyes of Irene, who is liable to wonder at the status of her friend's sudden yearning for "my own people" (182) [35]. In effect, therefore, *Passing* is able to translate the various anxieties associated with racial passing through the character of Irene, who voices them in the form of her own ambivalent censure of Clare's frank disclosure that she passes in order to acquire the wealth and social status that painfully eluded her in girlhood. Ambivalence, in fact, becomes a major theme of the novella, as Irene attempts (although with little success) to reconcile her fascination with and attraction to Clare with her discomfort at the various compromising positions that she feels compelled to assume in order to safeguard Clare's secret. Irene aptly sums up this ambivalent economy of aversion and desire— which could well describe the critical reception of modernist fictions of passing—in a discussion with her husband Brian: "It's funny about 'passing.' We disapprove of it and at the same time condone it. It excites our contempt and yet we rather admire it. We shy away from it with an odd kind of revulsion, but we protect it" (185–86) [39].

As Irene's remark hints, the notion of "race" loyalty constitutes an important basis of Irene's critique of Clare's passing, and thus of her ability to establish herself as superior to her friend. A self-fashioned "race" woman, Irene distinguishes between her own occasional passing, which she justifies as a means of circumventing racial segregation, and Clare's seemingly more opportunistic and deceitful (because permanent) commitment to passing in her marriage. The difference between herself and Clare, as Irene imagines it, is that whereas Clare is primarily interested in crossing the line as a means of self-advancement, Irene's interests lie in working to secure the happiness of others, not merely her husband and her two young sons, but the "race" as a whole. Repeatedly the text contrasts Irene's perception of Clare's "having way" (a phrase that encompasses Clare's knack for acquiring things as well as the possibility that she is "having her way" with Irene's husband) with her own philanthropic work on behalf of the Negro Welfare League, a racial uplift organization modeled after the NAACP and the National Urban League. Additionally, the discourse of racial uplift provides Irene a ready vocabulary for establishing the authenticity of her "self" through a series of racialized oppositions to Clare. According to Irene, she and Clare are "strangers. Strangers in their desires and ambitions. Strangers even in their racial consciousness. Between them the barrier was just as high, just as broad, and just as firm as if in Clare did not run that strain of black blood" (192) [44].

In order thus to see Clare as a stranger, however, Irene must also naturalize both her own passing and her status as a classed and gendered subject. Larsen hints at how Irene's censuring of Clare hinges on her ability to sustain a privileged relation to domesticity and to properly "domesticated" female sexuality. Notwithstanding her work for the Negro Welfare League, for example, Irene seems wholly unconcerned with the welfare of her black maid Zulena, and she exploits the fact of her marriage to Brian and the presence of their two young sons as a means of casting Clare's sexuality as "flaunting," "a shade too provocative," and "not safe." While she protests that Clare's passing irks her because it seems predicated on a blatant desire for gain, in fact Clare's rapid ascent up the class ladder violates Irene's middle-class belief in fair play and her tacit commitment to the American Dream of prosperity as a reward for sacrifice, self-discipline, and hard work. Like Amy in "The Sleeper Wakes" but unlike Brian, who harbors a "dislike and disgust for his profession and his country" (187) [40], Irene is loath to give up her attachment to a national narrative.

Such trust in her own entitlement allows Irene to overlook the fact that for Clare, passing provides a relatively sure ticket away from the domestic sphere of her white aunts, who exploit her as a source of household labor, and into the ranks of the upper class. In Clare's narrative, however, it is precisely their disparate class locations as children, not any fundamental difference in their "race consciousness," that primarily distinguishes her passing from Irene's. "You can't know," she tells Irene, "how, when I used to go over to the south side, I used almost to hate all of you. You had all the things I wanted and never had had. It made me all the more determined to get them, and others" (159) [19].

Through her depiction of Irene's growing animosity toward Clare, Larsen thematizes the clash between narratives of American individualism and racial uplift notions of collective duty and race progress.

More particularly, she symbolizes the contradictions within racial uplift ideology itself: its attempt, on the one hand, to construct a class-based solution to the problem of African American citizenship, and its recognition, on the other hand, of segregation as a "leveling" narrative that ultimately triumphs over class distinction. Irene experiences this contradiction at the level of an interiorized struggle between the fulfillment of her own self-interests and the satisfaction of what she perceives to be the needs and interests of the "race." Much like the ex-colored man, in other words, she feels forced to choose between apparently irreconcilable options of self-preservation and self-sacrifice, the second of which is tied to loyalty to "race"; only unlike Johnson's protagonist, Irene has Clare to make her sacrificial victim.

In drawing the narrative to a precipitous close, Clare's "fall" from an open apartment window suggests that Larsen could imagine no resolution short of death to the "dangerous business" of her passing (195) [47]. Yet it remains significant that whereas this finale to the story would seem to guarantee Irene's safe return to the domestic sphere, Clare's death ultimately is not conducive to such a happy ending. Instead, by leaving the scene of Irene's own "homecoming" to the domestic sphere outside the narrative frame of the story, Larsen seems to be acknowledging the inadequacy of domesticity as a solution either to the specific "problem" of racial passing or to the more general problem of the agency of the raced and gendered subject. Indeed, the darkness and heaviness that descend on Irene in the last lines of the book suggest that through Clare's death, something of her own faith in the redeeming and protective power of gendered domestic virtue has taken a blow.

* * *

CATHERINE ROTTENBERG

Passing: Race, Identification, and Desire†

In the second half of the nineteenth century, African-American writers such as William Wells Brown and Frances Harper began invoking the phenomenon of passing in their texts as a way of investigating the complexities and contradictions of the category of race in the United States.[1] The light-enough-to-pass Negro (but usually Negress) would play a central role in the imagination of African-American writers for

---

† Reprinted from Catherine Rottenberg, "*Passing*: Race, Identification, and Desire," *Criticism: A Quarterly for Literature and the Arts* 45, no. 4 (Fall 2003): 435–52, with permission of Wagne State University Press. Notes have been edited.
1. In this paper, race will be discussed in terms of the black/white divide, which I believe has, in many crucial ways, been the determining divide with regard to race discourse in America.

the next fifty years. Charles Chesnutt's *The House behind the Cedars*, Jessie Faucet's *Plum Bum*, and James Weldon Johnson's *The Autobiography of an Ex-Coloured Man* are perhaps the best-known examples. Nella Larsen's 1929 novella, *Passing*, the text under discussion in this essay, can thus be seen as inheritor and perpetuator of a long tradition of such narratives. In recent years, Larsen's text has become the most celebrated instance of a story about passing in African-American literature, eclipsing the tradition that preceded it. This is not coincidental, for Larsen is a master of ambiguity and intrigue, and the enigmatic finale of her novella has generated heated debates and countless interpretations.

Many analyses have attempted to determine whether or not Larsen's use of passing can be seen as a subversive strategy,[2] that is, whether the narrative serves to reinforce hegemonic norms of race or whether it ultimately posits passing as a viable survival strategy, which has the potential to disrupt "the enclosures of a unitary identity."[3] While this question still informs several critiques, in the past few years commentators have been concentrating more and more on how passing interrogates and problematizes the ontology of identity categories and their construction. Rather than trying to place passing in a subversive/recuperative binary, these articles and books use passing as a point of entry into questions of identity and identity categories more generally.[4]

In this essay I contend that Larsen's text can assist critics in understanding the specific and, as I will argue, *irreducible* features of race performativity.[5] That is, the novella can help us begin mapping out

2. See Corinne Blackmer, "The Veils of the Law: Race and Sexuality in Nella Larsen's *Passing*," *College Literature* 22, no. 3 (1995): 50–67; Michael Cooke, *Afro-American Literature in the Twentieth Century* (New Haven: Yale University Press, 1984); Priscilla Ramsey, "A Study of Black Identity in 'Passing' Novels of the Nineteenth and Early Twentieth Century," *Studies in Black Literature* 7 (1976): 1–7; Mary Helen Washington, "The Mulatta Trap: Nella Larsen's Women of the 1920s," in *Invented Lives: Narratives of Black Women, 1860–1960* (New York: Anchor, 1987), 159–67.

3. Martha Cutter, "Sliding Significations: Passing as Narrative and Textual Strategy in Nella Larsen's Fiction," in *Passing and the Fictions of Identity*, ed. Elaine Ginsberg (Durham: Duke University Press, 1996), 75.

4. Elaine Ginsberg, for instance, claims that "passing is about identities: their creation or imposition, their adoption or rejection, their accompanying rewards or penalties. Passing is also about the boundaries established between identity categories and about the individual and cultural anxieties induced by boundary crossing." "Introduction: The Politics of Passing," in Ginsberg, *Passing and the Fictions of Identity*, 2.

5. Quite a few recent articles on *Passing* having invoked Judith Butler's notion of (gender) performativity as a means of conceptualizing the way identity gets played out in the text. See, for example, Sara Ahmed, " 'She'll Wake Up One of These Days and Find She's Turned into a Nigger,' " *Theory, Culture & Society* 16 (1999): 87–105. Critics like Martin Favor (*Authentic Blackness: The Folk in the New Negro Renaissance* [Durham: Duke University Press, 1999]) and Jennifer DeVere Brody ("Clare Kendry's 'True' Colors: Race and Class Conflict in Nella Larsen's *Passing*," *Callaloo* 15, no. 4: 1053–65) [1992; reprinted in this edition, p. 393] have attempted to theorize the relationship between the different categories of identification such as race and gender in *Passing* so as to complicate Judith Butler's emphasis on *gender* performativity. While Favor and Brody provide convincing arguments regarding how gender and race norms are articulated through one another in Larsen's fiction, neither critic has managed to offer a sustained theoretical analysis of race as a unique *modality* of performativity, one that is different from gender.

the differences between gender and race norms since it uncovers the way in which regulatory ideals of race produce a specific modality of performativity. *Passing* is especially conducive to interrogating the modality of race performativity because, unlike other passing narratives of the period, Larsen's presents us with two protagonists who can pass for white; yet only Clare "passes over" into the white world. The depiction and juxtaposition of these two characters reveal the complexities and intricacies of the category of race. While Irene can be seen to represent the subject who appropriates and internalizes the hegemonic norms of race, Clare's trajectory dramatizes how dominant norms can be misappropriated and how disidentification is always possible.

This essay commences with a theoretical discussion of race. Although much has been written on the constructed nature of the category of race, very few analyses have offered a convincing and rigorous account of how race might be conceived of as performative reiteration. The second section offers a reading of "passing" scenes from the novella in an attempt to unravel some of the distinctive mechanisms through which race norms operate. On the one hand, the novella suggests that race in the United States operates through an economy of optics, and *the assumption of whiteness* is one of the consequences of this economy. On the other hand, the novella reveals that skin color (i.e., optics) does not really constitute the "truth" of race.

Invoking Homi Bhabha's notion of mimicry as a supplement to Butler's concept of gender performativity in the third section, I interrogate and theorize the ways in which the definitional contradiction of race ("can be seen" versus "cannot be seen") produces race as performative reiteration. While there are two idealized genders under regimes of compulsory heterosexuality, albeit with a very great power differential between them, there has historically been only one hegemonic and ideal race under racist regimes.[6] This difference, I argue, has far-reaching implications, one of which is the need to rethink the desire/identification nexus, a nexus that operates differently in race and in gender. Understanding the particular relationship between desire and identification in the novella also helps us begin to gauge the critical question of disidentification.

6. Two qualifications need to be made at this point. First, race is isolated in this essay so that the specific processes which have produced raced subjectivities in America can be examined. Although the separation or isolation of race is necessary for methodological reasons, in social practice (as in novels) the categories of race, class, gender, and ethnicity work simultaneously as a background for one another and often find their most powerful articulation through one another. Second, my inquiry focuses on the United States in the 1920s. Norms can and do change over time; race and gender performativity, therefore, cannot be theorized without taking context and history into account. However, I do believe that even a historically specific examination of performativity—such as the one I try to offer in this essay—can provide conceptual apparatuses and tools for theorizing the difference between gender and race norms in other historical settings and contexts.

At least one clarification is needed at this point, however. This essay focuses on the ways in which power—in the Foucauldian and Butlerian sense—operates on the hegemonic level and does not make a claim about the multiplicity of social practices per se. Hegemony, though, as we will see in the last section, is never complete, indicating that there are always counter-discourses and alternative norms circulating within any given society.

1. Race as Performative Repetition

In "Race as a Kind of Speech Act," Louis Miron and Jonathan Inda argue that "race does not refer to a pre-given subject. Rather, it works performatively to constitute the subject itself and only acquires a naturalized effect through repeated or reiterative naming of or reference to that subject."[7] The norms that constitute the symbolic order and create "the grid of intelligibility" are produced and circulated by the relations of power existing within a given society. In a white supremacist society, for example, norms work by constructing a binary opposition between white and black (or nonwhite) in which white is always privileged over black.[8] Subjects are thus interpellated into the symbolic order as gendered and raced beings and are recognizable only in reference to the existing grid of intelligibility. For Miron and Inda, the interpellation "Look, a Negro," famously addressed by Frantz Fanon, is parallel to "It's a girl!"[9] And once interpellated, subjects must, in turn, incessantly cite and mime the very race norms that created their intelligibility (and thus their condition of possibility) in the first place. In short, according to Miron and Inda, race performativity is the power of discourse to bring about what it names through the citing or repetition of racial norms.

The two critics cogently point out that norms or regulatory ideals which constitute and make social practices possible are produced through an "artificial unity" composed of a series of disparate attributes: "Physical features, namely skin color, are linked to attributes of intellect and behavior, establishing a hierarchy of quality between white and black."[1] The concept of race, like gender, does not denote a natural phenomenon, but rather "groups together attributes which do not have a necessary or natural relationship to one another in order to enable one to make use of this fictitious unity as a causal

7. Louis Miron and Jonathan Inda, "Race as a Kind of Speech Act," *Cultural Studies: A Research Annual* 5 (2000): 86–87.
8. Ibid., 99.
9. Frantz Fanon, *Black Skin, White Mask*, trans. Charles Lam Markmann (New York: Grove Press, 1967), 109.
1. Miron and Inda, "Race," 97.

principle, an omnipresent meaning."[2] Accordingly, a series of traits linked to whiteness (civilized/intelligent/moral/hardworking/clean) and blackness (savage/instinctual/simple/licentious/lazy/dirty) have been concatenated in the service of specific social hierarchies.[3] In *Passing*, Clare recounts how her white aunts, who took her in after her father died, thought that hard labor would be good for her: "I had Negro blood and they belonged to the generation that had written and read long articles headed: 'Will the Blacks Work?' "[4] The "lazy black worker" has a long history in American race discourse.[5] Jack Bellew, Clare's racist husband, also invokes and reiterates this kind of discourse when he tells Irene that black people are "always robbing and killing. And . . . worse" (172) [30]. Insofar as the performative repetition of norms is the condition of possibility for viable subjects, race performativity compels subjects to perform according to these "fictitious" unities, thus shaping their identity and their preferences. Performativity is, indeed, one of the most fundamental manifestations of the Foucauldian notion of positive power.

While "Race as a Kind of Speech Act" is one of the few articles that offers a sustained and rigorous theoretical analysis of the way in which race is subtended by performativity, I have serious misgivings about the simple transposition of Butler's notion of gender performativity onto race. Although I agree with Miron and Inda that we need to begin understanding race as performative reiteration and thus see my intervention as a supplement to their important work, critics must be careful not to ignore the specificities of race norms. Otherwise, we run the risk of eliding the particular mechanisms through which the subject comes to be "raced."

2. Assumption of Whiteness and the Contradictions of Race

The scene in which Clare Kendry and Irene Redfield reencounter one another after twelve years of separation serves to initiate the reader into the strange phenomenon of passing. When Irene initially escapes the searing heat of an August day in Chicago and enters the Drayton, there is no hint in the text that she is doing the forbidden, that is, ingressing white-only space. It is only once Irene becomes aware of another woman's stare that the reader understands Irene

---

2. Michel Foucault, *The History of Sexuality,* Vol. 1, *An Introduction,* trans. Robert Hurley (New York: Vintage Books, 1990), 154.
3. Miron and Inda do not provide specific examples of this concatenation. This is my intervention.
4. Nella Larsen, *Quicksand and Passing* (Piscataway, N.J.: Rutgers University Press, 1986), 158–59. All subsequent references to the 1986 edition will be cited parenthetically in the text. Bracketed page numbers refer to this Norton Critical Edition.
5. See, for example, Stuart Hall, "The Spectacle of the Other," in *Representations: Cultural Representations and Signifying Practices* (London: Sage Publications, 1997).

has been "passing herself off as white." The other woman continues to survey Irene, and this unwavering look forces Irene to wonder whether the other woman knows that "here before her very eyes on the roof of the Drayton sat a Negro" (150) [10]. Irene's fear of detection generates an inner monologue in which she admits that the other woman couldn't possibly "know" she is a Negro. Never, Irene assures herself, had anyone even remotely seemed to suspect that she was black. People always took her for an "Italian, a Spaniard, a Mexican, or a gypsy" (150) [11].

Clare's stare causes Irene to question her own (successful) attempt to pass as white. She is surprised by the possibility of being caught in the act of performing whiteness, for, as she tells us, she has never been found out. The stare does not, however, cause her to question whether the "languorous black eyes" of the other woman are part of a "black" and not a "white" body. Irene takes it for granted that the other woman is white. Even after Clare approaches her old acquaintance and insists that she recognizes her, Irene asks herself. "What white girls had she known well enough to have been familiarly addressed as 'Rene by them?" (151) [11]. Both Irene's admission that she has never been questioned when passing and her failure to register the possibility of the other woman "being" something other than she seems suggest that race norms work through assumptions of whiteness. As Sara Ahmed has argued, in a society in which white is the ideal or norm, one is assumed to be white unless one looks black. " '[L]ooking black' becomes a deviation from the normalized state of 'being white.' "[6] The invisibility of the mark of whiteness is exactly the mark of its privilege.

This assumption of whiteness is also dramatically exposed when Irene first encounters Jack Bellew. Clare's white racist husband. The tea party to which Clare invites Irene after their reencounter includes three women: Clare, Irene, and Gertrude. All three women are light enough to pass, although Clare is the only one who has completely "passed over." Bellew, who claims to know a "nigger" when he sees one, does not for a moment entertain the idea that one of the women sitting with his wife might be "black." He therefore feels perfectly comfortable acknowledging that he doesn't dislike niggers but rather hates them. "They give me the creeps," he admits, adding, "the black scrimy devils" (172) [30]. It appears that American racial classification assumes "that racial identity marks the subject in the form of absence or presence of color."[7] In other words, racial identity and classification seem to be constituted through skin color.

6. Ahmed, "She'll Wake Up," 93.
7. Ibid., 88.

But the category of race, it turns out, is much more complex, and these scenes bring to the fore the contradiction at the heart of race definition in the United States. On the one hand, as we have seen, race is assumed to manifest itself in the visible, in skin pigmentation. That is, it seems to operate in an "optical economy of identity."[8] But as Nella Larsen makes very clear in her text, the visible markings or lack thereof are not enough to tell the "truth" of race. After all, the three women at the tea party are not "white" but "black." One of the most rudimentary lessons of passing, as Amy Robinson argues and Larsen dramatizes, is that "the visible is *never* easily or simply a guarantor of truth."[9] Irene herself is aware that optics are not enough to gauge race as it is defined in the United States, averring, "White people were so stupid about such things for all they usually asserted that they were able to tell; and by the most ridiculous means, fingernails, palms of hand, shapes of ears, teeth, and other equally silly rot" (150) [11]. Jack Bellew also articulates the contradiction. His pet name for his wife is Nig, a strange nickname given that Clare has successfully passed into white society. He tells Clare that she can get as black as she pleases, since he "knows" that she is not a "nigger" (171) [29]. Once there is an assumption of whiteness, pigmentation does not signify in the same way. Melanin, it seems, is not the manifest truth of race, although it has played a crucial part in the construction of racial thinking in the United States.

The "assumption of whiteness" begins to reveal the specificity of race norms. In heteronormative regimes, one is assumed to be *either* a woman or a man, even if the standard and privileged position is male. The lack of visual markers "indicating" whether a given subject is male or female is destabilizing. In white racist regimes, the lack of visual markers is not destabilizing in and of itself. Rather, since whiteness is always privileged and the only desirable color, or, in other words, since there is only one ideal race, subjects are immediately assumed to be white in the absence of any telling marks of "color." But again, as *Passing* makes very clear, race construction is about much more than visibility.

3. *The Specific Operations of Race Performativity*

Juxtaposing Homi Bhabha and Judith Butler can help critics conceptualize some of the differences between race and gender as performative reiteration. Although Bhabha does not explicitly mention performativity in his chapter "Of Mimicry and Man," it seems that

---

8. Amy Robinson, "Takes One to Know One: Passing and Communities of Common Interest," *Critical Inquiry* 20 (1994): 719.
9. Ibid., my emphasis.

mimicry does indeed operate through performative reiteration, that is, through the colonized subject's incessant attempt to mime and inhabit the colonists' authority and hegemonic ideals. While Butler tends to concentrate on gender, Bhabha many times isolates issues of race ("white but not quite"). My goal, therefore, is to read these two theorists as potential correctives to one another, once again using "passing" as a point of entry into the question of race as performative reiteration.

In his now classic *Location of Culture*, Bhabha states that in the colonial situation mimicry emerges "as one of the most elusive and effective strategies of colonial power and knowledge."[1] The mimic man, the nonwhite native, does not "re-present" but rather repeats and imitates the discursive effects of colonial (or racist) discourse; mimicry is an effect of colonial discourse. On the one hand, the colonizer demands that the other approximate, through mimesis, the norms of the colonizing power, norms associated with whiteness.[2] On the other hand, in order to continuously naturalize, justify, and authorize his power, the colonizer must constantly maintain the difference between himself, as a white man, and the other. In other words, colonial discourse moves between the recognition of cultural and racial difference and its disavowal.

According to Bhabha, there is an ambivalence, a difference, at the "origins" of colonial discourse's authority. By rearticulating colonial "presence in terms of its otherness, that which it disavows," the mimic man can potentially disrupt the self-grounding assumptions of whiteness (and colonialism itself), disclosing the way in which otherness always inheres in presence. Mimicry can always turn to mockery; it is a hybrid site and can lay bare the way in which the colonial presence "is always ambivalent, split between its appearance as original and authoritative and its articulation as repetition and difference."[3] While Bhabha invokes psychoanalytic concepts such as paranoia and narcissism in order to explain the ambivalence which "grounds" racist identification, I would like to reposition his insights (even further) within a Foucauldian framework in the context of 1920s United States.

I believe that the ambivalence Bhabha points to in colonial discourse is similar to the contradiction that *Passing* exposes as being at the "origins" of race definition in the United States. The novella manages to reveal the paradox embodied in racist discourse, and lays bare how racist discourse attempts to produce desire in the black other to mime the ways of the whites (thus there is really only one norm),

1. Homi Bhabha, *The Location of Culture* (New York: Routledge, 1994), 86.
2. Ibid., 88. Bhabha emphasizes the racial aspect of mimicry: "almost the same but not white."
3. Ibid., 91, 107.

while at the same time this discourse assumes that "non-whiteness" has inherent characteristics that preclude black subjects from ever really becoming "white." In order to maintain the fiction of its own racial purity and superiority, racist discourse must constantly invoke and reinforce the "non-whiteness" of the other subject, whom it concomitantly encourages to live up to norms of whiteness.

Insofar as this is the case, white racist regimes create a particular bifurcation between identification and desire, one that is distinct from the divide characterizing heteronormativity. Taking the little boy as the standard measure of how the bifurcation of identification and desire operates, Sigmund Freud, in his *Group Psychology and the Analysis of the Ego*, states, "In the first case one's father is what one would like *to be*, and in the second [i.e., the little girl] he is what one would like to *have*." The little boy exhibits special interest "in his father; he would like to grow like him and be like him, and take his place everywhere. . . . At the same time as this identification with his father, or a little later, the boy has begun to develop a true object-cathexis toward his mother."[4] Identification and desire to have are therefore "two psychologically distinct ties"; desire to have is a straightforward sexual object-cathexis, while identification "endeavors to mould a person's own ego after the fashion of the one that has been taken as a model."[5] Identification, in other words, turns out not to be a sexual tie but rather an emotional one. As Diana Fuss points out, "For Freud, desire for one sex is always secured through identification with the other sex; to desire and to identify with the same person at the same time is, in this model, a theoretical impossibility."[6]

On the one hand, I argue that the difference between the "desire-to-be" (i.e., identification) and the "desire to have" is an ambiguous one, but one that is carefully maintained in the service of heteronormativity. Subjects are encouraged *to desire* to live up to the norms of a specific gender while concomitantly encouraged (and compelled) to desire the other. Thus, to complicate the usual psychoanalytic schema, in which identification and sexual object-choice are typically seen to be necessarily and essentially distinct for "normal" sexual development, and to build on Diana Fuss's and Ann Pellegrini's insights that desire and identification are always implicated in one another, I argue that desire in heterosexual regimes operates by

4. Sigmund Freud, *Group Psychology and the Analysis of the Ego: The Standard Edition*, trans. James Strachey (New York: Bantam Books, 1960), 46–47, my emphasis.
5. Ibid. As Shuli Barzilai (*Lacan and the Matter of Origins* [Stanford: Stanford University Press, 2000]), Diana Fuss (*Identification Papers* [New York: Routledge, 1995]), and others have pointed out, Freud's conception of identification is inconsistent and, at times, contradictory (see Barzilai, *Lacan*, 112–15). However, I do think it fair to say that *ultimately* identification and desire are distinct forms of attachment for Freud.
6. Fuss, *Identification*, 11.

engendering, encouraging, and *compelling* a specific type of relationship between two forms of desire: the "desire-to-be," which induces the subject to live up to hegemonic *norms,* and a "desire for," which induces a desire for sexual intimacy with the other gender.[7] On the other hand, I would like to further complicate this schema by arguing that the conflation of identification with the "desire-to-be" cannot be sustained. My comparison between the way in which identification and desire operate in heteronormativity and racist regimes will focus only on the identification/"desire-to-be" axis, since I believe this is where the crux of the difference lies.[8]

Like norms of gender identification, race norms operate by compelling subjects to assume or identify with certain identity categories. In the case of gender, subjects are interpellated into the symbolic order as either men or women and thus compelled to identify as either one or the other. By compelling *and encouraging* "women" to live up to norms of femininity and "men" to attempt to embody masculinity, heteronormative regimes reinforce their hegemony. There is a linking and thus collapsing of identification and "desire-to-be," which is fundamental to the operations of heteronormativity. In the case of race, subjects are compelled to identify as either black or white. But this is where the similarity with gender ends, since white racist regimes create a distinct bifurcation between identification and "desire-to-be," such that certain subjects are encouraged to privilege and thus desire attributes associated with whiteness, but concurrently these same subjects are *forced* to identify as black (which has gained its specific signification due to white supremacist discourse such as the one-drop rule). The assumption of whiteness that I outlined in the previous section is an effect of the way in which whiteness circulates as the ideal,

7. Ann Pellegrini (*Performance Anxieties: Staging Psychoanalysis, Staging Race* [New York: Routledge, 1997]) and Diana Fuss both argue that the separation that psychoanalysis has historically made between identification and desire is a problematic one, and they would both agree that this separation is an effect of heteronormativity. Identification for both Fuss and Pellegrini remains "a violent appropriation in which the Other is deposed and assimilated into the lordly domain of Self" (Fuss, *Identification,* 145). I will make a case for the need to delink identification and desire when analyzing the specific mechanisms at work in racist regimes.

8. Desire for, in racist and heteronormative regimes like the one described in *Passing,* is incredibly complex. Norms of heterosexuality alongside ideals privileging whiteness are inextricable when discussing how power operates to compel and encourage "desire for." Although Brian claims that he likes his women dark, his marriage to Irene (and apparent desire for Clare), who is light enough to pass, seems to undermine his assertion. However, to complicate things even further, I would argue that black women's "desire for" is constructed differently. Given the hierarchy and power differential, women's "desire for" in heteronormative regimes is mostly elided. As objects of desire for men, women's appearance is crucial; this is not true—to the same extent—for men under such a regime. For black-identified women such as Irene who strive for a nonmarginal existence, the man's class status seems to play a crucial role in their "desire for" and thus needs to be taken into account. Thus it makes sense that Irene would marry Brian, for his status as a doctor gives her respectability while allowing her to approximate the "angel in the house" ideal. Here we begin to see the complicated ways in which norms of gender, race, and class are many times articulated through one another.

while the one-drop rule and all of the prohibitions linked to trying to identify differently help ensure that subjects do not transgress racial boundaries. The ambivalence or contradiction underlying the assumption of whiteness can actually be restated in the following way: identify as black (or else) but aspire to be white. This contradiction, which actually constitutes the hegemonic category of race, proves to be a very effective way of policing racial borders.[9] The particular modality of the bifurcation, in other words, is simultaneously a product of power relations in a given society and that which allows power to operate effectively. This analysis diverges from a Freudian analysis not only because it underscores the different relationship between identification and desire in heteronormativity and racist regimes, and posits that identification and the "desire-to-be" cannot be collapsed, but also because in both regimes desire and identification are understood to be constituted by and through Foucault's conception of power.

Irene identifies as black despite the fact that she can pass as white. Due to the one-drop rule that was operative in the United States and inscribed in law at the time, it is no wonder that she does so. Irene's identification with blackness is described as a "bond," a "tie of race" (182), "the strain of black blood" (192). Although these descriptions can be read as having a positive valence, Irene's relationship to her identification with blackness is revealed when she suspects that her husband is having an affair with Clare. She describes herself caught between two allegiances—herself or her race: "Race! The thing that *bound* and *suffocated* her . . . the *burden* of race" (225, my emphasis). Race identification is ultimately described as something imposed.

All of the narratives of passing from this period underscore, in one form or another, how the category of race is forced upon the subject. All of these light-enough-to-pass characters, from Rena Walden [in *The House Behind the Cedars*] to the first-person narrator in *The Autobiography of an Ex-Coloured Man* to Angela Murray in *Plum Bum*, are interpellated into the symbolic world as black. The impact of the initial interpellation into the symbolic order is seemingly so great that the passing subject can never free him- or herself of its psychic effects.[1] Attempts to identify differently are always in relation to that first initiation into subjecthood. However, many of the

---

9. Using Eve Sedgwick's insight in a different context, one could argue that this focus on one drop of black blood is a tool used to control the entire spectrum of race organization. In many ways, it is the very arbitrariness upon which the distinction between black and white has been made that has lent "this distinction its power to organize complicated, historical transactions of power." Eve Kosofsky Sedgwick, *Between Men: English Literature and Male Homosocial Desire* (New York: Columbia University Press, 1985), 118. Therefore, difference—"white but not quite," or the one-drop rule—is a necessary part of the workings of racist hegemonies, and it is maintained and guarded as a means of ensuring that the white/black hierarchy retains its force.

1. The psychic effects of power within the context of racist regimes requires further research.

protagonists in these texts take the risk of identifying differently in order to access the privileges of whiteness, and most of them pay a high price or are punished for this "transgression."[2]

Punishment is an ever-present threat for subjects who attempt to identify differently. The "passing" mention of lynching is deceptive (231) [72–73], for despite Larsen's description of Irene's staid middle-class lifestyle, the threat of violence against black Americans who overstepped certain racial boundaries was ubiquitous in 1920s United States. Brian's answer to his son's question about why "they" only lynch colored people, "Because they hate 'em. . . . Because they are afraid of them, son," reveals some of the simmering racism that saturates Larsen's novella.[3] Through prohibitions and restrictions, the one-drop rule ensures that subjects conform to these constructed norms by compelling people with any African ancestors to identify as black. Irene is, in many ways, compelled to identify as black, although her "desire-to-be," as we will see shortly, lies elsewhere.

If *Passing* discloses that identifying as black has historically been a compelled identification, and not about the *desire* to usurp the other's place (to be or appropriate and thus become the other), then some of psychoanalysis's most basic assumptions about identification are put into question. Identification can no longer be understood simply as "an endless process of violent negation, a process of killing off the other in fantasy in order to usurp the other's place, the place where the subject desires to be."[4] Nor can it be understood as the psychological process whereby the subject assimilates an aspect, property or attribute to the other, and is transformed.[5] For identification with blackness under white racist regimes has historically not only been coerced, but it has also been coded as *undesirable*.

Desire and identification are not free-floating entities, since "we must understand power as *forming* the subject . . . as providing the very condition of its existence and the *trajectory of its desire*."[6] But in

2. James Weldon Johnson, *The Autobiography of an Ex-Coloured Man* (New York: Vintage Books, 1989); Jessie Redmon Faucet, *Plum Bum: A Novel without a Moral* (Boston: Beacon Press, 1990).
3. The anxiety expressed by both Clare and Gertrude about the possibility of giving birth to a dark child can also be seen as part of the prohibitions operating in racist regimes. For Clare, a dark baby would have spelled disaster; it would have "given her away." For Gertrude, a dark baby would have meant possible discrimination, discrimination that she is unused to due to her light skin (and thus the assumption that she is white) and white husband. "Being found out" becomes a constant site of anxiety for "passers." Moreover, to ensure success, the passer usually has to cut all connections to family and the past. Passing, as Irene Redfield points out in the text, is a "hazardous business" (157). And many passing narratives dramatize the dangers of race "transgression." See, for example, Faucet's *Plum Bum* or Charles Chesnutt's *The House behind the Cedars* (New York: Penguin Books, 1993).
4. Fuss, *Identification*, 9.
5. Jean Laplanche and Jean-Bertrand Pontalis, *The Language of Psychoanalysis,* trans. Donald Nicholson-Smith (London: Karnac Books, 1988), 205.
6. Judith Butler, *The Psychic Life of Power* (Stanford: Stanford University Press, 1997), 2, my emphasis.

contrast to Butler, who seems occasionally to collapse back into an originary desire, a *"prior* desire for social existence," which would help explain a subject's passionate and psychic attachment to subjugating norms,[7] I argue that the identification-desire dichotomy and its effect on subjects must be understood as one of the necessary productions of hegemony, that is, one of the most effective mechanisms of positive and negative power. As Butler herself says in her earlier writings, heteronormative and racial discourse are *formative* of desire and identification, and there is no reference to some prediscursive libido or amorphous desire that does not further produce the contours of that desire.[8]

It might seem that power should work to encourage black-identified subjects to approximate blackness as defined by the hegemony. This would operate as a mechanism of control because the subject's attempt to embody these norms would ensure that subject's subordination. But herein lie the paradox and the complex workings of positive and negative power. If a regime privileges certain attributes, then it must also encourage subjects to desire and strive to embody them. It can and does attempt to bar certain subjects from accessing privilege and positions of power through race differentiation and classification, or, in other words, compelling race identification, but it cannot completely control the effects of its own discourse. So long as blackness is coded as undesirable under white supremacist regimes, only those black-identified subjects who strive to embody attributes associated with whiteness will gain admittance to some of the benefits of privilege and power.

Thus, in racist regimes a concatenation that is very different from heteronormativity takes place. In heteronormativity (i.e., on the hegemonic level), identification with "being a woman" almost always implies (and is inextricably intertwined with) the desire to "be a woman," that is, a desire to live up to the norms of femininity in a particular symbolic order. Femininity is posited as desirable and as something that "women" should approximate; wanting to "be a woman" is coded as positive. The forced identification with blackness, however, is not linked with a desire to live up to norms of blackness. Rather, black-identified subjects, in order to sustain a nonmarginal existence, are compelled and encouraged to privilege and thus "desire-to-be white," that is, to live up to attributes associated with whiteness. As a consequence of the trauma of colonialism, Frantz Fanon asseverates that "The black man wants to be white,"[9] while Stuart Hall argues that "Blacks could gain entry to the mainstream—but only at the cost

7. Ibid., 19, my emphasis.
8. Judith Butler, *Bodies That Matter* (New York: Routledge, 1993).
9. Fanon, *Black Skin*, 9.

of . . . assimilating white norms of style, looks, and behavior."[1] This again is in stark contrast to heteronormativity, where women are never encouraged to live up to norms of masculinity, nor are men urged to live up to feminine ideals. Whereas female-identified subjects (subjects interpellated into the symbolic order as women) who desire to approximate masculinity (active, aggressive, etc.) are threatening to the powers that be, black-identified subjects who attempt to approximate whiteness have often been accepted by hegemony.

Although *Passing* is ostensibly about the dangers of passing over to the white world as manifested in Clare's enigmatic death, I would argue, along with many other critics, that the novella is just as much about Irene's attempting to approximate norms of whiteness.[2] Despite or perhaps due to her black identification, Irene is depicted as desiring a civilized and cultured life. "Irene didn't like changes, particularly changes that affected the smooth routine of her household" (188) [41]. Thus, Brian's dream of leaving the United States for Brazil is disturbing to Irene on at least two counts. It represents a change that would disrupt the "pleasant routine of her life" (229) [72], and Brazil, according to Irene's assessment of things, is decidedly not a civilized place. Irene's routine, it is important to underscore, consists of maintaining the appearances of white middle-class prosperity. She occupies herself with mothering, social obligations, and "uplift work"; and despite her declaration to Clare that she is "wrapped up in her boys and the running of her house," it seems that black maids do most of the arduous housework. As Jacquelyn McLendon avers, "Irene Redfield, in her strict adherence to bourgeois ideological codes, strives to mask any feelings or behavior that appears to be uncivilized or unladylike, measures herself by white standards, and lives in constant imitation of whites."[3] Irene strives to obtain "marginal acceptance and security," in American society," and this desire-to-be a viable and accepted subject in the United States forces her to "imitate the prejudices of the dominant society."[4]

Security is the most important and "desired thing in life" for Irene Redfield (235) [76]. Any and all attributes linked to hegemonic ideas of blackness—"the open expression of emotion and feeling rather than intellect, a lack of 'civilized refinement' in sexual and social life"[5]—are carefully policed by Irene. Her occasional

---

1. Hall, "Spectacle," 279.
2. See, for example, Blackmer, "Veils"; DeVere Brody, " 'True' Colors"; Jacquelyn McLendon, "Self-Representation as Art in the Novels of Nella Larson," in *Redefining Autobiography in Twentieth-Century Women's Fiction*, ed. Janice Morgan and Colette T. Hall (New York: Garland, 1991), 149–68.
3. McLendon, "Self-Representation," 158.
4. Blackmer, "Veils," 59.
5. Hall, "Spectacle," 243.

outbursts of temper and impetuosity are followed by self-admonishment (157, 190, 201). Even when Irene first suspects that Brian is having an affair with Clare, she refuses to display her emotions. Despite the shock and horror, Irene throws her already-planned tea party. She keeps up appearances: "Satisfied that there lingered no betraying evidence of weeping, she dusted a little powder on her dark-white face and again examined it carefully" (218) [63]. Rather than show any signs of distress, Irene "went on pouring. Made repetitions of her smile. Answered questions. Manufactured conversation. . . . So like many other tea-parties she had had" (219) [64].

Irene also ensures that any semblance of overt sexuality is checked; the stereotype of the lascivious, oversexed black woman was still very much in circulation during the period Larsen depicts.[6] At one point, she suddenly admits to herself that Clare is "capable of heights and depths of feelings that she, Irene Redfield had never known." But the clincher is in the next admission. Irene has "never cared to know" these feelings (195) [47]. Brian is her husband and the father of her sons, but as she ponders what to do with the suspicion of Brian's affair with Clare, she also tells us that she has never truly known love (235). The desire to approximate norms of civility is so powerful that Irene is willing to "hold fast to the outer shell of her marriage, to keep her life fixed, certain. Brought to the edge of distasteful reality, her fastidious nature did not recoil" (235) [77]. For to dissolve the marriage would no doubt bring the kind of notoriety that Irene tries so hard to avoid (157, 199). Moreover, if the marriage is already more about striving to embody the ideals of the white middle class, then it is not at all clear that the "substance" of the marriage would change after Brian's affair; the two already sleep in different rooms. In short, Irene strives to be as prim, as proper, and as bourgeois as (ideals of) white middle-class ladies.[7]

This desire to approximate norms of whiteness is reiterated in the other two major passing novels of this period. The protagonist in James Weldon Johnson's *The Autobiography of an Ex-Coloured Man* clearly exposes the "compelled desire" to embody attributes associated with whiteness. After witnessing a black man being lynched, he decides to pass. He abandons his ragtime career, which is associated with "black" culture, marries a white woman, and becomes a successful businessman. He expresses his anxiety of "being found out" but decides to take his chances anyway. And whereas Johnson's protagonist takes his

6. See, for example, Deborah McDowell, "Introduction," in *Passing and Quicksand* (Piscataway, N.J.: Rutgers University Press, 1986), ix–xxxv [reprinted in this edition, p. 363].
7. Ann DuCille, "Blues Notes on Black Sexuality: Sex and the Texts of Jessie Faucet [sic] and Nella Larsen," in *American Sexual Politics*, ed. John Fout and Maura Tantillo (Chicago: Chicago University Press, 1993), 197.

chances as a white man, Angela Murray in *Plum Bum* finds the strain of passing too much for her and ends up married to a light-enough-to-pass black man. And while both sisters, Angela and Virginia (who is not light enough to pass), are ultimately compelled to identify as black, they, just like Irene, are also depicted as striving to live up to white middle-class norms of respectability. In order to access privilege, it seems, subjects interpellated into the symbolic order as black must constantly endeavor to embody attributes associated with whiteness.

Thus, *contra* Miron and Inda, I would like to emphasize that the raced subject, in order to remain *viable* and to *not be completely marginalized* in a white supremacist power regime, must constantly and perpetually attempt to embody norms that have historically been associated and concatenated with whiteness. Although white racist regimes help create black subjects, the racial norms that this regime produces, promulgates, and compels subjects to approximate are invariably norms associated with whiteness. I believe that the delinking of identification and "desire-to-be" is key to understanding the particular mechanisms by which and through which norms of race operate under racist regimes. Moreover, desiring to approximate blackness, as it comes to be defined by this regime, means disidentifying with the dominant norms, can be dangerous, and can sometimes even lead to death.

4. *Identification Trouble*

By way of conclusion, I would like to introduce some additional complicating factors and qualifications. As mentioned, in white racist regimes, attributes associated with whiteness are always privileged. While such a regime would not necessarily discourage marginal black-identified subjects from striving to embody blackness, the splitting of identification and desire-to-be serves as one of the most efficacious mechanisms of control. This delinking ensures that the desirability of whiteness is reinforced, while black-identified subjects are simultaneously prevented from accessing many of the privileges that "true" whiteness grants.

Clare, however, disrupts this schema to a certain extent. Through her characterization, the reader is exposed to an interesting process of identification, disidentification, and a further disidentification. Interpellated into the symbolic order as a black woman, Clare "chooses" to pass over into the white world. Her marriage to a white racist who does not know that she is passing in many ways underscores the risk that this kind of misidentification carries. In her first identification crisis, Clare "decides" to perform race norms differently. Rather than remain a black-identified woman who strives to approximate norms of whiteness, Clare begins not only to approximate white norms but also to identify as a white woman. In the letter Clare sends to Irene after meeting her at the Drayton, Clare indicates that she had been on her way to "freeing" herself from her identification with blackness (145) [7]. We learn early on that Clare's decision to pass is inextricably intertwined with her determination to "be a person and not a charity or a problem" (159) [19]. In contrast to Angela Murray in *Plum Bum*, Clare has no loving family whom she has to break ties with and disown in order to pass. The risks she takes, like the ones taken by the protagonist in *The Autobiography of an Ex-Coloured Man*, are, according to Clare herself, "worth the price" (160) [20], for performing whiteness confers status and privilege.

Clare's desire to reclaim her initial identification as a black woman, however, is one that cannot be explained according to the logic of privilege. For this very reason Larsen's description of this further disidentification is fascinating. Clare knowingly courts danger and punishment when she shows up in Harlem; in many ways, she can be seen to be putting her social existence into jeopardy. In sharp contrast to the "status" she gains by performing whiteness, her appearance in black Harlem does not confer privilege.

Larsen's portrayal of Clare thus suggests that the preceding discussion did not fully capture the complexity of race performativity, and of performativity more generally. Hegemonic regimes, as I argued above, cannot completely control the effects of their own discourse. Even though whiteness is privileged over and against blackness in white supremacist regimes, the very repetition and circulation of different—and at times contradictory—racial norms create the possibility of subversion. As Judith Butler has reminded us time and again, because the symbolic order is dependent on reiteration for its very existence, it is also necessarily open to variation. Moreover, since it is impossible to fully inhabit hegemonic ideals once and for all, there is an irreconcilable space between normative roles and social practices. Subjects must *incessantly* attempt to embody norms, which, in turn, creates a continuous (and potentially discernible) dissonance; gaps and fissures can and do emerge within symbolic orders as subjects strive to embody regulatory ideals.[8] Due to the noncoincidence of ideals and social praxis, there is always the possibility that subjects will repeat norms in unpredictable and potentially contestatory ways.

In a sense, this is what Clare is depicted as doing when she attempts to approximate certain hegemonic norms of blackness. Unlike Irene, Clare does not police overt signs of sexuality. The

8. Butler, *Bodies*, 89, 124.

"shade too provocative" smile that she gives the waiter at the Drayton is one of the first things Irene notices about her old acquaintance (148) [10], and when the reader is first introduced to Clare she is with an unknown and never-named man; we find out later that he is not her husband. This linking of Clare and sexuality occurs throughout the text, from the gossip that Clare's disappearance from her aunts' house elicits, through the way she dresses in clothing deliberately meant to attract attention to her beauty, to Irene's suspicion that she is having an affair with Brian. Clare herself cultivates and performs this image; for example, during Clare's first visit to Irene and Brian in Harlem, she admonishes Irene for not writing by describing how she waited in vain for a response to her correspondence: "Every day I went to that nasty little post-office place. I'm sure they were all beginning to think that I'd been carrying on an illicit love-affair" (194) [46].

Clare is also consistently associated with theatrics, excess, and danger. Irene describes her as having a "strange capacity of transforming warmth and passion, verging sometimes almost on theatrical heroics" (144) [6]. Clare, who describes herself as lacking any "proper morals or sense of duty" (210) [58], is depicted as presenting a danger to the white middle-class conventions that Irene strictly adheres to (143, 181, 213). In effect, Clare's counterhegemonic performance of "blackness" can be seen as an attempt to reevaluate the desirability of "desiring to be black." But since white supremacist societies do not necessarily discourage subjects' attempt to embody norms of blackness, the importance of Clare's disidentification, for my argument, does not lie in the content of her desire. Rather, Larsen's portrayal of Clare points to some of the conditions of possibility of disidentification.

Although constituted through and circumscribed by norms, the fractured and competing nature of the ideals circulating in society seems to open a space for subjects to perform differently. Clare's second disidentification trouble, for instance, appears to be facilitated when she reencounters Irene. In the letter Clare sends to Irene after their meeting at the Drayton, she indicates that once she was glad to be free of her identification with blackness, but now she has a "wild desire" to associate with black people. Clare adds that it's Irene's fault, for if she hadn't seen the other woman in Chicago, the thought of escaping her "pale life" would never have occurred to her (145) [7]. What this points to, I believe is that confrontations or interactions between subjects can potentially lay bare the disjunctions and contradictions within the nexus of force relations. Clare, who had initially attempted to "perform" race by identifying and desiring to be white at the risk of "being found out," is suddenly confronted by Irene, who has "chosen" not to "pass over." This encounter, in turn, opens up a space of negotiation. It is not that Clare wishes to trade places with Irene; rather, Clare recognizes that other *configurations* of identification and "desire-to-be" are possible. Thus, a nuanced conception of agency emerges, one that derives, in large part, from the subject's ability to recognize and negotiate *between* the different possible configurations of identification and "desire-to-be" that help constitute the field of intelligibility.

Racial norms, to be sure, are spawned by a particular configuration of power relations, and these norms are both the condition of possibility of viable subjects and help produce and shape the subject's very preferences, aspirations, desire, and identification. Larsen's portrayal of Irene reveals just how powerful and effective these racial norms can be. This does not mean, however, that subjects are merely docile bodies, but rather that subjects can and do "perform differently." The depiction of Clare gestures toward the way in which identification and desire-to-be can be misappropriated and "assumed" in potentially subversive ways. Although Clare's enigmatic death ultimately precludes an unambiguously subversive or celebratory reading of the novella, tracing her identification and subsequent disidentifications can, I believe, give us insight into how power can be challenged through contestatory performances.

MIRIAM THAGGERT

Racial Etiquette: Nella Larsen's *Passing* and the Rhinelander Case†

I

In *Passing* Nella Larsen seems to suggest that identity is a hazy fiction one tells that outward appearances and surface events only partly confirm. Rather than directly stating their thoughts, characters communicate through an exchange of looks—particularly her two light-skinned female characters, Irene and Clare. These subtle forms of expression heighten the sense of uncertainty throughout the novel. The reader never learns explicitly the reason for Clare's fall out of a window, the reality of a homosexual longing between Clare and Irene, or the true nature of the relationship between Clare and Irene's husband. This indeterminacy extends to the racial identity of Larsen's

† From Miriam Thaggert, "Racial Etiquette: Nella Larsen's Passing and the Rhinelander Case," *Meridians: feminism, race, transnationalism* 5, issue 2 (2005): 1–29. Reprinted by permission of Indiana University Press. Bracketed page numbers refer to this Norton Critical Edition.

characters, an identity not always easily discernible because of the characters' mixed racial background and their inclination to "pass."[1] Without adequate markings or clues, any reading, whether of identities or situations, is flawed or incorrect.

A brief, almost offhand, remark Irene makes refers to a legal trial in which these issues of knowledge, passing, and the gaze combined in a process to interrogate the race and veracity of a woman. The *Rhinelander* case was an annulment proceeding in which wealthy, white Leonard Kip Rhinelander sued his wife, Alice Beatrice Jones, for fraud. Leonard claimed he did not know that his light-skinned wife was "colored," the daughter of a white woman and a dark-skinned cab driver.[2] Larsen's reference to the Rhinelanders occurs only once, near the end of the novel, after Irene suspects that her husband, Brian, is having an affair with Clare. Irene wonders what would happen if Clare's white husband discovered not the affair but that Clare has "colored" blood: "What if Bellew should divorce Clare? Could he? There was the *Rhinelander* case" (228) [71].[3] Married on 14 October 1924 in New Rochelle, New York, the Rhinelanders were featured in newspaper articles that described them as happy newly-weds and quoted Leonard's lack of concern about his wife's racial background: "[W]e are indeed very happy. What difference does it make about her race? She's my wife, Mrs. Rhinelander" ("Honorable Marriage" 11). It was not long, of course, before Leonard realized the "difference" race—and class—made to his prominent family. In late November 1924, at the demand of his father, Leonard filed an annulment suit, claiming Alice had lied about her race and deceived him into marrying her. Although this contradicted his earlier statement to reporters, Leonard filed the suit with the help of his father's lawyers, and the trial began on 9 November 1925. What escalated the trial to the height of drama was the role played by the nonwhite body. Alice's body literally became evidence in the case when she was forced to

1. Throughout this essay I am speaking of the specific issue of white and black miscegenation in the United States. As an anonymous reviewer noted, the contemporary terms "mixed" and "mixed race" have many meanings; in the context of *Passing* they imply the mixture of black and white, "a peculiarly North American mixture dilemma." In addition, I use the phrase "ambiguously raced" to describe the female characters in the novel; and the phrase is meant to convey people of color who may or may not be mixed with white (it is assumed, for instance, that both of Irene's parents are African American) and who appear more physically white than black or any other race. The difficulty of assigning definitive racial categories is, I argue, one of Larsen's central points in both *Passing* and *Quicksand*.
2. In newspaper accounts of the trial Alice and the Jones family members were referred to as "Negro" or "colored." Alice's lawyer, when it was necessary to refer to her race, used the term "colored." George Jones, Alice's brown-skinned English father, was at various times called "West Indian," "Negro," and "colored," and his immigration papers listed him as "colored" ("Rhinelander Annulment Suit," 3).
3. Nella Larsen, *Quicksand* and *Passing* ([1928, 1929] 1986). All subsequent quotations from this edition are cited parenthetically in the text. Bracketed page numbers refer to this Norton Critical Edition.

disrobe in front of the judge, lawyers, and the all-white, all-male jury to prove that she had never lied to her husband about her race, that in fact any man who had been intimate with her could "see" her color.

Although Irene's casual remark has been received as simply a historical reference, her citation is ironic, for not only are there uncanny similarities between the major figures of the novel and the trial but the novel also critiques the methods and conventions that assume a central import in the *Rhinelander* case.[4] Etiquette and performance, the forms of behavior on which the prosecution and the defense relied in the trial to authenticate race, are subversively used by Irene and Clare in *Passing*. Examining the trial in relation to *Passing* helps us to interrogate the cultural practices that enable and complicate the identity politics of race; both narratives illuminate the use of social and racial codes to evaluate, through the look, the female body. Abstract and elusive in the salons of *Passing*, the social and racial conventions are reified in practice in the courtroom, demonstrating the violence of such codes and reading processes in the creation of symbolic meaning.

The concepts of readability and representation are central to both Larsen's novel and the *Rhinelander* case. If, as Michel Foucault states, the body is an inscribed surface, "imprinted by history" and bestowed with what Judith Butler calls a cultural "intelligibility," *Passing* interrogates (while the case depends on) those meanings traditionally associated with the black female body (Foucault 1977, 148; Butler 1989, 605). Foucault's writing metaphor is, as Butler points out, problematic, for it assumes a prediscursive body that is "figured as a ready surface or blank page available for inscription"—a concept Foucault argues against in *The History of Sexuality*, Vol. I (Butler, 601). His statement offers a more disconcerting paradox when considered in light of African American bodies. Hortense Spillers's psychoanalytic "Mama's Baby, Papa's Maybe" is perhaps the most

---

4. The trial passed into obscurity until the recent publication of *Love on Trial*, a historical account of the events and people involved in the case (Lewis and Ardizzone 2001). In the 1986 Rutgers University Press edition of *Quicksand* and *Passing*, McDowell offers a brief explanation of the case (245 n. 8). Mark J. Madigan offers a short reading of the trial in relation to *Passing* (1990, 523–29) [reprinted in this edition, p. 387]. Near the final stages of copyediting, I came across Sarah E. Chinn's *Technology and the Logic of American Racism*. Chinn also looks at *Passing* through the lens of the *Rhinelander* case but for different purposes than mine. Chinn argues how the novel and case demonstrate the distinguishable reading practices of black and white spectators (67) and how "cultural texts show us how vision is segregated by race, by gender, by class" (59). Her interpretations of the trial focus on reading the skin as evidence, the belief that dark skin operates as "epidermal obviousness" (70) for blackness and on how the black spectator is usually more skillful in such reading practices than the white spectator. I focus less on how courtroom participants and spectators view Alice than on the assumption that the black female body can be easily read by any spectator and the role of etiquette or manners as a type of racial performance. We both suggest that certain white spectators are less inclined to question the knowledge assumed or obtained from looking (Chinn 2000, 64, 65).

insightful critique of the narrative function often assigned to black bodies, figures necessary for, but not full members of, a discourse Spillers refers to as an "American grammar," the "ruling episteme that releases the dynamics of naming and valuation" (1987, 68). Black bodies in these "symbolic paradigms" appear not too far removed from the blank pages Butler critiqued—only, in this case the exterior surfaces are inscribed to reflect a relation to whiteness. Portuguese slave traders, for instance, categorized captives as " 'white enough,' " "less 'white like mulattoes,' " and " 'black as Ethiops' "—a grammar of "declension" based on skin color (70). The black body is perceived as a vacuous object, given meaning and signification through a difference from whiteness. The paradox is that this empty object is, at the same time, all body, reflecting the negative value in the too familiar mind/body dichotomy, too much body to achieve privileged abstraction.[5]

Foucault's reading and writing metaphor suggests not only the visual appraisal of surface, readily apparent bodily attributes but also the process of making meaning and forming knowledge out of those physical clues, a process inherent in the Rhinelander trial and a strategy Larsen's characters employ. *Passing* undermines the grammar of racial language communicated through and by the body, those signs of "intelligibility" that help to enable meaning. Both the novel and the trial center on the assumption of an always decipherable, easily readable black body. The novel disrupts a racial and sexual "legibility," the meanings derived from stereotypes, by simultaneously hindering the reader's act of interpreting Clare and making the reader question the interpretative practices of Irene—just as the jury in the Rhinelander trial must decide to which racial category Alice belongs and judge Leonard's ability to "read" his wife. Reading the woman's body in both the novel and the trial is a delicate act because of the uncertainty of "race" of the light-skinned body. In *Passing* this uncertainty is further heightened by the potential for ambiguity of the decorated, stylized female form, the "masquerade" and remaking of the self available through fashion and cosmetics (Rabine 1994, 60). Indeed, as Larsen presents them, racial passing and fashion are curiously related; there is an easy confluence between the two because of their reliance on the subtleties of vision. Depending on the appearance of the mixed-race female body, the subject who passes can elide categories determined by race; and clothes can "camouflage" the body for those special times when "we don't want to be seen—or when we don't want our true selves to show through" (Fischer-Mirkin 1995,

---

5. In *American Anatomies* Robyn Wiegman argues that those whose bodies are marked differently from white masculinity, such as African Americans, are "prohibited" from "the abstraction of personhood that democratic equality supposedly entailed" (1995, 49).

12). Irene's and Clare's performance of a certain type of femininity, with fashion as their costumes and middle-class etiquette as their stage directions, helps the women to accentuate the ambiguous visual demarcations of the African American, light-skinned body and enables them to pass as white more successfully. Fashion and passing are forms of reinventing the self in the novel, ways to restylize how the black or the black/white female body can be read, or indeed, ways to deny any reading at all. As Meredith Goldsmith's article suggests, Larsen's heroines revel in the "pleasures . . . [of] bodily self-fashioning." This essay differs from hers by highlighting the adornment of the body not only to show the characters' "attempt at identity construction" but also to reveal how the characters strategically confuse the spectator of the black female body (Goldsmith 2001, 98).

This idea of performance is shaped by Butler's writings on gender performance, or "[t]he effect of gender . . . produced through the stylization of the body, . . . the mundane way in which bodily gestures, movements, and styles of various kinds constitute the illusion of an abiding gendered self" (Butler 1990, 140). But is race equally performative? Are there certain "gestures, movements, and styles" that are readily perceptible as an "effect" of race? Is it a subversive act or merely a type of performative essentialism when one acts out or plays up movements associated with a race? Larsen's novel suggests that, indeed, there are codes that are not "essential" qualities of a race but that are easily imitated, mastered, and performed and that easily signify one race (or gender or class) rather than another.

Expanding on Butler's ideas, Amy Robinson has written engagingly about sexual and racial passing. Directing us to view "identity politics as a skill of reading," Robinson suggests that we examine not the veracity of the passing performance but the appearance of veracity to others. This subtle distinction shifts the objective of reading the passing performance from an ontological to a spectatorial inquiry. Robinson's argument highlights just how intertwined the spectatorial and ontological positions are in relation to those women of color who do not pass (1994, 716). Alice's lawyer surprised Leonard's legal representatives by admitting, during the first day of the trial, that she had "colored" blood. But did she then withhold that information from Leonard? Could a man "know" his wife intimately yet not know her race? The fact that Alice had to disrobe, the belief that one could see her race and hence know her race, suggests how spectatorial knowledge constitutes ontological knowledge in relation to nonwhite femininity. For nonwhite women the two epistemological positions are violently aligned—Alice's disrobing situates her into a long line of women of color who have had their bodies, literally and figuratively, placed on trial. In addition, Larsen complicates any notion of readily interpreting the black or black/white female body. Indeed, as if punning on the difficulties of "reading" blackness, Larsen gives a crucial role to letters in *Passing*, just as letters played a significant role in the Rhinelander trial. In both there is a comparison of written letters to the body, but Clare's body and letters refuse a clear reading, whereas Alice Jones Rhinelander's body and letters are subject to the violence of the look. In the Rhinelander trial the body also takes the place of Alice's words, her testimony to the jury. More important, as I will show in my conclusion, the novel's concern with reading nonwhite women and the body elicits larger questions about the relation of black women to cultural "grammar" and about the status of the black female intellectual's work to literary theory and criticism.

One of Larsen's acquaintances once remarked, "Nella was an actress; she knew how to pose for a picture" (Davis 1994, 447). Her performative abilities equally excelled in her writing. Studying the facts of a trial suffused with the theatrical, indeed, a trial that summoned a major Broadway figure of the time, helps us to appreciate more thoroughly Larsen's lexical production. Her textual play conceals and reveals, tempts and teases not only Irene Redfield in her various acts of reading Clare but the novel's reader as well. By subtly referencing one of the most sensational trials that took place during the Harlem Renaissance, *Passing* dramatizes racial and social performance and reveals how to stage the ody to convey or deny a particular reading.

II

Visuality and appearance are central issues in *Passing*. An exchange of glances between and among women occurs repeatedly in the text—glances that the main character, Irene, can never fully comprehend. Irene's looks question her friend's "mysterious and concealing" eyes and admire her charm and "indifferent assurance" (161) [00]. Her evaluations of Clare are almost obsessively concerned with minute clothing details, and she frequently feels that she can never quite measure up to Clare's beauty and style, feeling "dowdy and commonplace" in comparison to her friend (203) [53].

Several discussions of women, fashion, and the fashion industry provide some clues to Irene's exceptional attention to Clare's attire and suggest the significance of fashion to women who occupy the boundaries of race. In Leslie W. Rabine's study of the "two bodies of women" (one caught in a system that negatively defines what a woman should look like and one engaged in a process of self-invention and transformation), she notes how clothing can mask the class of the wearer: "With the rise of commodity capitalism, workers could dress like the wealthy bourgeois, and so clothing became a masquerade that could *signify* any role in the absence of a referent, instead of *designating* a fixed place in a scale of positions.

It ambiguously revealed or concealed the social identity of its wearer" (Rabine 1994, 69–70, original emphasis). It is this "absent referent," the absent "markedness" traditionally associated with blackness, that both Irene and Clare play up through their use of fashion.

While Rabine points out the democratization made available by clothes and commodity culture, Diana Fuss in "Fashion and the Homospectorial Look" examines the processes of identity construction that occur when women look at the idealized, perfect women captured in the photographs of fashion magazines. Fuss uses Julia Kristeva's notion of the homosexual maternal facet to explain why women are attracted to these images. According to Kristeva the mother's face is the first object that the child looks at and identifies with while still in the pre-oedipal stage. As the child forms her own identity, the mother's face becomes a lost object: "For the girl, such a loss is a double [loss] since the mother's image is [also] her own" (Fuss 1995, 99). By looking at fashion magazines, particularly at ads that employ close-ups, a woman may get "special pleasure" from seeing the face of a woman, and this offers the "fantasy" of replacing the lost object, of recapturing the mirror image of the mother (99, 113). Fuss argues that the woman who looks is supposed to identify with the model and not have her; that is, these ads encourage the spectator "to desire to be the woman [in the ad] so as to preclude having her" (107). This leads her to conclude that "the entire fashion industry operates as one of the few institutionalized spaces where women can look at other women with cultural impunity. It provides a socially sanctioned structure in which women are encouraged to consume . . . the images of other women" (90–91).[6] Read with attention to the notion of an unarticulated desire, Fuss's argument supports Deborah McDowell's influential analysis about homoeroticism in this novel, that Larsen "flirt[s], if only by suggestion, with the idea of a lesbian relationship" between Clare and Irene (McDowell 1986, xxiii).

Just as clothes reinvent the exterior of the body, offering a type of costume, etiquette helps to finish the performance. Etiquette manu-

6. There is a significant class and racial component that Fuss leaves unexamined in her argument and that she acknowledges. Fuss omits how women of different racial or economic backgrounds would read these images. This aspect becomes significant when considered during the period of the Harlem Renaissance. In the beauty ads directed toward black women of the time, it was not just clothing that was being sold but also products to alter the hair and skin. Marketing of these items emphasized not clothes and jewelry, things that can be taken on and off, but physical aspects commonly associated with blackness. If, as Fuss suggests, the female spectator looks at the model to be and have her, how does the black female spectator be or have the white model? How do contemporary black women who read fashion images look at the white, Latino, Asian, or other black women who are portrayed within the pages? Do black women identify with these women? Do black women want to "have" them? Or do they merely want to have the objects that these female bodies display?

als offered instructions and prohibitions on how one moved or staged the body in social settings. With the proper awareness and training, anyone could occupy a certain desired social space or at least give the appearance of doing so. As Marjorie Ellis Ferguson McCrady and Blanche Wheeler put it in *Manners for Moderns*, "the behavior of the $12 a week stenographer can be just as becoming as that of the $50,000 a year lady" (1942, v–vi). One early etiquette manual "dedicated to the colored race" was the 1920 *National Capital Code of Etiquette*. In it, Edward S. Green advised his black readers on "How to Dress," doling out advice such as avoiding so-called loud colors "that fairly shriek unto Heaven" (14). Both *Passing* and Larsen's earlier novel *Quicksand* critique advice such as Green offered. As a teacher, Helga Crane tries to abide by her school's and Green's idea of "good taste" but rebels because of her love for rich colors (3). She considers marrying into a black "first family," but she flees her school and the South because "[s]he hadn't really wanted to be made over" (8, 7). Throughout *Quicksand* Helga tries to balance her wish for the appearance of social poise, as etiquette offered, with her more sensual, indecorous feelings.[7]

It is intriguing, then, to read *Passing* as not only a tale of black and white intrigue and discreet homosexual longings but also as a black modernist tale of manners, a subtle style manual that at times both promotes the black middle-class "performance" and displays the contradictions embedded in such acts. Irene, for instance, initially reads Clare through the language and lens of fashion. The first encounter between them reads like a descriptive excerpt from a women's magazine. Irene sits on the balcony of the upscale Drayton Hotel. When Clare first enters, Irene notices a "sweetly scented woman in a fluttering dress of green chiffon whose mingled pattern of narcissuses, jonquils, and hyacinths was a reminder of pleasantly chill spring days" (148) [9]. The correspondence between scent and color, between a woman's perfume and her clothes, is, as Goldsmith points out, reminiscent of the language of ads (2001, 113). Clare recognizes Irene first and bluntly stares at her. Irene is initially disturbed by the look but then feels guilty because she thinks the woman knows she is a black person sitting in a socially segregated space.

7. The equality etiquette offered would seem to be particularly significant for the class-conscious Larsen, who lacked the family, sorority, and church connections that provided the foundation for the black middle and upper classes in the early twentieth century. Larsen did, however, obtain a higher level of social status when she married Elmer Imes, a doctor who worked at Fisk University (Davis 1994, 128). Despite her characters' and her own ambivalence about the "strenuous rigidity of conduct" that the black middle class required (1), Larsen maintained an appearance of grace and elegance, particularly during the years of the Renaissance. Those who knew the writer have commented on her extremely poised social manners. As Bruce Nugent noted to her biographer, "her 'air' exuded social status" (Davis 1994, 142).

This use of clothing calls attention to what it can either hide or highlight beneath. Clare's look makes Irene conscious of herself; it is as if Irene "suddenly has a body" (Berlant 1991, 110). She becomes aware of her own attire and anxious about how she may appear to others:

> What, she wondered, could be the reason for such persistent attention? Had she, in her haste in the taxi, put her hat on backwards? Guardedly she felt at it. No. Perhaps there was a streak of powder somewhere on her face. She made a quick pass over it with her handkerchief. Something wrong with her dress? She shot a glance over it. Perfectly all right. What was it? (149) [10].

To Irene, Clare's steady look could only be the result of a blunder in her application of makeup, a lapse in her fashion sense. These assumed fashion and beauty faux pas force her to "verify herself endlessly," to reexamine her body and clothing in bits and pieces (Fuss 1995, 95). Fuss's homospectorial look, then, can also be a regimental tool. However innocuous the exterior look is, it can be internalized and operate punitively, especially for black women.

J. C. Flügel provides another reason why attention to clothes is so important for Irene, Clare, and other women who may pass. In *The Psychology of Clothes*, an examination of the cultural and psychological meanings attached to fashions, Flügel asserts that clothes augment one's identity, endowing one with a bodily presence: "clothing, by adding to the apparent size of the body in one way or another, gives us an increased sense of power, a sense of extension of our bodily [selves]—ultimately enabling us to fill more space" ([1930] 1966, 34). Fashion's ability to strengthen a sense of identity is important for these two women whose identities are so fragmentary and fragile. For Irene and Clare clothes are not only a metaphorical extension but also provide the means for deception: their well-dressed bodies allow them to occupy a privileged social space that, if they were recognized as black, would not be available to them. Although their fashions leave their racial identities in flux, their abilities to dress well enable them to heighten the perception that they belong to one race rather than another and to pass as white more successfully. In her analysis of the novel Butler remarks on how blackness is not an immediately evident way of classifying bodies, since "what can be seen, what qualifies as a visible marking, is a matter of being able to read a marked body in relation to unmarked bodies, where unmarked bodies constitute the currency of normative whiteness" (1993, 170–71). What the scene at the top of the Drayton reveals is that the "markings" can be concealed, played with, or heightened to achieve a certain effect. Indeed, Clare and Irene's fashion skills allow them to evade being considered "marked" at all.

This episode on the top of the Drayton is just the first of several scenes in which the women exchange glances, in which Clare's look imparts some knowledge that she has but that Irene, for some reason, cannot or will not understand. Additional scenes of visual exchanges reveal Clare's paradoxical status in the novel: that while everyone imposes his or her definitions on her, she remains unknowable, her gaze "unfathomable." Although she is always the center of attention, no one really knows her, both as a result of her objectification as well as not knowing to whom her "having" gaze is directed (Irene or Brian?). One scene of subtle reading and heightened unknowability occurs when Irene visits Clare's apartment for tea. Irene arrives, unaware that Clare has invited another former classmate, Gertrude Martin. What is most interesting about the reunion is what is not said but is merely implied or suggested about reading bodies and performing femininity and how the narrative communicates these issues through visual ambiguity, the light-skinned black female body passing as white.

This scene inevitably encourages comparisons, as Irene compares her life choices to her friends' and finds herself outnumbered, feeling a "sense of aloneness, in her adherence to her own class and kind" (166) [24–25]. For like Clare, Gertrude married a white man. And although she does not pass with her husband, Gertrude, in both her speech and actions, maintains a "dutiful eagerness" to be perceived as white (171)[00]. The quality that plagues Irene throughout the narrative, "loyalty to a race" (227) [71] and, implicitly, deception to one's race, underlies the scene and briefly rises to the surface in their discussion of a "black Jew" (169) [27]. Is one "authentically black" if one marries a black man and passes only occasionally, as Irene does? Or does one, like Clare, stay "true" to the race by periodically surrounding oneself with blacks? Or is the most "honest" position the one that is, in fact, represented by Gertrude, a position in which everyone, including your husband, knows you are black, although you try hard to convince others that you are white "in spirit"? Larsen makes us ponder these essentialist, although for her characters significant, questions through what is considered to be that most feminine of interests and perhaps the easiest and most superficial claim to legitimacy, clothing and decoration. The three women, through their attire and social skills, enact their own "performance" in an attempt to become "bodies that matter," bodies that not only give the appearance of having successfully contended with concerns such as marriages and children but also that have used racial ambiguity to obtain social status. Subtle, strategic, and unspoken alliances are made and unmade among the women as each seems to ponder the lives—and clothes and bodies—of the two others.

Larsen immediately sets up the relation among fashion, décor, and the body. Irene enters Clare's apartment and is confronted with "startling blue draperies" and "gloomy chocolate-coloured furniture" (165) [24]. In the midst of such an unusual color combination Clare manages to coordinate with her room by wearing "a thin floating dress of the same shade of blue, which suited her and the rather difficult room to perfection" (165) [24]. The other member of the tea party, somehow, does not harmonize as well. In fact, this person seems to disappear into the room, for "Irene thought the room empty, but . . . she discovered, sunk deep in the cushions of a huge sofa, a woman staring up at her." While Clare's body coordinates, Gertrude's body disappears. Irene subjects Gertrude to a thorough yet subtle look and judges her, in contemporary parlance, a fashion victim. Her former schoolmate wears an "over-trimmed Georgette crepe dress [that] was too short and showed an appalling amount of leg, stout legs in sleazy stockings of a vivid rose-beige shade" (167) [25]. Irene's gaze establishes a distinction between Clare's fashionable body and Gertrude's bodily extremes. Although her body initially disappeared, Gertrude seems on closer inspection to have too much body, for "[s]he had grown broad, fat almost," with aging "lines on her large white face" (167)[25]. What is significant about this scene is the subtle theory Larsen posits about the ability to read. Irene and Clare are women attuned to each other's class codes, with Clare able to read Irene better than Irene wishes. In fact, Fuss's homospectorial look can be redefined as a feminine-directed look or, as Brian succinctly describes Irene's feelings toward Clare, something "so subtly feminine that it wouldn't be understood by [men]" (215) [61]. Poor Gertrude, however, the woman who cannot read either fashion or people well, remains oblivious to the visual dynamics occurring between her two old friends.

This scene reveals another disparity between fashionable and unfashionable women and the significance of etiquette in the intangible skill of "class passing." Both Irene and Clare are women adept at social theatrics and etiquette, knowing the proper phrases to say and when to say them; and they are comfortable dispensing the banal amenities that count as social grace and poise in the world of Larsen's novel. Gertrude, however, lacks skill in hiding social discomfort: "She was, it was plain, a little ill at ease" (166) [24]. Indeed, Gertrude's biggest crime is that she is a shade too obvious, a shade too *readable*. Clare's illegibility is a part of her fascination. But Gertrude does not pass muster according to Irene's eyes, for she "looked like her husband might be a butcher" (167) [25]. If there is any doubt about this, about the difference between Clare and Gertrude, Larsen offers one of the few times when Irene becomes a reliable narrator, for to Irene, "it did seem to her odd that the woman that Clare was now should have invited the woman that Gertrude was" (166) [00]. Gertrude Martin, despite her strenuous efforts, simply cannot perform.

In this scene Larsen offers three competing visions of the black woman who passes, if only occasionally as Irene does. The women become reflectors of their husbands' wealth and positions, their husbands' success written on their female frames. But as Irene notes to herself but constantly fails to remember, "[a]ppearances . . . ha[ve] a way sometimes of not fitting facts" (156)[16]. Although Clare and Irene are both fashionably proper and socially skilled, beneath these surface appearances Irene may have more in common with the unknowing Gertrude than with the perceptive Clare; for Irene continually enacts misreadings of herself. Irene, for instance, never completely recognizes her class consciousness. Perturbed that Clare may show up at a black middle-class resort, she explains away her trepidation by thinking, "[i]t wasn't . . . that she was a snob, that she cared greatly for the petty restrictions and distinctions with which what called itself Negro society chose to hedge itself about" (157) [17]. But Clare, the most astute reader of them all, easily detects Irene's elitism while watching her contemptuous glance at Gertrude's "plump hands [that] were newly and not too competently manicured—for the occasion probably" (167) [25]. Irene's most significant self-deception involves her attitude about women who pass, women who, like Clare and Gertrude, lack "[t]hat instinctive loyalty to a race" (227) [71]. Yet Irene overlooks her own unfaithful moments when she tells a friend that she never passes, "except for the sake of convenience, restaurants, theater tickets, and things like that," as well as the fact that she is reacquainted with Clare at the moment she is passing (227) [70]. One cannot help but wonder if the resentment Irene feels toward Clare throughout the novel originates from her admiration of Clare's freedom from racial allegiance, the "thing that bound and suffocated her" (225) [69].

Only Clare emerges from this reunion scene with a sense of mystery intact. Indeed, there is an element of Clare's look that is so strange that Irene keeps thinking about it long after she leaves Clare's home: "Irene Redfield was trying to understand the look on Clare's face. . . . Partly mocking it had seemed, and partly menacing. And something else for which she could find no name" (176) [33]. Although she finally decides that the look is "unfathomable, utterly beyond any experience or comprehension of hers," it does not prevent her, as well as the reader, from continually wondering until the end of the novel, how should one read or interpret Clare Kendry?

Subtly playing on the notion of interpreting and misinterpreting blackness, of reading and decoding signs of race such as "finger-nails, palms of hands, shapes of ears, [and] teeth," the narrative seems to urge the reader to view Clare's body as an unreadable text (150) [11].

McDowell's analysis of *Passing* examines the relation that encourages a reading of the body as a letter and letters as a body. She notes that "the novel's opening image is an envelope," to which she refers as a "metaphoric vagina" (1986, xxvi). McDowell draws on both Irene's reluctance to read Clare's letter and what we will later know about Clare's "furtive" and "peculiar" qualities (143) [5; 9; 21; 22; 29; 42; 69]. Clare's inner femininity is concealed within the envelope and is not legible; and Clare's insistent letter writing propels the action of the story, just as her body attracts others' looks. This central and primary image of Irene reading Clare, literally and metaphorically, is significant because it is what Irene will attempt to do for the rest of novel.

But Irene's partial readings never allow her or the reader to develop concrete conclusions about Clare. Notably, Larsen delays revealing Clare's actual words in the letter, focusing first on the letter's surface qualities, its appearance. The letter, like Clare's fashion style, is "a bit too lavish, . . . a shade too unreserved in the manner of its expression" (182) [36]. When Larsen finally quotes this "second letter of Clare Kendry's" (181) [35]. (Larsen once again confuses the reader, beginning the novel not with the first letter but the second), it is not disclosed in full, but only in parts, as if Irene can contend only in sections with the intensity of her feelings for Clare. We never get the "full" Clare Kendry, even at the beginning of the novel. In fact, Irene's perusal of Clare's second letter mirrors her examination of Clare two years earlier at the top of the Drayton Hotel in Chicago, where she made only "instinctive guesses" about the woman before her (145) [7]. Irene destroys the letter, just as she will remove Clare from her life. After reading it, she tears it up into little pieces and "drop[s] them over the railing." Foreshadowing Clare's plunge out of a window, the letter "scatter[s], on tracks, on cinders, on forlorn grass, in rills of dirty water" (178) [34].[8] This technique of partial disclosure should be familiar to those accustomed to the representations of femme fatales, for the limited knowledge and visibility of a siren is a part of her attraction to others. Like the presentation of Gilda's body in Charles Vidor's film of the same name, Clare's words are alternately concealed and revealed. As Mary Ann Doane notes, "[t]he fascination of a Gilda is the fascination of the glimpse rather than the ambivalent satisfaction of the full, sustained look" (1991, 106). The erasure of words, a withholding, acts as a kind of lexical striptease; the presence and absence of certain words only heighten the erotic effect of the letter. As I make evident later, this "complex dialectic of

8. Jennifer DeVere Brody makes a similar argument about the cup that Irene drops at her party. The cup "foreshadows Clare's own broken body at the end of the novel" (1992, 1062) [Brody essay reprinted in this edition, p. 393].

concealing and revealing" is one of the novel's central reversals of the Rhinelander trial in which the "full sustained look" is imposed on Alice Jones Rhinelander (Doane 1991, 105, 106).

Clare, then, remains a perplexity even at the end of the novel. Although she is always the center of attention at various gatherings and in Irene's thoughts, she remains unknowable. Irene and the reader's shared inability to develop concrete conclusions about Clare allows her to depart as a puzzle, "indecipherable, unfathomable" (176)[29; 60; 33]. John Bellew has the satisfaction of at least knowing that Clare did in fact have some African American blood and of learning for himself one secret about his wife. When Clare does become "known," when her husband discovers her secret, she dies.

III

What would have happened had Clare not fallen out of the window? Although my reading suggests that Irene pushed her to her death, the ambiguity of the ending allows for the possibility that Clare chose this dramatic way to make her exit. Knowing the potential violence of her husband, a man who has a "latent physical power," Clare may have thought that the best solution was not confrontation but death (170)[28]. If we agree with Irene that Clare is inherently selfish, then her death is not an accident but a deliberate act that enables her to escape the explanations and recriminations of lying to her white husband.

It is the uncertainty of what would have happened to a woman such as Clare that makes one ponder about that fleeting mention of the *Rhinelander* case. The striking similarity between Clare's and Alice's positions brings history into the fiction of the passing woman. In his brief essay on the use of the trial in *Passing*, Mark J. Madigan notes that Larsen's reference to it is noteworthy because it acts as "a metaphor for the central concerns of the novel" (1990, 528). Although records do not exist that illustrate whether Larsen was deliberately trying to rewrite the trial, there is a more subtle and ironic significance to the reference to the Rhinelanders, for the novel problematizes the basic premises of the trial and undermines the concept of performing race or class through appearance or the codes of etiquette. As in the novel, clothes, or the lack of them, shape the perception of others. While Clare "dresses up" to conceal her racial identity and make it less certain, Alice must disrobe to prove that she was honest. In addition, letters exchanged between Alice and Leonard were introduced as evidence and contributed to the voyeuristic, sensational aspects of the trial. Although the two maintained a rigid distance in the courtroom, the Rhinelanders' correspondence with each other "embodied" their relationship, allowing the readers and hearers to peek into their bedroom. While Irene attempts to read Clare's body metaphorically through her unreliable vision, as if Clare were some undecipherable letter, Alice Jones's body is more literally read. Her body acts metonymically in the context of the trial. Because Alice never appears on the witness stand, her body, as well as her letters, stands in for her testimony. The Rhinelander trial, which occurred four years before *Passing* was published, centered on issues of racial knowledge, representation, and performance. As several crucial exchanges in the trial demonstrate, the outcome of the trial depended on not only Alice's body but also on Leonard's inability to "perform," through etiquette, the actions associated with wealthy, white masculinity.

Indeed, Leonard's marriage was considered a breach of proper decorum. His position in New York society was strong enough to get Alice listed in New York's Social Register of 1924, and then, as her race became known, ambiguously "de-listed." Responding to numerous complaints, including one from Mrs. Emily Post, the editor of the list somewhat embarrassingly stated that Mrs. Rhinelander was "in but not of the Social Register" and hoped that this qualification would settle the matter:"To an arbiter of social etiquette such as Mrs. Emily Post has proved herself to be . . . this should indeed be final, and yet now that a touch of the tar brush has dimned [sic] the lustre of the Social Register, who knows?" ("To Drop" 19). It was not, however, enough for Philip Rhinelander, the head of the Rhinelander clan, who reportedly threatened to disinherit his son. Several weeks after the marriage of Leonard and Alice, the suit for annulment was made public, and the trial took place a year later in 1925.

From the beginning the trial was a battle to represent the particulars in the best possible light. Both the prosecution and defense attempted to identify the aggressor in the courtship and marriage. While the defense argued that Alice was an innocent, hard-working "little girl," defiled by a wealthy playboy, the prosecution, led by Leonard's lawyer Isaac Mills, presented Leonard as a weak, easily influenced young man ("Kip Placed" 2). That he was "mentally backward" would help to explain how he was seduced and deceived by Alice: "We shall show that he was suffering from a physical ailment. He is tongue-tied. Sometimes he can hardly get a word out of his mouth." And yet although Leonard suffered from slow thinking, he was mentally alert enough to know not to associate his name with questionable people, refusing "to confer undying disgrace on the family by an alliance with colored blood" ("Calls Rhinelander" 8). The prosecution also attempted to show that Alice was more sexually experienced than Leonard, that she led Leonard astray. His team of lawyers relied on the stereotype of the sexually promiscuous black woman, arguing at one point that Alice lied about her age and "seduced" the younger Leonard.

Alice's lawyer, Lee Parson Davis, countered by questioning Leonard about Alice's attire before they were married. Leonard denied that "he had asked [Alice] to wear long sleeves" and that he carried a "powder puff" when they went on long trips ("Rhinelander Suit" 9). Her lawyer attempted to show that if Alice was guilty of deception, it was under the direction of a man who knew about her biracial background.

As with *Passing*, the trial was suffused with ambiguity and uncertainty. During an hour-and-fifteen-minute opening statement, Leonard's lawyer focused the trial on four key questions that surrounded the Rhinelanders' courtship, marriage, and case for annulment:

> Is the defendant colored and of colored blood?
> Before the marriage did the defendant represent herself as white?
> Did he marry her believing her to be white?
> Did he enter into the marriage with full knowledge of her
>   ancestry?
> ("Calls Rhinelander" 1)

The nature of these questions, their concern with ascertaining knowledge of a person's race and Alice's representation of her race to others, suggests the pressure to unveil the "vamp" ("Rhinelander Faces" 14). But the prosecution's case was hindered from the start, not only because of the statements Leonard had given to reporters after the wedding in which he acknowledged Alice's racial background but also because he frequently associated with the darker-skinned, African American members of Alice's family before the marriage. The prosecution tried to decrease the significance of these facts by focusing on what the *Chicago Defender* called Alice's and her sister's "independent" qualities: "Due to the independence acquired because of their early start in earning a living, Alice and Grace eventually became identified with that vivacious feminine set so often referred to as 'flappers.' They are said to have sought gayety [sic] and found it" ("Kip's 'Soul Message,'" 4). During the trial, the jury was informed of Alice's taste for alcohol and her expertise in poker.

In addition, Mills focused on a key point in the Rhinelanders' courtship to reveal Alice's familiarity with the opposite sex and to suggest her propensity for enticing and baiting a man away from his moral codes. In December 1921 Leonard and Alice spent several nights in a hotel, the Marie Antoinette, where they registered as Mr. and Mrs. Smith. Leonard stated that the hotel was Alice's suggestion and that it took only twenty minutes to convince her to let Leonard stay with her. Through his own lawyer's questioning, he revealed that they had sexual intercourse several times while they stayed there. Yet under cross-examination by Alice's lawyer, Leonard admitted that he lied when he stated it was Alice's suggestion. This crucial admission comes at an otherwise light moment in the trial, when even Alice laughs at the idea that he was sexually unschooled:

> Q[uestion]. You weren't so frightfully innocent when you met Alice, were you?
> A[nswer]. I was.
> Q. You made love to Alice.
> A. Yes.
> Q. You weren't so innocent about that, were you? (Loud laughter.)
> A. I was. (Alice laughed.) ("Young Kip" 12)

Taken literally, this exchange supports the prosecution's portrayal of him as a hapless young man led into lovemaking by a more experienced woman, but Davis eventually got Leonard to admit that Alice was "perfectly ladylike" until they arrived at the Marie Antoinette. The image of male innocence conveyed in his answers led to skepticism about both his veracity and his masculinity. In a crucial exchange regarding how Leonard's lawyers obtained Alice's private letters, not only did the defense question his manliness but Leonard himself seemed to question it as well:

> Q. You promised this little girl you'd keep them sacred?
> A. Yes.
> Q. But as long as it would benefit you to spread them on the record you were willing to break your promise?
> A. By the advice of counsel.
> Q. And you still consider yourself a man?
> A. I can't answer that. ("Young Kip" 12)

Both of these exchanges illustrate how Leonard's behavior during the trial contributed to a sense of emasculation, of a lack of masculine prowess. At times he "gave the impression of being driven indomitably by something outside of himself," although he was revealing the most intimate details of the courtship of his wife ("Rhinelander's Wife" 3). Leonard's hesitant admissions and erroneous testimony, and his frequent contradictions and weak, unmasculine presence, made him an unreliable witness. As the *Times* bluntly put it, "Rhinelander had been held up to ridicule on the very things which he might have been expected to know most about, little matters of social etiquette" ("Rhinelander Wilts" 6). The social and racial codes that assist Irene and Clare in Passing eluded the hapless Leonard. The conventions that would seem to validate Leonard's claims instead functioned to undermine his lawsuit. "Kip," a man in a position of not having to "class pass," could not perform the power of white masculinity attributed to men in his class. Under Davis's cross-examination, Leonard admitted that he pursued Alice, that he had frequent contact with the Jones family, including Alice's brown-skinned African American brother-in-law, and that his father's lawyers lied in written statements to the court.

While the dissolution of both Leonard and his case was achieved by placing Leonard on the stand, both the defense and cross-examination of Alice took place without her ever speaking a word. Her presence on the witness stand was not required. Her body, and her letters, would "speak" for her. Although I do not want to minimize the amount of attention Leonard received, Alice appears to have been not only more literally exposed but also more emotionally unveiled than was Leonard. Alice suffered through a dual exposure, the intimate revelations and expressions of her love for her husband by the prosecution and the viewing of her nude body by the judge and the jury. Even Leonard's letters opened her to inspection. Two letters Leonard had written that were read in court were so "shocking" that women were asked to leave the courtroom before they were read.[9] The *Pittsburgh Courier*, however, decided to let its readers protect themselves, and the paper printed excerpts from the "scarlet letters," which implied that Rhinelander sexually satisfied himself after reading Alice's notes: "Last night, sweetheart, after writing three full pages to you, I undressed and scrambled into bed, but not to go to sleep. No, baby, do you know what I did? Something that you do when my letters arrive at night" ("Text of Rhinelander's" 9). Read closely, however, the letter implies that Leonard only does what he has learned to do from his lover; and the revelations of Leonard's private letters further vilify Alice.

Unlike Leonard's notes, Alice's writings had a more unstable resonance within the context of the trial. The prosecution either read Alice's letters immediately after one of Leonard's weak testimonies, a point-counterpoint plan of attack, or read the letters without attempting to place them in context. Her declarations of love for the man she would marry sounded incongruous in the public courtroom. In an obvious attempt to make Leonard jealous, she uses exaggeration and hyperbole in several of her love notes. In one letter written while they were apart, Alice named the blackface entertainer Al Jolson as one of the many men who flirted with her and threatened to take Leonard's place in her affections. The prosecution brought in Jolson as a witness to refute this, showing that she was prone not just

---

9. The threat of soiling feminine ears was not that great for some female spectators. The *Times* noted that "[s]everal women left, but others who had been standing took their places" ("Rhinelander's Wife Cries," 3).

to embellishment but also to unmistakable lies.[1] Because Alice never testified during the trial, her letters to Leonard became the only documentation of her words and the first means by which the jury appraised her veracity.

Although the letters became an additional source of humor for court spectators and a diversion for the prosecution as Leonard stumbled through his testimony, they may have inadvertently helped Alice's case. According to a *New York Times* reporter, she wrote "poetry with a truly negro rhythm which was so superior to her ordinary forms of expression that it seemed as if she must have copied the lines from a popular song" ("Loved Rhinelander" 1) Alice's letters were framed in terms of the primitive, what the *Times* referred to as "unrestrained vulgarity" (3). To the reporter, they were "the fervid, illiterate letters of a woman to whom Rhinelander was a Prince Charming" (1)[2] Alice's writing became for others a confirmation of her racial heritage; her written notes became a sign of her race. Other excerpts of her letters demonstrated spelling mistakes and grammatical errors and were taken as both class and racial signs of her eight-grade education and her previous occupation as a maid.[3]

The appraisal of the letters became a preparation for the examination of her body—the disrobing scene took place as if one could visually authenticate race. Ironically, it was Alice's own lawyer who ordered that she display her body to refute any possible assertion that "Rhinelander was color blind" ("Rhinelander Jury" 3). Alice's lawyer sought to demonstrate that having had sexual relations with her before the marriage, Leonard would have had the opportunity to see her skin and hence know that she was relatively dark. Her body was offered as visual "proof" of her racial mixture and of the inability to misrepresent her race to him.

1. Jolson's appearance was one of the other sensational aspects of the trial. As expected, the entertainer lightened the tension in the courtroom, "smiling broadly" as he entered the witness stand. In response to Alice's claim that Jolson was a big flirt, the singer responded, "You have to be a flirt in the theatrical business." Discussing how his connection to the case affected him, he noted, "Every time I start for the dressing room the orchestra plays 'Alice where art thou going?' This is no joke" ("Rhinelander Says," 4).

2. Ironically, the words that seemed to have verified her race were actually from a song from a play, and the reporter seems to have overlooked the paradox of Alice being accused of plagiarizing "truly negro" yet inauthentic lines. The *New York Times* identified some of the lines as those sung by Alice Delysia, a stage actress, in the show *Afgar*. The music was by Charles Cuvillier and the lyrics by Douglas Furher ("Rhinelander Verses," 6).

3. In addition Phillip Brian Harper points out how Alice's lawyer determined her racial heritage from her writing. Davis read to Leonard one of her letters in which she referred to a "strutting party" and "roll[ed]" the term "out in the best negro dialect." Davis then questioned Leonard, "Didn't you recognize that as being a typically negro expression?" ("Rhinelander Says," 4). As Harper notes, through this particular exchange, Davis "imputed to her patterns of diction and intonation that clinched her negro identification" (Harper 1996, 135).

The moment of disrobing took only a few minutes, in the jury room, away from photographers, reporters, and other courtroom spectators. Although reporters were not allowed into the room, varying accounts of what took place appeared in the press.[4] The *Chicago Defender* offered the most vivid description of the event:

> The court, Mr. Mills, Mr. Davis, . . . the jury, the plaintiff, the defendant, her mother, Mrs. George Jones, and the stenographer left the courtroom and entered the jury room. The defendant and Mrs. Jones then withdrew to the lavatory adjoining the jury room and after a short time again entered the jury room. The defendant, who was weeping, had on her underwear and a long coat. At Mr. Davis' direction she let down the coat so that the upper portion of her body, as far down as the breast, was exposed. She then, again at Mr. Davis' direction, covered the upper part of her body and then showed the jury her bare legs up as far as the knees. ("Kip's 'Soul Message' " 4)

The reporting of the disrobing incident, as well as the court's and lawyers' decisions about what to allow to be read in open court, recalls the omissions in Clare's letter in *Passing*. The descriptions of what is concealed and revealed heighten the sensual elements of the trial for the trial's spectators and newspaper readers. But unlike Clare's body, Alice's body receives the "full sustained look" from the jury, the interrogative look available only to those whose bodies are denied abstraction (Doane 1991, 106).

More significant is what the act of disrobing suggests about the relation between "knowing" the black female and seeing her body. The disrobing act casts the ambiguous Alice as "black"—or at least affiliates her with other women of color who have had their bodies, or their words, on trial[5] Karla F. C. Holloway's pairing of Phillis Wheatley and Anita Hill illustrates the unreliability and duplicity associated with the black female in legal settings and the corresponding and paradoxical belief that the veracity of a black woman's text, her words or her account of an event, can only be determined in the

4. Alice's exposure in the jury room is only briefly mentioned in the *Times*. Referring to the strip incident as "the other sensation of the day," the paper focused more on Leonard's "smut[ty]" letters ("Rhinelander's Wife Cries," 3). The *New York Amsterdam News* presented only an editorial on the trial ("Rhinelander Trial Reaches Editorial Page" 16). The *Pittsburgh Courier* covered the trial in its "theatrical section" on 28 November and noted that Alice "[shrunk] like a frightened animal" ("Alice Tears Her Pride," 9).
5. Discussing Davis's decision in the context of past events of black women being objectified, Lewis and Ardizzone wonder if the lawyer thought the jury "would take pity on the unfortunate girl on display before them? . . . Or was he hoping that precisely that image of a sexually available, exotic woman would itself reinforce the blackness he was trying to emphasize" (2001, 157–58)? Lewis and Ardizzone link the scene to the exhibition of Sarah Baartmann, the "Hottentot Venus," the breast-baring of Sojourner Truth, and images of enslaved black women on the auction block, as Chinn does as well (2000, 76). My following examples of Truth and Anita Hill illustrate the assumed analogous relationships among black women's bodies, language, and veracity.

flesh. Holloway compares Wheatley's 1772 trial to prove she knew how to write poetry and Hill's 1991 testimony to Congress about her experiences with Clarence Thomas. In both proceedings the women's testimonies were "determined in a court of public and political opinion that had already judged the likelihood of their credibility to be in large measure associated with their gender and ethnicity" (Holloway 1995, 19).[6] Holloway's comparison suggests other unsettling examples of "voyeuristic encounters" that questioned or investigated the images of black women (19). Sojourner Truth, for instance, bared her breast to a white audience to end a rumor that she was a man (Painter 1996, 138–39).[7] This particular scene of disrobing, to which I will return shortly, has proven to be so useful that it functions as the "paradigmatic body" in discussions concerning black women and the body (McDowell 2001, 308). These scenes of verification highlight the need for the visual display or public disclosure of the black woman, either to prove herself or to justify her words, as if only through the sight of black femininity can one judge the black woman's truth, her "essence," her "authenticity." Alice's trial links her to other women of color who are judged in situations in which, like Hill's, "the black woman [appears] as mere body, whose moral and emotional sensibilities need not be treated with consideration" (Bordo 1993, 11). It is this association between visuality and the attempt to gain knowledge about the black woman, between public unveiling of black femininity and divination of a black woman's personality, sexuality, and experiences, that *Passing* ruptures with the presentation of Clare. Alice's jury room exhibition reified the assumptions of race, class, and gender into the factic, knowable, accessible black woman's body, a sedimentation of black femininity that Clare Kendry dismantles. Larsen's novel denies ready access to both the external and intimate aspects of a black woman, rendering inefficient any reading of black femininity based solely on a woman's body or appearance. The jury, however, did read Alice's body: the twelve white men ruled that Leonard had knowledge of Alice's race before the marriage and denied his suit for annulment. Alice's juridical success was ambivalent at best. One member of the jury, a Mr. Henry M. Well of Elmsford, revealed that the jury had a strong sentiment for

6. This discussion of indictments and words brings us back to Larsen. She was accused of plagiarizing her short story "Sanctuary," which appeared in *Forum* in 1930. The story had strong similarities to "Mrs. Adis," published in 1922 by Sheila Kaye-Smith (Davis 1994, 348–53). What adds to the enigma of these two publications is that *Century* was absorbed by *Forum* by the time Larsen's story was published. The stories were published in the same, although nominally different, magazine.
7. Painter provides a fascinating look at how Truth's image has been used in history: "We need an heroic 'Sojourner Truth' in our public life to function as the authentic black woman" (1996, 285). Painter also discusses in detail the "ain't I a woman" statement that Frances Dana Gage invented and that scholars frequently use (164–78).

Leonard, telling the *New York Times*, "If we had voted according to our hearts the verdict might have been different" ("Rhinelander Loses" 27).[8]

Notably, a historical sense of Alice Jones herself remains absent. Having been interpreted, read, analyzed, and perused, the woman at the center of the trial remains something of a mystery. Her reluctance to testify at her trial and the large cast of characters involved in the event keep her in the background. What becomes memorable is not so much the woman herself but what she represents—because of her blackness and femininity—to the spectators in the court, to the readers who followed the trial in the newspapers, even indeed, to the author of this essay. Reading through the newspaper articles, the "real" Alice Jones seems to be elusive, on the margins, not quite center stage. It is this unknowable aspect of Alice Jones Rhinelander that mirrors the obscurities of Clare Kendry and the ambiguities in Larsen's novel.

Despite critics' celebration of "undecidability" in the novel, analyses of *Passing*, including this one, often reveal the reader's complicit desire "to know."[9] In this sense the novel raises metacritical concerns of reading, language, and interpretation. There is a continual deferral of knowledge and facticity in *Passing*, unlike the disrobing event, which attempted to determine racial identity at the moment of disrobing. As Ann duCille notes, who one decides is the "novel's central figure" determines not only the interpretation of the ending but other aspects of the novel as well (1993, 108). With whose reading skills, for instance, does one wish to align oneself? One detects with Clare and Gertrude an opposition between two types of reading. Gertrude reads too literally, and Irene, according to one possibility that duCille suggests, never learns how to read at all until it is too late—she is " 'the last one to know' wife who has been blind to a friend's play for her husband" (107). Clare, however, almost seems to enjoy the havoc she creates by playing with her image and the visual signs and gestures of an upper-class white femininity; she knows only too well the multilayered, potential meanings of language, gestures, and acts. If there is anything that may suggest that this is Irene's story, it is the fact that Larsen continually places Irene into a position that is famil-

8. The Rhinelanders were legally divorced in 1930. Alice agreed to not use the Rhinelander name and dropped an alienation of affection suit against Leonard's father and a separation suit against Leonard (Lewis and Ardizzone 2001, 246).

9. In one of the most recent discussions of *Passing*, Brian Carr argues that scholars' analyses of the novel tend to "supplement" Irene's paranoid readings of events (2004, 287). Carr centers his discussion primarily on those interpretations of *Passing* that suggest that the novel "passes" as a text about homosexuality. While he focuses on the "nothing" of the "nonobject," the desire to know that cannot be satisfied by the text, my concern is with the act of reading and making meaning accomplished through the look, as well as who is permitted to make claims of knowledge obtained by looking.

iar, into the position of the questioning reader who must try to piece together a narrative based on partial clues.

Passing and the Rhinelander trial enable an analysis of reading and interpreting the disconcerting relation between black women and the body in symbolic culture and encourage one to question the larger theoretical implications of this alignment—why for black women, a test, a proof, a disrobing is so often needed to confirm entry into that symbolic realm of meaning and significance. McDowell, for example, questions why Sojourner Truth's disrobing moment is so frequently and briefly cited in feminist discussions of race. She argues that the name and the figure "Sojourner Truth" offer ways to deal easily with an unavoidable issue. Sojourner Truth is "useful simply as a name to drop in an era with at least nominal pretensions to interrogating race"; and the "ain't I a woman" question attributed to Truth is read as a nonnuanced, rhetorically powerful but theoretically incorrect inquiry of the category "Woman" (McDowell 1995, 162). But the invocation of Truth is disturbing on another level. As a familiar reference point, more "political" than "epistemological," Truth's breast-baring scene "captures graphically Truth's fixity in the body" (159). Discussing the claim about black female intellectuals' "resistance to theory," McDowell notes that the use of this scene has placed black women and the body in similar positions—in opposition to critical thinking: "It is precisely this earlier scene of verification that is being symbolically reenacted today. The demand in this present context is not to bare the breasts to verify black womanhood, but to bare the evidence that proves positively the qualifications of black feminist discourse as 'theory' " (162). Nella Larsen's work displays the problematics of statements that link black women and the "abundantly recognizable" black body (Barrett 1997, 318) or any reasoning that suggests that the black woman's body is always ready and available for whatever evidentiary or rhetorical use. Although the mind/body dichotomy has been "deconstructed" by scholars in the past several years, it still functions powerfully as a metaphor distinguishing the work of black female intellectuals from all others. To rephrase Amy Robinson's formulation, identity politics is a skill of reading, and academic politics is as well (Robinson 1994, 716).

In the only book-length treatment of the Rhinelander trial, Earl Lewis and Heidi Ardizzone note that when Alice died, her race remained unspecified. Alice's death certificate "left her race mysteriously blank" (2001, 254). Whether an accidental omission or a silence deliberately crafted, the absence is an unsatisfying but fit conclusion. For this finale to the *Rhinelander* case eerily echoes Larsen's ambiguous fatal endings in her narratives in which readers and spectators are denied complete knowledge and left on their own to contend with the gaps. If there is anything comforting about this delitescent conclusion, it is that it asserts, however slightly, Alice's prerogative to not reveal herself, even in her final representation.

Works Cited

"Alice Tears Her Pride to Shreds to Hold Her Man." 1925. *Pittsburgh Courier*, 28 November.

Barrett, Lindon. 1997. "Hand-Writing: Legibility and the White Body in Running a Thousand Miles for Freedom." *American Literature* 69, no. 2:315–36.

Berlant, Lauren. 1991. "National Brands/National Body: Imitation of Life." In *Comparative American Identities: Race, Sex, and Nationality in the Modern Text*, ed. Hortense Spillers, 110–40. New York and London: Routledge.

Bordo, Susan. 1993. *Unbearable Weight: Feminism, Western Culture, and the Body*. Berkeley: University of California Press.

Butler, Judith. 1989. "Foucault and the Paradox of Bodily Inscriptions." *Journal of Philosophy* 86, no. 11: 601–7.

———. 1990. *Gender Trouble: Feminism and the Subversion of Identity*. New York: Routledge.

———. 1993. *Bodies That Matter: On the Discursive Limits of "Sex."* New York: Routledge.

"Calls Rhinelander Dupe of Girl He Wed." 1925. *New York Times*, 10 November.

Carr, Brian. 2004. "Paranoid Interpretation, Desire's Nonobject, and Nella Larsen's *Passing*." PMLA 119, no. 2: 282–95.

Chinn, Sarah E. 2000. *Technology and the Logic of American Racism: A Cultural History of the Body as Evidence*. London: Continuum.

Davis, Thadious. 1994. *Nella Larsen, Novelist of the Harlem Renaissance: A Woman's Life Unveiled*. Baton Rouge: Louisiana University Press.

DeVere Brody, Jennifer. 1992. "Clare Kendry's 'True' Colors: Race and Class Conflict in Nella Larsen's *Passing*." *Callaloo* 15, no. 4: 1053–65.

Doane, Mary Ann. 1991. *Femmes Fatales: Feminism, Film Theory and Psychoanalysis*. New York: Routledge.

duCille, Ann. 1993. *The Coupling Convention: Sex, Text, and Tradition in Black Women's Fiction*. New York: Oxford University Press.

Fischer-Mirkin, Toby. 1995. *Dress Code: Understanding the Hidden Meanings of Women's Clothes*. New York: Clarkson Potter.

Flügel, J. C. 1930. 1966. *The Psychology of Clothes*. New York: International Universities Press.

Foucault, Michel. 1977. "Nietzsche, Genealogy, History." In *Language, Counter-Memory, Practice: Selected Essays and Interviews* by

Michel Foucault, ed. Sherry Simon and Donald F. Bouchard, trans. Donald F. Bouchard, 139–64. Ithaca, NY: Cornell University Press.

Fuss, Diana. 1995. "Fashion and the Homospectatorial Look." In *Identities*, ed. Kwame A. Appiah and Henry Louis Gates Jr., 90–114. Chicago: University of Chicago Press.

Goldsmith, Meredith. 2001. "Shopping to Pass, Passing to Shop: Bodily Self-Fashioning in the Fiction of Nella Larsen." In *Recovering the Black Female Body: Self-Representations by African American Women*, ed. Michael Bennett and Vanessa D. Dickerson, 97–120. New Brunswick, N.J.: Rutgers University Press.

Green, Edward S. 1920. *National Capital Code of Etiquette*. Washington, D.C.: Austin Jenkins Company.

Harper, Phillip Brian. 1996. *Are We Not Men? Masculine Anxiety and the Problem of African-American Identity*. New York: Oxford University Press.

Holloway, Karla F. C. 1995. *Codes of Conduct: Race, Ethics, and the Color of Our Character*. New Brunswick, N.J.: Rutgers University Press.

"Honorable Marriage Creates Furore." 1924. *Chicago Defender*, 22 November.

Kaye-Smith, Sheila. 1922. "Mrs. Adis." *Century* 103: 321–26.

"Kip Placed On 'Rack.' " 1925. *Pittsburgh Courier*, 14 November.

"Kip's 'Soul Message'; Notes Read." 1925. *Chicago Defender*, 28 November.

Larsen, Nella. 1928. 1929. 1986. *Quicksand* and *Passing*. Ed. Deborah McDowell. New Brunswick, N.J.: Rutgers University Press.

———. 1930. "Sanctuary." *Forum* 83, no. 1: 15–18.

Lewis, Earl, and Heidi Ardizzone. 2001. *Love on Trial: An American Scandal in Black and White*. New York: W. W. Norton and Company.

"Love Letters Spicy from 'Kip' to Alice." 1925. *Chicago Defender*, 14 November.

"Loved Rhinelander, Wife's Letters Say." 1925. *New York Times*, 13 November.

Madigan, Mark J. 1990. "Miscegenation and 'The Dicta of Race': The *Rhinelander* Case and Nella Larsen's *Passing*." *Modern Fiction Studies* 36 (Winter): 523–29.

McCrady, Marjorie Ellis Ferguson, and Blanche Wheeler. 1942. *Manners for Moderns*. New York: E. P. Dutton and Co.

McDowell, Deborah, 1986. Foreword to *Quicksand* and *Passing*, by Nella Larsen, ix–xxxv. New Brunswick, N.J.: Rutgers University Press.

———. 1995. *"The Changing Same": Black Women's Literature, Criticism and Theory*. Bloomington, Ind.: Indiana University Press.

———. 2001. "Afterword: Recovery Missions: Imaging the Body Ideals." In *Recovering the Black Female Body: Self-Representations by African American Women*, ed. Michael Bennett and Vanessa D. Dickerson, 296–317. New Brunswick, N.J.: Rutgers University Press.

"Millionaire's Marriage to Poor Girl Startles World." 1924. *Chicago Defender*, 22 November.

Painter, Nell Irvin. 1996. *Sojourner Truth: A Life, A Symbol*. New York: W. W. Norton, and Co.

Rabine, Leslie W. 1994. "A Woman's Two Bodies: Fashion Magazines, Consumerism, and Feminism." In *On Fashion*, ed. Shari Benstock and Suzanne Ferriss, 59–75. New Brunswick, N.J.: Rutgers University Press.

"Rhinelander Annulment Suit Jury Selected." 1925. *New York Amsterdam News*, 11 November.

"Rhinelander Faces Thorough Quizzing." 1925. *New York Times*, 15 November.

"Rhinelander Jury Warned." 1925. *New York Times*, 2 December.

"Rhinelander Loses; No Fraud Is Found; Wife Will Sue Now." 1925. *New York Times*, 6 December.

"Rhinelander Says He Pursued Girl." 1925. *New York Times*, 18 November.

"Rhinelander Suit Suddenly Halted." 1925. *New York Times*, 20 November.

"Rhinelander Trial Reaches Editorial Page." 1925. *New York Amsterdam News*, 25 November.

"Rhinelander Verses Familiar to Stage." 1925. *New York Times*, 19 November.

"Rhinelander's Wife Cries under Ordeal." 1925. *New York Times*, 24 November.

"Rhinelander Wilts; Gets Adjournment." 1925. *New York Times*, 19 November.

Robinson, Amy. 1994. "It Takes One to Know One: Passing and Communities of Common Interest." *Critical Inquiry* 20, no. 4: 715–36.

Spillers, Hortense. 1987. "Mama's Baby, Papa's Maybe: An American Grammar Book." *Diacritics* 17, no. 2: 65–81.

"Text of Rhinelander's 'Scarlet Letters' as Read to the Jury." 1925. *Pittsburgh Courier*, 28 November.

"To Drop Mrs. Rhinelander." 1925. *New York Times*, 16 March.

" 'Unnatural Practices' of Kip Are Made Known." 1925. *Pittsburgh Courier*, 28 November.

Wiegman, Robyn. 1995. *American Anatomies: Theorizing Race and Gender*. Durham: Duke University Press.

"Young Kip Stammers as He Tells of Pursuing Alice during Three Years' Wooing." 1925. *Chicago Defender*, 21 November.

Nella Larsen: A Chronology*

1868	Mother, Mary Hansen (spelled Hanson in some accounts), born.
1890	July 1, marriage license issued to Mary Hensen and Peter Walker.
1891	Mary Hensen marries Peter Larsen/Larson, according to census records. D. gives date as March 7.
	April 13, Nella is born Nellie Walker in Chicago (listed as born in New York in some sources and as born in 1893 and 1982 in others) to Mary Hansen Walker ("white") and Peter Walker ("colored"). Nella's birth certificate lists her as "colored."
1892	June 21, sister Anna ("Lizzie") Larsen is born. D gives this birthdate as 1893. Anna is listed as "white."
1898–1900	D surmises that Nella may have spent these years in the Erring Women's Refuge for Reform on Chicago's South Side, placed there to help the rest of the family pass for white. H reports, however, that in April and May of 1898, Nella sailed to Denmark with her mother and sister.
1898–9	Begins school at Moseley and moves with her family to 201 22nd Street in Chicago, according to H.
1901	According to D, Larsen is enrolled in Colman Primary School as Nellie Larson in September by Peter Larson, who lists himself as "Father." H gives the date of her Colman enrollment as 1903.
1903	According to H, Nella enters seventh grade at Colman primary School. The family moves to 4538 State Street.
1905	Nella is enrolled as Nellye Larson by Peter Larson, "Parent," in the Wendell Phillips Junior High School.
1907	The Larsens purchase a home on West 70th Place. According to D, Peter Larson changes his name to

---

* compiled primarily from Larsen biographies by Thadious Davis (D), George Hutchinson (H), and Charles Larson (L). As there is significant disagreement among Larsen's principal biographers about even some basic facts of her life, variant versions of her biography are noted as abbreviated above, when possible.

	Larsen. Nella enrolls in the Fisk Normal School in Nashville, Tennessee, as Nellie Marie Larsen, according to H and as Nella Larsen, according to D.
1908	According to H, the Fisk faculty vote not to invite Nella to return after her first year; D suggests she completed only one semester.
1908–12	D calls these the "mystery" years and suggests that Nella may have spent them in Chicago in an illicit, interracial relationship. According to H, Nella sailed to Denmark at least once and perhaps twice during these years and is listed on ships' manifests as returning from Denmark to New York in both 1909 and 1912.
1912	Enters Lincoln Hospital and Home Training School for Nurses in May.
1915	Nella is licensed as a Registered Nurse under the name Nella Marian Larsen on May 1 and attends graduation on May 13. In October, accepts position of Head Nurse at Tuskegee Institute Training School for Nurses, starting work in October according to D and early November according to H (This experience becomes the basis for descriptions of "Naxos" in her novel *Quicksand*.)
1916	Mary, Peter, and Anna Larsen relocate to 6418 Maryland Avenue in Chicago. In August, attends annual meeting of the National Association of Colored Graduate Nurses. On October 10, resigns from Tuskegee and, according to H, is released immediately from her duties, although she requested a month's time. According to D, returns to Lincoln Hospital as a visiting nurse.
1918	According to L, Nella works for New York City Department of Health. According to H, she sits for the "Healthy Drive nursing exam" and works for Health Department's Bureau of Preventable Diseases. According to D, Nella is appointed District Nurse in New York Department of Health and also is professionally active in a visiting nurse association dedicated to working with the Circle for Negro War Relief. Nella and Elmer Imes meet in late summer or early fall.
1919	Nella Marion marries Elmer Imes in the chapel of Union Theological Seminary. According to D, they move to Imes's apartment in Staten Island. H locates them at 984 Morris Avenue in the Bronx.

1920   Publishes "Three Scandinavian Games" and "Danish Fun" in *The Brownies Book* in June and July.

1921   According to D, Nella and Elmer move to 51 Audobon Avenue in Jersey City. H locates them living in Harlem at 34 W. 129th Street, apartment 17, that same year, in January. From May—September, Nella volunteers to organize New York's first "Negro Art Exhibit," which took place from August 1—October 11. According to D, Nella resigns from the Board of Health on September 15. H dates the resignation as October 4. According to H, Nella becomes "substitute assistant" at the 135th Street Branch of the New York Public Library (NYPL) in September. D dates this assignment as beginning in January of 1922.

1922   According to H, passes her library exam in January and receives a Grade I appointment. Because the appointment requires a high school degree that she does not have, Nella begins to fudge official forms, H reports. In the fall, takes a leave from the Library to enroll in Library School and intern at the Seward Branch of NYPL.

1922   Larsen family moves to California and Mary Larsen sells the house on Maryland Avenue. According to D, Mary does not join the family there until 1928.

1923   In June, Nella receives her library certificate and attends commencement on June 8. On July 1, returns to the 135th Street Branch of the NYPL as Assistant Librarian, Grade II, according to D. According to H, takes the NYPL exams in October and passes, then begins work in November at the Seward Branch of the NYPL in the Children's Divison. Becomes a regular at many Harlem Renaissance gatherings where she meets Walter White, Carl Van Vechten, Fania Marinoff, Donald Angus, and others. In May, Nella's review of *Certain People of Importance* is published in *The Messenger*.

1924   According to D, Nella is promoted to Children's Librarian at the 135th Street Branch.

1925   Takes leave of absence from NYPL in October and resigns in January of 1926, when her leave expires. Joins a Gurdjieff group organized by Jean Toomer.

1926   Publishes "The Wrong Man" and "Freedom" in *Young's Magazine* (January and April) under the name Allen Semi. In September, *Opportunity* publishes her review of *Flight*.

1927   According to D, Peter Larsen dies sometime between January 1927 and fall of 1928. In March, following revisions, Knopf formally accepts *Quicksand* for publication. In April, Nella and Elmer move to 236 W. 135th Street, apartment 5A.

1928   *Quicksand* is published by Knopf in March and is awarded the Harmon Foundation's Bronze Award for Literature in December. In May, Nella and Elmer move to the famous Dunbar Apartments, living at 2588 Seventh Avenue, apartment 6N.

Also in May, favorable reviews of *Quicksand* begin to appear and the NAACP hosts a tea for Nella that according to H, is rescheduled to May 20 and, according to D, Nella could not attend because of illness. By July, there are signs of problems in the Imes's marriage. By fall, Nella completes a draft of *Passing*, which is accepted by Knopf.

1929   In January, publishes a review of *Black Sadie* in *Opportunity*. In March, according to D, Nella goes back to the library for five months for extra income and does so again, briefly in October. According to H, these periods are somewhat shorter. In April, *Passing* is published; Nella is honored by a tea hosted by Blanche Knopf. Nella speaks at "Authors' Night" at the St. George Playhouse in Brooklyn with Walter White on April 14. In May, Elmer accepts an appointment as Head of the Physics Department at Fisk University, to begin in winter of 1930. In November, Nella applies for a Guggenheim Fellowship. In December, the NAACP publishes an excerpt from *Quicksand* in its Benefit Concert program booklet.

1930   Publishes "Sanctuary" in *Forum* in January and is accused of plagiarism. In March, receives the Guggenheim Fellowship. In May, goes to Fisk to join Elmer. Sometime in late summer or fall, Nella confronts Elmer about his affair with white, fellow Fisk Professor Gilbert.

1930   Travels to Spain on her Guggenheim. D dates her departure as September 9. H locates her leaving on the S. S. *Patria* on September 19.

While overseas, lives in Spain and France and works on *Mirage*.

1931   In January, requests an extension of her Guggenheim Fellowship. By March, a romance with Norman

Cameron has begun to sour and in April Nella leaves Spain for France.

In Paris stays first at the Hotel Paris-Dinard then moves, in July, to an apartment at 31 bis rue Campagne Première. In late summer or early fall, is informed that Knopf has rejected *Mirage*. In fall, returns to Spain with Dorothy Peterson and in November they travel to North Africa and then back to Spain again.

1932   In January, returns to New York and moves, in late February (H) or March (D), into brownstone apartment at 53 W. 11th Street. During this time, she is ill with pleurisy. In April (D) or May (H) joins Elmer at Fisk (L has him teaching at Vanderbilt at this time). In June, returns briefly to New York. In July, renews her passport and writes Dorothy Peterson that she is working again on *Mirage*. In September, Nella and Imes move into a new home in Nashville. In the fall, Nella is friendly, perhaps romantically, with Tom Mabry.

1933   In the summer, collaborates with Edward Donahoe, also a possible romance. Over spring and summer, Nella and Elmer's marriage deteriorates further and Nella either falls or jumps out a window of their home, inciting further scandal. Nella divorces Elmer on grounds of "cruelty," on August 30, in Davidson County, Tennessee. In September, travels briefly to Chicago before returning to New York, where she stays with Dorothy Peterson before taking an apartment on the Lower East Side. In October, the *Baltimore Afro-American* reports on the Larsen/Imes divorce and subsequently on the Larsen/Imes/Gilbert love triangle. In December, Nella lists her address as the Manual Training School at Bordentown and later takes over Dorothy Peterson's apartment at 320 Second Avenue. In December, Nella also works with the Independent Writers' Committee Against Lynching as Assistant Secretary.

1934–37   Friendships with her former friends continue to diminish; some express concern about her.

1940   Moves from 320 Second Avenue to 315 Second Avenue.

1941   Elmer dies on September 11. Nella runs into old friends on the street, sparking rumors about possible drug or alcohol abuse.

1942   June 17, Nella attends a memorial birthday celebration for James Weldon Johnson at the 115th Street Branch Library.

1944   February 14 is appointed Chief Nurse at Gouverneur Hospital.

1951   Mary Larsen dies in Santa Monica Hospital in September.

1954   Applies for a Social Security card in January. Resigns from Gouverneur Hospital in the spring but is rehired as Night Supervisor in the fall.

1959   In October, Nella writes a will naming her friend Alice Carper as beneficiary.

1960   Nella is mugged in front of the hospital and suffers a broken arm.

1961   In March, the City of New York tells Gouverneur to stop accepting patients.

1961   In December, applies for a position at Metropolitan Hospital and is interviewed on December 8.

1962   Accepts position as Supervisor of Nurses at Metropolitan Hospital, New York.

1963   In February, Nella is scheduled to begin working as the Night Supervisor in the Psychiatric Ward. In April, travels to Santa Monica to see her sister Anna, who refuses to acknowledge her. In June, found to be past legal retirement age, Nella is forced to take a three month leave and works her last shift on June 22. On September 12, Nella is officially listed as retired.

1964   March 30, Nella is discovered dead in her apartment by the building supervisor. Her funeral is arranged by Alice Carper and takes place on April 6 at the Miles Funeral Home. Nella is buried in the Carper family plot. On April 7 the *New York Times* reports Nella's death.

Selected Bibliography

By Ruth Blandon, with help from Lucia Hodgson

• indicates works included or excerpted in this Norton Critical Edition.

NELLA LARSEN: A BIBLIOGRAPHY OF HER WRITINGS

"Playtime: Danish Fun." *Brownie's Book* 1 (1920): 219.
"Playtime: Three Scandinavian Games." *Brownie's Book* 1 (1920): 191–2.
Review of Kathleen Norris, *Certain People of Importance*. *The Messenger* 5 (1923): 713.
• [Pseud. Allen Semi]. "Freedom." Young's Realistic Stories Magazine 51 (1926): 241–43.
• [Pseud. Allen Semi]. "The Wrong Man." Young's Realistic Stories Magazine 50 (1926): 243–46.
Quicksand. New York: Knopf, 1928.
Passing. New York: Knopf, 1929.
Review of T. Bowyer Campbell. *Opportunity* 7 (1929): 24.
• "The Author's Explanation." *Forum* 83 (1930): xli–xlii.
"Sanctuary." *Forum* 83 (1930): 15–18.

PASSING BIBLIOGRAPHY

Ahmed, Sara. " 'She'll Wake Up One of These Days and Find She's Turned into a Nigger': Passing Through Hybridity." *Theory, Culture & Society* 16.2 (April 1999): 87–106.
Allan, Tuzyline Jita. "The Death of Sex and the Soul in *Mrs. Dalloway* and Nella Larsen's *Passing*." *Virginia Woolf: Lesbian Readings*. Ed. Eileen Barrett and Patricia Cramer. New York: New York UP, 1997. 95–113.
Ammons, Elizabeth. *Conflicting Stories: American Women Writers at the Turn into the Twentieth Century*. New York: Oxford UP, 1991.
Baker, Houston A. *Modernism and the Harlem Renaissance*. Chicago: U of Chicago P, 1987.
• Baldwin, Kate. "The Recurring Conditions of Nella Larsen's *Passing*." *Theory@Buffalo* 4 (1998): 50–90.
Balshaw, Maria. " 'Black Was White': Urbanity, Passing and the Spectacle of Harlem." *Journal of American Studies* 33.2 (1999): 307–22.
Basu, Biman. "Hybrid Embodiment and an Ethics of Masochism: Nella Larsen's *Passing* and Sherley Anne Williams's *Dessa Rose*." *African American Review* 36.3 (Fall 2002): 383–401.
Beemyn, Brett. "A Bibliography of Works by and about Nella Larsen." *African American Review* 26.1 (1992): 183–88.
Bell, Bernard. *The Afro-American Novel and Its Tradition*. Amherst: U of Massachusetts P, 1987.
Bennett, Juda. *The Passing Figure: Racial Confusion in Modern American Literature*. New York: Peter Lang, 1996.
———. "Toni Morrison and the Burden of the Passing Narrative." *African American Review* 35.2 (Summer 2001): 205–17.
Berzon, Judith R. *Neither White Nor Black: The Mulatto Character in American Fiction*. New York: New York UP, 1978.
Blackmer, Corinne E. "The Veils of the Law: Race and Sexuality in Nella Larsen's *Passing*." *College Literature* 22.3 (October 1995): 50–67. Rpt. in *Race-ing Representation: Voice, History and Sexuality*. Ed. Kostas Myrsiades and Linda S. Myrsiades. Lanham, MD: Rowman & Littlefield, 1998. 98–116.

————. "African Masks and the Arts of Passing in Gertrude Stein's 'Melanctha' and Nella Larsen's *Passing*." *Journal of the History of Sexuality* 4.2 (October 1993): 230–63.

Blackmore, David L. " 'That Unreasonable Restless Feeling': The Homosexual Subtexts of Nella Larsen's *Passing*." *African American Review* 26.3 (Fall 1992): 475–84.

Bone, Robert. *The Negro Novel in America*. New Haven: Yale UP, 1958.

• Brody, Jennifer DeVere. "Clare Kendry's 'True' Colors: Race and Class Conflict in Nella Larsen's *Passing*." *Callaloo: A Journal of African-American and African Arts and Letters* 4 (Fall 1992): 1053–65.

Brown, Sterling. *The Negro in American Fiction*. 1937. New York: Atheneum, 1969.

Bullock, Penelope. "The Mulatto in American Fiction." *Phylon* 6 (First Quarter 1945).

Butler, Judith. *Bodies That Matter: On the Discursive Limits of "Sex."* New York: Routledge, 1993.

• ————. "Passing, Queering: Nella Larsen's Psychoanalytic Challenge." *Female Subjects in Black and White: Race, Psychoanalysis, Feminism*. Ed. Elizabeth Abel, Barbara Christian, and Helene Moglen. Berkeley: U of California P, 1997. 266–84.

Calloway, Licia Morrow. *Black Family (Dys)function in Novels by Jessie Fauset, Nella Larsen, and Fannie Hurst*. New York: Peter Lang, 2003.

Carby, Hazel V. "The Quicksands of Representation: Rethinking Black Cultural Politics." *Reconstructing Womanhood: The Emergence of the Afro-American Woman Novelist*. New York: Oxford UP, 1987. 163–75.

Carr, Brian. "Paranoid Interpretation, Desire's Nonobject, and Nella Larsen's *Passing*." *PMLA* 119.2 (March 2004): 282–95.

Caughie, Pamela L. *Passing and Pedagogy: The Dynamics of Responsibility*. Urbana: U of Illinois P, 1999.

Christian, Barbara. *Black Feminist Criticism: Perspectives on Black Women Writers*. New York: Pergamon, 1985.

————. *Black Women Novelists: The Development of a Tradition, 1892–1976*. Westport, CT: Greenwood, 1980.

Clark, William Bedford. "The Letters of Nella Larsen to Carl Van Vechten: A Survey." *Resources for American Literary Study* 8 (1978): 193–99.

Cobb, Michael L. "Insolent Racing, Rough Narrative—The Harlem Renaissance's Impolite Queers." *Callaloo* 23.1 (2000): 328–51.

Condé, Mary. "Passing in the Fiction of Jessie Redmon Fauset and Nella Larsen." *Yearbook of English Studies* 24 (1994): 94–104.

Craft-Fairchild, Catherine. "The Politics of 'Passing': The Scandalous Memoir and the Novel." *Illicit Sex: Identity Politics in Early Modern Culture*. Ed. Thomas DiPiero and Pat Gill. Athens: U of Georgia P, 1997. 45–67.

Cutter, Martha J. "Sliding Significations: Passing as a Narrative and Textual Strategy in Nella Larsen's Fiction." *Passing and the Fictions of Identity*. Ed. Elaine K. Ginsberg. Durham: Duke UP, 1993.

Davis, Arthur. *From the Dark Tower: Afro-American Writers, 1900–1960*. Washington, DC: Howard UP, 1974.

Davis, Thadious M. Introduction. *Passing*. By Nella Larsen. New York: Penguin, 1997. vii–xxxii.

————. "Nella Larsen." *The Gender of Modernism: A Critical Anthology*. Ed. Bonnie Kime Scott. Bloomington: Indiana UP, 1990.

• ————. "Nella Larsen's Harlem Aesthetic." *The Harlem Renaissance: Revaluations*. Ed. Amritjit Singh, William S. Shiver, and Stanley Brodwin. New York: Garland, 1989.

————. *Nella Larsen, Novelist of the Harlem Renaissance: A Woman's Life Unveiled*. Baton Rouge: Louisiana State UP, 1994.

Dean, Sharon and Erlene Stetson. "Flower-Dust and Springtime: Harlem Renaissance Women." *Radical Teacher: A Newsjournal of Socialist Theory and Practice* 18 (1980): 1–8.

Dearborn, Mary V. *Pocahontas's Daughters: Gender and Ethnicity in American Culture*. New York: Oxford UP, 1986.

Debo, Annette. "Changing Cultural Scripts: Nella Larsen's *Passing* and the Reconstruction of Modernism." *In Process: A Graduate Student Journal of African-American and African Diasporan Literature and Culture* 1 (Fall 1996): 36–52.

duCille, Ann. "Blues Notes on Black Sexuality: Sex and the Texts of Jessie Fauset and Nella Larsen." *Journal of the History of Sexuality* 3.3 (January 1993): 418–44.

• ————. *The Coupling Convention: Sex, Text, and Tradition in Black Women's Fiction*. New York: Oxford UP, 1993. 103–109.

Elbert, Sarah. "Reading the Unwritten War: Renaissance Tales. Nella Larsen's *Passing* and Louisa May Alcott's "M. L.," "My Contraband," and "An Hour." *Irish Journal of American Studies* 2.1 (December 1993): 34–127.

Esteve, Mary. "Nella Larsen's 'Moving Mosaic': Harlem, Crowds, and Anonymity." *American Literary History* 9.2 (Summer 1997): 268–86.

Fabi, Maria Giulia. *Passing and the Rise of the African American Novel.* Urbana: U of Illinois P, 2001.

Fuller, Hoyt. Introduction. *Passing.* By Nella Larsen. New York: Collier Books, 1971. 10–24.

Gallego Durán, María del Mar. *Passing Novels in the Harlem Renaissance: Identity Politics and Textual Strategies.* Münster: Lit Verlag, 2003.

Gates, Henry Louis, Jr. *Figures in Black: Words, Signs, and the "Racial" Self.* New York: Oxford UP, 1987.

Gayle, Addison. *The Way of the New World: The Black Novel in America.* Garden City, NY: Anchor, 1975.

Ginsberg, Elaine, ed. *Passing and the Fictions of Identity.* Durham: Duke UP, 1996.

Giorcelli, Cristina. "Intertextuality in Nella Larsen's *Passing.*" *Letteratura d'America: Rivista Trimestrale* 21.86 (2001): 127–47.

Golden, Marita. Foreword. *An Intimation of Things Distant: The Collected Fiction of Nella Larsen.* Ed. Charles R. Larson. New York: Anchor Books, 1992. Rpt. in *The Complete Fiction of Nella Larsen.* New York: Anchor Books, 2001. vii–x.

Goldsmith, Meredith. "Shopping to Pass, Passing to Shop: Bodily Self-Fashioning in the Fiction of Nella Larsen." *Recovering the Black Female Body: Self-Representations by African American Women.* Ed. Michael Bennett, Vanessa D. Dickerson, and Carla Peterson. New Brunswick: Rutgers UP, 2001. 97–120.

Goodspeed-Chadwick, Julie. "Sexual and Identity Politics in Nella Larsen's *Passing*: Women as Commodity." *Griot: Official Journal of the Southern Conference on Afro-American Studies* 22.2 (Fall 2003): 99–104.

Grayson, Deborah R. "Fooling White Folks: Or, How I Stole the Show: The Body Politics of Nella Larsen's *Passing.*" *Bucknell Review: A Scholarly Journal of Letters, Arts and Sciences* 39.1 (1995): 27–37.

Hanlon, Christopher. "The Pleasures of Passing and the Real of Race." *Journal X: A Journal in Culture and Criticism* 5.1–2 (August 2000–Spring 2001): 23–36.

Harper, Phillip Brian. "Passing for What? Racial Masquerade and the Demands of Upward Mobility." *Callaloo* 21.2 (Spring 1998): 381–97.

Harrison-Kahan, Lori. "Her 'Nig': Returning the Gaze of Nella Larsen's *Passing.*" *Modern Language Studies* 32.2 (Fall 2002): 109–38.

Haviland, Beverly. "Passing from Paranoia to Plagiarism: The Abject Authorship of Nella Larsen." *Modern Fiction Studies* 43.2 (Summer 1997): 295–318.

Henderson, Mae G. Critical Forward. *Passing.* By Nella Larsen. New York: Modern Library, 2000. xvii–xxxi.

Hering, Frank. "Sneaking Around: Idealized Domesticity, Identity Politics, and Games of Friendship in Nella Larsen's *Passing.*" *Arizona Quarterly: A Journal of American Literature, Culture, and Theory* 57.1 (Spring 2001): 35–60.

Horton, Merrill. "Blackness, Betrayal, and Childhood: Race and Identity in Nella Larsen's *Passing.*" *CLA Journal* 38.1 (September 1994): 31–45.

Huggins, Nathan Irvin. *Harlem Renaissance.* New York: Oxford UP, 1977. 159–61.

Hull, Gloria T. *Color, Sex & Poetry: Three Women Writers of the Harlem Renaissance.* Bloomington: Indiana UP, 1987.

Hutchinson, George. *In Search of Nella Larsen: A Biography of the Color Line.* Cambridge: Belknap of Harvard UP, 2006.

———. "Nella Larsen and the Veil of Race." *American Literary History* 9.2 (Summer 1997): 329–49.

———. "Subject to Disappearance: Interracial Identity in Nella Larsen's *Quicksand.*" *Temples for Tomorrow: Looking Back at the Harlem Renaissance.* Ed. Genevieve Fabre and Michel Feith. New York: Oxford UP, 2001.

Jarrett, Gene. " 'Couldn't Find Them Anywhere': Thomas Glave's *Whose Song?* (Post)Modernist Literary Queerings, and the Trauma of Witnessing, Memory, and Testimony." *Callaloo* 23.4 (2000): 1241–58.

Johnson, Barbara. "Lesbian Spectacles: Reading *Sula, Passing, Thelma and Louise,* and *The Accused.*" *Media Spectacles.* Ed. Marjorie Garber, Jann Matlock, and Rebecca L. Walkowitz. New York: Routledge, 1993. 160–66.

———. "The Quicksands of the Self: Nella Larsen and Heinz Kohut." *Female Subjects in Black and White: Race, Psychoanalysis, Feminism.* Ed. Elizabeth Abel, Barbara Christian, and Helene Moglen. Berkeley: U of California P, 1997. 252–65.

Joyce, Joyce Ann. "Nella Larsen's *Passing*: A Reflection of the American Dream." *Western Journal of Black Studies* 7.2 (1983): 68–73.

Kaplan, Carla. "Undesirable Desire: Citizenship and Romance in Modern American Fiction." *Modern Fiction Studies* 43.1 (1997): 144–169.

Kawash, Samira. *Dislocating the Color Line: Identity, Hybridity, and Singularity in African-American Narrative.* Stanford: Stanford UP, 1997.

Kent, George E. "Patterns of the Harlem Renaissance." *The Harlem Renaissance Remembered*. Ed. Arna Bontemps. New York: Dodd, Mead, 1972. 27–50.

Knadler, Stephen. "Domestic Violence in the Harlem Renaissance: Remaking the Record from Nella Larsen's *Passing* to Toni Morrison's *Jazz*." *African American Review* 38.1 (Spring 2004): 99–118.

Kubitschek, Missy Dehn. *Claiming the Heritage: African-American Women Novelists and History*. Jackson: UP of Mississippi, 1991.

Larson, Charles R. *Invisible Darkness: Jean Toomer & Nella Larsen*. Iowa City: U of Iowa P, 1993.

———. Introduction. *An Intimation of Things Distant: The Collected Fiction of Nella Larsen*. Ed. Larson. New York: Anchor Books, 1992. Rpt. as *The Complete Fiction of Nella Larsen*. Ed. Larson. New York: Anchor Books, 2001. xi–xxii.

Lewis, Earl and Heidi Ardizzone. *Love on Trial: An American Scandal in Black and White*. New York: Norton, 2001.

Lewis, Vashti Crutcher. "Nella Larsen's Use of the Near-White Female in *Quicksand* and *Passing*." *Perspectives of Black Popular Culture*. Ed. Harry B. Shaw. Ohio: Bowling Green, 1990. 36–45.

Little, Jonathan. "Nella Larsen's *Passing*: Irony and the Critics." *African American Review* 26.1 (1992): 175–82.

Lutes, Jean Marie. "Making Up Race: Jessie Fauset, Nella Larsen, and the African American Cosmetics Industry." *Arizona Quarterly: A Journal of American Literature, Culture, and Theory* 58.1 (Spring 2002): 77–108.

• Madigan, Mark J. "Miscegenation and 'The Dicta of Race and Class': The Rhinelander Case and Nella Larsen's *Passing*." *Modern Fiction Studies* 36.4 (Winter 1990): 523–29.

———. " 'Then Everything Was Dark'?: The Two Endings of Nella Larsen's *Passing*." *Papers of the Bibliographical Society of America* 83.4 (December 1989): 521–23.

McCoy, Beth. "Perpetua(l) Notion: Typography, Economy, and Losing Nella Larsen." *Illuminating Letters: Typography and Literary Interpretation*. Amherst: U of Massachusetts P, 2001. 97–116.

McDonald, C. Ann. "Nella Larsen (1891–1964)." *American Women Writers, 1900–1945: A Bio-Bibliographical Critical Sourcebook*. Ed. Laurie Champion. Westport, CT: Greenwood, 2000. 182–91.

• McDowell, Deborah E. *Quicksand* and *Passing*. Edited with an Introduction by Deborah E. McDowell. New Brunswick, NJ: Rutgers University Press, 1987.

McDowell, Deborah E. " 'That nameless . . . shameful impulse': Sexuality in Nella Larsen's *Quicksand* and *Passing*." *Black Feminist Criticism and Critical Theory*. Ed. Joe Weixlmann and Houston A. Baker, Jr. Greenwood, FL: Penkevill, 1988. 139–67.

———. *"The Changing Same": Black Women's Literature, Criticism, and Theory*. Bloomington: Indiana UP, 1995.

———. " 'It's Not Safe. Not Safe at All': Sexuality in Nella Larsen's *Passing*." *Gay and Lesbian Studies Reader*. Ed. Henry Abelove, Michele Aina Barale, and David M. Halperin. New York: Routledge, 1993. 616–25. Rpt. of Introduction. *Quicksand* and *Passing*. Nella Larsen. New Brunswick: Rutgers UP, 1987. ix–xxxi.

McLendon, Jacquelyn Y. *The Politics of Color in the Fiction of Jessie Fauset and Nella Larsen*. Charlottesville: UP of Virginia, 1995.

———. "Self-Representation as Art in the Novels of Nella Larsen." *Redefining Autobiography in Twentieth-Century Women's Fiction. An Essay Collection*. Ed. Janice Morgan, Collette Hall, Carol L. Snyder, and Molly Hite. New York: Garland, 1991.

McMillan, T. S. "Passing Beyond: The Novels of Nella Larsen." *West Virginia University Philological Papers* 38 (1992): 134–46.

• Michie, Helena. *Sororophobia: Differences among Women in Literature and Culture*. New York: Oxford UP, 1992.

Miller, Ericka M. *The Other Reconstruction: Where Violence and Womanhood Meet in the Writings of Wells-Barnett, Grimké, and Larsen*. New York: Garland, 2000.

Mills, Claudia. " 'Passing': The Ethics of Pretending to Be What You Are Not." *Social Theory and Practice* 25.1 (Spring 1999): 29–51.

Mullen, Harryette. "Optic White: Blackness and the Production of Whiteness." *Diacritics: A Review of Contemporary Criticism* 24.2–3 (1994): 71–89.

Nelson, Emmanuel S. "Nella Larsen." *African American Authors, 1745–1945*. Ed. Emmanuel S. Nelson. Westport, CT: Greenwood, 2000. 316–23.

Newman, Richard. "Two Letters from Nella Larsen." *Biblion: The Bulletin of the New York Public Library* 2.2 (Spring 1994): 124–29.

Nunes, Zita C. "Phantasmatic Brazil: Nella Larsen's *Passing*, American Literary Imagination, and Racial Utopianism." *Mixing Race, Mixing Culture: Inter-American Literary Dialogues*. Ed. Monika Kaup and Debra J. Rosenthal. Austin: U of Pennsylvania P, 2002. 50–61.

Pabst, Naomi. "Blackness/Mixedness—Contestations Over Crossing Signs." *Cultural Critique* 54 (Spring 2003): 178–212.

Petesch, Donald A. *A Spy in the Enemy's Country: The Emergence of Modern Black Literature.* Iowa City: U of Iowa P, 1989.

Pfeiffer, Kathleen. *Race Passing and American Individualism.* Amherst: U of Massachusetts P, 2003.

Pinckney, Darryl. "Harlem's Mystery Woman." *New York Review of Books* 49.7 (April 25, 2002): 18–21.

Rabin, Jessica G. *Surviving the Crossing: (Im)migration, Ethnicity, and Gender in Willa Cather, Gertrude Stein, and Nella Larsen.* New York: Routledge, 2004.

Rabinowitz, Peter J. " 'Betraying the Sender': The Rhetoric and Ethics of Fragile Texts." *Narrative* 2.3 (October 1994):201–13.

Radford, Andrew. "The Performance of Identity in Nella Larsen's *Passing.*" *South Carolina Review* 34.2 (Spring 2002): 34–42.

Ramsey, Priscilla. "A Study of Black Identity in 'Passing' Novels of the Nineteenth and Early Twentieth Centuries." *Studies in Black Literature* 7.2 (1976): 1–7.

———. "Freeze the Day: A Feminist Reading of Nella Larsen's *Quicksand and Passing.*" *Afro-Americans in New York Life and History* 9 (January 1985): 27–41.

Reesman, Jeanne Campbell. "Fiction: 1900 to the 1930s." *American Literary Scholarship: An Annual* (2000): 257–85.

Rooney, Monique. " 'Recoil' or 'Seize'? Passing, Ekphrasis, and 'Exact Expression' in Nella Larsen's *Passing.*" *Enculturation: A Journal for Rhetoric, Writing, and Culture* 3.2 (Fall 2001): n.p.

• Rottenberg, Catherine. "*Passing*: Race, Identification, and Desire." *Criticism: A Quarterly for Literature and the Arts* 45.4 (Fall 2003): 435–52.

Ryan, Katy. "Falling in Public: Larsen's *Passing*, McCarthy's *The Group*, and Baldwin's *Another Country.*" *Studies in the Novel* 36.1 (Spring 2004): 95–119.

Sato, Hiroko. "Under the Harlem Shadow: A Study of Jessie Fauset and Nella Larsen." *The Harlem Renaissance Remembered.* Ed. Arna Bontemps. New York: Dodd, Mead, 1972. Rpt. in *Remembering the Harlem Renaissance.* Ed. Cary D. Wintz. New York: Garland, 1996. 63–89.

Shange, Ntozake. Introduction. *Passing.* By Nella Larsen. New York: Modern Library, 2000. xi–xvi.

Sherrard-Johnson, Cherene. "A Plea for Color." *American Literature.* 76.4 (December 2004). 833–69.

Schockley, Ann Allen. "Nella Marian Larsen Imes." *Afro-American Women Writers, 1796–1933: An Anthology and Critical Guide.* New York: Meridian, 1988. 432–40.

Sisney, Mary F. "The View from the Outside: Black Novels of Manners." *Reading and Writing Women's Lives: A Study of the Novel of Manners.* Ed. Bege K. Bowers and Barbara Brothers. Ann Arbor: Univ. Microfilms Internat. Research P, 1990. Rpt. in *The Critical Response to Gloria Naylor.* Ed. Cameron Norhouse, Sharon Felton, and Michelle Loris. Westport, CT: Greenwood, 1997. 63–75.

Singh, Amritjit. *The Novels of the Harlem Renaissance: Twelve Black Writers, 1923–1933.* University Park: Pennsylvania State UP, 1976.

Sollors, Werner. *Neither Black Nor White Yet Both: Thematic Explorations of Interracial Literature.* New York: Oxford UP, 1997.

Stepto, Robert. "From Idlewild and Other Seasons." *Callaloo* 14.1 (1991): 20–36.

Sullivan, Nell. "Nella Larsen's *Passing* and the Fading Subject." *African American Review* 32.3 (Fall 1998): 373–86.

Sunderland, P. L. "You May Not Know It, But I'm Black: White Women's Self-Identification as Black." *Ethnos* 62.1–2 (1997): 32–58.

• Tate, Claudia. "Nella Larsen's *Passing*: A Problem of Interpretation." *Black American Literature Forum* 14 (1980): 142–46.

Teague, Rita and Colleen Claudia O'Brien. "Looking for the Other Side: Pairing *Gatsby* and *Passing.*" *Making American Literatures in High School and College.* Ed. Anne Ruggles Gere, Peter Shaheen, Sarah Robbins, and Jeremy Wells. Urbana: National Council of Teachers of English, 2001. 137–47.

• Thaggert, Miriam. "Racial Etiquette: Nella Larsen's *Passing* and the Rhinelander Case." *Meridians* 5.2 (2005): 1–29.

• Wald, Gayle Freda. *Crossing the Line: Racial Passing in Twentieth-Century U.S. Literature and Culture.* Durham: Duke UP, 2000.

• Wall, Cheryl A. "Passing for What? Aspects of Identity in Nella Larsen's Novels." *Black American Literature Forum* 20 (Spring-Summer 1986): 97–111.

———. *Women of the Harlem Renaissance.* Bloomington: Indiana UP, 1995.

• Washington, Mary Helen. "Nella Larsen: Mystery Woman of the Harlem Renaissance." *Ms. Magazine* (December 1980): 44–50.

————. "The Mulatta Trap: Nella Larsen's Women of the 1920s." *Invented Lives: Narratives of Black Women, 1860–1960.* Garden City, NY: Anchor, 1987.

Watson, Reginald. "The Tragic Mulatto Image in Charles Chesnutt's *The House behind the Cedars* and Nella Larsen's *Passing.*" *CLA Journal* 46.1 (September 2002): 48–71.

Wegmann-Sánchez, Jessica. "Rewriting Race and Ethnicity Across the Border: Mairuth Sarsfield's *No Crystal Stair* and Nella Larsen's *Quicksand* and *Passing.*" *Essays on Canadian Writing* 74 (Fall 2001): 136–66.

Wiegman, Robyn. *American Anatomies: Theorizing Race and Gender.* Durham, NC: Duke UP, 1995.

Williams, Bettye J. "Nella Larsen: Early Twentieth-Century Novelist of Afrocentric Feminist Thought." *CLA Journal* 39.2 (December 1995): 165–78.

• Youman, Mary Mabel. "Nella Larsen's *Passing*: A Study in Irony." *CLA Journal* 18 (1974): 235–41.

Young, John K. "Teaching Texts Materially: The Ends of Nella Larsen's *Passing.*" *College English* 66.6 (July 2004): 632–51.

Young, Vershawn Ashanti. "So Black I'm Blue." *Minnesota Review: A Journal of Committed Writing* 58–60 (2003): 207–18.

Zackodnick, Teresa. "Passing Transgressions and Authentic Identity in Jessie Fauset's *Plum Bun* and Nella Larsen's *Passing. Literature and Racial Ambiguity.* Ed. Teresa Hubel and Neil Brooks. Amsterdam: Rodopi, 2002.

DISSERTATIONS

Baldwin, Kathryn A. "The Color Line and Its Discontents: Passing through Russia and the United States." *Dissertation Abstracts International* 56.7 (January 1996): 2667A.

Bayliss, John F. "Novels of Black Americans Passing as Whites." *Dissertation Abstracts International* 37 (1977): 5117–18A.

Bennett, Juda Charles. "Translating Race: The Passing Figure in American Literature." *Dissertation Abstracts International* 55.11 (May 1995): 3509A.

Blackmer, Corinne Elise. " 'The Inexplicable Presence of the Thing Not Named': Intersections of Race and Sexuality in Twentieth-Century American Women's Writing." *Dissertation Abstracts International* 53.9 (March 1993): 3211A.

Boulware, Portia Danielle. "Black Love and the Harlem Renaissance: The Politics of Intimacy in the Novels of Nella Larsen, Jessie Redmon Fauset, and Zora Neale Hurston." *Dissertation Abstracts International* 62.12 (June 2002): 4163A.

Branzburg, Judith Vivian. "Women Novelists of the Harlem Renaissance: A Study in Marginality." *Dissertation Abstracts International* 44.10 (April 1984): 3063A.

Calloway, Licia Michelle Morrow. "Conceiving Class and Culture: Motherhood and the Domestic in Harlem Renaissance Era Women's Fiction." *Dissertation Abstracts International* 60.5 (November 1999): 1555–56A.

Conyers, James Ernest. "Selected Aspects of the Phenomenon of Negro Passing." PhD. diss. Washington State U, 1962.

Doherty, Amy Frances. "Reading American Self-Fashioning: Cosmopolitanism in the Fiction of Maria Cristina Mena, Willa Cather, and Nella Larsen." *Dissertation Abstracts International* 59.12 (June 1999): 4426A.

Dressler, Mylene Caroline. "Unmasking the Female Spectator: Sighting Feminist Strategies in Chopin, Glasgow, and Larsen." *Dissertation Abstracts International* 54.10 (April 1994): 3747A.

Edwards, J. A. Craig. "Creative Reverence: Self-Defining Revisionary Discourse in the Fiction of Jessie Fauset, Nella Larsen, and Zora Neale Hurston." *Dissertation Abstracts International* 59.5 (November 1998): 1570A.

Favor, J. Martin. "Building Black: Constructions of Multiple African American Subject Positions in Novels by James Weldon Johnson, Jean Toomer, Nella Larsen and George S. Schuyler." *Dissertation Abstracts International* 54.7 (January 1994): 2577–78A.

Grayson, Deborah. "Black Bodies/Black Texts: Critical and Cultural 'Passing' among Readers of Nella Larsen's *Passing.*" *Dissertation Abstracts International* 54.10 (April 1994): 3748A.

Hanlon, Christopher. "Pragmatism and the Unconscious: Language and Subject in Psychoanalytic Theory, Pragmatist Philosophy, and American Narrative." *Dissertation Abstracts International* 62.4 (October 2001): 1412A.

Harris, Laura Alexandra. "Troubling Boundaries: Women, Class, and Race in the Harlem Renaissance." *Dissertation Abstracts International* 58.8 (February 1998): 3131A.

Holmes, Thomas Alan. "Race as Metaphor: 'Passing' in Twentieth Century African-American Fiction." *Dissertation Abstracts International* 57.8 (February 1991): 2745A.

Kocher, Ruth Ellen. "Janus-Faced Women: Multiplicity and the Double Doorway in Larsen, Stein, and H. D." *Dissertation Abstracts International* 60.3 (September 1999): 743–44A.

Kosnik, Kristin Costello. "The Alien in Our Nation: Complicating Issues of 'Passing' and Miscegenation in the American Narrative." *Dissertation Abstracts International* 62.2 (August 2001): 574A.

Marren, Susan Marie. "Passing for American: Establishing American Identity in the Work of James Weldon Johnson, F. Scott Fitzgerald, Nella Larsen and Gertrude Stein." *Dissertation Abstracts International* 56.12 (June 1996): 4774A.

Mayhew, Kelly Shareen. " 'Nobody in Town Can Bake a Sweet Jellyroll Like Mine': Women's Expressions/Performances of Sexuality in the Twenties and Early Thirties." *Dissertation Abstracts International* 59.7 (January 1999): 2573–74A.

McCoy, Beth. " 'Do I Look Like This or This?': Race, Gender, Class, and Sexuality in the Novels of Jessie Fauset, Carl Van Vechten, Nella Larsen, and F. Scott Fitzgerald." *Dissertation Abstracts International* 57.2 (August 1996): 683A.

McDowell, Deborah. "Women on Women: The Black Woman Writer of the Harlem Renaissance." *Dissertation Abstracts International* 42.1 (July 1981): 215–16A.

McLendon, Jacquelyn Y. "The Myth of the Mulatto Psyche: A Study of the Works of Jessie Fauset and Nella Larsen." *Dissertation Abstracts International* 47.8 (February 1987): 3039–40A.

McManus, Mary Hairston. "African-American Modernism in the Novels of Jessie Fauset and Nella Larsen." *Dissertation Abstracts International* 53.7 (January 1993): 2372A.

Miller, Ericka Marie. "The Other Reconstruction: Where Violence and Womanhood Meet in the Writings of Ida B. Wells-Barnett, Angelina Weld Grimké, and Nella Larsen." *Dissertation Abstracts International* 56.12 (June 1996): 4775A.

Muhammad, Suzana Haji. "Voices of Disobedience in the Fiction of Charlotte Perkins Gilman, Kate Chopin, Edith Wharton, Nella Larsen, and Mary Austin." *Dissertation Abstracts International* 62.9 (March 2002): 3048A.

Nakachi, Sachi. "Mixed-Race Identity Politics in Nella Larsen and Winnifred Eaton (Onoto Watanna)." *Dissertation Abstracts International* 62.12 (June 2002): 4169A.

O'Banner, Bessie Marie. "A Study of Black Heroines in Four Selected Novels (1929–1959) by Four Black American Women Novelists: Zora Neale Hurston, Nella Larsen, Paule Marshall, Ann Lane Petry." *Dissertation Abstracts International* 43.2 (August 1982): 447A.

O'Brien, Alyssa Joan. "Gendered Disidentification in the Fiction of James Joyce, Virginia Woolf, and Nella Larsen: A Modernist Aesthetic of Mobility." *Dissertation Abstracts International* 61.9 (March 2001): 3559A.

Pavletich, JoAnn. "The Power of Emotion: Affect and Literature in Early Twentieth-Century United States Culture." *Dissertation Abstracts International* 57.1 (July 1996): 219A.

Pfeiffer, Kathleen. "All the Difference: Race Passing and American Individualism." *Dissertation Abstracts International* 56.6 (December 1995): 2240–41A.

Pines, Davida Beth. "The Paradox of Marital Failure in James, Ford, Larsen, and Woolf." *Dissertation Abstracts International* 60.2 (August 1999): 420A.

Rabin, Jessica G. "Surviving the Crossing: (Im) Migration, Ethnicity and Gender in Trans-National America." *Dissertation Abstracts International* 61.4 (October 2000): 1407A.

Ramsey, Priscilla Barbara Ann. "A Study of Black Identity in 'Passing' Novels of the Nineteenth and Early Twentieth Centuries." *Dissertation Abstracts International* 36 (1975): 1497A.

Royster, Beatrice Horn. "The Ironic Vision of Four Black Women Novelists: A Study of the Novels of Jessie Fauset, Nella Larsen, Zora Neale Hurston, and Ann Petry." *Dissertation Abstracts International* 36 (1976): 8051A.

Somerville, Siobhan Bridget. "The Same Difference? Passing, Race, and Sexuality in American Literature and Film, 1890–1930." *Dissertation Abstracts International* 56.3 (September 1995): 935A.

Stetson, Earlen. "The Mulatto Motif in Black Fiction." *Dissertation Abstracts International* 37 (1977): 5129A.

Stringer, Dorothy. " 'Dangerous and Disturbing': Traumas and Fetishes of Race in Faulkner, Larsen, and Van Vechten." *Dissertation Abstracts International* 64.3 (September 2003): 911A.

Thaggert, Miriam. "The Literary Picturesque: Gender, the Body, and Visual Culture in the African-American Renaissance." *Dissertation Abstracts International* 65.2 (August 2004): 522A.

Thompson, Carlyle Van. "The 'White' to Pass: Miscegenation, Mimicry, and Masquerade in Chesnutt, Johnson, Larsen, and Faulkner." *Dissertation Abstracts International* 58.9 (March 1998): 3530A.

Wald, Gayle Freda. "Crossing the Line: Racial Passing in Twentieth-Century American Literature and Culture." *Dissertation Abstracts International* 56.2 (August 1995): 555A.

William, Bettye J. "Nella Larsen: Shaping African-American Female Representation in *Quicksand* and *Passing.*" *Dissertation Abstracts International* 54.7 (January 1994): 2765A.

Witherspoon-Wallthall, Mattie L. "The Evolution of the Black Heroine in the Novels of Jessie Fauset, Nella Larsen, Zora Neale Hurston, Toni Morrison, and Alice Walker: A Curriculum." *Dissertation Abstracts International* 48.7 (January 1988): 1772A.

Yohe, Kristine Anne. "Vainly Seeking the Promised Land: Geography and Migration in the Fiction of Nella Larsen and Toni Morrison." *Dissertation Abstracts International* 58.4 (October 1997): 1286–87A.

Youman, Mary Mabel. "The Other Side of Harlem: The Middle-Class Novel and the New Negro Renaissance." *Dissertation Abstracts International* 37 (1977): 5836A.

Zackodnik, Teresa Christine. "Beyond the Pale: Unsettling 'Race' and Womanhood in the Novels of Harper, Hopkins, Fauset and Larsen." *Dissertation Abstracts International* 59.8 (February 1999): 2991A.